A

WOMAN

BY

DESIGN

A WOMAN BY DESIGN

Frances Kennett

RANDOM HOUSE NEW YORK

Library of Congress Cataloging-in-Publication Data
Kennett, Frances.
A woman by design.
I. Title.
PR6061.E6175W66   1988   823'.914   88-42654
ISBN 0-394-56544-4

Manufactured in the United States of America
Typography and binding design by J. K. Lambert
2 3 4 5 6 7 8 9

First American Edition

For my father, A. W. Kennett,

who told wonderful stories

ACKNOWLEDGMENTS

Some of the ideas on women's beauty and dress expressed in this book are taken from *Principles of Correct Dress* by Florence Hull Winterburn (Harper and Brothers, New York, 1914), notably the chapters written by Paul Poiret and J. P. Worth, the son of the first Parisian couturier, who continued in his father's tradition.

A

WOMAN

BY

DESIGN

CHAPTER 1

*D*eepwater Quay drew nearer. The
swaying and dipping of the ship's tender grew
stronger with the pull of the shore. All Alice
could see on the coast of Ireland was a milling
hubbub of passengers. They spilled out of the
train carriages steaming alongside the docks.

The tender would land Alice, her younger sister, Anne, and her mother, Louise, close to

1 8 8 5

Queenstown Station, in Cork harbor. It was the main point of emigration for the poor Irish, leaving their land forever. Behind the picket fences stood clusters of families wrapped in shawls and mufflers, with caps and bonnets, embracing one another tearfully or sometimes standing separate, staring out into the bay.

Their faces told Alice that they were setting out for America as unwillingly as she had left it. The cold and their lifelessness matched her own intense unhappiness. It unnerved her to hear so much crying. Though what could anyone do in such a windswept gloomy place but cry? She missed the sun. It was as if her new homeland was welcoming her with its own lament—for times past, hopes ruined and the prospect of worse to come.

The shiny white Cunard liner that had brought Alice and her family from America stood out in the bay of Cork at anchor in deep water. Tenders loaded with more well-dressed arrivals pulled away from the big ship. At the same time, the Irish were being rowed in local whaleboats to a rusting steamer at anchor much nearer the shore. The rich came back to visit; the poor fled. Freeing themselves from clinging relatives, the emigrants, mostly men and women in their twenties and thirties, piled into the ferryboat when they could not postpone their departure one minute more. They threw their string-tied suitcases and wicker baskets in ahead and jumped down. Many held sprigs of hawthorn, may, or bunches of flowers picked for the last time from some village lane. The whaleboat pulled away, just as the tender Alice stood in reached land.

Another wail rose from the crowd, and the flaglike mass of scarves, caps and kerchiefs rose listlessly in the air. Blank faces in the whaleboat drifted past Alice, tears and raindrops blurring their dark features. Metal-gray sky, white cloud, a boiling expanse of granite sea. The specks of clippers' sails, the foam of a paddle steamer, the angles of small yachts littered the bay. An untidy, gloomy scene, so many lives flung carelessly apart like flotsam on the sea.

"This way, ladies—help the little girls first." Hands lifted Alice bodily from her seat next to Anne and Mama and set her down on the quayside. She disliked being hauled through the air on so momentous an occasion. Doll-like, her legs stiff with cold, she waited while Anne, too, was deposited next to her and then the grownups followed in an orderly line.

Alice could feel the eyes of the Irish people behind her back. She turned to look more closely. A pinch-faced but handsome young man caught her attention because of the ginger-red of his hair. He hardly saw her, he was so deep in thought. Then, with his face still tucked into his mother's shoulder, he smiled absently at Alice. He saw a dark-eyed, white-faced child in an expensive black coat and new black boots. Alice did not smile back. It was only two months since she had said good-bye to Papa, and the remembrance of parting was still strong.

"Come along, Alice." Her mother sounded sharp.

"Where to? Is it much further?"

"To the hotel, the Queen's Hotel, to rest for a while, and then we'll be met and go on to Carrigrohane. Not very far."

Alice and Anne were insensitive to the bumping motion of the carriage as it rolled over the cobbles toward Westbourne Place, where the hotel looked out over the harbor. They had reached such a point of hypnotic fatigue with the endless traveling, that they felt they could journey on forever. All across the bluegrass plains from Denver, hot sun beating on the train, nights spent sleeping in a velvet-cushioned bed . . . New York, the smell of rotting vegetables and sewers, the rats on the sacks at the harbor . . . then the big boat, lit up by a thousand candles, where the grownups danced and dined . . .

Alice fell asleep. Along with the luggage, she was transferred to another, older carriage. She smelt carbolic, hay, and leather polish. When she woke up, all she could see in the dark interior was a large hat . . . a black hat. Her mother was talking to an old woman wearing mourning clothes like theirs. It must be their new grandmother. Alice fell asleep again, too shy to think of meeting someone so important yet.

She saw nothing of Queenstown, nothing of Cork City, which the carriage skirted, heading westward along the river on the upper bank. She sat up properly, sensing the end of the journey, as the great wheels clashed on the pebbled approach to Carrigrohane Hall. In later years, this memory of arrival at a house that seemed an isolated, enclosed ruin of a place, although it was a bare three miles from a bustling city, remained her abiding view of the Hardy home.

The low-brimmed black hat with a stiff spike of a feather loomed over her. All Alice could see under it was a thin, smiling mouth.

"I'm Grandmother Hardy. You are Alice and this must be Anne, still asleep, poor child. Welcome to Cork, my dear."

She took Alice's hand. The effect of her touch was warm, her grasp firm, and yet the gesture conveyed no feeling to the child. Alice looked up into dark eyes, the image of her own. But the black-brown eyes looked directly into her soul and seemed to know her entirely. She felt invaded by that strong, dark stare, more accused than questioned with any kindness.

"Do you know who I am? Your papa's mother. Are you shy?" The old woman sighed. "Not like your father. And you have my looks, too, not his. Not a Hardy, eh? A pity."

Alice was spared further scrutiny by the sound of a great fist banging somewhere outside the carriage.

"Open the door, Mary, the Missus is waiting at the front and freezin'!"

The coachman sounded angry. He wrenched open the carriage door, fled round the side of the house and let the forlorn child step down by herself. There was Carrigrohane Hall: ivy-clad walls broken by tall, churchlike stone windows and a castellated parapet fronting the gable windows in the roof.

Alice expected the front door to creak as an enchanted castle door-way should. But it swung back readily and four maids in white aprons flew out to line up in a practiced row. They curtsied.

"Here they are!" the new grandmother said. "My daughter-in-law, Mrs. Richard Hardy, and the children, Miss Alice and Miss Anne."

The maids curtsied again—to Louise. The youngest maid at the end of the line, with yellow hair, smiled at Alice, which made her feel less afraid. The coachman, a thick-built man who talked as if he had stones in his mouth and seemed to do all things in the household, reappeared behind the maids, this time without his livery. He helped Grandmother Hardy and Louise down from the carriage. Anne had just woken up and struggled, not to be carried but to climb down by herself; she swayed to and fro, rubbing her eyes with a tight fist. Alice hoped she would not cry, as she so often did when she woke up suddenly. But her sister was staring at another old man in the entrance hall. It must be Grandpa Hardy, Alice thought—he looked a little like Papa, but very old.

Grandpa Hardy, a tall gentleman with fat whiskers and a broad smile, came forward as quickly as he could. He leant heavily on a cane.

"Feeble leg—otherwise would have met you myself. All right? All right?" He bent creakily to Alice and Anne, huffing and smiling so that his whiskers went in and out conspicuously. Anne laughed. It was a sound long unheard in Carrigrohane Hall. The two youngest maids forgot their duties, and stood still, hands folded on their bellies, humming "Ahhh!" sentimentally.

But Alice was still nervous, still unhappy. The house was so dark inside. The hallway was dominated by a broad oak staircase. She was led into the Great Hall to the left, a room that ran the entire depth of the building, and consequently was filled with a pool of warmth by the fireplace, and darker shallows of cold in its corners. It was so old, very grand, but not at all friendly. Just then, the sun grew stronger. Light flooded in on three sides of the room, and drew her to a window with a stunning view of the river Lee below in the valley. It was not a home, Carrigrohane—it was a place to lock away an ogre, or a princess.

"I'll show you to your rooms," Grandma said. "I expect you would all like to rest. Follow me, Louise. The 'generals' will help the little girls."

Two pretty maids with freckles and frilled caps came forward to hold Alice and Anne by the hand and take them upstairs. Anne stamped her foot and screamed for Mama: Louise turned back to quiet her, but one of the maids had already picked Anne up, settled her on her hip and flicked her own bright yellow plait over her shoulder from behind, to tickle Anne's nose.

"Go on now, Miss! There's Mother, right ahead. Hold on to me piggy tail tight and we'll follow her up the stairs." Her voice had such an affectionate singing note to it that Anne stopped crying and did as she was told, holding the thick hair in her chubby hands and watching the girl's lips in profile as she talked.

Alice climbed heavily behind the second maid. She noticed the girl's apron was tied with uneven tails. Grandmaman in Denver would never have allowed that. Alice did not like the smell of polish and mustiness from the old mahogany furniture, or the long gloomy corridors hung with blackened paintings.

"Not that way—that's the mistress' corridor," the second maid said. "Up here, little miss." Another half turn and Alice found herself on a second corridor above the main apartments.

"You're to have the old nursery. When you grow big, one of you is to have the night nursery on your own. Do you know my name? It's Deirdre. I'm to be your nurse."

Alice had hoped that the plump girl with the blond plait was theirs. She did not like to show her disappointment, so merely nodded in understanding.

"Rosie, that's her, she'll help too, but she's a lady's maid. There's too much to do, of course, but they'll not do anything about that . . ."

Deirdre busied herself with the leather trunks.

"Rosie, would you look at these pretty things! All black, the pity of it! Look now, here's Mr. Lynch with the water. What about a little dip, ladies? Would you like to do it together? Come on then, in front of the fire. The turf's coming up nice and warm."

Deirdre chattered on, comforting Alice with her odd accent, the warm sound of her voice. The maid's curiosity at the sight of the fine clothes overcame her carefully trained servant manners. Mr. Lynch, the coachman, butler—and footman too it seemed—lumbered in and out several times, heaving pitchers of water up the backstairs.

Alice and Anne were soaped and washed in a hipbath in front of a peat-filled fireplace. The burning turf gave off a sweet, smoky odor, filling the bedroom with a light fog that added to Alice's sense that the day was dissolving into a dream of foreignness. Ireland was much stranger than anything she had imagined. Soon, she and Anne were tucked into a big four-poster bed, feeling sleepy again.

"Don't draw the curtains," pleaded Alice.

"So you *can* talk, Missy. I'm glad to hear you!" Deirdre left the bed drapes open and went away. The sheets were velvety stiff linen, with lacy eyelet holes along the edges. Alice threaded her fingers in the holes, and listened to Anne snuffling with her thumb in her mouth. They both realized they were alone together, something that had not happened for a long time.

"I want to be home home with Grandmaman, Alice. Don't you?" Anne said. "I'm frightened."

"Yes. I don't like it here. Oh, Anne, don't cry. You'll make Mama upset."

"Where's Mama? Where's Mama?"

"She'll come. She's getting dressed I expect. I wonder what Mama thinks of this place. Poor Mama."

Alice stared at the dark, blurry splodges of lilac flowers in the wallpaper, occasionally marked with brown rings, stains of damp. She was not very old, just ten, but she knew instinctively that Carrigrohane Hall was not a place her mother could be happy in. It was not her own house, and Louise was a bustling, creative person who filled the space around her with gaiety and activities. How could she do that in this old, dark place?

Alice drifted into sleep, but the smoky closeness of the room filled her head with images of disturbance and loss, then ambushing her between, so that she lurched as if falling—memories of happy days: Grandmaman, her real grandmother, on the porch at Adam's Creek, their own sweet house outside Denver City, where they had always lived till now. It was a square, white-painted, sturdy sort of house. On the east side cottonwoods and straggling evergreens rustled and sang when the slightest hint of a breeze encouraged them. Alice could see Grandmaman rising up from her rocking chair to wave at Papa coming home on horseback from the railway yard, riding over the gray-green prairie grass the way westerners did, tucked firmly in his saddle, his hips settled easily on the horse's back.

But suddenly there was another picture: Papa laid out on a wagon, brought home by Dr. Jencks from Denver City. Papa had been hit by some loose scaffolding on the railway station building as he stood nearby, checking the work with the architects. Papa, lying quietly in bed, while the pain in his head got better or worse, and the house kept silent. Alice turned her head restlessly—in her dream, as in life, she could not look at Papa's face for very long. It looked so unlike his soft self: serious, too noble, with that distant beauty she had seen in grown-ups' faces when they fall asleep in the sunlight. Alice remembered more clearly holding his hand, the long slim fingers that had shown her how to tie knots, fold paper kites, slipped silver coins from the ruffles at her chin. . . . And holding tight to Grandmaman too, the day Grandmaman had said good-bye. Now she would never see her again.

"Ssh! Alice! Don't! My dearest. You're safe now. We're home. This is Papa's home."

Alice broke free of her painful, trapping memories to feel her mother wiping her forehead with a cloth soaked in eau de Cologne.

"I want Grandmaman! Why couldn't she come?" Alice cried.

"Sweetheart, she couldn't travel all this way at her age. It would have—it would have been too much for her. And the climate suits her best in Denver. Better for her health, the dry air, you know. Grandmaman loves the warmth there."

Alice put her arms round her mother's waist, as she used to do with her grandmother. Louise was surprised, almost unyielding, but she made an effort and stroked Alice's head and cheek. Alice sat next to her mother on the edge of the creaky bed, and they both looked out of the window at the light on the river Lee. Alice watched without interest as the sun tried to break through a cloud, trying to give a more gold than silver cast to the landscape. In the light mist between the woods, the river wound slowly below Carrigrohane Hall, disappearing to its source at Gougane Barra, a small lake surrounded by high rocks.

"At Gougane Barra," Louise was murmuring in her ear, "there lived an enchanted eel; I've read about it in books. . . . The eel was wicked and often stole cattle from the fields, and swallowed them whole! But an ancient holy man, living on an island in the lake, used to work miracles, and heal the sick, and one day the enchanted eel grew so bold that he sidled up and licked the holy water from St. Finbar's own cup! So the holy man banished him forever, and now there are no eels or monsters in Gougane Barra, only waterfalls and streams, running down to the Lee . . ."

When Alice awoke, she remembered the strange sensation of being held close by her mother, listening to foreign words and magic stories about dark hills full of pookas and their spells. She made her own fervent wish that Grandmaman would always remember to put flowers on Papa's grave, as she had promised she would.

◆　◆　◆

Alice's first summer at Carrigrohane Hall passed quickly, and her new life began to take on its true character: dull and solitary. She worried about her mother, who occasionally appeared in the nursery and made a valiant effort to amuse her. But no one could replace Grandmaman. Alice did not want anyone to become her friend. Anne, by contrast, was like an injured animal recovered from a long sleep. She roused herself and set about sniffing her way through her new territory. The nursemaid Deirdre made a great fuss of her, plaiting up her long hair in complicated coils, taking her for rides in the dogcart round the gardens. Alice was determined not to give in to such advances so readily. Little by little, an anger took over from the misery of homesickness. Alice felt that everyone was part of a plot to make her revive: but she did not want a new life. She only wanted the old one back again.

Sometimes Louise would take her into Cork City, with Lynch driving the inside car. Alice was too small to see out of the window high up behind her head, and she found the stuffy two-wheeled carriage a trial to endure. She knew when Cork was near by the stench of the river—constant dredging to keep the channel clear for shipping all the way up to the city quays churned up a loathsome smell. But the city was an adventure. Louise would help her out, still groggy from the journey, and they would walk among the shoppers on broad St. Patrick's Street. Activity and sights revived Alice: striped awnings over the shop fronts and lettered signs over tall buildings were welcome novelties after the quiet of Carrigrohane.

On the hillside, above all the commerce, the pointed gables of Government House stood out. It was the residence of the officer in command at Victoria Barracks. Alice was fascinated by the English military people everywhere. Among the smart shoppers with their feathered hats, and the "shawlies"—old ladies with checked wool blankets draped about their shoulders—there were always soldiers or sailors, sauntering along in gangs. Once she saw a very handsome young man with a sword, hopping confidently onto a trolley bus as it moved past her, adjusting his pillbox hat more jauntily to one side. He looked like a tin soldier, but she also saw the leaden-eyed glances of the old men in the street, and the way they spat on the cobblestones at their feet.

The town conveyed an air of pleasant, humdrum bustle. Alice and her mother would first walk to the Lee Library for Mama's French novels. (Grandma Hardy disapproved, but Alice knew Louise still read them avidly in the privacy of her bedroom.) Then they would walk on to the Eagle Bakery, where Alice was allowed to choose something to take home for nursery tea—brown square cakes were her favorite. Sometimes they stopped at Bolsters', and Alice would compare the gilded lacquer tins and caddies to find the best pattern while Louise chose her teas.

If "The Inch" had time—her sister always mispronounced Mr. Lynch's name and so the nickname had been agreed upon—he would drive down the quays to let them both walk a little way, along Batchelor's Quay or by the Custom House, and see the tall-masted sailing ships making ready to journey downstream to Passage East, Queenstown and the great sea beyond. Then Alice would make the same wish, every time: *Please let someone in Denver feel sorry for me! Someone send a ship so we can all go home again!*

At home now, in Adam's Creek, she would be sitting on the steps, watching while Grandmaman marked her lesson book. It was always easy work—spelling, numbers, or coloring maps. Grandmaman was particular about the maps—she liked a close zigzag line of ocean in deep blue round all the outlines. If Alice had done well, she would be allowed to go round and feed the hens, or (if Grandmaman fell asleep) she could climb the trees, tearing her stockings or ruining her shoes. Papa would laugh when he came home, and be scolded for encouraging her. Then, to make the ladies forget their principles, he would tell them some shockingly exciting story about the railway camps and the wild men who laid the tracks out to the west.

One day Alice came home from Cork after an outing with Louise, as usual feeling slightly sick from her claustrophobic journey. She wandered upstairs, while Louise went to her own room to rest. Anne was not in the nursery—or in the bedroom they shared next door. Alice knew at once where to look. Every afternoon, Deirdre and Rosie were supposed to change into their dark afternoon frocks and rest up before their evening duties, seeing to the mending if there was any to do. Alice climbed higher to the attic floor where the live-in "generals," as Grandma Hardy called them, had their little rooms. From Deirdre's came the sound of laughter, the hiss and crackle of a fire and the smell of burning. They were making toffee for Anne! Pushing open the door indignantly, Alice found her sister sitting on Rosie's lap by the fire, while Deirdre stirred the illicit sugar (stolen from the pantry) in a pot over it. The maids were not allowed to cook in their rooms. Anne knew it was forbidden, and enjoyed the secret even more because Alice had missed the fun.

"And I bought you brown cakes for tea!" Alice accused her.

"Sure, Miss Alice, we was only keeping the poor wee thing company. Sit you down, and have a spoonful yourself," Deirdre offered kindly.

"No thank you, Deirdre."

"Oh, Miss Alice, let's be friends, why can't we?" But Alice was gone, flying down the stairs before the part of her that wanted to stay up there made her dissolve in tears and pull Anne's plaits as hard as she could. She slammed the door to the nursery. A few minutes later, to her surprise, Anne followed her in.

"You had a treat—me too." she said succinctly, sitting in the rocking chair. "I like Deirdre. I don't want her to be a nun. What's a nun?"

"You go and live in a convent and pray to God all the time and never go home again. Catholics do it all the time."

"What's Catholics?"

"I don't know, but it's different from going to church like we do. Why does Deirdre want to be a nun?"

"She says she's too old and there's no one left to marry. Look, Alice, I want to show . . . watch me."

Anne pushed Alice onto the bed and then turned away to stand on tiptoe and open the top drawer of their clothes chest.

"That's mine! Put it back!" Alice exclaimed.

Anne had pulled out a photograph of Grandmaman that Papa had framed last year—a long time ago.

"It's all right, Alice, let me, please! I only want to look at it. Now watch me, watch me!"

Anne sat on the rocking chair, swaying to and fro, staring at the picture. She held her breath, and set her mouth in a firm line. Alice watched, fascinated, as Anne's enormous hazel eyes filled slowly with tears that plopped on to her hands and smock. Anne increased the flow until her face was a perfect study in misery. Suddenly she stopped, put the picture on her knees and wiped her cheeks with the back of her hand.

"I just look at it, and I can cry really well," she said with satisfaction. "I liked Grandmaman. I like Deirdre too, though."

Alice was impressed. "Do it again."

"Only if you promise to be nice to Deirdre if I do. Promise."

"Promise."

"Very well then."

Anne took a deep breath, and repeated her performance like a china doll—the kind that swivels inside its hood to show a smile or a tear-stained face from one turn to the next. Her eyes brimmed, her cheeks crinkled, the effort disfiguring her agreeable face. But in midperformance the door opened and Grandma Hardy came in. Anne jumped and covered the picture quickly with her skirt.

Grandma Hardy looked at them closely. Anne pulled out her handkerchief and pretended to cough, to explain her flushed face.

"I thought Louise was in here," Grandma Hardy said, as a reason for her appearance in the nursery. She hardly ever visited them upstairs.

"Mama will come in later, but she's a little tired. Shall I call her to you, Grandma? Deirdre is busy preparing tea." Alice improvised.

"No, child, it's not important."

Grandma Hardy moved slowly round the room, arranging the wooden toys on the chest, straightening the picture books on the shelf by the fire. The girls looked at each other covertly and as if one body rose to their feet.

"Were you playing a game?" Grandma Hardy seemed in a friendly mood. "What do you like to do, Alice? And you, Anne? I should like you to feel at home."

"Thank you, Grandma . . . you are very kind," Alice replied obediently. Then she had a sudden thought. "Cards, please, grandmother."

"Cards?" For some reason Alice did not understand, Grandma Hardy's smile remained fixed.

"Then I could play with Mama—or Deirdre," Alice explained, with a hurried glance at Anne.

"Papa taught us," Anne added, with happy memories.

Grandma Hardy fidgeted by the door, and chose not to pursue an unwelcome suggestion.

"I think . . . there may be some things of that sort in the attic," she said slowly. "Alphabet cards—marbles—a few things I saved as souvenirs of Richard's childhood . . . they are old, but they might amuse you. And Lynch shall make a doll's house for you." She grasped the bell-pull in a decided manner. "I shall call Deirdre now. You two shouldn't be left alone like this." She studied the two obviously disappointed girls, now standing closely side by side in front of the chair. One was small and unnaturally flushed, the elder one pale and stiff, with a secretive, awkward manner. Grandma Hardy sighed, and shut the door behind her.

"Isn't it allowed?" asked Anne. "Can't we play cards any more?"

"No, I don't think so. She didn't look very pleased, did she? Now, give me back my picture."

"Here." Anne pulled the hem of her skirt off the rocking chair to reveal the picture of Grandmaman, with her still smile.

"Don't do it again," Alice said, firmly shutting the picture in her drawer. "I don't like it—and *I* don't cry."

"Why not?"

"Because Grandmaman wouldn't want me to. Nor Papa. So I'm going to bear it, and so are you."

"I don't want Deirdre to be a nun. She's my friend."

Alice relented for her little sister. "I'll ask Mama about it if I can. Don't worry."

But Alice knew she could not talk to Mama. Louise never listened. She nearly always had a headache or was too tired. And Grandma Hardy would never tell her anything. "It wasn't done." Everything "wasn't done."

Deirdre came in with the tea tray, winking at Anne to let her know she had not been caught with the toffee. Mama followed her.

"Stirabout and Miss Alice's brown cakes," Deirdre announced.

"Aren't there any eggs for the children?" Louise asked in a listless voice.

Alice and Anne stared at their yellow porridge.

"I'm hungry, Mama, and I don't want stirabout any more!" Anne wailed, as if she saw a chance of getting something better.

"Mrs. Keefe just gave me what the mistress ordered, ma'am," said Deirdre, but she bit her lip as she looked down at the table.

"I'll have to speak to Mrs. Hardy," Louise replied vaguely, as if to herself. "Cornmeal and cakes is hardly enough."

Deirdre's back, bent over the fireplace, was rigid. Alice knew what she meant: Mama could try but she would never win. Not another word was spoken as the girls spooned up their food. Alice felt the stirabout rise in her throat again and again.

The other maid, Rosie, knocked gently on the door.

"Ma'am wants to know if the young ladies can come downstairs now to repeat the hymn."

Alice saw her mother raise her arm to her forehead, leaning back in her chair as if shielding her eyes from a sudden wind.

"In a little while, Rosie. I'll bring them down." Mama said.

"Here, Deirdre. You have my cake." Alice felt sick. "I don't want any more." She turned a pleading face to her mother.

"Can you explain to Grandma? I didn't have time to learn the hymn properly because we went to Cork."

"Oh, it doesn't matter, child! Come and say it to me. Come! Come!" Louise pulled Alice round to her and held her hands. "Say it to me. Don't be nervous."

Alice thought her mother's hands were cold and rested heavy on her lap.

> "The trivial round, the common task,
> Doth furnish all we ought to ask;
> Room to deny ourselves . . ."

Alice stopped.

"But that's the second verse. Oh dear." She struggled not to cry.

"Run and fetch the hymnal, Deirdre." said Louise.

"Don't you know the hymn either, Mama?" Alice asked with surprise.

"I've no memory, sweetheart. No memory at all."

"You remember lots of things, Mama, you really do."

"Not now, Alice, not now." Louise had made her little effort, and sank back into lethargy again. Deirdre reappeared with the hymnal.

"Will you 'take' me, Deirdre?" Alice asked her.

"What? Downstairs?"

"No, I mean will you hear my words? Mama's a little tired."

Deirdre could not read, but she was too sorry about her deficiency to admit it.

"Haven't I got enough to do? I have to see to the bathwater while you two's gabbin'. . ." She stopped herself short of saying "Proddy hymns" and hurried out of the room.

Mama took no notice of this insolence at all, which dismayed Alice.

Mama just went on sitting rocking by the fire, with her arm up over her eyes.

"I suppose we'd better go down," Alice said reluctantly to Anne.

A little later, Alice and Anne appeared in the drawing room below. Both grandparents sat facing each other on either side of the fire. Alice looked at Grandpa James hopefully, but something in his *Cork Examiner* was upsetting him. He got up with a gruff murmur and left the room.

Alice turned to face Grandma Hardy, took a breath and started to recite, but the old woman interrupted her.

"You're both too young for deliberate wickedness. Misguided, misled behavior, perhaps. I will forgive the highly improper suggestion you made, Alice, about a devil's entertainment—card-playing indeed! You're only old enough to have the seeds of filth sown in you, not for them to have taken root. I'll weed them out. You can and will learn, and I'll be patient until you do. Now, Anne first. Wait outside the door, Alice, until she has finished. Then you won't be able to copy."

Alice's spirit flared only briefly at the injustice of this last remark. Grandma's cold face held her in a trance, until she accepted all she heard as gospel truth. Grandma Hardy was so stern and convincing. She must be right. She must have guessed Alice was bad and a cheat even before Alice knew it herself. Grown-ups knew so many things. They had all the power of the world in their words. Living with Grandma was like taking a long, arduous journey through an unknown, bleak landscape. Whatever Alice did, no good would come of it.

She sat on the stairs and closed her eyes, while the gabbled litany of her sister's words came muffled through the door. Shut out in the drafts of the hall, she hugged her body. Her grandmother's coldness edged its way into her heart, and she shivered. Soon it would be her turn, and she might forget, and Grandma Hardy would dislike her even more. She put her head down on her knees, pressing her eyes so that little suns shot about inside her eyeballs. She felt as if she would never see a real, strong sun again—never run about in a sweet-smelling air and hear a loving voice, like Grandmaman's, calling her name. She could not understand how she had become so evil. Ever since Papa had died . . .

Then she thought that perhaps she *was* wicked. After all, it had been so exciting to have a whole new set of clothes because of the funeral. New things, not faded country dresses and scuffed boots for playing in the meadows at home. It *was* very grand to be seen in a velvet-collared coat and matching muff for the journey all the way across America—and exciting too to travel in a luxury railway carriage that a friend of her father's had arranged for them. A real Pullman. She was only ten, but she traveled in a railway owner's *private* Pullman, all the way across America!

She stood up and tried to think of her hymn. She could not ask anyone to explain, least of all her mother, why Grandma Hardy criticized her all the time. Alice suspected it was something to do with her way of remembering all those happy times in Denver. But it would hurt so much to let those bright images fade away forever.

◆ ◆ ◆

Gradually Alice's repertoire of evangelical hymns improved, and she and Anne found acceptable ways to fill the hours. There were so many activities that Grandma Hardy did not allow—they all had "waywardness" in them. Not too many books, they agitated the mind, not too much music (though Louise still played for them in the hall when Grandma Hardy was away from home), no dancing and *no* card-playing. Alice was told that a governess would come from England at the end of the summer. She began to understand that Grandma Hardy was a rather grander person than Grandpa—she was English, he was Irish; her family had titled people in it, while Grandpa's, though an old Huguenot family in Cork, only had money. These facts explained why the governess had to be English, and why Grandma Hardy seemed not to have very many close friends in the neighborhood. Back home in Denver, Grandmaman had been famously popular. She was French, from San Francisco, and Alice considered her entirely much grander than Grandma Hardy. But grand in a different way—she held court, and all kinds of people came to tea with her, whether they were visiting railway men, actresses from the Denver theater, or local folk who just liked a gossip on the porch with her. Grandmaman knew everything and everybody in Denver . . .

At least a governess might be company. Both "The Inch" and Deirdre were under Anne's thumb already. Alice accepted this fact—Anne was younger, at the age when it was still possible to wind adults round her fat fingers. Alice would have done the same thing if she could have managed it, but being older and a lot less "quaint" made it difficult. She attempted to make Grandpa Hardy her ally, but as the weeks went by he seemed to grow disappointingly preoccupied with something called "the Monster Bank." Alice did not understand at all until Mama explained that it was something to do with his duties in Cork. The Munster Bank had suffered a crisis because one of its officials had stolen a great deal of money.

Her grandparents were not under personal financial pressure because of the bank's crisis; Alice knew that Grandma Hardy's deliberate and careful charity was not caused by lack of money. Everything at Carrigrohane was measured out, noted meanly, with none of the easy comfort of life back home in Denver. Grandma Hardy meant to do her duty by her orphaned relatives, but she wanted them all to be properly conscious of her goodness; when they were not, she disapproved of them.

Still, the attic floor proved a treasury of old toys and mementos. One wet day, Deirdre tied up her lace-capped head in a muslin cloth, rolled up her sleeves and rummaged in dusty boxes inside a cupboard under the skylight. Old books, hat boxes, buckled shoes and the promised marbles were pulled out. Then one very special collection was revealed: Alice's father's own butterflies. Deirdre sat back on her heels, peering at the mahogany-and-glass cases.

"When me Da was here as groom, he used to do that with Master Richard. They had chloriform and cotton pads—a smelly mess if you ask me," Deirdre said.

But Alice took the glass-framed boxes carefully, carried them down to the day nursery, and sat by herself poring over the butterflies. There was her dear Papa's tiny handwriting, so painstaking, with little flourishes everywhere. Her throat grew tight, and her eyes filled with tears. She kept staring at the bright colors, and her tears made them even more beautiful: a sea of blues and yellows and warm, soft reds. She blinked so that she could see more clearly. Some butterfly wings were almost iridescent—greens and lilacs, such handsome things. It all seemed to fit together in Alice's thoughts: the sunlight of Denver and Papa's vivid boyhood treasures, while all she had was dull days in gray cold Carrigrohane, sitting alone by the window, looking out at rainy mists.

Alice disliked being made to make things—Grandma Hardy always made her unpick her sewing, and Berlin woolwork was so tedious—but the butterflies inspired her. Paper, glue and scissors were allowed, and she had a small box of paints. Soon she was absorbed in making pictures of paper dolls, which she dressed in fantastic finery. Patterned paper scraps, colored wrappers from dried goods in the larder, torn pages from Grandpa Hardy's magazines, old bits of wallpaper from the attic stores—she used all these to assemble her masterpieces.

The butterflies came to life. There was Grandmaman, in her French gowns ("she always dresses very European," was what the Denver ladies used to say). Then one in blue, meant to be Mama in her Sunday best. That took a long time, but not so long as the gorgeous girls from the Star Hotel in Denver City: Alice knew they were wild women, but even Grandmaman used to admit they were pretty creatures.

"What's that, then, Miss Alice?" Deirdre peered over her shoulder. "Why've all them butterflies only got one wing, poor things?" She didn't understand at all—how could she?

"It's not a butterfly. Don't be silly."

"Well, don't be getting glue on yer clean pinny."

Alice looked down. Torn shreds, gluey lumps. "Go away."

"Friendly little person, aren't we?" But Deirdre did as she was told.

Only Anne understood. Tonight, when the pictures would be dry, they would sit up in bed and they would act out a play. The ladies could be propped up on folds in the sheets. She and Anne could have a conversation; she'd be Grandmaman and Anne could be that widow friend, Madame Lecler. Or they'd pretend to be Belle Rivière from the Star, or have the Mama doll sing one of those old songs that Papa liked to hear.

◆　◆　◆

The butterfly game stopped on the day that Mama gave Alice news that was worse than anything before. It was a light evening when Louise came up to see her, in the bedroom. Alice's conversations with her mother had become even less frequent as the summer months went by. Louise watched as Alice and Anne recited their prayers, coughing a little as if she needed to apologize for her intrusion.

"I'm a good girl, Mama, aren't I?" Anne said, climbing into bed with a slight doubt.

"Yes, my darling, a very good girl. For six years old you are very, very good. Grandma told me so again today."

"Do you think I'm good too?" Alice asked.

"Of course I do. How could you ask?"

"I didn't know it took up so much time being good. It didn't seem that way at home."

Mama laughed, a sound that reminded Alice of other days.

"You were a wild little girl, I know that. Grandma Hardy is right—you are old enough to learn proper ways."

"Did you? With Grandmaman?"

Mama avoided replying. "That's why I came to see you tonight. Grandmaman's latest letter! She sends her love, and look, a pressed flower for each of you. Here you are."

Alice held the precious cornflower in the palm of her hand. A sudden lightness of feeling made her breathe carefully.

"Now sweetheart. Listen to me." Mama's voice was light too. So light that Alice could hardly hear what she said.

"I'm going away for a while. Perhaps a month, perhaps a little longer. I haven't been too well, and—I feel a change of air would do me good. . . . Grandmaman sent me addresses in Paris, and first I go to London to see some colleagues of Papa's. I have to visit a lawyer about the estate . . . Adam's Creek. So I shall be very busy and get well again."

"When?" Alice asked, but she guessed already.

"Tomorrow, early. The Inch is going to take me to the ferry. Now, you must both be good girls while I'm gone. Remember your lessons, remember your prayers and remember—"

"I'll remember it all, Mama!" Alice exclaimed. She did not want to hear any more. *Remember me! Remember me too!* she wished silently. Yet she was glad. Mama was a shadow, not the intense laughing presence that had once filled their white house with an expectancy of happiness. Alice was relieved, even pleased to see her go, yet mortally upset to feel such a wrong response to her mother's news. It was wicked to be glad that Mama was going away.

Louise got up from the bed. Alice rose to her knees and flung her arms round her mother's waist, speaking quickly.

"When you come back, they will all tell you how good I've been. My hair will be long and straight and I will have read *all* the saints, and my sampler will be stitched."

"And Deirdre can go and be a nun," Anne added, without fully understanding why this would be a good ending.

"Pray for both your grandmothers," Louise said.

Alice and Anne nodded.

"I'll write and send you more flowers."

Alice looked at the blue cornflower in her hand, with its silvery-gray stem.

"Deirdre says in the old days they took witch hazel on the boats to touch the ground where they would have to sleep in the new land. Then they didn't get bitten by snakes. But we didn't get snakes in Denver, did we?"

"Adam's Creek. Because it was like Paradise." Mama looked tearful, but determined to laugh at her. "I don't believe there are snakes in Paris either! Goodnight, God bless you, my dears."

With that comforting thought, she left the room.

CHAPTER 2

A 1 8 8 5 – 9 0

lice was fourteen when she was
told that Grandmaman had died. "The piece of
lace you sent me was beautiful, my dearest,"
Grandmaman wrote, in the last letter Alice received. "It reminded me of the day we all dressed
up for Papa's birthday—do you remember? I was
a Gypsy, Mama was a grand Spanish lady with
a mantilla and you wore a headband with bright

red feathers, and Papa called you his little Indian. *Ma chérie,* such good days . . ." Alice did remember. It was all Grandmaman's idea, that impromptu party at Adam's Creek. The old lady had looked quite magical with her wide, lively face surrounded by the gold coins of a Gypsy scarf. She was always bold and full of fun.

Alice suffered dawns of sleeplessness because she had not replied to this last letter. She had lied to her governess, Miss Barry, and told her that she had indeed written; she had given the letter directly to The Inch to take to the post. But Alice had done no such thing, because she was cross with her Grandmaman for bringing back yet another good moment from the past, and ignoring her unhappiness at Carrigrohane.

The news of Grandmaman's death made a criminal's gloom fall on Alice. God, of course, saw everything, and now had punished her for her deception. She should have written. Waking to think of it, brooding through her schoolroom hours, she became immersed in an unhappy tedium. She felt half dead herself.

At night she lay stiffly in bed next to Anne (in spite of all Grandma Hardy's protests, they always slept together). Alice waited until she heard Anne's slow, sticky breathing become lighter. Sometimes she could believe those stories of Indian mystics, who said that the soul traveled out of the body at night, for Anne became so still and untroubled that she really looked as if she had escaped her existence.

Shivering, Alice slid to her knees beside the bed and tried again to be heard, by someone, somewhere.

I love you, Grandmaman. I hope you can hear me. I miss you. Are you near Papa? In the graveyard? Who is looking after you? Tons of people, I expect. Everyone in Denver brings flowers to you, don't they, to pay their respects. . . . Grandmaman. I'm sorry. *But you never told me where Mama has gone, and I wrote and wrote, so many times. You knew all the time and wouldn't tell me. That's why I got so cross.*

Alice began to cry, the quiet tears that expect no audience or sympathy, and seem to empty all hope out of a body. *Please God, please hear me, I've never meant to be a bad girl.*

Silence. Alice despaired. Because if God was the kind of person who thought Grandma Hardy was good, then she stood no chance of being heard or understood.

She had spent four years of virtual isolation at Carrigrohane Hall with only a governess and Anne for daily company. The occasional confused chatterings of the "generals" had helped to develop Alice's fertile imagination about her evil nature quite wonderfully. Whispered words about her parents, her grandparents, and the state of the world around her frightened Alice. Constant faint sounds of threat—though she had no idea what was being said.

If Grandmaman had really, really cared for her, she would have let her into the secret about Louise. All Grandma Hardy ever gave were excuses—lies even. Alice was sure she was hiding the truth. First it was Paris, then it was Vienna, then a spa treatment in Baden-Baden. Louise never sent a single card to Carrigrohane, let alone the promised flowers. Too busy. That meant that no one loved Alice at all any more—not even Grandmaman. Because otherwise she would have understood Alice's anxiety and told her the truth, however shaming it was.

Alice gave up praying and climbed back into bed, with the sudden terrifying thought that she had made Grandmaman die: she had stopped writing, out of anger and abandonment—and Grandmaman had died soon after. When Papa died, she had been punished. She had no idea why, and it seemed a harsh judgment. She had lost everything dear to her: her home at Adam's Creek, Grandmaman's love, even Mama. Alice had thought nothing worse could happen to her, and now it had—Grandmaman had died with no good words to connect them at the end.

It was all her doing—*she* was responsible! Alice sensed she was losing everything good inside herself, as well as all the goodness of her world. She was magical, satanic: all she had to do was think an unloving thought and the worst things actually came true. She buried her head under her pillow, half wanting to scream, half wanting to suffocate herself. It seemed the only way out. But her lungs forced her to breathe, and Alice whined, a thin, relieving sound.

Anne woke up. "Stop that dreadful noise! Shut up!"

"Shut up yourself! Leave me alone!"

They turned their backs on each other. Exhausted, dizzy, Alice fell asleep, trying hard not to touch her sister.

Next morning, Alice wandered through the house to a place of refuge, struggling with the fearful power of her evil nature. Anne was still downstairs in the nursery, having her hair braided by Miss Barry. It would take an age because Anne hated it so, and would wriggle till Miss Barry lost her grip and the braid slipped from her fingers. Alice decided Miss Barry should smack that child hard for once. She crept into her hideout on the servant's landing and buried her head in a pile of cushions. She did not want to cry any more, but her head was heavy, and she wished it did not ache so much.

Then she heard Anne's plaintive voice, calling for her through the corridors. "Where are you, Alice? Alice!"

Alice burst into tears. How cruel she was, wanting Anne to be punished . . . only a little sister, not really deserving her harshness.

"Where are you?" Anne pleaded. "Don't hide, it's mean of you!"

"I'm up here," she sniffed, "in the berdoyers." She heard Anne's thumping tread up the stairs, and her familiar little hum starting up now that she knew where her sister was. But when Anne reached the landing, she stopped singing and her habitual placid expression flattened with dismay.

"What's the matter? You're crying!"

"No I'm not." Alice wiped her cheeks with the back of her hand.

"You are so! Did Grandma Hardy call you in again?"

"No, it's not that. Oh, don't just stand there. '*Entrez Mademoiselle, mon berdoyer enchantée* . . .'"

Alice smiled, but neither of them were in the mood.

The "berdoyers" were relics of one of Alice's best make-believe games. She had stolen a novel from her mother's empty bedroom, a long time ago. She scarcely understood the plot, but was lost in admiration of the high drama in the illustrations. What caught her fancy was the idea that beautiful women spent a great deal of their day making themselves even lovelier and sharing secrets in private places called "boudoirs." Alice had told Anne, with big-sisterly authority, that these were a kind of retiring tent, where ladies kept their best jewels and their love letters.

On the top floor landing, further down the corridor from the generals' rooms and the attics, the girls had built their own "berdoyers" and filled them with cushions, biscuit tins rattling with broken beads, sealing wax and tangled hair ribbons. They played at "fine ladies," swooning in fainting fits, weeping over their broken hearts, admiring flowers and jewels showered on them by their lovers, all of whom they refused ever to acknowledge. Dolls were lined up on the cushions for tea, and told all the scandals. These inanimate creatures were the "confidantes" of Mama's novel. When the girls grew too old for the game itself, the "berdoyers" remained, a good place to be when either of them felt melancholy.

"Please talk to me . . ." Anne pleaded.

"You wouldn't understand." Alice sat up, clutching a cushion.

"No, I might not, but I'm frightened when you cry. I don't like it."

Alice sniffed, and pulled at Anne's arm so that she would sit close to her.

"Silly baby. I'm all right now."

"What is it? Please tell. After all, I'm ten now, two numbers since January."

"It's Grandmaman. I didn't write to her, and now I can't. I lied and said I had," Alice confessed.

"Oh dear. You were bad."

"I know. I've asked God to forgive me, but I don't think He does."

"Perhaps if you did something really good instead He might believe you were really sorry."

Alice sighed. "Haven't you noticed how hard I'm trying? I was nice to Deirdre, nice to Miss Barry—I was even nice to Sophie when she came to French today. But I don't think it's having any effect."

Together, in silence, they considered Alice's predicament. Anne understood what a tremendous effort Alice had made. Sophie was the curate's daughter, who came to share French lessons with their governess on Tuesdays and Thursdays. She was a plain, soft-spoken girl, hopeless at learning anything. For Alice to control her impatience with Sophie was a genuine act of penitence.

"It would be easy if we were Catholic," Anne commented. "All Deirdre has to do is go and tell her priest and he gives her a prayer to do and forgives her, every Friday." Deirdre's robust approach to life's problems was a frequent topic of conversation between the sisters.

"Well, it's not as simple as that," Alice corrected her like a Sunday School teacher. "You are forgiven for a venial sin, but for a mortal sin you never get forgiven and you go straight to Hell, forever and ever. I'm sure I'd always be doing those if I were a Catholic, not the forgivable ones."

"What does venial mean?"

"I'm not sure. I think it's something to do with loving, because it sounds like the word Venus."

Anne looked thoughtful. "You mean, like when Rosie got told off for kissing the man from Cork who brings the meat?"

"I think so," said Alice, in some doubt. "It doesn't seem so bad to me, to kiss someone. Anyway, Rosie said that butchers were the worst for it—it comes from always handling the meat. I don't think her young man could help it. I suppose if you're really good, you don't do anything like that. Like Grandma says, you just love God. No one else."

It seemed a dismal prospect to two lonely girls, whose only experience of earthly love with a family had ended long ago.

"I really did love Grandmaman," Alice said at last. "I really do want her to know that and for God to forgive me."

"Then you must do something to show God what you say."

They looked at each other, deep in contemplation of various episodes of flagellations, fastings and other bodily denials and tortures that came to mind. Their education in this area had been thorough, for Grandma Hardy allowed them to read an ancient copy of Foxe's *Book of Martyrs* in the library on Sundays.

"They wouldn't let me go on a fast," Alice murmured. She had privately explored the idea of some physical punishment—burning her hand, hurting herself so she would lie awake all night—something she could do in secret where no one could stop her. She had not acted on these thoughts because she was terrified of being found out. Somehow they would put her in the wrong even though she meant to do right. Self-punishment had a glow of excitement about it that made her certain of blame. Even thinking about it made her feel wicked.

"I know," said Anne. "We could make an Albert Memorial. Somewhere no one would find it—in the garden, perhaps. Then you'd never forget how naughty you'd been. God would like that."

The idea appealed to Alice at once. It was spring, the garden would be a good place to be forgiven, better than trying to punish oneself in a bedroom by candlelight. The girls ran downstairs. At the far end of the paddock, joined to the west side of the house by a pebbled path, was a small copse. Ostensibly it kept the lines of washing from being seen by the owners and their guests, but Deirdre had told them the real reason the washing lines had been placed there dated from the days when laundry girls were employed at the house: they could walk past the paddock and flirt with the grooms without being seen by anyone looking out of the windows.

Beyond the copse was an old gazebo originally built to give a vista over the wooded slopes leading down to the river Lee. Long neglected, it was the perfect place for the girls to realize their plans. They ran back to the house to ask for Deirdre's help in setting it to rights. She obliged, pleased to see them active out of doors. It never occurred to her to be suspicious. Girls liked to have private places, and Carrigrohane was hardly cosy for the sisters.

Over the next few weeks the girls worked hard on the gazebo. Alice, Anne and Deirdre cleaned the leaded windows, swept out the floor and dragged in an iron table left to rust in the copse. Old velvet curtains from the attics were smuggled out, one by one, to give the interior a funereal pomp.

Alice was happy in her new refuge. Sitting there on a horsehair mattress acquired from The Inch's stables, she felt at peace. She could read her stolen novels, now much better understood than in the days of the "berdoyers." Pride of place on the iron altar was given to her best china doll, which she had dressed to resemble Grandmaman, and decorated with garlands of ivy from the walls of Carrigrohane. Nightlights taken from the bedroom cupboard lit up the soles of the doll's feet, giving it a corpselike presence.

The blooming of early summer flowers brought the girl's designs to a grand climax. In a rush of religious fervor, they ran down the approach, gathering armfuls of wallflowers and irises for a special morning service. They filled the gazebo with them, rammed into cracks in the wood and up the sides of the altar. Anne stole a chamberpot from the maid's scullery where all the receptacles from the upstairs rooms were daily emptied out, washed and stored. It made an excellent votive bowl, brimming with rhododendron heads, blooms of a rich bishop-purple, gathered from where they fell under the bushes on the main drive.

Alice and Anne arranged every item to their satisfaction and then knelt down to pray. They had decided that Anne should "intercede"— it was a word Alice had heard in church and more or less understood. Besides, Anne demanded that she should have a role to play in this first memorial ceremony.

"We ask you God to bless Grandmaman, and forgive Alice her sin, and accept these offerings from us today." On numb knees, they waited. Only the sound of the river, the wind rattling a loose board in the gazebo walls, and a bird-call from the woods could be heard. Alice desperately wanted a sign from God. It was a suspended moment; in her act of willing for contact, Alice felt as if her whole body had emptied out. All that remained of her was a tight shell of skin, with listening ears, trembling closed eyelids and the dry flesh of her fingers and palms, pressed firmly flat. She hoped Anne felt the same, and on hearing a tiny release of breath, opened her eyes to look at her. Anne was staring at the doll, and jerked her head, to make Alice look at it too.

A fat brown snail was sliding up Grandmaman's bodice, leaving a silvery trail. Over the black wool, over the felt, up the side of her china neck. The girls watched rigid with fascination as the snail sucked at a pale pink cheek and nestled under the brim of the straw hat. Perhaps it was the dusting of rice powder Alice had given the doll's blond hair to make it look old that had attracted it. Miracles do not need explaining: it was a magical performance, given them by God. The glisten of slime caught the sunlight as it flickered through the windows. Tree branches scratched at the broken panes. Grandmaman looked rakish—almost exactly as Alice remembered her—determined, free-spirited, utterly lacking in cant.

"What are you doing?" A voice bellowed at them. Grandma Hardy stood in the doorway, with Miss Barry on one side and Deirdre just a step back. Alice and Anne jumped to their feet.

"Are you heathen worshippers? Or is all this intended to please the Pope?" Grandma Hardy raised her stick to knock the doll to the floor and tear the decoration from the walls.

"Unhealthy! Conspirators! Mocking God, mocking goodness!" she shouted. "No wonder your father sent you back to me!"

She turned on Miss Barry and shook her fist in her face. "Is this the reward I get for taking you in? I knew I should have sent to England for a new governess. Now I see that I was right!"

Alice could not bear this injustice.

"It's not Miss Barry," she spoke out. "We never talked to her about it. It was all my idea, just mine, and it's not even *meant* to be Catholic!"

"Typical of you to lie, to take the blame! You've been a natural fabricator ever since you entered this house!"

Grandma Hardy swept out of the gazebo.

"As for you two"—she rounded on the governess and the maid—"if it were not for the long-standing obligations owed by both your families . . ." Anger choked her before she could think of a threat. Anne seized the moment and burst into hysterics.

"Every wallflower picked!" Grandma Hardy shouted at Alice over Anne's screams. "You're a feeble, feeble girl to backslide into such infantile ways!" With a last hateful look she turned back to the house.

Alice was so tense she started to laugh. Grandma looked like a witch in a charity performance, disappearing through the flapping sheets. Somehow getting into trouble had cheered Alice. An event, at last! Besides, God had heard, and Grandmaman had forgiven her. She also thought Grandma Hardy had been very rude to her governess, and it was unusually satisfying to see a grown-up misbehave.

"Miss Barry?" she said hopefully, wiping the dirt from her face, "I don't know whether Grandma's more worried I might convert than angry about the wallflowers!"

"Alice!" It was Miss Barry's turn to be shocked. The remark was typical of the in-between world the girl lived in. At times she was as childish as her little sister, at other times as quick and impudent as any adult wishing to be irreverent. Alice's pale face and dark eyes made her look very strong-willed at this moment.

Miss Barry felt she had to do something, not merely to defend herself but to change the unhealthily limited existence of the girls. She led them back to the schoolroom, ordered them to stay there for the rest of the day with no food as Grandma Hardy would expect, then made herself ready for lunch. Luckily, Mr. Hardy was home that day. He was always an ally. Miss Barry waited while Mrs. Hardy related in shocked tones the morning's event.

James Hardy turned to her in a kindly way.

"You gave me your assurance . . ." he reminded her, embarrassed to mention the past.

"I've never discussed religion or subverted them in any way," she answered. "But they must know, from the maids or from their few contacts with friends, a little about the Catholic faith."

Esther Hardy shifted irritably in her chair. Her husband's liberal acceptance of local Catholic gentry had always been against her wishes.

"If I may offer a suggestion?" Miss Barry hesitated, not wishing to presume.

"What is it? Do you see a deficiency in some way?" Esther Hardy as usual grasped the point. Miss Barry asked permission to leave the table and hurriedly fetched a bag from a chair by the door. She took out the slime-tracked doll, much to Esther's disgust. But James exploded with mirth. Underneath the somber black of the doll's outer dress, Alice had stitched three fine lace petticoats—and beneath them, a pair of chamois-leather drawers. They were carefully made, an exact copy of the kind worn by sporty local ladies who rode to hounds. Esther had no idea what the presence of this item in the doll's wardrobe meant. Inconsequentially she protested:

"But the girl hates sewing!" It was all she could manage to say, faced with the embarrassment of a young governess revealing such an item, even in miniature, in front of her husband.

"Miss Alice hates most things she is forced to do, but she's not dull. Observant, inventive, certainly not wicked. I feel she needs more company, the friendship of her equals, to prevent her inwardness, and to coax her from her stubborn ways." Miss Barry tried hard to sound fair.

"I will *not* send the girl away to school. She's seen too much of the world already—is far too quick . . ." Esther waved at the doll as proof.

"I'm not suggesting that. She would be very upset to leave here, she genuinely loves you and Carrigrohane, as she should," Miss Barry said dutifully. "Miss Alice would be most unhappy to be parted from her sister too. But she's nearly fifteen . . ."

"Fifteen, d'say?" James was interrupted by the maids, and in sudden exuberance he called for Madeira. The sight of the perfect "shammy drawers" had put him in a good mood.

"Quite right, Susanna my dear. Needs company! I've neglected to think of these things, due to my problems," he apologized. "Mrs. Hardy: now the weather's better, I'll organize courts, on the old cricket pitch."

Deciphering his rapid decisive speech, a habitual task, Esther Hardy was faced with an unwelcome suggestion. James wanted her to act as hostess to the neighborhood youth for tennis parties. Alice and Anne had accompanied her occasionally on visits; they knew a few children from suitable local families. They met them at St. FinBarre's in Cork on Sundays, at bazaars, and sometimes they were called upon themselves. But there were no house parties at Carrigrohane, or guests who came to stay as in other homes. Over the years Esther had broken with all her family, and with those friends who fell short of her moral standards.

"I've no wish at all to drag young girls about," she said, rudely.

"It won't come to that dear." James seldom rose to her anger. "Susanna, ah, Miss Barry, is right. Needn't be a trial to you. Miss Barry shall draw up the lists, and you can help her—approve it."

Esther looked at him severely. He meant she could exercise her power of veto over anyone she thought fast.

James sat waiting for her response.

"Well, my dear? We don't want the girls to turn out odd—religion, causes, that sort of thing. . . . Jolly them up a bit."

Miss Barry was amused. For all his geniality, Mr. Hardy was an excellent negotiator. He was suggesting that Alice was just the kind of girl who might become intense about something "inappropriate." Catholicism was anathema to Mrs. Hardy—apart from common. The mere hint that Alice might turn to that religion, become a nun even, was enough to persuade Esther Hardy to agree.

"There is no need for jollification, as you put it, Mr. Hardy. But if Miss Barry feels that she cannot keep them sufficiently engaged in study and relaxation"—a warning glance at Miss Barry made it clear that she was on probation—"then I shall do my best to provide them with other reasonable outlets for their energies."

James Hardy finished his Madeira with relish and retired, satisfied on many grounds, to the library with the latest copy of *Forest and Stream*.

◆　◆　◆

Miss Barry had not expected Alice to be so unwilling to cooperate with the new scheme. The girl paled at the thought of company, and watched preparations in a state of nerves. The Inch summoned a red-headed handy-lad from his seemingly endless family to help him harness the donkey, putting the animal in leather shoes to drag the roller over the grass. When the lawn was a little less lumpy, they painted on fresh white lines.

"What will I do," Alice asked Miss Barry anxiously, "if 'it' happens, when we have company?" They were looking at the approved tennis guest list one afternoon in the schoolroom. At once, Miss Barry understood. Alice had her "poorliness" again.

"You need not play. You sit out, say you have a bad wrist or prefer to talk to others not in the game. It is generally thought advisable not to exert yourself and to avoid shocks of any kind when you are in that way."

"Does it really, really, happen to everyone?" Alice looked at her governess intently.

Miss Barry blushed and moved away from the table.

"I've already explained it. You must accept yourself, and not take a morbid interest in your body. It's sinful, and leads you to temptation."

"Miss Barry," said Alice, disheartened, "now you sound just like Grandma." She looked at her pleadingly, quite unguarded for once. "I don't want these people to come."

Miss Barry was sorry for her. All the child's defiance had crumbled.

"You must accept things as they are. You'll grow used to it. Besides, it will be exciting to make new friends of your own." She picked up the guest list to create a distraction.

"Sophie's elder brothers are coming, and the Fogartys, they're home from school . . ."

"Really? The Fogartys? How did you persuade Grandma to include them?" Alice was interested again. The Fogartys were a very grand Catholic family.

"The eldest was presented at the castle last autumn. She received the viceroy's kiss—on the cheek! It's said she'll be getting engaged, to a very important person."

"Elegant Elinor! On the cheek! Now, to be sure, *she* won't be coming, she's so important." Alice put on a mocking, gossipy tone.

Miss Barry kept her temper.

"No, but her good behavior means that your grandmother will let Tom and Patrick come."

"Who else?" Alice was beginning to cheer up. She had met the boys once. The younger one, Patrick, was good fun.

"The Boyle girls from Rostellan and the Stoneys from Montenotte . . ."

"Oh, Miss Barry . . ." Alice was wondering again which of these girls was afflicted as she was. She felt as if she were being introduced to a shameful plot, an underworld of feminine secrets. "I shall just pray it's not happening to me . . . Not that I'm anything but hopeless at tennis anyway."

Miss Barry looked wistful. "Make light of it all, Alice. You're lucky to have so many chances. Do be a good girl, and try your best."

"My best is never good enough for Grandma, it seems to me."

"Alice!" Miss Barry's patience was dwindling. "Your grandmother could have dismissed me and fetched you another 'Protestant paragon' from London. You've been offered a chance to improve, instead of punishment, which you deserved."

"*Ne te fâches pas . . .*" Alice rallied and attempted a little wit, a new game now that she was nearing fifteen.

"*Et n'oubliez-vous pas, mademoiselle, que je parle beaucoup mieux que vous. Laissez-moi tranquille.*"

Alice bent to her workbooks, knowing she had gone far enough. She loved making mischief, and Miss Barry was an easy target. But it did not do to make her angry. Miss Barry was a kind person, as close to a friend as she had ever had, apart from Anne.

Miss Barry had actually lived in Paris. When she was in a good mood, she would show Alice her scrapbooks of picture cards, in cosmetic colors, of wide boulevards and women in picture hats. Miss Barry had been to the Opéra, and several times out riding in the Bois de Boulogne. She could describe the life of a debutante perfectly to Alice, with every detail of the Dublin and Paris *beau monde* made splendid—because her one chance in life had failed. Her father was a Cork butter merchant who had lost all his money, his health, everything. Only the kindness of Grandpa Hardy had saved the family from ruin. Miss Barry's social pretensions fascinated Alice. If only Grandma Hardy knew that she had a perfect ally in her governess—but they never spoke to each other freely. A social gulf prevented the contact. Miss Barry lived now on the very edge of gentility.

◆　◆　◆

The day of the first "event" was sunny; no chance of a cancellation, which made Alice glum. She sat on the lawn guarding the lemon punch, though the dreaded physical affliction did not make sitting out necessary. The young people arrived; they all knew one another well, and Alice just a little. Miss Barry was in charge, but the boys soon organized the order of matches to suit themselves. The girls, dressed in sporting white linen and serge, flung their hats with an easy confidence on to the grass bank, ready to play. Full of laughter and jokes, Alice's guests all ran about, their teasing words hanging on the still, warm air. Sophie came dutifully to sit beside her, not speaking. Alice found her just as boring out of the classroom as she was inside it. Then, to her surprise, Sophie ran off, muttering something about promising Anne a ride on her newly acquired secondhand bicycle. It dawned on Alice that Sophie was afraid of her, and actually preferred to play with a girl who was four years younger.

Conveniently, Miss Barry appeared from the house, carrying a parasol to give to Alice. Alice found her presence suddenly most welcome and hugged her arm, peering into her basket as she sat down.

"What've you got there?" she asked.

"I've been drawing," Miss Barry replied, pulling out a sketch pad to show her. It was a quick cartoon of The Inch. His burly shoulders were hunched to one side as he steadied Anne on Sophie's new bicycle. He looked as if he were guiding home a drunken man with a will of his own. Anne's hair ribbons trailed over The Inch's black coat, a silly feminine detail on his broad back.

"Miss Barry! How lovely, how clever you are! It's just so perfect of them both—how they are, I mean."

"*How* are they? I don't feel I know your family at all," said Tom Fogarty, in his English public school voice, falling to the grass at their feet. Two balls had landed in the rhododendrons; the game was abandoned while Patrick and the Stoney girls searched in the bushes.

Miss Barry was about to hide her sketch pad, but he took it from her hands.

"Do let me look, Miss Barry. It's very good. I can see you studied."

"I did" she said, not really blushing, but her small features softening a little. "Here in Cork at the School of Art and in Paris, for a short while."

"And you, Alice, do you draw too? I can see that tennis is perhaps not your favorite pastime." Tom was trying to be friendly. Alice noticed that his soft black hair was rather long and could not decide if this was proper or affected.

"No, it's not that. I've never played before this summer, and I'm quite hopeless at it."

"Not at all, you just need practice," said Miss Barry, her voice resuming that impersonal encouraging tone she had perfected. Alice reddened, knowing that Miss Barry was dropping a hint to Tom. But he seemed not to hear her; he was idly turning the pages of the sketchbook. Alice was tongue-tied and happy not to make conversation.

After a while, Grandma Hardy sent word out that tea was ready and all the young people gathered in the hall. It was pleasantly cool after the heat of the lawns, with a few patches of gold-dusted sunlight to remind them of outdoors. Patrick Fogarty took Anne on his knee and fed her biscuits. Tom was showing off Miss Barry's watercolors to a little crowd of guests. The Stoney girls (by some divine punishment for their unfriendliness, Alice believed) were caught in a duty conversation with her grandmother. Sophie came and sat beside her, a little more at her ease with her older brothers close by.

"Your grandmother has invited my brothers to visit during the week. If you'd like to, that is—we could have tennis lessons," she said in a tentative voice.

Alice looked at Sophie with a sudden excess of gratitude. "Oh Sophie, that'd be lovely. We really must learn how to play—it's very kind of you all." She stretched out her hands in an impulsive, sporting way. "Shall we meet on Tuesday? It will be something else to look forward to, after French."

"Something else you will do better than me," said Sophie, as a matter of fact, not with bitterness. Fair and plain described her looks and her personality.

"Oh, I don't think so, Sophie," Alice replied.

In a new mood of inferiority, Alice was ashamed of her behavior in the past. She knew there had been days in the classroom when she had squashed poor Sophie, losing patience and calling out the right words in French to Miss Barry. It had been easy to excel in Sophie's company: now the field of battle was suddenly enlarged. With a characteristic urge to right a wrong the instant she perceived it, Alice made a silent promise that she would fumble at tennis on Tuesdays consistently until Sophie was appeased.

Besides, she saw how Tom Fogarty looked at Miss Barry, over the drawings. He did not need to pay attention to a governess, nor was it just well-bred manners that produced such kindness. Alice thought that such honest admiration would be a fine compliment. Not that she could hope to earn it from anyone. As a girl she observed it, but for a moment, sadness made her feel like a grown-up woman.

CHAPTER 3

A 1 8 8 5 – 9 3

lice's natural competitiveness, nevertheless, developed as much as it could in the
narrow social world of County Cork. Sophie became the perfect supporting partner in Alice's
social forays. Grandma Hardy approved of the
friendship, for she was anxious for Alice to learn
how to use with good grace the benefits of her
superior social position. The years blended into

one another, more marked by the change of season than by the change of number. The summer months passed in a pleasant round of tennis, croquet and impromptu picnics. In the winter, Grandpa James would organize breakfasts for the Muskerry Hunt, beefsteak and beer at four in the morning. The girls loved to glimpse that other social world, more adventurous than theirs. Local landlords mixed on jocular terms with spruce young officers from the Cork Victoria Barracks. A few visiting English guests at nearby houses added distinction, the ladies resplendent in silk high hats and white stocks, sitting sidesaddle in ample skirts on their hacks. Alice and Anne would drive with Miss Barry in the dogcart to the hills around Carrigrohane, up laneways and rough bawneens until they came to a summit with a clear view of the field. They watched as the hounds drew the coverts, and flushed out a fox; then the colorful stream of pink-coated riders would spill across the countryside at an irregular pace.

Alice had little idea of what was happening in the world beyond the demesne of Carrigrohane. Sometimes events filtered through the web of controlled innocence in which she lived: a conversation overheard outside St. FinBarre's in Cork on a Sunday morning; the end of a bitter whisper between Deirdre and Rosie in a dark corridor. Once, reality whirled so close to her that she was sucked in, helpless. It was in December, when Alice went to Cork to buy drawing materials and haberdashery with Miss Barry and The Inch.

It was a cold day; they huddled together in the inside car, glad for once to be so confined in the stuffy carriage. Going up Grand Parade, they were met by a large mumbling crowd; at times the murmurings broke out into loud cries and the multitude seethed in its path down the street. The carriage came to a standstill at the side of the road until the mob passed. Some band boys, trailing behind with their instruments, broke into a fight with their opposite numbers from a rival outfit. Alice could hear the crack of instrument cases mixed with the more ominous sounds of ribs punched, and the groans of the winded.

"What's happening, Miss Barry? What's going on?" Miss Barry was looking unusually upset and anxious.

"Your grandparents wouldn't like me to discuss this with you. I think you'd better ask them yourself when we get home. Mr. Lynch, is it safe to go on?" she called out of the tiny window.

"Seems clear now, Miss. Factions and fights—that's all we're in for, poor man . . . it's the end of the Chief."

Miss Barry tapped the carriage roof. "Really, Mr. Lynch! Drive on."

When she got home, Alice waited for a private moment to speak to her grandfather. He was out all day, and she did not find him until after supper in the library. She knocked timidly, in case he was asleep.

"Come in! Come in!" He looked pleased to see her. Luckily he was alone; Grandma Hardy had retired early.

"I'm just going to bed, Grandpa, but I wanted to ask you something."

"What is it? More secret money for a new hat, I suppose!" He had helped her out a few times in the past.

"No, it's not that now." Alice felt unusually apprehensive, for she seldom spoke on any serious topic to her grandfather.

"We went to town today. There was—some sort of disturbance. I believe Mr. Parnell had come to speak—I heard Mr. Lynch talk about "The Chief." That's Parnell, isn't it? What's happened?"

The jovial smile on Grandpa's face faded. He put down his paper and for once looked directly at Alice.

"I can't discuss such a matter with you. It's an entire disgrace. All I will tell you is that the man is a renegade, a traitor to his own class. That much we always knew. But now we know also that he's a man false to God, and to true friendship. He betrayed his friends and his party, with a great scandal. He thought in his vanity he could carry the party in spite of it. But no one could do that—not in a Church-infested country like ours."

"What do you mean, Grandpa? I don't understand . . ."

"I won't say more, Alice. Good-night child, go to bed."

But Alice was determined to find out. The maids would not tell her, for Grandma Hardy had strict rules about "the 'generals' communicating with the girls"—a rule that had become tighter ever since the disaster in the copse. It seemed to Alice that there was a world of action and power, a world of grown-up mistakes that Grandpa Hardy knew about, and which she was never expected to understand. All she could do was absorb the moral dimension—the weakness of one man and his public shame.

She went to bed, trying to fit these glimpses of other actions and emotions into some pattern. They belonged to a compartment in her mind where memories of Deirdre's horror stories were stored: cattle maiming, rick-burning, potatoes failing and babies dying of hunger. A jigsaw of dark images, with all the important pieces missing.

In the morning she looked for The Inch. She hoped to catch him in a talkative mood, so he would forget she was the child of the house and tell her everything. He was in the stables, his favorite place. There, while she sat in the hay listening, breathless with shock, he told her a discreet version of the O'Shea divorce: that Parnell, the leading figure in the struggle for Ireland's independence from England, had been found to have a dishonorable attachment to another man's wife. It was his sadness that made him speak out of turn. That and his loss of hope for Home Rule and the shambles now ruining Parnell's Parliamentary Party.

"The bitterness, the bitterness has been terrible," he kept repeating. "All the men that loved him feel so betrayed. If a man can't look after his private affairs, how the hell can he look after a country? Excuse me, Miss."

He suddenly realized he was talking to Alice, and turned his back on her, struggling with the coach harness.

"Go away with you, Miss Alice. I shouldn't be caught talking, the master will send me packing for me Fenian sympathies."

Alice trailed back to the house, to Miss Barry and Sophie, waiting to begin yet another boring French lesson. Alice looked at their pinched faces (the schoolroom was freezing) and slid into her place with an inaudible apology. Miss Barry sneezed into her handkerchief.

"We're supposed to be grateful for your presence, I take it." She spoke with unusual sharpness.

Alice was still too full of thought to realize her offence, or to notice that Miss Barry was low-spirited.

"I was talking to The Inch," she said, quickly, knowing it was hardly a good reason to be late for lessons.

"Talking to The Inch! How edifying!" Miss Barry looked sharper than ever.

Alice jumped up, her temper rising fast. "It was! All about Mr. Parnell, and his affair with Mrs. O'Shea, and the Land League, and I think he's right—Ireland should be governed by the Irish!"

Miss Barry closed her eyes as if she might faint.

"Out of respect for your grandparents' great kindness to you and to me, I will pretend those foolish words weren't spoken. You meddle in affairs quite beyond your powers of understanding."

Alice banged on the table, just as The Inch had banged his fist on the saddles. "But Miss Barry, when *will* I understand such things? Who's ever going to tell me? How can I form any opinions about anything, except perhaps that I look better in blue than does Sophie?"

"You shouldn't hold opinions. You defer to those of your betters."

Sophie shifted uneasily, embarrassed and a little hurt by Alice's comment on her looks. Alice could see it was no use expecting help from her.

She sat down, discouraged, and picked up her textbook. But one large question still filled her thoughts most urgently.

"Miss Barry, what will I do when I grow up?"

Miss Barry looked surprised, but quickly lowered her eyes to her own book.

"Nothing, of course," she said coolly.

"Nothing?"

"You'll marry and be a lady. You should consider yourself most fortunate, considering your poor efforts to develop any refinement."

Alice leant back in her chair, the finality of this "nothingness" looming like a prison sentence. She put an arm up to cover her eyes, to cover her confusion. She suddenly pictured Mama, who had hidden her face like that many times.

"Miss Barry? Mama was a lady, wasn't she?"

Miss Barry slammed her book down on her desk and walked quickly from the room. Everything then happened very fast. One minute Grandma Hardy was in the doorway, the next, towering over her.

"You're not here, in my house, to ask questions, air opinions, or create disturbance. You are here to be grateful. Do you understand me?"

She struck Alice across the cheek so hard that Alice had no time to protect herself. Grandma Hardy wore a heavy gold band, and a jetted mourning ring for her son Richard. Alice's cheek reddened and swelled up with the weight of the jewelry.

"Your mother is dead!" Each word was venom. "She wasn't a lady. I'm ashamed she ever bore my son's name! You will never, ever, do the same to me—bring shame to me!"

Alice looked up, trying to hear, trying to understand. But Grandma Hardy misunderstood the piercing expression in her dark eyes, and saw only insolence. She hit again, the back of her hand striking the other cheek, and this time her rings cut into Alice's skin.

Alice saw nothing else. Miss Barry suddenly pushed in front of her, and pressed her clammy hands on either side of Alice's face. Alice heard ranting sounds, but was too confused with pain to understand the words. She felt as if she were drowning in a roaring sea, hot waves covering her face.

When Alice opened her eyes, Miss Barry was still beside her, sniffing.

"She's woken up, Miss Barry!"

Alice heard Anne's voice, loud in relief. Then she realized she was lying in bed, with Miss Barry and Anne keeping watch beside her.

"How are you, Alice dear?" Miss Barry asked.

"I don't know. Why am I in bed?"

"Well, Mrs. Hardy thought you should be quiet for a while, till ah, um, till you recover," Miss Barry explained.

Alice remembered, and touched her cheek. A linen strip and plaster covered it. The pain came back. Deirdre knocked at the door just then and bustled over to her side.

"Don't you worry, Miss Alice. Amn't I putting me mother's special compress on it? Green things and moss it has in it, just like she makes for me." She leant over the bed and whispered in Alice's ear: "And didn't I say a prayer for you, all the time I was compounding it?"

"That will do, Deirdre."

"Right you are, Miss Barry." Deirdre moved slowly away again, emanating rebellion while doing what she was told.

Miss Barry fingered the lace edge of her wet handkerchief.

"Alice, I should explain I think . . ."

"I don't want to. I don't want to talk about it." Alice closed her eyes, feeling a terrible pain welling up inside. Grandma had finally told her the truth. That was an end to it. She did not want to cry about Mama, not now, not in front of anyone.

"Your grandmother suffers very much from—the strain. First your Papa, then your Mama, and all the troubles in the countryside . . ."

"Will Alice be sent away?" Anne's voice trembled.

"Oh no! Oh no, my child! But you both must understand that the world your grandmother knows is changing, and Mrs. Hardy is afraid for you. She only wants the best."

"Can I have some water, please?" Alice asked. Miss Barry's words meant nothing to her. They were no consolation: they did not explain the hatred or the violence, and they would not make Mama come back.

"Here you are." Miss Barry sighed. "Oh, by the way, your grandmother has suspended lessons for a while, too. You're to stay in your room until—until you feel better."

"So she's sent Sophie away."

"Sophie's to visit relatives."

Anne and Alice looked at each other—they understood this much: Alice was to be kept hidden, so Grandma need not see what she had done, and so Grandpa would not find out either. Alice derived satisfaction, even angry strength from this guilty avoidance. No lessons was an unexpected benefit. In the midst of her unhappiness, Alice grasped at very precise things for a little comfort.

"Oh, Miss Barry, do sit with us, and tell us a story." Alice guessed that Miss Barry would be feeling remorseful, and might do what they wanted for a while.

Miss Barry looked wan. "You've heard my stories so many times."

"But we love them! You know we do!" Anne clapped her hands. "Tell us the one about the ball you went to at Fota Island—"

"—and the room with the maids and the hairdressers all waiting to mend your curls." added Alice.

"You wore white satin and pink flowers." Anne started it.

"Yellow roses."

"And your favorite partner was an English officer, Henry Brown . . ." Alice knew it all by heart.

"Oh no! That was at Rostellan the month before! My partner at Fota was Captain Hollings . . ."

Alice caught hold of Anne's small hand, and, lying back, half closed her eyes. They'd both told wrong things just to get her started. An ideal, fantastical world of silken dresses, banqueting halls and wonderfully attentive men filled Alice's mind, blotting out everything else. After lunch, Anne would fetch Miss Barry's scrapbook, and they would all study the faded prints, the well-thumbed dance cards and the brown, crumbling pressed flowers. Alice decided not to tell Anne what Grandma Hardy had said about Mama; not yet. She was far too little and soft to bear it.

◆　◆　◆

Alice's respite from lessons and formal visits lasted for several weeks. Every day her bandage was changed, the swelling went down, and the gash on her cheek faded. The incident was never mentioned by anyone again—Alice herself was so stunned by her grandmother's action that she could hardly believe it really happened. Grandma usually showed her cruelty by simply not doing anything kind—she had never roused herself beyond hard words before. Alice peered anxiously at her own face every day. It wasn't vanity—she suspected that her grandmother would be much more disapproving of her if the marks remained visible. It would always be a reminder of how provoking she had been.

As for Louise: Alice thought very little about her. She was so preoccupied with surviving the day-to-day misery of not being loved that she had no energy to mourn her. Her mother's death was too bound up with Grandma Hardy's cruel act—all Alice could do was numb herself to any feeling for the past.

The winter months worsened; by December the fog was impenetrable, and cold crept into every corner of the house. Christmas was a joyless affair: Alice was given a new Bible, a new pair of velvet slippers by her grandparents, and some paintbrushes from Miss Barry. Anne, who was always more indulged, got hair ribbons from Grandpa, two new pinafores from Grandma Hardy and a cut-out book from Miss Barry. They all had lunch early so that the staff could go home to their villages for the rest of the day. While her grandparents slept in the library afterward, Alice and Anne were taken to visit Sophie and her family at their dark little house. But it was full of candles and cakes, and the sound of the brothers playing games.

It made Alice so envious that she was quite relieved when it was time to go to church and she could be quiet again, to recover herself. Besides, she hated the way Sophie kept looking at her with her big blue eyes and that flat, empty forehead. She could not bear to be pitied by her.

The next day Deirdre came back and announced she was giving in her notice. Her father had again failed to pay his rent to the agent for the smallholding, and was to be evicted. They were all going to leave Cork and join relatives in America. *America!* thought Alice—to her it was the image of freedom. Deirdre was one of the few fixed points of her life, from the beginning of her time at Carrigrohane. Both Alice and Anne were deeply distressed by this news.

"Me Da has lost all heart for it," Deirdre explained to them, while making their beds. "All this year's been so bad for him, and now, with Mr. Parnell's dying . . . he was a big man for him."

Dead: one of the dark pieces of the jigsaw fell into place. The punishment for sinning . . .

"Ssh, Deirdre. Don't ever say that when Grandpa or Grandma are near you. They're totally against that man."

Deirdre smiled. "What an unnecessary piece of information! I was only telling you because you asked me why, Miss Alice."

"What's to become of us, with you gone?" Alice's eyes filled with tears. Deirdre was so big and strong, and had been such a reliable presence at Carrigrohane.

"Don't be crying now, Miss Alice. There's nothing else to be done. You'll be fine with Rosie and Miss Barry, to be sure, and you're almost a grown girl." She was speaking with a deliberate calmness, an accepting cruelty that Alice found infuriating.

"It's so unfair!" Alice exclaimed, frustrated.

Deirdre's smile remained fixed. She stood by the window, folding sheets. She stopped with her arms full, looking down over the lawns of Carrigrohane.

"That's the word for it, Miss Alice. It is that—'unfair'!"

◆　◆　◆

Alice and Anne felt empty more than sad after Deirdre left. One morning they woke up and Rosie brought them their breakfast; Deirdre had gone. Her absence frightened them as well as causing them loss. They mooned about their rooms as if trying to hold on to the insubstantial traces of Deirdre's presence. To Alice, once again things seemed to have a terrible connection: the violence, the fighting in the streets, a great man's shame and death and her own small sufferings. She did not understand any of it, which gave her imaginative constructions on events all the more significance. It made her feel like a neatly dressed doll, left out and caught in the rain.

Perhaps it was just coincidence that made James Hardy fulfil a long-standing promise to an old friend in London, whom he invited over for a few weeks to shoot with him. They were to go to a neighbor's shooting lodge in the Wicklow mountains. In honor of the guests, Grandma Hardy was prevailed upon to arrange a supper party and invite a few other distant acquaintances from Cork. She seldom had to entertain, for James was very understanding about her preference for solitude. On this occasion, surprisingly, she agreed, even seemed relieved to have a little diversion.

The guests from London arrived on a crisp January morning. They were to stay one night before going on to Wicklow. Alice was allowed to stay up for the dinner party—the first event of its kind in her own home. Miss Barry was instructed to join them too, to make up numbers and keep an eye on Alice.

Alice wished she had a new dress for the occasion. Her wardrobe was always a source of discontent. Other girls had mothers who went about in Cork or Dublin. It was common practice for the mothers' grand clothes to be cut down for their daughters, making presentable gowns until they came out and were bought their own outfits, brand-new. Grandma Hardy had no such wardrobe; she wore only mourning crepe, so Alice had nothing to turn to. Twice a year she was allowed to buy a French print, a zephyr cloth or a cashmere from Grant's in Cork City, and with help from Deirdre she would make herself the simplest of things. None of her dresses could ever be eye-catching, as they all had to be worn so frequently, but now there was no Deirdre to help her.

On the day of the dinner party, Alice began to feel rebellious. It seemed so much worse that she should not be allowed to make a presentable appearance in the privacy of her own home. All day she sulked, having plenty of time for it as the house was a turmoil of domestic activity, with extra hired maids scurrying about seeing to the guests' needs. The very absence of Deirdre with her usual cold-water views of these goings-on added a bitter edge to Alice's mood. She heard The Inch cursing as he humped another heavy box up the back stairs—and suddenly knew how she could make a grand appearance at the dinner party.

With Anne's help, she dragged her mother's trunks out of an attic room where they had been stored and forgotten. Louise's dresses were old-fashioned bustled affairs with far too many trimmings. They had never been unpacked, because Louise too had worn mourning crepe in those months she spent at Carrigrohane. Grandma Hardy would never guess where any of these old silks and laces came from. Near the bottom of the trunk there was one dress of a bluish-lilac silk that Alice thought might do. If she did not tie the padded bustle over the petticoat, and if she filled out the unfashionably tight sleeves by stitching on a puffed oversleeve—it could be made beautiful.

All afternoon, Alice sewed. She hid the dress away when she was summoned to tea to meet the visitors. These were an elderly gentleman—Sir Warren Thomas—his wife, Evelyn, her brother, Edward, and a younger relative, William Wickham. Alice applied herself very well to making polite conversation with Lady Evelyn, who studied her with curiosity. Lady Evelyn saw a girl of about seventeen, who had just grown up to be attractive rather than pretty, small in stature, with fine hands and delicate features. A tiny scar marked her cheekbone, rather endearingly, as if she still got into girlish scrapes. Her small, dark eyes were too much in the Hardy family mold to be handsome. However, they did not pierce, like her grandmother's, but shone with vitality. Lady Evelyn was much entertained by Alice's chatter—she had an amusing naïveté, no doubt due to her sheltered life at Carrigrohane.

William Wickham wanted Alice from that first moment. He was captivated by her voice, a strange lilting mixture of American and English, with an elaborate use of French phrases and the odd local Irish word. She was striving for effect, he could see. Others might have found her artificial but William thought he saw a fantastical aspect to her personality. She seemed to him like a muse, a sylvan deity, a shy thing about to dart away into the haze of the woods around Carrigrohane Hall. When the mist cleared, he wanted to be the poet at her feet and own her totally.

Alice did not look at him at all. She was aware that there was a young man, tall, extremely slim, with reasonable good looks but rather thin soft brown hair, leaning against the fireplace. Grandma Hardy would be watching her like a priest from the pulpit, so she knew she should not stare. It was important to please Grandma Hardy with good manners. At six they all parted company to rest and dress for dinner. Alice sent the maid away, explaining that Anne wanted the fun of dressing her, and asked the girl to go to Miss Barry and help her with her hair.

Miss Barry would be pleased at Alice's kind thought, and leave her to get dressed with just Anne's assistance. The maid was so new that she would not put on airs and object to serving a governess. When Miss Barry was ready, she passed by Alice's bedroom door.

"Shall I wait and take you down?" she asked, her hand resting on the knob.

Scarcely breathing, Anne shook her head at Alice and gesticulated at her. "No, thank you, Miss Barry, I'll follow you in a minute," Alice said, following Anne's mimed orders. Anne hurriedly finished pinning up Alice's hair.

"I can just see her," whispered Anne, "making a grand entrance! Do follow her now, Alice, go on!"

Her heart thumping, Alice tiptoed out behind her governess, and watched her as she swayed elegantly down the staircase. She knew exactly what Miss Barry was thinking about: all those exciting days in her own girlhood when she had been presented to people like this. As they neared the foot of the stairs, Alice realized that everyone was staring at her. She had thought she might slip in behind her governess, but even Miss Barry sensed, with a sudden drooping of her shoulders, that no one was looking at her. She stood aside, and looked with mixed emotions at Alice.

Alice hesitated on the stairs, then gave up all hope of dignity and ran forward to the waiting guests.

She had stuffed the homemade lace sleeves with the heads of Bourbon roses from the garden, to puff them out. Roses were pinned to her black hair, piled high at the back of her head. A tight blue bodice revealed her promising figure. The skirt was hopelessly incongruous, even Alice knew that, but she liked the way it pooled at her feet. She looked at the men with obvious pride in her handiwork.

Grandpa Hardy raised his glass, with a cheer; Sir Warren Thomas echoed his hurrah with a more noncommital "I say . . ." and Grandma Hardy looked appalled. Alice read her thoughts: *Bare-faced effrontery . . . No modesty in her manner . . . That foreignness, that craving for incident that is shocking and dangerous . . .* She had heard it all before.

Young William Wickham took Alice's hand, indulging her with mock chivalry as he kissed it. It was all show—all fancy—Alice knew very well there was nothing more to it than that. Grandma was wrong to think that she did not know it.

But Alice and William caught each other's eye in the surprise of the moment. His glance of admiration gave her the victory she wanted. As for William, Alice's unworldly, romantic appearance strengthened the fantasy of her that was forming in his mind.

◆　◆　◆

The party left early the next day, and to Alice's surprise she did not receive any summons to the drawing room. Miss Barry said very little either, and finished lessons early, complaining of a headache. Fear and then excitement flickered inside Alice when she thought of the night before. She had been seated at dinner between Mr. Wickham and her grandfather, who paid most of his attention to Lady Evelyn Thomas, on his right. Alice had talked to the Englishman all evening. He was the nearest thing to perfection in manhood she had ever met. Now it occurred to her that he was simply the *only* example of true manhood she had ever met. He was at least five years older than the young men she met locally; soft spoken, gentle, not teasing or at all wild with physicality.

Alice and Anne sat in the berdoyers, recalling all the evening's glories. Alice had found out that Mr. Wickham was an orphan, as they were; that he had sizeable estates in England, which he had only recently inherited; and that he was very fond of his guardian, Sir Warren.

" 'I only came to Ireland to please him with my company' he said. Then you said—" Anne was listening eagerly.

"Then I said, 'But I hope you like Ireland, Mr. Wickham, even if it is a duty.' "

Anne clasped her hands and mimicked, in a deep voice: " 'Not a duty, Miss Hardy, but a pleasant surprise.' "

They collapsed into the cushions, laughing, but Alice secretly wondered if the Englishman had only been paying empty compliments . . .

She was left to herself for the rest of the morning. Anne went out for her regular ride with The Inch. With the visitors gone, an ominous stillness gathered into the house. The silence continued all afternoon, while she and Anne read, then walked in the garden. Grandma Hardy did not appear in the evening for supper, or call Alice to her room. Alice wondered if she had done wrong. She could not go to sleep without some kind of reassurance, so she went to see Miss Barry before she went up to bed.

"It seems so quiet, Miss Barry, with everyone gone," Alice began.

"Yes, it does indeed." Miss Barry would not be drawn.

"I expect Grandma is *toute bouleversée* after all the company."

"Tout *bouleversée,* if you must speak French."

"Miss Barry?"

"Yes?"

"Did you like my dress?"

"It was pretty, though obviously terribly old-fashioned."

"Is that what everyone thought?"

"I really don't know. A girl should never make an obvious bid for attention to her person. It's common." Miss Barry went back to her book and Alice understood that the subject was meant to be forgotten.

Nothing was said for several days. Alice spent most of her time with Anne between lessons. Grandma Hardy did not leave her room, at least not when Alice could catch sight of her. It was as if Alice were just a child again. She wandered freely about the grounds with Anne, both huddled under umbrellas, then hurrying in to their small peaty fire and drinking chocolate to get themselves warm.

Grandpa James and his guests returned on Sunday evening. Grandma Hardy reappeared, greatly improved after being left alone. But her face darkened when Alice made some excuse and went off to her room to have tea. Alice was not in the mood to see guests again— her nerve had left her completely.

After supper, the guests went to bed; Alice heard them disperse through the long corridors. Then Rosie came and told her she was summoned to the library.

"Now you're for it," Anne said, cheerfully. Alice went down nervously, prepared for a lecture about her rudeness to the guests.

Before she could explain, Grandpa James turned to speak to her, looking grave.

"I'm not sure if you deserve congratulations," he began.

"For what, Grandpa?"

"William Wickham has asked for permission to propose. I take it you would listen to him?"

"Grandpa! Has he really?"

Grandma Hardy shut her book and looked hard at her granddaughter. Alice sat abruptly on the music stool and steadied herself with an arm resting on the closed keyboard. All week, Esther Hardy had been wrestling with this possibility. Wickham was moneyed and well connected, so why was she doubtful? His lack of immediate family worried her, and there was something else, indefinable. Instinct told her that Wickham was not what he appeared to be. But James had come back from the hunting trip well pleased with the news, and brushed aside her misgivings. Both he and Sir William thought Alice was as innocent and charming as any bride should be. Esther worried whether a father might have felt more jealousy, faced with a suitor, instead of the relief James obviously found in a good offer. He only admitted to pride, that Wickham had been smitten so instantly.

Esther looked at Alice, glitter-eyed by the piano, her resemblance to her mother more marked in this important moment. She was transported with excitement by the attention focused on her. It was a good match, but Esther doubted that Alice was truly submissive enough to make a proper wife. She had done everything in her power to break the girl's spirit, to bring her up as sheltered from all outside influences as she could.

"What do you say child? Aren't you too young to contemplate marriage?"

"Oh no, Grandma! I'm nearly eighteen. Elinor Fogarty was engaged when she was only seventeen."

Esther was irritated, but could not show her reactions. The Fogarty girl had captured an English title, which was the reason her family agreed to a brief courtship and an early marriage. Was Alice entirely innocent in making the comparison? The truth was, girls often married very young, their parents consenting to the risk if the stakes were high enough.

"Good thing, marriage," said Grandpa James. "Steadies a man. Gives a girl a proper place in the scheme of things. Responsibility, eh?" He smiled at Alice, hoping for the best in her.

"I will *not* give my approval." Grandma Hardy said.

Alice stood up in alarm. Did Grandma Hardy intend to keep her locked up in Carrigrohane studying French grammar and playing aimlessly at tennis parties for the rest of her life?

"I don't believe you are steady enough. But I will allow you to speak to William. You can tell him that if he cares for you, he must wait at least a year."

Grandpa James was about to protest, but Alice was too quick.

"I'm sure you're right, Grandma." She lowered her head. She knew if she could just be allowed to speak to William . . . Grandma nodded, and Alice could just make out the wave of her hand. She walked as slowly as she could from the room, then ran across the corridor to the great hall where William waited. Alice shut the door and leant against it, her arms held tightly behind her back.

"Well?" he said, "Am I allowed to speak?"

"If you are sure that I shall be what you want."

She was so eager to please, so proud of his attraction to her.

"I will look after you, protect you—I adore you with all my heart."

"I'm not very sensible, Mr. Wickham, and Grandma thinks I am far too young to be a wife."

"Miss Hardy! Alice! Age has nothing to do with it—it is your spirit! You're so free—like a—"

He fell on his knees in confusion, and held her hand. Free! He could not have offered her a better word.

"Mr. Wickham! Please get up; I don't deserve it."

But he continued to kneel as if in worship and she dared to touch the top of his head.

"I would be very happy to be made your wife. Grandma Hardy says you must wait, but please, let it be soon—let it be very soon!"

CHAPTER 4

A 1 8 9 3 – 9 5

lice and William walked through the woods to the river Lee. He took a leap over a fallen trunk and turned to help her. Alice felt a little thrill of excitement as she gave him her hand; William was so manly and gallant.

"Of course, Sir Warren will persuade Mrs. Hardy eventually," he continued. "Though it would help if Lady Evelyn spoke up for me. I don't understand her."

"No, neither do I," Alice agreed. "Perhaps she's just being polite. But honestly, I doubt if there's anything anyone else can do. Grandma's always had a poor opinion of me. It's up to me to convince her I'm fit for you." She said it as a matter of fact. William held her close, and kissed the top of her head.

"How could she not adore you! How could anyone!" he murmured gently.

Alice was ecstatic. Every gesture of affection was enough to make her feverish. No one had touched her kindly for such a long time . . . her eyes filled with tears.

"Sweetheart!" Timidly, William kissed her on her lips, and brushed his thin fingers across her eyelids. Words failed them both.

William turned away, and stooped to pick her a few flowers. Alice realized that he was a little embarrassed by his show of feeling, and this endeared him to her. They both had so much to learn about each other.

William suddenly heard a fluttering in the grass.

"Snipe! By God!" He mimed the swooping movement of a gun aiming high as the birds sprang up into the air.

"I say, Alice, when I get you home, you'll see, wonderful hunting country. I'll give you the bay, a steady old horse, and we'll ride together. Oh Lord, I can't wait. I've been planting new coppices, on the eastern edge, soon have a fine spread. Just you wait and see. . . ."

"And shall we have visitors?" Freedom and gaiety beckoned her: a grand life on a country estate.

"Visitors?" He looked blank for a moment. "I expect people will call—done thing, you know." Impulsively, he gathered her in his arms. "But I want to be alone with you—honestly, Alice my dear, if you knew how much I want us to be married . . ."

"Oh, William!" He kissed her again, and Alice found this sensation so arousing that she pulled out of his arms and ran, pretending to laugh, back toward the house.

The truth was, all this isolation with William was unnerving her strangely. Grandma Hardy allowed them to be alone together only because she sincerely believed prolonged doses of Alice's company would bring William to his senses. The engagement was still unofficial—so neither she nor William seemed to be able to plan seriously, or become acquainted properly. It was all gasps and kisses, dreams and long silences.

"I'll see you at supper!" Alice called back. William striding after her, looked disappointed, and turned toward the stables.

Anne was still having tea in the schoolroom. Alice was suddenly relieved to be back in their shabby corner, and joined her sister in eating bread and jam from a thick kitchen plate.

"Where've you been?" Anne said, between mouthfuls. Food was never plentiful at Carrigrohane and they both ate like prisoners.

"Down by the river. With William," she confessed.

"Oh, Alice, how disgusting! I don't see why you're in such a hurry to be married. As soon as people get married they have babies and they're sick all the time. Why don't you wait—at least till you come out in Dublin?"

"You're just beginning to make visits," Alice remarked, "so that makes social life seem exciting. When I was thirteen or fourteen a tea party after cricket was the high point of my week! But now I want to get away—can't you understand?"

"I wouldn't get married to do it."

"There's no other way to leave Carrigrohane. Besides, you're too young to understand. I *love* William."

"Oh. All that . . ." Anne sighed. The future looked very dim to her. Men, kissing, and Alice leaving.

"Don't be jealous, Annie, you know how it upsets me. I'll always love you, you know." She moved round the table to sit with her sister, but Anne stuck out an elbow, and wielded her knife rather savagely at the bread.

"All right." Alice sat back in her place, and was silent. She would stay with Anne until her mood improved, because it was miserable not to be friends with her.

Besides, Alice had her own misgivings about the loving side of getting married. She found a totally new physical pleasure in being with someone—a man, that is—but her duties as a wife were a mystery. Alice wondered about her own parents, and though her memories were vague, confused feelings stirred in her. Papa had been handsome, playful, very kind to her, and he always made Mama laugh. As for Mama— Alice tried to focus her thoughts, but she could not remember how Louise had behaved as a "wife" at all. Or, to tell the truth, as a mother. She only remembered Mama's terrible despair after Papa had gone. She could not have been a loving person, otherwise she would have stayed to love her and Anne. All the same, a reawakened curiosity about the past made Alice summon the courage to face her Grandma on the subject, once more.

"Grandma," she began softly, "there's something we never discuss. . . . Now that I may be contemplating marriage, please may I ask you about something—private?"

She saw Grandma stiffen, and look forbidding.

"There are times when innocence is your best, indeed your only advantage."

"Please! I must know! What really happened to my mother? Will you tell me the truth now?"

Grandma Hardy seemed surprised—almost relieved—as if she had not expected a question of this sort at all. She hesitated, then chose her words cautiously. "Perhaps it is fitting you be told this much. After your mother left, your grandfather and I applied to be made your legal guardians. Louise relinquished her ties to you. I'm sure it was a great sadness to her, but for your future security she knew it had to be done. Not long after, she died of a serious illness. Abroad."

"Do you mean she intended never to return?"

"I'm afraid so, my dear. You must accept the truth. That is why I could not tell you before. You would have been hurt by the truth. Do you understand me?"

The old lady was looking at her fiercely. Alice was not sure what Grandma wanted her to say. It was as if she were daring her to answer honestly.

"I confess, Grandma—I gave up wanting her, I quite forget when." She grew bolder. "In fact it would have been a—a disturbance to me, if Mama had returned. I've been quite content at Carrigrohane." Alice wanted to stop, but something drove her on. "It's *you* I wanted to have love me, not her!"

If her eyes suddenly grew warmer, if tears lay behind them, Alice would not allow the sensation. Anger overcame guilt or even pity for her mother. Grandma Hardy was the one who had power over her. The old woman stood up and held out her hands to take Alice's in her own.

"I do love you, Alice. All these years I've fought with you, for you, to make you good. You've a very strong character—make sure it leads you on the proper path, and never into shame. You could make me very proud of you."

This blessing pleased Alice more than she could say. She had never received praise in all her years at Carrigrohane—now she suddenly felt brave and free, impervious to harm. It was as if the moral fiber that Grandma had wanted to grow in her had at last taken root, and spread quickly through her limbs like a framework of iron.

"I do understand, Grandma. I promise, I promise you will be proud of me."

They kissed, accomplices at last for a death had been brought about between them. All Grandma wanted was Alice's rejection of her mother and all she stood for. She had given what was needed. Alice was elated, and ran from the room. Grandma sincerely loved her, and wished her well. Perhaps freedom from Carrigrohane would be her reward for her good behavior.

She was right. In a matter of days, Grandma Hardy changed her mind and agreed to the marriage—but only in six months' time. Grandpa Hardy was delighted, and immediately arranged an engagement party to make the announcement public. Alice insisted it should be just a family affair, a reception in the hall with a marquee on the lawn for the tenants and servants—such as were left. She wished Deirdre was still with them to share the pleasure of it.

Lady Evelyn took the sisters into Cork, and ordered them both new gowns from Grant's. She gave them tactful advice about their fashion choices. Evelyn Thomas was more sophisticated than anyone Alice had ever seen—tall, with a not very beautiful face dominated by a wide mouth and bright intelligent eyes, she evinced self-possession, a sharpness matched by the cut of her clothes. Neither her wit nor her dress gave any appearance of effort. The girls' genuine excitement at being given so much freedom amused her, for Lady Evelyn had grown accustomed to having anything she wanted. Alice chose a slipper satin in blue, a color to remind William of the day they met, and Anne chose white muslin with pink ribbon trim.

On the evening of the party carriages began to arrive at nine. The Inch had found ancient knickerbockers; in musty velvet and white stockings, he stalked about the entrance hall like a cheerful Malvolio. The curate and his wife came early, as Alice had requested, so that Sophie could be with her as a special guest. William looked magnificent in his formal clothing. His slight build and his fair coloring against the severity of black made him seem even more aristocratic to Alice. The servants stood waiting at one end of the hall. Mrs. Keefe was a forbidding dowager in purple satin; Rosie was flustered from having spent all day dressing the girls—Anne in tantrums over the tightness of her curls and suddenly in crisis because she had no dancing shoes. The Inch's handy-lad, Sean, had been dispatched to Cork to buy a pair—a wonderful duty. He arrived back posthaste, with the horse in a lather and himself dripping. Once in her new shoes, Anne was happy, with an exuberance that made the evening brim with excitement before anyone else had arrived at Carrigrohane.

As the hall filled with the Hardy acquaintances, Anne whispered: "Don't you regret it, Alice? You'll have to dance with William all evening!"

Alice laughed and shook her head.

"No more games, playing one partner against another!" Anne persisted. She admired her sister for her conquests—she had learned how to flirt almost as well as Charlotte Stoney, which was high praise. She nudged Alice, as they stood next to Grandpa in the receiving line. "There's Henry Molyneux. Don't you feel sorry for him?"

Alice pinched her arm. "He's lucky to escape me—isn't that the truth!" But her hand lingered in Henry's clasp and she promised to dance with him before supper, to spare him waiting to say the delicious regretful words she knew he had prepared. This was her special day, and she meant to savor it. As she waltzed with William, she hoped everyone would think how finely matched they were. She was tiny, and William so tall and protective, yet delighted to see her receiving other men's praise. She loved him for this generosity, which made her grow in confidence.

"Oh look, there's Elinor, with her parents, and Tom Fogarty." Alice pointed them out to William. He did not seem very impressed by her Irish connections. "She's visiting from England, you know, because you are here, 'Sweet William.' "

"Such a common flower," he said, pulling an amused face. "How can you bless me with that name?"

"I only mean to draw comparison to the fineness of your person." Alice could see by his expression that he accepted the compliment, after tantalizing her for a moment with a frown.

"I'm supposed to pay *you* the compliments." He risked brushing her ear with a kiss as she turned her head in the dance.

"Then I shall be a hard mistress, and demand that you pay me one every hour on the hour, all evening. Now go away and think, William. The first had better be splendid."

"No splendor can match yours tonight," he said, taking the opportunity that instant.

Alice was enraptured. Their conversation was like every romantic book she had ever read.

"Oh, William!" she sighed. "Now, do go and dance with Sophie. She deserves your compliments so much more than I do!"

William left her, incredulous that such a pretty, vital girl would soon be his own, exclusively.

Alice surveyed the room, proudly acknowledging the smiles of the Stoney girls, and casting a bright look in the direction of Tom Fogarty—he looked so boyish and self-satisfied compared to William. She waited confidently for poor Henry Molyneux to take his place at her side. Soon she would leave them all behind, in the paltry, suffocating ritual of an Irish county. William would open doors to a real life: friendship, a place in English society. Alice was so eager to learn, and so very grateful to William for offering her a new world.

◆ ◆ ◆

When William came back to Carrigrohane Hall in the autumn, both he and Alice were even more determined to marry. They had filled the time in between with a rapturous correspondence in which they both promised each other the stars, adding to their fantasies of how wonderful their new life would be. Alice knew she had met a man whose sensitivity and imagination equaled her own—and William thought the same.

When it came to planning the wedding day, however, Alice had no desire to show off. She felt that her own and William's lack of family called for restraint—she did not want mere acquaintances from County Cork filling up her side of the church if the Hardy and Wickham pews were to be noticeably empty. She also stuck firmly to her preference for the chapel at Carrigrohane, rather than the Romanesque splendor of St. FinnBarre's. The cathedral's three spires dominated Cork city. It reminded Alice too much of the rigid determination of Grandma Hardy and her religion. She had no wish to make her vows in that austere building, filing in, half afraid, past the gloomy draped stone figures that lined the doorways, as she had on so many other Sundays. The place was altogether more suited to funerals than weddings. Besides, Sophie's father could perform the ceremony at Carrigrohane. Anne and Sophie were to be her bridesmaids.

"Is there no one else from England who will come?" Alice asked William timidly.

"Sir Warren, Lady Evelyn—I'd prefer it to be a small affair. I'm marrying *you*, Alice, not taking the world to wife. Do *you* need a grand occasion?"

"No. I hate the idea." She wanted privacy, a sense of romance, a feeling of being made precious. And lurking behind these wishes was a vague contemplation of the sacred nature of the marriage vows. She looked so serious for a moment that William felt the need to comfort her.

"How gentle you are, Alice. I do love you so." That was all she needed to be content.

Alice made her own dress of heavy, creamy-white satin. Even Grandma Hardy was impressed by her patient handiwork. It was not a difficult gown, because all the decoration Alice required was supplied by the finest piece of Limerick lace she had ever seen—a wedding veil, given her by Grandpa James. Then, just a day before the ceremony, Grandma Hardy produced the last of her family jewels: a pair of diamond clips and a set of sapphires. These last looked soft under the lace, and Alice decided to wear them for the ceremony.

The day came, warm and still for Alice. The Inch had refurbished the coach, and decorated it with flowers in little glass vases. Alice and Grandpa James drove the short distance via the approach and the lane to Carrigrohane church. It was such a comforting sight, the small, square-towered building filled with her family and close friends. Sir Warren and Lady Evelyn smiled benignly as she came in to stand beside William. Alice felt very shy to be the center of so much attention. Grandma Hardy was deep in prayer, and her gaze rested stone-eyed and unseeing on her.

Mr. Scott, Sophie's father, spoke the words in a mild English voice that echoed over Alice's head. She gave her responses just loud enough for William to hear—no one else. But William, mindful of his position, announced his vows calmly and clearly to the whole church. Soon it was over. Outside on the path, Anne was hoisted up high by The Inch and she showered rice over all the guests.

"Catch, Sophie!" Alice called out—"There's no one else should have my flowers!" Sophie blushed, but managed it precisely, as a girl with two big brothers should. Then Alice declared on impulse: "Don't let's go by carriage! I'd so enjoy to go the quick way—please say yes, William, it's such a glorious day!"

William looked disconcerted. "I say, Alice, this won't do. We can't all trail across the grass . . ." He began to look a little tight-lipped.

Lady Evelyn intervened. "Nonsense, William. We're only family, aren't we? It's a charming idea. Lead on!"

Alice darted away through the cemetery and everyone followed her lead. Hearing her laughter, William relented: she was after all, such a natural, unspoilt creature, and her whims were enchanting. She looked like an impudent angel, lifting her white skirts, her veil floating as she skipped on.

So the poor shawlies, the old women waiting at the gate clutching their scruffy barefoot grandchildren, were denied the chance to see the carriages bowl away, filled with all the grandly dressed people. The Hardys and their guests, a colorful parade, turned through the wicket gate at the far end of the churchyard and walked back to the Hall in private across the lawns. Alice was going away from Carrigrohane just as she had come to it. The house had been her entire, secluded world, and she left it as remote from that other Ireland as when she had first arrived.

William caught up with her as they reached the lawns.

"I'm so eager to return to Rutland," he whispered. "I want to see you in my own home."

"It's not much longer. I'll say good-bye soon."

After a wedding breakfast, proudly set out by Mrs. Keefe, Alice went to change and to say good-bye to Sophie and Anne, as briefly as she could.

For once Anne did not cry. The girls sat in the schoolroom, which looked strangely ordered and unused. They had had no lessons for weeks. Alice looked unfamiliar too, in a new suit of gray wool, ladylike and serious for once.

Alice stroked Anne's hair, and hugged her close.

"Don't be sad, dearest."

"Oh, Alice, I'm not. If you're happy, then it must be the best for you."

"You shall come and stay with me, if Grandma allows. You and Sophie shall visit me. Won't that be an adventure for you? Don't be lonely without me, promise!"

"I'll write all the time; it will be fun to get some letters . . ." Anne replied dolefully.

Alice laughed. "Annie, don't be so tragic. If I know you, you'll write to me three times in one month, and then you'll persuade Grandpa to take you to all the Christmas parties, and you'll forget all about us!"

" 'Us!' " Already Alice was lost to her, attached to William for good.

There was a knock at the door, and Miss Barry came in to say William was waiting and Alice should come downstairs. She took Alice's hand and gave her a small box.

"It isn't much. A token . . ."

Alice was surprised to see Miss Barry so affected by their parting. She opened the box: it held a silver locket.

"Dear Miss Barry. I shall miss you. I wasn't good enough for you, I know—you've been very kind."

She ran from the room, leaving Anne and Miss Barry to follow her downstairs, arm in arm.

◆　◆　◆

The journey to England was exhausting and awkward. First they had the carriage ride to the docks, then an overnight ferry to Liverpool and a long train journey across country to Rutland.

On board the ship, they sat out for a while in a stiff breeze. William was anxious, overly attentive, constantly offering Alice gloves, rugs or rearranging her cushions and calling the stewards for drinks or more blankets. Alice could not understand his awkwardness. Finally he accounted for it.

"I took the liberty of booking two cabins," he confessed. Alice blushed.

"I thought perhaps—the journey—you might feel seasick . . ." he continued desperately.

"Oh no! I'm a good sailor!" Alice contradicted him, unhelpfully. William could not possibly know what emotions stirred in her, to be on the sea, leaving Ireland far behind her. Elation, a tremendous lifting of spirits possessed her.

"Well." He was at a loss for words.

Alice kissed his hand with a childish, affectionate touch. It was all so new, this need to be tactful about something she did not even understand properly.

"You don't want our first night together to be—*mundane?*" she suggested. She felt very bold.

William's face was suffused with passion. Oblivious of the cold, the thickening air full of steam and smoke, he kissed her, drawing deeply on the softness of her mouth. Huddled in blankets, they stared at each other, and then out at the turmoil of the gray sea. Alice was so overwhelmed by her physical excitement that she was quite happy to sit out freezing all night. But eventually, William led her to her cabin, and in a prim way, showed her how to bolt the door from the inside. After another passionate embrace, he went away, and Alice had barely taken off her shoes, her suit and her stays before she collapsed into sleep.

Next day a special train took them from Liverpool to their destination. William had ordered it so that it stopped directly at Upton Halt, where a fine barouche was waiting to drive them to Upton Park, William's home. As they passed through the village, the pavements suddenly filled with local people, cheering.

Everything about Rutland appeared bookishly neat and attractive to Alice. At home, near Carrigrohane, there were no villages, just hovels and squalid smallholdings dotted about the landscape. Only Aghada, The Inch's village, was more prosperous, because of its railway line, and the trade of the coast. But Upton was a fairy-tale medieval place, with neat thatched cottages, and new tenants' housing with slate roofs. The villagers looked solvent—there was even a group of men in tweed suits who did not doff their hats with speed, like the rest, but acknowledged the passing carriage with a cooler curiosity and turned back to their own conversation. Alice was quick enough to see new grades of existence, quite different from Cork. She could not wait to have William explain to her what it all meant.

When their carriage turned into the curving driveway, Alice saw all the staff out ready to applaud again. She blushed to be the focus of so much attention, and was overcome by the magnificence of William's home. She stepped out of the carriage, and the staff were introduced; there were at least twice as many as at Carrigrohane. She thought the housekeeper, Mrs. Hadding, looked even fiercer than Mrs. Keefe, and the butler much less friendly than The Inch. A sudden wave of homesickness made her feel weak; she leant on William's arm.

"Poor girl, you're tired," he said in a loving tone. "The maids will look after you until you feel better, then perhaps we'll take a stroll round your new domain." He smiled so pleasantly that Alice recovered immediately. Reluctantly she left him in the Great Hall, and was taken up the gilded staircase to her room. William had had it decorated in gray-blue, her favorite color. The furniture, all French, was covered in an expensive brocade. William had neglected nothing in preparation for her, and she felt a renewed confidence in their life together.

While Alice was resting in her room, William smoked a cigar, lying on the sofa. After a while, he went upstairs to his own room, called his valet and washed vigorously to release the knot of tension binding his chest and stomach. He changed his clothes, dressing with great care. It would be soon, very soon . . . He lay back on his bachelor bed, dreaming of making love to Alice with a rising passion. Alice was so virginal, so pure. He would be patient and tender. He was experienced in sex—life in the Guards had given him ample opportunity to exercise his manhood. The charms of the Haymarket ladies were well known to him—one in particular—but William wanted no more of those energetic romps, that had to be followed by sluicing his penis with a pitcher of gin to ward off infection. Alice would yield to him, encased in white linen—well, something finer maybe—her eyes would open wide with surprise, and then his own darling muse would swoon and obey his passion. He pictured her, lying still, her face pale and damp with loving, submitting to his caresses, lost in admiration at his energetic devotion.

William got up hastily; his erection was positively uncomfortable in his well-fitting trousers, and he wanted to save himself for this first union.

He took her to see the gardens, a wide sweep of lawn stretching down to an ornamental lake, with avenues of beech trees on both sides of it. To the left of the house were stables, and below, between them and the lawn, a large walled garden where the vegetables and flowers for the house were tended. The grounds were immaculate compared with the wildness of Carrigrohane, and impressed Alice considerably. Later, they dined quietly, sipping champagne in celebration. Alice was amazed at the richness of decoration, the luxurious newness inside the house, so unlike Carrigrohane.

"How old is the house, William? You told me it was Palladian." She had not a clue what this meant, and felt incredibly grown-up.

William smiled indulgently. "A classical scholar built it in the 1840s, in the style that was popular then. My father bought it on his marriage, in 1865 I think. Perhaps it was 1866. I don't quite recall."

Then Alice remembered: William's father had made money from iron ore on this very land, and had taken his wife on a tour of Europe to celebrate. But they had contracted a fever and both died. William was eight when it happened, and had been cared for by his trustee, Sir Warren, until he came of age.

"I didn't live here very much—after my parents died. It's always been my ambition to make it my home again. I love the place dearly. With you here, as my own sweet wife—my dream is complete."

"We've so many sadnesses in common," Alice said, becoming intense. Tiredness, overexcitement, sympathy, champagne, all induced her melancholy.

"But we'll be so happy now!" William said, trying to deflect her mood.

He seemed particularly excited, Alice thought—more so than at the wedding. Her spirits rose, sensing his elation.

They went to bed, Alice a little dizzy from champagne. She put on her nightgown, then sat by the window expectantly. William had said he would come to her room in a little while. He knocked, and soon he held her fondly, kissed her lips, her eyes, her ears, no words being spoken. William guided her then to the bed and lay beside her, shaking from head to toe in ecstasy. Alice was lulled by his enfolding arms, his soft-haired head bending over her, kissing her neck, the bare part of her shoulder above her nightgown.

She sat upright in sudden alarm, her eyes wide.

"What are you doing?" He had pushed his hand between her thighs, pressing her legs to open. She drew herself up on the bed, her knees tucked up to her chin.

"Lie down, Alice. I won't do you any harm. When a man makes love to a woman, he must enter her being. Don't be afraid. Soon we shall be one."

Alice's throat was dry with terror as she submitted to him again. He seemed oblivious to her reactions, overcome by a mysterious force that guided his every motion. She closed her eyes . . . she quite liked his hands cupping her breasts, his sucking kisses as he licked her sweating skin. But when he entered her, she felt a sharp pain, and then he drew both her arms above her head, imprisoning her wrists in a tight grip, and moved up and down on her, demented. Something happened, a warm flood spread backward round her buttocks. William gasped and rolled off her, panting.

The pain was nothing compared to the misery of physical invasion. It could not possibly be that it was William's right to do this thing to her. He turned and smiled gently.

"Are you happy, my dear? We are truly, truly now man and wife!"

She fought back her tears; he was so pleased with them both. She nodded dumbly. So happy—such horrors! It was beyond belief.

Alice's excitement about Upton was eclipsed by the discovery of sexual misery. It went on and on, the daytime loneliness and the nightly ordeal. William quickly reverted to his squire's life, enthusiastically joining the last of the shooting parties. He had missed so many while he dallied in Ireland. Then it was hunting—each day he got up early and disappeared on his covert hack to wherever the meet was to be found. He often came back exhausted after dusk, ate a hearty meal and then fell upon her briefly, expending his last ounce of energy.

Just when her patience was nearing its end, William came home early one afternoon and announced his intention of holding a hunt ball to introduce her to his friends in the neighborhood.

"After all, my dear, people will talk if our 'romance' goes on too long! We can't hide away in total seclusion, though I admit I like it this way, with you as my own precious darling. . . ." He advanced on her as she lay on a couch by her bedroom window, reading.

Alice put down her book. " 'Romance!' " she said bitterly.

"What did you say?" William was affronted by her tone of voice, and suddenly Alice was frightened. No one had told her one word about this matter; William had provided her with a magnificent home, and was about to launch her on the wide, adult world. She wanted to be able to love him, if only she could make him understand that it was all so strange and new to her. "My book. I'm bored by my book. Do kiss me, William."

He lowered his head to her breasts and kissed them through her thin cotton dress.

"Carry me to the bed," she whispered, putting her arms round his neck. But he did not move. "Touch me very slowly . . ." she took his hand and guided it down the curve of her ribcage to her waist, and up the side of her breasts again. She felt herself relaxing, and a warm, giving energy rising up inside her. She pulled his hand to her chest, and lifted her face to kiss him while forcing his fingers to squeeze her breasts.

William stopped kissing her. He wrenched his hand away and stood up, straightening his clothes.

"Really, Alice." He sounded surprised, almost shocked.

"What's the matter?"

"Well, it's the afternoon," he replied, confused. Alice was slightly aroused, and did not hear the coldness of his voice. She slipped the shoulders of her dress down so that her little nipples were revealed, erect. She felt playful, unusually excited by her boldness. She moved in scared anticipation toward the bed, hoping that this time William would be a little patient with her.

But as she turned round and put out her arms toward him, she knew it was all a mistake. He stared at her, utter distaste in his face, and then turned his back on her.

"How can you entice me? Like a common whore . . ."

"Don't go, William, I want you to love me. Can't we be close?"

He fumbled with the door handle, so great was his disgust. He could not help glancing at her, his revulsion increasing. She saw herself then as he did: tousled, in disarray, ordinary, with tears in her eyes.

"Don't distress yourself, Alice. Think of the servants. It was my fault for disturbing you, when you clearly need peace." He left quickly, as if his reproving words would be enough to bring her to her senses.

Alice sat on the bed, trying to understand his reaction and her disappointment. Humiliation crept upon her, and then, in a sudden burst of fury, she threw her book across the room. The gesture frightened her. It was the first time she had ever raised her hand in anger.

◆ ◆ ◆

At the hunt ball, Alice did her best to perform as she thought was expected of her. It was a splendid affair, the sportsmen in their pink tailcoats, the women glistening in diamonds. Alice's feelings for William revived when she saw the pleasure it gave him to show her off to the local families who formed his circle—the men were all as affable as he was himself, the women drily well-mannered in the style of Lady Evelyn. But during the evening, Alice began to feel definably ill. She sat out several dances, though she adored dancing, and William was frowning at her for refusing the guests. His disapproval caused her to hide for a little while in her favorite part of the house: the Chinese room. William eventually found her there, sitting in semidarkness. She looked exotic, gleaming in her white satin dress, with the eccentric figures of the Chinese people grinning at her from the wallpaper, sprays of plum blossom above her head.

"I'm sorry, perhaps it's the excitement. I just feel a little dizzy and weak," she apologized.

William looked sorry to see her so pale. He believed her, because he knew she was overly impressed by his friends and at the prospect of being more accepted in her new life.

"I'll send for Dr. Briggs tomorrow. You've had these attacks before. There must be something wrong."

"No! Don't do that!"

"Why ever not?" he looked impatient again. How could she tell him that the maids in Carrigrohane had a terror of doctors, and only took their own medicines? Even Grandma Hardy had raised her in a fatalistic way, letting every illness run its course untreated. Alice had no belief at all in the medical profession. She began to feel like a primitive, in need of complete reeducation.

"Oh well, if you insist." She felt tired and anxious for his approval.

"Perhaps we'd better go back to our guests. Do they like me, do you think? I do want you to be proud of me . . ." Alice spoke plaintively.

"They all adore you," William said, pleased that she wanted to earn his praise.

"Who's that very large lady, with the bold laugh?" Alice was fascinated by a particularly richly dressed woman, festooned with jewelry. Her arms displayed a heavy shapeliness as she circled the ballroom, almost carrying the young man in her power. Her manner was not unlike some of the types she had met at dances in Cork—except that this woman seemed to command authority, and was not at all unsure of her position in the world.

"Daisy Panton. A terrific rider."

"Oh." One passion among many Alice did not share with her husband was fox-hunting.

He squeezed her arm. "I rather like your fragility, Alice. It's very attractive to come home to."

Alice shivered involuntarily. She had the feeling William almost wanted to break her like a twig.

But after their guests had left, William came and slept with her without making love, a gesture of tenderness that made her like him all over again.

Dr. Briggs arrived from Warkham next morning. He suggested they should have a consultation in the Chinese room, which seemed odd to Alice. She had kept her maid waiting in her bedroom expressly so that he could examine her there.

His manner flustered her. He addressed all his remarks at her while blinking at the top of her head.

"Can you oblige me, Mrs. Wickham, by telling me if you've ceased to be 'unwell' in a regular fashion?" He smoothed his whiskers and flattened the gloves that sat on the crown of his top hat.

Alice had noticed that her monthly flow had ceased, but had assumed that her new life might have disordered her functions, and had not worried about it.

"Yes, indeed, I had noted the fact."

"Once or twice? Can you recall—be exact?"

Alice drew herself up to a new height. "Only once. That's why I didn't think it was cause for alarm." He had a most condescending manner.

Dr. Briggs did not seem to acknowledge her reasoning, but gathered up his gloves and hat.

"Then it is highly likely that you are with child, Mrs. Wickham, although we shall only know for certain in about two months. I advise complete rest, no riding or severe activity. Try to avoid upheavals, shocks of any kind. I shall only be able to make a confirming examination when your condition is safely advanced. You alone are responsible for that."

He took leave of Alice without further words, pausing only to congratulate William in the hallway before climbing back into his carriage.

Dr. Briggs despised wealthy women in grand houses. In his younger days, he had seen births take place virtually in the fields. Many working women in the towns, even in the sculleries of these fine mansions labored at their jobs until their babies were born. He thought Mrs. Wickham looked like a real hothouse flower. But Dr. Briggs was ambitious too, and liked the fees he got from rich women and their husbands. He was the "county doctor," even if he did not like his patients.

The grating of stones under the wheels of Briggs' vehicle broke in on William's trancelike state. He stood alone in the Great Hall of his house, watching the carriage disappear through the chestnut trees. He was amazed, and then angered at his stupidity. He had looked for perfect union—mere domesticity was not part of his dream at all. He had an idealized notion of "Woman," fed by an utter absence of contact with girls of his own class. In his youth, before he came into his money, all was sex and flirtation: sex with the street girls, flirtation with the debutantes. He had grown entirely bored with both, until he met Alice. Something about her made him believe that love could be beautiful, ennobling to his very soul. Now reality had broken in on his fantasy. He walked slowly into the house, to Alice waiting in the Chinese room, but he did not come close to her, or take her hand.

She looked up, unsure of herself, quite as frightened as he was.

"I missed my poorliness, and the doctor says I must be pregnant. I should have guessed. Anne told me having babies made one sick."

All this talk of bleeding and vomiting . . . in a daze William began to look down on Alice as a mortal, feeble girl, not his muse any more.

"Are you pleased, William? I hope it will be a boy. Would you like that?" she said, looking for reassurance.

He wanted to hit her. She had the beginnings of a wan smile on her face as she sat there, picturing herself madonnalike with a child in her arms. A loving hope—and yet she was so uninspired by *his* devotion. Suddenly William thought of trying to make love on top of a distended belly and his anger broke out.

"I must say this is a fine mess," he said.

"What do you mean?" Alice's smile faded, giving William a small satisfaction.

"I had planned to take you to Europe. No point in that now. You'd only be nauseous all the way."

"Oh! What a pity! I should have loved that!" she exclaimed. "So much I wanted to see!"

"Well. I *was* of the opinion that your education was sadly lacking in certain areas . . ." William spoke with unfriendly honesty.

"I know! I know! And I should have been so happy for you to teach me!" Alice refused to hear his unkindness.

"Ah well, now you'll have someone else to instruct, won't you?" She had given him the perfect opportunity to hurt her again. "I'll fetch Lady Evelyn from London," he added quickly, almost ashamed of his retort. "I think you need her company in these first few weeks. You're sure to continue sickly and she will be good for you."

He set off for London that night, leaving Alice to her thoughts. She wandered about the polished corridors upstairs, through the barred squares of moonlight thrown onto the cold stone floors. Alice touched the unfamiliar ornaments, Oriental urns, gilt mirrors, silken tassels twisted round the drapes. Out in the blackness of the night was a still, ordered expanse of rural life, families taking rest before another day of labor. She had never been poor, but she was restricted in another way—Upton Park was only a grander version of Carrigrohane Hall, a prison in which she was expected to do nothing but suffer William's displeasure and cope with her own frustrations. She did not want to have a baby: she had barely stopped being a child herself. William reacted as if she had betrayed him. No romantic voyages anymore. Alice remembered Anne's words about marriage, and felt tearful. Rather than be plagued by regret she went to her room and fell into a restless, dream-filled sleep.

Lady Evelyn returned with William after a few days, and saw the undisguised panic in the tightness of skin round Alice's eyes. William left them alone—he had work to inspect on the estate.

"Well, this is good news," said Evelyn, striking a positive note. "Sir Warren and I are delighted. Poor William had such a miserable childhood, losing both parents so young. Domestic life will be all the more precious to him."

Alice did not believe her. William's hostility was obvious—Lady Evelyn was far too astute not to have noticed. Then Alice remembered that at Carrigrohane, Lady Evelyn was the only person who had not uttered a word for or against the match. As William's foster-mother, perhaps she knew of certain traits in her nephew's character that would make any wife's task difficult.

It was hard to confide in someone she hardly knew, but Alice's confusion made her desperate.

"Lady Evelyn, why is William so disapproving of me? What have I done? Has he spoken of me to you?"

"You're imagining things," said Evelyn soothingly. "Perhaps it's the process of pregnancy that alarms him. He has very little knowledge of family life, you see. I'm afraid that's partly my fault. If I had had children—he grew away from me so soon." She looked unhappy.

Alice kissed her affectionately and sat by her. "I'm sorry to be sad when I should feel excited. With you here, I shall be much more cheerful, I promise. It's just that . . . well, married life is still so very new to me."

"Yes, I know, but you get used to it. There are compensations. You'll see. I know that William can be very demanding . . ." She chose her words with tact, and watched Alice carefully.

For a moment Alice wondered if Lady Evelyn really was referring to the physical business, and tried to think of words sufficiently delicate to allow the conversation to continue.

"He seems to want something I can't give him. I don't know what it is . . . and sometimes he is very angry with me. Oh, perhaps it's just that being with child—it happened so soon, I had no idea . . ."

Lady Evelyn was silent for a moment. "When I was young, I was deeply ashamed that I did not have children. When William came to me, I was pleased to be able to be a mother, if only through a legal arrangement. Perhaps I was overzealous. We were never close, and he could be—how shall I say—sensitive."

Alice realized Lady Evelyn was talking of William in another way. She was actually confessing that William was difficult to love! Perhaps he had always been changeable, given to black moods. She felt relieved.

"It wasn't your fault, I'm sure!" Alice responded frankly. "Perhaps he was too deeply affected by his mother's death to be close to you . . . besides, how much freedom you have had, without children!" she added bitterly. "None of the awful 'conditions' that mothers are so prone to."

Lady Evelyn, perhaps feeling a little disloyal to William for her words, was not prepared to let Alice enlarge on her miseries.

"Children are the purpose of marriage, if you are fortunate," she affirmed, "and you should feel blessed."

"Oh, I do, Lady Evelyn—and I understand a little better, thank you. I shall just try to be more obliging."

Lady Evelyn decided to let the matter rest. Alice was such a strange, instinctive person, and the couple had a sort of bond between them, she could see. Whether it would change into a more solid partnership would depend on this very young girl's patience—and submissiveness. At least Alice seemed to understand that now. Lady Evelyn decided not to overemphasize William's "tempers"; Alice would have to find her own methods to deflect them, and perhaps family responsibilities would mellow him.

"Now we shall make lists of things you'll need and I shall order them from London. William should talk to the carpenter about making you a crib—they usually love to do that sort of thing when the mistress is having a baby. I doubt if there is a family crib in the attic here."

"I should like to find a nursemaid—perhaps from home, I mean, from Cork. And a midwife," Alice suggested.

"Never!" William, coming in, had overheard her last remark. "This is England, not the bogs. Dr. Briggs will attend to you. I don't want a gin-toper in my house."

"Of course not, William, I'm sure we shall be well organized, just as you wish," Lady Evelyn soothed him. "I shan't make any arrangements without consulting you first. Have you decided which room should be the nursery?"

William had a flashing memory: himself holding a wooden boat, picking at the paintwork on the window frame, while he looked out over the park, wanting desperately to go out to play. Why did he feel so unhappy, so uneasy?

"Wherever you think best. As a boy I used to have the blue room." He turned to Alice. "I have to go to London for a few days—things to see to. Lady Evelyn has kindly agreed to stay while I'm away. If you need me, you can send a message to my club. Good-bye, Alice. I hope you feel better." He bent to kiss her cheek, and Alice touched his arm with a light pressure.

"Thank you for bringing Lady Evelyn, William. You're very kind." She felt so vulnerable, in need of his support, and suddenly afraid of what might happen to her if William did not overcome his doubts about the baby.

She knew he was avoiding her, and so it continued. Lady Evelyn came and went over the next few weeks, organizing her. She found Alice a local lady's nurse, Hodge, who looked after her on the days when she felt sick and sleepy. Evelyn sometimes returned from London with samples for the nursery, but Alice felt sad choosing things for the house when William was away. His absences grew longer; Lady Evelyn suspected he was hardly there in the gaps between her visits. Both the women kept up a pretense that he had adjusted; somehow Alice sensed that it was her task to hold on to William, and that Lady Evelyn might blame her for his lack of interest.

At times Alice hated the life growing inside her. One day when Lady Evelyn had gone away, she rode her mare through the lanes, hoping perhaps for something to happen. That night she had backache, and was filled with remorse, praying that she would not be punished for her selfishness. Next morning she went out into the sun, thankful to be spared, asking for forgiveness. She passed under the arches of topiary that bordered the walls of the kitchen garden, slid open the old bolted door and went in—she liked the place, as it was sheltered from the strong, cool winds that blew across the open countryside. Alice sat against the mossed red brickwork between the espaliered fruit trees, warming herself in a patch of sun. William found her there, half asleep, her belly just beginning to round out. She was a fertile part of nature herself, he thought, like an animal, with her eyes closed.

"Why are you here? The gardeners will be embarrassed to work with you intruding on their patch."

Alice started up, then shaded her eyes. It was true: she could see the backs of Mr. Fellowes and his lads resolutely turned on her and bent low among the vegetables.

"I'm sorry, William. I'll go back to the house with you."

"I have some news for you." He took her arm. "I hope you'll be pleased." In his own way William was making an effort—he hoped she would understand.

"I want to have your portrait painted," he continued, "by a local man. He's a great animal artist, in the class of Fernely or Stubbs. Will you agree to it? It will occupy you in the coming months."

"I may not be able to sit for very long; I do become uncomfortable, and my back aches."

"No matter, I tell you. He's a local man, he'll come as often as he can—short visits—will that suit you?" William was insistent.

"Why an animal painter, William? I'm a little puzzled by your choice . . ."

"Oh, of course he paints portraits, too. It's just a phrase. I want him to show you in the Great Hall, by the window, with the hunt just assembling for the chase."

She was touched. It was endearing that he pictured her with his favorite pursuit.

"If it will please you, William, I feel I succeed so seldom in that these days . . ."

He shook his head. "Don't fret, Alice. Your concern is unwarranted." He patted her hand in the crook of his arm. In spite of his gesture, she could still hear a coldness in his voice.

◆   ◆   ◆

Alice sat thoughtfully in her bedroom one night while her maid folded away her clothes. Not for the first time she recalled Lady Evelyn's words, and tried to plan a new way of behaving. She began to see that she was as much at fault as William for their misunderstandings because she had failed to accept any responsibility for herself in their marriage. He could not be expected to do everything for her when he had already honored her with a good name, a grand home and a secure future.

Lady Evelyn had hinted that his selfishness was the result of loneliness and ignorance, for he had no brothers or sisters to moderate his whims. Perhaps coming into great wealth had made him a little overconfident—there were still times when he was as petulant as a little boy.

Tomorrow she would ask William to invite that large woman he liked so well—Daisy Panton and her husband. She would plan an elegant supper with Mrs. Hadding's help, to show him that he could be proud of his wife. She stood up, looking at herself in the mirror. Her condition did not show so very much, and with a corset under her evening clothes she might manage to look quite normal for the occasion.

William knocked on her door—a new custom, as if to emphasize that he did not like to see her *en déshabille*.

"That will be all." Alice dismissed the maid and turned expectantly.

William shifted awkwardly, as if he did not want to commit himself to entering the room. Alice could not help shivering, and he saw her do it.

"All right, all right, I'll shut the door," he said, irritably. "I forget, your delicate condition."

"Oh, William!" Alice wished he would be kinder to her, and struggled to think of words that would please him.

"Look here, Alice . . ." He paced in front of her, uncertain where to begin.

"When I have my picture painted, William, what would you like me to wear? Is there any gown you like particularly?" Alice broke in quickly, determined to remedy William's dissatisfaction.

He stopped moving, and stared, frowning, considering a number of different responses he could make to the question. Alice felt exposed to her naked self, for William gazed at her, impassive, as if he could dispose of her in any way he fancied.

Frightening, wild ideas assailed her. Perhaps he would announce that he did not love her any more, or that he loved her so much that he could not bear to share her with a baby. Suppose he said he would send her back to Carrigrohane until it was all over—a terrifying prospect!

"William?" she whispered, pleading for an answer. She felt so afraid of failing in her marriage that she knelt down by the bed and buried her face in the silky cover—William might think she was praying, but all she wanted was to hide from the blankness of his face.

She heard William move quickly beside her, and glanced up, wondering. He still wore a hard, conflicted expression as he bent forward and lifted up the dark coil of her hair, lying over one shoulder.

Quite slowly, William untied the braid, fingering her tresses and twisting them round her head, comparing the effect from one angle and then another, while he studied her face. Alice still did not understand his mood.

"I should like you to wear blue," he said, at last. "And I like your hair when it is full and wound above your ears—you remember, like when I first met you?"

Alice softened, a tentative smile on her face. "I'd no idea how foolish I must have seemed . . ."

"You were quite perfect. Unlike anyone else I had ever seen. Like something from a dream."

"Has the dream faded?"

"You could help me, Alice." He stroked her hair; she knew he wanted her to lose herself in him.

He was waiting for her to reach up silently, touch his hands as he twisted and fondled her beautiful hair. Seduce him with compliance. But Alice recoiled with a primitive refusal to take part in this eroticism: she could not raise her hands above her shoulders, for then the baby might strangle on its own cord. Deirdre had told her of a girl in her village who was too vain not to dress her hair when she was carrying—and her baby was stillborn.

William hurt her; he smoothed her head so fiercely that she drew breath aloud.

"I'm sorry. How careless of me. Good night, Alice."

"Don't go!"

"It's no good: I've no patience. I don't understand you, Alice—you always seem remote from me."

"That's not true—I worry for the baby, can't you see that? There must be some other way to please you . . . don't you want me to care for our child?"

He glared at her. Pride stopped him from declaring his own all-encompassing need of her. Alice suddenly understood how much William hated her for making him feel unrequited, jealous, out of control in his own domain. She was meant to be his finest possession, something he could cherish and admire. In return, he hoped for physical enjoyment at will—except that she could not surrender herself to him. Only now did she see that, to William, love meant power over her. She could not find it in herself to give in. His sexual hunger repelled her.

"Caring! You're not caring! Good-night, I say!" he shouted, slamming the door.

Only William was possessed. If that was love, she should never have married him. Someone should have told her; or perhaps William was right, and she was a failure as a woman and a wife.

CHAPTER 5

1896

When Lady Evelyn next came to visit, Alice was pleased to be able to present a cheerful face. There was a physical reason: the first weeks of sickness had passed. But Alice's happiness lay in other causes: one was Ned Fielding, the other a letter Alice waved at Evelyn as she came running out to welcome her. Lady Evelyn barely had time to climb down from the carriage (Alice still had not learned that Potter the butler should open doors and usher in guests) when Alice clasped her and jumped up to give her a kiss.

"Anne and Sophie are arriving on Friday! Isn't it simply wonderful? Wait till Ned Fielding sees Anne—he won't want to paint me any more, will he, Evelyn? You tell him, do, she's going to be the beauty of the Hardys!"

Alice ran up the steps to the Great Hall, where a bearded, shabbily dressed young man stood warming himself in front of an unseasonal fire.

"Lady Evelyn, may I present Mr. Edward Fielding? Do move from the fire a little, sir; you tease me about it, and then you find it is extremely pleasant!" She turned to Evelyn:

"Mrs. Hadding disapproves of fires at this time of the year but I've always hated being cold and I make an excuse of my condition. Then, of course, no one can deny me!"

Lady Evelyn had never seen Alice look so relaxed and blooming, not even when they first met in Ireland. Was it really only a year and a half ago?

"I understand you are to paint Mrs. Wickham's portrait, Mr. Fielding. Do you progress?"

Ned smiled broadly. "Present conditions inhibit that, your ladyship. Although I suspect Mrs. Wickham was always a jack-in-the-box."

"You can judge for yourself, Evelyn—this way. Do come!"

Alice again clasped her with unusual warmth and led her to the ballroom, where Ned seemed to have set up a permanent artist's studio. An easel, two large chairs, baskets of wilting flowers and the remains of a substantial picnic lunch suggested a gypsy's encampment on one corner of the polished floor. Ned and Alice glanced at each other— perhaps it did look a little too "picturesque."

"Mr. Fielding likes the light," Alice suggested.

"But surely it doesn't face north?" Lady Evelyn inquired with a hint of disapproval.

"Ah, no, but this room is not in regular use and as the canvas will be very large, I can leave my work here between sittings. I couldn't expect Mrs. Wickham to travel to *me*," Ned added.

"Indeed not." Alice could see that Lady Evelyn was doing her best not to be charmed by Ned, although he would defeat her in the end. How could he fail? He was completely without guile, a burly, brotherly fellow, who provided the companionship she had hoped to share with William.

"Look at Mr. Fielding's likeness of me, Evelyn. I like it—I hope you do, too."

Alice turned the easel; Evelyn was impressed. In a charcoal sketch, Ned Fielding had caught Alice just as she herself always thought of her, in that moment between girlhood and maturity. The dark eyes glittered, and the thin body tensed, as if the figure wanted to spring to her feet because someone had asked her to dance.

"It's only a preliminary. He hasn't started on my commission yet." A cool voice broke in before Evelyn could praise Ned. William had appeared to welcome her.

"Good afternoon, my dear." Alice watched disappointedly as Evelyn turned away to kiss William without saying anything complimentary to Ned.

"Shouldn't you rest, Alice, before we dine?" William ordered her. "I came home early to give Ned a game of billiards. Come on, old man. Till this evening, ma'am."

William bowed to Lady Evelyn and strolled out, his arm across Ned's shoulders. William was so tall and graceful. Ned was a good few inches shorter, his ginger hair was a shambles and he bumped into the doorway as he left the room. But it was Ned who could arrange cushions behind her back to make her comfortable. William's smooth white hands never touched her kindly any more.

Alice twisted her fingers in her shawl. She did not understand William. He did not seem to mind that Ned spent hours with her; he was never jealous, yet he chose such awkward moments to assert his authority. She hardly knew what to say to Lady Evelyn. To her surprise, Evelyn grasped her hands.

"It's going to be a wonderful portrait. If William doesn't want that sketch, then you shall allow me to have it."

"Won't Mr. Fielding like Anne! Don't you agree?"

"There are different types of beauty, Alice—let's wait and see how various are Mr. Fielding's tastes."

So Ned was ordered to be present on Friday when the groom brought Anne and Sophie from the train. Alice realized, with a little horror, that it was not just tiredness that made the girls look shabby. She had become used to the wealth of her surroundings and the style of the few neighbors she had met. Now she could see both the girls for what they were: genteel, but plain-mannered. But then Anne, a lissome fourteen, pushed off her bonnet so that her reddish hair fell down her back as she rushed to kiss Alice. Over her shoulder, Alice saw Ned fold his arms across his chest—something he did when his attention was captured. She was pleased, for Anne was even more beautiful than she had remembered.

"There, I told you! Mr. Fielding, this is Anne—and Sophie. How glad I am to see you both. I've been so—oh, I've missed you. How good of you to travel so far alone."

Sophie looked apologetic. "I'm not sure who needed the chaperone more. Liverpool bewildered me—and I was dreadfully seasick crossing over." Alice was amused; no one should talk about feeling ill in company. Such indelicacy in one so delicate as Sophie was incongruous.

"I kept telling her—how'll she endure it, all the way to Africa?" Anne demanded.

"Africa, Miss?—" Ned asked.

"Miss Scott."

"The curate's daughter! Of course! Forgive me! Mission work!"

Alice saw Evelyn's eyes shine with intrigue. Perhaps she was noting how familiar Ned had become with her.

"But it isn't true, is it, Sophie? I thought you were just dreaming when you wrote it to me."

"Well, there's nothing definitely arranged, but my father has agreed, if a position is ever offered . . ."

Alice felt earthbound. With her own particular worries, she had forgotten all about the wide world beyond Upton. Once again she resented the life inside her.

Anne laughed, and looked so knowingly at Alice that it was obtrusive. Alice was no longer accustomed to her closeness.

"You're picturing palaces, tribal princes offering Sophie priceless jewels!" Anne teased. "I know you are!"

"My dear young ladies, I'm sure you'd like to see your rooms. Potter—the bags—" Lady Evelyn soothed them before childish sisterly feelings stirred too strongly.

Ned watched, leaning against the fireplace in his usual spot as the little group progressed to the stairs. Lady Evelyn, in command, gave orders to Potter and Mrs. Hadding, for Alice was far too excited by her guests to bother. Anne was half listening to her sister's chatter, while bending over her hat boxes and darting him dark-eyed glances, bold but innocent coquetry. At least, he hoped it was. Sophie was trying to be ladylike and to keep her eyes fixed on the staircase, but curiosity and awe at her surroundings made her trip on the first step. As the three young women went up, arm in arm, it was Alice's turn to look back at him, her pale face unusually flushed with pleasure.

"Will you walk with us in the park?"

"Wouldn't you prefer to be alone?" Ned was conscious of Lady Evelyn hovering in the archway below the staircase.

"Not yet. We've plenty of time for that." Alice wanted him to understand, to help her keep up the pretense, just for a little while, that her life was perfect. She had great pride. She stood above him, motionless, pleading silently.

"I'm pleased to dance attendance on you, then. What man wouldn't be?"

Lady Evelyn moved like a shadow into the Chinese room, and the girls' high voices floated away along the gallery upstairs.

◆　◆　◆

When William next returned home two days later, he found the ballroom not only littered with Ned's paints, but with a pile of dresses and sewing paraphernalia. Indifference turned to irritation. Life with Alice was not at all what he expected. He could not bear the atmosphere of womanly activity that was invading his beautiful house. First there had been the business of the nursery, now the upheaval of these unwelcome intruders from Ireland. His home was hardly his own any more. He had already put a stop to Alice's plans to replant part of his spinney with a "wild garden." *His* forests were for pheasants, not for her to wander in like some Marie Antoinette. This was his predicament: he either stayed at Upton to control Alice and be driven mad with domesticity, or he took his pleasures elsewhere and left his precious home to be transformed.

William stood on the garden terrace, beyond the ballroom. Shading his eyes, he could see Anne and Ned on horseback galloping toward Upton across the water meadow. Sophie, Alice and Lady Evelyn walked back more sedately from the lake. William felt lonely, excluded from this company. He liked the idea of intimacy with Alice—he had imagined she would inspire his every thought—but "wife" was not "Woman," that magical erotic presence he had wanted to keep all to himself in his house. He still loved Alice intensely in that role of "Woman." Perhaps too much.

The party joined him on the terrace, and one of the grooms led away the horses.

"What's the meaning of all that?" William pointed to the disorder in the ballroom. He did not mean to sound unfriendly, but his thoughts prompted an abrupt tone of voice.

Anne, impervious to his manner, shrieked like any kitchen maid at Carrigrohane.

"Didn't we spend all morning letting down Alice's hems? She's grown a full inch taller since she left home!"

William felt spectacularly foolish to have a wife who had outgrown her trousseau.

"But—how unnecessary! You should order new gowns from London, Alice. What possessed you to be so—so *frugal*?"

Alice faltered. "I'm sorry, I didn't mean . . ."

"It will be all over the estate!" William muttered. "Think of your position—think of the servants!!"

"William, please—" Alice indicated Ned and Sophie, who were trying not to listen and were discussing the landscape "views" most earnestly.

"Why not take Alice up to London, William?" Lady Evelyn intervened. "I don't believe she's visited since she arrived. You've never accepted our invitations, at least."

"I can't possibly do that." He was adamant.

"Oh, why not?" Alice asked. "I know I've been unwell, but I'm so much stronger now."

"You have your guests. And you are in no condition for a journey."

Alice looked down at her rounding belly. William hated her pregnancy. How ironic—she hated it as much as he did, except for one thing: it meant William never came near her bedroom.

◆ ◆ ◆

"How much longer will they stay?" William asked. He had summoned her to the library after dinner to convey his disapproval. Alice heard a colder note entering his voice: more hostility than before. "Anne and Sophie have been here for four weeks. Time enough. Your lying-in could happen soon."

"Oh? The days have passed so quickly." she answered feebly.

"Evelyn's been back in London for over two weeks. Surely you must realize that I prefer your company alone, in my house, sometimes at least?"

"But you've been absent since last Sunday!"

"Of course I have! I have an estate to manage! Business affairs! And besides, the conversation of a trainee missionary and an impudent child are not to my taste!"

"That's neither accurate nor kind! Ned finds them both amusing—as do many of my friends!"

"Oh, yes—the Crawshays. Daisy Panton . . ." He tried to sneer, but in secret William was surprised at Alice's friendships. The Crawshays had distinction; they were an old local family full of "country good will." The Pantons were wealthy, sophisticated people with whom he had an acquaintanceship but who were much more attentive to Alice.

"Half of them are Ned's friends, not yours. He's the ladies' man. He's the sort of fellow—what d'ye call them? 'Darlings'—who prefer to play cards in the drawing room while the rest go hunting . . ."

Alice had no idea what he meant, except that he insulted her friend.

"You introduced him to me. I trust that anyone my husband presents to me is a suitable companion?"

"Take care, Alice. My patience isn't limitless."

"But what have I done? It isn't in truth that you dislike Anne or Sophie. Won't you talk to me, explain my failings? I'll try to make amends . . ."

Alice blushed as she spoke—William colored as he heard her, but neither of them dared to confront the truth.

"Do as you are bid, then, madam."

"I can't send Sophie or Anne home! I may never see Sophie again. . . . She's going so far away." Alice's voice trembled.

"No theatricals, please. Good-night, Alice."

William reached for a decanter on the sideboard and Alice was meant to be dismissed. He looked so angry, yet puzzled too. Alice hesitated. She studied his bare long neck as he leant forward. His soft brown hair was too tightly trimmed, still like a young recruit's.

"William—will you stay with me tonight?" He gulped his brandy, looked vacantly at her for a moment, then shook his head. Alice turned away, went to her room and fell asleep, tired of feeling sad.

◆　◆　◆

In the morning, William left early to go shooting. Alice breakfasted alone, for Sophie was in her room and her sister always liked to ride before the dew left the meadows. But today Anne appeared, still in her riding habit, while Alice was at the table.

"Is anything wrong?" Alice detected her embarrassment.

"The stables are locked. The groom says it's his orders."

Knowing what William intended, Alice took only an instant to invent an excuse.

"Oh, yes, that's true, the veterinary doctor comes today. I completely forgot."

"Oh." Anne looked relieved. They both knew what was happening, but neither wanted to speak of it. What good would it do?

"Ned will be here shortly for my final sitting. Will you sit with me, or shall you read?"

"Sophie's going to hear me speeches." Anne was having elocution lessons in Cork to get rid of her local accent. Alice considered her sister's poor pronunciation to be a deliberate act of provocation. When alone and confiding, Anne would revert to her naturally inflected voice.

"You're up to some mischief, I know it!"

Anne attempted innocence. "Not a thing. I assure you." She studied herself in the long mirror behind the tea things.

"Mm, well, I hope you'll tell me, when the time comes."

"When I'm certain, when I know it's not just dreams."

"Oh, do tell me now, please Anne! Let's have a secret to keep . . ."

"I'm going to be an actress," Anne announced.

"Grandma Hardy would die first!"

"You wouldn't tell, would you?" Anne had spoken so fiercely that Alice almost thought she might.

Alice shook her head. "I wouldn't do that, you know I wouldn't, but all the same, this must be just a girlish notion!"

"No, it's not!"

"Yes, it is! It's not at all the occupation for a lady!"

"What is, then, Alice? All this?" Anne waved her riding crop about rather wildly.

Without a word, Alice put her teacup down slowly, and stared into it. Anne regretted her words instantly.

"All I meant was—was—I couldn't do it as well as you do, Alice."

Alice looked up, and Anne saw disappointment and misery in her face just for a moment.

"I'll ring for some more tea." Alice said. "Do you mind if I just pick some flowers, before Ned arrives?"

She left Anne alone to consider the unpleasant consequences of challenging a grown-up sister's decisions in life.

When Ned came, he would not hear of work—Alice looked far too tired. Instead he rode over to the Crawshay sisters, who lived on the other side of Upton village. There he extracted an invitation to lunch and croquet, came back with the hostesses' little Victoria carriage, and drove Alice, Anne and Sophie away in it for the rest of the day.

William came back to an empty house. He was instantly ashamed of his pettiness in locking up all the horses. Evidently the gesture had not succeeded in causing any inconvenience. He stumped through the ordered splendor of the rooms (for Alice was careful now not to give any further cause for criticism) until he stood by Ned's near-finished portrait.

There Alice sat, calm and remote, by an open window, utterly at peace. Beyond her, through the opening, the vibrant colors of the hunt meet presented a noble contrast to her repose. William liked the painting so much that he wondered if, after all, he could still love Alice.

◆   ◆   ◆

"Good-bye. Write to me, Sophie dear."

Six precious weeks, and now they were leaving. The strain of defying William was too much for Alice. She was also on the verge of confessing everything to Anne, but it would do no good at all. Anne was not old enough to understand the real reasons, and Alice's deepest wish was for no hint of any problems to be taken back to Carrigrohane.

"Good-bye, Alice. I do miss you so. I'm so dull without you." Sophie, pale-faced and quiet as always, stood waiting by her side for Anne to come out to the carriage.

"You're so good!" Alice repeated. She had learnt just how valuable Sophie's quiet loving presence was only when she did not have it. "You will tell me when you go away won't you? I shall worry . . ."

"Oh, I won't be allowed to go for years yet. And besides, if God does ever send me, He'll look after me wherever I go." It seemed a matter of fact to Sophie.

"Your God is much kinder than the one I know," Alice commented irreverently.

"How can you say such things? When you have everything—and a baby to be born so soon!"

Alice shook her head, so that Sophie should think it was just a frivolous remark. She really wanted to scream about her terror at the birth, about her hatred of William's possessiveness. But Sophie was reticent, as she had always been. The memory of the violence at Carrigrohane still lay between them.

The carriage was brought round, and Anne hurried out with William, who had offered to take the girls to the ferry.

"I can't find my boater. Grandma will be cross."

"I put it in the basket already—don't you remember?" Sophie reminded her.

Anne clung to her sister, then drew back awkwardly. She had felt Alice's stomach against her in their embrace.

Alice pulled her shawl across the bulge. "Silly girl. Kiss me again."

William stood by the carriage, waiting for the travelers. "We must go. Give me your arm, Miss Scott."

Now that he saw Alice's unhappiness at parting from her visitors, he felt desperately sorry for his selfishness. Alice had a rare talent for making him feel guilty.

"I'll be back early tomorrow evening," he promised. "I'll bring you some books."

"French novels!" Anne suggested, then the carriage moved off, and Alice stood waving until she could not even hear the horses' hooves.

◆　◆　◆

"Nurse! Nurse! Where will the baby be born from?" Alice clutched the woman's arm as another terrifying pain twisted up through her belly.

"Lord! I've been visiting you all these months and you never asked me nothing! Bit late now, isn't it, Madam?" Hodge, the nurse, looked irritated to have to be direct—there was no time to find a discreet phrase. "From the same place where the master put it in!"

Alice was so shocked she forgot the pains.

"Here's Doctor Briggs." The nurse looked relieved to see him, and stood up to give him a nod of respect. He hurried past her, dropping his bag on a chair and not even bothering to remove his coat.

"Damned difficult. Any other night but this. Lift the bedding, nurse."

"What are you going to do?" Alice whispered. Sweat plastered the hair to her head and the nightshirt to her chest.

"I'm just going to see how near the world this infant is. Pardon me, Mrs. Wickham. What I'm going to do is necessary. I hope it doesn't distress you too much."

Unidentifiable sensations of injury spread upward into Alice. She shrieked as the doctor groped inside her. The nurse pressed on her stomach when Dr. Briggs ordered it. Alice felt as if the whole part of herself between her legs was going to explode outward, tearing her very self to shreds. Then, during a very strong surge of griping force, the doctor cut into her flesh. She screamed loudly.

"You shouldn't feel it—try not to flinch, Mrs. Wickham," the doctor said.

"Don't do it again! Don't do it again!"

"I hope it won't be necessary. Now, help us."

"Oh, what do you mean?" she wailed.

"Oh, good lord, Madam, do what it feels like—push!"

Alice pushed and pushed, but all that happened was a straining of the muscles in her arms, neck and face. Then Dr. Briggs began to suffocate her with a thick cloth. She could not struggle because the nurse had pinioned her legs. Again a pain, again, again, again . . .

Through a haze, she sensed the doctor's huge fingers working in her insides like red-hot pokers scraping round a burning furnace. And then suddenly, a sensation so urgent and dire that she thought she would remember it forever—Alice could only think of a cannonball roaring through her flesh.

"The head! It's done!"

Alice fainted. She drifted then, somewhere between consciousness and oblivion. She began to focus herself, and was able to see for a moment, a bundle of white linen held against the nurse's ample chest, with a fragile, puckered face inside it—an animal kind of life. But then she floated away, for hours or days—she could not tell how long. Her body caught fire. Her limbs shook. She poured sweat so that she seemed to lie on a bed of liquid.

◆　◆　◆

William and Ned Fielding stood in front of Alice's portrait in the Great Hall. Two days ago, a baby girl had been delivered with comparative ease due to Dr. Briggs' use of chloroform. But Alice was now dangerously ill: puerperal fever or milk fever was suspected. Dr. Briggs was noncommital about the outcome of the night. Puerperal fever was usually fatal. If it was the milder version, milk fever, Alice might survive.

"Look at her now, Ned, in the evening sun." William stood dreaming before Alice's image, as if the drama upstairs was happening to someone else.

"I never understood till now why you wanted me to paint her like that when she was pregnant." Ned looked at the sylphlike form of Alice, which he had had to paint from imagination, ignoring her condition.

"You wanted to remember her as she was—isn't that it?" Ned spoke with bitterness. His understanding of Alice and William's relationship had become clearer in the past few days, during the crisis of the birth.

William turned stiffly, not acknowledging Ned's remark.

"I believe she'll recover. Alice has great will."

Ned was about to comment on the irony in William's remark when a clattering of hooves made them both turn to the window. Mud-spattered and excited, Daisy Panton was reining in her horse and untying a large bundle from her saddle. She swung effortlessly to the ground and within seconds was striding into the hall.

"Mr. Wickham! Delighted with the news! Can I see her?"

Daisy nodded a gracious hello to Ned, making formal introductions superfluous. William was amused that a sixth sense had informed Mrs. Panton that Ned was a poverty-stricken nobody, possibly a tenant carpeted for some negligent act, so that she could safely ignore him. He experienced a particular satisfaction in seeing a woman who cam-paigned so vigorously for the Suffragettes in London revert to age-old hierarchical customs in the countryside.

"My wife is not well, Mrs. Panton. The doctor is a little concerned."

Hearing this cool description, Ned unwittingly confirmed Daisy's judgment by fumbling for his hat and rushing for the door. She was not to know that disgust mounting to rage made him leave so abruptly.

"Darling girl, how dreadful!" Daisy exclaimed. "She simply must pull through! Have you any idea what a little gem you have, Mr. Wickham—what a charming and sweet child your wife is? She has quite made the summer for me here!" Tears came to Daisy's eyes, and she thrust her bundle toward him.

"I must go; it's too distressing my being here at such a worrying time. My condolences, and do accept these—"

She fled, causing ripples in the air as if it were water, and she a muscular swimmer plunging through it. He opened the parcel. William was impressed but also intimidated by this evidence of great friendship. What on earth did a woman as rich and distinguished as Daisy Panton see in his simple Irish wife? Even as William thought it, shame made him reflect. It had all gone wrong between him and Alice, but she was still an unusual, affectionate person.

Hothouse lilies, gardenias and orchids, wrapped in damp linen: how typically extravagant of Daisy Panton. A smell of horse sweat and leather mingled with the fine scents.

How could he dwell on these things, when Alice might be dying? William did not believe it was possible she would die, and rejected

Ned's fears. Alice was as strong as—a peasant—he did believe she was. Dr. Briggs came down the stairs, and gestured to William that he would take his leave.

"I've done what I can for her. Tonight will see the illness reach its crisis. I regret that this has happened—in cases of emotional instability, however, it is often the way."

"What do you mean, sir?" William was quick to sense that Dr. Briggs was exonerating himself.

"A pregnant woman must at all times consider her child. Her condition is precarious—any shock or depressive state of mind can lead to an outbreak of infection, in the infant or in the mother. I question merely whether this could be the cause—was Mrs. Wickham prone to unhealthy nervousness, or to obsessive tendencies, during her pregnancy?"

William wondered if her constant desire for his company but not his favors could be construed as obsessive. He was in doubt, but finally shook his head. Her dissatisfaction with him . . . he felt too confused to lay the blame for that on Alice, to attribute her illness to it.

"No, Dr. Briggs. Alice is a remarkably vigorous and healthy person."

If Dr. Briggs noted a hint of ambiguity in William's reply, he thought it best to reserve his comment for a later time.

"I shall call again in the morning. I must see to another patient in the next few hours."

William did not care what birth or death or dread disease Dr. Briggs went into the night to attend. He closed the door, and saw Ned, who had come in from his agitated turn in the garden, and was impatiently waiting at a little distance for news.

"She's recovering. Dr. Briggs just told me so. Let's have supper, and I'll send you home later in my carriage."

But Ned preferred to walk to his lodgings in Upton village. William dined alone, surrounded by his hunting prints and his French girandoles. The candlelight flickered on the plain gray walls. William stayed at the table for many hours, drinking his brandy and smoking several cigars. His mother had died in this house, after a long illness. He had been so pleased to return to his inheritance, after so many years away. Now the house was infected again, as his childhood was.

◆ ◆ ◆

In the morning light, Alice lay quite still, peaceful at last now that the feverish pain had lost its grip on her limbs and her stomach did not hurt so much. For two days and nights every part of her had ached and shaken, and she had poured sweat from every particle of her skin. The nurse wiped her face with eau de Cologne. Once, another hand had done that when she was hot, and in a strange bed. So strange. The silken damask was gone, the bed reduced to plain linen sheets and covers. Once there had been little daisy eyelets that just fitted her fingers. Mama! Louise!

Her body had been torn apart, emptied out. Now she was separated. Alice rolled over to a more protective position, and rested her face on her two hands, palms together under her cheek. Her mother must have given birth to her with all the pain that she had just endured. She hated Louise for failing her, and then, as quickly, loved her for giving her life. But Alice thought that she herself would never, never desert her child as her own mother had left her. It all came back to her with an overwhelming force. She would never forgive Louise. She would never leave her baby, Laura. Nor William. It was only his inexperience, his loneliness that made him so difficult. She would have to learn to be more patient, more inviting . . .

She heard him slip into the room.

"William." In her own ears her voice sounded unusually low, not girlish as it had been.

"My dear! You're better—Dr. Briggs assures me that the worst is over."

He tried to keep the gravity of her illness from her. The strain of labor had left Alice's face swollen, with red blotches all over it. Moon-faced, with broken blood vessels, she looked like a drunken harridan after a fight. The nurse said it would subside—but no sooner had that happened than Alice succumbed to the fever. Every detail of her suffering made William recoil. He felt ashamed of himself, but there was no denying the strength of his repulsion.

"William. I'm sorry. I'm not what you wanted, tell me truly—am I? I will try to change. It all seems so clear; where we went wrong."

"Don't talk now, Alice. It's not good for you to be upset. I love you dearly—I always will." It was nearly the truth.

"How's my baby? Laura? Is she well?"

She could tell that William had not bothered to see the child since its birth. Yet he had wanted her named after his own mother.

"Well, quite well. Sound asleep—as you should be, my darling."

"I wish I could see her."

"We'll wait until Dr. Briggs returns. Wait and see what he advises.

Now rest, my dear. You've been rather ill, but thanks to God, you've been spared."

"I never heard you utter a prayer, William. It seems so strange. Was I as ill as all that? I didn't know."

He looked vexed. She was reviving, becoming interested in her own drama.

"I do pray. Often. There are many things about me that you don't know, or understand."

"But I've been spared to live my time with you, William, and I swear, I will try! I do promise to do better, for you and the child."

"Don't talk any more. You'll tire yourself, Alice, it will do you no good. I'd better leave you to rest. Good-bye, Alice, and God bless you."

William stumbled from the room. He did not know if he was crying in guilt over Alice's reprieve, or for all the years of unhappiness to come.

◆　◆　◆

Several months later, Alice was undressing in her bedroom. Fully recovered, she had had one of her well-planned days. She had spent the morning in battle for supremacy with the housekeeper, Mrs. Hadding, the afternoon riding with Ned and Sarah Crawshay, and taken tea in the nursery with her darling child. Mrs. Hadding, in the midst of defending her position, had informed her of William's return—he had been shooting for several weeks in the border country with the Duke of Buccleuch. Some instinct warned her that the long-dreaded confrontation might occur that night, and she was ready for William to make his appearance in her room.

It wasn't that she did not love him. She did, when she could, but it was as if a veil of insubstantiality had parted between her eyes and her view of the world. She didn't know much about life, but she knew about truth. Her grandmaman had loved her—she could start from that. Her mother had loved her father, and he had returned that affection. Grandma Hardy had—cared, and cared deeply, strongly, with her own brand of conviction, limiting, almost crippling her with its narrowness. Anne . . . Alice wanted to see her sister again, more than anyone else in the world. When all this was settled, she would ask her to come, very soon, to revel in Laura's babyhood.

◆　◆　◆

When William came to her room, that night, he thought she looked unusually pretty and calm, lying back on the bed. Quite her old self again. Was it possible she could be what he wanted, after all, now that he had given her a child? William came closer, expecting her to reject him after the long months of separation and illness. Yet she seemed as accepting and passive as he had ever wished. William's confused, old passion for her returned with force. Neither of them made a sound as he stripped and lay beside her, trembling as he used to.

"Alice," he murmured, "tell me I have the right to approach you now, after all this time apart . . ."

"I'm your wife, William. I'm duty bound, in love."

William lay on top of her, and roughly pulled up her nightdress. He could not help himself. No soft caresses of her skin, a desperate longing to possess her made him push into her at once. With a heartfelt sigh of lust, he moved deliberately in and out. Alice looked up at him with deep, calm eyes, exactly as he had imagined her once, pure, yet accepting.

William stopped. He withdrew in a fury, his penis turning limp. He pulled back the covers, and pushing his hand between her legs, searched for the telltale thread.

"You've got a goddamned sponge in there!" he shouted. He yanked the object out of her, and held it up in the moonlight.

"You're a whore! How dare you commit such a filthy act!"

Alice was unmoved by his fury. Worse still, she began to laugh.

"William! Put it down! You're making yourself look ridiculous!"

Limp in the shadows, shoulders humped in rage, he was a travesty of a classic statue, his trophy dangling from his hand.

"What is the meaning of this? Dr. Briggs was right—you indulge in unnatural acts! No wonder you were sick!"

Alice sat up abruptly, her manner changed, her voice cold and forthright.

"Dr. Briggs himself brought me that infection on his own person. If I had had a midwife as I wanted, I might have been in cleaner hands. Hodge the nursemaid showed me how to protect myself. The sponge only has quinine on it—it's quite safe. I don't want another baby yet. If I'm to be your wife—and I will try—then at least allow me that right."

It was the longest argued speech he had ever heard her make. No muse now—a harpy.

"Nothing of the sort. Only common whores, horsebreakers, indulge in such commodities. I know what I'm talking about!"

"Do you, William? Then you should be well pleased!"

"Don't speak to me like that! Such impudence, such accusations—you're meant to be my *wife*, not my mistress!"

"I would be your wife, if you had any notion how to make me one!"

"Are you sure it's not your own duplicity that makes you unfit for the part?"

William snatched up his clothes, and dressed hurriedly.

"If you persist in using these degrading objects, contrary to the spirit and intention of all marriage, I shall not consider you my partner—in any sense of the word."

Alice watched him leave the room with no weakening of her determination. He did not want a baby, yet he could not bear the fact that she was withholding herself even to this degree from him. He insisted on owning her exclusively. Perhaps she was terrified of giving herself to a man . . . anyone she had ever loved had gone: her father, her mother, grandmaman. Was William right to say she was deceiving herself? Grandma Hardy had told her she was strong. She would test her judgment now, on a most challenging path.

CHAPTER 6

1 8 9 6

*I*t was an irony to Alice that she was living a lie just when she had discovered the truth. A whole year had passed since Laura's birth, and she had learned how to present the image of a devoted wife to the outside world. But William found her impossible to love. He could not remove her from Upton, nor could he leave it entirely himself. Something always held him to the business on the estate: there were budgets to approve for new fencing, the reroofing of cottages and the upkeep of his stables to occupy him. But the reasons became less imperative as the months went by. Alice and William led separate lives, their paths hardly ever crossing. In the mornings, Alice breakfasted with Laura in her room, wrote letters or battled with Mrs. Hadding over household arrangements. At lunch, Ned Fielding or one of the two Crawshays, Lady Mary or her younger sister Sarah, kept her company. Lady Mary introduced her to local village life, took her on outings where she performed her "good works," and helped her to develop a sense of place in Upton. On other days, Daisy Panton would ride over without warning. She always looked vigorous, full of life, reining in a fine horse that trembled from head to toe with the pleasure of being exercised. Daisy would insist on Alice joining her, and set off at a canter with no allowance for Alice's lack of horsemanship, shouting blunt instructions about her riding style. After a fast stretch, they would plod along the bridlepaths, and Daisy would gossip. Alice began to glimpse the other side of Daisy's life—her "amours" and her dabblings in suffragism in London. She thought herself dull and simple compared with her new friend: Daisy was not only a large body but a large spirit, too, and made her feel very young.

On market days, Alice drove to Upton by carriage, making small purchases just for the pleasure of watching the world go by. Whole cheeses lay piled on sacks at one end of the street; strong-armed women tossed baskets of potatoes or carrots onto canvas cloths laid out on the cobbles. Local farmers suspiciously eyed the sheep penned in small squares at the other end of the way.

On "Statute Day" or Martinmas she watched the laborers lined up in their best suits, giving a proud look at the men who would take them on to work for the next twelve months. Each wore a token to show their trade: the shepherd a whisp of wool, the carter, a piece of whipcord, the cowman a plaited straw. When an arrangement was made, they removed the "favor" from their buttonholes and stuck it into their caps, under their ears or in a pocket flap, as a sign that they were bought. Then the men sauntered through the streets to find their womenfolk, and to drink to their new prospects on the "hence money" or shilling given them by the farmer as a sign of good intent. Some of the sweethearts were servant girls who had put themselves up for auction in the same way. After the day's hiring, the couples would dance to a fiddle in the street, throw coconuts at shies and buy gingerbread or trinkets from the stalls.

Even though the men leered in crude fashion at their favorites, and were seen off by the most handsome, Alice watched these ritual exchanges with envy for the freedom in them. But she did not sentimentalize for long. Lady Mary was on the Board of Guardians at the local Workhouse. Alice soon discovered that these stalwart boys, their thick hair wetted down, and showing off their strong muscles, might turn into gaunt, bent old men, enfeebled with labor, supping toothless on porridge. And the girls might die in childbirth, as she had nearly done, if a pox or consumption did not carry them off first. Rural unemployment was nowhere near the starving tragedy she had been kept from in Ireland, but discreetly urgent, a well-oiled vise tightening its grip with precision. The drift away to the iron-ore mining in Northampton was only an option for those who could give up country ways and endure the filth of the towns.

That was how life was, she had found out. Underneath the energy and the hope lay a mass of dry bones, white as the stones these boys would labor to draw to the edges of each field. In her confrontation with the rawness of life, Alice became obsessed with cruelty as well as with happiness.

Sometimes she longed for the cramping security of Carrigrohane. Anne wrote often, and wanted to return to Upton Park, but Alice made excuses, afraid that she would see even more clearly what was wrong and reveal her circumstances to their grandparents. Alice's pride held her back from such a fall.

It could not last, this artificial life, with no communication, no anger, no attempt to make it better or worse. William might be satisfied with keeping up appearances for his friends' sakes, behaving with ostentatious politeness in front of the servants. But Alice wanted more out of life. Ned Fielding agreed with her. He had started on another portrait, not a commission, but for his own pleasure: an iconic image of Alice with her child. His devotion was evident in every line, every brush of color on the canvas. He began by painting the surface entirely red, so that the whiteness of her complexion had a warmth behind it. For the background he chose the Chinese wallpaper of her sitting room. The ornate formality of its ceremonial figures under the twisting branches of the plum tree gave Alice a distant, precious look.

Alice sat alone for him while Laura was taken out in the bassinet by the nursemaid Hodge. Ned was finishing the outline of Alice's head, smooth black hair drawn up from the lace at her neck. He saw she twisted her hands nervously, apparently thinking he would not notice.

"When does Lady Evelyn arrive?" he asked.

"Tomorrow. About noon, I think."

"And William? Any news of him?"

"His last letter was postmarked the Isle of Wight. I imagine he will return at the end of the regatta."

"Foxes, pheasants, guns and boats—is there no end to his craving for physical fun?"

"These are the perfectly normal pursuits of a gentleman."

"You don't have to pretend to me, dearest lady. I've spent too many evenings with William in the library, watching him drink brandy till the cigar falls from his fingers. A good brandy and a cigar are the perquisites of a gentleman, too. It all depends how you choose to use 'em."

"I'm not pretending anything. William has made his choice . . . other men live otherwise. What am I to do? I have no control over him." She got up, moving about the room restlessly. Ned was quite unlike other people she had met. He was the son of a prosperous yeoman farmer, whose natural talent brought him many patrons among the landed gentry. She liked his independence; he did not care what anyone thought of him, and was never diminished by being short of money. In Alice's circle, wealth had always been counted a moral virtue, and she was beginning to discover how wrong that was.

"Hypocrisy! A man behaves like a boor and his wife feels responsible for him! You're as bad as all the rest—you treat the bounder like an absolute child!"

She knew it was not "done" to discuss her private life with another man—but Ned was different, a devoted friend, and she wished there was no harm in it. For a moment she was tempted to confess everything.

"Ned, don't talk so. It doesn't help me, you know. Put it aside—let's go into the garden. Wait, let me look first."

Alice came to stand by him. She was learning a great deal from Ned, and he found her an apt pupil.

"Look, Ned, this green."

Alice dipped a brush into a corner of his chaotic palette. Ned was profligate with paint: he mixed great coils of color into multicolored spirals, like tropical seashells. Alice dabbed a patch of color onto the back of her hand. "You see? How well this jade looks with gold!" Her bracelet fell forward over her wrist. "It's not a green in nature, at all, is it? An *expensive* green!"

"You have an instinctive sense of color," he remarked. "What would you put with that red?"

"A mauve. Like the fuchsias in the glasshouse."

"Or better, this orange, like a lily?" he asked.

"No. I think the red is too blue for that."

"You know best then, Madam."

She laughed, rubbing her hand with a linseed rag, sniffing it with relish. "I just love the smell. Come into the garden now."

They skirted the yew hedges and she took him her private way, past the door to the kitchen garden, down past the south face of the house, over the gentle slope of land between birch trees to the ornamental lake at the end of the lawn. Beyond, in the long meadow, catching sight of them, cows raised their heads, buttercups dangling from their slow-moving jaws.

Alice knew she was fortunate—in a special class. Her privileged existence should have been a blessing, not a prison sentence. Unhappiness was forcing her to compare her lot with others.

"I went to the Union House with Lady Mary and Sarah," she told Ned.

"How strange you are to tell me now, amidst such an idyllic, pastoral scene. You're an odd creature, Alice."

"It was frightful. Do you know, Ned, the warden told me that for every four old villagers who can manage, there is always one who is a pauper."

He shrugged his shoulders. "Did you take flowers to cheer them up?"

"It *is* offensive to patronize, if that is what you're suggesting," she replied. "But I don't see why their lives should be made so ugly."

"To deter people from entering."

"They're helpless—sick; they have no relatives. They already suffer. They have a communal tub where the new ones are stripped and scrubbed when they come in. The helpers walk among them, jangling those fat bunches of keys. It's a prison. There's no kindness or goodwill in the place."

Ned wondered if Alice intended "good works" to take the place of personal happiness. He had seen this happen to many women before. It did not always prove beneficial to the poor.

"Luckily it's small. They've no more than thirty people in the place," she continued.

"Luckily? Why?"

"Because it won't be difficult to economize on my allowance and provide them with their own proper clothes. To me that's one of the worst things. They were laboring, decent people, most of them. They've worn work clothes all their lives, and never once looked as ugly as they do now in those ill-fitting cast-offs. It's an affront to them."

"It's kind of you, Alice. I don't deny your good intentions, but don't you see, it's often much worse? Upton only has to deal with a small population, the rural poor. They're simple old souls, as a rule. Imagine the workhouses where the young, not yet depraved, are housed with broken families, adult drunkards, as well as the very old and senile. Imagine the scenes . . ."

"I can't, Ned." She shook her head in apology. "I don't know much about other people's lives. You can't expect me to learn all about the world at once."

"My dear, I didn't mean to sound critical. Far from it. I'm no rabid radical. I leave that to your famous Mr. Shaw. In fact, I place no hope in politics."

"Well, I count that a deficiency in myself, too. But I must start somewhere. I don't have many talents, or much experience. I don't even have the spirit for broader actions."

"You think too little of what you are."

"I know very well what I am, Ned." Alice laughed, an old, disillusioned sound. "I'm a complete innocent, faced with my first real challenge. My life may not be perfectly happy, but I shall have to make the best of it."

They walked back to the house together. The double windows in the ballroom were opened wide above the stone steps leading onto the lawn. As Alice walked in, she explained her plans in more detail to Ned, holding his arm. Occasionally she tapped him with her small fist for emphasis. Ned was saddened to see a girl, barely twenty, striving so seriously to come to terms with a failed marriage. The plunge from virginal innocence to responsibility was always precipitous.

When Lady Evelyn arrived next day, Alice was well rehearsed. She meant to impress William's foster-mother with her new sense of direction, her lack of self-absorption or "nerves." That would give less credibility to William's accusations, when they came, and she sensed they were not far off.

They took tea in the Chinese room, after Lady Evelyn had rested, and Alice explained her plans to help the villagers.

"I'm going to set up a sewing class; I shall call it a 'Dorcas Society.' I shall collect donations of old suits, and I'll teach the village girls how to make them over. Heaven knows, I have had to do that for myself often enough! And we can make shirts and underclothes. The old people can at least be given linen that's fresh, not that horrid coarse gray stuff."

Lady Evelyn was pleased. "I think it's a very laudable plan. It won't involve much expense, and it may give the girls a chance to learn a trade. Not all of them want to go into service these days, and now there's much less for them to do on farms."

"Why is that?"

"Don't you ever discuss these things with William? I'm surprised you're not more familiar with estate matters. It's because of the machines. Where *is* William, by the way? I do hope to catch a glimpse of him this time."

Alice flushed slightly. "He's at Cowes. I couldn't leave Laura on her own in the nursery—besides, the summer here has been glorious."

"Alice, forgive me if I intrude when I ask—was that wise? You shouldn't neglect your wifely duties for your child."

"William didn't ask me to go with him."

"Is everything as it should be between you and William?"

"I don't please him, as a wife. I don't think he loves me—not now, not in a way that I can understand or return."

"Love!" Lady Evelyn straightened her back, unconsciously adopting a defensive pose. "To be honest, very few well-regulated minds, how shall I say, succumb to that emotion. It's written about in books, of course . . . cheap romantic novels. But women, unlike men, can't choose what you could call their course of action."

Now Alice understood Lady Evelyn. It was perfectly clear to her that she was meant to submit to William's opinions on every issue, including the sexual. She just had to use her wits to make her situation endurable.

"I told you before, there are compensations," Lady Evelyn reminded her. "You have a beautiful home, your darling Laura, and I can see you intend to make yourself useful. That's the spirit! But don't be too neglectful of your duties as a wife. Remember, you can't build a partnership on infatuation."

"But Evelyn, when we married, there were other words. Not 'love'—perhaps you're right. I find all that an enigma, really. 'Obey'— yes, I will have to do that. I'm powerless. But the word I think of is 'cherish'—I don't think I can live without ever being understood . . . and I believe that William keeps to that other word, 'honor' only in the letter, not the spirit. He will honor our agreement, but he won't live with me or care for me."

Lady Evelyn had been turning to stone as Alice spoke.

"A distant husband is not always a tragedy." she said, each word enunciated without discernible emotion.

Alice did not notice the change in her companion. "Oh yes," she hurried on, "I'm sure he will be discreet . . . but what about me? When he returns, he avoids my accusations by attacking me. He says I'm cold, unyielding, that I strike a superior note . . ."

"Do you?" Lady Evelyn suddenly accused her.

Alice's nerve failed her. She did not dare tell Lady Evelyn the truth about her precautions and William's attitude. Perhaps, as Evelyn had never borne a child, she would not understand her circumstances. She might even agree that William was entitled to react as he did.

"You have less to fear than women did when I was a girl," Lady Evelyn persisted, somehow sensing the heart of the matter. "Good heavens, it's only been illegal in the last ten years for a man to rape his wife."

Alice looked shocked at the word. "You mean, women were forced to do it?"

Lady Evelyn had set her trap. "So you *do* refuse."

"No! Not exactly . . ."

"Beware, Alice, you have a lot to lose. Use your head, not your heart, in these matters. You have a duty. Now," she said, changing the subject, "that Pandora's box has to be shut tight again quickly! Take me to the nursery. I long to see my one and only grandchild!"

Alice felt so oppressed by Lady Evelyn's attitude that she let the matter drop and meekly followed her to the nursery. They both played with Laura, avoiding each other's eyes, taking turns to hold the child as she struggled to walk a few steps across the floor. Like Alice, Laura was a small creature, with perfect, fine features. For a moment Alice's spirits lifted. Whatever else William had failed to do, he had provided her with one joy.

Downstairs, Mrs. Hadding was about to take tea in her own parlor when the bell rang. She bridled at Alice's ignorance, to summon a housekeeper at such an hour, but straightening her lace cap, she moved confidently through the stone corridors, her sphere of influence below stairs. Alice was writing in the Chinese room.

"Oh, Mrs. Hadding. Please forgive me for interrupting your afternoon. I have an unusual request, however. Your sister from Upton is about to arrive, isn't she?"

How did Alice know that? Mrs. Hadding was disconcerted. Of course she had a perfect right to entertain her own family on a Sunday afternoon, but the question showed that Alice was becoming more informed about things than she had imagined.

"Yes, Madam."

"Then take these letters and ask her to distribute them for me, will you? They're nearly all on her way back and the last one is to the Cloughs. Well, her little boy—Billy isn't it?—could take it round for her when she gets home."

Mrs. Hadding looked at the letters in her hand. The Cloughs, the Bassets, the Suttons—how on earth had Mrs. Wickham found them out? And what did she want with them? Farm laborers, a quarryman, a journeyman blacksmith's brood . . . some charitable enterprise. That was it.

"I have a little more time to be organized, with Lady Evelyn so set on amusing Laura. I remembered Mrs. Grant told me she was coming today, which made me think to write. Thank you Mrs. Hadding. I'm very much obliged."

Alice arranged her desk, not looking at Mrs. Hadding again, hearing the swish of the housekeeper's gray alpaca dress. "If you only knew, Madam, if you only knew . . ." That was always Mrs. Hadding's dry comment on Alice's attempts to learn the system of the house, and the duties of the staff. The words seemed to echo in rebuff in her footsteps: "If you only knew . . ."

◆　◆　◆

When William returned two weeks later, he found Alice's latest innovation already well set up in the empty lodge at the east entrance. He cursed himself for not having replaced the iron gates before, so that he would have an excuse to turn out her protégées and install his coachman. He knew all the girls by sight: Minnie Clough, a fat girl in her early teens; Mrs. Basset's middle two, and Teresa Sutton, with a face like a pulled beet, a strong dark complexion and a frizz of hair scragged up on top of her head. The Basset boys sat with their sisters, being minded, each one wearing a hand-me-down girl's smock over heavy black boots, their caps stuck to their heads. A pile of shirts lay finished on the worktable. The girls were turning up the legs on various trousers. William looked closer: they were gentleman's suits, hardly worn, probably cast off as their owners' waists expanded with age.

Alice was being helped by Sarah Crawshay on this particular afternoon. They were laughing and whispering together as he came in. Alice was always so sweet, so fresh and charming with other people! William assumed the semblance of a loving smile as he greeted his wife.

"Good afternoon, my dear. Potter told me I'd find you here. It's all very well ordered, to your credit." He nodded at Sarah. "Good afternoon, Miss Crawshay."

"Thank you, William." Alice replied. "I think the girls enjoy it, don't you, girls?"

"Yes, Mam." What the girls really liked was Mrs. Wickham putting on an Irish accent when she told them what to do, and the butler Potter coming across the lawn with a maid who carried a basket of buns and a pitcher of milk. Perhaps Teresa Sutton and Minnie Clough saw more advantages in the situation. They liked sewing, and Mrs. Wickham had promised to give her "Dorcas girls" paid fine-work if they improved.

"Lady Evelyn has come back from her drive, Alice. We should go in and dress for dinner."

Through the window Alice could see down the path to the main doors of the house. Evelyn was just stepping down from the carriage. She sighed. Her peaceful hours were over. The ritual went on.

"Come on then, Sarah. My other guests will be arriving soon. We'll have to stop now, girls. Please don't forget, next Tuesday."

"Yes, Mam." Surreptitiously she nodded; the children took the remaining buns from the basket as they filed out of the side door. William stood with his back to them, on the front doorstep.

"It's disease I worry about, Alice my dear," he said smoothly, for Sarah was listening innocently. "I know how easy it is to pick up infections from the villagers. Ask Dr. Briggs." He smiled into the distance.

Alice looked at his stiff back with intense dislike. She enjoyed the girlish, gentle atmosphere of her "Dorcas Society" and now William had invaded it with his male arrogance, his superior selfish concerns. He never missed an opportunity to remind her of that night, when she had protected herself against his desire for sex. Ever since, it had been warfare between them.

"They're all perfectly healthy children—and I'm as strong as a horse. I can withstand most things," she replied, in warning.

"I was thinking more of your child. You have to consider your duties—I know you're devoted to her, and you can't be too careful."

She did not know how William had developed this ability to veil his insults with false concern. Sarah had finished packing her basket, and was listening to William with her usual ingenuous attention. It annoyed Alice to see her miss his meaning.

"How considerate you are, Mr. Wickham! My sister is just as anxious as you are, but she has more experience in these matters, and has assured us that the girls are all from perfectly proper families, poor, but very clean."

"Well, that's a comfort. I trust Lady Mary's judgment, of course I do."

Even in these words, Alice felt herself diminished as an immature hobbyist with no true commitment to her work. Not like Lady Mary, Sarah's sister, with years of committees and "good works" to her credit. It was unfair: she worked every afternoon with her little group of girls. They had made over trousers and jackets, donated by wealthy families in the area, so that all the workhouse inmates had at least one decent outfit in which to receive visitors or attend church. Now the girls were learning to stitch fine linens, and Alice was planning a sale of work that several neighbors had promised to attend. She felt quite proud of her first steps with the Dorcas Society, but William was not interested in hearing of these things.

"You'll stay, won't you Sarah?" she pleaded—the more company she had the better, if William was in a mood to taunt her.

"I'm sorry, I can't, but thank you, Alice. We have guests, too, this evening at Desthorpe, and Mary's expecting me back."

"Let me drive you, Miss Crawshay," said William in a kindly, protective manner that made Alice remember old days and feel sad. She watched as her friend and William walked arm in arm to the house. Potter was sent to fetch the carriage, and they had both left by the time she locked up the lodge.

William was away for quite some time. Alice dressed for dinner, then she and Lady Evelyn entertained the guests until he returned. Daisy Panton and her husband had come with the Master of the Hunt, Colonel Stebbings, and a newcomer to the area, a red-faced, desperate-looking curate whom Alice had met at the workhouse one day. She had invited him out of sympathy for his loneliness. Looking at her sporting company, she wondered if she had made a mistake.

At last William appeared, and Alice could tell at once that he had been drinking. William did not have a head for alcohol; it had a strong effect on him, perhaps because of his slight build and his highly strung nature. Alice felt a pang of sympathy for his improper condition; they were both so hopelessly incompetent at sharing their lives.

Colonel Stebbings, an old friend of William's, noticed at once and adjusted his conversation so that he could keep his host in good humor. Alice hurriedly rearranged the table seating so that the colonel was placed close to William, and the curate a little nearer her.

The young curate, Mr. Glass, had recently returned from South Africa. Paling slightly, Alice introduced him to her drunken husband, to Lady Evelyn, tight-lipped and distant, then to Daisy Panton, covered in pearls and talking of horses in a loud voice. Her husband, "Panton," and Colonel Stebbings were clearly both bored by the young man's presence. Mr. Glass suddenly regretted accepting Alice's invitation, and his thought was apparent to her at once.

Out of sheer nervousness, he launched into an explanation of the trouble brewing with the Boers between Cape Colony and the Transvaal. Alice tried to listen, but William's barely controlled outbursts of hilarity at the other end of the table made it difficult. Colonel Stebbings was finding it harder to keep William quietly amused.

"It must have been frightfully hot," she commented in a vague way to the poor curate. A sudden lull in the conversation gave the remark an undue audience.

" 'Frightfully hot'!" mocked William, making her sound like a mad duchess. "Wouldn't suit you at all, with *your* cold blood." He paled, knowing well enough what he said was unjust and an insult. He threw more wine down his throat.

To make matters worse, Daisy had not quite caught his words, but was sharp enough to sense that she was missing a vital exchange.

"What *did* he say?" Daisy asked the curate in a loud voice, heaving her strong shoulders in confusion.

Mr. Glass began mouthing words devoid of sense, his red forehead mottled with suspicion.

"I said she has cold blood," William persisted, stupidly. It was the first time he had shown his hostility in public. Alice did not think she could conceal her shame.

Lady Evelyn spoke up with a sudden brilliance.

"Imagine! An Irish moss rose transplanted to the plains of Africa! I'm reminded of another Irish friend of my mother's, from an ancient line in Kerry, if I remember right. She was wondering what to take with her to the Cape, and I distinctly recall her words: 'Should I take me tiara, d'ye think?' "

She captured the accent perfectly, and the whole gathering burst into laughter. William thought it funny too, though Alice disliked this mockery of the Irish. It made her feel unexpectedly homesick.

Lady Evelyn continued to carry the burden of the evening till the guests left, for Alice was far too upset, and hardly able to converse. Both women went to bed without any further reference to the hostile incident.

Next morning, Alice was playing with Laura in the nursery while Lady Evelyn looked on. Neither of them wanted to discuss what had happened. Then Mrs. Hadding came in with a large bouquet of flowers, and a note. Expectantly, Alice took them both. The flowers were from Daisy Panton, a generous mass of camellias and lilies. At first she thought the note came with them, but Mrs. Hadding shook her head.

"The Master left that with me last night," she explained, with unction in her voice. "He said I was not to give it to you, Madam, until you were well rested, after such a long evening." Even Mrs. Hadding spoke in William's double-speech now; the habit was contagious. Alice read the letter in silence, then passed it to Evelyn. William had left her for good.

"It's outrageous!" Evelyn said at last. "I shall go up to London at once. I'll speak to him."

"No, no! Don't go!" Alice demanded. "Don't do that, please! Let me think first!"

"But Alice—do you realize what this means? If he takes up residence in London and leaves just his agent here to run the estate for him, it will advertise to the world that he cannot stand to live with you. My dear girl, what have you done?"

Alice was stung. "You see? Even after what happened last night, you still believe that I'm in the wrong!"

"I don't believe William would behave in such an unseemly manner without provocation. You have as much as acknowledged to me that there had been cause . . ."

Little Laura struggled to her feet and tore at Daisy Panton's flowers, babbling anxiously and trying to hand them to Alice and Lady Evelyn. Their angry voices upset the child, and she toppled over, bursting into tears. Hodge hurried in and swept Laura up in her soothing arms.

"Don't do that!" Alice screamed at Hodge. "Leave her to me!" She grabbed at Laura, who reacted to her violence with even louder cries.

The noise invaded Alice's senses. It was as if Laura were her own self, screaming for attention. There was a sound, a sudden draught, and Alice shivered. Clutching Laura, she turned to look at the door but no one else had come in. Lady Evelyn and Hodge stared at her as if she were mad. Then Alice understood that the door opening was inside her, an almost audible sensation, as all her stored-up misery broke out.

"I won't allow anyone, ever again, to spurn me!" she hissed, quite unthinking of Hodge's presence. "I've more right, more value than ten Wickhams! You'll see! I'll never, ever forgive him!" Grasping Laura tight, with the baby's head buried under her chin, Alice ran out of the room. Down the stairs, out of the house, over the lawn. She hid in the kitchen garden, knowing Lady Evelyn would never look for her there. Mother and daughter sat under the raspberry canes, picking off the soft fruit. Laura forgot her tears. Soon her lace bib was stained a brilliant pink, as she squeezed the juice from the irresistibly ripe berries. Alice picked and ate mechanically, the way Deirdre and Rosie used to do at all their meals. The first thing she would do would be to go to London and find that lawyer—what was his name? Layton Stayce. The one her mother had visited in London, all those years before.

◆ ◆ ◆

She had never been to the city, so Lady Mary took her. Alice made up an excuse about financial arrangements for the Dorcas Society, to explain why she was visiting a lawyer. Lady Mary escorted her to London as far as her own town house in Anson Street, Belgravia, then sent her on in her carriage to Mr. Stayce's address. Lady Mary's tiger stood waiting by the horses, whip in hand, in the street outside the chambers—a witness. Alice knew she must keep a good account of herself now, all the time. She climbed a cold stone staircase, where every step was worn into a smooth dip by the trudging feet of applicants for justice. She did not feel inspired to believe she would find it in such gloomy surroundings. It was also a strange thought that her mother had climbed this very staircase, years before when she had left Ireland, to discuss the settlement of her affairs, and the sale of Adam's Creek.

Layton Stayce did not look very welcoming. A bony-headed man with cold eyes and elongated parts: his nose, fingers, even his limbs all hung from him.

"Before we begin, Mrs. Wickham, on the instructions you gave me by letter, there is something I must clarify. You say you found my name mentioned in correspondence of your mother's at Carrigrohane Hall?"

"Yes. I apologize for not explaining all that more clearly. Years ago, I found an old letter, in a book, merely your confirmation of a date to see my mother, Mrs. Richard Hardy, when she visited London. I just remembered your name." (She did not tell him that she and Anne used to invent stories about a "Layton Stayce" in the berdoyers. Those fantasies were entirely out of keeping with the man.)

"I see. That explains the— It wasn't possible that there was any recent connection, obviously."

"No, quite so. But I've no wish to go over the past now, Mr. Stayce. I came to you because I had no one else I could consult for advice, and no wish to approach my own family in Ireland on this matter."

"Well. We have obeyed your instructions and discovered what you wished to know. Are you quite sure that you want me to tell you the result of our enquiries? We could abandon the matter, if you want to change your mind now."

Alice wondered how many women had sat opposite lawyers like this and decided to shrink from the truth.

"No, I'm decided. Please go on, Mr. Stayce."

"Your husband is seen a great deal at his club of course, for his own social reasons. But he is cohabiting with a music-hall singer in Maida Vale."

"That's preposterous!" Alice exclaimed. "So vulgar! William would never endure such a person's company!"

"Our enquiries confirm that his acquaintance with the 'prima donna' in question began before your marriage and recommenced a few months after you arrived at Upton Park. We have traced the girl's history. Mr. Wickham first met her at a house of—forgive me, Mrs. Wickham—convives in Windmill Street. She was very young—barely thirteen. It was due to your husband's patronage that she left that house and got a job at the Alhambra in the chorus."

Alice held back tears. His absences, his coldness were explained. He had given up hope of subjugating her, and returned to a former liaison. William's efforts to dominate her were pathetic . . . he only wanted to control people. This young girl was his inferior. Perhaps that made it easier. She despised him.

Layton Stayce paused, looking up from his notes for the first time. "It could be worse for you, Mrs. Wickham. A 'semi-domestic' situation like this is less injurious to you than other forms of vice."

Alice realized at once that he was talking of disease. How much more could she endure? Perhaps her illness when Laura was born was due to . . . It did not do to dwell on these things. Alice could not help being fascinated by how quickly she understood the facts of life when anyone gave her new details.

"However, Mrs. Wickham," Layton Stayce went on, "You can't sue for divorce on these grounds, which I imagine is what you intend to ask."

"I don't understand."

"Adultery is not sufficient. If *you* were adulterous—forgive me if I speak plainly—Wickham could divorce you. But a wife must show some other cause: desertion, extreme cruelty, unnatural habits—that sort of thing."

"But he *has* left me!"

"Desertion without cause must be for a minimum of two years. Also, it would be very difficult for you to prove. He visits occasionally, he keeps you in his house—very comfortably too, I imagine."

Alice was desperate. Should she tell Layton Stayce the truth?

"There's something else." She could not begin. She had no words to describe it.

"Yes?" Layton Stayce, world-weary, tried to convey that there was no sin known to man that he had not encountered in his time.

"I took precautions. After my daughter was born. He disagreed with that. He was—physically abusive. Need I explain?"

Stayce closed his eyes. He could not, or would not bring himself to imagine the incident. Alice took his sudden remoteness as a hopeful sign.

"It's an interesting point," he murmured, half to himself. "It's never been raised in a court of law, of course. Could a husband divorce his wife on the grounds of failure to agree to full sexual rights? Alternatively, could he sue for restitution of those rights? Mm . . ."

"No, Mr. Stayce, you've misunderstood me. I would sue for his refusal to—"

"No. I have *not* misunderstood."

The cold gray in his eyes gave her an unpleasant shock.

"Mrs. Wickham. My advice to you is to drop this suit. Do not mention what you have told me to anyone. Do you realize how drastic your course of action will be? There are no more than five hundred cases of divorce a year, and only a mere handful in—Society. It would ruin you financially, and you would lose caste. If your husband were to use the facts you have just conveyed to me to defend himself against you, imagine the disgrace. The newspapers would have a field day—

there's no law to stop them printing your name and all the details. There would be no means in anyone's power to prevent you from being the center of a public scandal."

"But I can't endure his desertion, his adultery, his occasional insulting visitations for the rest of my life!"

"There are many women who do, Mrs. Wickham. For the sake of their good names, and their children's futures. To be cut off by the world is a wretched life. I want you to go home and consider my words before you do anything else."

There was nothing left to discuss. Alice went directly to the station in Lady Mary's carriage. When she arrived home at Upton Park late that night, she paced the house in a fury.

She could not go back to Carrigrohane. To do so was an admission of defeat. She would not immolate herself for Laura's sake. She had never been first in anyone's life—not even her own mother's. Why should she be self-sacrificing? Most important of all, she would not condone what William had done. She would not let him erode her sense of her own worth—newfound, in anger.

Alice wrote a frantic letter to William that night, telling him she knew all about his "prima donna" and begging him to release her in whatever way he could without causing a public scandal.

Days, weeks passed, with no response from William. Alice could not make any decisions until he answered her. To keep herself busy, she concentrated on her new duties with the village girls at the Dorcas Society. Her venture had expanded, and Alice spent her time organizing a move from the lodge house to an empty grocer's shop in Upton village, where the girls not only made linens for the local union workhouse and hospitals but finer embroidered pieces for petticoats and nightdresses. Alice now sold these regularly for profit to her wealthy friends. She even considered going back to London to find a shop—like the National Linen Company in Fleet Street perhaps—that might give her orders.

The number of seamstresses had risen to twenty-three. She had taken on a sewing teacher, a Mrs. Burns, to help train the younger ones. Alice gave them all lunch and paid them a decent wage, up to three shillings a week in some cases. An outworker spinner at the local mills could make about two or three shillings a week, but worked much longer hours than Alice's girls.

She was thankful for her "good works." No one came to call on her now. It was as if everyone knew what was happening. Daisy Panton had not visited for weeks, Lady Evelyn had returned to London, and Ned was busy somewhere in Somerset on another commission. Alice had no one to confide in.

Lady Mary and Sarah Crawshay remained close to her, but she did not consider it at all appropriate to discuss such a shocking subject as divorce with either of them; they were such naïve people, despite their connection with the lower orders—or perhaps just because of these charitable works. They refused to acknowledge the bad in anyone.

A few weeks later, Layton Stayce wrote again, asking Alice to visit him. Alice did not wish to travel up to London alone, so Sarah went with her, the ostensible purpose of the trip being to get supplies for the Dorcas girls on Mrs. Burns' orders.

Alice had no knowledge of the city at all. To her, it represented William's world of vice, with a smart corner inhabited by women such as Daisy Panton and Lady Evelyn. Another dark corner was inhabited by the arbiters of the system, the laywers.

On her second visit, however, Alice responded to Sarah's girlish excitement at being in the center of the fashionable universe. Alice was meant to be in charge of the outing, but was just as lost and impressionable as Sarah herself. They managed to get a hansom cab from St. Pancras to the lower end of Regent Street, and delved into the sewing department of Swan and Edgar's. Soon they had bought quantities of lawn, linen and machine-made lace.

"Oh, Alice, it's costing us a fortune. Are you sure we should buy all this?" Sarah looked anxious as the counter boys wrapped up their purchases.

"Please send them to this address," Alice ordered, giving that of Lady Mary's town house in Anson Street. She was enjoying a sudden freedom. "We've got work enough already to cover these expenses. If I don't buy stocks now, we'll run out of supplies, and then the girls will lose interest." A bold idea came to her. "Sarah! Let's celebrate! Let's take tea! Oh, don't pack that"—hurriedly Alice stopped the sales assistant—"I'd like to look at it myself." Alice had bought sewing manuals for the girls, but also on impulse the latest copy of *Le Moniteur de la Mode.* Sheer caprice, and escape from her worries.

"This way, ladies." Alice tried to look casual as she walked through the tea room, with its paneled walls, tinkling spoons, pink-covered tables. The waiter seemed to judge her exactly and gave her a table not quite in a corner, but not too exposed.

"Oh, heavens, I've never been out like this!" Sarah exclaimed, overcome by the menu card and handing it over to Alice. Alice would have preferred a bolder ally in the adventure, such as her sister, Anne, but Sarah's background gave her sufficient poise to prevent her making a fool of herself.

Bathed in the department store's electric light, surrounded by women in ostrich feathers, flowers and chiffons, Alice tasted the delights of self-indulgence for the first time. She was wearing a dress from her trousseau, ordered from the dressmaker at Grant's in Cork. It was made over, and out of date. The hostility of her life with William had driven all thought of personal vanity from her head. Even Ned's admiration had not revived any spark. But Swan and Edgar's did. Perhaps it was the event, taking tea in a public place for the first time in her life that made her want glamour. Seated among the palms of the sedate restaurant, Alice was aware of being in the midst of a throng of women dedicated most happily to making the most of themselves. Grandma Hardy would have died of disgust, but Grandmaman, her dear Grandmaman in Denver, would have smiled maliciously and pointed out a particularly ugly hat.

Sarah was staring at a woman with a large feathered hat, her face swathed in spotted veiling, who was being ushered to her seat by the maître d'hôtel.

"Look at her retinue! A page boy, two whippets, a maid with a hatbox and two shop assistants! She must be very rich!"

Alice looked closer at the extravagant figure clouded in net. She suddenly noted wrinkles on the woman's neck, mottled marks on the back of her hand. Turning away, disappointed, Alice saw a girl at the next table crooking her finger over her teacup and taking a large, unseemly bite out of a cream cake. The girl dabbed her mouth in a coquettish fashion, as if she were acting a part. Alice felt shivers of perception tingling through her scalp. She watched another middle-aged woman trying to catch a waiter's eye, and turning pink with embarrassment. She, too, was unaccustomed to commanding attention: Lady Evelyn would never be flustered like that.

Alice saw that these ladies were not quite as grand as she had first imagined—some were respectable, but perhaps from out of town like her and Sarah. Some were another breed. Perhaps William's "prima donna" looked like one of these pretty creatures in silk and lace, with cherries and birds sitting on the brims of their hats. Alice wanted to be able to observe this world correctly—to be intimate with it—because, like her, all the women were struggling to maintain some dream or image of themselves. That touched a sense of longing in her, to find the right part for every person on this worldly stage.

After tea, Alice and Sarah took a cab to Anson Street, where Sarah was expected. Then Alice went on with the coach and tiger as before, to Layton Stayce's chambers. The excitement of the day faded as she climbed the gloomy staircase in Lincoln's Inn Fields. She had no idea what news had caused his sudden summons.

When she walked into the room, she gasped in surprise. Lady Evelyn and Sir Warren Thomas were waiting for her. Evelyn rose to take her hand, a gesture that reassured Alice that she was still a friend.

"I'm so sorry . . ." Lady Evelyn whispered, guiding Alice to a wooden bench. Sir Warren occupied the leather chair facing Layton Stayce, half excluding the two women. The men were in charge, and would conclude the matter like any other business transaction. It was all very quick. Alice heard the facts in a blur of fright, her heart thumping. William had greeted her request for a divorce with great indignation. He had written to the Hardys at Carrigrohane complaining of her impertinence. Her grandparents were willing to buy the divorce, but only on condition that Alice did not return to Ireland.

"Why?" she asked, tearfully. "I didn't want them to be consulted! Why did he do that—and why do they refuse to see me? I'd never go back, but they have no reason to forbid me!"

Layton Stayce looked grave. "William Wickham threatened to cross-petition, citing Ned Fielding. He accused you."

"That's a lie! You know it! A lie!"

"Your husband only *threatened* to cross-petition. We dissuaded him from acting on impulse," Layton Stayce added. He was like a schoolmaster who strikes a pupil and then asks kindly if the red mark smarts. All three adults sat staring at Alice, and she felt like a naughty child. Alice started to protest to Lady Evelyn, who looked away, shaking her head.

"I told you to be more circumspect . . . of course, I don't believe a word of it, but you were too open—I tried to warn you. I understand your grandparents. After all, Mr. Fielding isn't *known* to your family."

This was a polite but killing way of reminding Alice that Ned Fielding was an artist, not truly one of her class.

"The costs will use up most of your family's intended legacy to you. Are you still determined to end the marriage?"

Alice could not reply. She fought back tears.

Sir Warren spoke for the first time. "I'll make provision for Laura.

William refuses to do that." He looked disgusted, both with Alice's failure to manage William, and with William's dishonorable behavior.

"He thinks he will force me to accept his terms for the marriage." Alice stated it as a fact. Lady Evelyn and her husband exchanged a glance: they knew all too well how high-handed William could be with his money, as with everything else. "Well, I won't go back, and I thank you, Sir Thomas, at least for offering me a means of escape."

Layton Stayce continued, relentless. "Your grandmother thinks it would be better for you to remain in England."

"I might pervert my own sister, you mean." Alice was so hurt she spoke rashly.

No one responded to her words. Lady Evelyn tightened her grasp of her hand and whispered an explanation. "Think of Laura. You wouldn't want her to grow up there, would you?"

"No!"

"Well, your grandfather has a brother here, in London. A doctor, Edward Gayott Hardy. He's offered to look after you, take you in."

Alice had never heard the name mentioned at Carrigrohane. Perhaps Grandma Hardy made a habit of breaking ties with all relatives. . . . What an odd condition—was she meant to be an unpaid housekeeper, in return for this unknown man's protection? She half wished she could stay with Lady Evelyn but realized, sadly, that Sir Warren would never agree; he was far too loyal to William to shelter her.

"I'm not very well-disposed toward doctors," she said bitterly.

"Alice!" Even Lady Evelyn was losing sympathy for her. "You cannot afford to say such things. He's a distinguished man, with a practice in Harley Street and a house in St. John's Wood. You're not in a position to have strong preferences. The last time you followed your inclinations, you married William. You didn't succeed very well then, did you?" Instinctively, Evelyn let go of Alice's hand.

Sir Warren made an effort to say a last kind word. "Don't be too bitter, my dear. William's behaved like a complete cad. I regret your action, but I know you're not entirely to blame for this family disgrace. You'll lose your place in Society, but it is how you conduct yourself in the future that will make the world forget your past. Your grandfather James is a good, kind man, and I'm sure any brother of his will be just the same."

Alice knew she had been educated to be ignorant, because the world judged that best. Now she had to live in straitened circumstances, because of someone else's wrongdoings. She wondered how she was ever going to learn "Society's" rules when they kept on changing, like a game of chance in which someone marks the cards.

"I'll take my leave now, Mr. Stayce. Good-bye, Lady Evelyn. Good-bye, Sir Warren. I am indebted to you."

Lady Evelyn was too conflicted in her loyalties to speak or to give her a parting kiss.

Alice went down to the waiting coach. She would have to tell Lady Mary the truth now—and Daisy Panton. It would be the end: she would lose all her friends with her change of status. It had been irksome at times to have a position to live up to, but now she would disappear into the shabby backstreet world where women fallen from gentility hid themselves.

How could William have accused her and Ned, when he had introduced them in the first place! Did class rules allow him to say what he liked of a supposedly lesser man? Was there no room for innocent friendship between men and women? Ned of all people, so simple, direct, and above such hypocrisies! She realized how very much she would miss his companionship. Alice wanted to see Ned Fielding, to reassure herself that were some truthful, loving beings in the world. She would say good-bye honorably, with no hint of shame attached to her. She would write to him in Somerset and explain that she had news she could only convey to him in person. She did not want anyone to pass on William's disgraceful accusations without Ned knowing the truth for himself.

CHAPTER 7

1 8 9 6

*M*innie Clough watched Alice pinning the pink flowers to Sarah's waist.

"No, Mam, better without," she said. Otherwise, the dress was beautiful: lilac satin with deep flounces of scalloped fabric at the hem. Minnie was very pleased with these flounces; she had taken the silk to the undertakers in Warkham herself. She took a ride into the town early one morning on her father's cart, as he journeyed to farms for blacksmithing jobs. The undertakers in Warkham had a pinking iron for the silk that lined their coffins, and for a few pennies neatened the edges of fine fabric for ladies' gowns.

Back at home, Minnie had laboriously folded the silk by hand and stitched rows and rows of the scalloped strips to the edge of Sarah's dress, following Alice's design.

Miss Crawshay was going out to India to join her intended husband. They had been promised to each other for a long time, and with his recent promotion to captain in the British army, Mr. Rupert Firth had written home for Sarah to join him. Alice had asked all the Dorcas girls, including Minnie herself, to work together on the trousseau.

"I think you're quite right, Minnie." Alice agreed. "Turn a little, Sarah; I just need to adjust the train."

Alice felt such strength of purpose at this moment. Quietly, she pinned and fluffed out the fabric, adjusting its fall. Nothing was as bad as she had feared. She had confessed all to the Crawshay sisters, and they had not deserted her. She had written to Ned, to Daisy Panton and to Dr. Gayott Hardy, accepting his offer. She had moved into her own future.

Lady Mary and Sarah stood by her: they were delighted with her suggestion that she should undertake the design of Sarah's wedding clothes with the Dorcas girls, as a parting gift. Clothes did not interest Lady Mary at all and she knew that Alice took an interest in fashion without being wildly extravagant. It never disturbed Lady Mary that Sarah was consorting with a woman in the throes of a divorce. Out of loyalty to Alice, both sisters assumed she was blameless and never asked any questions.

"Mama would have been delighted," Lady Mary pronounced. "She always said I'd be a spinster and that Sarah would make a good match. She'd be so happy to know the gel's going to do the thing in style. Spend what you need to, Mrs. Wickham dear, within reason of course!"

Alice felt the compliment of Lady Mary's confidence; she gave affection sparingly, but it was of sterling quality, a characteristic Alice found very English. The matter was settled. Lady Mary went back to her committees, while Alice and Sarah bought India outfits from all the right stores. They explored a little further afield on each London visit. There was hardly a shop in Oxford Street, Bond Street, Regent Street or Piccadilly that they had not visited in the past few months.

The wedding gown and the bridesmaids' dresses had been fitted, the going-away suit already done and the dresses for Sarah to wear during the Simla Season had been packed away in her tin trunks. At the bottom of one such Sarah had, with a blush, hidden a complete layette; all the shops sold them for ladies going out east, as part of their trousseaux. Alice was touched by Sarah's bright confidence—her own marriage had been by comparison inauspicious.

She helped Sarah out of the last dress, and the maid brought her day clothes. She rang the bell: "Potter, have Minnie driven back to Upton village with the dresses, will you?" Minnie left grandly, her arms full of tulle.

Sarah tidied her hair. "It all seems so extraordinary—here I am going to the other end of the earth, knowing perfectly well exactly what will happen to me, and you're just going north to St. John's Wood, and we have no idea what will become of you!"

"Well, Rupert's been promising you married bliss for years and years. I've had only one letter from Dr. Hardy, just today."

"What did he say?"

"That he's looking forward to meeting me; that he used to be very close to my grandfather before his marriage to my grandmother Esther and that he has plenty of space for me in his house. He's a specialist doctor—he's spent many years in Germany, which I suppose is why he never visited us in Ireland. Although I suspect he never liked Grandma Hardy very much."

"Are you quite quite sure you must do this, Alice? It seems so frightful to leave your husband."

"He left *me.*"

"I'd simply die if Rupert did that."

"He won't. You've known each other since you were children. You know his family, he knows yours. You've told me so a hundred times . . . Rupert loves the army, and he loves you. He always has. Besides, there's something else."

"What's that? Do tell." Sarah waited expectantly for Alice to define some other positive aspect of her marriage. It was always nice to hear such things.

"You bowl extremely well for a girl! At mixed cricket you'll be the star, and Rupert will be even prouder of you!"

Sarah laughed at the picture of sporting bliss that Alice presented, but Alice could tell that she hoped that was exactly what would happen.

"Hold still, I'll finish your laces," Alice said. "Now give me a kiss, Sarah. Oh dear, I shall miss you so . . ."

At the door, Potter's voice rang out. "Mr. Fielding, Madam." Ned came in as they stood with their arms clasped round each other's waists.

"Charming picture! I could paint you both, just like that. Miss Crawshay, how do you do—and Mrs. Wickham?" Ned bent low, but smiled as he looked up. "Miss Crawshay, forgive me, but your hat is crooked."

"So it is!" Sarah looked in the pier glass and realized that in the enthusiasm of the moment, Alice had knocked her straw boater out of place.

"Ned, don't tease! Congratulate Sarah—she's to be married!"

"Well done! Splendid! Rupert has claimed you at last!" He shook Sarah's hand as if she had won a race. It amused Alice to see Ned's chameleonlike charms at work on another. With her, he relaxed into something of an aesthete, showing her books of Japanese prints and teaching her about color and composition. With Sarah, from one of the oldest local families of Upton, and whom he had known from childhood, he would soon be discussing his last visit to Hurlingham or the Ascot races. The Crawshays were not the kind to stand on small social differences, unlike new money: the Wickhams and the Pantons.

"It's wonderful to see you again," Alice said, not looking at Ned but picking up bits of silk, and revealing an endearing gap between her striped blouse and the tight belt of her linen skirt. Ned could not believe that this happy woman, flushing as she bent forward, was in the midst of the domestic crisis she had mentioned briefly in her letter.

"I'd almost given up hope of seeing you again. Why didn't you write to me, Ned?" Alice forgot she meant to be cool and correct. Sarah moved toward the open window, but Alice ignored the hint that she ought to be less direct.

"I went walking on the moors when I finished my commission. It took three weeks for correspondence to catch up with me."

"But it's been three months!" Alice could not help herself.

Ned's explanations, so carefully planned on the journey to Upton, suddenly dropped from his thoughts. The truth was, Alice's letter had made him wonder what he wanted from this friendship, and he was confused. Irritated not to find a suitable reply, he turned away to look at the garden.

"Wonderful to see this view again—so comfortable after the west. Tell me, Miss Crawshay, have you been to Somerset?"

"We visit relatives in Gloucestershire sometimes, but that's as far as I have ever been."

"An intrepid traveler! India will hold no surprises for you then!" Ned teased, and Alice laughed with them both, thinking that she was very happy that Ned had finally come back to her.

"Here's tea—on the terrace, Nellie—and will you ask Hodge to bring Miss Laura down?"

"My favorite child. How is she?" Ned enquired.

"Very angry, because she wants a pretty new dress. Everyone else seems to be having one made . . ."

"Does she know yet about—you and William?" He could not help asking directly. Now Alice was embarrassed. It was always the same. Close friends would try to avoid the topic, but everything reminded them. She was glad Sarah was leaving for India soon. She hated her friend's happiness being marred by these whisperings about divorce. It made Alice feel even more tainted when her difficulties touched the lives of others. She wanted to go through the process as quickly as possible, preferably alone.

"No. Laura has no idea what's going to happen. It all depends on my meeting with this Dr. Hardy. We have corresponded, but he had to go away to a medical conference in Germany, and delayed our arrangements. The lapse of time only makes me more determined to press on."

"Laura!" exclaimed Ned, as she ran out to them. "How you've grown."

Alice laughed. "They do, Ned, quite normally." His lack of domesticity was one of his charms.

"Tickle tickle!" the child demanded, as he lifted her up. He brushed his red beard over her cheek, till she drew up her knees and squealed with laughter. "Tick tock?" she asked: the old tricks were not forgotten. He pulled out a large fob watch and opened the lid. It played a tune, and Laura put her thumb in her mouth and laid her head happily against his chest.

Something remarkable occurred to Alice. She did not believe that new memories could come to her now, after so much sadness, so many long nights of bitter reflection. A healing vision came to her suddenly from the past. She was a sick child, she was hot, and afraid to be in pain. A man heard her, and lifted her heavy body in his big, strong arms. They sat in a deep chair by the fire; she could see the flames dancing before her, fuzzy through half closed eyes. A big body, a wide chest to lean on, the smell of a cigar . . . Papa. She could even hear his voice: "You'll be better soon, poppet. Daddy knows."

"Men." She said unexpectedly. "Men are wonderfully *big* to little girls."

Ned smoothed Laura's smock down over her knees to her kid boots, a proprietorial gesture. He reveled in assuming fatherhood for a few minutes.

"Men hope to capitalize on that favored view for the rest of their lives," he joked, looking with enquiry at Sarah, and avoiding Alice.

"Oh, I agree! I think Rupert is an absolute hero! But he does disappoint me sometimes. He can't dance, and he falls asleep standing up in church on Sundays."

Sarah was surprised at their laughter, but enjoyed being thought witty.

"If those are all his faults—and I'm sure they're his worst—then you'll be very happy!" Ned commented.

Sarah had to go. Alice hurried her parting words, feeling saddened. "Now, I shan't see you till we go to town on Friday. I'll call for you at ten." On Friday Sarah was leaving for London and her sea voyage, and Alice was to visit Dr. Hardy.

People were always leaving, thought Alice. It was pointless to be close to anyone. She ignored the fact that she had left her own sister, Anne, and a dear friend, Sophie, to pursue her new life in England. Unhappiness made her veer between painful sympathy for others less fortunate, and a sharp perception of herself as a victim.

"Oh, I nearly forgot!" Sarah interrupted her thoughts. "Mary and I want you to have this. We found it at home when I was sorting through my room . . . I hope you like it, it seemed the perfect memento." Sarah could not make a farewell speech; she pushed the book into Alice's hand instead. Alice understood, and held the gift as if it were very fragile, turning the pages with care. It was a collection of color plates, studies of English wildlife: birds, butterflies and finely detailed flowers.

"It's beautiful. Thank you, Sarah."

"I don't want to take it with me. I'd hate to be nostalgic. I thought you'd like it, for the colors."

"I do. It's perfect. It will always remind me of the best days I had here at Upton—with you and Ned."

"Good-bye, Mr. Fielding."

"Good-bye, Miss Crawshay, and good luck."

"Till Friday, Alice." Then Sarah bent down to kiss Laura's head as she lay asleep in Ned's arms and hurried away.

Ned turned to comfort Alice, reaching out to touch her arm.

"She'll come back. Rupert will look after her. Firth's a good chap. Sit down. I want to know the meaning of all this."

Alice called the maid. "Nellie, ask Hodge to take Miss Laura in now. She's so sleepy, I think it's the heat." A late summer haze covered the lawns, a green mist rising from the lake. Laura did not protest when she was carried inside.

Alice was unsettled by Ned's touch. His hand had rested longer than it should. She wondered, not for the first time, if he had stronger feelings for her than friendship. It made telling the truth much more difficult.

"It's been decided, while you were away. I'm divorcing William and I shall move to London."

"My God, Alice, it will ruin your life!"

"Don't say that to me—you of all people! Resorting to propriety!"

"It's one thing for a man to fly against the rules—quite another for a woman!"

"But you wanted me to be happy!"

"Yes, but that's not the way! How will you live? You have no idea how to manage on your own. I hope William's paying you off handsomely. He should, the—"

"Don't—don't. I won't hear it. And I won't have you thinking of me as a waif and stray!"

"If only I could offer you something more than my—" Ned's love of freedom pulled him up short of committing himself. The words were lost in a mumble. He cleared his throat. "Shameful!" he muttered, standing up and folding his hands awkwardly behind his back.

"Oh, Ned!" Alice laughed at his self-deception, and liked him even more than she always had. He might lie to himself, but he was hopeless at concealing his thoughts from others.

"You know I adore you, Alice!" he protested.

"Of course you do. But listen, there's something else. Be serious for a moment."

Ned sat down again, and Alice felt all too aware of his proximity and drew back.

"William accused me, to my family, of having an affair."

"You don't say—the—with whom?"

"With you."

"By God!"

"I wanted you to hear it from me first. I'm sure we should ignore it, but obviously you should know. You may wish to dissociate yourself from me in the circumstances. I think it would be best. I had to tell you . . . it would have been wrong not to." Alice heard herself run on. It dawned on her that perhaps an affair with Ned had been more in his mind than she liked to admit.

The same thought came to Ned, too. He had an urge to fulfill the accusation and have done with it. In that moment they were both tempted.

"Why not?" said Ned, with a dangerous grin.

"I don't love you like that. No. I don't know. Perhaps I do." Alice really did not know. She thought she loved Ned like a brother, but she felt so happy to see him again that perhaps she could care for him in that other way. She felt her heart jump, her longing for love drawn out by Ned's boldness.

"Come to me." Ned pulled her to her feet, and kissed her full on the lips. His mouth was juicy and firm, his beard soft and caressing on her cheeks. His whole body seemed full of energy; neither of them could breathe. Ned was so solid, it was like falling to the ground, thinking she was hurt, then loving the soft earth and the damp smell of the grass. He held her very tightly and spoke in a deep muffled voice into the curve of her neck.

"Love me, Alice. I could make a go of it. You're wonderful. If you throw up your marriage, I'll give you love. I'll be devoted."

"Will you, Ned?"

"With all my heart. I've never said that to another woman. There's no one to compare with you, Alice, my dearest angel, in my heart."

If only it were true. Alice pushed him back a little, but he held her still. It was ridiculous: Ned was a bohemian, perhaps a great artist. Even William in his saner moments had genuine respect for the man's work. But Alice knew he would never thrive with responsibilities.

"I can't take the risk. There's Laura, and there's your work. You want to love me forever, but you know you couldn't do it!"

"I would, I swear! Don't try to limit yourself, Alice!"

"No. Let me go, Ned."

"I will not. You're more beautiful than I have ever seen you before."

"You mustn't say such things! I want my freedom, too. I do so!" Alice struggled to be free, and found herself growing furious as he resisted. A wail rose in her throat, a long cry like an animal at night, and as it came out, she hit him hard across the neck with her arm, and then on top of his head. But Ned was a simple person, and he knew at once that he should not break his grip. Alice's mood had shifted from a momentary yielding to hysterical defiance. He held on, with an odd determination, while she flailed at him as hard as she could.

"Let me go! Goddammit! Jesus! Joseph! Mary! I hate you! I hate you! I wish I were dead!" The strength left her, she was faint, and she slipped through his arms and fell on the terrace.

"Alice, are you hurt? Let me look—don't move. Don't lift your head."

With no trace of sexual interest in the contact, he touched her body to make sure she had not injured herself. Kneeling down, Ned calmed her without words. He rubbed her sore elbow, stroked her shoulders and made her lie still with her head on his lap. They lay like children across the terrace steps.

"Ned, you will forgive me, won't you?" she whispered. "I—I don't know what happened."

He smiled. "I don't usually refer to the Queensberry Rules when I propose. I'll have to remember that next time." He propped his head on his elbow, looking at her sideways and laughing to himself.

Alice knew it would all be forgotten. He had not proposed "marriage" after all. Perhaps frustration had made her so violent: she did not have the courage to defy all conventions at once. Better to have Ned as a friend for life—or at least until he found another woman. She rested against his body, closing her eyes from the strong sun.

♦ ♦ ♦

That Friday, Alice's cab drew up outside a high wall in Lime Road, St. John's Wood. Sarah had come with her for company. They clung to each other for a moment. "Good-bye! Good luck!" Alice stepped down and Sarah drove back to Anson Street to make ready for her departure. Now Alice was completely alone. She pulled the doorbell and waited. Limes and maples along the pavement soughed in the breeze. The splodgy colors of blown roses disordered the mansion lawns on each side of the street. A butler appeared, wasp-striped in a waistcoat, unlike Potter's forbidding tails, and led Alice up the path to the front steps and through a hall lined with marble busts to a sunny drawing room.

"Doctor Hardy will be with you in a moment, Madam. A patient is just leaving."

Alice stood still, looking down through the bowed window onto a small low garden. Trellises covered with creepers lined all the walls. On the steps leading down from the house, a large marmalade cat slept under a stone urn, the white hairs on its belly ruffling in the wind. As Alice waited for Dr. Hardy, the cat's tail lifted, a hint of its wild dreams.

"Good afternoon, Mrs. Wickham, I'm so sorry to have kept you waiting. Please sit down, then we can discuss our plan."

Dr. Hardy was smaller than she expected, quite unlike his brother, Grandpa James, who was bulky and impressive. But he had the same humane cast to his face, the same beady half-concealed intelligence in his expression. His eyes were deepset with a kind light, and he had those familiar abundant white whiskers.

"Now," he said, with a directness that made her feel shy. "I'm a busy man, and I don't need all this space. My man Norton comes in daily, and the housekeeper, Mrs. Bacon, lives downstairs. Quite frankly, I live almost entirely in my study upstairs. I sleep little—I often use the couch in my room rather than bother to go to bed. So what I propose is, you use these rooms here on the ground floor for your own purposes, and the entire top floor. As long as you don't mind having to confine yourself to the back stairs during the day, so that you do not disturb my patients as they arrive and depart . . . will that be acceptable? Otherwise, it's comfortable enough—there's plenty of space up there. There's even a little attic above for a nursemaid, if you wish."

"I see," said Alice, an inaudible response.

"Now, I'll show you your rooms. They haven't been used for the past ten years, but this was a child's home once. I inherited the house from a patient."

They climbed the dark servants' staircase, and its twists and turns made Alice feel anxious. It was a distinguished, not very old town house, but even so, much smaller than Carrigrohane or Upton Park. Panic at what she was abandoning became tangible on the narrow wooden steps. She felt gloomy and terrified at being enclosed in such a small space.

On the top floor, the bedrooms were small but had an attic charm. She could hear a blackbird through the skylight. One room was papered with a pattern of faded cherries and blue ribbons. The other had a vast brass bed and an equally faded but beautiful patchwork quilt. There was a rocking horse, so old that its teeth had yellowed realistically with age, and its rough mane was missing in chunks, as if it had been ridden into many battles. It was all very cosy, but the shabbiness made her sad.

"It's very pretty," she said, making an effort. "Laura will love this room, I can just see her in it."

"Good. This way, then. I'll show you my quarters and the front stairs. Up there is the maid's room—" He pointed to another half-turn on the stairs. "My patients are harmless," he continued, "but they could cause you or Laura alarm. They suffer from nervous disorders, forms of mental disturbance that keep them from a full life. I try to help them with my little 'sessions.' During the day, when the bell rings twice, keep your doors closed for a few moments. That will give Norton time to show my visitors upstairs. At the end of each session, I will ring a second bell twice, and the process will happen in reverse."

Alice was mystified, and a little afraid. Dr. Hardy showed her his study, his bedroom and library before leading her downstairs. She had an impression of mahogany, mirrors and plush. The curtains were all drawn shut and a slight scent of orris filled the rooms.

"Here's your dining room. I haven't used it in years." Dr. Hardy drew back the curtains so that sunlight refreshed the room from both ends when he opened the double doors opposite the window. Adjoining was a small morning room, overlooking the walled garden. It was all more interesting than elegant; compared to the cluttered shabbiness of Carrigrohane and the cold splendor of Upton, the place felt like a haven. Alice had not been in such modest surroundings since her childhood at Adam's Creek.

Mrs. Bacon appeared, a kindly, plump woman, gray-haired under her lace cap and with a fine pink complexion. She shook hands with Alice, and her skin felt soft and dry, as if she were covered in talcum powder.

"I thought I'd give you a sherry in the drawing room," she suggested to Dr. Hardy, very much as a mother persuades a child.

"Good idea!" said Dr. Hardy, leading the way, but then he stood by the fire, staring at the chairs as if he had entered a strange hotel lounge and could not choose where to sit. Alice realized that he hardly ever socialized; he was utterly caught up in his work. She thought she would be very lonely living with this kind, dedicated old man.

"Dr. Hardy," Alice began, after a sip of sherry to give her courage, "I think I should explain to you, about the reasons for my change of—"

"I don't think you need to do that, Mrs. Wickham. Your letters told me enough to satisfy me, and I'll learn the rest all in good time. You're divorcing your husband. That's a very difficult and brave thing to do. You have a child—almost a grandchild to me in fact! And just enough finances to support her and begin a new life. I think that's sufficient for me for the moment."

His words convinced Alice that she had been right in guessing that Grandma Hardy had never approved of her brother-in-law. Perhaps the dislike was mutual. Dr. Hardy had nothing in common with his brother's wife: such a harsh and judgmental woman would not have appealed to a man of his attitudes. Perhaps that was why the brothers never visited each other, and grew apart.

But Alice wanted Dr. Hardy to know of her unhappiness, the physical miseries, the totality of her failure—all the struggles that had brought her to this crisis. It welled up inside her, and she thought she would burst with it, or cry forever.

Dr. Hardy observed her, with a controlled expression. His voice however lowered to a pitch of vibrancy she had never heard in anyone else.

"I have every sympathy for your unhappiness, my dear lady. It is hard."

"It is." Alice nodded, struggling to remain composed. She closed her lips tightly and blinked away tears.

"You can rely on my protection. I'm busy, but always on hand. Trust me." Alice heard and believed every word.

He leaned forward and took her hand. Stiffly perched on the edge of her chair, Alice could not think of any way to respond to his kindness. She struggled not to reveal her distress.

"Your grandfather tells me he doesn't believe one word of the stories he has been told. Don't speak. Just hear me out."

Her head jerked in the semblance of a nod, and she quickly brushed something from her eyes.

"Some people are so afraid of their own weakness, their own capacity for sin, that they respond viciously to any sign of it in others. You must see that this is a deficiency in their nature, not in yours. Do you understand me?"

Grandma Hardy . . . she believed it all, no doubt! Alice was sure of it. She nodded, feeling the weight of her mistakes, and not knowing how to endure it.

"Courage! I'll help you!" He shook her hand to bring her to her senses. "Now," he said, resuming his other, "normal" voice. Alice realized how he must have developed these two modes of speech: it came from years of talking to people who were always teetering on the brink, and pulling them back.

"There's just one detail. Mrs. Bacon, my housekeeper, suffers from pains in her joints. There's one request I could make, if you'd agree as a condition of your residence!" He twinkled at her—at least, that was the effect she thought he was trying to create.

"Of course, anything."

"I rise very early. I have the impression you do too—because of your child?" He knew very well that was not the reason why she lay awake in the early hours of the morning. Alice realized she must look quite haggard.

"I'm a fervent believer in certain dietary aids to longevity," he continued. "I've made a study of the Russian system of drinking koumiss, or mare's milk, to detoxify the system." As she listened to his precise little speech, Alice felt the tensions within her ebbing. "It's one method; there are several others . . . so, with your permission, I'll ask you to prepare my special early breakfast. It will mean Mrs. Bacon need not climb the stairs until she has unlocked her limbs, poor dear. Of course when you find yourself a maid, she'll live downstairs and do the task."

"I'd be pleased to help. What do you take?"

"Warmed oats, goat's milk, cabbage juice and a fresh-grated onion. Mrs. Bacon will show you how to prepare them, and then you can do it for her. I work best at dawn—thank you!" He was pleased with his scheme, though Alice secretly wondered if he had not devised the whole plan just to make her feel welcome.

She left Lime Road with unfamiliar hope. Perhaps, in time, she would be able to rebuild her life. St. John's Wood was an oddly fashionable quarter; Lady Mary told her it would *almost* do. There were dubious kept ladies in small white villas in the area, it was true. But a number of well-considered artists and writers had built their homes in its salubrious air, away from the city. It was only on the fringe of her previous social world. Alice hoped that this would not necessarily add to her ill-repute. There was another advantage besides its modest claims as an address: Dr. Hardy expected no rent for her share of the house. Alice's next challenge was how to deal with her sudden lack of funds. She had thought of little else for the past few weeks.

Sir Warren had agreed to give her a thousand pounds annually to support both herself and Laura. It would pay for necessities, like education and clothing, and allow Alice to insist on making some small contribution to Dr. Hardy for their keep. Up until now, Alice had never handled money with her own hands. Her purchases for the Dorcas Society were all charged to William's accounts in London stores, and repaid to him by handing over the checks she received from her customers. On a few occasions, payments for the linens had been made direct to William's bank from the husbands of friends.

If she wished to be independent, she would have to earn some more money.

The carriage met her at Upton Halt, and Alice rode back to the Park, suddenly alive to her surroundings. She was leaving, there would be no more sad journeys homeward to Upton again. Alone in the carriage, she stared out at the landscape of Rutland, absorbing its familiarity, trying to imprint its beauty on her memory. The enlarged fields, the thick thorn hedges that were the great attraction of the hunt; the steely wide sky where larks shot upward like sparks over a bonfire, swirling and circling in alarm at the sound of the carriage wheels; the cool wind that never seemed to leave the deep folds of the hills—all these were noble things, to be remembered when the dishonor of the moment had passed. As soon as she reached home, Alice wrote a last letter to William.

Dear William,

You know the pain and remorse your recent actions have brought me. But my mind is settled and my future plans no longer uncertain. I shall leave Upton Park at the end of September, three years almost to the day since I came here as your wife. Potter is left in charge of the staff until you tell him whom to dismiss. I am to be in good hands thank God, and so is Laura. I beg you, for her sake, not to attempt to contact us. I ask this in recompense for the injury you have done me, and for the sake of my child's future happiness. I cannot forgive you, but I don't wish you unhappiness.

In sorrow, Alice.

Two weeks later, Alice was ready to leave. She told Potter she would want the carriage at six in the morning, so that she could take the earliest train. She had no wish to be observed on her last journey from Upton Park. When she came downstairs with Laura in her arms, who was wide-eyed with excitement at the thought of a long journey, Alice found Potter and Mrs. Hadding waiting in the hall in their Sunday-best clothes.

"Potter's ready to accompany you, Madam. It isn't right, you leaving like this. If I may, I should like to see Miss Laura to her new place." Mrs. Hadding spoke kindly for once.

Alice was grateful, and they all climbed into the carriage, a funereal group in the foggy light of early morning. Alice had refused all offers of company—Ned least of all would she allow to go with her on a day like this. In fact, she had forbidden him to contact her at all until the divorce was settled, for fear of giving William grounds for his suspicions, or, (as Lady Evelyn had insinuated) in case she gave in, out of sheer fright at her isolation. The kindness of stiff old Potter and the formidable Mrs. Hadding reduced the desolation she felt, without imposing some other intimacy on her.

They delivered her like undertakers with a coffin, on the doorstep of Lime Road. Mrs. Hadding gave no indication of her opinion of the neighborhood. Potter did not utter a word either, except to issue instructions about luggage and minding skirts. The couple would not go into the house, in spite of Mrs. Bacon's friendly invitation. Alice hoped that the gifts she had left behind at Upton Park for all the staff would be some reward—it was impossible to thank them with words, they would be too embarrassed. Mrs. Hadding and Potter were nonplused by their own good deed, and escaped from her as soon as they could.

Mrs. Bacon had filled the drawing room with flowers, and upstairs in the second attic Norton had already unpacked Laura's trunk of toys, sent on ahead. Alice hoped Dr. Hardy would appear to welcome her, but was told he was away from home. She was disappointed, but soon realized he wanted her to find her way into the house by herself this first time.

"Come, Mrs. Wickham. If you don't mind the informality, will you sit with the child in my kitchen, while I give her a hot drink? I have coconut drops, if you'll allow it. It's the cosiest corner of the house, and you both look a little pinched. What a dear thing the little girl is! About three, I'd say?"

Alice sat by the fire, her heavy skirts steaming. She had never been belowstairs at Upton: she was reminded of days with Deirdre at Carrigrohane. How tired she was, not so much from the journey as from her constant swings of mood from sadness to hope. She felt alone and unaccountably old—as old as Mrs. Bacon looked. Alice thought of all the days ahead that she would spend listening to Laura's prattle and the old woman's simple talk. She was too young to be reduced to such a life. She wanted to beat the walls.

She roused herself. Dr. Hardy had been far too kind for her to think of his home with such hostility.

"Laura, I'll go upstairs and see to our things. Will you stay here by the fire with Mrs. Bacon?"

Laura had a cake in each hand, and was stretching her arms high over her head so that the cat could not reach them. Intent on saving her morsels, she nodded at Alice's words and seemed unconcerned to be left in these new surroundings.

Alice forgot her as she unpacked her bags and walked slowly through their new rooms, touching surfaces and opening doors. Mrs. Bacon had taken care of all the trunks forwarded during the week, and Alice's clothes were laid out neatly on the tallboy shelves. She opened her jewel box. There were the earrings from Grandma Hardy, her wedding present; then a silver locket with a curl of hair—three strands, her own, Anne's and Miss Barry's, a touching gift from her governess; and a bracelet sent to her by Anne on her last birthday. Twenty-one! She had not celebrated it, but spent the day at the Dorcas Society . . .

She heard a scuffle on the stairs. Laura had crawled all the way up to her, with Norton one step behind in case she fell.

"Brave girl!" Alice said, and took her in her arms. They investigated the rooms again, Alice beginning to feel more enthusiasm, as she held Laura on the rocking horse, pulled open all the drawers to reveal their belongings and helped her pile her Noah's Ark animals on the oval sill below the skylight. They lay on the quilted bed to rest for a while, happier and more peaceful than Alice imagined possible. How did Laura know instinctively that she was in a good place? The rooms had the aura of happy childhood, past days filled with games and whispers that still lingered under the eaves.

In the afternoon, a messenger boy delivered flowers from a smart shop in Piccadilly, and a note from Ned, wishing her well in her new home. Alice had given her address only to him and Lady Mary for the present. She was still uncertain what to do next, whom of her acquaintances she might want to continue seeing—or, more critically, who would consent to call on her. She was glad Ned could not come. It was not only prudence; she did not want him to see her in this new setting. He was so much a man for visual impressions that these "reduced circumstances" might destroy the charm she held for him. He had sent her ridiculously expensive lilies from Solomon's. The gesture pleased Alice; it was optimistic.

Tranquility began its healing work on Alice in those first few weeks. Each day she woke early, sometimes forgetting where she was, remembering only when she heard the flutter of pigeons' wings under the roof quite near her bed. The animal closeness brought her to reality with a start: at Upton all nature's sounds had been carried to her from a distance on a constant cool breeze, the northeast wind as it traveled across the land. She dressed quickly, and went to prepare Dr. Hardy's eccentric breakfast while Laura still slept.

Occasionally, through the kitchen window, she glimpsed one of his patients. Wealthy, reserved people, who avoided anyone's gaze. Just once she saw obvious distress: an old lady, moaning and clutching her head as she climbed into her carriage. The sound upset Alice profoundly. It made her realize how fragile her new calmness was, and deterred her from questioning Dr. Hardy more closely about his work.

During the day, she wrote copious letters to Sarah, Lady Mary and Mrs. Burns, the new supervisor at her Dorcas Society. She wanted to write to Sophie, to find out about her mission plans, and to Anne especially, but these last two were impossible. It was perverse, she knew. She did not want to go back to Carrigrohane, but Grandma Hardy's downright refusal to have her wounded Alice unspeakably, and made her cut all communication—even with those parts of her old life that were of value to her.

Instead, she limited her life. In the afternoons, she walked with Laura in Regent's Park. At night sometimes they could hear the roaring of the lions when the sound carried in their direction. It was most clear on Sundays, for it was rumored (by Mrs. Bacon) that the animals went without food on the keepers' day off. It was Alice, not Laura, who imagined the beasts would break out in a rage of hunger, and carry someone off. Laura was too small for such a terrifying thought; Alice still close enough to raw feelings, to wonder.

Returning home to Lime Road from one of her walks, she was greeted by Norton with the news that she had visitors. Lady Mary was waiting to see her. Alice was delighted to see her kind friend. It made her realize how much she had missed her Upton circle.

Lady Mary rose in her usual brisk way as Alice came into the drawing room. There was someone else: Daisy Panton.

"How could you rush off like that, only a letter telling me you'd gone?" said Lady Mary. "Apart from your abruptness, most unlike you, it caused me great inconvenience, for I had a plan to discuss with you before you left."

"I had to do it." Alice said. "It seemed right."

"Good heavens, what do you think we are?" said Daisy, adding her condemnation. "I went off to Scotland with Panton, never dreaming you were in such trouble. I've only just returned, to find Upton Park all locked up and my newfound friend disappeared! Though I must say, looking back, I was very dim not to realize . . ."

Alice was tired and muddled by their chatter. It seemed so odd to hear Lady Mary's ringing, privileged tones in Dr. Hardy's quiet home.

"Sarah's dresses," Daisy persisted. "I've heard all about her trousseau. So what we thought was, why don't you make some clothes for me too? I'd rather pay you than Madame Rose in Bond Street. And if you like, I could tell the others—Belinda Hall for one is constantly complaining about her lack of just the right thing. She hasn't a clue of course, poor dear, that's her problem—only looks well-dressed on a horse."

"Daisy, do let Alice have time to think—you'll quite deafen her with too much talk, as always! What do you say, Alice? I have a genius for schemes, but I do think this is one of my best ideas . . ."

"I don't know . . . it was a pleasure to do it for Sarah, because I knew her so well. I didn't feel nervous."

"Courage, Alice!" Lady Mary interrupted. "That's all you need. And don't think only of yourself. If you succeed you could provide further work for the Dorcas girls. It doesn't seem to me that you will fail. And you have Laura to think of. At least you'll earn the respect of those former friends who'll only too readily see guilt in you if you hide your face!"

Lady Mary provoked defiance in Alice with these words. It was unintentional: Alice had seen her do it to others many times. Lady Mary always found strong arguments by instinct, often giving offense, but always for a good cause.

"I think you've given me enough reasons. No more, please!" Alice wanted to refuse outright, but then she reconsidered. "I suppose there's no harm in trying. . . . I could use the morning room for fittings, it has quite a good light. I'd have to buy a new sewing machine of course—I left my other one for the Dorcas girls in Upton." It was pointless; how could she finance such a venture?

Lady Mary was pleased. "You agree? Good. Then I shall send the latest Singer machine round to you from Harrods. No—I won't listen, Alice. You can have it on loan, if you insist, and repay me when you're better established, but not for a year at least. Now, Daisy, tell her what you want. I have to get back to Anson Street soon."

"I'd just love a new ballgown for the Duchess of Argyll's—and do you think you could make me a tea gown, just like Sarah's? Something really *comme il doit être*—and what color do you think best? I thought pale yellow, perhaps . . ."

"Yellow is the worst color for nearly all complexions. I remember Ned telling me that once—I mean, Mr. Fielding, the artist . . ."

"*The* Ned Fielding?" Daisy was fascinated.

"Yes—you know him, of course." Alice explained, but Daisy looked puzzled. "William asked him to paint my portrait once," she added. Remembrance dawned: Alice could see that Ned had finally "arrived."

"My dear! I just saw his work at the Burlington, such a price!"

That explained the extravagant flowers, thought Alice. How frustrating that she could not see his exhibition or enjoy Ned's success openly, in friendship.

"Well, then, Alice, what do you suggest?"

"What? Oh. Colors. Well, be true to your name, Daisy. I'll make it in white with green trimmings—and rich in lace, I promise!" She spoke quickly, still thinking about Ned.

"Wonderful! Can you do it by next Saturday, the tea gown at least? I'll be back in town properly then—that's my first week with guests. I'm sure it will be perfectly splendid! Make the ball dress however you fancy, but in the same colors—I like the idea very much. Come, Alice, shouldn't we take measurements?" Daisy might be absent-minded and given to hurling herself at enthusiasms, but she was certainly wholehearted.

Alice sent Norton for her sewing box. She thought how strange it was to make such luxurious, frivolous objects like tea gowns and ball dresses at a time like this.

"I'm sorry, but I will have to ask you to give me some money to buy the materials. An advance? Would ten guineas be possible?" Alice apologized.

"I haven't got it!" said Daisy, in surprise. The three women looked at one another—not one of them had a penny about them.

"Put it on my account at Harrods. I'll write you a note," Lady Mary offered, sitting at the writing desk at once.

It was settled. Daisy insisted she wanted both designs to be a complete surprise. The tiger at the door rang the bell to remind Lady Mary of her next appointment, as instructed.

"Don't let her pay you less than twenty guineas for the ball gown!" Lady Mary whispered quickly as they left. "Cheap at the price!"

Twenty guineas! Alice woke up—the whole conversation having taken place while she was in a trance. Could she really charge so much? Tomorrow she would go to Bond Street and find out what would be a fair sum. Nothing in Sarah's trousseau had been half as expensive. She still had copies of material costs in her desk. They might be worth checking.

Some time later, Mrs. Bacon found Alice deep in thought in the drawing room, sitting at her desk, twisting the tape measure in her hands.

"Shall I bring you a little supper, Madam? Laura has had her tea with me, downstairs."

"I forgot all about her, Mrs. Bacon. You must forgive me—I'm so thoughtless!"

"No matter, Madam. I like to have her with me. She's a sweet child, brightens up the place. And you'll be busy—is that a dress you're going to make yourself?"

"Mm? Oh no, Mrs. Bacon, it's for a friend. In white satin and chiffon, with tassels of green silk perhaps . . ."

Alice was drawing little sketches on sheets of writing paper, the words "Upton Park" hastily scratched out on the top of each page.

CHAPTER 8

1 8 9 7

*D*ressing Daisy Panton was a trial of nerves. Alice's original scheme of green and white survived Daisy's prevarications, but every other detail was accepted, rejected, then accepted again a hundred times. Several special delivery letters arrived each day with new instructions. Alice, who had no patience, thought she would never endure the life of a dressmaker if all her customers were as willful as this one. Daisy's money and position created in her a fretful desire for attention—far too much, in Alice's opinion. After several days of contradictory orders, Alice decided to ignore all other messages and make both dresses exactly as she pleased.

The tea gown was the simpler of the two. As time was limited, Alice boldly placed an order for several yards of fine Brussels lace, several more of satin ribbon and a heavy silk chiffon for a lining. She also walked the length of Oxford Street to find the materials and trimmings for the ballgown, so that when Daisy returned for the first fitting, not a single detail would be left in question.

Alice had never drafted a pattern or made up a dress single-handedly in her life. Mrs. Burns, the seamstress for the Dorcas girls, had cut out all the dresses for Sarah's trousseau; Alice had merely suggested the designs and done the stitching. Sarah had attended frequent fittings as each model was sewn, but all Alice had now was a list of measurements from a woman who was much more endowed than Sarah, in every sense of the word.

Daisy had a generous embonpoint—a mature plumpness that had to be set off by her clothes. She was the shape that all men loved—or that all women currently saw as the desirable ideal: broad-chested, narrow-waisted, and wide in the hips. Daisy would have been wearing a day corset when she visited Alice with Lady Mary, but for a soirée at the Duchess of Argyll's she would sacrifice all thought of comfort for true elegance. Her waist could be made at least three inches smaller with tight-lacing. Given all these difficulties, it would be almost impossible for Alice to achieve a good fit. To give herself a little more confidence, she cut out a pattern in newspaper, and then in old sheeting, donated by Mrs. Bacon. She used instructions in one of her magazines, the *Lady's Companion*, for a bodice and a plain, bias-cut skirt with a simple train which she could extend without difficulty. She tried to fit the skirt on herself, but it was hopeless. She could not alter the fall of the back—she had only one long mirror—and besides, Daisy was at least three inches taller than she was.

"Mrs. Bacon! Help me!" Alice did not ring but ran downstairs as fast as she could. The housekeeper was making cakes with Laura in the kitchen.

"Lord, what's the matter? Is there a fire?"

Alice laughed. "Merely a desperate solution. Stand still: thirty-eight, twenty-nine, oh no, forty-two. You won't do . . . but you *are* the right ·

height." Alice stood hands on hips, having measured Mrs. Bacon without ceremony while the housekeeper's hands still worked the flour in the bowl.

Mrs. Bacon turned round, holding her whited hands up like a puppet. "This is on account of her ladyship's gown?"

"I'd like to get the underskirt and the bodice pinned by Saturday at least . . ."

Mrs. Bacon drew herself up a little. "If it's my waist that concerns you—let me put on my best stays. I had a fine figure, once. But you'll have to help me. I can't do it by myself with these old bones." She rubbed her hands clean and untied her apron.

Half an hour later, Mrs. Bacon stood regally in her petticoat and stays (ancient but effective) while Alice darted at her with pins, and snipped at the sheeting. Mrs. Bacon was patience itself and offered constructive criticism. "Drape the bodice—leave a little more room round the midriff. She'll breathe heavy after dancing. . . ." It was touching to see her looking in the mirror, as a young girl might, tilting her white-haired head gently to one side, and smoothing the linen with her age-softened, bent fingers.

By the appointed day, a froth of a tea gown lay ready on a chair, and a half-finished bodice, underskirt and overskirt were ready for the real essay.

Daisy was impressed. The tea gown was a mass of loosely draped honey-colored lace, with green silk chiffon underneath and white flowers caught into pale green bows, all down the front opening—very alluring, and clearly made with only one purpose in mind.

"You must have worked all night to finish it! You are a miracle of labor, Alice—did no one help you in this?" Like many rich people, Daisy relished the details of other people's service on her behalf.

"Oh yes, Mrs. Bacon was invaluable! But never mind that—it's the ball gown I'm so anxious to fit. You are wearing your evening stays?"

Daisy's lashes fluttered, hiding her clear blue eyes. "A twenty-two-inch waist! I was nineteen in my younger days, alas!"

Alice did not bother to correct this self-deception (twenty-eight reduced to twenty-four was nearer the truth). Daisy was statuesque: the white bodice, elongated into a point at the stomach, fitted like a second skin and her bosom swelled dangerously out of its casing. Daisy, however, was pleased with that effect.

Alice pinned swags of stiffened silk marguerites across the shoulder and down the front.

"I chose marguerites because field daisies would be on much too small a scale to make *any* impression," she explained. A little mockery was irresistible. Alice was beginning to enjoy herself.

"It's heavenly! But isn't it a little plain?"

"Wait. You haven't tried on the overskirt."

Alice poured three layers of chiffon in three shades of green over the shining satin. Caught back with clusters of daisies to one side, each color ended at a different height from the hem. The idea was simple— all that she could do in the time—but the movement of the colors made the gown luxurious and original.

"I think I see the idea . . ." Daisy liked the dress, but wanted yet more persuasion. Alice knelt down to pin decorations to the train.

"Now, a last detail—you could have tassels, like this, or if you prefer, seed pearls, or even prettier, crystals—dewdrops, do you see?"

"The crystals—how clever of you—that's perfectly rustic and romantic!"

"And you must wear a stiff taffeta petticoat under the silk underskirt. I haven't time to make one, but the sound of silk on silk is so delicious— *chou-chou*—such a luxury! I wore my first one for the hunt ball—do you remember, Daisy, when we first met?"

The memory came back to Alice unclouded. It was when she still hoped that she could be happy. Alice sat back on her heels, holding the crystals in the palm of her hand. This was perhaps the way to redeem the past—make use of it.

"Oh, I do indeed." Daisy helped her to her feet. "I thought you were an extraordinary child—quite unique. William really should have looked after you. You're totally blameless, Alice. Whatever anyone else should make you think!"

"Ssh! Please! You'll make me cry, and tear marks quite ruin satin!" Alice did not want to spoil her very first commission.

◆   ◆   ◆

Just as Alice feared, some days after the ball Daisy came back. The dress had split entirely up one of the bodice seams. Alice was embarrassed and started to apologize but Daisy interrupted.

"I couldn't care! It lasted till the polka, and I burst in my partner's arms. He had to take me home . . . of course he thought it was all designed to entrap him—which it did. After months of intrigue!"

Alice was amused, and greatly relieved, but also surprised by Daisy's immodesty. Then she realized, with a certain dismay, that perhaps she was only a *dressmaker* now, the traditional recipient of all confidences. She had no place in Society, for she earned money, and being in "trade" broke more rules than getting divorced. *She* would never be invited to grand occasions, so Daisy had no need to be discreet.

"Will you mend it—and will you see Cecily Day? She's walking in the park, but I could soon bring her here, if you agree."

"Mrs. Cecily Day? For a dress?" Alice repeated stupidly. She knew the name, of course—a beautiful woman who had been in the Prince's circle for a while.

"Perhaps I shouldn't tell my friends; you might become too busy for me." Daisy hesitated.

"That couldn't possibly happen."

"Will you see her, then?"

"No, I think not. I'd be foolish to make more mistakes. You're very generous, Daisy, but let me make you a perfect dress to prove myself to you, first. Besides, I couldn't possibly do more work without getting some basic "blocks"—you know, pattern pieces, cut for me by Mrs. Burns. And then there's the problem of the house—Dr. Hardy has patients coming here during the day, and he may not want to be disturbed by such comings and goings."

"Surely he won't disapprove if you're earning your own living! What do men expect these days! After all—"

Alice prevented Daisy from giving her a speech on women's rights. "He's entirely supportive, Daisy, but for that very reason I must consult him."

"Well, be sure to tell him that I'm determined you shall succeed, and that I was paid dozens of compliments on your beautiful gown! And look here, no more of this twenty-guinea nonsense. Cecily Day spends hundreds a season in Paris—I see no reason why you shouldn't start as you mean to go on."

Alice was amused: to Daisy all of life's decisions consisted of making up one's mind. Alice envied that sublime self-confidence.

"If I *were* to charge more, I could afford to hire a seamstress to help me . . ." she murmured.

"Look, make me another ballgown—anything! Use the same base skirt and just cut another top, with the same décolletage, of course!" Daisy was rather wildly grabbing at Alice's box of trimmings and draping strips of sequins across her broad bosom. She was a natural manager—such a pity she exercised her talents only on young men, thought Alice.

"Very well, Daisy, I'll do as you say." Daisy kissed her enthusiastically and left to go riding in the park with her friend Cecily Day.

Dr. Hardy listened attentively when Alice broached the idea of a small dressmaking enterprise that evening.

"So all these fine ladies would have to come here for the dresses to be tried on?" he repeated. He folded his hands on his knees as if they were discussing a theory of the universe. Alice found his interest deeply affecting: he had an almost childlike readiness to be interested in anything, seldom passing judgment or imposing his own values on other people's concerns.

"Yes. They'd only come in the afternoons of course, if that would be convenient for your work. I know it sounds frivolous but—"

"Dear lady! Women have adorned themselves since the world began! You must make a life for yourself . . . and if this is your talent, then I hope you succeed. Though I must say, your friend Mrs. Panton quite terrifies me when she is all 'on display,' shall we say? She's altogether magnificent."

He spread his thin old arms helplessly, and they both laughed at the picture of Dr. Hardy expressing passion for a woman of Daisy's voluptuousness. He looked delighted: and then Alice remembered that she had not laughed so freely for a very long time.

◆　◆　◆

Alice did not regret her caution. After a few months, her small enterprise began to expand into a flourishing concern. It was all due to Daisy. As her romance blossomed, so did her her need for beautiful, seductive clothes. The excitement of a new affair made her even more attractive; friends commented on her good looks, and Alice benefited with more customers.

Lady Mary also tried to persuade Lady Belinda Hall, a Rutland acquaintance, to bring Alice a young niece who needed a Presentation dress. Although Alice did not imagine that she would ever advertise herself, the title "Court Dressmaker" would have been useful, so she welcomed the chance to master the formal evening styling required by debutantes for their first visit to the palace. But Belinda refused, and Alice was disappointed. She knew from her own girlish circles in Cork exactly how perfect a Court train should be; how to make the right headdress for the traditional three white feathers; but then she wanted to add a little imagination, some original detail to make her dresses exciting as well as becoming. If Belinda had scruples about supporting her, there would always be others.

Slowly, more commissions came from society families, for word of mouth mattered more than any other recommendation. "Elegant Elinor," the Fogarty girl, now Countess of Wenham, came to her, but Alice pretended not to be recognized, and received her order for a dress with an unbending remoteness. The countess did not call again. But there were many such women in Daisy's world who pitied Alice, or who were curious about her, and that in itself kept her busy with orders. Alice had to learn how to be flattering but formal, developing a certain grandeur in her manner as self-protection.

Every day, Laura disappeared into Mrs. Bacon's room downstairs, while Alice worked long, hard hours. In the mornings, she sketched new designs, cut out or sewed, while the light was at its best in her room. Mrs. Burns in Upton had been able to suggest a pattern-maker, and now she had two young assistants from the Dorcas Society, Minnie Clough and Teresa Sutton, one to do plain sewing, the other to stitch the trimmings. They arrived after lunch, for in the mornings they left their lodgings early and went about the city "trotting" or "matching"—finding fabric samples and haberdashery for Alice's new designs. (She had stopped buying her supplies at expensive West End shops now that she had trained helpers.) It was still inconveniently unacceptable for a lady like Alice to wander round backstreet warehouses by herself, but her young assistants did it, protected by their poverty, by the cheapness of their clothes and their lack of class.

When the two Dorcas girls arrived, Alice was free to turn the sewing work over to them, and to receive any customers. All day long the old house in Lime Road echoed with bells. In the mornings, Dr. Hardy's patients called, and the coded rings informed the household who was in and who was out. In the afternoon, no one was in doubt: Dr. Hardy retreated to his study to write, while loud, light voices and womanish laughter filled the house.

Alice learnt quickly that stunning looks had nothing to do with a blatant display of riches, but with the assertion of wealth in quiet ways. Some of her dresses were simple *fourreaux* of velvet or satin with a minimal decoration at the neck, hem, or waist: sheaths of rich fabric that revealed the outline of a body. Wives or mistresses could wear them nakedly, if they had the confidence of beauty, like Daisy Panton, or with the family jewels if all they had were imperfect figures and the material attributes of their class. The shapes Alice created were not extreme, although the sleeves were sometimes wider than she would ever have dared to wear herself, and the skirts a little tighter across the hips. The general effect that both Alice and her customers were agreed upon was one of subtle confidence and discreet sexual appeal.

◆　◆　◆

As Alice's new life took shape, she began to look back to those attachments that she had been forced to give up. Foremost of these was her sister, Anne. After a silence of eighteen months, she wrote to her once more.

My D M L S —
My Dearly Missed, Loving Sister—can you forgive me? I've been so sad, and at times unwell. But now all is past, long forgotten. I couldn't face you before, but I'm better, and so very happy! When you come, perhaps I'll explain it all—no, I think not. We shall start again. A bad dream, that's all. Here I am—do you think Grandma might soften just a little, enough to let you visit me? Perhaps you could tell her that London is a historical place to visit in this, the year of the Jubilee. . . . You *do* want to come, don't you? I have written Grandma under separate cover to ask her kind permission . . .

Anne was astonished. Alice's writing was barely recognizable. She had covered large sheets of sketching paper with hurried sentences, full of exclamation marks and dashes. Cartoons of figures filled the margins: beautiful women in frilly dresses, a little baby on the floor in a tangle of ribbons; Dr. Gayott Hardy smiling as he ate onion rings; Mrs. Bacon, with a cat, both asleep upon the cushions.

The girls began a detailed correspondence, Alice writing during her long hours of solitude at night, when Laura was asleep. She would be too tired to sew, and too involved in her dreams of success to think of bed. Anne wrote back at equal length during the dreary days at Carrigrohane, between her formal visits to country houses or her unusual trips to Dublin with "Mrs. O'Brien," her voice teacher. There was less chance that they would be recognized than in Cork, so they went to the theater all the time, and even visited some of Mrs. O'Brien's raffish theatrical friends in dilapidated rooming houses.

Alice could tell that these illicit excursions were a rewarding contrast to her sister's more conventional social activities. She imagined the obligatory calls Anne would make to the Stoneys, the Boyles, the Patersons, or even just to Cork with Miss Barry to purchase unnecessary things.

"I practise 'acting' the obedient granddaughter, never to upset Grandma, never to arouse her suspicions, so that my great plan can become a reality," Anne confided in one letter. "Here it is: Mrs. O'Brien has promised me a letter of introduction to theatrical personages in London. If only, if *only* I can persuade Grandma to let me come!"

Unexpectedly, Anne succeeded. Grandma Hardy decided to go to Marienbad to try the mud cure for her rheumatism; the damp beds in Carrigrohane were finally claiming her. Anne rightly complained that she would be bored by invalid company all summer. Her patriotic sentiment for the Jubilee disposed Grandma Hardy to hope that a visit to Alice *was* reasonable. Slightly mistrustful, she made Anne write to say that it was only expediency that made her agree, not any relenting toward Alice.

Alice wondered if Dr. Hardy perhaps had written to Carrigrohane in confidence, reporting on her good progress. She had lost caste entirely by going into trade of course, but at least she was becoming a success. In the Hardy bones, particularly in Grandpa James', a respect for commercial initiative still lurked.

Anne traveled to London with a military family (friends of Grandpa Hardy's) who were returning to England on leave. She was elated by the sight of the capital decked out for the festivities. Shopkeepers made window displays all red, blue and white. There were piles of objects in honor of the Jubilee: tin trays, portraits, transfer mugs, china busts—just like the trophies of an African trading post. Union Jacks and bunting filled the streets—cheerful, vulgar trimmings on staid gray edifices.

Anne's chaperones placed her in a cab heading north from the railway station, and Anne rubbed the dusty window pane, leaning forward to catch every glimpse of these jollities as she passed by. There is nothing so exciting as London on a bright summer day. The stone buildings gleam with unusual brightness after months of being shrouded in smoke, fog, and gritty rain. More often than not, a breeze dispels any staleness or sultry heaviness in the air. Smart, important people are out of town, a hint of vacancy in the streets makes adventure possible. To a young stranger like Anne, London suggested a city of fairy tales. It lay dozing, like a giant warrior in loosened armor, with a chink in its social steel. She felt she was slipping in, an unnoticed lady Gulliver, and might hide comfortably before she took the enemy.

But the further she rode, the more timid she became. She lost all sense of direction, for London was laid out on a vast scale compared to Cork or Dublin. Then, arriving in Lime Road, and seeing Alice again, she suddenly knew that she was coming to a real home.

Alice, in a blue gown, sat by the window sewing. A pretty child was hiding with her dolls under a grand piano; trails of ribbon and lace covered the floor. Alice stood up, slimmer than Anne ever remembered. Her cheekbones stood out, wide and fine beneath her deep brown eyes, which were unchanged, alive with pleasure at seeing her. No pallor, no dark circles spoilt Alice's features, as Anne had feared.

"Oh, Alice! I've missed you!" They kissed and hugged each other without reserve. For many years, the only warmth they had known came from the closeness of sisterly contact. "I've so much to tell you, but first I want to know all about—unless you don't want to tell me, of course. I'm sorry—are you feeling faint?"

Alice sat down abruptly. "No. It's just—seeing you brought it all back. That summer—the baby. Oh, don't let's talk of it. Look, there she is—say hello to the little one!"

"Oh my. I don't believe it. My sister's baby." Anne crawled under the piano, whispering in a voice that imitated the "generals" at Carrigrohane, full of "Lord love ye's" and other strange phrases. Laura gave an intense stare at the beautiful laughing creature who spoke so comically, and yet seemed to be known to her already. Just then, Dr. Hardy came in, following the sound of laughter to the bunches of skirts under the piano.

"Poppa! Better now . . ." Laura showed him her doll, its head mysteriously fixed back on again by the visitor.

The girls stood up and Anne came nearer to be introduced. Dr. Hardy was fascinated. How strangely different, yet familiar too: everything in Alice written a little larger, more wildly in the younger sister. Anne had the same pale skin, emphasized by the candor of her expression, and amber eyes, much lighter than Alice's. Her height and a mass of awkward reddish hair contrasted with her elder sister's smallness, more fragile bones and smooth black coiffure swept upwards. But their tiny firm mouths were the same, thin Irish lips, and they both had small straight noses. Loyalty made Dr. Hardy prefer Alice's delicate looks, but he was impressed by Anne's more classic beauty.

Anne liked Dr. Hardy on sight. She knew from Alice's letter that this was the man who had helped her sister through bad times. Besides, Anne liked older men, and soon had Dr. Hardy flattered, if slightly bemused, by her attentions.

Alice was elated to have someone to impress, too: not with her beauty, but with her efforts. In the following days she indulged herself. She could not help performing for Anne, watching her eyes widen with excitement as yet another titled woman came into the room and kissed her in greeting—or introduced a friend who wanted Alice to dress her. It *was* vastly impressive—Alice behaved with supreme nonchalance when Mrs. Cecily Day (now a regular customer) ordered a dress to be ready in three days and sent to the country for a weekend party where "royalty" was expected.

"That means she's back in favor with the Prince," Alice informed Anne, who listened as if she were telling Arabian Nights' tales.

When the house was quiet, Alice sat working at her desk, showing Anne her sketches, ten or so designs thought out in the space of a few hours. The pictures were so detailed that the sewing girls could work from them exactly after the cutting and fitting was finished. Swatches of fabric were pinned to the corner of each drawing, and samples of all the trims were laid on top for final choice.

After a few days of adjusting to Alice's pace and amusing herself with Laura, Anne was ready to explore London. Dr. Hardy did not keep a carriage, so Daisy Panton sent round her barouche with instructions that Alice and Anne were to tour all the sights at their leisure. It was a perfect day—the sisters could wander in arcades, galleries, all the monuments and parks, for as long as they pleased. They decided upon a strange list of favorites.

Anne wanted to see Beerbohm Tree's new theater, opened for the Jubilee and named Her Majesty's. It dominated the Haymarket, an Italianate stone and granite façade that suited its owner's grandiose style.

"I'm going to see him act as soon as he returns," Anne vowed, "*and* Ellen Terry in *Madame Sans Gêne* at the Lyceum—just as soon as the doors reopen!"

Then Alice took her to a more curious attraction—the new moving staircase at Harrods'. They were children again, sailing up and down, from floor to floor, trying not to laugh at prosperous shoppers, apparently floating, looking glum. From Knightsbridge they rode to the City, glancing into back lanes, spying out corners just as Dickens had described them. They climbed the Monument so that Anne could see the whole of London. In an act of unusual boldness they ate oyster pie in Leadenhall Market, ignoring the stares of all the lunching clerks who peered round the edges of their wooden cubicles to admire them.

The afternoon was spent in Bond Street, in Burlington Arcade, and at the Academy in Piccadilly to see the new exhibition by Lord Leighton.

At last they drove home, via Park Lane and Regent's Park. Dusk fell, but they could still see each other's familiar profiles. Relaxed and happy, they exchanged the first full truths about the two years since they had last met at Upton. Alice told as much as she dared about William and his mistress, about Laura's birth and her illness. Anne admitted to a few romantic attachments, but seemed entirely obsessed with her theatrical ambitions.

Laura was already asleep when they got home, so, deep in conversation, they both crept into Alice's bedroom and made ready for bed. Anne borrowed a nightdress, reluctant to leave Alice even for a minute when they were so near to their old intimacy again. They brushed each other's hair, cuddled together, and finally told each other all their dreams.

"I'll be a famous actress. I just know I will."

"And I'll make you beautiful gowns, and men will send diamonds and roses to you every night." Alice teased.

Anne was too self-involved to hear the mockery.

"Ah yes, Alice, but I have to be very strict. I've no intention of—um—ruining myself. I only want admirers, for men to flirt, to be in love with me! I mean to be a serious actress, and any scandal would ruin my chances . . ."

Alice did not think for one minute that Anne would keep her word. She was so young, just eighteen, but she looked abundant, and much older. Alice's opinion of the stage was entirely based on Grandma Hardy's views, and her bitter discovery of William's theatrical mistress.

"Not vaudeville," Anne seemed to read her thoughts, "*Real* theater, I shall be a *grande dame,* you'll see."

"And what about me, sweetest, what will happen to me?"

"Oh, you'll marry someone else, someone even grander than William was."

Alice shifted in disagreement, pulling the sheet up so it brushed her lips and half hid her face. She was thinking of Ned. The divorce was all settled, but he had not come to see her.

"I don't want to," she said. "I just want to be left in peace. I know other women have happiness with men—I see the way they smile when they put on a pretty dress, and I can imagine them parading for their lovers. I like that. It does give me pleasure to think about it, but only at a distance."

"But aren't you lonely, even sometimes, Alice?"

"No, strangely, I'm not. My ladies keep me busy, Dr. Hardy is kindness itself, and I have my own plans. I *will* make a success of my new life. I hated having to do what William wanted—he thought I should be grateful for marriage, and he never cared to make me happy. I should like to be no one's property ever, ever again."

A silence ensued, both the girls drifting in and out of sleep, dreams, the excited awareness of each other's presence in the big brass bed.

"Are you awake?" Alice whispered. Her declaration to Anne had brought her a sudden clarity, a little surge of energy that broke into her peace.

"Mm?"

"Are you serious? About being an actress?"

"Mm. Yes."

"Grandmaman would have loved that . . ."

But Anne was too tired, hardly remembered the name, and could not rouse herself to ask Alice what she meant.

◆　◆　◆

In the weeks that followed, Anne did as much as she could to help Alice, who was especially busy because of the Jubilee. Parties, fetes, Jubilee balls and receptions meant more than the usual number of summer gowns, and Alice was very happy to have so many orders.

Anne hated sewing, so her help took the form of creating diversions for her little niece, Laura. One day she took the child and Mrs. Bacon down to Chelsea to see the Colonies' soldiers encamped there for the celebrations. They had never seen men so tall, wild, small, red or black, performing their military duties with a domestic calm under all shapes of canvas tenting. Laura stared in amazement at the men, but buried her face in Anne's skirts when a Hausa soldier smiled directly at her.

For Jubilee day itself, Alice half wished she could go back to the village, to Upton. Lady Mary would have open house, stalking about the lawn in her usual heavy silks. She would try to be gracious and friendly, but terrify the villagers with her autocratic manners. Only the older village people knew her goodness well enough not to be cowed by her eccentricities. There was going to be a banquet, laid out in the Market Square, and a tree-planting ceremony on the green. The Dorcas girls were to have a display and sale of work, and both Minnie and Teresa were going home ("Hadn't they worked for weeks on their finery?" Anne mocked). Alice thought it would be utterly inappropriate to go so near to William's territory on such a public occasion.

A gesture of détente from William's relatives brought Alice a reward for her tact. Lady Evelyn sent an invitation for the sisters to watch Queen Victoria's procession from the windows of one of Sir Warren's properties in Mansion House Street. They accepted instantly, and went early by cab to avoid the crowds converging all along the route of the royal parade. Lady Evelyn had laid out a champagne breakfast for her guests, to sustain them while they waited. She greeted Alice and Anne with her former affection.

"How attractive you both look!" She kissed them before turning away to welcome other guests.

"Thank you for asking us . . . and Laura sends her love. . . ." Alice just managed to whisper this before Lady Evelyn disappeared.

"She comes to Lime Road to see us," Alice explained to Anne, "but Sir Thomas doesn't approve . . ."

"Doesn't Lady Evelyn ask you for dresses? She's very smart," Anne asked.

"Oh no. That would be most improper—can you imagine, any one of her friends might enquire for her dressmaker, and Evelyn would be so embarrassed!"

Anne did not understand these vagaries of class at all. She shrugged her shoulders prettily and followed Alice into the reception room.

Stripped of all office detail, the wood-paneled boardroom had been turned into a gala hall. High windows opened out on to three long balconies, swagged with bunting and bunches of flowers. Streamers were draped between the chandeliers, and an army of servants had staggered up the stairs with palm trees, water fountains and gauzy drapes to soften the masculine decor.

Eventually the parade began. The sisters had an impressive view of that memorable display of imperial majesty: the riotous colors of foreign uniforms, the turbans, plumes, pillboxes and fezzes, bobbing up and down below, interspersed by the clashing brilliance of brass bands.

A gold-printed issue of the *Daily Mail* informed them that there was an empress, a crown prince, twenty-three princesses, a grand duke, three grand duchesses, four duchesses and forty Indian rulers in that cavalcade.

Looking up at the tops of the buildings across the street, Alice saw one wild youth scrambling up between two attic gables, waving a giant Union Jack as the men marched below. For a second she imagined him plunging down onto the giant African warriors, onto their fringed spears, held so stiffly upright. But with the mad energy of one caught up in an unforgettable event, the boy placed his feet deftly on the rooftiles until he reached a chimney. He looked ecstatic aloft with his flag—and she admired his courage.

Lady Evelyn joined them on the balcony, apologizing for not introducing them to more people, and for Sir Warren's temporary absence.

"He has other special guests to attend to. I'm sure he'll find you." Alice doubted it, but smiled agreeably. Lady Evelyn had already done more than she had expected of her.

"You've been so kind. I'll prove to you . . ."

Cheers drowned Alice's words. Another grand army passed below. Alice was glad that Evelyn had not heard what she tried to say—it was impulsive and foolish, perhaps. But Alice wished she could explain her sudden thought: that she and Anne were their own little army, too. They were allies, climbing a little higher with their dreams, like the boy who waved his flag over the rooftops.

◆　◆　◆

Alice began to see real dedication in Anne's apparently foolish plans. Few other girls of eighteen would have the courage to search out theater offices and demand interviews as she did, clutching Mrs. O'Brien's dog-eared letter of introduction. Alice helped in the best way she could, by making one or two startling outfits, tight-waisted suits in brilliant worsted plaids, with jewel-colored velvet at the neck and cuffs. With her emphatic hats, all spotted veiling and quivering feathers, Anne was certainly remembered wherever she went.

It was to no one's great surprise, therefore, that Anne came home one day with the news that she had been offered a very small part in a short-run subscription theater production. Mrs. Bacon cooked a splendid duck to celebrate and ordered Norton to produce a good wine from the cellar to accompany it. Dr. Hardy was instructed to present himself properly dressed (no slippers) for supper that evening, and to reciprocate, both Alice and Anne wore their best gowns.

Alice and Dr. Hardy sat like pupils, while Anne explained the importance of her chance.

"It's summer, you see, the big companies are still touring out of town. But Miss Lily Lavelle—you must have heard of her! No? Oh, you are such dull folks! Well, she's taken a short lease, to try out a newly written play—written just for her, imagine!"

"Lily Lavelle?" That's an Irish name." Alice said.

"It is so! I know—from Dublin, that's how she knows Mrs. O'Brien, my voice trainer. They acted together just once . . . ," Anne laughed with a touch of malice. "Mrs. O'Brien always tells me how successful she was, but she was only a nurse then, in one of Lily's touring plays . . ."

"A nurse?" said Dr Hardy, puzzled. Too much food had made him less attentive than usual. "She was your throat specialist, this Mrs. O'Brien?"

Anne looked exasperated, so Alice quickly explained once again that Mrs. O'Brien had taught Anne "voice" but had been an actress herself, in her youth.

"So this is a favor, to an old friend." Alice was quick to see and criticize Anne's ingratitude. "Mrs. O'Brien's letter was at least your way in."

"Oh yes, quite, but I do get paid, imagine! A salary! Five pounds a week!"

Alice had to resist passing an irreverent comment. Anne's hat alone would obliterate three weeks of those wages.

"Oh, of course, I do have to provide my costumes . . ." Anne added quickly, hoping that Alice would agree without thinking.

Dr. Hardy was most amused. "My dear, I'm not quite sure who succeeded in this audition—you or Alice!"

His loyalty was so touching—but now Anne was on the verge of tears because they were teasing, when the small part meant the whole of her life to her.

"Don't take on so, I'd love to do it," Alice agreed. To make amends, she sat with her sister that night and read through the play, letting Anne speak her own part. Alice was intrigued; it was a "New Woman" sort of play, about a governess, a fallen woman who searches for the man who ruined her. Years after the episode, she takes a position in her former lover's family household, at the time when his younger sister is being forced into a marriage of convenience by her ambitious mother.

Of course, the governess defends the daughter, confronts her former lover, and fills him with remorse. But the play had a good ending, in Alice's opinion. With his admiration reawakened, the lover proposes to the governess, but she refuses him, preferring to remain in the nursery with the young siblings, unrevealed to the women of the family. Alice liked the severity of that.

The Governess was an attack on women's status, and particularly the attitudes of genteel families to their sons and daughters. Convention gave the eldest sons all the money, all the education, and all the freedom to do wrong. Daughters were property for disposal.

Alice was disturbed by the play. So much of its content related to her own understanding of the world's ways, but she found it shocking to think of her sister taking part in it. Her upbringing made her baulk at the idea of challenging the "way of the world," which seemed immutable to her. She also found it odd that a West End actress, as Anne described Lily, should want to play such a pathetic, severe character as the governess. Anne was to be the beautiful affianced girl. A small part: with her fine looks, careful débutante's manners, and Alice's expensive clothes, Anne really was perfect for the role. Lily Lavelle was not taking much of a risk.

Any misgivings Alice felt about abetting her sister were swept aside by Anne's wild joy. Alice noted a little sadly that although *she* might find an unconventional life hard, a disregard for social rules was vigorously developed in Anne. She behaved just as she wanted, not on impulse but because any other way of life was impossible for her. It was like trying to stop a beautiful butterfly from opening its gaudy wings.

"Tomorrow, you shall give me Miss Lavelle's notes on the costume. I'll make you something perfect."

◆　◆　◆

The play was only performed eight times—six nights and two matinees—at the Moonlight Theater in Bloomsbury, late in August. Anne got a "highly commended" mention in a review that concentrated mostly on the immorality of modern playwrights, who depicted fallen women as blameless victims.

Alice thought this was a a dishonest criticism. Lily Lavelle, with her golden hair, thrilling voice, and physical magnificence, could never be convincingly downtrodden, however well she acted. She had an extraordinary appeal, a magical vitality even when she was completely still. Anne looked suitably ingenuous—her auburn coloring certainly contrasted beautifully, deliberately no doubt, with Miss Lavelle's blondeness. The silky crinoline Alice had made satisfied her as appearing reasonably authentic in the limelight.

Dr. Hardy sat beside Alice during the first performance—almost ruining it for her by staring at her throughout the evening, observing her reactions. Alice was particularly glad therefore to be asked to the Moonlight again as a last-night guest. She could watch Anne more critically, and better still, meet the famous Miss Lavelle at the reception afterward.

Lily hired a restauranteur to bring in tables and chairs and lay them out on the stage, and had even summoned pink cloths, carnations, candles. Champagne for the whole company probably finished off her meager profits; Alice, with her newfound interest in finance, could not help being prosaic about this needless extravagance.

Later in the evening, Anne introduced Alice to Lily, and they acknowledged each other with mutual curiosity. Alice reckoned they were both about the same age—but she could not help responding with pleasure, not rivalry, to Lily's unusual physical perfection—her pale, dense skin, her beautiful proportions, and her clear, grayish-green eyes.

"Thank you for your letter about Anne's costumes. My first venture . . . how relieved I was to know that you were pleased."

"Not at all, Mrs. Wickham. You had some fine ideas. I particularly love the simplicity of the engagement scene dress. You painted on the satin, did you? Such exquisite butterflies . . ."

"I enjoyed it!" Alice could see Lily's attention wandering as she glanced past at other guests. Lily had the manners of someone intensely vain, used to being watched.

Lily waved gracefully at no one in particular. "Well, we shall part ways now, Annie and I. There's only room for one Irish actress in any company! Ah—there he is!" She gestured to a late arrival. "No, don't leave me, Mrs. Wickham. I want you to approve!"

A brilliant smile summoned an athletic, imposing man to her side. He moved deftly through the crowd.

"Do something for me, Hubert. You are going to take that little Irish girl, my adorable Miss Hardy, on tour for me, aren't you? Show her the ropes. Mrs. Wickham, may I present Hubert Kerrick? He's been training actors and actresses in Shakespeare since you and I were children, but I swear he looks fresh enough to be my younger brother!"

The look Hubert Kerrick gave Lily made the idea quite untenable.

"Mrs. Wickham is Annie's sister, and a wonderful designer of costumes."

"Oh yes, I see the resemblance. . . . I'm to convince you of Miss Hardy's moral welfare, is that it?" he teased. He was ridiculously handsome, perfect and dark, but with vacuous eyes.

"Oh no, not at all. . . ." Alice wanted to protest but decided it was simpler to accept the role in which she was cast: that of overprotective guardian-sister. Was she really so unused to socializing that she looked like a devoted relation, a dull chaperone? They were not talking to her, but at her, anyway.

"Oh yes, Mrs Wickham. I know Anne values your judgment most highly." Lily shook her fan at Mr. Kerrick, commanding him to explain himself.

"Well, then let me assure you—the male team plays cricket or rugger on tours, to keep fit. I have chaperones for my girls, and we have our own trains for journeys—segregated compartments, too. Between sports and rehearsals, there's no time for intriguing. It's a sacred enterprise, taking Shakespeare to the provinces! As Miss Lavelle will tell you, I believe in it with all my heart." He blinked rapidly, to indicate his sincerity.

Alice tried to envisage Anne, with her fine airs, traveling round England in this sportsmanlike entourage. "Kerrick's Players" sounded more like a school's first cricketing eleven than a company of theatrical artistes.

"I'm sure it's a wonderful opportunity, Mr. Kerrick." He bowed, kissed her hand and then bowed over Lily's admiringly before turning to another conversation.

Lily prevented Alice from leaving her by sporadic whispers and touches on her gloved arm, yet she constantly turned her head, waved to other guests, or called out to someone.

"He speaks Elizabethan verse appallingly, does Mr. Kerrick! Look, there's Mariana—Dearest! But he is a great professional, Hubert, I mean, of course. And excellent company. Supper's delicious, do try the fish. . . . If Anne means to continue, nothing could be better for her. At last, a full glass! Thank you, my angel. Give one to Mrs. Wickham too."

"Thank you, it's really too kind of you to—"

"Why do I care, do you ask?" Lily interrupted, totally aware of Alice's thoughts in spite of appearing inattentive. "She's very young, and full of promise. A tour will show her if she's hard enough for this life. She needs to discover that for herself. No one can tell her. This is no favor, Mrs. Wickham. At times, she will be *very* lonely and unhappy!"

Lily was so amused that for a moment Alice was not sure if she had entirely kind intentions toward her "adorable Miss Hardy."

CHAPTER 9

1 8 9 8

Two months passed before Alice received Lily Lavelle's letter asking for a meeting. Lily arrived long after the agreed time, looking radiant as she always seemed to. Her clothes invited the gaze of admiring crowds, who enjoyed looking at her whenever she stepped out of a carriage, a restaurant or theater stage door. Today she wore an outrageous hat with ostrich feathers dyed cornflower blue drooping over the brim of black velvet. Her suit of vivid blue cashmere showed her nipped-in waist, and a three-quarter jacket with tucks at the hip matched the tucks on the widening gores that swept the floor. A rustle of hidden delights, layers of petticoats, filled Alice's room.

Of course Alice hoped that an order for an outfit might be the reason for Lily's visit, but the sight of all that Parisian splendor made the idea ridiculous. Lily was far too smart to offer her custom. So Alice was even more surprised when Lily announced that she wanted her to design costumes for a forthcoming stage part.

"I'm sure you have just the talent for it. It's a new farce, for Christmas—it's light, quite thoughtless. Of course, I prefer the kind of work we staged at the Moonlight, but I have to earn a living, and so these things must be done."

She handed over an envelope. "I've drawn something basic. I'd like a flowing dress, the kind of thing that Sarah Bernhardt wears, though of course on me the effect will be rather different. I have such a womanly figure—it's a frightful handicap. . . ." Lily sighed, as if her fashionable curves were an obstacle rather than the source of her fame.

"Loose, yes, flowing robes . . ." Alice was studying the sketches Lily had made on the back of a theater program. They were more than competent.

"Tell me about the part—better still, may I read the play?"

"I knew you'd ask me that, you're such a thorough worker! Now where did I put it? Oh, what a bore, I left it in my carriage. Just a minute."

Before Alice could offer to go for her or send one of the girls, Lily had run down the steps. Her lack of ceremony when she was immersed in her work made Alice like her more than she had at their first meeting. She smiled, hearing Lily cooing in passionate tones to the dogs waiting in her carriage.

"Now, look," she said, reappearing with the same involved haste: "I can't stay, I'm due at the theater in half an hour. Read this, and give me whatever you like—here are my measurements, and I swear they are accurate! I can't afford to tell lies, in spite of acute vanity on the matter. Otherwise I'd look ridiculous . . . When shall I come back?"

"Shall we say the end of the week? I'll have designs and samples of fabrics for you by then. I hope I can satisfy your faith in me! I am honored!"

"Nonsense. I've no doubt you'll do splendidly. I don't think you quite realize . . ." Lily paused, and thought better of her remark. Alice flushed, realizing that Lily was on the brink of praising her again, and had decided against it.

"Have you heard from my dear little Annie Hardy?" Lily asked, as she hurried to leave.

"She's very happy," Alice answered. "I must say I hardly expected her to cope with a traveling player's life, but it does seem to suit her. I miss her already, but she'll come home for Christmas. The first time we've celebrated together for ages—with friends, in Rutland."

"I hate Christmas. The theater is closed, and I become bored with parties . . ." Lily arched her neck as if her bones ached at the mere thought. "No doubt your husband will spend his Christmas hunting," she continued, "so you will be able to rest in peace, and eat crystallized fruit all day! I'll send you some, I have them delivered from Paris. Manette's—they're quite the best. Now I must go . . . Good-bye, dear Mrs. Wickham, till Friday."

After she left, Alice wondered why she had assumed there was a hunting husband. Lily was by nature inquisitive, she supposed. She found she liked her more and more, all the same. She was an extravagant woman, and her manner seemed contrived, but Alice began to recognize that this was the result of her efforts to hide an intelligence that was not welcomed in her profession—not among the women, certainly. Alice rather wanted to believe this was so, for she wished to find a friend of her own age. She had been without companionship, except for Anne, for a long time.

It was hard not to be able to socialize with her customers. There was good reason for it: even the well-intentioned among them lived entirely on credit, their husbands or their husbands' agents settling accounts at certain intervals when it suited. Only dear prodigal Daisy and Lady Mary thought to give her cash. In order to get satisfaction from the rest, she had to keep her distance. On paper, her business was now worth over three thousand annually, having grown from nothing in less than two years. In practice, she lived with a pressing burden of debt. Salaries were not a problem. The Dorcas girls received one pound a week, the cutter was paid per piece. But Alice had to buy whole bolts of fabric from silk and velvet importers, and carry stock of many trimmings so as to have supplies ready for her customers to make their selection. Her one advantage over other dressmakers, those model gown purveyors, was that every dress she made was unique, not remotely like the next one. A popular French design by Worth or Paquin would be published in a colored sketch, then meticulously copied many times in one season—and women who had paid a hundred pounds for it in Paris might see a tolerable version of their outfit on sale in Bond Street in a dressmaker's shop.

Alice had no head at all for figures, with the result that sometimes she had no money to pay for the materials she needed, while her customers owed her several hundred pounds. Polite letters requesting payment were ignored. So in the end, she resorted to the only method available to her. She had to turn away orders from any woman who owed her more than three hundred pounds. As she was very much the favorite in particular circles, this usually produced a speedy settlement. But in order to make the threat of such action convincing, it was essential that she kept her distance from her patrons. No wonder there was a social gulf between "trade" and "clientèle"! She could hardly refuse to make a ballgown for someone, if she had accepted an invitation to the dance! Alice began to see that the rules were not merely an invention of the upper classes. Perhaps the lesser folk, the "traders," preferred it that way too.

Lily strengthened Alice in her ambition. The actress was eccentric, self-indulgent, but she had a dedication and a total self-reliance. Alice envied her that, but wondered if she were lonely, too. Anne said she had many lovers. Alice was curious to know if this were true, and how much of herself Lily gave. To her, it seemed impossible to live that double life—subjugated by emotional attachment, yet continuing on an individual path.

She thought of Ned, not for the first time recently. If she had accepted him, she wondered if he would have encouraged her plans, and if he would have been as understanding and cooperative as Dr. Hardy had been. For all his easy-going charm, Alice imagined he might have preferred her to pose for him, and then to clean his brushes . . .

In the evening she sat by the fire studying Lily's play, while Dr. Hardy indulged in his evening ritual of reading to Laura. It was a light farce, ineffably silly, full of comic embarrassments and surprised fools. The main part, that of the countess, was flattering in every detail, though in a vapid way, and Alice could see why Lily might want to raise funds through such a piece to finance her more radical modern plays. Alice found her thoughts wandering from the script to a voice in her head—the moaning sound of the old lady, one of Dr. Hardy's patients, whom she had glimpsed again in the morning, stepping sadly into her carriage.

"Can I ask you, Dr. Hardy, about a little mystery?"

He looked up from his chair, over Laura's head, while the child studied the picture book.

"Yes?"

"I know I shouldn't ask about your patients, but—what do you do, exactly?"

"I think the best way to describe it is 'the talking cure.' When people tell me about themselves, it has an affect on their difficulties . . ."

"But the old lady who came this morning—she's wealthy! Not an invalid, which at her age is a blessing . . ."

"Oh yes, an interesting case. She was a teacher in Africa, with her husband. A good family, loving relatives. But having to retire and come back home has upset her. Her husband died, so she could not go on alone. Though it was many months before her family found her and insisted on her return."

"What happened then?"

"An obsession took hold of her. She worried about her pupils constantly. How would they learn without her? Of course, the authorities have supplied a replacement long ago. But my patient fancies that the children still need her, and that she must keep in her head their names, the register, till she gets back to them. Even worse, the weight of the worry makes her believe that her head is in danger of falling off. She holds it up all the time, like this." He propped himself under the chin, as Alice had seen the old lady do.

"How does she manage to do anything—eat, or dress?" Alice asked in disbelief.

"By exchanging hands, so that she can free one arm, then the other."

"Poor lady. Can you cure her? I don't see how . . ."

"We make progress. Yesterday when we were looking at a map of the Gold Coast, to find the location of her home, she forgot for a moment and pointed at the atlas quite freely. . . . But I've made you sad, telling you all this."

"She's worked hard all her life. It seems cruel she can't enjoy her old age in peace."

"But that's the point. She was yoked to responsibility for so long she can't live without it."

Dr. Hardy frightened Alice. She often felt her loneliness and cares acutely. Perhaps her busy life was abnormal, and would drive her to madness too.

"My poor head," murmured Alice.

"Quite so; her constant words. We often think of a phrase like that when we're burdened with cares. 'My head could burst'—something like that."

"But you're a doctor, not someone who deals in images!"

" 'Shadows we are, and shadows we pursue.' . . . Now it's time for this child to have her story. What is it to be? 'The Princess and the Pea' or 'The Three Bears'?"

Dr. Hardy's world seemed not so far away from the fantasies in Laura's books. Perhaps that was why he enjoyed the child's company so much.

Alice left them to their tales, put aside her trivial script and turned to her letters. Anne was now with Mr. Kerrick's "Number Three" company, a "fit-up" touring smaller towns off the main circuits. "Fit-up," Alice learned, was the name given to a touring group that took its own lights, scenery—even proscenium arch—and set them up in town halls or corn-exchanges in country places. Anne described her days learning small parts and gaining experience as the best she had enjoyed in her life. Alice wondered if Anne, too, had received a letter like the one she herself was holding now. She could not bear to have to forward such news.

My Dear Alice,

It is with great sadness I have to tell you of your grandmother's recent illness. When we returned from M'bad she seemed greatly improved. But various circumstances have weakened her spirit. The Dr tells me she must be kept very quiet. It is her heart. Someone sent us a news cutting with a review of Anne's first theatrical performance in London! It came unsolicited, in a plain envelope, not sealed. It was a gt shock. Fate decreed that Anne's own letter explaining to us her choice of life did not arrive until much later—2 weeks. She had failed to pay the postage. Poor darling, she was careless but well-intended to write. I cant approve, you know that. I had different expectations for my Gd-daughters. The strain on my beloved E shall not be allowed to overcome her. For this reason I prohibit either of you from any further communication with Carrigrohane in any form. I am unable to find forgiveness in my heart for you both at present but with God's help in time it may come. Yr grandfather

James

Alice's thoughts darkened; she barely heard the comfortable voice of Dr. Hardy reading to Laura. She crumpled the letter and threw it in the fire. She had no idea who had sent the cutting to her grandparents, and regretted that neither she nor Anne had been brave enough to write sooner to confess their actions.

The "proper path" that Grandma had once pointed out for her seemed impossible to follow now. She felt that her egotism, her fantasies of some richer kind of happiness, were leading inexorably in a new direction. It was not a path strewn with roses and temptations of the kind Grandma feared. There were certainly pitfalls and monsters, but the dangers were "compromise" and "weakness," the enemies "self-pride" and "false ambition." Worse still, this unfamiliar path led through dark tangled places, where she would feel lonely, or possibly become neurasthenic like Dr. Hardy's patients. All these terrors were hers, because she had broken out of marriage, and turned to building a life all on her own.

Alice watched the flames in the fireplace die down, flickering blue and green over the burnt letter. She realized that she could not turn back, however feeble she felt. Little castle archways glowed in the coals, and the fire warmed her.

◆　◆　◆

The dresses for Lily were exceptional. Alice had combined the current theatrical *grande dame* fashion for loose flowing robes with a transparency that was very daring outside a vaudeville show. The neckline of one peach chiffon tea gown looked as if it would fall off Lily's shoulders if it descended another inch. Alice held it up by stitching gold chains in the back, between the shoulder blades. The powdery texture of the chiffon added beauty to the warmth of Lily's white skin; her firm body was emphasized by a sash tucked with flowers at the waist, underneath the chiffon. Another dress had a cummerbund covered in pearls and crystals that shone through an overdress of cream lace. A cascade of frills, also trimmed with crystals and pearls, fell from the neck to the hem.

Lily was pleased, and knew she would be a great success in these outfits. Even before the play opened, she used them to create publicity for herself. She had herself photographed so that picture postcards of her wearing Alice's dresses were on sale all over the country to coincide with the first night. She also asked Alice to make line drawings to give exclusively to the society newspaper *The Queen*. They were unsigned, for Alice had no public name as yet. But then Alice too had a brilliant idea, and suggested that Ned Fielding might be persuaded to paint Lily in one of the dresses.

"You must be mad!" Lily exclaimed, causing Minnie to drop her pins (they were in the midst of yet another fitting). "Do you have any idea how expensive that man is? He had a portrait of Frances Warwick in the Royal Academy show last summer—imagine what he charges a countess!"

"But I think he might do it for me," Alice insisted. "He's an old friend, and if we succeed with these designs, it will help my business substantially. Ned will see that. Let me write—I'd like to see him again. It's such a pleasure to be able to do something for *you* too, after all you've done for me . . ."

Alice was indeed grateful, but learning rapidly from Lily that mere talent was not enough. Self-advertisement was essential. She knew Ned would not be offended by her request; on the contrary, he might be amused by her new venture. She was glad to have an unusual reason to write to him. It was almost two years since they had met. She wrote, but received no answer. Her days were too full of work for her to dwell on her disappointment.

Several weeks later she found herself sitting in a plush theater near Piccadilly, surrounded by a group of Lily's admirers. In the stalls she recognized many faces—other clients, figures from county life she had not seen for a few years, and in their midst, the "PBs," as they were known—"the professional beauties" of the Marlborough House set, Prince Edward's own circle. Alice knew they came to gather ideas for their own wardrobes, as much as they did to show off their beauty or have their fine jewels admired.

It amazed her to think how high her ambitions were reaching. She was in no doubt now that she wanted to be the most sought-after *couturière* in London, not merely a dressmaker or a *modiste* who simply copied fashion designs. Like Worth, or Poiret in Paris, she wanted to have the title because it suggested she defined the fashion, not just followed it. With Lily's patronage, she was a little nearer her goal.

She barely followed the play. All her senses were caught up in listening for the gasps of admiration from the audience. She watched how effortlessly Lily moved across the stage in her beautiful gowns. The peach-colored chiffon caused a sensation—at first glance Lily looked half naked as she lay on a daybed, fanning herself in a pool of light.

After the performance, Lily was given a supper party in her honor by an admirer, the Baron de Falbe, a great patron of the theater. Alice was invited, and savored the irony of being announced in one of London's most sought-after drawing rooms for something she alone had achieved. All thoughts of her shameful divorce and her exile in St. John's Wood began to recede. When she arrived, Lily called out her name in dramatic tones to make everyone pause for a moment, acknowledging her. Then Lily applauded and everyone joined in, pressing round Alice to make their introductions and to compliment her. The novelty of a "lady" (albeit a divorced and therefore a disgraced one), working as a dressmaker was a topic of interest to many in the room. Alice refrained from explaining that with her poor education, sewing was all she could develop as a means of living.

Then there was Ned. He had not replied to Alice's letter about the portrait; he hated to write to anyone—fearing to expose his lack of an elegant social style. He always preferred his exchanges to be personal. But he had responded: by presenting himself at the theater that night to watch Lily and judge for himself whether he could record her performance or not. All this Alice divined as he stood, arms folded, watching her cross the room to meet him.

"Well!" he said, kissing her hands, "this is a surprise indeed."

"Will you do it?" she asked. Alice tried not to pass judgment on his avoidance of her. She tried to see only the best feelings, not the selfishness. Now that she was a success, he was proud of her.

"Of course I'll paint her! The difficulty is to decide which dress characterizes her best. You've an extraordinary talent for capturing personality, Alice, in colors and shapes. The hidden pearls, the heavy beaded edges to that lace, the movement—it all made her look unconventional yet aristocratic at the same time. Remarkable!"

"Well, I have you to thank for many of my ideas."

"I don't believe you, Alice. For one moment. You must have known always that your spirit would find its own expression—surely you did?"

"No. I didn't know that." Alice was amused by his lack of understanding. Ned had no idea how slim her hold on her own identity or self-confidence was. Perhaps men never felt like that, or never admitted it.

"Well, we shall all benefit, now that it has." He bent again to kiss her hand, and as he did so, Alice saw Lily's observant eyes as she fluttered in her circle of admirers. She seemed to signal: "Are you impervious, Alice Wickham, or not?"

Alice was uncertain if her pleasure would have been quite the same without Ned's approval. She was angered at the possibility that his admiration made it much sweeter. But then, when he took her arm in his, and led her to a table of his friends, she thought her antagonism to his flattery was unjust. Ned admired her for what she was—not a great artist, as he was, but at least a good designer. Perhaps it really was possible to enjoy a man's affection without losing one's self-respect or freedom. By the end of the evening, Ned had promised to come to the Crawshay home, Desthorpe, to see everyone during Christmas.

Anne came back to London from her tour a great deal thinner, and with a bad head cold. Mrs. Bacon did what she could to nurse her, but only Alice had the knack of improving her bad moods. Anne was an impatient invalid, bored to distraction by books, unable to knit or embroider—and she exaggerated all her aches and pains. The very real threat of a killing influenze epidemic that winter made the whole household strive to humor her. Now Alice had two reasons to be glad to go to Desthorpe: first, the promise of Ned's presence, and the enjoyment of company to entertain Anne, who would certainly flourish with an audience. Alice looked forward to this reunion with her close friends, to showing off Anne's grown-up beauty. For the moment her best method of improving Anne's temper was to sketch some new clothes for her and look after her costumes. Anne not only supplied her own clothes for the tour, but was supposed to keep them repaired, a job she loathed.

"I'm a hopeless seamstress," she complained, sitting up in bed. "I don't know how you have the talent for it. I only do it when I must."

"I think it's all the making over we did at Carrigrohane."

Anne fell silent, thinking of the grandparents, unwilling to ask Alice for news.

"I haven't heard from them again. Or from Sophie. I wonder what has happened to them." Alice replied, answering her thoughts. She stitched steadily, avoiding Anne's eyes. "I wish there was something we could do to please them. We must be such a disappointment."

Anne lay back, suddenly exhausted. "I don't feel beholden."

"Well, you should!" Alice was surprised to hear Anne laugh at her.

"You do love to moralize, dear sister. Be true to your heart—you hated Carrigrohane!"

"I did so." Alice admitted it, feeling wicked all the same. "But they did what they thought was best for us."

"What was best for *them*, so that we would bring credit to *them*!" Anne replied. "That's why Grandma was so shocked to see the news in the paper. All her friends would read it. She thought of herself all the time."

"You do too," Alice argued.

"That's different. I want things to change for women, so I have to be strong in my own views. Lily feels the same—you'll see. Freedom!"

"You sound like Daisy Panton when she tells me about the Suffragettes."

"There are many ways to that end. Mine is a different one."

Alice sewed thoughtfully, aware that Anne was trying to be opinionated to impress her, as she was the elder. Alice guessed that Anne had picked up these new ideas on her tour—from the other girls, and from the circumstances of being alone. Alice pictured her life as she had described it, going back after a performance to some boarding-house room, sniffling with cold, barricading the door for fear of intruders. It was a hard way to find a new life, and certainly not "free," as others would define the notion. Yet in spite of the difficulties, Anne wanted it.

◆　◆　◆

Just before their departure for Rutland at Christmas, Hubert Kerrick invited the sisters to a celebration at Blanchards restaurant in New Burlington Street. Anne was eager to go now that she was recovered. She wanted to be seen in London by all the theatrical figures she knew, not to be forgotten in the provinces.

Lily queened it over the lunch as one of London's currently successful starring attractions. Once again Alice took a professional interest in her clothes—she could not help being envious of the unmistakable cut of Paquin from Paris: a sheath of white grosgrain, worn with a gold-buttoned basque jacket covered with red and gold military braid, and a white pleated chiffon blouse lightly puffed out at her waist. When Lily wore stays, her narrowness made everyone else hold their breath.

Ned Fielding was there too, and dancing attendance on Lily. This came as a great shock to Alice. She knew that the portrait was nearly finished, and had been paid for by the Baron de Falbe. He intended that it should hang in the foyer of the Moonlight Theatre as an acknowledgment of Lily's contribution to modern works on the London stage. Perhaps Ned always cultivated the company of his subjects, so that they would be at ease with him and reveal more of themselves . . .

Alice looked round desperately for someone else she could talk to, rather than interrupting Lily and Ned. Patronizing the theater was becoming socially acceptable, it seemed: at the Baron's table, Alice saw Sir Philip and Lady Belinda Hall, acquaintances from Rutland. She wondered if they would cut her—it had happened before. But the sight of her and Anne, both so boldly turned out (Alice in gray velvet, with an enormous fur collar, and Anne in red with an astrakhan jacket), seemed to encourage the Halls in their wanderings in Bohemian circles. They half rose, delighted to spot someone they knew. But Alice saw Ned and Lily advancing toward her, and could not escape.

To her surprise, Lily took her aside to talk privately, and left Anne to practice flirting rather expertly with Ned.

"I expect Anne thinks she has been invited here so that Kerrick will make her the offer of her dreams," Lily said, directing Alice to a bow-window table. They looked out at the bustle of Christmas shoppers turning in Regent Street. "Well, he won't."

Alice was instantly worried for her sister.

"What do you mean? Don't you think she has talent enough?"

"Of course I do! But she hasn't served her time yet. *You*, my dear, are another matter."

Lily's attention wandered, as it always did, waving at her friends, watching new arrivals, keeping an eye on Ned. She saw that Alice caught her glancing in his direction all too often. Boldly, Lily blew a kiss at him.

"We talk about you a great deal," she said, comfortably.

"I'm flattered!" Alice was very sharp.

Lily was amused to see a spark of rivalry at last.

"So you should be! We both have your interests at heart, Alice. That's why I have something to propose to you. I want to move you into your own premises."

Alice was amazed. How could Lily suggest such a thing?

"The show is a great success. Half of London will be wearing oyster chiffon this Christmas for their *robes d'intérieur*! But you can't possibly expect me or anyone else to continue to plod out to the suburbs of the north to do business. Wouldn't you like to be nearer the center of things?" Lily gestured at the street.

Alice looked out. No snow yet, but a light fog. Street lamps were lit early, and a chestnut-seller's brazier glowed bright on a corner. A child with a fur muff stood beside her nursemaid, staring into a shop window filled with jewelry and lit with candles. At the center of the display a tiny ballerina turned on a silver music box. Outside the hat shop next door, a collection of pink-nosed grooms chatted, while they waited for their mistresses and kept their horses quiet.

"Of course I should!"

"That's settled then. When you come back from Rutland, you can find a suitable house and my solicitors will deal with the lease. Make sure it's something stylish. Appearances are everything in this. Quite honestly, you can't continue to do the quality of work you can produce under such odd conditions . . ." She did not refer specifically to Dr. Hardy's strange practice, the mysterious visits of "neurasthenics" to his rooms upstairs. Lily had no concept of such psychic misery. She was too positive, too full of life ever to succumb in that way. Alice understood why she spoke disparagingly, yet she was indignant at hearing the doctor's dedicated efforts so dismissed.

All the same, Lily was right: Alice knew she had to set herself up in the West End if she wanted to expand. Three or four fittings were needed for most dresses. Only the faithful would come out to St. John's Wood. She was just too far away from the idle rich, who would only bother to visit a dressmaker close to their haunts.

"Besides," Lily said, "I think my investment will turn to profit. You may as well agree to the proposal while I'm in a position to make it. Next year, I could flop!"

"But I don't think I can possibly agree to your offer." Alice suddenly felt the weight of it, and she was also far too angry about Ned's defection to accept. It was just forgivable that Ned had not revived their friendship out of respect for her reputation (her own wish, after all). She had never challenged his decision—never written to summon him again. But suddenly seeing him with another woman changed her view of him. Alice was smitten with jealousy—piqued by the idea that he had become successful, all too soon forgotten her and now fallen swiftly in love with her own particular friend.

"That's foolish." Lily said evenly, not realizing how truly her words applied to Alice's private thoughts. Alice flushed. "Don't be rash. Besides, I enjoy being a fairy godmother. It's the best Christmas I've arranged for myself for a long time!"

Lily gestured to Ned for him to join her. He appeared to be deep in conversation with Anne and the Baron de Falbe, but as soon as he saw Lily needed him, he made his excuses and came over. Alice was disgusted by his obedience.

"Champagne! Alice, let's seal our agreement! Ned, do come here, help me to persuade her!"

So he knew all about the plan. He had probably told Lily all about her marriage, their—friendship—everything. Perhaps she should show Ned how little she cared: be brilliant, be stylish, make him regret the loss of her. For he had most certainly lost her now. She knew she had no reason to be so angry, for she had no rights in the matter at all. Alice drank her champagne rapidly, dizzy with the prospects that opened before her, but mostly envious of Lily.

"Oh! My head is going to spin!" She tried to laugh, while Ned and Lily took turns to link arms with her and sip from each other's glass.

CHAPTER 10

L 1 9 0 0

ike many covetous ladies, Alice often lingered in front of Mme. Delphine's little shop in the Burlington Arcade. Veils, necklets of lace or ribbon, a pile of chiffon collars and artificial flowers filled the curved glass bay. Mme. Delphine was going to help her find a French fitter, an urgent requirement for Alice's new salon. The excitement Alice felt in presenting herself in that corner of Piccadilly for a professional reason was quite unlike her former pleasure as a casual shopper, idling and staring at pretty things. A great adventure was beginning for her, and the beauty of the handiwork on display almost made her eyes prickle. Inside the salon, she could see tea gowns and dressing robes in chiffon or accordion-pleated cashmere. A toque of mink, caught up at the side with twisted loops of white satin, was discreetly labeled "21s. 9d." Alice thought that was a mistake. In her establishment, nothing was marked with a price.

"Good afternoon, Alice."

She looked up, startled, to see Ned standing beside her. For a whole year Alice had watched the progress of his affair with Lily, and Ned had never sought her out in private.

"How curious!" she said dryly. "For three years I've been living in London, and visiting Mme. Delphine's almost every week. Yet I've never bumped into anyone here before. How very odd that we should meet!"

"I knew you had an appointment this afternoon."

"Oh?"

"Yes. Lily told me."

Alice felt herself redden. She had maintained a coolness toward Ned, for a whole year, out of pure jealousy. She did not like herself for it, but had no control over her feelings.

"I'm so glad you accepted Lily's offer. Wonderful woman, Lily." Ned flapped his hat against his coattails, out of nervousness.

"Yes. I *adore* her too."

"And it's turning out very well, isn't it?"

"Oh yes, I'm expanding quite steadily. I love my work."

"But you don't feel affection for me anymore, do you, Alice?" Ned stood squarely beside her, looking into the shop window. Alice stared straight ahead.

"So vulgar, that price label," she said, irritated. "Don't be silly, Ned."

"Look here, Alice—"

"I don't want to talk about such things! Don't be indiscreet! Consider my feelings!"

"Listen to me." Ned leaned closer, determined to have his say. "I'm not indifferent to you. But—I was very close to you, closer than I've been to anyone. Grant me the truth of my feelings. . . ."

"You never visited me when I needed you!" Alice's true emotions welled up in an instant. Pretence was impossible; she was near to tears.

"You told me to stay away!" he protested, indignant. "You didn't even write!"

"If I had, you wouldn't have answered—and you could have decided for yourself to overcome my fears . . . or was it just so much easier to find other entertainments?"

"You're being entirely unreasonable."

"You didn't come to Desthorpe." She had stored up this grievance for a year.

"Ah, no. I am sorry for that."

"Ha! Sorry!" Alice was aware other people were looking at them with interest. But then the shop door opened, and Mme. Delphine greeted Alice:

"Well, Mrs. Wickham, *enfin!* And I've such good news. Mme. Blanc will do for you . . ."

"Oh! That *is* splendid. . . . Excuse me—good-bye Mr. Fielding. We'll meet at Lily's on Thursday—unless of course we bump into each other by accident again."

Ned gave a curt nod and strode off without another word.

"*Ma chérie,* you weren't very nice," Mme. Delphine commented, following Ned with admiring eyes. "I watched you through the window. I couldn't hear—but that man was sincere, to look at him, and *désolé.* "

"Oh, not at all." Alice was flustered, offended by Mme. Delphine's interference. "A simple misunderstanding."

"A handsome man." The dressmaker sighed, trying to look French and experienced, neither of which she was.

"About Mme. Blanc?" Alice reminded her, refusing to gossip.

"Yes. I couldn't use her of course, she's a little slow for me, but she worked at Callot Soeurs in Paris for years and years. *Soyez-vous gentille,* and she'll do very well for you."

Alice was aware of the condescension. Mme. Delphine's business was select but very brisk. She obviously thought that Alice was one of those "society wonders" who made their friends a few robes for the pin money and gave it all up when another enthusiasm took hold. There was no point in arguing with this opinion, for Mme. Delphine would only be convinced by deeds. Alice hurried back to her new home in Conduit Street, to write a letter offering the job to Mme. Blanc.

Past "Lewis and Allenby, Furs and Opera Cloaks"; Messrs. Redfern, a tailoring house with a branch in Cowes for the summer season, yachting and Riviera clothes; then past Miss McGhee, milliner, and the brass plaque for "B. Marcus, Ladies Tailor and Habit Maker." Further down the street was Kenneth Durward, Ulster House, "Suppliers of topcoats and carcoats." In Bond Street were her rivals-to-be, Worth and Redmayne, and, in Dover Street nearby, Kate Reilly. Alice was at the center of the marketplace in London fashion, trying to convince herself she belonged there.

When she opened the door of her little salon, its ordered reality gave her a shiver of energy. Lily had been generous with her money. Alice had a small sitting room, bedroom and bathroom at the top of the house. A workroom, kitchen and the usual appointments for the staff were on the middle floor, and here on the ground floor a large showroom and fitting places. Instead of single pier glasses she had mirrors fixed to the walls and to the doors of the fitting rooms, so that clients could see themselves from every angle. The room was decorated with Louis Seize furniture, no cut flowers, but more formal plants in antique jardinières. In the spring she would have bowls of hyacinths, narcissi or lilies.

Her little helpers, Minnie Clough and Teresa Sutton, had taken lodgings together with a tailor's family in Soho. They could walk to work, and had Sundays off, with a family to keep them company. Both girls had graduated from "trotting" for fabrics to being "improvers." Soon they would be fully trained hands and take their place alongside the three new girls upstairs—a bodice hand, a skirt hand and a finisher. Minnie wanted to be a finisher too—she could do pressings, buttonholes and trims. Teresa was a good fine sewer and could become a bodice hand. But Alice still could not cope with her orders and sent a great deal of work out to a middlewoman, Mrs. Vine, for making up. Mrs. Vine had been a seamstress in the West End for many years and now ran a small workshop making up model dresses for her various former employers.

She wrote an eager letter to Mme. Blanc, asking her to consider employment with her as chief pattern cutter. Then she settled to some sewing, completely absorbed in her task. She looked back over her first year in the new premises with pride—perhaps to compensate for the unsatisfactory outcome of her talk with Ned.

Conduit Street would always remind Alice of her wedding designs. War had broken out in South Africa the previous autumn. The Boers invaded Cape Colony and Natal in long-anticipated assertion of their rights. It was all very glorious—everyone had a relative who had volunteered to join the war. Alice could still not understand why the girls showed their patriotism by rushing into marriages before the conflict was over, although everyone had said it would all be sorted out by the New Year. The brides looked sweet and brave, the young officers positively epic in their devotion to country and matrimony. Alice remembered her first wedding dress for a military bride as it had been reported in *The Queen: A princess gown of white crêpe de chine, embroidered in white and silver. A court train of white panné, falling from the shoulders, embroidered in silver and mother-of-pearl sequins and trails of lily-of-the-valley. A wreath of orange blossom under a tulle veil, the only decoration a handsome diamond crescent in the hair . . .*

That October, when the first field marshals slipped into Waterloo station to begin their journey, in flapping ulsters and carrying their umbrellas, their casual departure set the tone of confidence shared by all their officers.

There had been few balls in that winter season. Alice recalled it had seemed inappropriate, but people gathered together to share the information they received in letters, the newspapers, or from friends in high places. After a short stay at Desthorpe, made less happy by Ned's absence, Alice had come back to the city responding to the common feeling that it was good to be near the source of news. Theaters were half empty, but the restaurants were full of war chat. During December, the severity of the fighting became public. Lord Roberts was sent out with reinforcements on Christmas Eve itself and the year ended with the severest fighting at Mafeking. The full horrors of casualties were revealed in the press . . . no relief was apparent in the sieges of Kimberley, Mafeking or Ladysmith. When subsequent waves of soldiers and officers set out, fear leaded all hearts. Sarah and her husband, Rupert Firth, sailed from India to the Cape, for he had been appointed to General Buller's staff.

In her workroom, Alice planned, stitched and cut all winter. She read newspapers anxiously, caught up with the worries that her clients discussed with her. The *Daily Graphic* contained "artists' impressions" of the Transvaal scene—alongside a sketch of a howitzer arriving at Modder Camp was news of fashions from Paris: "A furore of pleats this year" the paper said, complimenting Mlle. Cécile Sorel at the Vaudeville and the pretty actresses at the Gymnase on their new clothes.

Alice could not resist escaping. In January, she and Anne had made their first trip to Paris, staying with the Baron de Falbe's mother on the Île St. Louis.

Alice spied discreetly at a few couture establishments in the rue de la Paix, and the rue de Rivoli: Worth, Paquin, Doucet and Felix. The black-jetted baroness acted as her introduction. These salons were awe-inspiring in their grandeur and solemnity. Frenchwomen had no reservations about taking fashion seriously, and were much more discriminating than her own customers in London. Alice came home full of inspiration.

Then in March came the news that Ladysmith had been relieved. Londoners went mad in the streets. Alice barely had time to look up at what was going on: Anne was understudying the lead in a play at the Coronet, a small suburban theater in Notting Hill Gate. Alice had to make costumes for this, as well as something for her sister's appearance in Princess Christian's concert in support of the Rifleman's Aid Society. It was the closest Anne had come to appearing on the West End stage. She was featured in one of the tableaux at the Haymarket late one afternoon. Alice visualized the costume in every detail: *Stone-gray cashmere, smartly trimmed with green velvet and paste shamrock buttons, the whole tucked and embroidered with Swiss Muslin, also tucked to form the yoke of the bodice* . . .

Anne's appearance was so memorable that several other charitable ladies came to Alice as a result. Mrs. Arthur Paget and her friends chose costumes for "The Masque of Peace and War," yet another fund-raising event for the widows and orphans of the Household troops, at Her Majesty's theater. Alice then made the acquaintance of the Duchess of Buccleuch (wife of one of William's hunting cronies), a tall, distinguished woman with impeccable manners who managed to have the entire showroom staff at her beck and call whenever she visited. As the duchess was close to the royal family, she gave Alice the final accolade—an introduction to the Court. No dressmaker could consider herself truly established until she had royal patronage, not merely clients who went to the Palace to be presented. The irony was that Alice had married before she ever formally "came out," and now, divorced, would never be allowed to be presented.

In May at last came the news of Mafeking—the Boers' siege was lifted. Alice heard the news in the early hours of the morning, still hard at work on Presentation dresses at the time. The news was posted up on the gates at Mansion House: it spread through the city in one great shout. Hansom drivers bawled it as they drove through the town, then people flung up their windows at the clatter of hooves and the hoarse shouting, and the word passed on.

The season began, brilliant but subdued; the men were still absent. For a reception at the Foreign Office, the Duchess of Buccleuch ordered a ballgown—how was it? Alice paused in her stitching to see it in her mind's eye, quite perfect: *Pink satin, covered with shimmering white satin worked all over in medallions of point d'Alençon lace, embroidered with diamonds. The edge of the skirt had a flounce of pink mousseline de soie with diamond-embroidered lace falling over it from a garland of roses and silverwork. The bodice had a full lace berthe with sleeves of chiffon and pink roses on the right shoulder . . .*

Then one day, she had been working upstairs when she recognized a familiar, long-unheard voice outside her room. Minnie burst in, startled and excited, leading Sarah and her Captain, Rupert Firth, recently returned from the Cape. One look at the soldier had revealed to Alice that he had suffered a common fate: he had been wounded, and it would take him a long time to recover. How sad she had been to find this young man, of whom she had heard so many confident and happy stories, for the first time, looking so drawn and remote.

Alone in her workroom, Alice bent her head, and the needle flew across the silk. The voices of the friends echoed round her in her solitude.

"We couldn't wait till you came to Desthorpe. I just had to call and see you!" Sarah's clear voice called out.

Alice had to show her the salon at once, all her sketches, her fabrics, then Minnie had somehow lost all her manners and blurted out gossip about all the Dorcas girls.

Rupert asked permission to smoke, while Sarah tried on hats and boas. "Do you know, Alice," she prattled, "there are seven thousand guardsmen in South Africa—London is practically manless! I'm so glad Rupert was made to come home with me. It was just the same in Simla in ninety-six or was it ninety-seven? When you all went up to the North-West Frontier—do you remember, darling?"

How Sarah had tried to be cheerful, trying to keep Rupert's attention fixed! His injuries were not physical, Alice realized. He smiled, encouraging Sarah's performance, grateful for her love.

"Imagine! I didn't like to tell you in my letters, Alice darling, because it was my first season and I wanted it to sound so grand."

"What, Sarah?" Alice heard herself laughing, trying to play her part.

"It was so *drab*, that Simla Season; they called it the 'Anybody's Year.' Imagine!"

Laughter . . . echoing round her room. Alice regretted their pretensions, yet how much they had wanted to show Rupert that in spite of all the ugliness in life, some good remained—friendship was there, and the comfort of home.

That light, careful enunciation of his words: his voice was dry with nerves.

"When I went out to South Africa"—Alice could hear him, a ghost suffering, just as he had stood before her in this very room—"only thirty out of the hundred horses we had on board survived the storms round the Cape. We threw the carcasses overboard—didn't have time to shoot the poor devils." He knocked his cigarette repeatedly on a china dish: *tap-tap; tap-tap.*

"My best hunter cracked both her legs sliding into the bulwark: the stablings all broke. Some of the horses snapped their necks, slewing about the wet deck."

"Rupert! No more! Rupert!" Sarah's sad voice.

"No, wait, it's a joke, don't you remember, darling? When we got to Durban, we found our regiment was known as the 'Four Seven Eleven Boys.' Do you see? Eau de Cologne . . . for the Cavalry Gentlemen . . ."

"Let's go home! We're far too late!"

And Alice had chided Sarah: there was no need for them to run away, for she did not mind in the least if Rupert wanted to tell her all about it. Her little room was full of such whisperings, sad confessions came to her many more times than happy secrets.

"Don't hurry, not on my account," she had said. "I'm so sorry, and I do understand."

"Do you? I'm glad," said Rupert, his gray eyes old in a young and would-be handsome face.

"It's not over, not by a long mark. They'll fight on and on, those Boers. I saw one dead once, Mrs. Wickham." *Tap-tap; tap-tap.*

"This one was a farmer, you could see that by his hands, great brown mitts, crossed on his rifle, on his chest—just like a man holds a hoe. And staring up into the sky with a steady eye, seeing him anywhere else, you'd have thought he was just a man pleased to see a spot of sun come at last from behind a cloud. But not there, of course . . . sun all the time, and besides, his stomach was blown out."

"Rupert!" Sarah had begun to cry.

"Let him say it!" Alice comforted her. "You think this is the first I've heard of it? I sit and stitch, give my ladies tea in little china cups, and when I hand them sketches to look at, they pass me letters, or even read them out loud to me. As if they must hear it said."

Alice looked out at the *va-et-vient* in the street below. She had meant every word she said to Rupert that day, and lived by it now: "Of course we keep up appearances, 'Keep the flag flying,' as my ladies say. But sometimes, in quiet places, things come out. I'll never forget. That's what you want, isn't it? For that one Boer man not to be forgotten. I'll help you to do that."

Rupert did not reply. The voices in Alice's past faded away. He had gone back to Desthorpe, to be nursed by his family, a wounded hero returned. Alice still believed he ought not to fight his memory. She kept that promise among the thoughts that sustained her as she worked on in solitude.

◆　◆　◆

Mme. Blanc duly arrived a few days later, and Alice knew that she was lucky to have found her. Silver-haired, stiffly corseted in widow's black, Mme. Blanc was beyond fashion because she was all technique. Nothing surprised her and nothing was impossible. Alice showed her her newest ideas. Mme. Blanc thought she could make patterns, but needed time to work them out. Alice decided that the best solution was for the old lady to take up residence in her own rooms on the premises, while she herself moved out to a hotel in Dover Street—a reckless extravagance, but all she could do in the circumstances. Mme. Blanc was going to help her realize her greatest ambition—to stage a whole new "Collection" for the Autumn. Orders *à mesure* were fine, but she wanted to be in advance of current fashion.

Alice bought a little whippet for company, and was soon a familiar figure in the streets of Mayfair, hurrying to her workrooms every morning on foot. On weekends she went back to St. John's Wood to see Dr. Hardy and to prise Laura out of Mrs. Bacon's all-encompassing care. They went out for the day to Mme. Tussaud's, Barnum's Show at Olympia, the galleries in Mayfair, or just to the zoo in Regent's Park, like in old times.

Sometimes she went to Desthorpe Manor. Rupert was improving slowly, and Sarah was happy to be at home again. They forgot their responsibilities and talked about their plans as if they were very young, at the beginning again. But nothing could keep Alice away from Conduit Street for long.

She aspired to make women new, to individualize their clothes. Creating a new dress for each female form, releasing all its latent beauty, was her talent and her life, and she wanted to do it with perfection and originality. Others might find her world frivolous, but Alice was utterly dedicated to her beliefs. She invented clothes that were exotic, unusually loose but not ornately decorated as the current taste dictated. They were unlike the "artistic" robes of Paul Poiret; less grand than Worth or Doucet.

Three themes ran through her first collection. "Tunis Tunics" were for the Lily Lavelles of her world: gorgeous bodies to be sheathed in silk, with wide cummerbunds of pearl or other shining substances, and a gold esprit net overdress to veil the curves. Arabic jewelry worn like a collar around the neck; a key pattern embroidered at the hem with velvet ribbon. The bodice would be close-fitting, trimmed with ribbon and narrow lines of embroidery, with little straps of black velvet at the shoulders. Alice intended these dresses to have a timeless womanly quality.

There were "Symphony Dresses," very loose, clouds of draped chiffon in several shades of one color, intended to reflect the personality of the wearer. Violet, lavender and pale pink were mixed for a Titian beauty; layers of brown with gold for a more confident brunette; apricots and corals for a young blonde.

For debutantes and ingenues, there were "Painted Pastels"—each one with a theme that sprang from the wearer's own inclinations (Alice had derived these from the butterfly dress she had painted, Anne's first costume). As an example, she hand-painted milky muslin with colors that would suit an imagined girl, a girl with green eyes and reddish-gold hair and a passion for dancing: Shaded reds of poppies on white, with a red band to tie in her curls, and red slippers to complement the flowers.

Mme. Blanc studied her pictures, and cut the patterns for the Painted Pastels first. The Tunis Tunics took more thought. Alice decided to save time by delivering copies of the master patterns to the woman who took work from her when her own girls were too busy. Mrs. Vine ran her sewing workshop on the outskirts of west London. With these extra seamstresses, or "outworkers," starting work on the designs at once, she might still be ready for the Autumn season.

A hansom cab took Alice further west than she had ever traveled before, past Harrods, past the museums, past Olympia, long past the tall houses isolated by the river where Beerbohm Tree once lived. Eventually she came to a tree-shaded suburb where an old Elizabethan manor house had been half torn down. Its once prolific kitchen garden was now used as a yard for wagons. There was a duck pond in front of a few old Georgian cottages, and on the other side of the green, a new Gothic church, its deep red brick standing out intensely against the small firs planted in the churchyard.

Further on, down the main road, the neat, solid houses with looped chains at their gates ran out and were replaced by terraced homes in long narrow streets, with tiny patches of garden in the front. Washing hung out behind them, two lines, up and down, a telltale sign that these speculatively built properties, intended as family dwellings, had already been turned into lodging houses and were probably very crowded. The cab stopped in Woodhouse Road, just in front of an alley leading down from the house at the gable end.

"Twenty Woodarse Road" said the driver, and Alice stepped out. The workroom was a low shed behind the house, down the alley. In the back yard between, Alice saw children and chickens scuffling in the dirt. A luminous blonde girl was sweeping fluff out of the shed door as she approached.

"Is Mrs. Vine here?" Alice asked, feeling like a traveler in a foreign land.

The girl took a quick look at Alice's smart tailored suit, her velvet hat, and was terror-struck.

"You're not from the 'Ealth, are yer?"

"No, I'm not." Alice could hear the steady vibration of treadle sewing machines inside the shop.

"'Oo shall I say, then?"

"Mrs. Wickham, and I'm not the factory inspector either, there's no need to be afraid. I should have let Mrs. Vine know I was coming. Can you tell her I'm here? It's awfully hot."

Twenty girls sat stitching gowns at tables that stood on the hard earth floor. The contrast between the fine fabrics and the poor clothing of the girls was stark. The dresses were kept carefully on the tabletops, away from the dirt underfoot. The light was good: the roof was half glass on one side and there were windows along one wall. Alice imagined it would be bitterly cold in winter, just as it was stiflingly hot now. But what she had never imagined was this absorption in exhausting work. No one seemed to notice the filth or the tedium. Fingers flew over gauzes, turning out yards of hem or ruffles in minutes. At the back of the room a huge old gas stove added to the intolerable heat, for it was loaded with pressing irons; sudden spurts of steam shot into the air as the girls lifted the irons off and banged them down on their pressing boards.

Mrs. Vine appeared, surprised and anxious to make a good impression. Alice knew that her business was valuable to Mrs. Vine, but that she had made a blunder in appearing in the workroom. Mrs. Vine liked her trip uptown to pick up orders, and did not enjoy close identification with her dismal setting. She called an impromptu tea break and the girls rushed out, breaking into animated chatter.

"I like to provide them with soup or tea," Mrs. Vine explained, "though of course they bring their own meals." Alice nodded. It would be pointless to express her shock at the monotonous labor being sweated out in that ugly room. Mrs. Vine had come well recommended: she was sought after in the West End for her good "hands" and ran an organized shop. Alice knew she was not the worst in an industry full of unscrupulous slave drivers.

"Here are the new pieces; Mme. Blanc's worked them out." Alice handed them over rather helplessly. Mrs. Vine looked at the stiff card patterns and the made-up *toile*—a prototype in cheap fabric. She was an experienced cutter herself and could have worked from Alice's sketch with no difficulty but she did not have time to do it. She had to keep her girls constantly busy to make her shop pay. She put the sample dresses on a stand in the middle of the room and studied the patterns.

"Mm. I see. Though I don't know that the belles will be happy to give up their lacings and their waists. Elegant though. I like the drapery."

It did not matter to Mrs. Vine that these muslin fantasies might fetch eighty guineas in Alice's salon, and that she got five pounds per item, and her girls a pound a week. These were good rates for everyone concerned, and, more important, Alice tried to keep her in a regular flow of orders. Still, Mrs. Vine was careful not to take in jobs exclusively for one person. The time was coming when Alice would have to set up her own workrooms on a bigger scale.

Alice was appalled. It was one thing to know that such conditions existed—and these were good by general standards—but to confront such drudgery was a shock. "I don't want you to work overtime," she said, in a fit of remorse. "Please let me know if you can't manage it all in the time."

Mrs. Vine gave her a long look. "I do send work home sometimes with girls who need it. There's two or three here who'd sooner go on after eight at night, with their mothers helping, for the extra pennies. I can't do overtime here, see. Being a gable end, a light can be seen from the street. It was different in Stepney. Inspectors couldn't see into the back of them buildings. Still, the air's better out here. Though it costs me a lot, what with going up and down to the West End."

It simply had not occurred to Alice that when Mrs. Vine came to Conduit Street to collect work, the fare came out of her profits.

"My dear, and what about the messengers? You should have charged that to me—that's even worse!"

Mrs. Vine shrugged. "I'm doing all right. You're fair, Mrs. Wickham—it's when I'm kept waiting for hours on end for the patterns and stuffs in other houses that I really lose out. You don't do that."

"Mrs. Vine, when I can, will you come back and be a head of workroom for me? You know it may come to that if these dresses catch on. I'd pay you handsomely."

Mrs. Vine shook her head. "I can't. I have to be here. There's the kids, and my husband's not well. He has to be minded." She spoke quickly so that Alice understood she would not discuss the idea in further detail. "I like my independence and trade's good. You'll give me a reference, won't you, Mum, when the time comes for you to move on?"

As Mrs. Vine spoke to her, Alice looked at her tired face and realized Mrs. Vine was no more than Lily's age. That ripeness of thirty or so hung slack about her body, with no vitality, except for her forehead, stubborn and shiny with the steam from the irons.

"Of course I will. Be sure to come and see me when you need help. I've been very pleased with your work."

Mrs. Vine was satisfied, looked quickly at the girls, and ordered them back to work. There was no more to be said—Alice felt she was being dismissed, sent back to her proper place. Mrs. Vine did not want her sympathy and it would be self-indulgent of Alice to be upset. After all, she wanted the dresses made, and this was the system. A hidden heap of labor made many others, like her, very rich.

By September, Alice was ready. In spite of great nervousness she sent out her cards:

> *An Invitation to a "Ko Kwei Party."*
>
> *No one is to eat or smoke for half a day, and then come with sachets of perfume for the other guests to guess. . . . Crystallized violets, ice wafers and China tea will be served with the prizes, and a little entertainment afterward.*

The response was dramatic, and the word spread. Over the next few days, Alice was deluged with requests for more invitations. In the end she arranged a whole series of showings, every two hours through the afternoons of a whole week, and hired two footmen to prevent lines forming at the entrance. The whole point of her "Oriental tea show" was to induce a receptive mood, and she did not want her new customers, who were running into hundreds, to have to put up with any tiresome delays.

Of course Lily was one of the privileged circle who were received first, and Ned came with her, as Alice had expected. But she was so preoccupied with making her day successful that she quite forgot she was angry with him—indeed, she was glad to have him give her an opinion she would value. He tried to say calming things, and that helped a little, too.

"Your invitation was so mysterious you've stirred everyone's curiosity," he said. "Lily can't wait to see what you have in store. Good luck, Alice." he added sincerely.

"Definitely patchouli, my dears," Lily cried, pulling the silk scarf from her eyes and clapping her hands. Musk, orris root, lily of the valley . . . Alice was beginning to feel very, very excited.

"Look," she whispered to Ned, absently tugging at his sleeve. "I don't have a sister in the theater without learning something from her!" She could hear her own voice sounding sharp, not as nonchalant as she wished. She signaled to the two footmen, and curtains parted on a small stage at the far end of her salon. A gasp came from the tea-tasters.

Alice had arranged all her dresses in a tableau on a platform. They were worn by twenty life-size models cast in plaster of Paris, their blank faces swathed in gauze. Alice had pinned each dress in place, with Mme. Blanc's help, so that they suggested different personalities.

In the middle of these still, rapt figures, a Japanese musician began to play: pipes, bells, and strange stringed instruments.

"My God," said Ned, "they'll love it! What a brilliant idea, Alice!" He began to laugh, and Alice found herself sharing his amusement. Society loved to have "creators" at work for them . . . like her, like Ned. He took her hands, in a kiss, and then, before she could resist, held her in a warm embrace.

"Really, Ned! In front of all these people!" But Alice was pleased to see him so enthusiastic and happy for her—and no one was looking at them anyway. They were all staring at the tableau and the musician.

"I told Lily you'd be a success! You've done it!" he said, and Alice could see nothing but the warmth of admiration in his eyes. Her disapproval of Ned, of his very physical reaction to all women, was blotted out. Suddenly she could accept that he regarded her as an equal, a woman he might have tried to love, not treated as a casual mistress. She had misjudged him because she was too young and too inexperienced to see his qualities. Lily was a much better choice for him.

Ned held her arm for a moment longer, and she knew he would blurt something at her.

"Don't!" she whispered fiercely. "Not now!" She wanted to say all was forgiven, forgotten in the excitement of this moment. In honesty, she didn't want to think of anyone else, even Ned, at all. Perhaps Ned understood; he nodded, as if realizing that he could not intrude on her, and slipped into the crowd of guests, who were beginning to crowd toward her to pay their compliments.

"Do please go and look close! Do say you like my dresses, otherwise I might just faint!" The women laughed, but they did as they were told.

By the end of the week, after many more tea ceremonies, Alice was sure that her collection was *"le dernier cri pour la saison d'automne."*

◆　◆　◆

Orders for the Tunis Tunics alone could have kept Alice's dressmakers busy till the end of the year. There was a barbaric splendor about them that caught the fancy of London's society women. Alice found that she had created a classic, and believed that she would continue making these models with a little variation for many years to come.

No one knew, not even Anne or Ned, where her idea had originated. Alice had a distant memory: Grandmaman's boxroom in Denver, stuffed full of foreign treasures. There was a portrait there—a brother of Grandmaman's who had been a soldier in the French army, in Africa. A leather trunk held his gold-braided uniforms, and cracked photographic plates of weird and wonderful sights: soldiers on camels, women in silks and jewels sitting cross-legged on striped mats; palm trees, rows of soldiers between them on horseback. Sometimes Grandmaman would lift out of boxes silvery lengths of fabric, still impregnated with spicy odors . . . this was one of a handful of images Alice still cherished of the old lady. Alice sometimes suspected that there was more to remember, especially in quieter moments, when she touched fabrics, or pinned braid to a new dress. But she would resist. Not yet. It was not the time.

It was obvious she would have to move from Conduit Street. Old Mme. Blanc complained bitterly about what an upheaval it would be, and began to pack her bags, muttering with disdain rather as Alice imagined old French countesses did when they fled to their country châteaux before the Revolution. Luckily, she was spared a great search for a new home, as one of her customers, Lady Ventry, knew of a property belonging to a relative that was standing empty. Alice now had the money to organize a quick move, and very shortly she was established in a large house in Berkeley Square, with a beautiful staircase and several reception rooms on the first and ground floor that suited her purposes without much alteration.

Mrs. Vine, the sweatshop manageress, did not change her mind about Alice's offer of work, but she found Alice a younger unmarried woman to be her first head of workroom. Alice discovered it was the custom for heads to find their own hands in each department, so she was spared much of the detail. But she had to hire a separate head for a skirt room and a bodice room, as well as for special gowns. Emboldened with success, she took on a total of eighty hands in one month—all along the scale from trotters and improvers to trained finishers, pressers and a host of special workers to do beaded embroidery, lace appliqué and the painted muslins that were becoming almost as popular as the Tunis Tunics. Each head of workroom had her own forewoman to supervise the girls, clock the work in and out at various stages and see to supplies.

That was not all. Downstairs Alice hired her own *essayeuses* to wear the dresses for visitors; a second head fitter to help Mme. Blanc; two *vendeuses* or show-women to wait on the clientele; a showman rather like a *maître d'hôtel* to keep appointments running smoothly; a doorman, and two pageboys to run errands.

Ever since her visit to Mrs. Vine's sweatshop Alice had determined to do all she could for her own girls when the time came. Full of idealism, she started with unusual regulations. The girls were all to wear aprons and black velvet ribbons to neaten their hair—these were supplied free to encourage the girls to take care of their appearance. She gave them a free meal at midday, and tea all the time (the quality of which seemed to be a burning issue in every department). Girls were fined sixpence a week for unpunctuality, but Alice paid sixpence a week extra for good timekeeping, too. This device enabled her to spot the girls who were desperate for extra money. These were the ones most likely to be working overtime for other fashion houses to keep their wages up (although at twenty-five shillings to two pounds a week, the trained hands were getting top rates). But Alice ruled that none of the girls should work elsewhere—for secrecy, but also so that she could find them the extra work if they needed it.

Her plan was that in slack time—January to late spring, when most of her customers were abroad or in the country—she would send some of the girls to Upton to work at the Dorcas Society, and help train the younger ones. Some would also go to the country houses of her friends for a week at a time, to do making over or plain sewing. In this way they could keep up their incomes and be in the fresh air at the same time.

There was always theater work, too: with Lily's faithful patronage, and Anne's improving reputation, it would be possible to even out the seasonal nature of her work with stage costumes, particularly in that other slack time, late summer, when everyone went to the moors.

"Everyone": that circle of the privileged who had closed ranks around Alice. She was intoxicated with her acceptance. Alice gave back Lily's investment with interest. Lily took it, not because she did not wish to continue with her support, but because she admired Alice's desire to be free from obligations. Besides, she needed the money for another try at management.

Lily came to Berkeley Square before Alice opened her house to the public: October 1900. The rooms were painted a silvery-blue, Alice's favorite color, which was becoming her "signature." The interiors had been furnished in the Louis Seize style that she favored. Ceiling murals shone out richly against the new white paint on the plasterwork.

"Do you approve?" Alice stood with hands clasped as if in prayer, waiting for Lily's judgment.

"It's quite incredible! I don't know how you have the nerve to carry such an establishment on your tiny shoulders," said Lily in genuine amazement. "Twenty-five—you're such a baby!"

"Oh, Lily, you do understand, surely?" It seemed quite simple. "I *have* to do it—in the same way that you must act."

"I don't believe you," Lily said in a cool voice, shutting the door as they walked into Alice's private sitting room.

"How can you say that?"

"Don't you know yet? Well, perhaps I should not disillusion you . . ." Lily stopped, tempted as always to delve into Alice's ambition, share her secret thoughts.

Alice was puzzled, but she had grown used to Lily's fragmented way of speaking, assuming that she was thinking about too many things all at once, and waited to see if she would explain herself. But Lily had seen Ned's painting of Alice and Laura, hung for the first time in a place of honor over the fireplace. Lily studied it with interest. Then Alice guessed that a whole series of questions was about to be directed at her, and turned away. She adored Lily, but she did not want anyone ever to know how stupid she had once been, or that she had cared for Ned. She had only recognized how much when it was too late.

"Won't you come with me? There's something else downstairs that makes me more excited than almost anything else in the house. Do come, Lily, it's such a delicious idea, and I designed it all by myself."

Succeeding in diverting Lily, she led her down the stairs running ahead of her more like a schoolgirl than a woman of business. There was a small storeroom in the hallway under the staircase. Alice opened it to reveal all her store of stationery and wrappings. Cards in pale blue, tissues in soft colors, boxes piled high and covered in blue and silver stripes were printed with one word: "Alys."

"Do you like it?" she asked. "The design isn't too showy, is it? I should simply hate to look commercial. But I think it's important to change my name, have a label, like they do in Paris. 'Alice' sounds too childish, don't you think? 'Alys'—that's me now—will it do?" She was glittering with excitement.

"It's a brilliant idea, so romantic. Very French, too." Lily did approve, yet at the same time she thought her dark little friend looked more like her true self at that moment than she did in Ned's portrait.

CHAPTER 11

1 9 0 2 – 3

The "Tunis Tunic" soon came to typify the new Edwardian woman, along with the swan-bend corset, the Alexandra fringe, and the marble shoulders of the king's belles. When Queen Victoria died, propriety gave way to self-indulgence. The odor of smelling salts was wafted away by the smoke of fat cigars. Alice stood among the crowds of mourners at Hyde Park Corner, watching the vast pageant as it passed through the streets. Spiky, black-fringed trees reached up to a wintry sky. The railings and lampposts were hung with horse-shoe shaped wreaths. The same magnificent cream-colored horses Alice remembered seeing a few years before at the Jubilee parade were used to pull the coffin on its gun-carriage. The only difference in their trappings were the purple ribbons braided into their manes.

Yet Alice felt great hope. She felt she was being released by events, enabled to enter with full spirit into a new life. As she stood among the crowds, in the cold air, she said a prayer of sorts for another death: Grandma Hardy had finally given up the struggle against ill health. Perhaps she wanted to die with the end of an era that had suited her so well. Neither Alice nor Anne had been sent any details of the funeral arrangements; just an announcement card. They had to assume that they were still not welcome. So Alice stood in Hyde Park, obscurely hoping that Grandma Hardy would have been pleased with her for that. Carrigrohane Hall loomed in her mind, a bleak old castle, absorbing its few last ghosts.

Berkeley Square was freedom in contrast to that place. Now Alice could delegate the day-to-day work, she sent for Laura to live with her and hired a governess. She had a home of her own, above her workrooms, for the first time. She and Laura still went back to St. John's Wood for the weekends to see Dr. Hardy and Mrs. Bacon.

Alice was not at all sure what led her from one decision to the next in her new world. Ideas seemed to filter through a gauze—on one side was reality, on the other her private, creative world. It was like looking out of a window through net. Shapes could be seen clearly, just the detail of the foreground was blurred. What she saw prompted new ideas: a "line" was suggested. Alice knew that her success was due to her enthusiasm for making women look beautiful, not only handsome, but individual. Inspiration came from many sources not always readily identified.

Perhaps it was a growing awareness that women wanted to change their lives. She was not unique in her experience—Daisy financed suffrage activities; Lily tried to stage new plays; Anne wanted complete independence—but they too had a clear understanding that appearances mattered in the world, and that if women could be made to look assured and confident, they would be well treated.

One of her customers, the Duchess of Buccleuch, was Mistress of the

Robes, carrying the Queen's train at the Coronation of Edward VII. Alice thought that the admiration and respect her clientele received was confirmed not just by state occasions, but by many public rituals, including all the lesser ones—being seen in the right places. She was conscious that her work in the salon was evolving into something more than mere dress designing. She had grown used to her power to transform people. An idea would take shape, and just as in the theater, actresses were helped to become their parts with her costumes, so perhaps would "real-life" women, when they wore her designs.

In Paris, on that first visit, she had been overawed by the stiff grandeur of the couture houses. *Essayeuses* encased in black crepe, hiding all bare skin, showed the dresses, barely moving. The sight of inferior flesh—a showroom girl's bare arms—was considered improper to everyone. A matron might bring a young son, a woman her fiancé or lover to help her choose clothes. A half-naked girl of a lower class would cause offense. Or was it that a man's roving eye might find the poor *essayeuse* appealing in her fine clothes? An invisible working girl might for a moment become a highly visible woman. The hypocrisy Alice saw on all sides urged her to be daring. Perhaps she could show others how to put on airs, and be accepted for entirely acquired charms . . . She decided to find a handful of beautiful girls and train them up to be her mannequins. In France there were *mannequins de ville*—society women who were dressed for free by couturiers because they were good advertisements, seen in all the right places. Hers would be somewhere in between these women and the black-covered salon girls.

Besides, Alice sensed that women were being elevated to a new status. The King's flirtations were the subject of endless gossip in her circles, and her own friends seemed to conduct their love affairs with less furtiveness than in the past. In was a kind of freedom, to admit to sexual adventures. Alice had given the subject very little thought recently. No, that was untrue—she had thought about being in love many times. Her salon was redolent with the possibilities of attraction between men and women, but she forced herself to keep all that at a distance, too hurt, too proud to admit the need of anyone's love for herself. She found it quite easy to divert her energies into work, and she had Laura as an outlet for tenderness and intimacy. She felt unloved, of course, all the time. But that was a safe, familiar feeling. Not being loved was like sharing a room with an old friend—comfortable, convenient, limiting.

Moving about in the world diverted her mind from her personal inadequacies. She began to search for her girls, wondering if the common belief that beautiful women were rare was true. People always gathered on the pavements when creatures like Lily Lavelle or Mrs. Cecily Day stepped out. Alice knew only too well why loveliness was such a valuable commodity that a "professional beauty" could make a good life if she chose to sell it. The working conditions, poor health and bad diet of the majority of people in London made women ugly whatever their natural good qualities. Alice remembered the shock of truth she had felt on reading a French novel in which the hero fell out of love because his childhood sweetheart had to work in a shop. Her family were suddenly made poor: the sight of her, pale in the face, with a slight stain of sweat under the arms of her bodice, killed his devotion.

Her first choice was an easy one. She went back to Mrs. Vine's to find the blonde who had been sweeping the doorstep of the dingy sweatshop.

"She left me about six months ago," Mrs. Vine explained. "But the family live not very far from here, over a shop in the High Street."

Alice found her way past a pie shop, a pawnbroker's and a hardware store piled high with brooms and buckets, to the cobbler's on the main west road. She was determined to interview each girl in the presence of the family, so that no suspicion of immorality would be aroused. For the same reason, she had decided to give all the girls pseudonyms. Like her own name, Alys, it ensured privacy. French names would make them sound like whores, so she settled on Greek.

The blonde, Florence Nuttall, lived with her cobbler father and two younger brothers above the shop. She was to be "Phoebe." Mr. Nuttall was surly, and for a while Alice wondered if he intended asking payment to compensate him for the loss of his daughter's wages. He seemed reluctant, even when she told him how much extra she would be earning. Something troubled him, but he would not tell her what it was. "So it's agreed then, Mr. Nuttall?" she persisted. "Florence can begin her training with me on the first of August, and I'll pay her wages a month from that date. A guinea a week during training, plus fares and food. Two guineas after that."

"She's got to be in by seven every night."

"Do you want her sent home in a cab?"

"Don't be daft—she'll get too big for her boots. The bus will do—but not after seven. You give me your word. And no men at all." Florence's mouth gawped briefly as the money was mentioned, which made Alice wonder if she had made a wise choice. If nerves made her do that at the Autumn shows . . . she realized she was being far too critical and left the arrangement as it stood.

Minnie Basset led her to her next address, a discovery that encouraged her very much. There were flats in Silver Street, not far from Minnie's lodgings, largely inhabited by Russian or Polish Jews who fled from the pogroms in eastern Europe. They formed a commercial colony in Soho, continuing their longstanding tradition of work in the tailoring trade. Mr. Szenkier was one of these, and had twin daughters who were employed with him in his brother's establishment. The girls had beautiful faces, long straight noses and bold eyes, partly hidden under fringes of thick black hair. Kitty, the more forceful sister, was instantly attracted by the idea of not half blinding herself on buttonholes for the rest of her days, and dragged her less willing twin, Tina, behind her. Mr. Szenkier did not need much persuading.

They were both quiet, cultured girls, needing only confidence to make them "project" as Anne would put it. Alice decided to call them her "Diana" and "Daphne."

"Zoe" was the name that came to mind for Betsey, the daughter of Alice's paper-box makers, who lived in a Shoreditch court. Alice gave the family work because the father had been crippled in the Boer War, and lost all chance of better employment. Betsey was the eldest of eight children. Her parents were trying against all odds to run a decent home. Alice nearly retched when she smelt the suffocatingly stale air in the dark alley that led to the common yard where the washhouses for the flats stood. Dirty stone staircases led up to the public balconies— door-banging communal lavatories were easily found by the smell on the corner of each landing. But Betsey's family flat had clean net curtains, and a row of pot marigolds in a triangle of light by the wash line.

Stanley Hill set the tone for his family: self-help and self-improvement.

"I'm not one of yer working-class conservatives, Mum, hoping for patronage or charity." Alice had heard his speech many times and was quite prepared to hear it again. "I'm Liberal. You've been good to give me work. But all the same . . . what guarantee of security will you offer Betsey? We don't want fancy favors. She'll not have a future in your lark. What'll she do when her looks are gone and her head's been stuffed with fancy notions? I'd rather get her into a Borough school for

ıt's what I think. We'd have saved enough for it next

you what, Mr. Hill. That's an excellent suggestion. Let Betsey
ɔ for three years, and she can have lessons in typing at the same
ın return. An insurance policy—would that do?"

Alice surprised herself at her bargaining, necessity forcing her to
think quickly. She particularly wanted Betsey to join her team. She was
a strong, big girl, with a longish neck and probably a fine pair of
shoulders, if only they could be seen. Alice was not so bold that she
dared ask for that. Mr. Hill would have been quite rightly affronted.
And Betsey's hair was a handsome coppery gold.

Mrs. Hill swayed the argument. "There's no harm done—we know
Mrs. Wickham's house, don't we? And why shouldn't Betsey enjoy her
looks? I'm sure I'd have wanted to, if I'd had 'em. Go on, love, have
a bit of fun. I'm pleased for you, don't mind your Dad."

"Thank you, Ma, but I won't go if Dad doesn't say yes properly to
me. You will, Dad, won't you?" Betsey did not bother to look winning.
She understood her father too well to try that. It was yes or no on the
logic of the proposition.

"No fancy ideas. That's all I ask." He gave in.

After her promising start, Alice ran out of luck. She made it difficult
for herself by refusing to ask for help outside a small circle of contacts,
for fear of losing her element of surprise. Gossip could spread fast in
Soho, and her rivals might seize on the idea for themselves. Alice
became obsessed with her search. Every time she traveled about London, she peered into the crowds, hoping to find a girl that she could
use in her salon. There were so many kind, sweet faces, on all sides.
Alice often thought she had found what she wanted, but the girls
disappeared, refused her offers out of moral shock or timidity, and
sometimes out of hostility for her upper-class manners. Alice was not
offended by this. After all, in every walk of life she met with some form
of disbelief, if not direct disapproval. Some of her friends' husbands
refused to accept that she did not have a backer (they meant lover),
directing her enterprise. They rejected the idea that a woman could
work alone as she did. At the other end of the scale, these angry
working girls thought she was philandering with their lives, even
though Alice tried to convince them that she might be creating a new
career for them.

Once she came close to her own origins in her search into other lives.

The Duchess of Buccleuch had given her the address of a velvet maker, one of the last craftsmen left in London able to hand-loom the fabric. He had supplied lengths for the royal robes at the Coronation: amethyst velvet for the Queen, worked in gold with all the national floral emblems branching from the Plantagenet crown. Alice was interested in seeing his work, and went to his address, in an old street in Spitalfields near the beautiful Hawksmoor church. The house was built on gracious lines, dating from the days of the Huguenot silk merchants who had lived in that area. It had a classic portico and a winding balustraded staircase. Now the house was sublet to a mixture of nationalities, French, Irish, Polish and East Enders among them. On every floor, whole families lived in each room. The velvet maker lodged at the top of the house in a long attic that still had the sloping tall windows that had been installed for the silk weavers more than a century earlier. Mr. Allen was a descendant of those Huguenots himself; like Grandpa Hardy. His grandfather had anglicized the name Allenet: her own name, Hardy, was originally "Hardi" in French. He lived with his wife and one surviving daughter. In that young girl, Lisa, Alice saw her own family's heritage once more. Lisa had the same soft looks of Alice's father, and his father, Grandpa James, before him. Long features, a romantic, open expression, a strong spirit that poverty could not diminish. The physical similarity moved her.

Alice had not expected to find someone so perfect for her new idea—she had come only to see the velvet. The coincidence made her believe she had luck on her side again, and she made her offer that very afternoon. Like the tailor, Mr. Szenkier, Mr. Allen was interested in her suggestion—anxious to get his daughter out of her poor surroundings. When he called his wife to come in and meet her, Alice understood why. Mrs. Allen had been sitting on the kitchen roof at the back, to get some sun and a dose of air, even if it was smoke-filled. Alice recognized her pallor and her panting breath as the common signs of infection—tuberculosis. Every time she worked with Lisa at the frame, chatting, sighing or even giving her own daughter an affectionate kiss, she was increasing the risk of the girl's own decline.

Alice knew so little about the course of the disease that she could not take any risks.

"Wouldn't you prefer to think about my offer?" she said, hurriedly. "Why don't you take my card and call on me in a few days' time?"

She hoped that by then she could find out from Dr. Hardy whether she would endanger the health of her other young protégées by taking Lisa in.

For several weeks Alice drilled the other new girls in the correct way to walk, turn at corners and hold up their heads. They giggled, grew bored, complained of headaches, but sometimes, especially when they saw some of Alice's dress designs, became enthusiastic. Soon progress was being made. The girls practiced in a room at Alice's hotel, away from Berkeley Square, so that no one would ask questions. Then, one by one, Alice took them to her salon, and positioned them in a discreet corner so that they could peep into the world of "Alys." Florence, or "Phoebe" in the making, suddenly stopped gaping at everything Alice said. She sat stiff and upright on a stool watching the customers, particularly a blond girl far plainer than herself, and very gauche, being forced into an unsuitable heavy green brocade dress by her mother. Phoebe was sorry for the girl, and pointed her out to Alice.

"*Reelly* ugly. An' now she's cryin'! All this to choose from, and she's in an awful state! It's impossible. Reelly, it's *not* possible!" Phoebe was working herself up into quite a state: Alice told her to be quiet, and turned to the girl and her mother, just as they were preparing to leave.

"Ah, Madame Alys!" The mother was pleased. "I asked for you but they said you were engaged."

"I was, Mrs. Smalley, but I finished early just to be sure to have a word with you. The *vendeuse* took all the details, I hope? You want the green brocade, is that so?"

"Yes! It's a perfect match for the family emeralds. For Julia's ball in September—don't you agree?"

"Oh yes, the green is quite splendid . . . so this is Julia, is it? Hello, my dear." Alice gave the girl a kiss. "Mother's quite right of course, brocade is just the thing for emeralds."

"Oh, no, not you *too*! I shall look perfectly hideous in it," Julia moaned.

"Wait a minute. Take off your cloak."

Julia did as she was told. Although her face was undistinguished, she was slim built, and stood straight. She twisted her gloves shyly. Alice laid her hand over her fingers and said, "Look!" pointing down at Julia's feet. "Pretty little feet, and such darling hands . . . angelic!"

Mrs. Smalley smiled as if she alone were responsible for her daughter's good features.

"Do you know," said Alice softly, just to Julia, "I've seldom seen such beautiful hands." She stroked Julia's fingers. "The rule, Mrs. Smalley, is always, 'the more nature does, the *less* art has to do.' Why don't *you* wear the emeralds and the green brocade? After all!," she dared to add, "if prospective suitors need to see the family jewels they can admire them on *you* much better than on Julia! Let her wear silk—so much better for the young—long sleeves, with a point over the wrist, seed pearls along the edge, up the seams, to a peak here, adding height by her face . . . wouldn't that do? Diamonds in her hair, if you insist, but no more than a single piece, a crescent or a spray, like this . . ."

Alice pinned a length of silk tightly to Julia's arm, wound the rest of the bolt round her figure, and fixed an aigrette in her hair. She stood behind the girl, holding up a pleat of fabric to both her shoulders, to give a clear impression of the finished effect.

"I suppose I could . . ." Mrs. Smalley was considering the brocade again, much tempted.

"It really does need a little *authority*, that brocade," said Alice. The word was enough. Mrs. Smalley listened eagerly to Alice's suggestions for her own ballgown. Both customers were satisfied.

Alice went back to Phoebe, who had paid close attention to the conversation.

"Are you going to make dresses for me, like that?" Phoebe asked. "Just for me, like that?"

"Yes. So the Mrs. Smalleys of this world have a clear idea in their heads. They can't see, from fabric alone, or from a sketch, whether a line will suit or not."

"I'll be beautiful," Phoebe murmured.

"No, Phoebe, you are beautiful *now*, don't ever think otherwise. I'll make the world take note of you, that's all—don't ever forget the difference. Stand up straight, Florence! Now say it!"

"Say what, Your Ladyship?" Phoebe looked alarmed.

" 'I am beautiful.' This minute, now!"

"What do you mean, Your Ladyship?"

"Oh, never mind, girl. Florence, I mean, Phoebe, that will do."

Alice turned away, and Phoebe went back to the other girls in Dover Street. Alice was sorry she had been so short-tempered. She ran upstairs to her own rooms, interrupting Laura, who was reading with her governess, Miss Dalton. Confusion made her abrupt. She descended on Laura, and covered her with kisses. Laura was used to these sudden displays of affection from her mother, and took it in good part. She settled comfortably in Alice's arms, pleased to be held.

Alice hummed to herself.

"I'll only stay a moment, Miss Dalton."

The governess sat by the window, slightly disapproving of Alice's interruption. Alice sang quietly to Laura, an old Irish song she had picked up from Deirdre at Carrigrohane. Memories of her solitude, the overbearing disapproval of her grandmother, mingled with images of wan, unappreciated faces: the two girls downstairs, one rich, one poor. Out of the randomness of her thoughts, another face came to her. It was Lisa's. She was the source of Alice's unease. Dr. Hardy had told her it was unwise to employ the girl until she was sure that she was healthy. Alice had sent her to Upton village for a while, to lodge with Mrs. Burns and build up her resistance.

Ever since she had met Lisa in Spitalfields, recollections of her grandfather and father had flitted, shadowy, in her mind. Alice suddenly decided that she would have to go back to Carrigrohane to make her peace. She sat humming, her lips brushing the top of Laura's head. Lisa's face evoked images of others, so similar: Grandpa James, and the idealized rather than truly remembered warmth of her father's expression. The more successful "Alys" became, the more the past rose up to remind her who she was, and make her unsure of her gains.

Now was no time to think of leaving London. The autumn collection was nearly ready, but the salon needed alteration. Risking the anger of those clients who imagined "Alys" was there to satisfy their whims day and night, she closed the house for a week, while builders, painters and carpenters built her a small Greek temple in the center of the main salon, and covered the walls with new drapes of blue silk. The girls were to present the new dresses in this setting, as if they were Muses, inspirational figures. They would parade along a narrow platform walk, then pose like statues among the classical pillars. It was the most expensive piece of self-promotion Alice had ever conceived.

The excitement of the day carried the entire staff except Alice herself, who was so anxious for success that she was sharp with everyone, particularly the doorman, who seemed unable to cope with the crowd pressing at the doors even before they were opened.

"What are you doing!" she snapped. "Let them in! I can't have my ladies waiting on the street!"

Daisy rushed forward to kiss her. "Isn't this exciting? I can't wait. What are you going to do—I hope it's very daring!"

"I suppose it is, quite," said Alice, nervously.

Her worries were unfounded.

"Ladies and gentlemen," she announced in a thin, shaking voice, "here are my latest 'creations' . . . Phoebe, will you step forward?" Small hands parted the silk curtains, and the girl stepped out, walking gracefully down the length of the room. A warm murmur of praise rose on all sides.

"Phoebe" from a suburban workshop, "Diana" and "Daphne" from a Soho tailor's room and golden "Zoe" from an East End courtyard justified all Alice's efforts. They slipped in and out of their model gowns with practiced efficiency, then glided in front of Alice's audience whenever their names were called out, as if they were being presented at Court. Alice's guests were fascinated; Daisy Panton was trying to spot family resemblances. (They must surely be this year's debutantes, everyone thought.) Many a real debutante's mother, Mrs. Smalley among them, regretted that their own daughters had so little poise. The anonymity of the girls added to the excitement. Alice had once again presented London with a novelty, and her success was assured.

The "parade" was well under way when Lily made her own grand entrance. Ripples of interest made heads turn toward her—feathers, wide brims, ribbons, bobbing as if seaborne. Alice realized at once that the room was so crowded Lily would be forced to wait by the door for lack of space to find her seat. She stepped forward, holding up her hand for a moment so that Zoe stood still in the middle of her "performance." Then Alice walked across the room, smiling at her friend.

"Darling!" Lily cried, kissing her cheek in apology. The audience stared: it was just like a theatrical début. Alice was amused, not at all angry. "This way, Miss Lavelle," she invited, and guided Lily across the floor to the front row, where her seat of honor had been reserved.

But Lily's sharp eyes had noticed a row of very excited faces peering at her from behind the stage drapes. She smiled gaily at them, and they could not resist fluttering their hands back at her—for she was a favorite celebrity in the world they came from. At that moment Lily was the only woman who guessed the truth. She was their idea of a "great lady"—the quiet social distinction of most of the women in the room meant little to Alice's mysterious mannequins. They were nobodies, young outsiders.

Not for long! After the performance, Alice hustled the girls away, for the audience were fit to beseige them with questions. She was determined to keep the secret just a little bit longer, relishing the curiosity she had created.

Mrs. Smalley sailed over.

"Stunning! That Zoe creature—not one of the Foxwell girls, is she?"

Alice laughed out loud. "No, a far sight prettier than either! Hello, Julia, I want you to have a "Painted Pastel" in lilacs . . . just perfect for you. I hope we can convince your mother!"

Mrs. Smalley was unsure how to receive any of these remarks, and towed her daughter away. Alice made an effort not to allow her excitement to lead her into more irreverence, and retreated to the dressing room to congratulate her girls.

Within a few days, Phoebe, Zoe, Daphne and Diana had their separate circles of admirers. Some of the husbands, brothers—even lovers—who attended Alice's showings sent flowers and enthusiastic letters. Most were innocent or naïve expressions of admiration, but there were a few who offered more material rewards for their success. "Diana" and "Daphne" attracted a little less attention from the men because they were Jewish—a prejudice that Alice was astonished to find still counted even in such lighthearted matters as flirting.

"Not one of you is to answer these letters!" she insisted. The girls were gathered to hear her verdict on their performance a few days later. The chief *vendeuses,* Mary and Rose, were standing guard.

"I gave my word to your families! It's part of your contract of employment that you don't associate with clients and their acquaintances!"

Looking down at their happy faces, Alice felt it was pointless to rant at them. They were so excited, so full of dreams. She sighed.

"Promise me at least to be good. I'd never forgive myself if one of you came to harm. You must be—discreet. After all"—the thought came to her—"I don't mix business with pleasure myself."

The girls glanced at one another, blushing at Alice's honesty. But their looks also communicated that they thought she was making a fool of herself, being so irritated and overprotective.

Phoebe, surprisingly, was the first to speak up.

"Oh, Your Ladyship! You are hard on us. We do have *brains* you know. I like it here—we all like it here." She did not bother to look at the others for agreement. "No one's going to muck about. Honestly, it wouldn't be worth it."

"Thank you, Phoebe. I did not mean to suggest that I didn't trust you . . . if I implied that, I apologize. I worry for you, that's all."

To Alice's dismay, these last words seemed to make everyone embarrassed. The girls glanced at one another shiftily. Rose quickly dismissed them, and they hurried away.

"Well?" Alice asked.

Rose spread her hands, asking to speak freely, and Alice drew breath with impatience. "Come along, Rose!"

"You explained yourself. That's going far enough, but please, allow me to be frank, Mrs. Wickham—there's never any need to *apologize.*"

◆　◆　◆

Alice felt deflated after the excitement of her shows. Trade was demanding, but almost tedious now that her little house was professionally organized. All the workrooms were fully occupied with orders for her new collection, and her staff was well able to turn out numerous variations according to her specifications. (In fact the workroom heads were more competent than she was when it came to creating small differences to satisfy that "uniqueness" she insisted upon.)

Alice found herself with time on her hands—time to sit with Laura after months of neglecting her for more pressing matters. Time not to worry about finances, because she had an order book worth many thousands of pounds, an overflow of orders to pass on to Mrs. Vine and a constant demand for the fine linens being supplied to her by the Dorcas girls under Mrs. Burns. In fact, she had a little empire, and she was just twenty-five years old. . . .

"Who's that pretty lady, Mama?" Laura's voice interrupted her thoughts. She was sitting by the window, looking down over the customers going in and out of Berkeley Square.

"That's Mrs. Cecily Day. Smart, isn't she?"

"I don't like ladies who wear wild things round their necks. Who's that one now, Mama?"

"She's a real duchess! The Duchess of Buccleuch! She picks up the Queen's clothes for her, just like Miss Dalton does for you . . ."

"Laura's a good girl. She tidies herself."

Alice laughed, and hugged the child. At least she was happy, not living in dread of constant wickedness, so different from herself at the same age. Persistent thoughts of Carrigrohane spoilt her pleasure; Alice began to suspect that she was incapable of contentment, and that she would always live dissatisfied, in pursuit of something else.

That night Lily and Ned had invited Alice to a late supper at the Ritz after the theater, to celebrate Lily's new venture—a tour of the provinces with *The French Countess*. She imagined the party would include some admirers for her to reconsider. The Baron de Falbe, small and balding, but quiet, attentive and rich, would continue to pay suit.

As she dressed herself that evening, Alice realized she had no desire at all to attend. She studied herself in the mirror: her black hair swept up high over her wide forehead, her dark eyes somber when they ought to be gleaming. She knew she was not beautiful, but striking when her face was lit a little happily. All at once it became clear to her that she had to stop striving and dreaming, because events were moving too quickly for her. Success, even wealth, was in her grasp, yet she still felt lost in herself. She wanted to run away from her position, her confident, lonely place in crowded rooms. She had never imagined it would ever happen, but she yearned to see Ireland. She had something important to take back there, now.

A week later, she left "Alys" in the hands of Mme. Blanc, Mary and Rose, and took Laura with her. She did not write to tell Grandpa Hardy of her plan in case he refused to allow her to come. Once she had decided to go back to Cork, Alice was filled with eagerness to see Carrigrohane Hall. She thought of so many questions to ask her grandfather. Then, at other times, she could not think of anything she really wanted to know. Many things confused her. On the one hand, she felt there was nothing she had done that needed his pardon; on the other, she would have done anything to win back his approval.

Anne would not go with her. She was on tour again with Hubert Kerrick, in his Number One company this time, and did not understand Alice's sudden wish to return home.

"What a mad idea," she wrote. "Where's your pride? We did nothing wrong. I *do* feel badly about Grandpa, but I can't do it, can't go back. Are you wise, Alice? Just when everything is going simply brilliantly for you?"

When they reached Cork, Alice hired an outside car, as a treat for Laura, to take her from Cork City to Carrigrohane Hall. It was an open carriage with two bench seats that folded out on each side. She and Laura sat together, facing the landscape, with a thick rug over their knees. The driver, standing on the other side, whipped up his horse, and they swayed disconcertingly into movement. Laura was a composed six-year-old, just a few years younger than Alice had been when she first arrived in Ireland. Alice held her a little tighter as they bounced through the countryside, landmarks coming back to her through years of unremembering. She realized with surprise that all these scenes were still there, imprinted on her mind.

Riding up the approach to Carrigrohane Hall she felt apprehensive, cold in the sudden shadows thrown by unkempt bushes on either side of the drive. No one opened the door when they arrived.

"Wait—just in case we have to go back with you!" she warned the driver.

"Right you are, Milady."

Alice banged on the door. The old bell pull was broken. She could hear the noise it ought to have made in her head, but not in the air. When no one answered, she took Laura's hand again and went round to the kitchen entrance through the old stone arch. There were weeds growing in the brick path.

Just as she turned into the coachyard, Grandpa James appeared from one of the stables, smoking a pipe, with a sporting newspaper in his hand. He looked as if he had been lying in the straw with his dogs—which, in fact, he had.

"Alice, m'dear. Good to see you. Seen Lynch? Want him to go to town on an errand."

Lynch opened the kitchen door and stuck out a grizzled head. He did not quite see Alice.

"No more bets! That's three this week already. You've had your quota, or I'm a—Jesus, Miss Alice!"

He was amazed and pleased in equal measure, then a hope came to him.

"I don't suppose you brought the other one with yer? Never mind, single blessings is the best . . . and who might you be? Are yer goin' to tell me, or has the cat got your tongue, young lady?

"Laura, sir." She was under the impression that The Inch was her grandfather, Alice realized. Well he might be, she thought, for he had given her and Anne just as much care.

"Well now, this *is* a surprise! Come this way, come this way. You'll see we're not used to visitors these days, but you're family, so I don't suppose you'll mind. This way—follow your master."

Alice could see that The Inch was doing his best to maintain order. Mrs. Keefe's clutter had been taken away—the kitchen was empty, spotless, all the boards and tiles gray-cold with disuse. Grandma's drawing room was bare of ornament. Only the furniture remained, and the piano, shut and covered. Alice was glad that the doors to the Great Hall were closed. To see that room now would destroy her recollection of its grandeur, the light flooding in at the long windows, the view over the Lee, the sun's atoms dancing in the corners. Dust on the oak staircase made Alice think no one had gone upstairs for weeks, if not months. Grandpa's library was another matter—the setting for his whole life, day and night, with a daybed in the corner, newspapers, pipes, clothing on every surface.

The Inch paused in the doorway, surveying the mess.

"Now, where am I going to put you all for the night?" he worried.

"Oh no, not possibly!" Alice reacted at once. "We'll go back to Cork tonight—I asked the driver to wait. Please, Inch, on account of Laura, it would be best . . ."

His grin at the old name overcame his disappointment that she would not stay. He was relieved to think that former grand times would not be compared to the current state of affairs.

Grandpa Hardy had paid hardly any attention to their conversation. He was riffling through piles of magazines all over his sideboard and desk. "The form's here somewhere," he said. "The horse is a winner, Lynch."

While his back was turned, Alice looked questioningly at The Inch. "Always?" she whispered.

He shook his head. "Since he retired. Took her going fairly hard. Nothing to do, makes it worse. Bad winter, bad chest." He tapped his broad body, making a noise like a full barrel.

"What's that, Lynch?" Grandpa asked.

"I was just telling Miss Alice—"

"Alice! Such a surprise. And you must be Laura. Pretty girl. Take after your mother—No, not the eyes . . ." he suddenly paid attention to the child.

"I really shouldn't stay long, Grandpa. We had a long journey today." Alice wanted very much to go away.

"Oh? So soon? Well. Whatever you think best. Lynch, you could drive her back to town and—"

"No bets! And she has wheels of her own."

"Oh? Oh well, just an idea." He looked downcast.

"We'll come tomorrow, Grandpa, shall we?" Alice suggested. "For a picnic, perhaps, like the old days. Inch, I'll bring a hamper. Shall we do that? Like the old days."

"Ah, that would be grand." The Inch was mentally picking which spot he would scythe. On the front lawns, where the courts used to be, perhaps.

A knock at the door reminded Alice of her driver.

"The lady's just leavin'." The Inch bellowed through the front door.

"Good-bye, Grandpa," Laura said politely, waving at The Inch as the outside car lurched off. Alice was too wrapped up in her impressions to correct her mistake.

Next day, revived after a good rest, Alice returned to Carrigrohane with a hamper supplied by the hotel, supplemented by purchases she made purely out of nostalgia from the Eagle bakery, still there after six years. No brown cakes any more, but familiar barmbrack—a currant loaf to remind her of Sunday teas. She was more prepared to accept Grandpa's decline than she had been the previous night. He had been the outgoing partner, Grandma the recluse. Now he no longer had the contrast to spur him on. The Inch's stoic acceptance of his master's new ways impressed Alice, and comforted her. Besides, Grandpa seemed to have forgotten that he was angry with her or Anne. She decided not to question any of it, to let things move along their destined course, which was how The Inch seemed to be dealing with the situation.

The picnic was an unforgettable happiness for everyone, perhaps because Alice had decided not to revive the past. She sorted out Laura's mistaken identification of The Inch for Grandpa James. The Inch was enormously flattered, and sat with them for lunch, which Grandma would never have allowed. He spread out blankets on a freshly mown patch, and they all ate with pleasure, inside a circular wall of uncut meadow grass, clovers and cow parsley. Emboldened by Laura's familiarity, The Inch took her on his knee, and told her all the naughty stories he could recall from Alice's childhood. She was fascinated by his strongly accented voice, his long, winding stories full of the repetitions that children hope for and seldom get.

Then Alice described her work and her salon, unselfconsciously, not expecting disapproval, and none came. Grandpa James occasionally paid attention, but lapsed at other times, reading his newspaper or arranging another combination of tasty morsels for himself and his grandchild.

It was so peaceful. Swallows dipped down from the castellated walls, flying over their heads and disappearing into the woods. After lunch, Alice took Laura for a walk round the gardens, to see the old gazebo, then the orchard and the stables with the water trough where she and Anne used to fish for snails.

They walked down the overgrown path to the churchyard gate, to pay their respects to Grandma's grave. There was a simple plaque inside the church, and an ornate grave outside it with a winged angel leaning over as if to say "lower your voice." The grave was not well tended. Somehow Alice could not picture Grandpa visiting it for sentimental conversations with his dead wife. Under dusty glass domes a few floral tributes from the funeral still survived. Alice tried to read names, but most of the ink had run in the rain or faded. The Stoneys, the Boyles . . . Alice was drawn back in time just by the names. Another headstone stood near the wicket gate, the only other recent grave. Curious, Alice read the inscription. It was for Sophie, her childhood friend, who had died the past winter. She had never reached Africa or India.

"Let's go, Laura."

"Aren't you going to say prayers?"

"I forgot. All right." They stood, heads bowed.

Then they walked back to the house. Laura seemed content to be surrounded by mysteries.

"Won't we see the house, Mama?" she asked.

"No, I don't think so. It might upset Grandpa, bring back memories." It was a convenient answer; Alice did not wish to see any more: the gloomy bedrooms, the schoolroom, the attics, the "berdoyers."

The Inch found them wandering in the remains of the herb garden, where mint, balm and rosemary spread haphazardly over the clay pie-crust edges of the paths. They all walked slowly back across the lawn, to where Grandpa Hardy lay asleep with *The Field* over his face.

"Tell me about Miss Sophie," Alice whispered to The Inch.

"Tragic, it was. A weak heart. They'd suspected it for a long time. Then they left here, the curate and his lady, this Christmas."

"Did they go far?" Alice could guess the answer.

"They did. A school in Lahore. That's a wonder."

Alice merely nodded. Sophie's timidity, her reticence, was explained. She felt a deep sadness, but an awareness of her own great strength and fortune at the same time. She knew that Sophie would have understood that, and felt very close to her.

"You'll be coming back for longer, next time, won't you, Miss Alice?" The Inch asked, trying to cheer her. "And bring herself with you—that bold girl."

"I'm so sorry that Miss Anne could not visit this time," she answered. "She was rehearsing, you understand." Anne had meant so much to the old man—she wished her sister had come. To please The Inch she told him all about Anne's career and her ambitions to appear in a play in a West End theater. He listened intently, as if such concerns were quite familiar to him.

"All the same," he concluded, "I couldn't abide a big city. Even Cork frightens the life out of myself."

"Neither of us could leave London now. Miss Anne has her theater, and I have my salon."

Grandpa James sat up. He had been listening, not sleeping at all. "Stop blathering at her, Lynch. Of course she has to stay in London. It's her profession she's talking about."

He drew out a cigar and leaned back when The Inch had lit it.

Alice felt a softening, a yielding sensation inside her. Grandpa James had offered the best acknowledgment she could ever have wanted. He had recognized her efforts, and her success, in that one remark. For a man of his generation, it was a radical change of heart, overcoming many of his assumptions about women, divorce, trade and social life. But the softening that Alice felt was also dismay, because his words made her suspect that he too was close to death, just when it seemed she could love him very much.

It began to grow cooler as the sun dropped west of the house and long shadows moved across the grass.

"We ought to go," Alice murmured, reluctant to move.

The Inch went across to get the wagonette and take then back to Cork. Alice sat in companionable silence with Grandpa James while Laura picked flowers to take home and press. Eventually Grandpa James lumbered to his feet and put out his hands to help Alice up. He held her at arm's length, observant as he had been in the old days, when his whiskers would have bristled.

"You're a pretty girl," he said, but his face clouded.

"What it is, Grandpa?" she asked.

"There's something I should tell you perhaps, about—"

"Sophie?"

"No, that's not it. Though that was very sad. Sweet girl." He began to fumble for his watch, looking distressed. "There was something important—not about a death, not a death . . . You've lost so many dear ones, haven't you? It wasn't right to leave you all alone like that. Your—your poor mother—and then your grandmother—my darling Esther—poor dear Alice, it wasn't right!"

He grew so agitated and confused that Alice became apprehensive, and tried to stop him from making such an effort. "Don't upset yourself, Grandpa, it doesn't matter now. You've made me very happy. And we shouldn't dwell on the past, should we?" She patted his hand.

For a moment, Grandpa James looked aghast. He passed his hand over his eyes, trying to clear his thoughts. The rumble of the wagonette wheels diverted his attention.

"It's Lynch," he said. "Time to go, my dear."

"Yes, Grandpa. Time to go."

CHAPTER 12

I
1 9 0 5

t was "Alys" who closed the door to her
workroom. After five years of successful business, her new identity had replaced all others. She
was hardly ever called "Mrs. Wickham" and even
her close family friends had taken to her created
name, especially when they saw the pleasure it
gave her.

She had an afternoon of freedom to work on

some new designs for her autumn collection. Expectantly, she opened a box of trimmings delivered to her that morning, looking for a beaded edging to decorate a dress she had nearly completed. Zoe stood quite silent in her workroom, while Alice draped strips of one kind or another across her bodice, looking for the best effect. No words were spoken; Alys knew well that Zoe could stand still as a statue, daydreaming for hours while work continued. She leaned forward and the sweet smell of Zoe's warm skin and cachou-scented breath reached her. It pleased her that all the girls had become so beautiful, looked so adorable in their finery, and Alys smiled at her. She was happiest at these times, absorbed, dedicated and encouraged by the calm pleasure that Zoe found in her role. It was, after all, beauty that gave Alys her starting point.

A knock at the door. Zoe jumped, and Alys pricked her with a pin. "Oh, I'm sorry, dear! How clumsy of me." She called out: "I thought I told everyone I wasn't to be disturbed!"

"I know, madam, but the gentleman says he has an appointment."

Alys paused, distracted. She liked designing so much more than attending to business that it was entirely possible she had forgotten some unpleasant appointment. She wrote down every detail required by her customers, and never forgot colors or matches, but financial affairs were different. They were beginning to loom as a real anxiety and she had to force herself to think of solutions. Perhaps this caller was a creditor.

"I don't know who it is. There must be some mistake. What's the man's name?"

"The Duke of Wye, madam. I gave him tea in the blue room."

"Heavens, Lilian. Thank you. Convey my apologies and say I'll be there in an instant. No. Better still show him up here. Hurry, Zoe, off you go."

Zoe shed the skirt and bodice and disappeared through a second door while Alys tidied away the trims. Then she thought it might be better if he saw her at work, not sitting calmly at all. She was angry that she had forgotten about this appointment. The Duke of Wye had written at least two weeks ago about the lease on the house and specified a day and time when he would call on her. Only the possible unpleasantness of his news had made her forget the date.

Sir Edward walked in and Alys hurriedly finished with her dress. He was obviously unused to seeing a woman looking so busy. Alys nervously arranged the toile on the dressmaker's dummy, a fold of brown velvet in her thin hands. She was a little conscious that her body looked straight and tense as she did so, and became more rigid, sensing his gaze. She gathered her poise and looked at him, instantly aware of his appraising eyes.

"I'm sorry, Your Grace," she said quite simply, putting down the velvet. "I have so little time to myself, I forgot. Please forgive my rudeness, keeping you waiting—at least I am here! Do take a chair."

"Madame Alys, delighted. I realize your time is precious," he replied, glancing round the room with what appeared to Alys a polite effort not to seem amused. "Although I must say I had no idea of the scale of your enterprise. I'm afraid my plans will cause you some inconvenience."

"Nonsense!" said Alys, with more firmness than she felt. "It was always understood to be a short lease. If you need the house back you shall have it. I'm pleased that you need it for such a good reason. You didn't tell me the name of your bride-to-be. Would I know her, do you think?"

The Duke of Wye was not sure from the tone of Alys' voice if she was feigning ignorance of his widely acclaimed match, or was anxious to make the social connection. Something in her manner even suggested that she was about to confer a privilege by acknowledging his fiancée's existence.

"Charlotte Day," he replied.

"Oh yes, I know her aunt, Cecily Day, very well. I've designed her gowns on many occasions."

Sir Edward was surprised. Mrs. Leslie Day was one of the most elegant women in London and reputedly spent a fortune in Paris every season. He had no idea why she should choose a dressmaker in London.

"I'm not a dressmaker," Alys interrupted, as if reading his thoughts. "I am a *couturière*. There is a difference, as my customers know. Their husbands usually notice it at once—by the results, and by their bills!" she added, glancing at him with a lively gleam in her eyes.

Alys regretted her words at once. She had meant to flirt, but she had not meant to talk of money. She knew that Sir Edward was assessing her situation and her pride was piqued. How strange to be consulted eagerly by half the aristocracy in London, confided in by some of the wealthiest women in the country, and yet for this pompous middle-aged man to have no idea of her success or achievement.

If Alys were honest with herself, which she seldom was in these matters, her irritation was also caused by the deep impression her visitor had made on her. She thought the Duke of Wye was a fine figure of a man—dark-haired, florid-featured, but with a confident handsomeness. His presence filled all the space in her little room. He sat as casually as he could on a too-small gilt chair, everything about him out of proportion to the surroundings.

"Do they, indeed," Sir Edward replied. "I have no idea what a dress from 'Alys' would cost."

"Well, that would depend on the fabric, the style and so on, but for several of this season's models you would have to pay at least fifty guineas."

The Duke stiffened visibly and Alys was pleased to have impressed him. Fifty guineas would buy him a good hack or pay his valet's wages for a whole year. "I had no idea that fashion was such a profitable trade," he replied.

Alys decided to ignore his use of the word "trade." She knew exactly what he meant by it. "Would you like me to show you round your house?" she offered. "Just for your interest?"

Alys grew more and more nervous as she went down the staircase, the Duke's heavy tread behind her. If he only knew how fragile her little empire really was. If only he did not notice how feeble she felt, confronted by his self-assurance. At first she had found him threatening in his strength and presence. But he spoke with a mild, deep voice, and moved with almost effeminate gracefulness. She found this physically provoking, and realized she was entertaining quite specific sexual thoughts.

Yet Edward's threat was a very real one.

He was a man with a fortune and an army of servants who could dismiss her from his house with no regard for her concerns. Somehow she had to make a friend of him, and be granted more time. But alongside her desire to soften him, Alys felt an equal determination to impress.

Sir Edward followed as she took him down from the second-floor room, once his father's study, to the basement by the back stairs. The servants' hall had been converted into a dining room for the work force. Places were laid for about forty people, and maids ran between the scullery and the old laundry, where an ample supply of vegetables and meat were being prepared. As soon as Alys appeared a hush fell on the room. A small boy sitting at the corner of one long table paused, a steaming potato halfway to his mouth. He looked up anxiously, and slid the cap off his head. Alys walked across the room to the front entrance without a glance at any of the bobbing heads or the dipping and curtseying going on behind her back. Sir Edward followed, feeling a mixture of mild curiosity and irritation at this foreign system operating in his house. They came to a separate entrance in the side hall, next to the front stairs.

"I took the shortcut to show you this," Alys explained. "You can come in there"—indicating the main hall—"and pass upstairs or out this way, unnoticed by other customers. Discretion is very important."

Moving into the main hall, they came to the reception and fitting rooms to the left of the entrance. Among the clusters of women in the room, Sir Edward recognized an acquaintance of Charlotte's studying a mass of deep mauve feather boa. She held it to her face with a jeweled hand, in front of one of the mirrors. In the reflection the Duke caught sight of that distant, dispassionate look he had seen on Alys' face when he walked into her room. He felt out of place, and backed quietly away from the doorway before being seen.

Alys took his arm and gestured to the right of the hall. "We fold back the doors when we have our fashion displays—my girls come down the staircase here, you see, and turn into the salon like this." Alys left his side, opened the doors, and glided between the empty rows of silver chairs, raising her arms as if arriving like a princess at a ball, her fur wraps being taken by unseen hands. The walls of the drawing room had been lined in blue silk. Silver ribbon hung in festoons across the folds of the blue velvet curtains. The room had a theatricality that was pleasing but not overdone.

"Now I will show you my pride and delight," Alys said. "But first let me just see if the room is empty . . ." She smiled freely at Sir Edward and his whole body lightened. She was the oddest little creature—it hardly seemed possible that she was the center of such an impressive concern.

"Look!" On impulse she pulled his arm to direct him into what had once been his parents' morning room, overlooking a small courtyard at the back of the house. It had a pink marble fireplace, and a curved bay window. All round the room stood French seventeenth-century armoires, white and gilt. In the middle was a circle of silk damask chairs, surrounding a low table. Spilling from the cupboards, heaped on the table and draped over the chairs was a froth of underclothes, night things, gloves, hats, silks and wraps, all colors of silk, crepe de chine, hand-embroidered voile and net. It was an intimate disarray that struck Sir Edward as deliberately erotic. Alys was studying him with an expression like an Egyptian cat.

"It's delightful, isn't it? I believe that my dresses are so pretty they also need becoming things to go with them. Otherwise what a disappointment my customers would be when they undressed for bed."

Alys spoke in a light, firm voice that avoided any hint of impropriety. No sudden flush came to her cheeks—it was as if she had never been moved by sexual feelings but understood they could be aroused in others. Sir Edward recalled someone else who talked to him like that. A Batavian madame in a house in Paris: the click of her ivory dominoes as she waited at the red plush-covered table in the anteroom; a light enquiry as to his preferences . . . the tiny hands arranging a rose in his lapel as he stepped out into the night.

"Would you like to see the workrooms?" Alys asked, embarrassing him for his thoughts. "This way. May I present this dear girl, Lilian? You met her just before; she is my showroom *directrice.*" Alys always used the French terms when she wanted to create an impression. "And these are my chief *vendeuses,* Mary and Rose."

The women came to the head of the stairs. Was it intentional that she had chosen women to act as interesting comparisons with her own fine looks? Lilian was tall and fair, simply dressed, like a Puritan. Mary was friendly, plump and wide-smiling; he could imagine her paying ladies compliments. Rose, a little younger, had an ideal figure, but seemed not to notice her attributes, studying her notebook and giving him the briefest of acknowledgments. Edward was discomfited by the manners of these women—the salon seemed to give them an aura of self-importance that spoilt the pleasure of their looks. Pretty shopgirls pleased him, as a rule.

"Lilian has a head for figures, and as I'm hopeless at that, she is very valuable to me," Alys said, turning to her to explain her companion's presence.

"His Grace the Duke of Wye is my landlord, and he's come to tell us that we have to move soon. It's a pity, isn't it? Now, don't tell the girls anything yet. And Rose, I saw Mrs. Fielding downstairs. Tell her

to come for her fitting later, at four, as I've been unavoidably delayed."
She turned to him, sensing his restlessness at not being attended to.

"I'll show you the workrooms, then."

From the landing she led him along a wide balcony to a long room overlooking the square. Under tall windows, clusters of women were busy hand sewing half-made dresses, laid on long tables covered with clean sheeting. The light fell across their shoulders at a perfect slant.

"It matters to me that the girls have good conditions," she explained. "I know what it's like to sit up half the night in gloom, trying to finish an order. While it's possible I minimize the strain. Besides, dresses as pretty as these should be made with love, not tears."

Alys lifted a fold of chiffon to show him the fine work. The Duke glanced briefly: it looked like one of those seductive tea gowns Charlotte wore when resting at home before dressing for dinner—when she often complained of a "headache" and he flirted with her.

Alys had moved to the far end of the room, where she chatted to an old woman who was pinning a soft creamy fabric to a tailor's dummy. Alys laughed, and he took a great fancy to the sound.

"This is Cecily Day! We have all our best clients' measurements kept on a form, like this!"

Was Madame Alys teasing him, as she poked a finger at the felt pads filling out the horsehair body? Cecily Day was much thinner than—at least, he had always thought so . . .

"Nun's veiling," she added confusingly, and he knew she was teasing him. He thought she had far too much self-assurance for his liking.

"We use it to work out the draping of a dress in a soft fabric, and for something crisper, we'd use mull or muslin—here. You see the difference? It's much stiffer, and heavier."

Alys glanced at his profile and realized he was growing bored. How disappointing. She loved to talk about her work.

"That's enough, I think. I'm sure all these feminine sciences should be kept secret . . . *A toute à l'heure, Madame.*"

They went to her own rooms to conclude their discussion. Alys sat by the window, rather conscious that next to the bowl of lilies she made an interesting composition. She hoped to be appealing, for she did not want to move house at all. It would cause no end of disruption.

Edward suddenly remembered the name. "Alys" was Mrs. William Wickham. He had been abroad when his cousin, Lady Ventry, sent a letter asking for his permission to let the town house for as long as possible to a Mrs. Wickham, for a discreet commercial venture.

She had written, "Wickham, you remember—Sir Warren Thomas is his guardian. He was in your brother's house at Eton. No scandal attached to dear Alice, such a lovely creature. Hardy's the name, Irish I believe."

"Irish" covered a multitude of possibilities, he thought. He decided to be firm, although he was beginning to find Alys intensely interesting.

"I hate to be the cause of such upheaval, but as Miss Day will no doubt wish to make changes, I have to get vacant possession in plenty of time. I realize it will be difficult for you. Shall we say a month, or six weeks?"

Alys was astonished. Six weeks in which to prepare for the Courts, finish all her orders and find a new house! In September she would also show her new collection. It was impossible to think of house-hunting in the midst of that.

"I'll do my best, Your Grace, to comply with your wishes. But I have to admit that a suitable property isn't easy to find. I do have very specific requirements, you see—a reputation . . ."

"A reputation?" asked Sir Edward, wondering what kind of complication she had in mind. He began to think of several and found himself responding to her with a physical pleasure, part of which was due to the fact that he could not decide whether Alys was a lady or a tradeswoman.

"My clients expect a certain standard from me. An atmosphere. I have to charm them, make a visit to 'Alys' an experience. I must have light, space, dignity in my surroundings."

"Ah, I see," said Sir Edward, heavily. "Well I'm sure that won't present you with too much difficulty, someone of your ability. Take your time, take your time. We can always review the situation at the end of July."

July! Still only six weeks! He had every intention of getting his way, Alys realized. The Duke of Wye was a man accustomed to being obeyed. She began to feel rebellious, and determined to make him compromise. It was all for the sake of extending her lease, no other reason.

After a few more words about her requirements, Edward left her alone again. She hurried back to her workroom upstairs, and rang for the housekeeper. Mrs Booth appeared, heavy-breathing from the stairs.

"Mrs. Booth, there was a boy in the kitchen."

"Yes, Ma'am I'm sorry. Betty's brother." Betty was a finisher in the blouse room.

"If he's still there, let him sweep the garden for his meal. If he's gone, deduct a farthing from Betty's pay this week. And find out her circumstances before this goes any further. Carefully, mind—I'm not going to fire her. I'll find the boy work, if necessary—but I can't house and feed everyone's relatives without being consulted—where would I be?"

"Yes, Ma'am." Mrs. Booth knew better than to offer explanations when Alys was fractious and needing to settle to her work. Alys turned back to the box from Mr. Lowenstein, and Mrs. Booth shut her door.

In the weeks that followed, Alys and Lilian investigated many addresses given to them by letting agents but none were suitable. Most were too small, inconveniently located or very plain. The few that had potential were double the rent that Alys was prepared to pay. She realized that Lady Ventry had arranged an unusually favorable lease for her on Berkeley Square.

Three weeks later, Sir Edward called again. Alys was unaccountably nervous, and although he had no appointment and she was deep in her work she let him in. She gestured to the windowseat in her workroom, while she offered her apologies for slow progress.

"As I told you, it is quite difficult. Most places are so mean and ugly. We did see something in Grosvenor Square yesterday . . . quite spacious, but inelegant. No ceilings worth noting, and a very poor stairway."

As she spoke Alys continued pinning and cutting, barely glancing up at the Duke. When she did, she noticed the irregularity of his profile, which she liked, and his firm lips.

"But did it have *light*?" he asked with irony. "I thought it was light that was all important."

Alys' admiring look faded. She bridled at the obvious lack of concern in his voice. He watched the street below, idly tapping on the windowpane. He wanted her out, and expected her to go; none of her requirements was taken at all seriously.

"I'm sure you think I'm entirely frivolous," she said, "but this is my livelihood. My custom will suffer if I move too hastily. I'm not being particular on my own account, because I can live in the simplest surroundings, personally. But 'Alys' is special, and I'm determined to see that it remains so."

Alys stuffed laces into the drawer vigorously. "Your Grace, Cecily Day tells me you'll be traveling in Europe after the wedding. Couldn't we complete all this by the spring instead? I'd be able to manage the Courts and all the Presentation Balls, and it will be quieter after that." Alys spoke quickly before her nerve gave out.

Sir Edward stood up. This woman, "Alys" Wickham, had a way of speaking that infuriated him. She was a presuming nuisance, and in his own house, yet instead of putting things to right straight away, she attempted to reorganize his plans. Spring would probably do, but it certainly was not her place to suggest it. Livelihood indeed. She must have made a fortune out of her divorce from Wickham. She even extracted information about his plans behind his back. Cecily had acted inappropriately to discuss him with a dressmaker, for that was all she was, it seemed.

"I'm sorry, but that just isn't possible. The house will need a lot of work."

"But I've no objection to Miss Day coming in whenever she likes with her architect. It could all be planned and executed in her absence during the winter. You have an agent, Wills, isn't it, Your Grace? I'm afraid there's no one behind me, you see, to take care of these things. I have to do everything for myself, and that's why it takes such a long time. But your man Wills could oversee the work while you're away."

Alys hurried on, determined to wear down the Duke's resistance with commonsense. But she also wanted to win a point, and make the move on her own terms, not his.

"No." Sir Edward confronted her. "You're a woman of exact tastes. So is Miss Day. She'll want to supervise her own house, just as you wish, it seems, to run your own affairs."

"I do, Sir Edward. I do indeed!" They stared at each other, neither one certain whether anger or attraction caused this argument. Alys saw she had met her match. Sir Edward was as implacable as she was, yet she wanted his attention and respect. Alys could not know that Edward suddenly wanted her admiration just as much, not merely her obedience. He had been surprised to hear her say so frankly that she was alone, entirely unsupported in her venture at "Alys."

He had no idea what made him relent. On a sudden inspiration he saw how he could resolve the deadlock and please them both.

"What Wills *could* do is find another house for you. I'll put him on to it straight away. As you say, Wills really should manage my estate."

Alys almost smiled at the ruefulness in Sir Edward's voice. If Wills had managed Wye's affairs properly he would never have allowed Lady

Ventry to persuade him to let the house in the first place. Alys knew that she had charmed Lady Ventry and the agent, too—everyone—to get her way. Sir Edward was beginning to guess as much. She slammed the drawer of laces shut triumphantly.

"What a simply wonderful idea! So helpful, so generous of you! It certainly will relieve the pressure on my time. Shall we go down and have some champagne to celebrate? I do so love the death of a problem!"

She took him lightly by the arm and led him downstairs to the blue room. Sir Edward watched as she summoned her order, fussed about the room, tilted her head as she raised her glass. Why he should dispose his servants to do her bidding, he simply did not know.

"To our new homes," he said.

Alys felt devious, but barely in command of the situation. She was flirting, trying to protect her enterprise, but wanting more from this man at the same time. Partly she was just deeply grateful to him for a realistic, helpful suggestion, for support was as rare to her as a paid bill. She had trained herself not to rely on anyone, except for the one occasion when Lily had given her the deposit for the first workroom. Without that she would never have started, and it was difficult enough to go on. Without a husband or a family behind her to act as guarantors to a bank, money was impossible to find.

That was why Sir Edward was so attractive, she decided, smiling at him over her glass. He represented systems, connections, power, all the things from which she was excluded by sex. She was very glad to be a success on her own terms, but the thought of his support was enticing. Charlotte Day was a lucky woman . . .

◆　◆　◆

Sir Edward kept his word. Over the next few weeks he returned to Hanover Square several times with details of other large houses to rent. Lilian was surprised at how easily he got an audience with Alys at any time of day. No one else was allowed to interrupt the work schedule in such a way. Lilian often found him perched on the window seat in Alys' workroom. While Alys adjusted a model, he would read out details of houses supplied to him by the agent Wills; Lilian liked to see Alys laughing, chatting so freely. It softened her fierce ways.

Lilian thought of those other times when Alys would attend to a client who had brought in a husband or lover to approve the choice of a dress. Alys would enthuse, dramatize the effect of a garment in a sparkling manner that would leave her audience thoroughly enlivened, but herself tired and sharp. Lilian liked the way that after Sir Edward left, the ripples of ease took much longer to fade in the house.

Edward Wye was also growing more attached to Alys. He had truly never imagined that her work was so essential to her. The idea that she was independent in every sense of the word fascinated him. Her self-involvement of course diminished her sexual appeal when he was with her, because she did not treat him as if he were more important than she was, but whenever he left her, he immediately wanted to be with her again. The idea of an affair occupied his thoughts only briefly. He had had enough liaisons in his time to satisfy his vanity, and Charlotte certainly was no disappointment. She was a demanding fiancée—a beautiful woman who knew how to amuse and inflame him in equal degree. He looked forward with confidence to consummating his marriage, for it was late enough in his life to be a matter of personal choice, not necessity. His brother was providing an heir, and his mother had died four years previously, so Charlotte was spared her censorious ways. She was, ironically, all that Pamela, Duchess of Wye might have wanted in a daughter-in-law: wealthy, of good family, handsome, healthy. Reserved, perhaps, even cold to outsiders, but Edward knew that in spite of her ways she could respond. All she needed was winning with fine things.

Alys was completely different. The beauty of her life came from her own creativity—a few yards of filmy fabric around a mannequin seemed to make her happy for a day. Luxurious surroundings were only an enticement for her customers. All she ever seemed to want from him was his interest, his presence, which he gave unstintingly.

They both found objections to many of the houses that Wills put forward. After the third rejection in one week Edward realized that he had left Berkeley Square pleased to see that Alys was so particular. When his note arrived asking to see her again the very next day, Friday, Alys at last came alive to the idea that their reasons for meeting so often were entirely spurious. He could have sent Wills alone with the details.

The Duke's carriage bowled up as appointed. Alys happened to be in the first-floor sewing room, learning a few new details from Mme. Blanc, and she stooped over the balcony to watch him arrive. Edward bounded onto the pavement and shouted impulsively up to the window.

"I've found it!" She had to admit an instant's disappointment. He wouldn't call again once she found the right house.

Whatever her feelings about losing his company, the news made her excited. "The perfect answer!" he declared, waving a letter above his head as he came in. "Heard from Wills in confirmation today. Right across this very square, my dear. No difficulty for your established customers, more space for you, a double staircase and a very long lease. There's even the possibility of a freehold. There's more, but I want to show you the place myself first."

Alys took her wrap, and they walked arm in arm through the sunlit square. They made an unusual pair: Edward, tall, broad-shouldered, noticeable for his heavy, dark features that looked at variance with the quiet taste of his gray morning coat. Alys was in confusion. She had not been able to decide whether the situation called for glamour or not. She had covered the loose tunic dress she liked to wear for work under a velvet cloak, and added an egret-feathered hat borrowed from her pink salon. Her whippet followed at an obedient distance, on a length of satin ribbon.

Passers-by stared, but the local work force eyed them with a more professional detachment. Some thought she looked too old, too cool to be his mistress. Others considered he was too attentive to be her husband. A delivery boy sniggered at her strange loose garments.

"Shut up! That's Madame Alys," the flower girl standing near him said, with more asperity than he thought he merited.

"Airs, all airs, you lot here," he muttered, pushing his bike away.

The house was impressive, with a pillared portico, a narrow porch with a bay window to one side. At first Alys thought this was too confining an entrance, until she stepped through to see the staircase. Centrally positioned, it curved down on both sides to a tessellated marble floor. Through a wide passage to the side she came on another surprise. About fifty years previously a ballroom had been added to the back of the house, taking up the space that two reception rooms would have occupied. The leaded glass dome arched above her head. Iron pillars with candelabra stood at intervals round the rectangular room, making an oval shape of the roof. The light was clear; even on a dull London day the effect on her clothes would be flattering.

"I thought it would make a perfect showroom, don't you agree?" Edward asked. Alys was so pleased that he had paid attention to her exact requirements.

"Oh Edward, it would be magnificent. But surely, the rent on this house must be exorbitant!" Her heart thudded too obviously as she said it. Alys guessed what he had in mind and was afraid of it. If he lent her the money, she would be compromised. What if she failed, what then? In a partnership, she would have to support his investment in her . . . worse than that, his faith. What would Charlotte think of such an arrangement? But Alys knew that the house was perfect.

CHAPTER 13

1 9 0 5 – 7

*E*dward did not call to see Alys again for a very long time. He did not know how to deal with his intense feeling for her—friendship was not enough, he realized. He knew that he had to possess her physically, that she represented something too maddeningly unattainable for anything else to satisfy him. Once he had decided that, old habits of conquest came easily to him. He had no intention of making an advance until he was quite certain he would win. He let Wills organize her removal, and simply sent her flowers on the day the new house opened.

In a mood of sexual perversity, Edward renewed his attentions to his fiancée. Charlotte was surprised at his sudden interest in her; it seemed odd that the physical side of their relationship should become an issue. After all, Edward had avoided marriage on many occasions, and had obviously enjoyed a bachelor life for many years. Charlotte supposed that he dealt with his needs . . .

Edward stood in the morning room of his house in Berkeley Square, only half listening to Charlotte's detailed description of her plans for decorating the interiors. There were no traces of Alys' presence left in the place. She had been meticulous in moving out on time and leaving everything exactly as it had been before. Edward was irritated. It would take a long time before he could enjoy the house as his own and his own wife's home. He found such obsessive thoughts of Alys irksome.

"I don't approve, you know," Charlotte was saying.

"What? Of what, darling?"

"This used to be such an elegant square. Once you let trade in . . ."

" 'Alys' you mean?"

She was pleased that she had tricked him into mentioning her name.

"Oh no. I meant a whole *host* of shopkeepers encroaching in the area. No one in particular. Still, it is a fine house. Do you like this green?"

"It's perfect. But honestly, sweetheart, I'm hopeless at these things. You should ask your Aunt Cecily. All the taste is on your side, my dear."

Not so hopeless that he could not spend weeks tracking down just the right house for his former tenant, Charlotte noted. But it did not upset her deeply. She rather expected Edward to have a past, perhaps even a present, certainly a life separate from her. His obvious interest in Alys put the woman in her rightful place—much more successfully than anything Charlotte herself could have devised. All the same, she was curious about her.

"I think I'll do that, Edward. I'll ask Aunt Cecily to give me some ideas."

But her aunt did not give Charlotte the kind of information she hoped for. Cecily Day cultivated a fine sense of intrigue. She upheld family loyalties, but had a care for Alys. She admired her, placing her among a small group of women she valued for their nonconformity. So, to Charlotte's annoyance, Cecily also walked through the empty rooms of Berkeley Square pretending interest in the decorations, but really determined to protect her friend.

"She's an original," she explained. "A bit hard, perhaps, quite distant with people sometimes. But how that woman works!"

"Oh come, Aunt Cecily, surely she must have assistants who actually run the business . . ."

Cecily shook her head, dismissing the idea. "You don't understand. I do, because clothes are a passion with me. Alys is a perfectionist, she thinks out every last detail—for people who care, that is. That's why I go to her. It's extraordinary to find that attention anywhere else but in Paris."

"But she is an exhibitionist. And her sister is an actress! It's all so vulgar."

"Well, I don't object to the unconventional. Extreme people often have a serious side . . ."

"Fashion! It's preposterous to talk of her like an artist! Really!"

"Oh darling, of course you're right. I've no sense of proportion. I never did have."

Charlotte thought her aunt was ridiculing her, and that made her even more annoyed. But she knew she was delving into odd allegiances among older, more worldly people than herself. She would have to be patient and endure everyone's slightly superior ways until she found out what she wanted to know about Alys.

She would never buy a dress from her. All her wedding outfits were coming from Drécoll in Paris: white crepe de chine embroidered in white and silver, and a court train of white panné with silver and mother-of-pearl embroidery. Luckily Aunt Cecily had set a certain style for the family. Charlotte's own mother thought dressing in Paris very "fast," and Charlotte, who had ambitions of becoming a great society hostess, had been worried that she would have to wear some family heirloom and look undistinguished. Her parents might have money, but they loathed ostentation. However, pride at Charlotte's good match had softened them and she was allowed to have her French gowns.

When Charlotte went to Paris some weeks later to try on her trousseau, Edward felt a welcome release of tension. He was unused to fitting in with someone else's plans. He knew that once they were married, Charlotte would be less demanding. It was only the social pressure of the event, the preparations for the day, and the work on the house that made her so time-consuming. Still, he was grateful for a week's respite, without consultations on guest lists and all the rest.

Of course his thoughts turned to Alys. It was over two months since he had seen her. She had written one short note thanking him for all his help and acknowledging his gesture in sending her flowers. Since then, nothing. "The house really is wonderful to be in," she wrote. "I am very sensitive to atmospheres. I feel there are good spirits in the corners, and my work flourishes . . . thank you for all your concern and kindness."

As he climbed the steps to her front door in the middle of the afternoon, he wondered if Alys would understand why he was calling. He could not resist making her aware of his interest. The doorman took his card and Edward waited expectantly in the showroom. Anticipation of pleasure was improving his mood. But Alys sent him away. She was busy with a customer and could not see him. At first Edward was furious, but then he realized that Alys had made a mistake. By not seeing him, she was admitting to him that to do so would be the ultimate temptation. He was winning.

Alys tried hard to concentrate on her client. She did not allow herself to move about the room as a pretext for nearing the window, so that she could catch a glimpse of Edward leaving. She sat resolutely paying attention. She had formed the habit of spending a good half hour with each newcomer, to find out how she lived, what she enjoyed doing, to form an impression of her personality. How her customers smiled, moved and spoke all added up to a picture that helped her in her designing. She also gave them advice on their style of dress, and charged a fine price for the interviews. It seemed the more she asked, the more people were prepared to pay her.

"Go on then, Mrs. Lyttleton. I'm sorry we were disturbed."

Edith Lyttleton was the wife of a young Liberal politician. She admitted quite openly to Alys that she loathed "dressing" and felt most at home in her riding clothes in the country, or in a simple "tailor" doing her round of charities and committee meetings.

"But look," she added, "the suffragettes dress up to the nines! It's effective. I never bothered about it before. I've always supported Arthur, but up till now, only from the wings . . ."

"It must be a trial to you to make public appearances."

"It is. But if that's what Arthur wants me to do, then I must."

"I think we can do something for you, to give you a little more confidence." Alys liked her loyalty.

"Now, absolutely nothing showy. I couldn't carry it off. But everyone tells me you make such becoming clothes, and I do need flattery!"

In spite of her preoccupations, Alys laughed. "Nearly every woman who comes here tells me that. Whether they're beautiful or frankly homely."

"Homely. Hm." Edith examined herself in the mirror, doubting.

Alys looked at Edith's soft face, full lips, and girlish, intelligent expression. She was pretty but undefined, with a shapeless frizz of fringe hiding her eyes.

"Mrs. Lyttleton. I can promise you that there's not a hint of homeliness in you! Wait and see. Rose, take Mrs. Lyttleton's details . . . You see, if you have taste and sense, you can make yourself look pretty. If you have money, you will make yourself look elegant! But leave it till Thursday, and I'll show you some more sketches. Good-bye."

Alys ran upstairs. Lilian, watchful as always, saw her slam the door to her retreat, the workroom. She had seen Sir Edward arrive, leave a note, and turn away. Lilian had a sudden fear of impending disaster. She knew Alys worried about money, and the move to the new house had stretched her resources. But Alys always coped. She always had.

◆ ◆ ◆

That evening, Alys sat in her drawing room upstairs in Berkeley Square, looking out over the trees at Edward's house. All afternoon she had barely concentrated on her work, disturbed by his sudden arrival at her door. She knew exactly what it meant. It also happened that Cecily Day had cancelled a fitting because she was chaperoning Charlotte on her trip to Paris. Edward was alone.

Alys watched the Wye carriage leave the square at nine o'clock. She went back to her letters and bills and tried to work. Around midnight the carriage came back and a cloaked figure went into the house. She had a mad impulse to run across the square and burst in on Edward, tell him how much she wanted him to love her—make her feel desired. She had been given his attention and his admiration, but it was not enough. For the first time in years she felt like crying, but anger won over tears. She was being quite pathetic, she told herself sharply, besides immoral, to have such feeling for a nearly married man. Alys forced herself to go to bed and dismiss him from her thoughts.

Next day a disaster brought her back to reality. Daisy Panton was waiting for her in the blue room, shaking with fright.

"Quite ghastly!" she said. "I don't know what I'm going to do. If it ever gets out, I'm ruined!"

"Calm down Daisy, you must tell me from the beginning, otherwise I can't follow you . . ."

"You know how hopeless I am about bills, money, that sort of thing. And it was simply marvelous to be able to help you—isn't that so, Alys? I did help, didn't I? At the beginning?"

"Of course you did, dearest! I would have been lost without you and Lady Mary to spur me on."

"And then it just grew and grew. . . ."

Alys began to guess at Daisy's predicament, and felt a sudden chill, nervousness in her very skin.

"I think I'll just sit down, Daisy. You can't pay me, can you?"

"Well it's worse still. I hid half my bills and sent you money on account from my own resources for those—you know, from housekeeping, the odd dividend and so on. But somehow the last account got through to my husband, and the truth is . . ."

"Howard Pechell's name appeared on the list of amounts paid in."

"Yes. And Panton simply does not believe that Howard paid for those things just to help me out."

Neither did Alys. Pechell was Daisy's lover, and had been for several years.

"I don't know how Lilian could have made such a terrible mistake!" Alys was distressed. "It's intolerable. My God, half my customers could provide their husbands with grounds for divorce if this sort of thing happened all the time."

"No, no, Alys. That was my fault. I asked her to make up a detailed account because I didn't dare ask Howard or Panton for more without remembering who had paid what. I simply left the thing tucked inside my housekeeping ledger by mistake—just when Panton had one of his rare moods to check my records for himself. He doesn't trust me with much money. I don't blame him."

"Daisy, this is a calamity. You promised to settle this quarter. I'm going to be in difficulties myself very soon. There's you, and Lily—I can't possibly press her, with the American tour—or Lady Ventry. And I sent a whole group of 'Painted Pastels' to Paris, a speculative venture, on consignment. The money only comes to me when they are sold. Oh, Daisy! I'm sorry, I shouldn't say all this when you are in such deep water. What will you do?"

"Panton's made me promise to spend all this season in Rutland. I'm not allowed to see Howard again. Everyone will know, Alys! That's the worst."

"Not at all. Don't think of that. Occupy yourself well and you'll make everyone think you're bored with London. It happens from time to time. People have very short memories."

"But I'm not as organized as you are. What will I *do?*"

"Well, you'll have your horses . . ."

"Good God, Alys, I can't spend a whole summer in the stables! What shall I do for company—gossip—amusements?"

"Just for a while, Daisy, it will only be for a season. Besides, you'll have your sons for the summer: spend time with them for once—they'll be grown up so soon . . . and I tell you what—why don't you take over the management of my Dorcas Society for me? It's not an onerous task—you just have to visit them once a month, perhaps a little more, discuss any problems with Mrs. Burns, interview new girls who want to join—do you know, Daisy, the salon here keeps all thirty girls fully employed now with lingeries and blouses? I'd willingly relinquish the responsibility to you, as I really don't have the time—and if you do it properly, I'll reduce your bill."

"Frightfully generous—you know you don't charge me properly anyway." Daisy smiled at her.

"Oh, I don't have much choice!" Alys laughed.

"Well, then, I'll do as you say and be a devoted mother and a doer of good works. I must: I really must. Panton's been too good a sport all these years."

When Daisy left, Alys considered her financial situation in detail. She needed to raise £2,000 by the end of the year. She was as fully extended as she could possibly be, with many outstanding bills, not only customers' unsettled accounts, but debts she owed to her suppliers. She sat back in her chair. For some reason, she was not beside herself with panic. She had been managing her business single-handedly for three years—longer, if her apprentice time with the Dorcas Society was included. Someone or something always seemed to turn up when she needed help.

It was all too tempting. There was Edward, obviously interested in her. Many other women would have given themselves for less. What was the difference between marrying for money and having an affair in order to protect her own little empire? Alys had no doubt at all that Edward intended to be trustworthy in his dealing with her. Men in his position conducted their *amours* as well as their marriages by a code of rules. Daisy was not the only one to have a financial arrangement with her lover—many of her customers expected loyal support for their favors, and were given it with respect.

It was the day for important visitors, Alys decided, as she heard another knock at the door. She felt so near the brink of crisis, in her heart and in her work, that a fatalistic calm spread through her. Lilian held a card: "The Duke of Wye requests the pleasure of your company at supper September 15th . . ." Tonight, while Charlotte was still in Paris.

"I can guess what Mrs. Panton came to see you for." Lilian had to speak. 'I'm very sorry, Madame Alys, if I acted wrongly."

"No, Lilian, it wasn't to be helped. Poor Daisy, she does so hate staying more than a week in the country!"

"What shall we do? At the end of the month?"

"Oh, something will happen. I have a few alternatives. I think I shall call my solicitor, Stayce, for advice. He might be able to arrange short-term finance."

"Miss Anne sent a message to say she will be a little late, but looks forward to seeing you on Friday evening."

"Good!" It was easy to imagine what Anne would say. Alys was not sure she wanted sisterly encouragement to launch into an affair.

◆　◆　◆

It was all so simple, just to let it happen. When Edward's guests left the house, Alys declined their offer of a lift; she had barely fifty yards to walk to her own front door. Edward publicly announced that he would escort her, and they waited, cloaked, in the hall, while the others left. The servants were occupied in the dining room. Edward sent the butler away to supervise, and as soon as he disappeared, glanced at Alys. She knew what to do. She moved swiftly and noiselessly to the staircase that led up to the first floor at the side of the house—her own device. He had judged her exactly. Edward waited until Alys had time to reach his bedroom. Knowing the house as well as she did, she would know where to go. Dust sheets, paint and ladders indicated it was now Charlotte's domain, being put in order. Edward had insisted on his own paneled room remaining as it had always been. He had a sudden recollection; for Charlotte's sake he had to be careful.

"Jones." He called the butler back, as he stood by the half-open door.

"Tell Peters I shall take a stroll after I see Mrs. Wickham to her door. I don't want him to wait up for me."

"You have your keys, Your Grace?"

"Yes I do. That's all. Good-night, Jones."

Once again the butler bowed and Edward waited until the hall was empty before shutting the door and following Alys.

He pulled her into his arms and kissed her for a long time on the mouth. She was shaking from head to toe with excitement and fear. Edward was surprised and drew back; for all her quick response to him, she felt as untouched as a young girl. It was hard to believe that a woman in her position had not taken other lovers since her marriage. Her intensity suggested she had not.

"You surprise me. You are bold, and yet—"

"I never wanted anyone before."

Edward did not need to hear more. He picked her up and carried her to the bed. Turning back, he locked the door, then pulled off his clothes and slipped into a velvet dressing gown. Alys, propped on her elbows, grew even more excited at the casual way that he undressed in front of her. He meant to take his time, and she could hardly wait to begin making love.

Those words took on an entirely new meaning. Edward undressed her with great deliberation, kissing and stroking every part of her body as he uncovered it. He did not expect her to be passive. At first she was taken aback, even shocked, by the way he took her hands and showed her what he wanted—his chest to be caressed, his nipples to be fondled, his penis to be held firmly and stroked. She found all these demands disgustingly animal, far too intimate. For several moments she did what he seemed to want out of confusion. She did not know how to convey to him that all this was new, repulsing rather than stimulating her.

But then Edward stopped, leaning up on his arms, over her.

"You are sure, aren't you?" he asked. "You want to love me, Alys? Tell me you do. For my part, I must have you."

"Yes, I do want you."

"Then there must be no guilt, no misery. Only pleasure, and love. Trust me, Alys."

He bent down and kissed her gently on her cheeks and then more sweetly just behind her ears. Alys found a sexual power rising through her, and new foreign words were suddenly understood. His body was not strange anymore, but the body of someone with whom she had been secretly communing since the day they first met. When he placed his weight upon her, she willingly opened herself up for him to enter her. She clasped her arms and legs about him, pulling him onto her, eager for more weight, more masculine strength to fill up the sudden void inside her.

They made love several times; at first to explore each other's bodies, their special responses, then because Edward wanted to woo Alys with concentrated attention and give her pleasure, just for herself. He soon realized that she had no idea what he intended. Not that Alys was aware of her deficiency—she was far too excited, too new to this level of physical awareness to go further than she already had.

They slept for a while, then woke up with an instantaneous shared exultation at finding each other side by side. They made love again slowly, describing their pleasures and laughing at the difference of their skins, their proportions, their sexual whims. Edward could not stop touching Alys' tiny body. He gathered her up for the pleasure of her smallness, her perfection, her femininity. She bit his chest, pulled the graying hairs curling on his breastbone, licked the sweat on his arms, covered him with kisses. At last she fell asleep again, holding onto him so tightly that she woke up for a moment with a pain in her shoulders. Then real sleep absorbed them both, the deep sleep of two people who have abandoned suspicions and made the final commitment to share each other's defenseless, dream-filled hours. Alys had never been so close to anyone in her whole life.

At six, Edward woke her and they dressed quietly in order to leave the house before the servants discovered she was there. Edward found a cab, and they took a long drive round the streets of London and the parks, with the shutters drawn. Kissing, holding each other, half sleeping, with Alys' head resting on Edward's shoulder, they listened to London waking.

He held her face in his hands. "I've never known such ecstasy." No one had ever spoken to Alys in such direct physical terms. She guessed that Edward had had many mistresses. She felt prouder than she had ever been, to be so sexually pleasing.

"I've never known love," she replied, a sudden realization.

He felt a moment's pity, but more than that, a powerful desire to make Alys mad with love—to have her love him with all the wonderful intensity he knew she was capable of giving.

"It's inconceivable to me that you have not," he murmured. "You're so full of feeling."

"Not everyone has the chance to show their love."

"Then you'll share it with me, and I shall treasure it."

She wanted to say, "Always," but changed her mind.

Then the cab stopped at her house. It was past seven, and Mrs. Booth was unlocking the doors for the servants. In a sudden fear that Edward would be seen, Alys did not say good-bye but jumped out and slammed the door behind her.

"My! You've been to a fine party, Your Ladyship!" Mrs. Booth stood admiring Alys' sparkling evening gown and cloak.

Alys heard the cab draw away, and with it the joy of her life. Nothing had been decided. He would never come back. It was impossible to go on.

"You must be tired, Your Ladyship. Shall I get you some breakfast or will you sleep?'

"I don't know, Mrs. Booth. I can't think." Mrs. Booth picked up the cloak as Alys let it drop in the hall.

"Oh well, pleasure always goes to the head. I'm glad you had a good time." Mrs. Booth had a vicarious satisfaction in Alys' irresponsible behavior.

"I did, Mrs. Booth, thank you. I did."

CHAPTER 14

1 9 1 0

*E*dith Lyttleton was admiring some pale, tweedy Irish cloth—bainin—which Alys had suggested for a summer suit.

"I'm looking forward to this holiday," she said, holding up Alys' sketch and picturing herself wearing the loose jacket and straight skirt. "I simply love to have Arthur to myself. Though after the fifteenth there's ten of us at *Roches des Lilas.* I'll do as you suggest, Alys. I like this fabric."

"Good! It's very becoming."

"Are you sure you won't accept my invitation and join us?"

"I've already promised to go to Paris with some friends at the same time." Alys was lying. Nothing would make her leave London.

"Another year, perhaps. I want you to know Arthur rather better. He's not at all at home when he comes here!"

Alys laughed. "No! Only certain men revel in their women's atmospheres. There are those who do, you know. Many of my ladies don't buy anything without their husbands' final approval. For taste, not for the price."

"Well, Arthur has neither the time nor the talent for these things, but he does notice your dresses sometimes. Especially when so many people pay him compliments about me—aren't you pleased?"

Alys considered Edith's satisfied profile, as she buttoned her coat and arranged her hat. Edith was wearing one of Mme. Delphine's feathered toques at a new assertive angle. It pleased Alys to see a woman emerging in style.

"We're going to Windsor this weekend," Edith continued. "I'm so nervous, but pleased for Arthur, of course. Oh, Alys, are you all right?"

Alys slumped into a chair, feeling faint.

"I'm fine. I'm sorry. I don't know what's the matter with me."

"You work too hard for all of us. You're very pale. I do so wish you'd come to Cannes. You need the rest."

"I'm sure you're right, Edith, and I shall do as you say, and take better care of myself. Now do hurry—I don't want Arthur to think I'm making you vain, and he simply hates waiting downstairs!"

But as Edith rushed out to meet her husband, that wave of despair returned to Alys. It was the open pride, the honest ambition Edith had for her marriage that cut Alys to the quick. Her own life was full of such secret desires. Under her velvet dress, Alys could smell the odors of sex rising up from her skin. Her whole body ached with heat and tiredness. She had slept barely three hours the night before and had a full day of consultations before she could rest alone upstairs.

Alone: Edward went home to a house full of activity, interest, another's waiting arms. She was amazed at herself for continuing the affair, but could not imagine it ever ending. Charlotte and Edward had been married for six months, and in that time, since the honeymoon, she had seen Edward almost every day. They were addicted to each other, requiring each other's presence daily as if it were the only reason for continuing to live.

Alys had never needed anyone so much. Separated from Edward she felt dead, as if all the color had drained from life and left her with faded images. It was only her experience and the goodwill of her customers that enabled her to continue with her work. Fortunately she had Lilian, who was growing used to her perfunctory orders and passed on a more detailed version of her ideas to the heads of workrooms.

Alys could see control slipping away from her, and almost welcomed it. Layton Stayce had been very helpful about her finances; Edward too. Just as she had expected, Edward stood as her guarantor for a large investment of capital for her business and advised her to set herself up as a limited company. Stayce and Edward and a financier connection became her directors. It was not the way she would have liked to bind Edward to her, but it was all she could do. Now she had a manager to keep her accounts, a young man whom Stayce appointed, who swiftly set up stock control systems and managed the books.

It was Lilian who knocked discreetly at Alys' door and reminded her that Lily was waiting downstairs.

"Oh damn. She wants the designs for her new play. I haven't done them. I completely forgot."

"No you didn't, Alys, remember? You've only put them out of your mind. You made roughs in pencil and asked me to find fabrics and color them in for you after. I left the sketches there for you, beside your notebook, last night."

Last night Alys had told everyone she was working late but she had slipped out to meet Edward at their apartment in Dover Street. She was so well-known in the area that no one questioned her solitary arrivals and departures at all hours of the day—she could easily be visiting customers somewhere nearby. The block of flats had a flower shop in the lobby. During the day, the scent of irises, lilies of the valley, roses, wafted about Alys as she arrived for her secret meetings. The flower shop was always cool, with the smell of peat and the water sprayed on the flowers. Its welcoming atmosphere gave Alys the illusion that she was entering a world of simple, natural pleasure as she passed by and climbed the stairs to her rooms. She arrived with her senses heightened, but was always oblivious to that sweet perfume when she left, dragging her unwilling body into the cold world outside.

Alys went down to meet Lily and show her the sketches. Lily was choosing a robe in the pink room, and looked indestructibly gorgeous as usual. Alys was beginning to understand how she did it: Lily knew what she wanted and made sure she was gratified. She planned for herself a whole series of small victories, every day. Alys felt a thrill of recognition as she watched Lily hold up a beautiful silk *robe de chambre* and run it carelessly through her fingers. She dropped it, turning to Alys with a gesture of welcome.

"Lovely lace. Perfectly horrid color for me. Pink would be simply exquisite." Lily put her gloved fingers to her mouth, almost in a kiss, making her choice. She pointed to another silky slither on a gilt chair. "That color—this design. Can I have two of them made, and sent to me?"

"Of course, Lily. Now come and look at these. What do you think?"

They went to her private room, Alys walking ahead. Lily noticed how she braced her shoulders, as if making an effort to clear her thoughts. Then Alys' hand wandered in a desultory way up the back of her head, and she smoothed a loose dark curl in place behind a comb. In that instant Lily knew that Alys had taken a lover. She was piqued that it had taken her so long to discover the reason for Alys' exhaustion and her faraway looks. She was determined to find out who it was.

"I think this one for Act Two is simply lovely. But we couldn't use the red for Act One. Awful to light and clashing against the other colors, much too obvious for me."

"Of course not." Alys did not tell her Lilian had chosen that color. She would never have suggested it herself.

"I like the lavender, though. I'll have this one." Cautious Lilian! She had attached three or four other scraps of fabric to each card. Alys was pleased with her assistant's thoroughness. At the same time, she realized she would have to make a great effort to stay in control herself, or give up that personal contact which had made her a success. How would "Alys" continue without that? It was impossible to think of it.

With laborious attention to all the details, Alys finished the costume designs with Lily. Written notes were her only defense against forgetfulness. As she wrote, she did not hear what Lily what saying—something about Anne, who was also in New York.

"What did you say, Lily?"

"That Kerrick's tour is going frightfully well, I've heard Philadelphia sold out, Boston was almost as good, and now they have two weeks in New York."

"Anne's not a dutiful correspondent. It's very good to have news of her," Alys said.

Lily put all the sketches together, fastening them with their silk ribbon. "Do you think she'll marry him?"

Alys remembered one last confiding conversation she had with her sister before she left, and blushed.

"Oh, forget about Kerrick," Anne's words came back. "If I stay with him, I shall play supporting roles to his star parts for the rest of my life! I don't even want to discuss it! We must talk about *you*, Alys. I was glad at first that you had a lover, but this is too serious! Do be careful. I wish I hadn't encouraged you . . ."

"One has to be so careful, don't you think?" Lily was observing her kindly, with an innocent interest in her voice.

"What?" Alys started.

"I mean, Anne has such a promising career. I knew it from the first, of course. It's a difficult choice. Perhaps Kerrick isn't right for her. All the same, he's very well liked; it would be an admired match."

"Anne doesn't think of her future in that way." Alys sometimes wondered if Lily had deliberately placed Anne in Hubert's path so that she could be free of him, free for Ned. The powers of sexual intriguing were new to her, alternately fascinating and repelling her.

"Do *you?*" Lily paused, watching carefully for Alys' immediate reaction. "I mean, do you think Anne should marry? Or do you share her view that modern women should avoid it?"

"Anne is very strong, but a dreamer. No, that's not what I mean . . ."

"She has fantasies," Lily said sympathetically. "Her image of herself changes constantly. I understand that in her very well. She's an actress. Do you see it like that too?"

"Well, yes. What Kerrick offers is too fixed, too tangible." Alys struggled to be tactful. After all, Kerrick was one of Lily's oldest theatrical friends, whatever other relationship once existed between them.

"Is that what she says? Well then, she certainly doesn't love him. When you love someone, all your dreams reside in that person. It's a mad, overwhelming sensation—don't you agree?"

Alys felt the persuasion of these words so fully that she burst into tears. Lily felt a little remorse for having forced a confession from her. For a while there was a silence between them, then Alys poured out all her secret, her ambition, her passion for Edward, how she could not live without him. "Oh, Lily," she said at last, "it's wonderful, but quite impossible too."

"I'm happy for you, that you have known such feeling, but I'm very anxious for you too. You can't succeed in being discreet forever. There are people on all sides looking for a scandal to fill their emptiness. Envious people."

"I have a horror of it. That's what I fear more than anything. Fame—infamy! They seem so close! I know I court disaster. I can't help it."

"You're not living as you should, my dear friend. Once you said to me, before, that you worked because you had to. Well, you don't. You work to escape, which is different. Perhaps in time your own life will mean something more real to you. But unless you give up matters of the heart, you will suffer. The alternative is to live more joyously, as I do, *never* to be destroyed by love."

"I don't quite understand you . . ."

"My dear, it's simple! You *suffer* so! What's the point of a love affair if it causes you as much distress as this! If you can't accept your lot, then you must end it, before you become quite ill with your burden. You're being very self-indulgent. Go away, to the country, or France—take a cure in Switzerland. Anything. In most cases"—Lily looked reflective—"distance is all that is necessary."

"I can't do it!"

"Well then, introduce Sir Edward to me." Lily laughed.

Alys was incredulous and very angry. The moment of understanding had passed, Lily had been revived by it, and now she was being heartless.

"But not until the end of March!" Lily added cheerfully. "You must finish all these dresses for me—they simply wouldn't be the same if you left them to someone else."

Alys could not believe that Lily was so selfish, or that she could treat a friend so wilfully.

"I've never failed you before, Lily, and I certainly don't expect to now," she replied stiffly, taking up her sketches and notes.

But Lily's hand restrained her, and she came very close. Her intimacy was powerful, just as her expansiveness was strong enough to fill a crowded room with gaiety.

"No, of course you won't fail me, or yourself either. You are a creature of discipline. Don't lose yourself in this affair. It's a mistake." She left Alys, her last words full of conviction.

Alys wandered round her room wild with tears. She hated her womanish predicament, and yet she did not have the strength of mind or purpose to act as Lily—or even Anne—would have done. She had worked so hard to build an honorable life out of her feelings of need, and it all seemed in danger of collapsing, all because of her uncontrollable passion for someone unattainable.

But then Alys remembered how natural and peaceful she could be with Edward. It was not always illicit desire that made them long for each other. There were gentle conversations, confessions of hope, a sharing of secret thoughts—love as well as lust. How could Lily think she was in danger of losing herself? In Edward's company, Alys felt more at one with her conflicted nature than she had with anyone else.

Alys did not make an end to the affair, but allowed herself to become more deeply involved. Months passed by; one season after another, while her work never ceased to develop and bring her new victories. It cost her enormous efforts of energy to lead a double life as a mistress and a couturière. What Lily said was true: her sexual liaison did not add to her creativity, but drained her of potential. Meanwhile, her appointment book for consultations was always full, and she had more orders than she could comfortably handle in Berkeley Square.

The "Painted Pastels" were a *succès d'estime* in a corner of Paris—discerning customers liked their Englishness, and Alys supplied increasing numbers to an agent there. In Berkeley Square, Lilian assumed more and more responsibility. Her knowledge of Alys' taste improved, and she found herself able to say to women, with authority:

"Madame Alys never advises red near the face—it creates a coarsening effect; wear it only with a touch of white" . . . "Black alone dulls the skin. Use a hint of something pale, a touch of gold or blue perhaps, to soften it . . ." But customers missed Alys' special attentions. Alys was a lady, one of their own class, while Lilian would never be anything more than a competent valued servant. Lilian was too clever to miss the distinction, and far too proud to alter herself by assuming a false voice or by dressing out of keeping with her station.

After a whole season in which Lilian had almost sole charge of the salon, Alys appreciated how well her assistant had overcome the world's prejudices. Without pandering, Lilian impressed the clientèle. Her professionalism and her dedication won her admirers. Lilian always reminded customers that she was operating strictly under Alys' supervision, and that gave them confidence. They began to speak of Alys' "awfully sweet girl, Lilian," and then to ask for her by name.

Lilian's success only gave Alys more time to fritter away, demented in her workroom, waiting to see Edward. She would have laughed at any of her friends indulging in such predictable signs of infatuation. She lost weight, her absent-mindedness increased, and her temper shortened. Her "girls," her mannequins, guessed what was happening, but they were young and enjoyed romances. Alys' intensity frightened everyone, including herself.

After the spring season, many of Alys' friends left London for the country, and she began to dread the prospect of Edward's departure again. He always refused to discuss his plans, desperate at the thought of parting from her and hoping that something could be arranged so that he could stay in town. Alys was still convinced that Charlotte had no idea what was happening. Edward's financial involvement in "Alys" provided the perfect explanation for any occasion when they had to meet in the daytime, or for the occasional delivery of a letter, usually a frantic declaration of love, from one or the other, after a misunderstanding.

When Mrs. Leslie Day suggested that Alys should visit her in August at Melbury in Derbyshire, Alys at first refused, out of her long-standing reservation about socializing with clients. Her rule was nothing more than an excuse to turn away unwanted invitations these days. She did not feel at ease in the country anyway—large house parties were not to her taste. Only Lady Mary's home at Desthorpe was enjoyable, almost a family setting where she could relax.

Yet, Cecily Day's invitation was flattering . . . one of the best houses in England, the scene of some royal intrigues, by all accounts. Alys suddenly wanted to force her way back into the enjoyment of society, be frivolous about gossip, wear riveting clothes, no longer stand on the sidelines of life. As soon as she thought of it, her picture of Desthorpe changed from a comforting, secluded retreat, where she would sit peacefully with Sarah, and read out loud to Rupert—it became a dull avoidance of the gusto of life. Alys thought of the poor man's enfeebled body, the whiteness of his hands, folded limply over a blanket. Rupert had never regained his former vigor, was inclined to nervousness and melancholy, and spent his days reading quietly or helping Sarah and Lady Mary with their charities . . . he had refused all offers of help, even the idea of a consultation with Dr. Hardy. And the Firths had never had children.

At once Alys repented. She had no need to think unkindly of a man's broken spirits, just because her own were so fully charged with passion—and she had forgotten about Laura! The child hardly ever left London, never visited Desthorpe because it was uncomfortably close to Upton. The correct and sensible plan would be to accept Edith

Lyttleton's invitation, and take the child, with Miss Dalton as chaper-one, to the South of France.

With a complete lack of conviction, Alys forced herself to go to her bureau and write a note to Edith, asking if it would be feasible to include her daughter Laura in the house party at *Roches des Lilas*—if the Lyttletons were traveling *en famille*. If so, then Alys might find it possible to rearrange her Parisian trip, and come on to join them.

She felt virtuous as soon as the note was dispatched—but in her heart, she knew she would never go through with the plan. Then Cecily Day came for a fitting, and revealed exactly the detail that made Alys succumb.

"Oh, Alys, how can I persuade you? All your friends will be at Melbury at some point during the month—Daisy, surviving her disgrace and longing for company—Panton of course, the bore—the Baron de Falbe, who has a soft spot for you, and because Edward loves to talk politics, and he knows all about Europe . . . who else can I mention to tempt you?"

He had not told her: Edward had promised to go to Melbury and had not even consulted her. Alys' anger gave her the energy to be very collected in her reply.

"To be honest, I'd thought of joining the Lyttletons in France. Or to go to Florence; I've never been to Italy. But perhaps I could fit in a week or so—can I think about it for a while?"

"Of course, I understand, but please don't refuse me. Shall I see you this evening at Beatrice's?"

"You *are* wearing my black lace for it, aren't you Cecily?" Alys loved to be domineering with her favorites. Lady Ventry's gatherings were elegant and a good place for her work to be seen.

"Of course I am! I wouldn't dare go otherwise! *A bientôt*, then!"

Alys dressed herself with meticulous care later in the evening. Laura came in to watch her, sitting on the edge of her bed and admiring Alys as she arranged flowers, silk Banksia roses on a yoke of Brussels lace. Alys caught her daughter's adoring expression, reflected in the mirror.

"Do you like it?" she asked, smoothing the satin skirt down from a tight-fitting basque. There were very few quiet times these days between them.

"Oh yes, Mama! Your waist is so tiny! Miss Dalton says she thinks you are very pretty in a French sort of way. Did you know that this is the only house that Miss Dalton has had a position, where the family has no title?"

"Well. We're honored to have Miss Dalton, then."

"I think so." Laura agreed in all seriousness. "She has excellent taste, Mama. She's teaching me such a lot of things about painting and music and—"

"I have to go, darling. Kiss me."

"Miss Dalton says you have a natural refinement, just like a Duchess."

"Hm! I think a better word for me is *finery,* not refinement. I've plenty of that. Now off to bed. I never stayed up late when I was your age."

Laura kissed her and went to bed obediently. She was developing into a proper little lady, Alice thought, with her own pretensions. Alys suddenly realized that she had been so preoccupied with her own changing life that she had scarcely noticed Laura developing from a child into a girl. Laura was happy, and that was all that mattered.

◆　◆　◆

Across the table at Lady Ventry's, Alys saw Edward deep in conversation, seated between his cousin Bea, the hostess, and a new de Falbe debutante—Alys could not remember the girl's name, although she herself had supplied her dress. The Baron sat opposite his niece, at Alys' side. De Falbe was invited everywhere because he enjoyed company and was a kind listener. But placed beside Alys, who could hardly stop looking at Edward, let alone converse, his social deficiency was all too obvious. De Falbe had long given up any amorous intentions toward Alys. They ate in almost complete silence.

He roused himself to make one more effort.

"Miss Lavelle tells me that Miss Hardy has decided to remain in New York, after her tour. She has received an offer. You must be very proud of her. What sisters! You both have such talents."

Just at that moment, Alys saw Edward laugh at a remark from the debutante. The girl looked embarrassed, then pleased to have been considered witty. Edward leant toward the girl to reply, and with a sudden tenderness, brushed a finger along her cheek. No offense was caused; the young girl recognized the caress of a man admiring her as a fine object, as one would touch a flower, or a china vase.

Alys felt sapped of vitality. He was so free with his charm, so certain of her that his love spilled over, to everyone else's benefit. She wanted to kill him—better still, drive him to despair with some act of inordinate cruelty. He seemed to flourish in love, while she was being destroyed by it.

She spoke quickly, "How kind of you to say such sweet things, Baron de Falbe. I had rather hoped Anne would be back in time to join us at Melbury—it's my first visit; I hear it's a fine house."

Edward looked sharply at her, unaware of his offense. He was puzzled by the loud, bright sound of her voice. He heard enough to understand that she meant to follow him to Cecily's and frowned at her. She acknowledged the silent message: Edward would be staying at Melbury with his wife. Alys looked down the table at Charlotte, who was listening attentively to a very beautiful young man, reputed to be the debutante's conquest: Charlotte and the admirer were about the same age, both rich and fully aware of their value to the others in the room. Alys felt no guilt at all about Charlotte. She seemed so perfectly attuned to her role as an older man's wife, so buoyed up by her newly acquired title. Alys doubted if even knowledge of her affair with Edward could pierce the armor of complacency that shone on her, like the gilding on a lily.

◆   ◆   ◆

Of course Alys knew it was commonplace—the careful arrangement of bedrooms at these country gatherings. No hostess planned her guest list without making sure that lovers were positioned within easy reach of each other's rooms, and that unimaginative conventional couples were left to their illusions on other corridors. At Melbury, Cecily had plenty of scope. The house was a crumbling Elizabethan mansion, with additions providing ungainly wings and extensions at the sides and back of the house. It stood low down in a valley, surrounded by beech trees and elms all shorn to an even line by the deer that roamed about the park.

Cecily Day enjoyed the intrigues of her friends. Alys felt she was excluded from these frivolities: Cecily intended her to have a rest. Also, she liked to provide her wealthy circle with a few artists or with promoters of good causes, to patronize; just one or two distinguished guests to enliven the evenings. Alys supposed that Cecily would be forever an enemy if she found out she was being deceived. It was a question of losing face rather than offended morality. Possibly it could lead to a breach of her patronage, her friendship too, which made Alys feel more regret. Cecily would realize she had been made to look foolish, and that was unforgivable. That first night, Alys waited in her room impatiently, pushing aside guilty thoughts of moral shabbiness, waiting only for the sound of Edward's stealthy tread outside her door. She had kept him from seeing her for two whole weeks in London before joining him at Melbury.

At last he came. He hurried to the bed, drawing the curtain round it quickly to drown out any sound that might be heard by someone else passing on a similar errand.

"What are you doing to me, Alys? Why did you refuse to see me? I've been in torture!" He grabbed her, stroking her hair so fiercely that it hurt to the roots.

"Let me go. Selfish brute! Don't you touch me—beg me to forgive you first! Or I'll send you away forever! At once, do you hear me?"

She knelt up on the bed, pushing him away from her but clutching at his clothing in a passion, willing him to submit to her possessiveness.

"What have I done?" He never looked so impossible to tame or to own as he did now, protesting his innocence.

"You can't, you simply can't flirt like that in front of me! I won't have it! I will kill you first!"

Remembrance of their last meeting dawned on him and he laughed.

"My God, woman! Have a sense of proportion! She was a mere child—are you so mistrusting of me that you think— I never meant to hurt you, Alys."

"Never again! Never again will you do that in front of me! Touch someone as you touch me! Promise!"

But Edward said nothing. He sighed, and the fight left him. Alys began to cry and flung herself against his tired body.

He spoke slowly. "I can't promise not to hurt you, because you see offense in so many things. You don't believe I love you."

"I do! I'm sorry. Love me, forgive me. Please."

He turned to her with all the practiced, familiar tenderness he could give. Their eyes were shut, their bodies touching, naked and certain of each other. Edward lay on her hard, trapping all her limbs with his own, as if he wanted to engulf her, once and for all. When he entered her, they both sighed with relief: they were one again, all mistrust and anger forgotten. Then tenderness too was left behind; they moved against each other with a greedy appetite for sexual gratification. When Edward sensed that Alys' body was totally taken up by her hunger for satisfaction, he came out of her and kissed her, with his teeth biting and sucking into the wet purplish folds of her sex. She shuddered into orgasm, then pulled him to come on top of her again, growling with pleasure as he moved hard on her to heighten the enjoyment of her last moments of release. Then Edward pleasured himself, lifting her hips to his body with a possessing firmness in his hands, so that he could be even more deeply part of her, responsive as one person. Alys pressed up to him with an animal hunger for his satisfaction. When he came, it was a second, encompassing sensation that made him cling to her with devotion and gave her a moment's freedom from the tyranny of his love.

It was a unity of pleasure, of taking and receiving love that they had perfected, and which restored them just for a while to some secret world of peace. Only after making love did Alys see the fractured moments of her life fall into place. It was as if the splinters of a broken mirror had been magically restored to a smooth reflection of the truth: how she really was, how everyone and everything was intended to be, found, not lost.

They rested, without talking at all, then Edward got up and dressed. Alys did not ask him if he would go to bed in Charlotte's room—she did not care if he did, because it made no difference. Tonight, or tomorrow night, he would make love to his wife, perhaps with as much physical pleasure as he had with her. Alys knew Edward could do that—love other women as he loved her. All she cared for was that he wanted to share a bed with her, as much, perhaps more than all the rest. She wanted love, and was wanted in return.

"You can't stay here, Alys," he whispered.

"What do you mean?" Alys felt in control, certain of her rights and her power to carry on the deception. She found it hard to believe that Edward felt guilty or upset by her presence in the house. Across the square, a few streets away, or down a corridor, it made no difference.

"It's too close. Too dangerous. If Charlotte were to suspect any-thing . . ."

"She's used to your staying up, playing cards, drinking brandy, going for walks. I shall be immaculately good, I promise. I can't leave as soon as I've arrived. It would look obvious."

"Of course not. But as soon as you can."

Alys felt anger rising, but did not want the peace and intimacy of their past moments to be driven off so soon by her temper.

"You needn't come to me again, while I'm here, if you like. I'm quite happy just to be in your presence."

She lay back on the bed, stretching her arms above her head and brushing her wet hair back from her face, against the pillows.

Edward looked down at her with a wooden expression. She knew he was thinking of how soon he could have her again. She waved her fingers at him, not even lifting her hand from behind her head.

"Good-night, darling," she said.

Edward flung his jacket off and fell on her again. He did not stop to undress: he knew Alys loved the thought that he had to get into her at once. She tugged at the buttons of his trousers until she could clutch at him, his penis already hard with his need to enter her again. This time Edward paid no attention to Alys' pleasure, which excited her: she had had satisfaction enough, all she wanted now was to savor the effect she had on him. Edward moved on her in a passion, until she forced him to lie down so she could hang over his chest, digging her finger-nails into his arm muscles, driving herself lightly up and down on him. Then, before it was too late, Edward threw her back on the bed and pressed her knees up hard to her ribs so that he could thrust himself much deeper into her. She wanted to laugh at the glorious desperation of this act of sex: she wanted him to go on trying to be one forever. It was over quickly. Edward clenched his teeth and hissed as he came, a sharp sensation that was near to pain. He rolled off her abruptly and lay beside her, exhausted.

In the distance, they heard raucous laughter. Some of the other men were going to bed.

"You must go," Alys whispered.

She sat up, straightened his clothes and playfully fixed his buttons.

◆　◆　◆

Alys was only in control for two blissful weeks. She was careful not to avoid Charlotte completely. They rode together after a late breakfast with Daisy and Bea, who both had enough conversation to fill any awkward gaps. The women walked across the fields to join the men for picnic lunches, an attempt to divert them from their sporty pursuits. Alys often went alone with Cecily, deep in consideration of other women's clothes, the likelihood of hat feathers being banned altogether to protect the birds and the latest in orientalism from Paris.

Once Alys made love to Edward in the fields when they were sup-posed to be joining the others for an afternoon shoot. It was a frantic, terrifying experience, in a copse, not at all comfortable, and only saved from disaster by their sudden perception of how comic their despera-tion to make love was. Afterward they lay in the grass, watching in the distance the servants from the house trooping back disgruntled with the remnants of the picnic: a table, six chairs, a wine cooler and various heavy baskets of food and linens. Alys' unpleasant memories of country life at Upton Park began to fade as she took fresh pleasure in the sunshine, the meadows and her idleness. She felt happy and healthy, with a fullness of being that was new to her. But she knew she had to leave. Too long a stay was a strain on both of them, and she had to think of her work at the salon, much neglected in past weeks. She forced herself to announce her departure to Cecily.

"I won't go!" she cried on Edward's shoulder on her last night. In spite of his intense relief at her departure, Edward was beside himself. He simply adored Alys' company; she made him happier than anyone else he had ever loved.

"Look, I'll come to London on Friday—we'll spend the weekend alone. Is that a comfort?"

"Oh, Edward, how can you do that? It will look suspicious."

"I'll arrange it very carefully. Don't worry."

Alys did not allow herself to think of the attention that Edward would pay to Charlotte for the next few days to make her happy enough for him to leave.

"Make love to me again," she murmured, and spread herself on top of him, kissing him into submission before he could go back to that other bed.

Next day, Cecily was sorry to see her go. Alys had been an affectionate companion, a pleasure to look at and a popular guest. Her outfit for the train journey was impossible—a vivid emerald green Eton jacket with a high collar, tight sleeves, and a deep red skirt, shorter than Melbury village had ever seen before, revealing high red boots buttoned up the sides. Alys' whippet leapt around the coach wheels while her trunks were loaded—for her first stay in the country Alys had come more than well prepared.

Charlotte joined Cecily on the steps to wave good-bye to Alys.

"She's very stylish," Charlotte offered, as the carriage disappeared.

"Stylish! Oh yes." Cecily laughed at Charlotte's faint praise.

"I don't know what you see in her, Aunt Cecily. She's not particularly intelligent, or a brilliant conversationalist. I find her rather formal and arrogant, actually."

"She? I didn't know, dear Charlotte that anyone of my female acquaintances was important enough to be 'she' *tout court.*"

It was harsh of Cecily to rebuff her niece's attempt at confidence. But she did not feel that Charlotte needed her support or her sympathy as much as Alys did. Cecily knew very well what was happening, and that

Alys would be the loser. Edward had been intensely selfish, and, as usual, others would suffer. Cecily hoped that, with her connivance, the affair would reach its inevitable conclusion a little quicker.

Cecily's manipulations were not the answer. Alys went back to London more certain than before of Edward's love for her, happier in her memories than she had ever thought possible. Once she had needed all her perseverance to put the past behind her. Now there were images in her mind she could treasure, call back with a rush of joy whenever she had a quiet time. It struck Alys that some people had little else in their heads but good memories—what on earth was important to them?

Lilian was waiting in Berkeley Square. Alys thought she looked very appropriate, standing in the hallway—a composed young woman, happy in her work, grateful to Alys for her unusual opportunity. She led Alys to her little office behind the fitting rooms. From seamstress to business woman, in zibeline serge, silvery gray Lilian was a fine-looking girl—did *she* love anyone?

"Madame Alys, I have some sad news," she said slowly.

"Love! Love!" The words clanged around the room as Lilian told her in a few words what had happened. Florence, her Phoebe, her mesmerizing pale-skinned blonde, had found she was pregnant.

"She's been dosing herself with powder to get rid of the baby." Lilian went on with her explanation. "The doctor, on examining it, found it was a poison—it contained white lead. She lost the baby, but she is very likely to die."

"But Florence was such a proper girl—she never had callers—I can't imagine her with lovers! No one ever paid court to her here. A few flowers, a few notes . . ."

"No, that's right. She always went straight home." Lilian weighed her words carefully so that Alys would be sure to catch her meaning. The crude truth dawned on Alys. It was someone in the family.

"Are you sure? Who knows? The doctor?"

"No. He mustn't know because of the police. Florence told me herself. I sat with her. She was delirious."

Alice remembered the surly, possessive little cobbler presiding over his household, his two pinch-faced sons and Florence, pale and obedient, standing by them all in the kitchen, at the table, waiting for her father to give permission for her new life.

How her face had lighted up at the thought of freedom, working for Alys, being taught how to carry herself like a lady . . .

"Where is she?"

"At home." Lilian said it finally, her head lowered.

"At home!" Alys exclaimed. "Why on earth is she still there?"

Lilian raised a hand to calm Alys. "Please listen, Madame Alys, it's not how you think. They're devoted to her. Her father and her brothers love her. They're desperate about what has happened. They won't be parted from her. Not one of them is admitting who was responsible. I think it must have been the father. But perhaps the boys were part of it, too."

"It's evil, revolting!"

"It happens all the time. Whole families in crowded conditions . . . *that* is revolting."

"What shall we do?"

"Look after her—you will pay the doctor, won't you, Madame Alys? I took the liberty of arranging all that, it was so urgent, I couldn't wait for your—"

"Of course. I must go to her."

"I don't know." Lilian looked hesitantly at Alys' extravagant clothing. "I think we need to be very discreet. If the newspapers found out—they might invent all kinds of stories. I don't know. We have to protect Florence, but also the other girls, and ourselves."

Alys understood at once what Lilian hinted at. No one would publish the truth, for that was too obscene to contemplate. But the notion that Florence had been "ruined" by her connections in high places—even her own family might turn to that distortion to cover their guilt.

"Her father wouldn't dare," she murmured.

"No, but the brothers might. Be careful if you visit, and do let me come too."

"Be careful! Be careful!" That was all people said to her, all the time!

◆　◆　◆

Next day, Alys and Lilian went to Florence's flat in that dismal high street. The doctor was waiting for them at the door and stood in attendance in case questions were to be asked of him.

"She's very poorly," he said, "but I told her you were coming and it pleased her."

Mr. Nuttall was not in the shop at the front of the house. Only one of her brothers sat in the kitchen, his arms folded on a green oilcloth, waiting for the kettle to boil. Several pairs of dingy men's combinations were festooned over the fire, steaming. The kettle lid rattled. Alys went upstairs. Through the thin floorboards, Alys could hear the rhythmic *tap, tap,* made by the other son, who sat mending shoes at the back workbench. The boy in the kitchen followed her.

"Tell your father not to worry about the doctor's bills," Alys said to the boy, hardly able to look him in the face. "I have put it all in a note. I'll take care of Florence's medical needs."

"Thanks." He stood up, shifting uneasily, as if he needed to say something. "When you got 'er—I think we was afraid she'd leave home. We never thought it would come to this . . ."

"It's not my fault!" Alys glared at him. The boy had the same fine, wan features that Florence had. An open, simple face, and now he gawped.

"Oh no, Your Ladyship. I never said—not your fault."

He stood awkwardly in the doorway, trying to order his thoughts, torn between idle accusations, and revulsion at the truth. Truth broke through for a moment. "She was pleased to be with you, Mum. Best times she's had, she said."

Alys had no wish to torture him. She went into the bedroom. Florence was still and lovely as a marble figure, like a knight's wife on a church tomb, with her hair pulled back, her white forehead shining.

"Hello, Your Ladyship. Fancy you being here."

"Call me Alys, dear Florence." She bent low to kiss her.

"Oh, I couldn't ever, you know I couldn't, Your Ladyship. I'm ever so sorry I let you down."

"Don't say it, child. You were the first one I wanted. I'm so glad you came to me. The first one I chose."

"Really?"

The light in her eyes made Alys disbelieve all she had been told of the hopelessness of her condition. Florence could not die with that spirit in her. It was against nature.

"I bought you these flowers, and something special, from the girls. Look, Lilian's opening the box."

Inside was a white lawn nightdress, tucked and ribboned, folded in layers of tissue.

"Look at that! Yards of insertion!" Florence breathed.

"Well, it had to be very fine for someone who knows about these things." Hours and hours of handiwork had been put into it, to stitch the lace in panels at the hem and bodice.

"Ooh, Your Ladyship, it's ever so pretty." Florence had forgotten about her disgrace. It was all a terrible accident to be left behind while there was still time to be forgiven and to forgive.

"Thank you! Thank the girls for me!"

Alys held her breath, watching Florence carefully. She did not want thoughts of her former life to make her sad. But Florence had forgotten about "Phoebe" and her splendor. She was herself again, at home, released from an unbearable secret, free.

"You will tell me if there is anything you need?" Alys asked. "I shall talk to your—family about the housekeeping. Don't worry about—"

"No," Florence interrupted. "Don't do that. Dad's managing it all very well, and I have a lot put by, you know. My brothers take turns with the shop and looking after me. It's not necessary for you to help us, Your Ladyship, *Miss Alys,* I mean, *please* let us be. Thank you, though, for everything."

The doctor came to the door, and signaled that it was time for them to leave.

◆　◆　◆

Alys went back to Berkeley Square struggling with her emotions. Different reactions swam to the surface, black writhing forms in turmoil. "Guilty!" one dark mouth cried out at her. "You altered a life with no thought for the consequences!" another accused. Then she heard laughter, the indulgent, maddened sound of herself and Edward rolling in each other's arms on down-filled pillows—in secret, above a flower shop in Mayfair. She felt as if she too were drowning in wrongdoings. She had lectured all her girls on temptation, yet had given in to it herself, with less cause.

She went slowly upstairs to her own apartment. Laura had been out all day at Dr. Hardy's, and was content enough. Her mother's unexpected return made everything perfect.

The sight of that small face filled with unalloyed pleasure at her return made Alice even more ashamed. How could she have been so reckless when she had a child's future in her hands? She stared at Laura as if she were a stranger. A composed child, Laura seemed far more content than she had ever been herself. Alys suddenly did not want to be in her company.

"Laura, I've had a change of plan—well, shall we sit in my room, while we talk?"

"Oh yes, can I look in your boxes?" Laura's favorite pastime was to try on all her mother's jewelry while they had a "real conversation" (all the more valued for its rarity).

Alys sat behind her, watching as she pinned big diamonds in her ears and hung pendants round her neck. The diamonds were a gift from Edward. Suddenly she knew she had to get away from him completely, to end it.

"Darling, I may have to take a trip."

"To Ireland again, Mama? I liked those old men."

"No!" Alys wanted fresh vistas, no contact with the past. "What about—America? New York! Yes, that's it! We'll go on a big liner, and have pretty cabins, and—"

"We could see Aunt Anne in her play . . ."

"Yes—of course, that's perfect!"

"But what about my lessons?"

"Well, perhaps Miss Dalton could come with us." Alys had not arrived at practical details. She had only just thought of the trip.

"Do you know, Mama, I think you could make dresses for Americans. Miss Dalton says they're very rich, and the girls are always coming over here to marry dukes and earls."

"What an extraordinary idea . . ."

"She says they love the Europeans, because we are so full of history. She's always being offered work there, but she likes to stay here with me . . ." Laura was very satisfied with her governess's compliment.

"Do you know, that may be just the answer. How clever you are! I should have thought of it myself!"

"Mama?"

"Yes?"

"May I speak?"

"Don't be afraid of me. Whatever it is, you are permitted to say it."

"Would you be very unhappy if I asked to stay here with Miss Dalton instead? I could visit Uncle Hardy and Mrs. Bacon, and Lady Evelyn will come often, and I have my lessons, and the summer—"

"Don't be so dull, Laura! There must be something else. What is it?"

"Well, I know you want to go away, and it would be an adventure, but I won't see you, will I? You'll be getting famous, and going to balls, and I'd rather be here than in a hotel waiting for you . . ."

"Oh Laura, I didn't see it like that. Opening a salon was *your* idea, remember! Though it is a very good one indeed."

Laura knew her better than she knew herself. Alys was amazed she had been blind to her own opportunities. If Worth and Redfern could come from Paris to open in London, why should "Alys" not succeed in New York? She would do just as Lily suggested: escape, but with a strong personal motive to leave.

Laura was smiling at her patiently. She did a sweet thing: she looked up in enquiry, and waved at her, curling her fingers softly. "Mama?" Alys realized that for several moments she hadn't heard a word the child had said. She kissed Laura tenderly.

"You look like a little angel, granting a prayer," she said, hugging her. "Or perhaps a fairy, because I don't think angels wear jewelry."

"Why not? They might."

"Yes. I suppose they might."

"Mama. Are you going to be very rich, if you go to New York?"

Alys was amused. "Rich enough to pay Miss Dalton and turn you into a well-educated miss. That pin is meant for your hair, not your collar, darling."

"Put it on for me, Mama. Now I look like a fairy queen. Can you tell me a story?"

Avoiding all her troubled thoughts, Alys invented stories in a well-loved series they called "Miss Barry's adventures in Paris," embroidering on the truth.

◆　◆　◆

Alys had no call to go back to the cobbler's shop again. When Edward came to spend the weekend with her, she told him nothing about it, and loved him as wonderfully as she knew how, for the last time. She was amazed that he did not guess that she was lost to him. When he told her he could only spend one night with her and had to return to Melbury on Sunday morning, she pretended unhappiness, and convinced him. It was the only time they had spent a whole night together, and Edward was relaxed, intimate and mellow.

They dined in Berkeley Square, then took a hansom to their rooms in Dover Street. The flower shop was locked and dark. Alys had never seen the place on a weekend night. As she reached the top of the stairs ahead of him, she looked down on Edward's bent head, and a tenderness for him made her fling her arms around him as he reached her height. He stopped two steps lower. Their eyes met.

"There," she said, kissing him. "Isn't it strange, we never came here together like this, till tonight?"

"Never? I didn't know that."

Edward unlocked the door, pleased at her romantic thought. Alys knew then that she was free of him, because his indifference to a loving detail did not hurt.

Curiously, the luxury of a night together seemed to dull their excitement. Making love was a slow, lingering pleasure, fulfilling Alys with an easing warmth, not a feverish climax. How faithful her body was, even though her conscience and her heart had withdrawn from Edward's love. They slept for many hours, and on waking to find they still had each other, made love again sleepily, without needing intense gratification. In all this time, Edward guessed nothing of Alys' thoughts. He left her lazing on the pillows, refusing to wake up properly as he said good-bye. It was a gentle way to part, cowardly perhaps, but how Alys had chosen to do it.

"Good-bye, my darling. I'll send a message as soon as I can arrange another 'escape,' he comforted her, stroking her hair gently. "Aren't you going to speak to me?"

Violently, Alys turned to him and flung her arms round his neck. She kept her eyes shut tight.

"Poor darling. You do so hate farewells . . ." He caressed her slowly, making the moment endless. Edward sighed, then laid her down and tucked the covers round her bare skin. The door shut, and Alys pressed her face into the pillows as hard as she could so that he would not hear the wild groaning noise she made as his footsteps died away. She cried out not because her heart was sad, but because his very tenderness had made her body ache for him to touch her again.

Terror ensued upon sorrow: how could she have given up the one man in existence who had made her come to life, made every inch of her flesh and soul take on a value, a purpose unknown to her before? Alys flung herself on her back, flailed out, crying uncontrollably, her body stiffening with one urgent need—"Come back! Don't go! Don't leave me! Love me!" Her arms dropped, her hands clutched her belly: it was still damp with the sweat of their bodies' union. Supposing Edward never lay there, never pressed his weight upon her again? The thought was unbearable, and she wanted to die.

Tears drained away. She opened her eyes, gasping and hiccuping, aware of the hard truth of this moment. She had broken with the one person in the whole world who loved her, and for whom she was intended. God, if he existed—or more probably, a malign fate—had created her for just this moment, just to know the full measure of her futility. Without Edward she was nothing: a deadened, suicidal nonentity.

She stared despairingly at her surroundings as if discovering where she was for the first time. The ceiling had cracks in it: the cornice work ran into a blank wall at the far corner, where a once-fine room had been partitioned for this tiny apartment. Alys shivered, for as Edward's presence faded from her body, the bed grew damp, and the room cold and unsavory. She had never lingered in it before, always left hurriedly to return to work. It was seedy, impersonal, and made her feel disgraced.

A Sunday morning: bright sunshine slit through the shutters, knife blades of light. Few footsteps on the pavement: the jingling of a harness and the desultory orders of a groom as a carriage in the mews behind the building was made ready for a morning ride. Other women with their husbands were rising for breakfast, going to church, meeting friends in the street. Edward would go back to Melbury—be there in time for sport in the afternoon, and a convivial supper with other guests and *his* wife. She, Alys, meanwhile, would spend this momentous day striving to find reasons not to kill herself.

Her heart would never beat again to the rhythm of love—a pulse that made hours of work and other encounters illusory, while the one true time of the day approached: that moment when she fell into her man's arms, and allowed her whole being to be filled with love.

His wife. Alys thought then of her own marriage. Only now did she realize why William had hated her so much. He knew about such feelings, in a choked and inexpressible fashion, through lust. He had yearned to share ecstasy with her. His immaturity and selfishness made him cruel, quite impossible to love—but now she pitied him. She had been totally unawakened to desire; never once wanted him to penetrate her, let alone have him see her rise to passion. Even now the idea disgusted her.

Alys got up and dressed, slowly covering her nakedness as if she would never see her body in this light again: in the shadows, occasionally transformed by a sunbeam from the narrow window. With a last look at the turmoil of her bed, she locked the door and pushed the key back under it.

In the street, she almost collided with a waiter from the hotel nearby, where she had once stayed.

"Morning, Madame Alys! Lovely day for a stroll!"

He was on his way to work: extra pay for a Sunday, and his girl would come up to town and call for him at six. She knew all this because her mannequins used to chat to the waiters at the hotel between their deportment lessons. Dearest Florence . . .

"Good morning, Billy, how nice to see you."

"Late as usual—shocker aren't I?" he grinned, and hurried past her toward an alley and the hotel kitchens.

Ordinary things went on: the boy looked so busy and pleased with himself. Alys swayed and almost fell. She clutched an iron railing for support, while an urge to run her head against the spikes rose up in her and just as quickly vanished . . .

Never again. She held on to those railings, straightening her back, wondering how that cheerful young lad made love. With joy, for a diversion, perhaps! Then she began to cry again softly to herself. It came to her that she did not just admire the awesome beauty of masculinity—the thrilling muscles of Edward's arms, the transfixing foreignness of his sexual organs—she envied male confidence, its self-importance. And then, in cold misery, as if saying good-bye to the best hope of her heart, she decided to fight for that sense of identity in her own life, and never again to crave for it between someone else's sheets.

Alys held the railings in the manner of an old woman whose heart has made her stop for breath. Then, with great effort, she made her way down the quiet street toward the park. She would walk among the beautiful people, feel the sun on her face, then go home and take Laura out to lunch. Her steps were slow and deliberate, like a thief's stealing away from a burgled house: Alys had her love wrapped up, clutched to her, and she was taking it away from Edward. With every step, like a burglar, she experienced a surge of relief, a sense of willed-for freedom, a release. The madness which had put her whole life at risk was over.

She would never want anyone, ever again. She would become "Alys," not "Alice," to her own design: successful, imperturbable and rich.

◆　◆　◆

It took her a long time to compose the letter she sent Edward, to explain she could not go on, and that for the sake of future happiness they would have to learn to be friends and nothing more. Alys had no doubt that her business relationship with Edward would continue. He was a man of honor about such things, and besides, her business was flourishing.

A week later, Alys heard that Florence had died. She sent flowers, but did not attend the funeral, for fear her presence would cause too much idle curiosity. The girls went for her, in their real selves: Kitty and Tina Szenkier, Betsey Hill and Lisa Allen.

The following weeks were filled with work, finishing the latest autumn collection, hiring a ladies' maid to accompany her to New York, explaining all the special orders to the staff, finalizing details in meetings with Layton Stayce regarding payments and the management of Berkeley Square.

Lilian was the only one Alys confided in about her possible new venture in America; Lilian reacted with a rather too serious expression to the news, making Alys blush unaccountably. It occurred to her Lilian understood her real motive for the trip.

"Why don't you take the new models with you?" Lilian suggested, anxious to make a practical contribution and to camouflage the moment of understanding that neither she nor Alys wished to expose further. "Perhaps—not merely for your own wardrobe, but just in case you decide to show them. You never know . . ."

Alys' muted face lightened perceptibly at the thought of such a positive step.

"Brilliant, dear girl! Can they manage? The workrooms are so busy . . ."

"I'll see to it, Madame." Lilian was determined: she wanted to help Alys back to her old self, whatever means were used. After another three weeks' cutting, stitching and overtime payments, six tin trunks of model gowns were added to Alys' luggage.

When all Alys' plans were laid, she sent Anne a cable:

SAILING FOR NEW YORK FRIDAY 21 AUGUST
CUNARD LINE. HAVE BOOKED A SUITE AT THE PLAZA
DMLS

"Dearly Missed Loving Sister." The words that had been used in their erratic correspondence for many years. This time Anne would be the one to show Alys her new world.

Alys heard nothing from Edward. She assumed he was fighting his disappointment in the countryside, for the house across the square was still shuttered.

Her own rooms were to be closed in her absence. One Sunday Alys drove to St. John's Wood with Miss Dalton and Laura, and left them in Mrs. Bacon's hands. Dr. Hardy was delighted to see her—particularly as this was her first visit for many weeks, and the last time before a prolonged absence.

"I'm going to miss your Sunday visits, my dear," he said, pressing Alys' hand to his lips. "Though I have to admit, the pleasure of Laura's company every day will be more than a comfort—a joy that I did not expect!"

"Are you sure it's no burden to you?" Alys asked.

"It's good for an old man like me, set in his ways, to be shaken up sometimes. I expect we shall manage." Dr. Hardy spoke with such satisfaction that Alys could see it was pointless even to pretend to worry. Her freedom was not being won at Laura's expense.

The three of them traveled northward to Liverpool together; Laura was excited to see the ship that was to take her mother to America. Alys could not leave England without causing ripples of interest among her circle of friends; her stateroom on the *Silver Star* was crowded with well-wishers who had come to see her off. It was a disorganized, wonderful party, with old friends and new acquaintances arriving and journalists from the London newspapers trying to describe the extraordinary spectacle of Alys' dress: white velvet, bordered with fur at the hem and sleeves; osprey feathers trembling a foot over her head; diamonds (the present from Edward) like fiery drops in her ears.

Dr. Hardy sat in a corner, tired after the effort of the journey, with Laura close at his side.

"Ooh, look! There's Ned! And there's Lily, Mama's friend, you remember her, Uncle, don't you?"

"Of course I do, my dear. And who's that fearful-looking woman with a bird on her head? In spite of your mother's lesson I still don't understand why women enjoy these dead things . . ."

"It's Mrs. Leslie Day. She's ever so rich. That's her friend the Baron, what's his name? I don't know the other lady with him, though—isn't she pretty?"

Alys stood face to face with the de Falbe debutante. With clear eyes, no longer filled with jealousy, she saw how very appealing the girl was. But that did not stop the dislike that welled up in her. She half acknowledged her, then turned away.

"Baron de Falbe! How unexpected all this attention is! But how welcome—are you too going to give me your cards? I have enough introductions to see me through a year of paying calls!"

She could not help presenting a glacial shoulder to the niece—what was her name? A lovely dress from Doucet in Paris . . .

"So sudden, Madame, you gave us no choice—we've all come scuttling up here to say good-bye. Why didn't you tell us all before? What will the ladies do without your endless ideas? The Americans don't need you, Madame. . . . *On dit qu'elles sont très sportives* . . ."

The Baron was unusually talkative. Was it champagne, or did he have Edward's confidence, and chatter at her in this way out of embarrassment?

"Oh, heavens, I'm only going to see my sister's new play. I shall be back, Baron, in time to save London's wardrobes. Oh, Lily, how sweet! Laura, come and open this for me!"

Laura ran over and sat at her feet, unwrapping the small basket that Lily had passed to her mother. It contained a patent corkscrew, a telescope, a punnet of strawberries, a box of Manette's crystallized fruits, and a letter in Ned's handwriting addressed to a Mrs. Adelaide Hay.

"Who is she, Ned?" Alys asked.

"Please see her," he replied. "She's bought several of my paintings over the years. You'll like each other." He sidled her into a corner. Her friends, with their usual mixture of tact and furtive interest, melted away—as best they could in a small room bursting with flowers, luggage, waiters and chattering new arrivals falling on old friends.

"We'll miss you." he said. Alys was so tense that she wanted no more emotion, and shook her head.

"Nonsense! Why does everyone talk to me as if it's the end of the world! I'm only going for a month, or two at the most!"

Ned as usual persisted. "Don't run away, Alys."

"What do you mean!" Alys' cheeks flamed. He obviously knew all about Edward from Lily. She could see it in his eyes.

"Excuse me, Ned. I have to say good-bye to my guests."

"No, wait. That was too crude of me. What I meant to say was, Alys, be forgiving. You forgave me, and I have been grateful for your friendship ever since."

"Forgiving?" Alys spoke the word as if it was an introduction to the language. "There's no one to forgive this time. It was all my own doing."

But Ned spoke out of friendship, and she found herself lingering.

"Don't be too hard on yourself! Be human, like the rest of us! We all make mistakes . . ."

"How true. And very few pay for them." She shuddered, thoughts of Florence with her all the time. She smiled at Ned. "Aren't I lucky, Ned? No harm done."

Ned wondered if it were true. So did Alys, feeling particularly brittle.

The sirens started to sound, and the porters hurried along the decks to warn all visitors to leave the ship. Laura kissed her mother one last time, then clutched at Dr. Hardy's hand as they were hustled down the gangplank by the chattering, slightly drunken mob of Alys' friends. Laura looked up at her mother, standing on deck and waving a scarf at them all, as they dispersed on the quayside.

"Doesn't she look tiny, Uncle?"

"It's a very big ship, my dear. She'll be quite safe."

"Oh, I know. People do it all the time. I've been watching in the newspapers. Miss Dalton reads out who comes and goes."

"That's very kind of her."

"Is my mama really famous?"

"Not really dear. Well known perhaps. Well respected for her work." Dr. Hardy would have added "well loved" if he could.

Looking up at Alys' stiff, bright little figure by the ship's rail, he wished that someone stood there at her side. For all his progressive work, there were certain areas in which Dr. Hardy still thought as an old-fashioned gentleman.

CHAPTER 15

1 9 1 0

When Alys saw New York, she lost all sense of proportion. A madness, a desire to startle and impress rose inside her. She clung to the rail of the *Silver Star,* watching, lost in thought as the ship ploughed the filthy water and slid to its mooring at the dock. She wanted to do something, anything, to obliterate the shame of her liaison with Edward. The distaste and pity she had felt for Florence were suddenly repellent emotions. Looking up at the city skyline, its very height announcing a new world to conquer, Alys became desperate and lonely to the point of hysteria. She stared at the crowd on the quay waving to the other passengers beside her. She wanted to plunge down into that cheering mass—to touch, to belong, to be attached to everyone there. Impossible. But another gratification—success, a name—that would satisfy her. Alys was savage about it.

First she had to find her maid, lost below decks saying good-bye to her new servant acquaintances. Alys battled through the customs, and the complications of her arsenal of trunks. Then she faced the alarm of noise, dirt and thronging traffic on her cab journey across town. But, all at once, she was gladdened by New York. The city captivated her with its adventurous beauty. Soaring buildings on wide avenues, the cosmopolitanism of the people on the streets excited her, bringing her new energy. New York forced her to look up higher than ever before. The tops of buildings always offered a surprise, a gargoyle's head, some glittering Eastern tiling, a spiky rail of twisted ironwork. It was simply that in London a lady was used to lowering her gaze. In New York it was impossible to do that. The "El," the overhead railway, thundered above the avenues, a reminder that people were constantly on the move. In the streets motor omnibuses and horse-drawn carriages jostled for space—rivals like everyone else in the city. One had to be alert, even watchful, to take on this world, Alys realized. New York looked brash, wide open, beckoning anyone with spirit to respond to its challenges. That was the general opinion that she had already absorbed, but now she saw the city for herself, a little differently. It was stiflingly hot—the streets shimmered with heat. Canvas awnings on the block-sized hotels flapped like impromptu flags, and water carriers hosed down the pavements. Alys saw a raffishness displayed in this populous, bursting metropolis that stimulated her. New York suited her perfectly.

On arriving at the Plaza, Alys sent a message to Anne at her new theater, Galliani's. She had not expected to be met, for she knew that rehearsals for the new play might prevent her sister from coming at the last moment. Anne, of course, was far too self-involved to think of leaving a note of welcome for her at the hotel. While Alys waited for a reply, she occupied herself briefly by admiring the rococo splendor of her rooms overlooking Central Park. Then out of restlessness she ordered up copies of all the city newspapers and periodicals, taking note of the editors and addresses she might need for her "launches."

Much to Alys' relief, a messenger boy arrived with the news that Anne would join her for lunch at two o'clock. Alys had not eaten all morning, and suddenly realized how hungry she was. Soon she would have company! Anne had elected to stay behind when Kerrick's Players returned to England. Alys still did not know whether her sister had been forced to leave because she had refused to marry Kerrick, or whether this "Mr. Galliani" had poached her away. Anne had an inventive approach to self-advancement; any number of explanations were plausible.

Alys rested, and spent the rest of her first morning writing letters to all the society connections supplied to her by such London friends as Cecily Day, Lily Lavelle, Ned and Daisy Panton. She intended to exploit to the full her special position as "society *couturière*," and her connections with Court circles. Not once did her hand falter as she scribbled those confident notes, assuming friendship with the grandest names in New York's Social Register.

She had spent two weeks locked in her cabin, weeping about Edward until her body rebelled against misery and did not respond to her thoughts. She had avoided other passengers, taking walks on deck at dawn, before anyone was about, or late at night, after the dancing had stopped. Slowly, other thoughts had revived her. The voyage was an emptying out of bitterness; all vicious thoughts of Edward seemed to dilute to nothingness as she observed the oily boredom of the sea. A few positive notions remained. She had inspired love: there had been many other times in her life when she had considered herself unlovable. She had also inspired devotion, for many people relied on her implicitly for their work and happiness. Alys only half believed in her own good qualities, but by the time she reached New York she had decided to act as if they really existed.

Alys put down her pen, remembering those cabined days on the ocean. She reread her letters, signed with such a bold flourish. They were nothing more that pathetic appeals for friendship and connection. Suddenly her noble shipboard theorizing seemed unreal, too ideal to put into practice. Her brave mood of the early morning faded. Struggling for acceptance in this enormous city would be a daunting task— establishing a clientèle among the "Four Hundred" would need more than "lovableness" and "talent." A friend of Cecily Day's was holding a small reception for her that very evening. Alys wondered if she had the energy to be seen. She wanted to throw herself into a new life, and yet she could not bear the idea of being a stranger, of having to prove herself. Alys lay on the couch, deflated, depressed. She longed for Anne's arrival, because her head buzzed from thinking too much and not reaching any conclusions.

The bell rang: Anne rushed in, and within seconds Alys was full of laughter and energy again. She hugged her sister. They touched each other's curls, admired each other's fripperies, turning round and round, delighted to be together again.

"You look so grand! What a robe!"

"And you're so thin! This Mr. Galliani isn't taking care of you well enough!"

"Horrid little man! A genius but odious!"

"Be patient! If you leave someone as kind as Hubert, everyone else will seem monstrous by comparison."

"Don't let's talk about him—I want to know why you're here—this isn't a holiday, is it? Are you really going to open a salon? And how's Edward? How are you—"

"Don't let's talk about that. Lunch at Delmonico's, and then I have to be back here to change because a dear friend of Cecily Day's is giving a reception for me, and I'm to be ready at six."

"Six? Do you really need the whole afternoon here to change? Don't you want to see New York for a few hours?"

"All in good time. I have to make a grand entrance tonight, so I shall rest and dress with care. I've found a charming little girl, through an agency, and she loves to put up my hair. Irish, too! Millie, my cloak!"

Alys wore white fur and a jeweled turban for lunch at Delmonico's. Anne was a little dismayed by her sister's exhibitionism. She had always considered herself to be the glamorous one, and Alys far too impatient, too dedicated to her work to make an issue of her looks.

Alys ignored the curious glances from other tables, describing her summer and the end of her affair with Edward, waving her arms in large gestures.

"It simply couldn't go on! Me! Above a florist's shop in Mayfair! I suddenly woke up, and it was done. Finished!"

"Well, you don't seem to have broken your heart over it, as I feared."

"Oh, Anne, don't be silly." Alys' eyes filled with tears, the champagne and the pleasure of confiding in Anne making her soften unexpectedly. "You know me better. I simply had to do it. Having any part of Edward's real life was unbearable, and I didn't enjoy being so squalid."

"But he loved you!" Anne sighed at the romance of it. A dark obstinacy appeared in Alys' expression; Anne remembered it from childhood.

"Not enough."

"But that wasn't his fault—there was too much at stake: his marriage, your name—I don't understand why you're so angry," she persisted.

"I'm not sure myself, but other things happened; I was reminded that we were very wrong. I blame him, but I blame myself too. Oh, Anne, I do so want to escape from all that."

"Then I think you should do what everyone expects you to do, and be horribly successful."

"I intend to."

"Women here do dress quite appallingly at times," Anne continued. "If they have wealth, they wear it on their backs—so ostentatious! You'd make a fortune. 'An English Court Dressmaker'—there's a lot of money in that title."

How strange it was, thought Alys, that the person she had created for herself now seemed to run her life. "Alys."

◆　◆　◆

Alys was impatient. Her London friends certainly opened the right doors for her—by the end of the first week Alys had succeeded in obtaining an invitation to tea with a Gould, and a reception hosted by a Vanderbilt. One or two women were enchanted by her own costumes and flattered when she offered to make them replicas. Alys went to an employment agency to find the address of a workroom that could execute her orders, a little seamstress' shop not far from her hotel. But she was not content to wait patiently for a patron, and to slide inconspicuously into some small niche as a "society dressmaker." She wanted the word that went back to London to be that she had taken New York by storm. Most particularly, she wanted Cecily Day, Charlotte and Edward to hear she was an astounding success. Sometimes the thought of her London circle made her cry; but in a minute her mood would change and she would become defiant.

Gritting her teeth against the vulgarity of her action, Alys plunged all her accumulated cash profits into a month's campaign of nonstop advertising. Whole pages in *Vogue* and *Harper's Bazar*; photographs of her celebrity clients in the lesser journals; neat long columns in the evening press on the imminent opening of her New York salon. (Not a word as to its location.) Mistrusting her ability as a copywriter, Alys kept the wording of her advertisements baldly simple:

"ALYS": COURT DRESSMAKER.
PATRONS: THE DUCHESS OF BUCCLEUCH,
LADY DE VENTRY, MRS. CECILY DAY,
THE GREAT ACTRESS LILY LAVELLE;
VARIOUS CROWNED HEADS IN EUROPE WHO EXPECT
DISCRETION. CONSULTATIONS GIVEN;
SALON OPENING SOON.
ALL ENQUIRIES TO THE PLAZA.

The hints of fame, blue blood and gossip were intentional, but the promise of an opening was quite false. Alys doubted if she could afford the lease on any suitable address by the time she had finished with the advertising pages. She took the risk of such extravagant publicity knowing well that it might lead to triumph or to downfall.

Alys sifted through the resulting letters of enquiry, ruthlessly rejecting names she could not find in the Social Register, and inviting all those who were "acceptable" to a reception to see her latest collection. That was cynical enough, but not so calculating as the letters she wrote to all the magazine and newspaper proprietors of note, offering to make their wives any "Alys" gown of their choice "as an experiment: to prove that I can release the truly individual beauty in everyone—for which I will charge nothing." Alys included the guest list of those society ladies whom she had invited as further bait for the press.

"I think New Yorkers like boldness," she declared to Anne. "If I fail completely, it doesn't matter. I tried."

This fatalism surprised Anne. She found Alys' frame of mind too forced, too desperate to last, and her cold determination even a little unattractive. Alys knew this was so, but she was in no mood to soften or take Anne fully into her confidence. No one, no one would know how much happiness she had known and lost with Edward.

On the appointed day, Alys waited. Half an hour after the prescribed time still no one appeared. If nothing came of this exercise, Alys had no money to carry herself through the next season's expenditure in London. Her "collection trunks" lay open, and twenty sparkling, lacy, sprigged and blossomed dresses hung limply on the walls of her room. Alys suddenly realized that she ought to have retained a proper advertising agency, found new model girls, hired a theater, gone to all possible lengths to launch herself professionally in New York. Her pathetic effort at self-promotion had failed.

Eventually, Ned's acquaintance Mrs. Adelaide Hay appeared, accompanied by Mrs. George Gould, whom Alys had met just once at a tea.

"How d'you do," said Adelaide Hay, monumental, plain, bluff and awkward (though Alys had established from her society studies just how wealthy and influential she was).

Mrs. Gould wandered about graciously. 'Look, Adelaide, how clever of you to persuade me to come with you. I love this mauve—Madame Alys—I could do with that."

"Mauve isn't your color, Mrs. Gould."

Astonished eyes dwelt on her. Alys did not flinch. Mrs. George Gould was wearing a strong, vividly mauve suit.

"Not for that design . . ." Alys held her ground. "I think you would look far more stunning if I translated it into gray and silver."

For a few seconds, approval and rejection hung in the balance. Alys' success depended on a rich woman's whim. Mrs. Gould studied her hard.

"Very well," she said, at last. "Make me look stunning."

The details of the conversation that followed were lost on Alys—she spoke as if she were outside herself, acting a part she had rehearsed. Still, she had the presence of mind to triple her London prices. Alys wrote every order down, knowing she could not trust her memory of this event. Six dresses; three ballgowns; six *robes de chambre.* Thousands of dollars from Mrs. Gould alone. Then Mrs. Hay added her own kind and even more generous requests, and Alys stopped adding. Suddenly they were interrupted. The doors opened wide, and a hotel porter announced the press. Mrs. Hay and Mrs. Gould left instantly—but fortunately were recognized as they sailed past the crowd.

"Mr. and Mrs. Dagworth of *The Tribune! Mr. Duffy of The Examiner! Ladies' Home Journal!* Mrs. Rose of *McCalls! Pictorial Review!* The ladies from *Vogue!* Mr. and Mrs. Beatty of *Town Topics!"*

Alys wandered through the crush, answering questions with a great deal of bold lying. It seemed an easy game now to be so self-aggrandizing. Buckets of champagne were emptied, replaced and emptied again. Handsome men and women, ugly men and women, wealthy scions of good family, and self-made opportunists—a motley crowd were assembled to take notes from Alys. The foreignness of their manners, their accents, their odors, perfume and smoke, titillated Alys' senses. She found herself perched on a corner of the bay window overlooking Central Park. Her curious audience gathered round her.

She tried to look composed, but excitement made her features taut (though she knew that made them seem finer) and her voice was breathless. She fancied this made her sound more seductive to the men at her feet.

"What do you think of American women's fashions?"

"I think American women dress with wit and taste."

"Oh, Madame Alys, give us a little more, please!"

"Well . . . how can I express it . . . they display a certain jauntiness, a neatness, a freshness in their attitude to clothes that strikes me as very un-European."

She wanted to sound authoritative—somehow critical and yet encouraging at the same time. Alys forced her natural reserve to become a slightly challenging aloofness. She would invite these people to warm to her, to please her, if they could. She hoped to intrigue them, but she did not want them to consider her cold, typically English and a snob— just remarkable.

Alys caught sight of the reporter from *McCalls*. Mrs. Rose was white-haired, brisk in navy-blue gabardine for a suit with a striped satin blouse. She looked less like a working woman than a society wife trying to enter business. She was listening intently; then Alys saw the woman's hand slide quickly up to her collar, like a caress, as if the hand belonged to some other person, a lover perhaps. Without taking her eyes from Alys' face, Mrs. Rose gave her blouse a little tug to make it stand straighter at the nape of her neck. Alys warmed to her theme after that glimpse.

"All American women have a natural *espièglerie*, an alertness that makes any one of them a pleasure to dress. Give one a handsome gown and she wears it with distinction."

"So you don't think we're vulgar?" challenged a male reporter from one of the papers.

Alys looked at him like a schoolteacher. "I think you employ a very English word, which doesn't suit your country. I think it's a fine thing when anyone can amass a fortune, instead of a few inheriting wealth. If a woman chooses to dress with style, then it shows that she values herself."

"But surely, women dress to please their husbands?" Mrs. Rose interrupted.

"If that were true, then I would have no customers! I don't think men are interested in the changes that it pleases women to study. A really beautiful woman is aware of fashion but she dresses to suit herself, and enhance her looks . . . My loveliest clients create their own style, and modify that with my help, from year to year. Choose a style, Mrs. Rose, and I'll tell you if you're right . . ." Alys was in business.

◆　◆　◆

From that near-miss of a start, Alys began to receive customers. Anne was often on hand to encourage her, and for that Alys was grateful— her grip on reality would have loosened altogether without it. She found New York energizing to the point of fantasy. Alys used her London associations shamelessly to introduce herself to all the best families on the Social Register. Working down the list, she sent out invitations to those known to her friends, then used their names in turn to write to a second set of guests, and so on until her diary was filled with consultations. Old-established families came to her because she had cachet; new ones because she offered very good advice on how to dress and behave on formal occasions.

Finding seamstresses was difficult when she hardly knew a soul in the city, but she explored the employment agencies in New York's garment district, establishing itself on the west side of Fifth Avenue in midtown. Soon she had orders, and a whole team of outworkers, pattern cutters, silk importers, bead merchants and the rest, ready to do her bidding.

Needing another event to keep her in the public eye, Alys decided to ask Mr. Galliani if she could design the costumes for Anne's first major role in his little Broadway theater. Anne lent her a copy of the script, and Alys set to work to produce a whole range of sketches to convince him of her ability.

A gloomy, arrogant Italian, Galliani was already beginning to regret his enthusiasm for the promising young English girl he had stolen from Hubert Kerrick. When her sister appeared, dressed from head to toe in painted muslin with a whippet at her heels, his doubts turned into exasperation.

"The cost! A Society dressmaker! We gotta wardrobe. Do you and your sister want to ruin me? This is not a Vaudeville theater with the spangles and fans, Madama!"

A few words about Lily Lavelle, Alys' other commissions for Kerrick's company and her file book of photographs from London began to make him look a little more favorably on her. Alys finally won him over by offering to dress the whole company, not just Anne, for a modest sum. It was primarily the publicity she wanted, rather than the financial gain.

Anne was hard to please; she had become impossibly fussy as her confidence in her abilities increased. They argued as sisters, not working women, over colors, shapes, every detail of the designs, with old unsettled scores dinning in their words.

"You always want me to look sweeter than I am! Girlish!" Anne accused.

"She's meant to be sobered by her experiences at the end of Act One. I thought the frilled petticoat would add an appealing touch."

"Well, I won't wear it. Galliani just wants me to look beautiful and vapid, and you're playing into his hands with this outfit. Goodness' sake, I can act it. I don't need frills."

It took all the patience that Alys would have given Daisy Panton to deal with her. The task was made harder by Anne's constant alterations as her reading of the part developed in rehearsal. The petticoat, like a symbol of all else, was thrown out and then back into her dressing room many times. Slowly the costumes were finished: 1880s midwestern clothes for the men, an assortment of "tub frocks" for the women in muslins and specially dyed calicoes. There were also middle-European costumes for Bohemian homesteaders, in a scene at a summer fair.

While working on the designs, Alys spent many days touring New York looking for suitable premises to rent for her own salon. She could not go on working out of the Plaza—she had only a little parlor, bedroom and bathroom. Twenty dollars a day for that suite was expensive; although orders were coming in, Alys needed to increase the volume of her work in order to be financially secure.

The opening of *The Bohemian Girl* drew near. Alys had never had sole charge of a company before; as a rule, only leading actresses had their own designers. But Galliani insisted on his money's worth, and Alys worked hard on the entire company's wardrobe. This produced a freshness and visual harmony unlike other costuming she had seen.

"Galliani specifically said yesterday you're to wear the headdress vertically. Do you want to spoil your first entrance, and all my hard work, just to get your own way as usual?" First night: the sisters vented their nervousness on each other.

"My ladies!" Mr. Galliani steered Alys out of Anne's dressing room and up the dark stone stairs. "Time to see whether all our efforts have been justified," he said, a spasm of a smile crossing his face, as if he could not wait for disaster to make him happy again.

"Oh! I forgot to wish her good luck! I must go back!" Alys said, but Galliani blocked the stairs and took her arm forcibly to lead her to his box. She sat down, enraged, and he sat in front of her, slightly to one side, willing the lights to dim.

Then Alys spotted several of her new acquaintances down below in the orchestra seats, and leaned forward, nodding, flicking her program in acknowledgment. At this activity, Galliani hissed and clicked his teeth, without turning his head.

"Mr. Galliani! I've half filled your theater tonight. I don't respond to people's support with churlishness, as you do!" Alys whispered fiercely. He gave no indication he had heard a word. The lights went down and the play began.

The Bohemian Girl was a perfect vehicle for Anne, whose natural facility for accents turned her into a convincing middle-European. It was a rural romance, set in Wyoming in the 1880s. As soon as Anne appeared in her traditional costume, with ribboned headdress, embroidered skirts and red boots, a cheer rose from the audience.

Galliani reacted like a stone statue toppling. His shoulders fell, his head tilted back, his whole body seemed to collapse, and he ran a hand over his face as if he were remolding his features. He was safe: the play would be a success, and he would have a full house for weeks.

After the play, Alys held a reception at the Plaza for the cast, her new friends, and a handful of journalists. The playwright, Turner Hamilton, a sandy-haired young man came over the thank her for her efforts. He had a wonderful slow voice, not a New York accent at all.

"Where are you from, Mr. Hamilton?" she asked.

"A long way from here, Ma'am, Chicago. It's a fine city. I don't enjoy New York by comparison."

"Oh? Why is that?"

"Too European, too trying to impress. Chicago's my idea of a real American city. But it's all a question of taste," he added, in case Alys had taken offense.

"I was born west of Chicago myself." She smiled.

"And Anne?" he asked, with curiosity, a flush rising as he mentioned her name. He should have referred to her as "Miss Hardy," he thought to himself. Alys would guess he was an admirer, if she noticed.

"Oh yes, in Denver. But we both left when we were very young."

There was an exclamation of pleasure: Mrs. Millsom and her husband had arrived after having dinner elsewhere and had brought the morning papers.

Elsie Millsom was one of Alys' most colorful customers, entering society on the strength of her husband's oil findings. She wore Alys' sequinned black net, bordered with moonlight-blue paillettes in the shape of lily flowers, and a parure of sapphires. "You just tell me what color I should wear and I'll send Millsom round the corner to buy me something at once," she had said, as if they were discussing a spray of flowers. The "shop round the corner" was Tiffany's. "Green? Emeralds? Turquoises? Aquamarines? No, too pale for me, I think. How about sapphires . . ."

Now she swayed into the center of the room, a glittering figure, jewels at her neck, wrists, ears and breasts. Her Parisian black gloves covered arms that had been plunged in soapsuds until two years before, in the yard of a Texas farm.

"Now just listen, everyone!" she called out—and no one ignored Mrs. Millsom.

"This is the *Globe*'s review—this is *us*! *'The audience was not in one of its exacting and captious moods—they found the piece pretty, witty and inoffensive . . .'* " Mrs. Millsom glanced at Turner Hamilton, who raised his glass, looking slightly ill, and buried his face in its contents. "*Inoffensive*" had ruined the night for him. " *'Miss Anne Hardy played the character of Magda very cleverly and charmingly. She is a genuine comedian—many of her lines were spoken with a really remarkable justness of accent.'* Well there, isn't that nice!"

Hamilton was the only unhappy person in the room. Galliani drank steadily until the early hours, engaging anyone who passed in unintelligible conversation.

The room eddied with waves of Alys' expensive, hard-won connections: a Vanderbilt daughter, Mrs. H.M. Twombly; the art collector Louisine Havemeyer; Edith Gould, from the railroad family, who had been an actress herself before her marriage; and Princess Marie of Rumania, who was present simply because she had the suite next door at the Plaza, and had once invited her new English neighbor to tea.

The Princess had once told Alys that New York's "Four Hundred" was defined by the number of people who fitted into Mrs. William Astor's gold and white ballroom, at her Fifth Avenue mansion. Now aging, disapproving of the arrivistes, Mrs. Astor had lost her grip on society. But Alys could number at least twenty names that Mrs. Astor would have accepted at one of *her* parties.

She enjoyed the counting because it would mean success for her new salon. English society had the power to wound her, because she was attuned to its subtle rules, its degrees of acceptance. New York was more open and ostentatious, less important to her personally. But it was not necessarily more vulgar, as everyone assumed. Some of her American acquaintances were as kind and philanthropic as their English counterparts, conscious of their good fortune, generous to others. Some spent their newly made, tax-free money with blatant enjoyment, and thoroughly educated themselves into good tastes. A few were much more original, more to Alys' own liking, such as Mrs. Adelaide Hay, Ned's patron. He had been a good friend to give her this introduction, and judged well that they would enjoy each other.

Next day, it was to the Hay brownstone mansion on Fifth Avenue that Alys made her journey. She drove in one of the Plaza's own fleet of auto-cabs, for Mrs. Hay lived unfashionably high up the Avenue, on the corner of Seventy-fifth Street. An isolated edifice, her house resembled a Byzantine church or a medieval jail, depending on which angle was seen first. Mrs. Hay spent many hours a day at the bay window of her parlor, observing life below on the street. She had confessed to Alys a secret she shared with only a few trusted friends: she had a passion for photography and had installed a small studio with a large plate camera in her basement. Adelaide Hay would send out the butler to drag in the iceman, the chimney sweep, the knife grinder or the coalman—anyone she fancied—to be photographed on the spot.

Alys had looked forward to this visit for some time; conversations in her salon at the Plaza inhibited the old lady. Adelaide rose eagerly when Alys arrived: she stood like a curio amidst a jumble of treasures, French paintings, Italian marbles, Oriental lacquered screens and Chinese *famille rose* porcelain. The photograph albums were already laid out on a table, and tea beside them. In spite of her great wealth and the prestige of her name, Adelaide was lonely, and a visit from someone she liked was a treat.

"I pay my subjects, of course," Adelaide explained, as Alys turned the pages, but Alys did not think it was the power of the dollar that gave the boys' eyes such a direct gaze, and the older men their upright backs. Staring figures, imposing in stillness. The pitted, smudged faces, all variety of ethnic types, had an unnerving presence. It was a dignity that came from being singled out, thought worthy of attention for a few minutes. Vanity could be the worst of failings, but it was also a source of beauty in Adelaide's pictures.

"I read about your sister's play," she said. "Though I hope the two of you girls will give up all this nonsense and settle down, now you've proved you can do it. Terrible lives. You should be ashamed of yourselves."

"But what about my lovely gowns?" Alys laughed. Adelaide smiled in regret. Nearly sixty, a large woman with heavy features but lively eyes, she had worn dark, matronly clothing with pads and boning, until Alys persuaded her to wear new loose robes. Now she looked irredeemably plain but magnificent, and enjoyed the discovery.

Alys found it ironic that a woman who had outlived two husbands, one a gambler, the other a drunk, should still believe in matrimony. Her men had depleted her inheritance and left her with no more than a house empty of life filled with rare objects. Only this secret hobby had any sense of reality. Yet Adelaide still dismissed herself, and did the same with other women's efforts. Not quite: she had invited Alys to see her pictures.

"Do show me some more, Adelaide, and explain to me how you develop these darker ones . . ."

Soon they were deep in conversation about photography, and Alys liked her friend more and more. As she herself matured, she felt a growing interest and sympathy for women older than she was. She wondered constantly what it was like to be so old, with a life in the past. She had seen Adelaide frequently at public gatherings, in ballrooms, restaurants, theaters—uncommunicative, conscious that her mere presence was value enough. From now on, in such scenes, Alys would compare the dutiful society matron with this animated companion of an autumn afternoon, revealing her ageless qualities.

In the following week, Alys found her house: a small brownstone on a tree-lined street just west of Fifth Avenue, and near the garment district. Round the corner stood the new building of B. Altman, a store that had moved uptown to the block between East Thirty-fourth and Thirty-fifth streets. Gorhams, the jewelers, was also close by, as well as Tiffany's. The little house was big enough for workrooms and a salon, and Alys had it decorated in blue silk just like Berkeley Square. Carpenters built a replica of the little stage in the long reception room, so that she would be able to inaugurate her little "shows."

Weeks flew by in glorious haste. Alys looked for that humming, energized harmony in work that would keep all thoughts of Edward at bay. She would have to go home soon—perhaps she would return with Anne when *The Bohemian Girl* closed—but the longer she remained in New York, the happier she became.

Alys felt she was floating, like some kind of mad invention, an airplane, a dirigible perhaps, an engine of creativity driving her above the heads of everyone else. She felt her spirits soar, not least because she was beginning to make inordinate sums of money from clients like Adelaide Hay and Mrs. Millsom. They were willing to pay thousands of dollars for her dresses, where in London even her most extravagant customers never spent beyond hundreds.

She refused to work for Galliani again, in spite of the praise she earned for *The Bohemian Girl.* All New York was a stage! Everyone wanted glitter, diamonds, gold, silver, to display their wealth and status. She could not resist exaggerating her ideas, and the more lavish her gowns became, the more successful she was.

There were also personal admirers. Free of all restraints, emboldened by sudden wealth, Alys flirted carelessly with a growing entourage. Anne began to criticize her for her frivolity.

"*You* dally with everyone you meet, too!" Alys retorted. "First Hubert Kerrick, now Galliani and that poor besotted young man Turner Hamilton. You always take admirers, yet swear to me that your acting career is paramount. I'm simply following your own philosophy . . ."

They were driving to Sherry's restaurant for a Thanksgiving banquet hosted by Mrs. Adelaide Hay.

"But you've never toyed with people. Think of Ned—think of that dear old man, the Baron de Falbe! You never raised *his* hopes falsely."

Alys shrugged. "Everyone in New York thrives on hopes. It amuses me to create a few more. Besides, Adelaide Hay is determined to match-make. I have a southern gentleman, a relative of hers, tonight."

"Have you decided to come back with me next week?" Anne suddenly felt afraid for Alys. "I'm sure Laura misses you—and aren't you concerned about the salon?"

Alys laughed in a forced way. "I find it most amusing that you remind me of my obligations, when you've avoided being tied down quite assiduously!"

"Oh, Alys, don't be horrid—you always were the thoughtful one . . ."

"Well then, give me the credit for running my own affairs properly. Lilian writes to me from London every week. The salon workrooms are still working from the book of designs I left prepared for them. As for Laura—she's being spoilt to death by Dr. Hardy and Mrs. Bacon, and although I do miss her, of course, she knows this is important to me . . ."

"So you haven't chosen to come back with me."

"No, I confess I haven't." Anne recognized her sister's cool tones; it was hopeless to pursue the subject.

A few hours later, Alys knew fate had planned that she would not go back. After dinner, across the tables at Sherry's just cleared of flowers, silver, sweetmeats and candles, she saw Edward, deep in conversation. She did not love him at all any more: one glimpse of him proved that. Instead she remembered only the pure sexual hold he had exercised over her. She had no idea it could last so long. She had hoped it was all behind her, but desire was still alive, coursing through her like an injected drug.

There were three hundred people at Adelaide's party that night; perhaps Edward had not seen her. Alys knew she should leave at once, but a terrified curiosity to pit herself against his charm made her stay. Adelaide found her waiting by the water fountains for her escort, and looked questioningly at her.

"Well? How is my New Orleans nephew? Where is he?"

"Fetching my wrap. He's charming, Adelaide, but I happen to know that he's in love with Natalie Gould. He told me so before the soup."

"What frightful manners."

Alys merely laughed. Nearby, heads turned. She could not help laughing louder, and the jewels at her throat shimmered. Then she saw Edward, moving directly toward her. Within twenty paces of her, he stopped. Alys stared, gestured to Adelaide as if she had to leave, then ran from him into the crowd on the stairs. She tripped, twisting her foot sharply, and a hand caught her under the arm to steady her.

"Allow me." A tall, thin man stood next to her.

"Thank you."

"Mrs. Wickham, isn't it?" The man had a curiously precise English accent. He studied her face with interest.

"Yes. How do you—?"

"Sir Alec Colvin. I came to your sister's reception at the Plaza. With the Millsoms. After the play—clearly I made a deep impression on you!"

Alys could hardly breathe for the sudden crush leaving the banquet to dance. She found herself pressed against the stranger's side.

"I'm so sorry."

"Not at all. Step this way. Let the crowd pass." He steered her to one side of the landing, and she stood fanning herself, protected by his tall frame, while the animated throng filed past. In their midst was Edward, straining over the heads of others, tight-lipped, looking for someone.

"Ghastly crowd," Sir Alec said. "I don't dance, fortunately. Shall I find your partner for you? Aren't you with James Regius Hay? 'The New Orleans Nephew?' "

"Yes, I am!" She replied, with a laugh. "But I don't think I can walk very far—at the moment." Alys sank onto a sofa.

"Splendid. Then we shall sit here and amuse each other till he finds you. To lose a partner as beautiful as you are bespeaks a gross lack of talent in Regius Hay. I always suspected it."

Alys sat still, trying to pay attention, though it seemed to her that Sir Alec Colvin was talking nonsense as if it were his habit. He continued to chat, pointing out faces he knew as they passed on the stairs, and making quick observations that were affectionate but often cynical.

However, the more he talked, the more Alys relaxed in his company. He was light in every respect: light-blue eyes, pale-brown hair, light-skinned, and spoke in such soft, quick words that she had to incline her head to hear him. He was relaxed and intimate, as if he had known her for a very long time. Alys felt as if she were at the end of an interminable journey.

By the time Regius Hay came to claim her, Sir Alec Colvin had made her agree to go boating with him in Central Park the next day. Such an simple invitation could hardly be refused. Luckily, Alys' ankle showed no sign of permanent injury. She hurried away with her escort before Edward could retrace his steps and find her.

◆　◆　◆

A letter from Edward arrived next morning.

Dearest Alys,

I know why you turned from me. I have respected your wishes and made no attempt to contact you since you ended it in the summer. Dear friend, can we not be fond of each other? I did not come to New York to seek you out. I came for the cruise with Charlotte, Cecily and her husband, who has business interests here. I was certain you had already sailed back to London, as you told Layton Stayce that you would be absent for only six weeks. I was as surprised as you were to see you at Sherry's. May I call with Cecily to see your new venture, at five tomorrow? Everyone is talking about your success in New York. Well done.

Alys did not believe him for one moment, but intended to show him that there was no hope of regaining her.

She canceled her appointment with Sir Alec Colvin, because nervous anticipation made meeting anyone new unthinkable.

Cecily and Edward arrived on the hour, and she showed them round her silk-lined salon. Cecily talked endlessly of the glamour of New York society, closely questioning Alys about the friends she had made in the past few months. Alys told her all her news, grateful to Cecily for having introduced her to a Vanderbilt and to the Havemayers. It was also a relief to have a neutral topic of conversation.

"How will you run these two salons, Alys?" Cecily asked. "I do so admire your courage."

"I am considering hiring an assistant designer, to run New York under my name, and perhaps asking Lilian to move over from London to manage the new salon for me. She understands my approach very well after these past few years. Then I could travel back and forth, perhaps once or twice a year. It's just that the profits here are too tempting—even with extra staff I could treble my business. Why, Mrs. Gould's bill last week was four thousand dollars."

Alys mentioned these details quite deliberately. She was a woman in trade, in earnest, not obliged to keep to drawing-room notions that money was never to be discussed. And Edward was her business partner . . . if nothing else.

"Be careful about credit . . ." Edward warned her.

Alys smiled. "I learnt my lesson about that once. I've improved in my bookkeeping, I do assure you! Your advice has been invaluable." Alys tried to apologize, to show gratitude, hoping he would understand her real meaning.

"I should enjoy any enterprise that required me to undertake an Atlantic crossing regularly. Very bracing." Edward stood up, walking behind Alys' chair as he spoke. The closer he moved toward her, the more agitated she felt, particularly aware that Cecily was watching. Alys turned her head so that Cecily could not see her expression and for a moment pleaded silently with Edward. He remained close to her, as if to say, "We must be easy with each other. Do not draw back." Then he smiled, and she was reassured.

"This photograph of you, Alys, it intrigues me. Come and look, Cecily."

Cecily responded, placing herself between Alys and Edward, and all three stared intently, too intently, at the picture above the fireplace.

"A friend gave it to me," Alys said, at last. She did not intend to reveal Adelaide Hay's secret hobby.

Alys had posed for Adelaide one day in her studio, wearing a fur hat, a wide-caped coat, and holding her whippet on her lap. Black hair was pinned up from her small, pointed face: thin lips curved in a secretive smile. Dark eyes, as black and shining as ever, glanced with a little pride at the onlooker. Thin fingers held the whippet perhaps a little too consciously, a little too tight . . . and the subtle shades of monochrome coloring made her look unusually severe. All the same, Alys liked the portrait.

"It makes you look rather serious." Cecily commented.

"No, it doesn't." Edward disagreed. "It's very interesting, Alys. It captures your—elusive quality. You have the look of a woman of indomitable will and aspiration, who has never been subjugated. Which of course, is perfectly true, and why people admire you so . . . Isn't that correct, Cecily? Because dear Alys is so very much her own woman."

Cecily, tight-lipped, nodded agreement. Neither woman mistook his desire to be honest and his meaning was clear. Cecily was never to divulge what she knew; and Edward accepted the end of the affair.

"But are you sure you are wise to display it in your salon?" Edward went on, as if to confirm that he expected always to be on open, friendly terms with Alys. "I only want you to succeed, and I'm not certain that your clients will approve of that gleam in your eye, as you look down on them here . . ."

"Oh? Why not?" Alys could not help being curious.

"Because many women are not like you, and might find your expression disapproving, even intimidating. Don't you want them to be weak? To be tempted? Surely you do, in your salon, of all places!"

Cecily laughed. "How little you know of Alys." She loved dangerous conversation, her pretty, hard features enlivened for a moment. This was a confrontation she had anticipated with pleasure. "Women find her most encouraging and sympathetic!"

"I want them to choose to look beautiful out of pride, not out of vanity or weakness, Edward. There is a difference." Alys spoke from her heart, hoping he too understood.

Edward turned back to the photograph. "They will envy you, then—is that what you mean, Cecily? They all want to be like her?"

"Oh, my dear friend, the complexities of women's thinking are too much for me. It's enough that Alys likes her own portrait—and to tell you the truth, I am fascinated by the way it has caught her, too."

"Then we are agreed, Alys. We shall leave you with your mystery, and I won't ask what your thoughts were when the photograph was taken."

Edward took her hand, and kissed it. Alys hardly dared look up at him, but when she did, his eyes had a kindly light; her rejection had been accepted.

◆　◆　◆

Alys did not see Edward again, she had taken care to avoid social occasions to which he might have been invited. Two weeks later, she saw his name in a society column, on the listing for a Cunard liner leaving that week, and felt glad.

A time would come when they would meet easily as friends, but she was not yet ready to do so. She kept in touch with him in London over the following weeks, confining herself to news of her business. Lilian agreed to move to New York to manage the salon permanently, and Alys hired enough staff to cope with her current work.

Her successes in New York were more varied than in London, which gave her pleasure. One of the newspaper editors who came to her first gathering suggested she might like to write short articles on fashion. Alys went to the offices of the New York *Examiner* to deliver her first piece, dressed for conquest as usual. Fortunately the editor was amused by her erratic spelling and punctuation, to which Alice confessed with good humor rather than embarrassment. It would have been satisfying to send her articles to someone, but Alys could not think who would see the victory in the printed, ordered words. In the end she pasted them all into an album for Laura, together with postcard views of New York, and sent the present back to London with Anne, when she returned at the end of her run at Galliani's.

"Be sure to tell Laura that I miss her very much, but that she was a very clever girl to tell me to open the salon. You will tell her how much I love her, won't you?"

"Of course I will. Can't you picture Miss Dalton's face when she sees this album!"

"Yes I can. The silly woman doesn't know how much it costs me to be so 'famous.' Up all hours with a dictionary, I am."

"You *will* be home for Christmas, won't you?" Anne asked, as Alys saw her on board her ship.

"You've asked me that every day this past week. I've promised, haven't I?" Alys laughed.

"But it would have been fun to travel together . . ." Anne pouted, for she hated to be alone for very long.

"I'm sure you'll be given a lovely table, and make friends on the very first night. You know you always do."

"Thank you for the dresses."

"Don't be grateful—just make sure to tell everyone that I made them for you!" She kissed Anne good-bye and left her studying the first-class passenger list.

Traveling crosstown, Alys felt lonely, and regretted her decision to stay on. She had defended herself against low spirits by taking her notebook and sketch pad with her to the port. Now she told her cabdriver to head north up Park Avenue to the east side of Central Park, where there was a conservatory in which she liked to sit quietly and sketch shapes: flowers and leaves, useful for dress embroideries. The glasshouse was dense-aired and warm, a place for self-absorption. Concentrating on her patterns might restore her equilibrium.

It was difficult, at first, not to dwell on her mistakes and losses. Anne had made her wistful, reminding her of home. Alys thought of Laura, chatting with Mrs. Bacon, playing with the cat, sitting at her bedside in Berkeley Square, trying on her jewelry—these images made work seem unimportant. She would go home soon—but not yet! She did not feel strong enough to be back in all those places that would remind her of loving Edward.

Irresistibly, the scene of Edward's visit came to her mind. Alys allowed herself to think of that final meeting and how good he had been to abide by her decision without protest or any attempt at seduction. Possibly, in her absence, Lilian had told him about Florence. Perhaps he understood her own feelings of shame, and her desire to live better than she had previously.

Both Cecily and Edward had sung her praises all over New York while they were in the city, and sent many new customers to her salon. That was Edward's way, of course: he was never a man for extremes, and had found just the right way to behave decently.

Perhaps Edward had been just as overcome by his passion for her as she had been! Alys sat quite still, making an effort to concentrate on this new idea. Emotions frightened her—she avoided them until they were so powerful that they overwhelmed her or made her act with no thought for the consequences. Perhaps she had been very harsh with him: Edward might be an honorable man, surprised by desire, just as she had been.

Sympathy for Edward brought her peacefulness. She sat still, enjoying the silence and her solitude among the plants. The heat lulled her into a very private state of mind. Gradually the textures and colors of the tropics stimulated her imagination, and her fingers found their sureness as she began to sketch. She lost herself in work, in new ideas for sinuous dresses, bodices like calyxes unfolding, and skirts wound round with trailing flowers, encasing hidden limbs.

"I'm just closing, Madam." The conservatory attendant interrupted her, in apology.

"Is that the time? I must hurry!" Alys left, well-satisfied. When work absorbed her so that hours were lost, she felt she was winning her struggle for independence.

A good humor was important, because she had invited Anne's playwright, Turner Hamilton, to escort her to the Millsoms that evening, knowing that he too would be sad that Anne had gone home.

After supper he sat beside her in a quiet spot between a medieval altar screen and an Italian statue.

"Is Millsom taking lessons in art history?" he asked, disapproving of his surroundings. "Does he know what he's buying?"

Alys laughed. "A man who has a million dollars to spend on art is an expert already!"

Turner was shocked. "You can't mean that, Mrs. Wickham."

"Oh dear, of course I don't, Turner. You've lost all sense of humor today . . ."

"Oh gosh, I'm sorry. Would you like to dance?"

"No. Tell me about Chicago. Tell me about the West . . . I just remember blue-green grass . . . Pike's Peak, the huge mountain above us . . . and a house surrounded by cottonwood trees. My father worked on the 'Baby Road'—do you know? The small-gauge railway; I've forgotten its real name now . . ."

"The Denver and Rio Grande."

"Yes, that's it, a lovely name, I think." Turner grew attentive, keen to improve Alys' scant knowledge of the West, and as he did so, she was able to create a frame for those bright images she had cherished since childhood. Turner forgot all about Anne, or perhaps he fancied that by pleasing Alys he remained linked to her, even if tenuously. This thought occurred to Alys without jealousy. Everything the young man told her made her feel closer to her first and best home, wooed by memories into a stronger sense of her identity.

When Sir Alec Colvin stood beside her, she looked up at him with an enchanted face.

"Oh, I'm so pleased to see you again! Have you forgiven me for breaking our appointment? Come and sit down, I'm hearing all about the real America . . ." Without thinking, Alys took his hand, looking back at Turner again but holding Alec captive as he sat beside her.

Alec saw that she had no idea what she was doing; she was so involved in Turner's stories that she behaved unthinkingly. He sat back, feeling the softness of her skin, the momentary tightening of her fingers as Turner's tale of the West reached a moment of drama. Her taking his hand like that was a gesture of natural affection, raising his hopes unexpectedly. Alec prayed that she would not come to her social senses too soon, and realize that she was not flirting with him. She would be embarrassed by the contact.

She was: Alys became acutely conscious of the hand she held, the proximity of this virtual stranger. She could not move, for she sensed Alec smiling at her, and to change her position would reveal too much awareness of him. Turner had no notion of her confusion, for he was still concentrating on history. But after a long discourse on the plains of Montana, the big "die-up" of the cattle in the mid-eighties, he ran out of themes to amuse her.

"Gosh, Mrs. Wickham, I hope that wasn't boring," he concluded, falling into a depression again.

"Not at all. You couldn't imagine how I value what you've told me. Look, they're dancing again!" Alys said, rather obviously.

"My turn, Hamilton? With your permission?" Alec stood up, leading Alys to the floor without releasing her for a second.

"But you don't dance," she said, surprised.

"Just turn round twice and then I'll be able to sit down with you alone."

"And will you tell me stories too?" she said, laughing, yet Turner's reminiscences had made her soft-hearted, and she rather hoped he would.

"I think I could tell you stories for the rest of my life, if you always looked at me as you do now," he replied. Alys had no doubt he spoke the truth. It was the warmth of her mood that allowed him to say it.

"Have you heard the one about Mrs. Millsom's new car?" he continued, to cover his genuine emotion. "She drove it into a store window on Madison, shouting 'Whoa!' " Alys laughed again, but then he trod on her foot and tore the hem of her dress.

"I'm sorry—how fortunate you're a dressmaker," he said, recovering quickly. "I imagine this is not the calamity for you that others would make of it."

"Well, thank goodness they do, or I'd have no profits!" she retaliated, making him smile.

Alys was amused by his nerve, to make a joke at her expense when he had just made a complete fool of himself. She kilted up the torn skirt in her hand, took his arm and spent the rest of the evening listening to the misdeeds of New York. Alys was in a very good mood, free from guilty thoughts or any sense of threat, drawing confidence from the well-being she had experienced in the afternoon. Her happiness took on a new quality in this man's company: she felt lighthearted, and that in turn had a very positive effect on her wit.

The following day a small box was delivered for her at the Plaza. Inside was a flounce of antique Chantilly blonde lace, and a note of sincere apology from Alec for his awkwardness. But by that time Alys had a notion of how adroit he really was.

CHAPTER 16

1 9 1 2

Alys sat dismally on the edge of her bed, watching her maid sort out her trunks. A familiar scene: only this time she was in London, not New York, and not concerned with her business. For two years she had lived a high life, fulfilling all her dreams of money and independence. There had been worries and setbacks, of course—but no one had interfered with her single-mindedness. Until this: Miss Dalton, the governess, had sent a cable to New York forcing Alys to book passage home the moment she read it. Laura had absconded—to live with William Wickham.

With every dress unfolded, her sadness increased. Each one reminded her of another coup—the black jet she had worn for someone's birthday dinner at Sherry's; the striped silk for a visit to the offices of the New York *Examiner;* the blue chiffon she had worn for tea with Mrs. Adelaide Hay on the day she had ordered sixteen dresses. Hat boxes, fan cases, piles of monogrammed linen bags for Yantourney's expensive shoes . . . it all resembled a general's accouterments laid out on display after victory in battle. All that flitting to and fro across the Atlantic, making a name and a fortune. For what? So that she could return home to these empty rooms, dim without her daughter's shining face.

A letter slipped off the bed—Miss Dalton's final missive, which Alys could not bring herself to read. At least orders had been followed and Miss Dalton had already removed herself by the time Alys arrived home. But Alys suspected the letter contained some bitter words about her performance as a mother, and she did not need anyone else's criticism to add to her own sense of failure.

"I'll do that, Millie. You can leave the rest till morning. Just ask Mrs. Booth to send up some tea, will you? Good-night."

"Are you sure you won't want supper as well, M'am?"

"For goodness' sake, don't fuss. Just tea. That will do."

Alys wanted to be kinder, but anger and loss filled her chest with such a tight pain that she could not speak easily. She fiddled with her boxes until the girl had left the room, then she began to sense a new emotion breaking through her unhappiness. Like a fire-flame it spurted, a current of energy running through her so that she shuddered. Jealousy of William—or was it utter hatred? What right had he to steal away her child?

Miss Dalton had sent a detailed explanation, which Alys received on board the liner bringing her back to England. William had married a wealthy widow and was living in suburban content in Richmond. He had been introduced to Laura quite by chance; she had visited him a few times, until suddenly, two weeks ago, she had refused to return to Berkeley Square, and William had not made her go. Miss Dalton had been powerless to do more than write to inform Alys.

Alys supposed William had suddenly decided he wanted a child to complete his connubial bliss—it was too late to father his own—and now he had stolen hers. He had made no effort to contact her at all for fifteen years. Alys' name had appeared frequently in newspapers during that period; so he must have been aware of her existence—since Laura had been six years old, at least.

That was when she had moved to Berkeley Square. Alys pondered on the last few years, opening a small box on her lap. The two pleasures of her life—Laura and the salon—were like the fan she opened now: spangled lace on firm wooden struts: glamour and security, the one pointless without the other.

She dropped the fan quickly, and tore open Miss Dalton's final, bitter note. Snatches of sentences came at her. "Busy . . . constantly preoccupied . . . I feel it is only my duty to convey Laura's feelings of loneliness . . . a mother who is so ambitious . . . demanding . . ." She crumpled the letter up and threw it in the fire, shaking with anger. She would never forgive the woman for allowing Laura to be taken from her.

It was difficult for Alys to see the world as others did. Her own vision of life was now so strong and directed that sometimes she lacked truly compassionate understanding. Her imagination expressed itself in rapid bursts of discovery—in the inspiration for a design, in the sudden glimpse of another woman's potential beauty. Now it turned to Laura. Alone in her room, surrounded by her finery, Alys had a sudden realization of herself as a mother.

Where she had wanted to be close and confiding, she had been overbearing. Instead of setting an example by her independence, she had only undermined Laura's confidence. Most damning of all the truths in the letter was that she had *not* struggled so hard "for Laura's sake." Alys knew she had deceived herself. Right from the start, long before the added imperative of finishing with Edward, she wanted conspicuous success entirely for *herself*. Personal unhappiness was the spur, not the cause, of her ambition. Even now the idea of her self-imposed goals made her shamefaced. It was half exciting, half deplorable to want so much success and so much praise. Laura had only been the justification of her aims. The shock of this perception made Alys feel sick with herself. Laura's loneliness had never entered her thoughts—she had been too busy pursuing her own ends to let any inconvenient doubts interfere with her plans. Alys shivered again, and lay down on her bed, exhausted by the surges of emotion that ran through her. She fell asleep at once.

◆ ◆ ◆

Alys heard a bell, and someone talking. It was morning: barely awake, she recognized the voice as William's. She hurried out of her room and stood on the curve of the stairs. William was leaving a card with Mrs. Booth. He saw her, and was obviously deeply embarrassed by the intimacy of her clothing. She pulled her crumpled dressing gown closer to her body and moved down a few steps.

"What are you doing here? I can't talk to you, I'm too upset."

She could hardly see William's face because he stood against the light in the hallway and her eyes were blurred with sleep and the soreness of crying. His outline looked familiar, but a little more stooped.

"Forgive the sudden intrusion. I wanted to explain, talk to you quietly. Avoid a—"

"You still hate the thought of 'scenes.' Poor William. Don't worry. By tomorrow I'll be very calm. Is your wife agreeable to my visiting then? I don't have to see Laura, if you don't wish it." She spoke barely above a whisper, and appeared to him quite strained and ill. William felt less defiance and more pity toward her.

"Well, I do think it might be better if you didn't, at least tomorrow. We should discuss the matter first, I'm sure you agree. I'll send my car for you. I hope you'll feel better; I realize this is your first day at home." William shifted nervously, as if he wanted to say more. The very movement made him hateful to Alys, just like so many times before. She dismissed him before he spoke again.

"Till tomorrow. Good-bye, then."

William had to go, all his prepared speech undelivered. Women simply could not be spoken to when they were ill, he knew, but it was typical of Alys to get her own way even when she was in distress.

Alys went to her room and lay back on her bed. Richmond: Laura was there at this very moment. She conjured up another vision to add to her misery: Laura walking up the hill to a white-walled house. Perhaps she had spent the morning peering over the bridge into the river's flow, or discreetly watching young scullers on the banks . . . Laura, knocking at the door of that white house and being received with a welcoming smile by William's new wife, Madeleine. Or worse,

William, attending to her with conscious paternal charm, taking her rowing, or for a Sunday walk at Marble Hill. A sincere admirer, an ageless escort, a man of the world, a discovered father. All masculine delights in one . . . for a daughter.

Alys made herself sit up before her thoughts drove her mad. It was fortunate that her physical feelings for William were so close to disgust that the idea of seeing him again, remarried too, did not upset her. A wife: an old, mediocre woman who had wheedled her way into Laura's affection! It was also, Alys considered, an unforgivable disloyalty in Laura to do what she had done.

Even as she accused her daughter, Alys knew she was being unfair. The truth was, she had done exactly as she pleased, without thought for anyone else but herself. On the rare occasions in the past few years that she had spent time with Laura, the child had appeared to be perfectly happy—but now Alys forced herself to think of little hints she had ignored. Whenever Alys traveled, Laura went back to St. John's Wood. Dr. Hardy was aging, becoming a little frail and definitely more eccentric. Mrs. Bacon was almost bedridden and should have gone off to her family ages ago. She only stayed on at Lime Road because of Laura. The girl spent much of her time sitting with her dear old friends, reading books to them, winding wool for the housekeeper, or just stroking the cat and being peaceful. It sounded cosy, but now Alys could see that it must have palled.

No wonder rediscovering her father had excited Laura. Someone who would make a fuss of her—make her feel valued first above everything else, and stop her from missing Alys.

"What about me?" Alys wanted to cry out. She missed Laura with all her heart, thought of her constantly, and struggled against loneliness of another kind, too. Tears of self-pity fell on her cheeks, and the band of pain tightened round her chest. Constant work had been the only way to enjoy her own company. Alys realized that she had driven her own softness so far inside herself that it hardly existed.

Someone *had* offered to care for her in New York. Sir Alec Colvin was her close companion, but she only allowed him to amuse her, and would not listen if he tried to make serious declarations to her. When Alys received the cable about Laura's defection, she had packed her trunks and fled from New York at once, rejecting all his offers of help.

Now she was back in these familiar, deadening English circles, both angry and frightened. Nothing truly mattered except loving Laura, and she had neglected to do it, out of self-interest and the misplaced effort of being invulnerable. Alys willed herself to go to sleep; oblivion was the only way to avoid the awful truth of her thoughts and make tomorrow come quicker.

She woke early in the morning and fussed with her toilette. William's car was coming for her at noon. She was ready long before it arrived and stepped outside, impatient to get to the house. A bright sun made her head thud, and as the car drew near its destination, her heart and stomach began to lurch. Alys wished she had laced her corset more tightly for moral rather than physical support. She had dressed in a grayish-white suit, trying to look subdued. Now she regretted her choice—it only heightened her pallor and was a little too chic, which was not the appearance she had intended.

She walked up the brick pathway to the front door, which was opened by a maid before her hand reached the bell. The second Mrs. Wickham came hurrying forward from the garden, sunlight streaming round her. Wearing an expensive but old-fashioned dress, she exuded a comfortable, upholstered femininity. Madeleine Wickham looked like a woman of character with a warm heart.

"I'm sorry, Alys—may I call you that?" Madeleine spoke protectively as a favorite aunt might choose to. "This must be so difficult for you. If there's anything I can do to help you understand—"

"Help me?" Alys replied quickly. "It's obviously Laura who needs help."

"Laura's very well," Madeleine said in an even tone. "Blooming. She's out riding with the groom. Come in, please—shall we take your hat?"

A cloud of white chiffon was passed formally to the maid. Even Madeleine could not hide her surprise at the old, drawn appearance of Alys' small face.

Alys walked into the drawing room and looked out across the felty lawn, Madeleine's ordered garden. Treetops swayed above its trellised walls. Richmond Hill suited Madeleine. It was a well-kept, gracious home.

"May I ask where William is?" said Alys. "Will he join in this discussion of Laura's future?" She tried unsuccessfully to avoid a rush of sarcasm in her voice, as if William could not decide on anything beyond his own selfish needs.

"It must be very difficult for you to believe in the sincerity of William's affection for his daughter. He understands that—as I do. But you can't in all honesty deny him the chance to make amends."

"Make amends." Alys sounded dangerously flat. William heard her as he came in and saw her standing at the window with her back turned. She still held her shoulders tense and square, he noticed. Her two words propelled him back to another sunlit house, many years ago. Alys had sworn that he would never be able to make amends for what he had done. William blinked slowly, fixing his eyes for a moment on the face of the other woman who had succeeded in giving him love. Then he called out, "Alys" firmly, and waited for her to see him.

She wheeled round like a clockwork doll, and stood still as if the mechanism had stuck. But time had not: William thought she was much more beautiful in her maturity than she had been as a girl. Even more vital, arresting and proud.

Alys too was surprised that William looked different; it took her an instant to see how ridiculous such surprise was—after all, fifteen years had passed. He was still slim, but nearly gray-haired, which startled her, as he was only forty. William did not look weak and mothered, as she had expected, but kindly. Kindly! Alys was out of her depth. There was something in the atmosphere between him and Madeleine, a conniv-ance, an understanding, that she sought out with an animal curiosity.

"This is all very strange," he murmured. "Very hard. Please believe me when I say I had no intention of weakening the bond between you and your daughter. Laura's decision to come here dismayed us as much as it alarms you. But we'll find a solution. I only want the best for Laura—for you too, of course."

Alys stared at the wallpaper over his shoulder. Wreaths of laurel, curled round sprays of pimpernel. Pink and green, but not the green of grass—harsh, dyed coloring.

"How kind of you, William!"

William and Madeleine glanced at each other again. Alys' mechanical responses unnerved him, but Madeleine was cooler.

"I think we should have lunch," she said. They walked silently into the dining room, heavy with mahogany furniture and silver bowls of flowers. Mingling odors of sweet peas and beeswax polish made Alys feel slightly nauseated. The shiny opulence of the table was oppressive, but gradually the quiet efficiency of Madeleine's household began to placate Alys. It was strange how the simple actions of sitting down and being served food made it impossible to stay angry, but it was so. Madeleine wore down opposition with an unforced kindness, talking only about Laura's summer activities as the meal continued.

It worried Alys that she liked the woman. Madeleine had a strong, bony face, with a good profile and an old-fashioned, straight-backed dignity. Her thick hair was coiled up and needed many tortoiseshell pins to hold it in place. This abundance pleased Alys in spite of herself. Even the lunch had an Englishness about it that combined delicious tastes with simplicity: clear soup, cold salmon, and Dresden pudding, all cream and coconut. Piles of fresh strawberries from the garden, spiked with mint and served on ice, bled onto Alys' fingers.

"I didn't seek her out," William was explaining. "It was perfectly simple, strange that it had not happened sooner. Lady Evelyn has always kept her word to you not to discuss Laura with me. I knew, of course, that she visited the child unofficially. But recently, with your longer absences, Lady Evelyn has taken to giving Laura outings. I met them by accident in Hyde Park."

Alys could not blame her old friend. Lady Evelyn had tried to divide her loyalties between William and Alys as best she could, and only unwittingly caused this unwelcome relationship. Alys noted the criticism that she had failed to provide enough amusement for Laura while gadding about herself. It was not entirely the truth.

"There was no plot to take Laura away from you," William went on, in a most equable tone. "It was tempting, I admit, but quite wrong. I see now that I treated you very badly, and I've no wish to compound the error." He almost laughed! Warmly! Alys' anger flared up again.

"Besides," he went on, not noticing her reaction, "I value my new life far too much to cause more disruption." He gave Madeleine a benevolent look. "This is all a temporary state of mind—Laura's intoxication. She thinks she has a family at last! She's discovered me, she's devoted to Evelyn, and of course she adores Madeleine, too . . ."

"It's all so easy!" Alys cried out, words tumbling, accusations, insults, pleas, curses, in no order in her head. "Easy to say, but quite wrong! You acted intemperately when you revealed who you were to my daughter without consulting me. I'm sure Lady Evelyn did not introduce you: 'Darling Laura, this is you father!' Did she? Did she? *You* did it, didn't you, because you couldn't resist the chance to take something precious and innocent—just like the last time!"

Alys' eyes were wide and shining. Anger made her judge both William and Madeleine with deadly accuracy. She suddenly saw that they were both very little people, little, mediocre, sentimental people, in spite of their position in the world. Alys smelt complacency and dullness in the air as powerfully as she would react to beauty, power or exceptional talent in other settings. Madeleine made an art of it; William was spoilt, idle and wallowed in it; and it had attracted Laura. No wonder her own marriage to William had been such a total failure, no wonder it took someone as ordinary as Madeleine to make William happy. Alys' recognition of their limited natures made her feel sure she would win Laura back, though it might take some time.

Her anxiety disappeared as quickly as it had possessed her. All agitation drained from her body.

William had not replied to her accusation. Her cold words had the same numbing effect on him as they had had in the past.

Making use of this advantage, Alys pretended to be sorry for her outburst.

"This is no good. I think I should leave things as they are. May I call back, next Sunday, perhaps to see Laura when I've had time to reflect? I think, perhaps, nothing too abrupt . . ." she tried to sound amenable.

"An excellent idea, nothing too sudden, I agree with that." William was relieved.

"But William, if I were to consent, to say that she could stay with you a little longer, you must for your part make it clear to Laura that her rightful place, in fact her legal place, is with me."

"Of course. I give you my word." His face grew dull, his expression lifeless.

Then Madeleine saw that William's intention, half confessed, half hidden even from himself, had been scented out. She had not realized that he wanted to take Laura from Alys permanently. She had a new understanding of why these two people still hated each other.

"Of course we shall make it clear," she agreed with William, but added her own threat. "But I do think it right that Laura should know she can come here whenever she wants, and that Richmond is to be considered—a special place for her, for ever."

This was hard for Alys. She wanted to cut William out of Laura's life, as he had once cut her. But she could not make that decision for Laura.

"I shall let her decide that for herself." She did not pity William in his anxiety. Let him suffer the fear that she might persuade Laura never to come back. There were facts she could use if she wanted to . . .

When she took her leave, the image of that still handsome, gray-haired man, bending with solicitude to listen to Madeleine, remained with her. She regretted her vindictiveness. Alys did not like herself as she traveled back to London.

The appointed day arrived. Sunday morning was beautiful, far removed from the stunning heat of New York, where even the thinnest cotton lawn seemed to weigh on the body. Alys loved London sunlight; it had a liquid quality that reminded her of the sparkle in water. There was always a breeze that rippled the trees of the city parks even on the hottest day. She chose a linen suit for her visit to the country.

"Damnit," she decided suddenly, "that's not how Laura thinks of me." Out came the plumes, and a guipure-sleeved white lace dress. Even Samson, her whippet, had his collar changed, and on a whim Alys also took his newly acquired mate, Delilah. "I mightn't have a horse, but you two are a match for anyone's affections." Alys twittered encouragement as much for herself as for the dogs, who scrambled into the motor, Delilah tucked into a corner of her traveling rug for comfort.

Laura look more childlike than Alys had anticipated. In place of a defiant young lady, Alys saw a pink-cheeked fifteen-year-old in a high-necked cotton dress. It was upsetting to see Laura wearing something unfamiliar, something that she not chosen for her. William and Madeleine had absented themselves. Perhaps that was why Laura was more emotional than Alys expected: she flung her arms round her mother's neck, exclaimed with pleasure at her beautiful clothes, and fingered the lace sleeves with that infantile sensuality Alys remembered so well.

"Dear child! How I've missed you! You've given me such a terrible shock!"

"Mama—please! I'll try to explain—won't you come into the garden, and talk to me? Please don't be cross with me—you haven't come to take me away, have you? I couldn't bear it . . . come on, come on, you naughty creatures, this way!"

Laura ran off with the dogs to the garden, calling to her mother to follow round the pathway. Bees hummed in the lavender, night-scented stocks fell aside from her skirts as she moved uncertainly round to the back of the house. It was painful for Alys to ask for love; to beg for her daughter's company was deeply humiliating. She was hurt that Laura feared being forced to leave—she would never do that—how cruel! Though she wanted to . . .

She wanted to talk about New York, to tell Laura about her latest exploits, but she was afraid to mention it in case Laura was not interested. She could not think of anything else to say. Laura took command, chattering about the river, the horses, the groom, Peters, and his store of equestrian knowledge—currying and other vital matters. It took Alys back to her days at Upton Park. She started to worry. Could Laura really be happy with all those empty, boring activities that she had herself abandoned in sheer frustration all those years ago? How ironic. She laughed unexpectedly.

"What's the matter, Mama, did I say something odd?" Laura was instantly nervous that she was being mocked.

"Oh, nothing you said, my dear. I'm just rather amazed to find you so devoted to this country kind of life . . ."

"Oh, but I simply love the river—and I'm learning to ride in Richmond Park."

"*I* was just remembering a time at Upton Park when I went out riding with Daisy, trotting madly behind her, trying to keep up, and I fell in a ditch below the orchard. The groom had not checked the saddle girth. You hadn't forgotten that I used to ride too, had you? The ditch was full of soft old apples. I don't think I ever told you much about those days. I know I told you about Cork, but not so much about Rutland."

"Do you mean where you lived before I was born, when you were with Papa?"

The word spoken: Laura had mentioned her father. There would be no return ever to the days before William had made himself known. Now that man would have to be a character in the stories Alys and Laura shared. It was a bitter moment for Alys, one in which she hated Laura for causing her mortification. But it passed, and she made an effort to recall some happy times in those brief years she had spent with William. Just for Laura. At least her horse had been a good mount. She could talk about that.

"He was called White Spot I remember—terribly boring name, but there you are. After you were born, I rode him all the time—and people were shocked that I did. In Cork, the countrywomen simply had to work, babies or no, and I knew it did them no harm. But it wasn't thought suitable in Rutland— *un peu paysan.*"

In spite of her good intentions, Alys could not help negative memories rising as she spoke. She persisted, however, and made Laura laugh delightedly at her stories about life at Upton Park. Laura was thrilled by her mother's confidences. She always loved Alys' stories and now they were about her own beginning.

Delilah shot past them, with an untypical agitated bark. "What's that?" exclaimed Alys.

"Rabbits!" Laura giggled. "There's hundreds of them down the hill. Papa gets cross, because they're so bad for the walls."

Let the little beasts pull down the entire foundations! Alys prayed hard, watching the dogs tearing through the flowerbeds and throwing up earth, mechanical diggers. It was an irresistible thought.

"Mama, you're wicked," Laura said, smiling because her mother's hopes were so evident.

"I don't know what you mean," Alys replied in a grand manner, but she leaned forward and pulled out Laura's satin bow, so that it fell down over her face. Then she turned away, jumping up and clapping her hands for the dogs to stop.

"Come here, you bad things. Stop it at once!"

She wondered if Laura would be angry with her for being mischievous and showing her dislike. Alys could not bear to look back. She walked toward the dogs, pretending to be cross. Suddenly she felt Laura's arms reach round her waist from behind.

"I love you, Mama! I do, I do!"

"Then what is all this?" Alys turned on her. "How could you, Laura? How could you desert me? After all I've—"

"There you are! You'll never understand. It's always you, you, how hard it is for *you*! I don't want it to be hard! Why can't we be ordinary, nice and normal, like it is for other people!"

"Normal? Are you being disrespectful, girl?"

"Oh no, I didn't mean that. Mama, you're very special, of course, and I love you so—but—oh, I can't explain, I just wish, I just wish . . ." Laura clasped her mother's hands, but could not continue. She was short of breath and shaky. Alys was alarmed by these sudden signs of hysteria.

"Laura, do try to calm down. What on earth to do you mean— normal?"

"Like it is for other girls. They go to school, they have brothers or sisters, they have dogs, cats and, oh . . ."

"But Laura, we agreed you wouldn't go away to school because we'd miss each other. Don't you remember?"

"But I didn't know then how much fun it was for other families. I'm so alone, Mama, when you're not there. And I love company so . . . Oh!"

Alys suspected Madeleine had stirred up all this talk of "other girls," and hated her.

She hugged Laura, who cried pent-up tears for her empty nursery days. The child had always been so composed, reserved even. Alys was angry at her own selfishness, her stupidity. At Carrigrohane, she had had Anne. They had wandered through upstairs corridors, whispering, chattering, living in each other's imaginations all day long. Alys held Laura closer. The one aim of her life was that her daughter should never feel deprived of motherly love as she herself had been. She was sure that she had loved Laura devotedly, but in her effort to give the child a more comfortable existence, with none of the humiliating deprivations she had known, she had been too determined and self-involved. She had given love, a defiant, rather desperate sort of love, but she had come very near to depriving Laura of all childish fun.

"We don't have a Sunday lunch at home," Laura wept, "and we've never had a midnight feast."

Laura defeated Alys completely. She sank down to the ground, cradling Laura until the tears stopped.

"No," she said at last, "no, we didn't have a feast. But in fairness, Laura, we used to go to Dr. Hardy's, and there was nothing you liked better than Mrs. Bacon's funny oaty puddings—remember how you liked to stir the honey in and make a wish? Sunday in St. John's Wood was like Christmas all over again. We used to say."

Alys was near tears herself, trying to say comforting things. She cuddled Laura even closer. "I do understand, I understand more than you think, and we'll be friends now, won't we? I won't ask you to come away just yet. You enjoy your summer here, and we'll both have time to think. It will be better now, dearest, I promise. Give me a kiss."

She smoothed Laura's forehead, and stroked her hot cheeks.

"Do let's stop those naughty dogs. They really are going too far."

"I'll call Peters. He'll know what to do. Peters! Peters!" Laura ran away to the house, glad to be diverted from her muddled feelings.

Peters came out, with a tactful nod in Alys' direction, and offered aniseed balls to the dogs. Samson and Delilah fell on his hands, all murderous thoughts of rabbits forgotten. The whippets flopped on their bellies, and Laura patted their clammy backs, scolding them for their bad tricks. Alys bent forward and carefully tied up her daughter's satin ribbon.

◆　◆　◆

The bright transparent days of August passed, and the full warmth of September settled in the air. Alys grew accustomed to her new ways.

Each day she woke early, awareness of Laura's absence returning with the light. The only way not to miss her was to immerse herself in work. Her little refuge at the top of Berkeley Square became a virtual cell, where she locked herself away from company and tried to find some release from her worries. There were hundreds of things to do. Besides supervising an autumn collection, there were individual commissions for the London Courts, and various new models she wanted to ship to New York.

All Alys had to do was sketch a whole series of designs to be submitted to her clients by the showroom *directrices,* Mary and Rose. Nowadays she left the construction of them entirely to the heads of the workrooms. Every now and then, Alys took a tour of her establishment, to make sure that systems were in good order, and to put in an appearance for her most demanding customers. Occasionally, she would entertain a client for a private session, in which she gave advice on the general style and type of costume best suited to the individual. (She charged fifty pounds for this, as much as she did for a gown, but whenever she came back to London, there was always a waiting list.)

Meanwhile, in New York, her assistant designer took over some of the creative work, taking instructions from Lilian, who as the new *directrice* had succeeded just as well with the American ladies as she had with the London customers. This young man supplemented her ideas with his own originals, sometimes taking inspiration from the imports Alys sent over, and producing different models (for American fashions were always required to be more elaborate and showy than London clothes). In this way Alys' "handwriting" was present in all the gowns sold from both her salons.

One of her tasks in London was to finalize her export list. All shipments from Europe to America were taxed. Every piece in every consignment had to be itemized and valued, and Alys liked to do this herself, as she had the best sense of what they were worth. It was a tedious, undemanding task that suited her mood.

One day she found a large package waiting for her, from Lilian in New York. Her *directrice* did her best to justify Alys' confidence in her, sending constant reports and magazines, carefully annotated, like these. Alys was pleased to have a diversion, idly turning the pages of *The Delineator,* which gave all the latest ideas from Europe and was much used by American dressmakers. She liked to see how many of her own innovations were featured in its pages—though she would not have admitted to anyone that she was keen to see how she stood up to competition from rivals. Alys kept up a front of total indifference to other people's work.

The package also contained recent copies of *Vogue* magazine, covered with Lilian's comments. Its unusual mixture of society gossip, high fashion notes and class-conscious features fascinated Alys. Quite accurately, she judged, the magazine aimed at a prosperous new group of middle-class women who needed to be told how to dress and behave, because they had no society background. Their husbands wanted them to show off how much money they were making, but the women wanted to do it with taste. Alys flipped through the magazine, lost in her world of fashion.

She came upon a photograph that gave her an unpleasant shock. Under the title, "Society by the Sea," picturing many of her American acquaintances besporting themselves at Newport, Bar Harbor and Southampton, Alys spotted Sir Alec Colvin. She knew he was to be a summer guest at the home of Mrs. Millsom, and would have visited the house herself if she had been able to stay on. She felt quite homesick for her other life, seeing it displayed so glamorously.

Tall, thin, immaculate in white flannels and a striped blazer, Alec was leaning too attentively over the shoulder of a young blonde at the quayside in Aiken. Alys slapped the magazine shut and picked up another copy. There he was again. On a double-page spread, featuring the latest society wedding, "Stillman-Jay" Alec could be seen raising his glass with a winning smile to a Brazilian heiress, newly arrived in New York: María-Elena Monteira de Barros. Alys was upset, but refused to acknowledge the reason. They had been good friends, nothing more: he was entitled to make himself pleasant to other women, as she had always refused to allow him to become anything more than a casual friend ever since their first meeting. But Alec had never given up hope—and now she wondered if her long absence from New York had finally persuaded him she never would be closer. She threw the magazines in a heap and turned back to her desk. She would be more disciplined about her time, she decided; but she could not help thinking that Alec had always made days seem pleasurably long, and that life was for happiness, not just scoring victories.

Laura was quick to notice the change in her mother's atmosphere when she visited Richmond that weekend.

"Are you feeling quite well, Mama? You look tired," she commented, slipping her hand into Alys' as they set off. They were to go out for lunch, perhaps take a boat trip.

"I'm perfectly well," replied Alys. "It's just a little colder than I expected. We should take the rugs from the car when we get to the river."

Laura ran ahead to tell the chauffeur. She looked forward to these days, more keenly as the weeks lengthened into months. It was almost the end of September, and she was back at her lessons. It was such a relief that Mama had agreed she could stay in Richmond and go to a small school there for a while.

"Come on, Mama!" Laura was sure her mother was worrying about something. Her moods were all-encompassing. They sat together in the car. "Are you still happy about me being here a little longer, Mama? You look so sad today."

"Of course I am, sweetheart—happy about it, I mean. It's what you want; I know it will please you."

"I know it will, Mama, though I do miss you too."

Alys patted Laura's cheek and they held hands contentedly under the fur wrap. On these Sunday outings, Alys had come to know her daughter better than ever before. Laura was a quiet but endearing companion—often they did not speak very much, just walked together or sat in the garden. Laura's hysterical outburst seemed an isolated moment in the past, though it had shaken Alys badly. She had toyed with the idea of sending Laura to a finishing school in Paris, but saw that it would have been useless. It might have been a way to force a separation between Laura, Madeleine and William, but the girl would have been miserable—quite possibly it would have made her even more nervous. She was a shy, gentle person, with no wish to be daring or sophisticated, and Alys had to respect her qualities. Laura's obvious improvement in health and the new closeness between them confirmed that she had been right to give up her own wishes. But Alys felt it was all such a slow process toward reconciliation.

Alys wanted to win back Laura's happiness and love, not merely her physical presence. She was shocked by the girl's defiance, but it did not occur to her to take a stern line, as many parents would. Isolated from more conventional families, she would never have insisted on her legal rights and simply ordered Laura to return. Besides, it was convenient—she had to admit it. Much as she adored her daughter, she did not have time to spend with her every day. As Laura grew up and became a young woman, this was going to present a problem. It worried Alys, but she did not know what to do. The threat of Madeleine replacing her compelled Alys to find a solution.

It was all so difficult: even the comfortable privacy of her workroom had been invaded by that glossy pile of magazines and the smiling faces of her friends hidden in the pages. She longed to accept one of the many invitations she received to house parties in the country, to go back to Cecily's or to the Lyttleton's, but felt that Laura came first on weekends.

The car left Hampton Court, and they had lunch in a small hotel before taking a boat down the river. The journey was cold but pleasant, and Alys was grateful that Laura seemed brighter than ever, chatting about her new school as if she understood that Alys could not entertain her much. On the way home, she had a request to make.

"Do you think, Mama, next Sunday I could bring a new friend from school, Elizabeth Smith, with us?'

"Don't you like going out, just the two of us?"

"Of course I do, but you've never met her, and I talk about her all the time."

"That's true." Alys had taken a dislike to the idea of Elizabeth Smith, but made every effort not to let Laura know it.

"Better still, perhaps you'd like to bring her up to town on the train—no, I'll send the car—and you could come to Hanover Square, and then have tea with me."

Laura did not reply. She did not want to go—Elizabeth would be thrilled, and somehow Laura did not want her to be so impressed.

"On second thought, Laura, perhaps it's not such a good idea. You're quite right. We'll go to Kew and have tea there instead." Alys had sensed her objection with a little sadness. However, Laura had a right to make her own circle of friends.

"Oh yes! Thank you, Mama! I'm so glad."

"Here we are. Look, there's your father at the gate. I won't stop now, Laura, it's getting dark already. Oh, I nearly forgot. I brought you some lace collars. Choose the ones you like."

The parting was hurried, but Alys returned home feeling an unusual satisfaction that she had managed to be tactful, and that she and Laura were understanding each other better than ever before. She reached London just as the sun was setting behind the trees of St. James's Park.

She told her chauffeur to stop and he followed her at a distance while she walked a little way into the park.

She could see the tops of the old palace still catching a glint of the sun's brighter rays, while the trees nearer to her sank into a soft red. It was a romantic, medieval sight. The color of the sky was deep and rich; what she had to offer Laura was of that hue. Somehow, they would be reconciled.

It was almost as if Mrs. Booth intended to give her a reward. She stood beaming on the doorstep when Alys arrived back.

"You've had a visitor," she said, with unusual familiarity. "Such a charming man."

"What do you mean, Mrs. Booth?"

But Alys knew who it was before she looked down at the card displayed in glorious isolation on a silver plate. "Sir Alec Colvin." He had turned down the left corner, jokingly presenting himself as a close friend who had left a visiting card "in person."

"The gentleman was very disappointed not to surprise you himself, Madam, but hopes you'll lunch with him tomorrow. He's written the telephone number of his hotel suite on the back."

"Well, if I needed another reason to get a telephone this is certainly it." Alys spoke with clipped loudness to the doorman hovering in the hallway.

"You can call on the company tomorrow, Andrews, and have a receiver put in, a private line, without delay."

Mrs. Booth nodded agreement and slipped away.

Alys decided it was excellent that Alec had forgotten how slow these things were in London. After so long in New York he would naturally assume she had a separate phone connected to her apartment. She hesitated. Perhaps she should send the chauffeur to his hotel with a message tonight. She thought better of her impulse and went to bed.

If only Lilian had been there to see her at work the following day. She would have recognized her agitation at once. Alys missed Lilian's unspoken understanding of her moods. She was filled with misgivings. The last time she had given in to any similar emotion, it had ended in disaster. Her affair with Edward had almost driven her out of senses. She was still afraid of being taken over by sexual feeling. Even when she saw Alec's face in the pages of *Vogue* she had refused to accept what her dismay told her. Now that he had followed her to London, she knew what she felt. It had been cruelly hard to withdraw from Edward's passion for her, not least because it was the first time she had felt such physical pleasure. A long time had passed since then, and truthfully, Alys wanted someone to be kind to her.

The next morning she was as busy as ever. Edith Lyttleton came in her usual fluster, demanding three new "tailors" for the following week. Her husband, Arthur, had to tour the country drumming up support for a new "Buy British" campaign, particularly to help the depressed textile trade in the northern provinces. Edith was needed to travel alongside him in something appropriately patriotic. It was always a challenge to Alys to design something less extravagant than her usual models, and yet to make it elegant. Alys was amused to see how Edith's quiet taste was now turning into flamboyance. Edith picked out a bold check in purples and browns.

"No, Edith, believe me, it will muddy your complexion. Look at this bird's-eye cloth. Huddersfield too, just the thing! With velvet facings, some buttons on the skirt, and a new, slightly shorter length—very practical for travel and public assemblies."

Fitted skirts and jackets always looked well on Edith's tall, slim figure. She was still not very interested in clothes, in spite of the success that Alys' outfits had brought her with the public.

"Not too short, I can't be too daring! Choose two other fabrics, Alys. I leave it to you. I'll call back for a fitting tomorrow."

After Edith left, Alys worried about her own appearance, pinched up her cheeks, and fiddled with her hair. Eventually she gave up the effort to suppress her excitement and took Samson and Delilah to the square, much to the surprise of her staff. When she returned, she ordered the car and announced she would not be back that afternoon. Mary and Rose stood respectfully at the door as Alys pulled on her kid gloves and pinned on her toque. She looked at herself one last time, as objectively as she could. Rose stepped forward and on impulse adjusted the spotted veil a little lower, more coquettishly over Alys' cheek. "Thank you, Rose." Alys nodded, and a flushed smile slipped across her face. Rose felt sudden affection for the small straight figure stepping hurriedly down the steps to her waiting car. "Good luck, Madame Alys, good luck!"

◆　◆　◆

At first, lunch at the Savoy did not go at all well. Alec greeted her with an over-large bunch of flowers.

"How wonderful to see you, Alys."

"Irises! But I'm wearing blue!" she could not help remarking.

He laughed, undaunted, "I should have known! Pink or yellow would be better, of course!"

His confidence only made her more flighty and distracted. Alys' manner became indifferent, and she eyed the tables round her with more concern than she gave her companion.

Alec had forgotten that Alys always inspected the company to see who was present, who was wearing what, before she would pay him any attention. Out of nervousness, her professional scrutiny went on a little longer than usual. But her manner relaxed when she spied a well-known figure entertaining his mistress, who was wearing an unspeakable hat. The man had a wife who was one of her customers, and paid his bills more punctually than most. Of course, he was invisible to her in the company of his mistress, as opposed to his wife, and would not expect her to acknowledge him. But catching sight of him and the ugly hat (not one of hers) set Alys at her ease.

"Alec, why didn't you cable? Why on earth did you leave the coast at the height of the season?"

"Oh, because I adore long ocean voyages with no acquaintances. Don't be coy, Alys. I came to see you. I've made up my mind you'll marry me."

He folded his arms and leaned back, with confident good humor in his face.

Alys did not know whether to stifle a laugh or a shriek. It would have been romantic to clasp Alec's hand, and whisper "yes" at once. Inexplicably, she wondered if she liked him at all. His humorous manner struck her as suspicious, untrustworthy. She suppressed her contrary thoughts as quickly as they rose up.

"Alec, are you quite, quite mad? What on earth would you do with a wife like me?"

"Spend a good few years in a state of physical exhaustion and mental anguish, I expect. But it does seem it's the only future I look forward to with pleasure. Everything else seems to pall by comparison. I didn't realize until you left New York so abruptly how much I cared for you. Haven't I any hope at all that in the past few months I've been in your thoughts too?"

Alys twisted the stem of her empty glass in case the honesty of her eyes would give her away. Still looking down, she replied, "I've missed you, yes." If only he would talk about something else, in case she gave in at once. "But I've been very preoccupied lately."

"Laura. How is she?"

Alys sighed. "I think we're making progress. She looks forward to my visits, and has agreed to spend Christmas with me. But she remains in Richmond. Sometimes I just want to take her away with me . . ."

"Have you told her about me?"

"Good heavens, no. Why on earth would I do such a thing?"

Alys realized what she had said at once. She had not meant to sound so dismissive, as if his friendship had been nothing to her. It was just the habit of years not to include anyone in her plans.

Alec stayed silent. Clearly, he was going to have a subdued autumn.

"Have I hurt your feelings, Alec?" Alys was genuinely sorry to have disregarded him. All at once it occurred to her that she loved him very much.

"No, not at all, not at all. Waiter, we'll have some champagne now."

"Alec, how lovely! We had such wonderful times in New York—just the same, isn't it? I'm *very* pleased to see you."

"Darling Alys. It would take a mind-reader to know. Perhaps I should take up phrenology as training for our life together."

"I haven't said yes."

"You will, Alys."

She was encouraged by his certainty. Perhaps it could be a successful partnership. Before Alec could embark on any further declarations, Alys shook her head mischievously and changed the subject.

"No more. Tell me about Newport. I want to hear all the news. How did Ida Stillman look in her Vionnet? What's your golf handicap? What did you wear for Adelaide Hay's fancy-dress ball? I saw a picture of her in the most alarming outfit. I think she saved it from Black Ascot. Please, please, Alec, don't be serious. We've got plenty of time for all that . . ."

She wheedled and cajoled until Alec found himself laughing at her flirtatious manner, and responding with scandalous tales from the summer season. A famous stockbroker had cheated him in a game of golf. Alec had won three thousand dollars from a banker at bridge and still he had not paid up. "I don't blame him for being forgetful. His wife's having an affair with a bandleader." Adelaide Hay had looked like an ocean liner at her charity ball—*not* in one of Alys' gowns. "Streams of bunting, and a billowing hipline . . ." The Buckett birthday party had been a calamity: "Poor Florence looked hideous in polka dots, they matched her spots . . ." The final tally of European titles at the Stillman-Jay wedding was thirty-five. "I didn't include the Russians, they don't count."

"And who are you having an affair with, Alec? Tell me about the de Barros girl . . ." She tried to sound teasing.

"I've always wanted to have an affair with you, if you remember."

"You're so persistent! And you haven't answered my question."

"Waiter, we'll have our coffee upstairs."

"I'm not sure if this is a good idea."

"Well, then let me try to persuade you."

◆　◆　◆

In spite of her reservations, Alys found her defenses weakening. Alec's loving voice, his affectionate closeness after months of worry warmed her heart. Coffee was left to turn cold: Alec led her to his bedroom, and Alys discovered she was all too ready to be stirred by his advances. It was always exciting to make love in the afternoon. Alys had forgotten the heightening of all the senses that sexual arousal brings. The sight of his long, lean back when he pulled off his shirt was such a luxurious glimpse of masculine beauty that she had to avoid looking at him until he was safely in the bed, next to her, alive with wanting.

They met as strangers physically, yet in all other ways she responded to Alec as if he were the friend of a lifetime. His smile, his humor, his light speech were familiar to her, and now, when he touched her, that felt perfectly known too. She did not feel the violence, the druglike need for his penetration of her, which was all that was left of her memories of Edward. There was no craving, but more an anticipation of a slow pleasure that perhaps would last for longer than it ever had before.

Alec kissed her hair, her cheeks, her hands with tenderness. Her body came alive to a male touch for the first time in years. Curious mixtures of thoughts floated in Alys' mind as she slowly dissolved into physical intimacy—the charged present-time of the sexual act. The first day she was kissed, in the woods above Carrigrohane. Squeezing berries among the fruit bushes at Upton Park. The rain one day, dripping off an archway in front of Layton Stayce's office . . . It was always like that when she made love. Random moments of physical intensity, moments when her sense of self had been very strong, came back to the present.

Alec ran his slim hands down her shoulders, down her back, across her buttocks and thighs, relishing the curves and the smoothness that he had long imagined and could now touch. Alys was happy to be held.

When he lay on top of her they looked at each other, and almost at the same instant smiled.

"I love you, Alys."

"I love you too, dearest." she said.

Not entirely skillfully, they made love, Alys still nervous and a little shy, Alec having to make an effort to control himself until Alys whispered that he did not have to wait. He was surprised by her sensuality, and the knowingness of her touch. She had been loved very much already, but Alec was not envious. It meant that Alys had also lost someone, and he understood now why she had been so cool toward him when he tried to woo her in New York. Her body was no longer firm; it had its shadows and softness, yielding skin on her stomach and arms. Suddenly Alec was pleased to love a woman who was rich in experience, prepared to risk herself again in loving him. More than anything else, he wanted her to be happy in his arms.

Friends in New York had told Alys that Alec had a reputation as a charmer, a ladies' man. She sensed that she alone was special to him, for now at least. He had never married, but assured her that she was the only woman to whom he had proposed, and she believed him. But they did not share too many secrets, saving them up for other times.

Later they walked together in Green Park in the cool of the evening, then had a light supper in Mayfair. Reluctant to part after such intimacy, they strolled slowly back to the hotel.

"I expect you to decide very soon about me," Alec reminded her as they walked along. "And I insist that you invite Laura to lunch with us both on the weekend."

"I can't, there's Elizabeth Smith." Alys was apprehensive, but touched by his offer. It complicated her responses. Alec judged correctly that these two demands on her emotions were so strong that they would have to be confronted together.

"Well, I do think you could move that to another weekend. I really want to meet Laura soon. I can't understand why the poor girl had to be taught at home anyway, before this new Richmond establishment. In New York, the children of my friends go away to school, visit their friends on trips and holidays—they lead a full life, the girls as well as the boys. But I'm sorry if I intrude. I know how much Laura means to you."

Alys did not answer him.

Alec had many doubts about asserting himself in this paternal role. It felt quite out of character. He knew only too well the difficulties that lay ahead for Alys and Laura when the girl attempted to enter society. He was surprised to find his own conventional upbringing coloring his views. His love for Alys made him want her to fulfill all her ambitions—and for no doors to be closed on her.

"Having no social life is bad for a young girl." Alec could not resist trying again.

"She's not supposed to have male friends at her age. She'll come out soon enough." Alys felt very possessive.

"Well, she could start by getting to know just one other male. Me." He called the car, and helped Alys to settle herself in it.

"I've always been successful with the ladies," he teased Alys. "I'm always nice to young girls. You never know who they will marry. When I make an effort to be charming, I think few women fail to see my intentions."

"This from the man who has just proposed to me!" Alys exclaimed with a laugh. But as the car drew away, she looked back with an open face of love at Alec, and left him very happy.

CHAPTER 17

1 9 1 2 – 1 4

For the first time ever, Alys had some sense of continuity in her life. She rebuilt her friendship with Laura, by slow degrees, over the next two years. Marrying Alec (very quietly, with no public announcement) only a few months after he had followed her to England certainly helped. Laura was proud that her mother had become Lady Colvin. This amused Alys; her governess,

Miss Dalton, had turned her daughter into a most conventional young lady, and the Wickhams were continuing with the task.

But Madeleine and William were nonplused by the news. Their reaction helped Alys' cause. Laura could not help noticing that her father and stepmother were taken aback by her mother's late and highly successful marriage, and this had the effect of making her gravitate slightly toward Alys again.

Now the pieces of the jigsaw fitted almost perfectly. Laura spent her schooldays in Richmond and the rest of her time in London with Alys, unless business in New York took her mother away. Every time Laura came to London, Alec did his best to charm her, behaving like a sophisticated godfather.

Alys reluctantly accepted that Laura should have some other fixed base. She needed friends her own age, and someone to look after her as she developed from a girl into a young lady. Alys was far too restless and ambitious to provide such constancy, although she knew all too well how much it was needed. Laura did not miss her, and now Alys had Alec, the perfect companion with all the resources necessary to "endure" a demanding wife.

It did not matter to him that she moved constantly between salons, between Berkeley Square and the Plaza, or between the coast at Newport or the homes of her friends in the English countryside. He was careless with possessions; an itinerant childhood made him indifferent to a need for place.

This suited Alys perfectly. They created a sense of belonging just between themselves. To the outside world, Alec looked a roué, a clever man who dabbled in stocks and shares, gambled heavily on horses and cards, and could only be relied upon to amuse everybody. Alys saw his interior life, his affectionate loyalty. He had wooed her for a year—and then wooed Laura too, to make both of them trust him completely.

Alys' first trip back to New York after her marriage filled her with optimism about her life with Alec. They sat in their comfortable bedroom adjoining the small stateroom on board the *Arcadia*—Alec had chosen the ship just for its name. They were playing a game: for every kiss, Alec had to give her a truthful answer.

"What do you love the most?"

"What? Or who?" Alec put his arms round her.

"Don't be grammatical with me, Alec. I can't bear it."

"Passion: My wife. Hatred: Women who smoke in public. Ambition:

To win the Derby, or keep my wife happy. Both impossible." He kissed the side of her neck.

"Very good. What do you fear the most?" Alys laughed.

"Being beaten at poker by my wife." He slid his hands under her skirt.

"No fear of that, darling," she replied, slipping her arms round his neck. "Do you think, if I ever have the wit to learn the game, that I'd let myself win?"

"I'm damn sure of it," he replied, kissing her softly in the crook of her elbow. Alys slid out of her clothes and into the bed. She found traveling with Alec physically arousing. The unusual closeness of their quarters and the enforced leisure of a long sea journey made her feel more than usually responsive. At home she was often very distant from Alec, anxious about her work, worrying about Laura, difficult to talk to, even insulting to him at times. He left her alone then, knowing that she would take her time to come to him. Lovemaking had grown less frequent over the past months, but even more satisfying. Alys would suddenly create a free day and they would stay in bed together, frantic and romantic at the same time.

"I have you captive for more than two weeks," he murmured. "I'm not going to play cards, and you're not going to send cables."

"Oh, Alec, but I have to . . ."

"It's all arranged—you can't do more. If I know anything about you, you'll need all your strength."

"How did you find out?" Alys had already made arrangements to create a stir when she arrived.

"About your plans for New York?"

"Yes—about the reception at the quayside when we dock."

"You just told me."

"Sneak! Trickster! I hate you!"

"Then why are you untying my dressing gown, may I ask?"

"Because I love you too."

◆　◆　◆

Their arrival in New York was heralded by the most ludicrous fanfare Alys had ever received. Rising to the occasion, she walked down the gangplank of the *Arcadia* dressed in daringly short white crepe. She announced her delight in returning to New York, promised to surprise them all with completely original new fashions and to invite them to a whole series of parties and shows at her little salon. Then, hugging

Alec and giving a most unconvincing portrayal of a "devoted little wife" for the photographers, Alys summoned the Plaza limousine sent by the hotel, and disappeared in it with her husband.

Alys giggled as she glanced back and saw the hordes dispersing.

"You're impossible, Alys." Alec said.

"You don't mind, do you?"

"Not in the least if it helps you. As long as I don't have to do anything except look handsome and worthy of all your devotion— which, of course, I am."

Alec and Alys dined quietly in their suite at the Plaza, surrounded by banks of blue and white flowers, a present from the hotel to one of their most frequent and popular guests. It was such attention to detail that made the Plaza a favorite haunt of the European beau monde—that and the decor. "French-American Rennaissance," Alec called it, a dazzling, vulgar display of plunder from châteaux, churches, palazzi all over Europe. Alys could see his objections, but still liked to stay there because it reminded her of her first fond impression of New York, and gave her a delightful view of the park, over treetops. At Carrigrohane and at Upton, woods could be so oppressive and dark.

Next morning, the papers all took note of her doings. "Lady Colvin Returns to Salon Alys" ran one small note. "Titled *couturière* for New York" ran another. More wittily: "Salon Alys Under New Management." The publicity was creating quite an effect.

The enthusiastic response of her clientèle over the next few days left her in no doubt that the joke had been properly understood. "Lady Colvin" was much more sought after than "Alys" had ever been. Whenever she reached the hotel lobby, photographers and reporters lurking there would turn to her for pictures and quotes. Alys made a point of giving them alarming statements, partly out of devilment, partly because she understood from experience that this was what New York needed. "I've come to see what the chauffeurs are wearing this summer" she quipped. "The gossip's more fun than in London" she told another, speaking truly. When asked as always to comment on American fashion, she had an answer prepared that she knew would make a good story. "American women think to be well groomed is to be clean first and expensively dressed second. The Parisienne cares less about either, and only wants to look chic. American men don't like chic—it isn't their ideal of womanhood." It was true: Alys considered that American women were much more admired and petted for their femaleness than English women. It led to a certain tyranny, a power over men that English women did not possess. Mrs. Millsom, for instance, was the power of her household. "Millsom," whatever he was christened, had lost his first name when he gained a fortune, and happily trailed behind his wife from salon to salon, party to party after long days with his stockbroker.

But now that she herself had a title, Alys was amazed at the commercial possibilities opening to her. Over the following weeks a stream of petitions poured into the suite. She was promised hundreds of dollars to sit in certain restaurants. An agency offered her a handsome commission if she would engage her titled friends in London to act as hosts to summer visitors in their own homes.

"Imagine asking Lady Mary to open Desthorpe, or Cecily Day to do it!" she exclaimed to Alec, disbelieving.

"I don't know," he replied, thinking quickly. "Lady Mary would do it if she wanted the money for one of her charities. I agree Cecily might not, but Daisy Panton would, given the right inducement . . ."

"You're trying to shock me. I'm shocked." Not only did Alec know his adopted New York and all its weaknesses, but he knew her circle in London just as well.

"How do you find the time to be so *au fait* with so many people?" she demanded.

"Alys, my darling, I was born with money and I've spent twenty years doing nothing other than amuse myself. It is, as you very well know, a tiny world."

Perhaps his disregard for it was the reason that Alec paid no attention at all to her antics. New York had always been a money-fevered place that heated Alys' dramatic sense, her tendency toward extremes. She felt positively encouraged by Alec's lack of reaction to her public life. He knew she had worked hard for her success, and that she would stop performing when she tired of the applause. Meanwhile, he amused himself and gave her a secure sort of freedom.

They hired a "cottage" at Newport, a strange name for the fourteen-bedroomed, smart stone mansion near the sea, and Alys filled it with Eastlake furniture and her collection of paintings, including several by Ned, and some wild modern things that Adelaide told her to buy. *Vogue* magazine came to photograph her, publishing the picture with a biographical note that Alys had half invented. She did not want anyone to know about Carrigrohane or her mother, or about Laura. Her reconstruction of events was so convincing that everyone believed her. She became "One of London's most successful society hostesses, who has discovered another talent in her life, and dresses the most beautiful women of the capitals and the stage."

Alys tried not to be impressed by her success, but it was difficult, for she felt she had been blessed with good luck.

One day she had a meeting with Lilian at the salon to go over accounts and see to current work. Alys listened gravely as Lilian told her all about the recent Triangle Company fire that had taken place a few months before her arrival in New York. In spite of frequent requests for improved safety and health conditions, the managers of this shirtwaist factory had refused to act. The girls went on strike, but it made no difference. And then, one day in March, a hundred and forty-six girls died in a fire that blazed through their decaying workplace.

"Many of them jumped to their deaths from the upper floors," Lilian told her. "There were no fire stairs, and the doors were all locked."

Alys saw how easily it could have happened. On those few occasions when she had ventured into lower Manhattan to visit a textile warehouse, she had been oppressed by the neighborhood's squalor, made worse by the New York climate. Whether freezing cold in winter or steaming with summer heat, the streets were a harsh reminder that for every dream of fortune in America, including her own, absurdities, there were a hundred nightmares of poverty.

"It couldn't happen here, could it, Lilian? My house is safe, isn't it?"

"The building was not designed for so many people to work in it," she admitted. "We carry considerable stocks of expensive fabric in the basement rooms. We should make alterations, I think. The fire department came to inspect us last month—there's been a general tightening up of regulations, as you might expect."

"Well, we must get architects to check every room and if necessary add an iron staircase or new doors—whatever is needed."

"Thank you. I'll see to it, Lady Colvin. I'm sorry to tell you such unpleasantness. It's just that it's on everyone's mind, at the moment—and it's so hot."

Alys shuddered. It was insufferable to spend long hours in the city when the temperature rose to such an oppressive strength. The thought of burning, of suffering death in such horrific circumstances, momentarily shook her out of complacency. Life was full of such harsh contrasts—by degree much sharper than she had known in London.

'Get Mr. Brown, the agent, to call in Ross and Wilson. They handled the conversion for me. They're very good, and they'll know what to do. Now I'll go and see Mrs. Millsom."

She ran downstairs, glad to escape duties.

"What is it today?" she asked, planting a vigorous kiss on Mrs. Millsom's cheek. Contact with her solid flesh was quite welcome after the depressing thoughts of mortality she had shared with Lilian.

"I'm having a musical evening next Friday, to which you and your charming husband are of course invited. Some dancer girl, Ruby Mayer, is coming to give a demonstration of her 'classic style.' I hear she's a little like Isadora, but more prim. More leg and less 'corporeal expression' . . . so I thought that gray chiffon we picked out last month would do."

"I'll call someone to help with the fitting. But promise me first, no diamonds. It will ruin the effect."

"Don't you like my diamonds?"

"I do, I do, they're magnificent. It's just that your gown will do very well on its own."

Her crestfallen face made Alys less insistent on good taste. Mrs. Millsom had spent many thousands of dollars at Alys' salon, both on clothes and advice over the years, and her position in New York society had moved up accordingly. She could afford to be a little more adventurous.

"Wear a few diamonds in your hair, then, and more camellias, with laurel on your shoulder. It could all look quite classic." There was a hint of the Roman matron about Mrs. Millsom's heavy profile. "Your servants could wear togas and serve wine from silver jugs," she added.

"Well done! That's just the sort of nonsense they all like!" Mrs. Millsom was relieved of the need to be original again. Alys had a flickering image of Neronian splendor on Fifth Avenue while the city burned, but the thought quickly faded.

◆　◆　◆

Later in the year, all Society moved back to Manhattan, and Alys' designing days became busier than ever. It was routine for the salon to be at work on more than thirty different commissions each day. All new orders were now well handled by her staff, but Alys could not help looking over her assistant designer's shoulder, and accompanying Lilian to see what was going on. Whenever she was in town she still liked to have all sketches submitted to her for approval, often altering ideas to make them more in keeping with her own. At other times, as an exercise for her team, she would draw a swift "line" on a page and give all the apprentices the chance to interpret it as they chose. A *toile* would be made by each one, surprisingly different in interpretation, and she would pick out the most attractive model to be presented to her clients. Gradually her assistants learnt her preferences. Alys herself had had no formal training, and could only pass on what she knew by practice, without knowing exactly why certain things succeeded.

One weekend she returned to Newport with a small group of friends, including Adelaide Hay, María-Elena de Barros and her brother, Leopoldo, a most authentic species of lounge lizard. She understood a little better why Alec had spent time with the Brazilian heiress in her absence. He had certain connections in that country himself, had been sent there for months in his boyhood to see his family's estate and visit doting relatives. A few wealthy English aristocrats had invested in the Brazilian cotton trade—the Colvins had made some of their money in textile machinery.

Alys liked María-Elena better on acquaintance. She was beautiful but trying very hard to be more than just a glamorous heiress, and had an eager, enquiring mind. Unfortunately, like Leopoldo, she played every card game with cunning, and Alys still had not mastered a single one.

"You never play?" Adelaide asked her, as they sat on the terrace. In the room behind them, cards clicked and bets were murmured in a rhythm. "I should have thought a 'New Woman' like you would enjoy it—beating men at their own pursuits."

"Mm. I'm never sure whether it is better to persuade men using the charms at one's disposal, or to force them to change."

"You've managed very well by the first route," Adelaide said.

"Not always . . ." An exclamation behind them indicated the game had ended. María-Elena came out to join them, and Alec took Adelaide to admire some new painting.

"I want to ask you something," Alys said to María-Elena without preamble. "I hope you'll be complimented. What I'm intending is more a European custom than an American one."

"Oh?" That in itself recommended anything to María-Elena.

"Will you let me dress you? Exclusively? As a gift?"

"What an extraordinary idea!"

As Alys anticipated, María-Elena found the idea far too close to charity, even dishonorable for someone of her standing.

"Let me explain. I have many reasons. Firstly, your beauty is the best advertisement for my work that I could imagine. Secondly, you have the time to be seen in all the right places. Thirdly, every time you wear one of my dresses, there will be at least three women at my door asking for one just the same!"

María-Elena could not help being flattered.

"How can I refuse?" She paused. "On one condition . . ."

"I know what you will say. Complete confidentiality. No one will ever know. I promise."

If Alys was pleased to have found a way to disarm María-Elena, she did not think of it as anything more than good for business. She trusted Alec implicitly. Cultivating María-Elena had no other significance.

◆ ◆ ◆

The following year, Alice spent the autumn in London, so that she could supervise her daughter's Presentation and Coming Out season. For someone who had defied all conventions so publicly, she had a curious ambivalence to her daughter's way of life. Sometimes she despaired of Laura's caution or lack of spirit, then at other times she would be more protective than Alec or Laura herself could accept.

In Berkeley Square one evening, Alys came in upon Alec as he was settling himself for an early evening drink in her private room. She closed the door quietly so that she could surprise him. Stealth was unnecessary, for Alec had just put a ragtime record on the phonograph and was busy mixing a cocktail. Alys covered his eyes, then shook a piece of paper at his head.

"You knew all the time!" she said.

"What? What is it now?"

"William's opened the house at Upton! Here's a letter from Laura saying she wants to go there instead of spending the summer touring Italy with Lady Evelyn. Don't pretend you don't know all about it."

"I don't quite understand, darling."

"Look here, it's Jonathan Barclay, isn't it? Just because I refuse to let Laura get engaged—this is just a plot so that they can be together all summer long!"

"Don't see the connection. You can't possibly think that Laura would defy you, after all you've done for her."

"Of course I don't. But the Barclays have an estate practically next door to Upton. They'll be picnicking and canoodling all summer long."

"Sounds all right to me. You only said they couldn't get engaged yet—you didn't forbid her to meet him."

"You *are* behind it. How could you!"

"Look here, Alys, most of your working life is spent dressing young girls for the Courts and preparing their trousseaux when they've made their catch. You're one of London's experts at setting up a young girl so she'll entice some harmless young man. How can you possibly react so violently when your own daughter fulfills that same ambition?"

"Because she's mine, and barely eighteen, and she's different!"

"You were married at that age."

"That's no recommendation."

"But Laura's different from you, my sweet. She's quiet, affectionate, simple. She longs for stability, always has. She even likes horses, the dear girl."

"Will you please be serious?"

"I'm *perfectly* serious. You can't mold her. Remember how much you helped Anne find her own way? Can't you do that for Laura? Or is it just that her way bores you slightly?"

Alys drew breath to spit out a sharp retort, then gave up. This alliance between Alec and Laura was too unforeseen and firm for her to break it.

"Now don't fret. You've done wonders for the girl. I never saw a more assured and lovely thing in my life. But you've got to let go."

"It's Madeleine who's had this deadening influence on her. Fancy preferring Upton to Venice. She's mad." Alys sniffed.

"No, she's in love. You remember, Alys, that lovely little feeling when someone you long for is close by your side?" He moved close to her, kissing her earlobe, breathing into her hair so that her scalp tickled and she shivered.

"Don't, you're impossible!" But she was excited, in spite of wanting to stay angry. The music stopped, Alec pulled off his tie and walked away from her to the bedroom.

Such self-confidence was quite intolerable, Alys thought, as she followed him into the other room.

◆　◆　◆

Continuity: months later, the idea presented itself in an entirely unexpected form. Alys and Alec had spent the summer in New York, a few weeks in the South of France at *Roches des Lilas* with the Lyttletons, and then Alys returned to London refreshed for her busiest season. Laura was in town too, amusing herself with her small circle of friends. She looked unusually happy, with more vitality than Alys had seen in her for some time. One day, Lily called for a fitting, just as Laura went out visiting.

"When is she going to marry that Barclay boy?" Lily asked, as Alys adjusted her new loose theater coat. (Lily's firm and beautiful curves were thinning away as she grew older. She looked even more striking as age toughened her.)

"I wouldn't hear of it." Alys said through pins. She had no need to stoop to Lily's hem any longer, but she liked to do it.

"I think you may have to." Lily's clear gray eyes sparkled with mischief.

"What do you mean?"

"I think she's pregnant. Ask her—and do ask her if I can be the godmother. No doubt she'll elect that stepmother of hers, but a young person in today's world needs a progressive model. Like me."

"I have no idea what you're talking about, Lily. How dare you suggest that—"

"It's not a suggestion. It's a fact." Alys sat back on her heels, astounded by the idea.

"Don't be so Victorian, Alys." Lily helped her up.

"Laura! Of all people." Alys was at a loss for more words.

"Oh come, dearest, how many young girls have you prepared for marriage, right in this room, knowing their delicate condition?"

"How could I not notice such a thing? Alec is right. I lose all wits where my child is concerned . . ."

"You know it is a love match. Be thankful for that."

Lily left her to consider her course of action. Those last words mattered most: a love match. Alys had dressed so many rich girls who were being married off to titles or defunct estates to please their families. At least Laura was in love with a personable young man of good family, who had outlasted all other acquaintanceships in the past months.

For once, Alec kept out of the way when Alys confronted her daughter. Laura admitted it was true, most happily.

"I was going to tell you myself, very soon," she said. "But Lily is so knowing and loves to be in on every drama," she added.

"I'll never forgive Madeleine!" Alys said, inconsequentially.

"Oh, Mama, she was as beady-eyed and strict as anything! I promise she did her duty."

"How could you. The disgrace!" Alys found herself saying quite inept things.

"I certainly never expected to give you cause to say that to me, Mama." Laura actually laughed. Alys was amazed.

"We want to get married—soon—and this was all my idea. Jonathan was intent on impressing you, sticking to his word of honor and all that. I simply seduced him, honestly I did."

Alys felt her cheeks go white with surprise.

"I say, are you all right, Mama? Shall I call Alec? Are you going to faint? Do sit down, Mama, it's the shock."

"No, I'm not going to faint." Alys recovered quickly. Was it possible to be so wrong about a person one loved so very much—blind to their potential when it was all there, under one's nose? She had always thought of Laura as a deeply conventional person, but now she had swept aside all her reserves and shown her determination, her own form of courage. Laura knew how she wanted to live.

"Come here, darling. Forgive me. I treated you like a child—me, of all people." She buried her face in Laura's curly hair, and leaned back to look at her fully. "I think you will be very happy. Although of course, I can't condone what you've done."

All she could think of in secret, however, was how glad she was that Laura had experienced such happiness in her loss of virginity.

Alys set to work on a beautiful gown for Laura's marriage. It was a strange sensation to be alone again in her workroom high above Berkeley Square, a vaguely blue light from a November evening touching her paper. She pictured Laura playing with ribbons and dolls on the floor, under the heavy chenille cloth that covered the piano in Dr. Hardy's room. She had been an obedient, peaceful child, and throughout her nursery days had only wanted to please all those around her. Alys was proud of the flowering of her delicate little girl into a woman of purpose.

It seemed appropriate that the gown she created was cool white, not the soft colors of pink, blue or gold often favored by Laura's contemporaries. It had a long lace train, and high shoulders tilted with fur. Laura would look like an ice maiden.

The oddity of this inspiration did not occur to her. Just as she hoped, Laura was flattered by her choice of something formal, even a little old-fashioned, for her special day. She had secretly worried that she would be made to model one of Alys' more extreme "pagoda things" as she described them in private to her fiancé. Alys was too good at her work for that. Layers of skirts might have led the wedding guests to suspect Laura's condition.

Plans for an early and quiet wedding were soon laid. One person would not be able to attend: Dr. Hardy, who was suffering a weakening illness and confined to his home, so Alys and Laura went to visit him a few days before the ceremony.

Alys had mixed feelings as she entered that garden of windblown roses, climbed the steps to the old house and was shown in by Norton, still serving his old master. The quietness of the place had comforted her once; but now she saw how stifling it must have been for Laura to spend so many days there. She was very lucky that her daughter had remained so essentially stable and good, when boredom might have produced wildness in someone else.

But Dr. Hardy's affection for them both was a comfort. He was not at all shocked to hear that Laura was pregnant, and about to be married. He had met Jonathan on several occasions, had acted as a host for their secret rendezvous, Alys was amazed to find out. He knew that Laura was doing just what she wanted, and was happy for her.

"You'll live in the country, then." He wanted to know all the details, encouraging Laura to talk of her dreams.

"Yes, and you'll be able to come and stay; you'll like Jonathan's father, Maurice, I think he is about your age, Uncle, and won't it be nice to send for Mrs. Bacon so she can nurse the baby?"

"I don't know if that will be possible, my dear, she's getting even stiffer these days. I send her money, of course, but she seldom comes in now."

Alice felt out of touch. "Where is she?"

"With her sister in Hastings," Laura explained. "I went down to see her in the summer, Mama; we had a lovely day together."

"How nice of you to keep in touch with her," Dr. Hardy murmured. "Old ties, family ties . . . I wonder how long our peaceful little world will continue."

"What do you mean, Uncle?" Laura asked. "I hope you don't mean Germany and all those troubles."

Alys was even more perturbed. She had paid close attention to political events that summer, listening to the Lyttletons and their friends in France. They were not unduly concerned—why should Dr. Hardy want to spoil this visit with Laura with gloomy worries?

"My friends, doctors and professors in Germany, write to me, you see," he explained. "People are feeling so frustrated, full of grievances. Yet everywhere else in Europe life goes on so carelessly. I'm not alone in finding the current pace of life too swift, too self-indulgent. I fear for you young people." Only genuine concern could make Dr. Hardy talk so openly, Alys realized, with increasing apprehension.

"Uncle, don't say such things." Laura, glancing mischievously at her mother, dared to go on. "Mama is the wild one in our family. She's bobbed her hair and wears short dresses, while I prefer tweeds and still pin up my curls! Jonathan and I will look after the tenants, raise our babies and be thoroughly boring. You'll see, everything will be just the same as it always has been."

"I hope you're right, my dear," Dr. Hardy's childlike eyes looked so innocent, yet Alys wondered if his honesty and intuition made him see the future more accurately than all the sophisticated politicians.

Norton appeared. Dr. Hardy had to rest, and he was evidently growing tired, for he would not have spoken out if he had felt stronger. His thin hands moved restlessly over the blanket on his knees—he had never been much concerned with his physical needs, and Alys could see how much his infirmity irritated him. Dr. Hardy had spent his life comforting others, and disliked his own weakness.

"I think we should go, but I shall come back next week, after the wedding, and bring you books and some wedding cake," she offered.

"How kind, my dear. God bless you both—and may all your dreams come true, sweet child." He kissed Laura, and Norton wheeled his chair through the hall so that he could wave at them from the door.

Alys drove back to Berkeley Square in a pensive mood. Once before she had spent years designing wedding dresses for brave young brides. Suddenly she experienced a moment of _déjà vu_. She thought of Sarah and Rupert Firth, forced to live in retirement at Desthorpe because Rupert's health and prospects had been blasted by war. It could not happen again—surely people would remember the waste and prevent it reoccurring?

She tried not to let these suspicions spoil her pleasure in Laura's day, nor the other small obstacles to her enjoyment: divorce and remarriage meant that there was conflict in who would give the bride away. In the end, Alec refused, as gracefully as he could. He did not discuss his decision with Alys, for they were both so close to being upset by the denial of their preferences that they avoided talking about it altogether. William would have his moment, and they would have to stand back.

Grandpa James was too old to come to England; Anne was permanently engaged in theatrical tours, but promised to try to come. Jonathan too had few close relatives, only a widowed father, a younger married sister, and several grand but impoverished aunts. Alys made up for the lack of family by inviting all the closest members of her distinguished circle: Daisy Panton, Cecily Day, Sir Edward and Charlotte, Lily Lavelle and Ned Fielding, Bea Lady Ventry, the Baron and Baroness de Falbe; Lady Mary, Sarah and Rupert from Desthorpe, Edith and Arthur Lyttleton. It was wicked of her to upstage the Wickham troupe with her own company, but no one could blame her for doing so.

When the day came, Alys fussed around Laura, adjusting her heavy lace train and puffing her hair. She found it hard to talk to her daughter, although she had listened to so many other confidences in a similar situation. Alec knocked on the door.

"May I come in?"

"Oh yes, Alec, do!" Laura called, anxious for a quiet moment with her special friend, as Alec liked to be considered.

"How serene you look. Your happiness gives you a wonderful confidence . . . Look, I'm no good at making speeches. Bless you, my girl!" He winked, and drew out a package from his pocket just as he had on all her birthdays and Christmases for the past few years.

"It was my mother's. One of the more interesting pieces from the Colvin inheritance. It was willed to my daughter, but I never had children. The trustees have agreed that I can give it to you." He clasped a very fine collar of small diamonds round her neck.

Laura admired it in silence. She took Alec's hand between her palms, a distinct and tender gesture.

"Thank you, Alec. It's an honor."

He slipped away, leaving both Alys and Laura happy not to say anything else to each other.

The ceremony took place in Richmond, but Alys had her way for the reception and arranged a supper ball in Berkeley Square. The ballroom was filled with candles and braziers, and a clear winter sky sprinkled stars over the glass roof. Laura drove away to Rutland late that same night, nestling in Jonathan's fur wraps.

Alys would have lingered behind to dwell on the success of the day. She began to walk through the ballroom where so many debuts had been made. She heard Alec's step behind her and felt his hand on her bare shoulder.

"Alys, come away. This is no moment for gloomy reflections, you will make yourself miserable." He put a cloak round her shoulders. "In fact, I have an announcement. We're sailing back to New York on Friday."

Alys turned to remonstrate, but he would not listen.

"Christmas in New York? The Astor Ball? New Year's Eve at Sherry's?" he invited. Alys was tempted.

"Oh, if you insist!" she said, and they went upstairs to their own room.

Seven months later, Laura gave birth to a son, and cabled her mother in New York with the news of his name: John, as English and plain as anything. Alys decided she would always call him Jack, and ordered a trunk full of toys to be sent to the country from Harrods.

◆　◆　◆

Alys was in New York the following summer, too, in the months that led up to the declaration of war. She watched the mounting tension with concern, yet few of her American friends seemed to take account of it. They continued to throw their untaxed fortunes to the breezes of Madison and Fifth avenues as if the world could never change. But Alys always kept Dr. Hardy's words in mind.

In spite of her misgivings, Alys found her workload doubled. It was a sad irony that the "troubles" of France, which meant so little to her clientèle, dried up the flow of continental models to America, so that her own designs were even more in demand. When war was declared, her customers took on charity work with their usual vigor—it was as if the struggle in Europe was to provide the biggest fund-raising challenge they had ever seen. Fancy-dress balls, gala plate dinners, amateur spectaculars filled the social calendar. Laura wrote to say Jonathan had joined his father's regiment, but for the moment was still at home. Alys wanted to go back; she discussed the future with Alec, but for the first time found him indifferent to the increasing pitch of war fever.

"How can you ignore it?" she asked. "How can it have become so serious so soon?"

"Because no one bothered to look at what was happening. Blind selfishness on the part of the Allies. Germany was boxed in and no one paid any attention."

"For heaven's sake, Alec. You sound as if you think they had a cause. You must be terribly careful not to say such things in public. It would be misunderstood."

"So we shall endure mindless slaughter just to teach the Boche a lesson? Alys, surely you're too intelligent to believe all that."

"I don't fully understand what you're saying. You're worrying me."

"That's just what the government wants to do. They've lied very carefully about all their moves in these past years while gradually committing us to support France in this war. Somehow they've succeeded in whipping up fantastic support for the prospect of a fight. People seem to be almost grateful to the politicians for having the courage to make a decision for them."

"We must go home, Alec—I haven't seen the baby, and all this dressmaking seems so stupid at a time like this. I haven't the heart for it."

Such conversations were repeated for weeks, in their rooms at the Plaza or in the house at Newport, yet Alec seemed reluctant to tell her what he wanted to do. Alys had never been separated from him since their marriage; for four years they had never been apart. She could not travel back to England without him, but she could not persuade him to come with her this time. That sense of belonging that meant everything to Alys was being threatened on all sides.

"Lilian, do you want to go home for the war?" In her preoccupation, she asked her manageress for an opinion.

"Not particularly. There's only my mother. I think I'm more use to her here." Alys knew that a great part of Lilian's savings went back each year.

"What about—do you have a young man?" It was the first time Alys had asked the question. Lilian had always been very discreet about her own life.

"There's nothing of the sort. Not for the moment, anyway." She sat up straight, a little nervously. "Lady Colvin, perhaps you don't realize the chance you've given me. If I stay here, and work well, I can become somebody. There's more hope for me here than in England, you must see that. It's different for you, but I'm a nobody."

Lilian was right; at home her highest expectation might be to work for a few more years and then marry a shopkeeper or a respectable clerk. Alys had convincing experience of Lilian's managerial qualities, and understood why she was so frustrated with her social disadvantage.

"Well, you are somebody now, Lilian. I understand your view. I believe work is one way for women to achieve status. Yet, do you know, I was not allowed to be presented at Court when I became Lady Colvin? Not because of my divorce, that was forgotten long ago, but because I am in trade! And that beastly snob Madeleine Wickham presented my own daughter!"

"Yes, but Miss Laura, she wore your gowns all season, didn't she? And she's married very well."

"Marriage!" said Alys, bitterly, aware that her conversation with Lilian was only adding to her own confusion. She would simply have to get Alec to come back with her to London. With Lilian quite happy to stay in charge of the New York salon, there was no reason to stay on.

◆　◆　◆

For a few weeks Alys tried to ignore the worrying difference of opinion that was growing between herself and Alec. Life continued in much the same round, only now social activity was increased by the craze for fund-raising, to send money for the needy in Europe. She tried to interest him in her work; she asked his advice about an offer she had received to stage a special charity fashion show at her salon, sponsored by Mrs. Rose's magazine, *McCall's*. Tickets were to sell for a hundred dollars, or twenty pounds each.

"Should I do it, Alec? She wants us to have a soldier band, to play waltzes during the show and patriotic songs while everyone leaves— I'm not at all sure it is quite in good taste."

"Taste!" He laughed, but the sound lacked warmth. "I don't believe making a few rich ladies more comfortable about their security is altogether worthwhile, no."

"Well, honestly, if that's how you feel, why don't we go home? There's no point in staying here if it makes you so angry. My salon will run quite well without me. In fact, business is booming, and Lilian is in her element, dear girl."

"It's even worse in London—everyone rushing to join up, newspapers full of the horrors of the Hun. I won't take part in all that madness. You do know that, Alys, don't you?" He looked very grim.

"Oh, Alec, what are we going to do? I can't bear to hear you talk like this. I don't know what's right at all. I share your feelings about war, but can we just stand by? I don't know what is the right thing to do."

"Something will turn up. It always does." He spoke lightly, but Alys began to suspect that he had a plan. She knew Alec well enough not to press too hard for an answer until he was ready to confide in her, but her sense of foreboding grew.

As news filtered through of German successes in the first stages of the war, Alys found it increasingly difficult even to mention them to Alec. His normally calm expression would stiffen with anger. In deference to his views, she refused to plan the fashion show, causing some offense to Mrs. Rose, although that did not matter to her. Everyone in New York spent their time discussing the pros and cons of the war, whether America should go into it, and yet there were still many "neutrals" who would argue the Kaiser's side, if pressed. She was not the only person with mixed feelings.

But Alys missed the enjoyment of the unity and trust she had always shared with Alec, and longed to come to some understanding with him. One day she returned to their suite determined to discuss their future. Sensing that the time had come for conclusions, Alec escaped onto the little balcony of their rooms at the Plaza for a quiet cigarette.

Alys called out to him, as he stood looking absently at the view. Not facing him directly made it a little easier to speak.

"Isn't it odd, to feel so concerned about the war, when I'm American-born and Irish-bred?" she said.

"You mean, *I'm* the disloyal one."

"I didn't say that. How could you suggest it?"

"I don't believe in 'duty to one's country.' That's foolish. We're all connected. I've lived abroad most of my life, Alys. Why should I condone the work of fools just because I'm English?"

"Do you mean to stay here, no matter what happens? I really want to be at home in England." Alys looked at the blowing curtain, the shadow of Alec behind it. "Come in. Please talk to me."

Alec turned round, and Alys felt quite sick with fear. He was going to tell her something quite different from anything she had anticipated.

"We should go to Brazil. María-Elena wants me to go into a partnership with Leopoldo. Be a mentor for the lad. He has huge financial responsibilities, and not a clue what to do."

"He's an idiot." Alys said, harsh and disbelieving.

"No. Immature, maybe. He'll improve."

"Leave everything? Leave my work? Laura? What about the war? Our friends?" She could not believe what he was saying.

"Everything is going to change, anyway, Alys. Believe me, the world is never going to be the same."

"That's not what other people say! It's not what other people are dying for!" she shouted.

"Pointless! Don't you see, refusing to participate is even harder? I *have* a moral code. I just don't choose to discuss it with every lightweight I meet."

"Do you mean me?" Alys was angry.

"Don't be ridiculous. You know I don't. I've always admired and supported you. But you must have some respect for my feelings, too."

Alec made no move to come nearer to her. The space between them was already an ocean, a void. She could not accept what was happening.

"Do you mean, if I don't agree to give up everything here—everything in England too—you would leave me? Go without me?" Alys slid to the floor, almost fainting. She reached out for Alec's trouser leg, but he was so appalled by her gesture that he grabbed her in his arms and hauled her up.

"You've got to come too! I love you—don't force me to choose! Haven't I been your partner in everything?"

"Yes." she whispered.

"Then don't be willful. You said yourself you could not bear to go on making dresses for the idle rich at a time like this."

"But *you* will make money for the idle rich!"

"No. I'll build a new life!" Alec looked suddenly transformed, and Alys realized that what she was seeing was a new sense of purpose, revealed in every line of his face. He let go of her with a sigh, and shrugged. "Some changes in one's life are inevitable. I hardly know myself how this process began."

She could hardly credit that the man speaking to her was the man she had married. He did not care one jot for the loss of the world she had created. It was as if he had been playing an elaborate game, hiding his seriousness so completely that even she had been excluded from his private thoughts.

It made sudden sense, of course. Alec's passion for gambling, his success on the stock market, his acute observation of all those around him, all evidenced a clever man merely cruising. What Alys could not understand was why his apathy, so completely hidden by his charm, had turned into this need to destroy everything, including her life, in order to begin again.

"You said yourself," he added carefully, "Lilian will manage everything perfectly well without you. And don't be surprised if in London your business falls off anyway. The war will change everything, believe me. It's not just a boys' adventure that will be over in a few months. It's the end of an era, Alys. Wake up. Face the truth."

She had unwittingly fed his plans by telling him how well New York would manage without her. Yet Alys could not be angry with Alec, because he was deadly in earnest, and did not want to lose her.

Those horrible memories of war that hung round her early days in Conduit Street leapt into her mind. The golds, the "Alys" blues and flame oranges of her glamorous years turned to flares over a scene of horror in her thoughts. The war would bring an end to her world, amongst so many others.

CHAPTER 18

1 9 1 4

Alys sailed back to England alone. She left Alec behind in New York, planning his departure for Brazil and waiting for her to make up her mind whether she would go with him to South America or stay behind in England. She simply had no idea whether she would go with him or not. Her first action when she got back was to travel up to Rutland, to see Laura and Jonathan at their home, Bladeshill Manor.

The countryside was so peacefully familiar, it seemed unthinkable that the sloping fields, hedged with ancient ash and rowan in berry, could be intruded upon by war. Alys could hardly bear to look out of the train window at the young workers laboring to bring in an early harvest—the first one of the new war.

When she arrived at Warkham, the town nearest Bladeshill, she saw groups of new recruits, fresh-faced, tanned, with cropped haircuts, strolling through the town after a hard day's training. Children offered them sweets, and old men tipped their caps to them. As she drove from the station by taxi, Alys saw that the houses were marked with white circles, to show that they had the army billeted with them. Not a house was empty of guests. Alec's sickened words kept echoing in her head. He was right: how could mothers and fathers who professed to love their children allow such a thing to happen?

Laura and Jonathan made her see another point of view. The Barclays had been army folk for generations. The hallway and corridors of the old house were full of portraits of whiskered uniformed men, English versions of Alys' dim memory: Grandmaman's soldier brother, Pierre, in his ornate French uniform.

Jonathan took an entirely different, robust attitude to the war compared to Alec. He launched into his explanation that first evening of her visit.

"When I accompany the chaps to Waterloo, I feel proud, really I do. We had no choice about all this, inevitably, once Russia had mobilized. The invasion of Belgium was the last straw." He looked most unsoldierly, a sensitive-faced, blond young man, more equipped to plod the fields with a pair of binoculars, looking at birds, than to carry a gun. But as Alys compared him to his father, Maurice, who had a distinguished record of service too, she could see an identical sensitivity, and an equal devotion to duty.

What was also manifest was how methodically a mental preparedness for war had been building up among people in her absence. As a result, Laura and Jonathan were utterly shocked when she explained Alec's views, and could hardly discuss the problem with her. The subject hung in the air like a noxious gas. A potential source of great conflict was avoided by all parties. But the little silence that followed any mention of Alec (and of course his name seemed to crop up with even greater frequency because of the strain) made Alys miss her husband even more.

However, it was wonderful to see Laura so happy in her new home. She shared Bladeshill with Jonathan, her son, Jack, and her father-in-law, Maurice, who had obviously developed a deep affection for Laura, and made her mistress of his home. Alys was touched by the way that the old man would look round in irritation when Laura left the room for longer than he expected. He covered his gesture by making some critical remark about a draft or the servants, but everyone knew what he wanted. Maurice's other great pleasure was his grandson, Jack. Alys felt a little shy about the infant, not quite so willing to embrace the doting grandparent role as eagerly as Maurice did.

She was puzzled too by Laura's quite unshakeable serenity in the face of the gloom around her. All this patriotic confidence was quite beyond Alys' understanding. Mother and daughter spent a few days together, wandering about the farm, trying not to discuss the war, concentrating on gossip and other trivialities—the chickens, the vegetables, the impossibility of the staff. Finally, Alys could bear it no longer, and on her final evening, attempted to talk frankly to her daughter.

They took a turn toward the orchard before supper.

"Are you sure you want to go with Alec, Mama?" Laura said, knowing full well that her mother needed to talk, but almost at a loss what best to advise her.

"Well, the thing is, I feel I must go. I owe Alec so much, and I—well, I can't bear to be parted from him. Silly, but he's the very best friend I have ever had—my very best companion." Her eyes filled with tears, and she swished at a fruit bush pointlessly with her parasol.

"Would you have to give up the salons?"

"Of course I wouldn't! I'd certainly try to keep them going. After all, they run by themselves for months now. I'd have to take on another designer here in London, of course. Lilian and her American team do wonders in New York."

"But you put in appearances, and give your 'consultations,' don't you? Supposing your ladies felt neglected, because you'd left?"

"But I've got excellent assistants! I owe them all a living, and it's been my life too! I can't just throw up all those years of work! And there's the Dorcas girls. There's many who can't leave their families down here, and they make a decent wage from home, sewing for me . . ."

"Yes, but, Mama, they'll probably have other work to do now, with the war."

"So you think I'm redundant too." Alys was sad.

Laura shook her head vehemently. "No. Don't take offense, I'm only trying to think of reasons to help you go! I find Alec's attitude not disgraceful, exactly, but—"

"Unsympathetic. Go on."

"Yes, Mama, but remember, I love Alec too—he understood me just when I needed him most. I love him for loving you, Mama. You're so special to each other. It's very hard, but I think that standing by him would be the right thing."

Alys did not wish to hear any of this. She wanted someone to help her justify staying in England. But that was a task she could not expect Laura to fullfil for her.

"Never mind. I'll make the best of it—I always do. Tell me—are you happy, Laura—in *all* ways? After the baby—are you quite well again? I mean, is everything between you and Jack . . . ?" Alys had personal, longstanding reasons for her concern.

"Oh yes," Laura said. "It's wonderful. It always has been, Mama."

"Good!" Alys exclaimed with such relish that they both laughed. "Thank goodness you have Jonathan here, safe with you!"

"Not for long, Mama. I doubt it will stay so. He's constantly asking his regiment to send him."

"He's mad! Quite mad! Oh, Laura, what will you do!"

"Mama, don't worry. I have so many things to do. There's baby Jack, and Maurice. Then all the farm boys going off to fight means the indoor staff will have to finish the harvesting, and then there's the Red Cross . . . I want to do a nursing course."

Alys looked quite stricken at this agenda of events. Laura could not resist teasing her more.

"The only thing I miss is my horse. They've all gone to the regiment instead of being left here, roughed up for the winter."

"Well! Thank goodness for that. I never liked you hunting very much anyway."

Laura smiled. "I'm all right, Mama, don't fret. I'm living how I want to live. Isn't that what you want for me?"

Standing under the gnarled old apple trees, her hair curling out of its tight little pins, Laura looked so rooted in happiness that Alys gave up. Laura had convictions that were entirely beyond her, but thankfully that did not stop them from loving one another.

"And—sweetheart—if I were to go, you wouldn't think I was deserting you? I never want to lose you . . ." Alys' eyes filled with tears. A mood of guilt assailed her, as if a big black bird had flapped its wings and swooped, making her afraid. She had the feeling all this had happened before: the need for sexual love overcoming the duties of a mother.

"Mama, I'm a grown woman—you're not abandoning a child! Don't be silly. You're just creating a drama that doesn't exist."

"I'm sorry! Sometimes I feel like a blind old mole, worrying through the earth, throwing up little mounds of unhappiness wherever I go," Alys said. "It's just that you are so precious to me—now more than ever before."

"Don't. Jonathan is certain the war is going to be over very quickly. It's all a ghastly attack of madness, but the Germans will be defeated, you'll see, and then he'll come home again, and you and Alec will be able to live in peace, and it will all be just the same."

"I wish I could believe you, darling. Now look, I can't bear to say good-bye to you all again in the morning before I go back to London, so please don't get up for me tomorrow."

"You never were very nice in the morning, Mama." Laura agreed as they walked back to the house together.

Alys laughed. "You know me too well sometimes, my girl! Let's just have a wonderful evening together, shall we?"

Maurice looked particularly elegant that night—he had dressed with care for Alys' benefit, and she was glad that she had done the same. Jonathan gave her a watercolor of Laura and Jack as a token of her visit.

"Something to remind you how pretty she is, Alys, and I give it to you with my sincere good wishes—for whatever you decide to do."

"Write to us, Mama, won't you? Give us plenty of warning so that we can come to see you off."

Laura's generosity touched Alys; her steadfastness brought comfort.

◆　◆　◆

Back in London, all Alys' conflicts returned. It was impossible to leave when the whole nation, but particularly the city itself, was in a ferment of activity, engaging in the struggle. On all sides there was war talk. The newspapers carried daily bulletins on the front in Europe, with confusing maps showing the movement of the Allied and German lines; to Alys the black arrows writhed like snakes in some nightmarish board game. This view of the war as some great prank was reinforced by the stirring war poems printed every day in the *Times* to encourage young men to enlist:

Lad with a merry smile and the eyes
Quick as hawk's and clear as the day
You who have counted the game the prize
Here is the game of games to play. . . .

The parks, still bright with autumnal sunshine, were the scene of endless parades as Kitchener's young men, wearing their own clothes for lack of army stocks, were drilled by men in khaki. Alys read in a newspaper that in one weekend alone, ten thousand men had joined up.

The salon in Berkeley Square became once again a small arena for the battle between despair and hope. Many of Alys' regular customers came for something special to wear when they said farewell to sons or husbands. "So he'll remember me at my best," they would always say, and Alys' hand would fumble for her pins. In the late autumn, she had the saddening task of comforting many of these same women again, when they lost their men at the battle of the Marne. They turned to her, as they had so often done, for a few words of consolation. It was as if the intimacy of the salon made it easier for them to drop the front of bravery that they had to keep up at home. More and more, Alys felt that she could not leave her friends to follow Alec, but that she should do something to contribute, to alleviate the misery as best she could.

Occasionally, work at the salon brought her a little pride. A young woman whom she had not met before came to order a wedding dress.

"I don't want anything very elaborate," she explained in a diffident way, "but it was always my ambition to have a wedding dress from 'Alys,' and my godmother promised me I should."

"Does your godmother come to me, too?"

"Well, no. But actually, I knew your daughter very slightly. My name is Elizabeth Smith. We were at school together for a short time."

"And your godmother is Madeleine Wickham."

"Yes, how did you know?"

"Never mind. It doesn't matter. When is the wedding taking place?"

"The day after tomorrow."

"The day—? Oh. I see."

"He's going away, and we've got a special license."

"Well, then you'll have a special dress, too. It will be just as beautiful as I can make it in two days. But tell me—do your parents agree to this marriage? You're very young, not yet twenty."

"Well, there's only Father, and he says that making a choice for someone you love is making a choice for humanity. But then, he misses my mother very much."

Alys did not know whether to feel a crying sympathy for this simple girl, or a screaming protest at such sentimentality. All codes by which she had lived so far were being stirred up into some highly colored travesty of the truth, an intoxicating mix of duties, sacrifices, and excitingly noble gestures. She began to miss Alec more and more.

"I'm pleased to make your dress, my dear, but I don't want you to pay for it. I'll be your *fairy* godmother."

The girl was surprised, but very pleased, and left in a hurry to tell her fiancé all about her luck. Alys worked on nothing else but that wedding dress for the next two days, as if she were making her last special effort.

She was not the only person to wonder how to make her contribution—everyone she knew was of the same mind. Lisa, her beautiful mannequin, left to take up war work. Charlotte Day (she heard through other friends in the salon) was organizing fund-raising, and Lady Mary and Sarah were looking after the first convalescents at Desthorpe. But to Alys' great surprise, Anne turned up—a quite markedly changed Anne since their last encounter. Two years of touring all over England had matured her, turned her into a seriously dedicated actress. Her growing popularity and reputation made Anne determined to offer herself to the cause. Before Alys had any time to discuss her own difficulty, Anne had launched into her great scheme.

"Lily and myself, and a few other people—Hubert Kerrick, of course—are going to form a volunteer group to travel round the camps here at home, and when we get permits, we'll go to France perhaps, and give concerts, recitals, act out scenes. Cheer people up—especially the girls in the factories and people in hospitals. Will you help us, Alys?"

"How can I? In what way?"

"Well, you're so very good at advertising, that sort of thing—and raising funds through your rich ladies—couldn't you spread the word, raise some money for us?"

"Why don't you ask me outright, sister dear? How much do you need at this moment?"

"Well, about three hundred for the 'fit-up' staging, and ideally a motorized van for traveling between appointments . . . that would get us started, I think."

"Three hundred!" Alys turned to her desk. Lily had started her out on her path, once. She never expected she would return the favor in this grisly way.

"Here's five hundred."

"Oh, sweetheart!" Anne hugged her. 'How good to have your support . . . how's Alec? Why didn't he come over with you?"

"He's—I don't know how to explain it, he's sick of it all. I don't understand him. He keeps talking wildly about disappearing to Brazil." The old habit of elder-sister superiority rose again for a moment, stopping Alys from telling the whole truth.

"What will you do?" Anne asked, puzzled.

"I seem to be staying here for the moment. I can't decide what to do." Alys' voice trembled.

Anne looked sharply at her sister. Although their lives had been forced apart by their careers, she knew from Alys' letters how attached to Alec she was.

"I'm sorry."

Alys shrugged her shoulders, making an effort to stay in control. "There will be many other casualties. I'm not alone, I imagine."

"I'm not sure I understand what you're saying . . ." Then the full significance of Alec's behavior dawned on her.

"Alys! You don't mean Alec is a 'pacifist' do you? Have you told anyone—Lily or Ned for example—about this?"

"Not yet. I can't bear to discuss it," Alys admitted, not contradicting Anne, but dreadfully shamed by the tone of her sister's voice.

Anne looked somber. "Well. I don't approve, of course. I can't advise you. But I tell you what I suggest—why don't you talk to Edward?"

"Why on earth do you suggest that?"

"Not to discuss Alec. No doubt he'd be horrified. Honestly, Alys, you're so confused! Edward still has shares in your company, doesn't he?"

"Well, yes, he does, and Layton Stayce, too."

"Well then, they should be consulted so they can decide if their investment in the salon is at risk."

"You think I'll go!" Anne had never given her heart to anyone: and in some ways, Alys felt, despised anyone who had, even her own sister.

"Don't you understand!" Anne retorted with impatience, "I'm not criticizing your loyalty to Alec! You don't seem to realize that you're bound to lose many, many customers if this gets about!"

"Do you think so?" said Alys, bridling.

"Don't you sense it? And besides, Alys—half the theaters in London are already closed—what if the authorities decide to shut your house? Who knows? Edward has connections. He might tell you what to expect—he's sure to be in the know. Talk to him. You need him now."

Alys suddenly realized that Alec had spoken the truth: nothing would ever be the same again. All over London, all over England, critical decisions were being taken about businesses and livelihoods. Old grievances were being aired and settled; old relationships redefined, and newer friends were being tested for the right beliefs . . .

Alys was suddenly terrified. "You don't think the war will end soon—do you? You think it will go on and on, that hundreds will die, and all we care about will go up in flames."

Anne shook her. "We have to do what's best. I've found something, so will you." She embraced Alys warmly, then hurried away to a committee meeting: " 'The Little Theater of War' we call it," she said, laughing.

Alys wrote to Edward, asking for a meeting if he could possibly spare the time. She was sure he would be on active duty, and possibly unavailable, but fortunately Edward was still based in London, with the Queen's Own. His life was now spent in bureaucracy at the War Office, so her letter soon reached him. The butler from his house in Berkeley Square walked over two days later with the promise that he would lunch the next day.

Edward looked a little thinner, but fit and calm when he arrived in an army car at her door. They had not met for many months—not since her last reception at Berkeley Square for "Salon Alys" in the spring.

"How is Charlotte?" Alys asked dutifully, as they walked through the streets to the Ritz. They had not been out together in this way for a long time.

"Dismayed, of course, but she's very involved in the Queen's Charitable Fund for Unemployed Women. Goes on visits, raises funds, that sort of thing."

Edward did not ask her about her plans, as if he knew something of them.

"Edward, I need your help and advice as a director of 'Alys.' "

"I thought you might. Look, let's have lunch first, talk later. It's been a long time since we had a pleasant meal together. Good plan."

How easy it was now to be good-natured with each other. He took her arm through his own, and moved her closer to his side. Alys felt that immediate pleasure in contact that had never failed to draw her to Edward. The contrast between his heavy, muscular body and her own small frame had always disturbed them both; only actual contact made them feel comfortable. Touching him now, though, brought the dread of war so close. She could not bring herself to imagine anything happening to him. Edward had to remain indestructible, she felt, or the whole world would collapse.

Although they tried to talk about pleasant matters, family and mutual friends, it was impossible. Alys looked round the quiet dining room and realized that many tables were also occupied by couples, the male in uniform. The new clothes were awkwardly worn; unyielding serge and creaking boots. The men ate self-consciously, like schoolboys out for Sunday lunch.

"What worries me," Edward explained, "is that all this indiscriminate volunteering won't help in the long run. We've let trained workers run off and get killed in the trenches—thousands already. I'm very much preoccupied with supplies. We won't have the shells to fight with if this goes on."

"But it won't, will it? The papers talk constantly about the Allies turning the German front."

"I hope they do. But it looks very bad. I think new policies from the Government, not the generals, will be needed, even though I'm an army man. Otherwise the loss will be tremendous."

Alys lowered her head, afraid to tell Edward what Alec thought of it all. "Alec refers to it as 'pointless carnage.' "

"I know." he said abruptly. "I heard from friends in New York what Alec was saying. Doesn't surprise me."

"Why not? Don't you consider it unpatriotic?"

He shrugged. "I've known Alec for a very long time. Before you met. Behind his cynicism he's an idealist." Such connections no longer disconcerted Alys. The upper class in England was a family.

"I don't judge," Edward went on. "Actually, it surprises me that the pacifists aren't gaining more ground."

"Then you don't see it as cowardice." Alys was very grateful to Edward for his lack of condemnation.

"It's not for me to do so. There are plenty of others who will. I remember the lines from some old school poem or other. I've need to recall them often at present: 'All service ranks the same with God— With God, whose puppets, best and worst, Are we; there is no last or first.' "

Alys' eyes blurred with tears as she listened to Edward. It upset her, but also added to her alarm to hear a man being so grave and reflective.

Edward was not given to analysis as a rule; blind confidence had given way to doubt and reflection.

"Don't worry about Berkeley Square," he said, "to turn to practical matters. You'll think of something, Alys. You always do, and I'll support any decision you make. Layton Stayce won't have to fight—too old, so he'll keep an eye on things."

"And you don't think he'll want to withdraw his money? I'll need the capital if business falls off."

"We've all done very well out of you, my dear—we owe you something! My annual dividends have run to several thousands for the past few years! We stand firm."

"Thank you."

"I don't think they'll close you—not yet anyway. It's a question of morale at home. Such measures cause alarm. But it might happen later, no denying. You've got wonderful women working for you there, Alys. How the world will change for them now."

They walked back to Berkeley Square, and Edward left her at the steps to her house. Alys had an impulse to remind him of the first day they had visited it together, but superstition made her hold back. Edward kissed her, then, with a sudden, painful formality, he drew back and shook her hand. "Good luck, my dear. God bless." Alys nodded silently. Edward was thanking her for a memory of beauty and emotional adventure that he would cherish through all the hard days to come.

◆   ◆   ◆

Shortly after her meeting with Edward, Alys was interrupted in her work at Berkeley Square by the appearance of Rose and Mary, her two chief *vendeuses*.

"I'm sorry, Ma'am, but may we have a word?"

"Of course, Rosie."

"It's just that . . . we were wondering what you were going to do, Ma'am. Business is falling off, and the girls are all wondering what will happen."

"Nothing at all, Rose. You must reassure them. No one's going to be let go. For the moment there's work enough already on the books and if necessary we shall just have to broaden the scope of what we find acceptable to do. Fill in the time—I've never seen so much knitting going on!" She tried to laugh, but it was forced. Pathetic, multicolored scraps . . . they would all be reduced to the color of mud.

"That's just it. We were wondering about the war effort."

"What do you mean, Rose? All the girls are free to leave if they wish—Lisa's gone. Do you want to go too?"

"No, it's not that—though I should tell you that Kitty will be the next to go—she's getting married, and the family want her to give all this up."

Alys smiled ruefully. It was a good marriage for Kitty—and that meant putting her career behind her.

"Have you something in mind? You've already thought of a scheme, I think."

"Well, we're all seamstresses, cutters—there's no one here thinks they'd be much good at nursing or the like. But business is bound to get slack. So why can't we make clothes for the war instead? Shirts. Army shirts and things. They need tons of them, it says so in the papers. Couldn't we do that?"

Alys was cross that she had been so preoccupied: the obvious had not occurred to her. Anne had mentioned the possibility of closure—at some point the Government would want all enterprises to be geared toward the war effort, and nothing else would be permitted.

"Well, it seems unlikely that a couture establishment specializing in fine handiwork could be found useful in such a scheme, Rose, but I'll try to find out. I'll have a word with Edith Lyttleton. She'll tell me what to do."

"Thank you—we all think it would be best, Ma'am."

"I understand. Have you heard anything yet?"

Rose's eyes grew bright.

"Not a word since August. It's lucky I'm working, because I haven't seen a penny of pay from him for six weeks or more. There's many in my neighborhood in the same boat—only they have to wait for the soup kitchens. Thank goodness we never had a baby." She blew vigorously into her handkerchief and hurried out.

Mary stood by the door. "I'm sorry, Ma'am."

"No need to be," Alys replied, turning away.

Edith was at once responsive to Alys' suggestion. She put her in touch with one of the Supplies Officers, Hodgkin, in the War Office, who agreed to order five thousand shirts to be delivered as soon as possible. He sent her a requisition order and the cotton fabric within a week, together with a letter suggesting that as she had a large, skilled work force, she might consider bringing in new machinery to speed up her output. Mary and Rose were happy to investigate.

Before the end of October, six webbing knitting machines arrived, crated up, from Manchester. A Mr. Handley traveled down to show the girls how to operate them. He looked like a weaving frame himself, a man of sturdy build, in a thick worsted suit, with hands of a powerful, square plainness that showed more effectively than words how the machines were to be managed. Girls were allotted in shifts to the new enterprise. Alys' staff could produce 10,000 webbed army belts in a month with this system.

Her New York experience helped her; Alys watched her American profits dwindle alarmingly as she instructed Lilian to ship over the very latest cutting machines, buttonholers, overlockers, and all the other new devices to speed up manufacture. But this laudable effort only made her feel that her own establishment was changing forever. "Salon Alys" was hardly recognizable, with the carpeting in her beautiful ballroom stripped away so the machines could be bolted to the floor, and the steady hum of treadles turning all day.

◆ ◆ ◆

All these activities diverted Alys, comforting her with the knowledge that she was doing what was right to ensure work for her staff, and barely leaving her the time to dwell on the alternatives. But when Alec left America for Brazil without her, and started to send her letters about his new experiences, her irresolution made her sad. She simply could not take the final step and give up responsibility for something she had established entirely by her own efforts. It was all a question of exercising control: going meant yielding up her independence. Alys could not bring herself to do it, yet every time she thought of the distance between her and Alec, she grew sick at heart. Life was joyless, where it had once been a great adventure; there was no one to share the victories and the frivolities. No one would ever give her the happiness she had had with Alec. He had allowed her to be entirely herself and never passed judgment on her.

He wrote to her at Bladeshill, where she spent the first Christmas of the war:

Life with the *grā-finos* is amusing, strange, full of potential. I miss you. How did I fail to make you understand how much you mean to me? Give me your heart again, Alys, be my life's partner, as I have been yours.

P. S. I forget you don't speak Portuguese. *Grā-finos* is the upper crust. I'd love to teach you, perhaps I would succeed where I failed at poker . . .

How remote his bantering voice sounded to her, now that she was accustomed to the cheerful, laconic style of the English at war. It only confused her; she and Alec were changing, as their experiences molded new aspects to their characters.

On her return to London, Alys volunteered to stage an exhibition for Ned Fielding, as a fund-raiser for the "Little Theater of War." She used her beautiful lingerie room—the only one large enough for the event that was not already filled with industrial machinery.

Ned had traveled to France as an artist-observer, and produced a portfolio of sketches that he was determined to exhibit. They depicted the mud, the camps, the nurses tending the wounded; the ruins of villages, church spires rising like broken twigs against gray skies; the first truthful images of life behind the front that Alys had seen. There were also portraits of Lily and Anne, reciting to small groups of wounded men as they lay on stretchers at their feet, or hanging their "fit-up" curtains at the edge of some camp.

"It has to be a private showing," Ned told her dourly. "There are some people in official circles who would prefer some of these pictures not to be seen. But Lily needs the funds, and she wants everyone to know what she's doing."

Alys chose carefully among her acquaintances for those who would appreciate Ned's work, and support the actresses' enterprise. She did not ask Daisy Panton, for instance, because her own two sons had volunteered, and the drawings might upset her. Sarah Firth and Lady Mary would come; so would Cecily Day, and to her surprise, Charlotte Wye promised to attend, in lieu of Edward who had left for France. Numerous other customers supported the event, and it struck Alys that they were just as delighted as her friends in New York had been to normalize the idea of the war by continuing with their ritual events.

Ned was late arriving, but as transport in London was becoming a great difficulty, Alys was not very surprised. Her guests began to circulate, and she watched with interest for their reactions. They obviously found great curiosity value in some of Ned's sketches. To see actresses as glamorous and well-known as Lily Lavelle, and her protégée, Anne Hardy, in informal portraits, dressed in boots and loose coats, squelching through mud or sitting on sandbags, was diverting. Other pictures were quickly passed by—only the "personality" ones sold quickly. Most of her acquaintances did not want to see the war as it really was. "The struggle" was some abstract battle against the forces of evil in which their menfolk were engaged. The detail of it was to be avoided.

Alys hovered by a window, waiting for Ned to arrive. Even though he was growing old, less energetic, and even more devoted to Lily, Ned had lost none of his openness with women. For his own sake she hoped he would turn up soon, because he would sell many more sketches if he flattered the ladies in his usual easy fashion.

Charlotte Wye came over to her, blinking and looking slightly over her head in the way Alys knew so well from the more exclusive patrons of her salon.

"Remarkable! Edward would have been most interested, Lady Colvin, to see these. I know he would like me to support your cause—I thought I would take this one. Do you agree?"

Charlotte picked out a view of a village at dusk; almost a rural idyll, were it not for the charcoal skeletons of the trees.

Cecily Day joined her. "Don't be morbid. Edward won't want to look at that when he comes home! Don't you agree, Alys?"

Alys looked at Cecily; she *would* play with people like a cat with its claws in a tangle of wool. It was her only form of mental exertion besides deciding on her wardrobe. Charlotte was trying to be gracious, and did not merit such a response.

She was about to defend Charlotte's choice when Ned arrived, shaking raindrops from his coat before handing it to the doorman. He looked odd; he was staring at his coat as if he needed all his concentration to know what to do with it. Alys moved toward him, knowing that he had awful news.

"I got a message from the War Office. Lily's vehicle was in a collision near Abbeville. The van slid off the road, turned over into a ditch. She died at once."

"There must be a mistake—it can't be Lily!"

"It is true. Anne is safe—bruised, but otherwise unhurt."

"Anne! Thank God for that."

The room turned still; heads bobbed, whispers were exchanged. Alys and Ned soon found themselves alone, as all the guests realized what had happened and chose to leave.

"You see?" Ned whispered to her. He was gripping her hands painfully tight. "No one in London can talk about death. I've lost her, Alys. She was mad to do it—I told her. You must stop Anne."

"You know I can't. Everyone does what they consider best."

Ned straightened a little, acknowledging that she was right.

"Lily never did anything she didn't want to do," he said. "That's why I loved her. Somehow the things *she* wanted made everyone else happier. It was a gift in her."

"You must try to be proud that you knew her. I know I must sound so cruel, trying to make you accept it. But pride is the only thing that will help you to endure it. Better to have known her than—"

"Quite. Quite so, dear girl. Oh damn!" Ned lurched away from her before he broke down, and ran off into the wet streets to get drunk at his club.

Alys stood in her smart little room, the setting for so many conversations with Lily—kindly, intimate moments. Sometimes Lily had challenged her views; sometimes she had told her unpleasant truths, but concern and loyalty were always there, in everything she had said. Alys wrapped her arms round herself, for comfort. She had an awareness of magnetism, as if thinking of Lily, with love, could make her materialize. Desolation overwhelmed Alys. Then, in her misery, she decided to do what Lily would have been capable of, too—she would give everything up and go to Alec. They loved each other as perfectly and oddly as Lily and Ned, and she did not want to waste any more time away from that.

◆　◆　◆

Alys did not see Ned again. By the time Lily's memorial service was arranged, she had made her plans to join Alec. Ned did not stay in London for the service either—he went back to France as soon as he got a permit.

Alys wrote to Ned to explain why she had decided to go, and why she would not be at the church:

They'll all be there, sentimental. The people who filled her theaters, who wore copies of her clothes. The Lily I commemorate is the one who traveled out of her world to find me, and to help me start a new life. The one who was always so curious and warm about her friends that she knew my daughter's lover before I did! Who loved you better than I ever could . . . Lily would know why I give it all up. You do too, Ned?

He did not reply, but Alys knew that meant he accepted what she said.

She had no intention of doing anything by halves. If she were to join Alec in Brazil, then she would not merely leave the business in a caretaker's hands. Who, after all, would be her substitute? Laura had declared she was irreplaceable, and Alys liked to think she was. No: she would sell everything.

Finding a buyer for the salon proved to be surprisingly easy—and close to home. Kitty Szenkier's father, formerly a tailor in Soho, had risen to be the owner of several manufacturing companies that were thriving on war orders—uniforms, greatcoats, shirts. He made a reasonable offer for Alys' name, the lease of Berkeley Square and her share of the company. She agreed without hesitation, had the figures checked by Layton Stayce, got Edward's agreement to a change on the board and signed away her business. It took just three weeks.

More farewells: how Alys still hated partings! So, it seemed, did her daughter, when the moment finally arrived:

Dearest Mama,

I'm sorry we can't come to see you off, though to be honest I'd rather not. Remember the day in the orchard? We'll always be close in our thoughts. Jonathan is called away, and there's so much to do, and Maurice has been a little ill . . .

Good-bye, dearest Mama, have a safe journey. I'm so worried for you because of the *Lusitania* being sunk! Please send word when you are safely arrived. Jack and I have looked in the atlas and found out where São Paulo is. All my love, a kiss from your grandson. Good luck, and please tell Alec we love him very much.

Laura.

Alys in turn wrote a farewell to Anne, but did not attempt to dissuade her from her activities. Lily's death would only spur Anne to continue even more energetically with "The Little Theater of War." Both her daughter and her sister had accepted her decision, and these were the only people, at such a time of crisis, whose understanding Alys needed. While the war lasted, they all had different challenges.

Once the decision was taken, it seemed to easy to put into effect. Work at Berkeley Square continued unchanged by the new management. Mr. Szenkier had a young assistant who was itching to try his hand at designing the couture work (while it lasted) and Tina Szenkier herself, having served as one of Alys' faithful mannequins, was certain she could bring a little hint of Alys' personality to the designs. Alys decided not to interfere, but to let the Szenkiers have a fresh start. All the workroom girls were engrossed in the war orders, with a few private commissions to provide relief from the routine of the machines. They were so grateful for fulltime employment with their men away, that the shock of Alys' resignation was shortlived. Alys, too, was happy to have provided for her work force, for the alternative, closing "Salon Alys" completely, would have been too hard. She preferred to leave without a fuss, imagining the familiar bustle in the workrooms carrying on after she had left.

Her two *vendeuses* presented her with a parting gift: a fashionable brooch in the form of a dove with a gold heart held in its beak, set with turquoises, the symbol of fidelity . . . If Mary or Rose spared a thought for past glory, it was with fleeting pride and without much regret for a lost world of luxuries.

◆　◆　◆

Alys' ship, the *Verdi* of the Lamport and Holt line, was crowded with refugees. Sometimes they conversed in low, flat voices, about their escapes from Europe. Once the ship sailed, the decks were frequently filled with their high-pitched chatter, near hysteria, as rumors ran among them that German cruisers had been sighted. Alys spent most of the early part of the journey in her cabin, writing letters to the other friends she had not seen in person before she left. A tremendous elation at the thought of being with Alec again buoyed her up; she wanted to be peaceful, to let go of the past and be fully ready for her new life.

The ship docked at Lisbon on the way out, and a new crowd of emigrant families brought the vessel to full complement. Alys made the acquaintance of Paul Ogden, an American businessman, who increased her optimism with his knowledge of Brazil, and the eminence of the Monteira de Barros family in São Paulo life.

"Brazil is at your feet," he declared. "It's an exciting country, doing even better because of the war. With the de Barros family behind you, you'll get the best treatment—the best *despachantes* too."

"What are they?"

"People who get things done—dispatch, you see? In practice it means bribery. Nothing works without someone exerting a little influence on your behalf. And influence costs money. Every office, every ministry is full of them. The *senhores* with the fat palm."

Alys' achievement in building her own business seemed remote and of little consequence. She had succeeded in a woman's world, and now she was stepping into a world run by men, for men. She looked across the stateroom at the huddle of feathered women, the chatter of French and Portuguese filling the air with unfamiliar musical sounds. Alys did not relish being nothing but a bird of paradise: it was one thing to dress kept women, quite another to be one.

◆　◆　◆

Alys' first images of Brazil were as confused as the memories a child has in sickness. Colors, smells, apprehensions followed in quick succession. All her senses blurred into one reaction of feverish excitement. Her first view of Rio de Janeiro excited her beyond anything she had imagined—this was not a wild tropical jungle, as some of her friends had predicted. She could not wait to see Alec, to share her first impressions with him. The ship drew near just as a rainstorm broke over the coast. Alys saw rings of white foam turn crescent-shaped as they spread into several silver-white sandy bays near the horizon. Palm trees rocked this way and that as if they would fall down in the thunder and rain, but each time they touched the ground they bounced straight up again, with tossing fronds.

The small area of the city she could see as the *Verdi* drew nearer shore reminded her of Cannes or Biarritz, with sedate French-style houses, shuttered and decorated with curls of white plasterwork. The navy blue of the storm clouds increased the appearance of order by outlining all the buildings in neat, contrasting precision. It was seductive, a painter's view, and Alys delighted in it.

The twin peaks of the Pão de Azucar and the Corcovado dominated the bays, as unreal as giants. Although Alys was to travel on to Santos to meet Alec, she could not resist exploring this exotic city, and accepted her American companion's offer of a short carriage ride.

The sticky wet heat instantly drained her of energy, though not of excitement. The skin tones of all the people came to her like the colors of some child's illustrated adventure story: blue-black, plum-purple, coffee-pink. She felt drained of color, and her sensitivity to shade and hue disarranged, affronted. The black, fat *"Mamães,"* the candy sellers, wore white as if it blazoned color against their dark complexions. The crimson of a porter's old shirt appeared a faded flatness in the harsh light of the sun.

Paul Ogden summoned an old fiacre, drawn by a bony horse, and they drove through quiet streets, wide avenues planted in orderly fashion with trees. Their names were as musical and magical as the words of childhood tales: *palmitos, mangoes* and *jacarandas.* Just before returning to the ship, they paused for a view over the bay from Copacabana, a small seaside resort. Alys sipped herb tea and tasted little sugary Portuguese sweetmeats at a hotel facing the sea.

She returned to the *Verdi* and bid Paul Ogden good-bye. That night she slept fitfully, dreaming of seas, birds, and foreign voices, not quite sure where she was, in reality or in her imagination.

Santos, two days later, was entirely different. Alys was terrified. The port was small and jammed with traffic. The fetid odors of the harbor assailed her, mingled with the acrid sweat of crowds of porters, shouting and dragging sacks of black beans across the quays to waiting ships. The sweet burning stench of coffee hung thick in the air.

Gangways were let down, beggars roughly shoved out of the way by deckhands so that the passengers could descend. Staring at the mass of brown-stained shirts and wild dark eyes, Alys nearly fainted with fright. And then, like an apparition, Alec stood before her—dressed in a white suit.

Alys threw back her head and laughed out loud. "What on earth are you wearing? What do you have on your head?"

With his eye for the stylish, Alec had taken to wearing the *bandeirante's* wide-brimmed straw hat. He thought it appropriate, and was mildly put out by Alys' hilarity. But it was wonderful to hear her laugh, to have her running to his arms at last.

◆　◆　◆

Alys tried to pay attention to the scenery, except that Alec kept kissing her and her head was buried in his shoulder for a good part of the journey. They took a train past banana plantations, then climbed up a steep escarpment to the plateau of São Paulo. (The train was known as *A Inglesa*, "the English one," very well named, for it looked exactly like the engines on the suburban lines from Waterloo Station, with padded leather seats and brass lamps.) As the train climbed higher, Alys looked down on the jungle—clotted trees, like broccoli, she thought. They had to change to a cable car for the highest part of the climb, resting for a while at the stationmaster's house, sipping sickly-sweet *cafezinhos* and admiring the orchids around the stationmaster's windows.

Finally they arrived at the *Chácara Santa Emília,* Alys' new home in Santo Amaro. On the advice of the Monteira de Barros family, Alec had chosen a big old mansion south of the city that was surrounded by orchards. It had an atmosphere that he hoped might remind Alys of

England. She surveyed the gardens, laid out formally with flame-red poinsettias, rose verbenas, hibiscus and orange trees.

"You're pleased with it, Alys? It's a little dark, but you'll find you need to keep cool."

"The gables! the little arches—and I love the pink walls, like marshmallow!"

"My God, Alys, if you knew how I've missed you."

"I'm so tired, Alec—do let's go to bed."

But after such a long separation, their first night together was sleepless with love and conversation. They mourned for Lily, remembering her in fond detail. Then Alec questioned Alys about the sale of her salon, amazed at her impetuous, grand gesture.

"I hope you won't regret this, my darling. I hope you will think the sacrifice worthwhile."

"You mustn't say that! You've always teased me with your perfect right to expect devotion—don't tell me you didn't mean a word of it!" Alys tried to make light of his words, but she needed reassurance, not doubt. She had left everything just to be with him, and needed to draw strength from his conviction.

"Mm. I'd forgotten how quick-witted you are. I adore you Alys. You'll never regret this, believe me."

Alys' new dependency on Alec made her hungry for his attention and he responded eagerly, though not knowing why she was so passionate.

Next day Alys insisted on visiting the city to call on the Monteira de Barros family, but the moment she left the house, she realized she was not ready to face the challenge. It was insufferably hot and everything looked quite alien. As they drew nearer, São Paulo rose like a city of circles, reaching up to the glaring sky. Around the foothills lay many villages like Santo Amaro, with ordered populations of European artisans. Then came the forested suburbs, where richer *arrivistas* were building houses of stone and marble. Up and up their car traveled until they came near the Avenida Paulista and the center of the city. The jumble of architectural styles reminded Alys of Fifth Avenue, but this was all so new, gouged out of bare red earth, and still unpaved. As they approached the main part of the city she glimpsed older streets, their splendor now fading. These were the residences of speculators: twenty years ago coffee had boomed and made São Paulo a city of the world. But coffee prices rose and fell, some fortunes were lost, and the houses declined. The wearing climate, constantly alternating heat and rain, claimed back men's constructions as soon as they were neglected. Green streaks of moss stained the old white walls. Plaster moldings fell away from tall windows.

"Here, we're nearly there. Here are the *palacetes* of the old families—grand sight, isn't it?"

Cheek by jowl, the mansions of the coffee barons leaned on each other, heavy with age. The gateways and walls were encrusted with iron railings. Doormen in livery, mercenaries in a colorful army, stood on guard in the entrance halls.

"They look so—barricaded," Alys said, a certain enthusiasm draining from her voice.

"It's just a custom. Old Brazilian families are very private people."

"Exclusive, do you mean?"

"I suppose so." He shrugged, unwilling to be negative.

Alys stepped out of the car with difficulty. She could see servants scurrying into the house. María-Elena soon appeared to welcome them. She looked wonderfully modern to Alys—so familiar in her gestures, after all their meetings in New York. She walked with vitality; all the rest of the family women appeared silently from the shadows in stiff frocks, in silence. Pale and plump, they moved like armchairs gliding on wheels.

"Alys! How wonderful to see you! Mama, may I present Lady Alys Colvin? My mother, a Senhora das Dores, and my sisters, Evangelina and Herminia."

'*Enchantée, Madame,*" the women responded.

Then Leopoldo appeared, his big-city suavity totally suppressed by contact with his doting household. Alys hardly recognized him as the same chic young man whose passion for clothing, cars and gambling consumed a fortune in New York. He seemed reduced to the status of a naughty schoolboy in his own home.

"Alec," Alys whispered. "I don't feel at all well." She had a premonition that she was going to hate Brazil. But Alec's warmth, his comforting arm round her shoulders dispelled the notion instantly.

"My poor thing, we spent far too much time awake last night, when you should have been sleeping . . ." Alys laughed weakly and flirted with him.

" 'Awake' is a good term for it," she whispered, so that only Alec heard. He tried to ignore her suggestive tone, leading her to a chair in the cool tiled hall.

"Is anything wrong?" María-Elena asked with concern.

"I'll just sit down for a moment—I feel a little dizzy," Alys apologized, still trying not to dwell on the splendors of making love to Alec all night long. But it was no use, she was feeling weaker. To her embarrassment, Alys slid gently off her seat to the floor.

"*Coitadinha!* Poor thing! But she'll be all right—look, she's recovering." Alys heard María-Elena's crooning voice through a haze of weakness.

"Goodness! I've never done such a thing in my life before!" Alys said, as Leopoldo and Alec lifted her to her feet. She started to giggle, for Alec was trying to look innocent, but certain lingering thoughts made his eyelashes flicker just a little, and every time they did, she laughed again.

María-Elena stiffened, aware that something secret was the cause of all the embarrassment.

"Would you like to sit quietly here for a while? We'll leave you alone." She opened the door to a blue-tiled room.

Alec pushed Alys none too gently into the small parlor, while María-Elena shooed her family back into the shadows of the house. Alec wrapped his elegant long arms around Alys' tiny body, so that her laughter would not be heard. He kissed her with passion, till her nervous quivering subsided, and she was still and loving in his arms.

CHAPTER 19

A 1 9 1 4 – 1 8

lys changed totally—even physically—in her first months in Brazil. The heat, the luxury of freedom from pressure, made her plumper, shiny-eyed, and almost childlike in her lack of cares. She did not deliberately forget about the war, for there were constant reminders in newspapers and in everyone's conversation. But for a while she wanted just to enjoy Alec. She had missed him for so long. And Brazil, with its wondrous colors and exclusive, high-walled life, was the perfect place to intensify her relationship with him.

The *Chácara Santa Emilia,* the pink stucco house set in its orchards in Santo Amaro, was Alys' refuge from the world of *grã-finismo.* São Paulo's upper crust staged a continuous show. These people never spoke Portuguese, only French; they read imported newspapers, wore imported French clothes (though the men favored English silk shirts and Clarks' leather shoes), and drove at great speed in American cars. Leopoldo, María-Elena's brother, jokingly explained to Alys that his family was suffering a crisis of identity, shifting their allegiance from *La Belle Epoque* to "Fordismo" as he put it. "Fordismo"—the mad energy to manufacture things modern and fast, in factories that swallowed up hundreds of shift workers, day and night. It was true that in the *palacete* of the Monteira de Barros, the grandsons rode their English bicycles through the corridors unheeded, and sat on their saddles through the family lunch. They could do what they liked. The Monteira de Barros were one of the *quantro centão,* or four-hundred-year-old families in São Paulo state. The "four hundred" were permitted to attend Mrs. Astor's balls in New York. It took four hundred years to become one of the Brazilian elite. Alys found this coincidence poetic yet cruel, as if four hundred were the magic number for those who wished to exclude others.

Alys admired how well Alec had slipped into his new life. Every day he had meetings with financiers, mill managers and heads of staff, dragging an unwilling Leopoldo behind him, and trying to teach him how to live up to his responsibilities. Alec's knowledge of Portuguese was helpful, but more important was his nationality. There was a widely held belief that Europeans were far better administrators than Brazilians. Leopoldo explained it to Alys (*he* was far better passing judgment on other people's actions than being active himself):

"We're mere *fazendeiros*—farmers who love the life of the old estates. But we do believe that the future lies in the factories. Alec will help me with European ideas, American systems—'*a lingua do bife.*'" He laughed.

"Cattle talk"—in other words, harsh economic realities. The Monteira de Barros were short of actual cash; in 1913 credit had been tight in Brazil. Now that she had time to go into the details of Alec's affairs, Alys realized what a unique opportunity he had been offered. While in New York, Alec had agreed to put up the capital for a cotton mill, but under Brazilian law, partnerships were risky for a nonresident. That was the reason Alec had decided to go into business with Leopoldo and move to Brazil. She realized that, with all his wealth, Alec was growing mortally bored with his easy, nomadic life and had needed a challenge. Like many Englishmen, he was happiest making a commitment to a world miles from home, with a culture entirely foreign to his own. Just as he had enjoyed the extreme in her behavior when they lived in New York (though he would never behave so outrageously himself), Alec liked the chaos, the opportunism and the exotic luxury of Brazil.

Alys had not expected Leopoldo to become such an intimate friend— at first it was to María-Elena that she turned for support, and for introductions to a circle of friends. But María-Elena led a very different life in São Paulo than she had in New York. She became the self-appointed head of the household, dominating an old-fashioned, retiring mother, and making all major decisions about her younger siblings' lives. Leopoldo gravitated toward Alys as a sort of insurance—just in case he failed to live up to the family's latest expectation of him, and not take to the business.

So while Alec became increasingly involved in work, it was feckless Leopoldo who found a few hours to take her to the cinema in São Paulo for the latest Douglas Fairbanks, or for English tea at the Casa Gavraux, the bookshop for the best families. There they bought French novels, china vases, old prints and Parisian stationery. Leopoldo studied the notice board listing all the "exchanges" that rich bibliophiles wished to make. Exchanging rare editions was more to his taste than gambling on the stock market.

However, María-Elena's position in society and her great beauty made the subject of dress still important to her, whatever her other duties. She took Alys to *La Mascotte*, the city's smartest fashion house, for her professional opinion of Paulistano clothes. It was an imposing Art-Nouveau building, and the windows were filled with bronze sculptures: a child with a basket of fruit, a bacchante with a bunch of grapes. Inside all the best names of Paris were represented: Doucet, Martial, Huet and Callot Soeurs. Alys wondered just how many of these dresses were genuine imports—if New York could not get them, then how did Brazil? She suspected women were paying through the nose for carefully copied work. María-Elena was a little offended by this suspicion, so Alys did not pursue it.

"Wouldn't you like me to make you some things, while I'm here?"

she volunteered. "It would be something to do, and perhaps you could bring me some of your friends."

"Oh no, Alys, that would never do! It was possible in New York, but we couldn't have—I mean, Alec is being so helpful to us, with his background and experience and we do have to consider our obligations . . ."

"Propriety. I think that's what you mean, isn't it?" Alys suggested. "I suspected as much from the first moment we came to your home. I understand."

Alys did understand, but as the door of *La Mascotte* closed behind her and she glanced back at the gilded, falsely imposing statues in the window, she realized that giving up her business was going to hurt her more than she had allowed herself to think.

The news from home did not help. An influenza epidemic swept England that winter, and Dr. Hardy became fatally ill. Alys wished she could be at home to comfort him. Laura nursed him, and wrote as often as she could, but the end was inevitable. Dr. Hardy died alone at home, when Laura had returned to Bladeshill thinking he was mildly improved. The influenza had weakened his heart.

Like a constant nagging reminder of her abandoned world, the death bells tolled. First Daisy Panton lost her two sons. She tried to keep going, but the Dorcas Society had to be disbanded, and all the girls went into wartime posts. Daisy wrote from her country home, apologetic and at a loss. Alys was shocked by the wavering tone of her letter, unable to believe that such an indomitable woman would not recover her spirit. Hurriedly she wrote a letter of comfort, reassuring her good friend that she had been expecting the closure of the Dorcas Society ever since she left England. No more letters came from Daisy . . . another link with the past severed.

Edith Lyttleton's younger brother died. The Smalley girl, Julia, one of Alys' first and most faithful customers, was widowed in her first year of marriage. Soon after, Rose wrote from the salon to say that her husband, George, was missing, presumed dead after the battle of the Somme. Mary, her *vendeuse*, lost her fiancé in the German spring offensive in Flanders. Alys began to dread the arrival of mail from England, for it always brought new disasters.

But there were many things to divert Alys, to make her forget the miseries of others. Alec was as loving and appreciative as she had ever wanted, and life was an adventure. On days when everyone else was busy, she would summon the chauffeur-driven Dodge from the Monteira de Barros family, and make a voyage of discovery through the city.

This was the other São Paulo: corners where Syrian merchants congregated to do business; alleyways of Japanese restaurants and vegetable shops, filled with red and gold banners. German streets, lined with beer taverns, assailing her with the salty-rich odor of cooking meats. On other corners, Armenian women with colored petticoats and headscarves sold bazaar trinkets. Alys glimpsed but never dared enter these varied worlds, and the chauffeur always took her back to the same few doors for proper calls.

The ritual of São Paulo life began to pall after a while. María-Elena knew (or chose only to know) a handful of women from other families as distinguished as her own. It soon became clear to Alys that she was expected to conform. Her traveling companion on the *Verdi*, Paul Ogden, had been right in describing the Monteira de Barros family as a powerful influence in the city. Alys was attached to them, and other people were afraid to make independent friendships with her because of that connection.

Of course it was not exactly the world that Alys would have chosen, and the *grã-finos* were adept at social warfare. But Alys did her best, and the *Chácara Santa Emilia* soon filled with the most interesting mix she could manage; María-Elena's old friends, a few new millionaires known to Alec and a sprinkling of literati.

Alec became a founding member of a new polo club in Santo Amaro. Most of the other members were immigrant Germans, whom Alys found hard to like, but Alec soon took her to task for her prejudices. She discovered that some were Austrian or Swiss, as well as German, and many had left their countries for the same reasons Alec had left New York. On saints' days and other festivals, Alys and Alec would mingle with these new friends, and dance in the chalet-style clubhouse to the strains of a Blue Danube band. At such times Alys would find her new life so remote from everything she had cared about in England that only two responses were possible: great sadness, or the fullest awareness of joy in the moment. With Alec at her side, laughing, telling her jokes and making her feel adored, the choice was a simple one.

Early Sunday morning Alec and Alys rode together through newly planted columns of eucalyptus trees, at the Clube Hípico. Although she did not like horses with Alec's passion, she enjoyed these rides, being close to Alec when he was in his best mood.

"When shall we visit the *fazenda?* Has it all been arranged?" she asked. This was a treat Leopoldo had been promising her for some time.

"At the end of the month. I do admire you, Alys. You were never a country lover, yet you are quite prepared to face the wilderness."

"Well, of course! It's an adventure. Besides, I'm curious about 'The Coronel'—did you know, Leopoldo tells me he has a black mistress, and a son by her, to whom he has given a European education and publicly acknowledges?"

"Yes, I did know. It's not uncommon. Don't be so shocked, Alys. Would it be better if he never saw the fellow?"

"But Madame María must be mortified. Her own father—and she's so religious. Imagine what Grandma Hardy would have done if my father had married a black woman!"

" 'Doña María das Dores.' Come now, darling, your Portuguese should be good enough for that. What does her name mean?"

"Mary, Mother of Agonies."

"Clever girl! Madame Marie rather enjoys suffering, being a martyr and good enough to make up for her wicked old father."

"I can't wait to meet him."

In a month, she did; the whole Monteira de Barros clan packed its bags for a summer trip to the family farm. The first part of the journey, in a private train, was easy enough, but somewhere in the countryside, the train stopped, and they all shifted to carts, squeezed between high wooden wheels and lumbered with the baggage across endless fields. As far as Alys could see, coffee bushes and cotton trees spread across the *"terra roxa,"* the fertile Paulista red earth. The jungle had been slashed and burnt back to provide this vast acreage. In the distance, Alys noticed that some tall trees had been left standing to provide shade round the ancient *fazenda*'s country house.

The Coronel Alfonso Ariños came to the front steps to welcome them. Apart from the darkness of his skin, and a hooked, fleshy nose, he had the refined, sporting appearance of any country gentleman—not unlike Grandpa James.

Alys and Alec were shown to their bedrooms, which were surprisingly monastic, with plain wooden furniture and jugs of iced water. Alys changed out of her traveling clothes (grateful for the layers of muslin veils that María-Elena had recommended, and which were now stained with thick red dust). She slipped downstairs ahead of Alec to look at the salons, before joining her hosts. The rooms were filled with a genie's store of luxuries: Gobelin tapestries, Oriental china, cabinets made of filigree ironwork and Venetian mirrors. She found the Coronel sitting on the verandah, under the wrought iron tracery that supported some ancient vines.

He knew exactly who Alec was. He had been acquainted with Alec's now-deceased relatives, and had even met him once, when as a child he had visited his estates. Now Alec was a member of the Monteira de Barros *parentela*, the extended family network—a mixture of kinship, expediency and personal loyalties—that kept the old families supreme in the Brazilian hierarchy. Alys suspected she was not so readily included. She watched while his white, exhausted daughter, Madame Marie, introduced her, with explanatory notes in a rapid undertone of Portuguese, before disappearing into the domestic quarters. Only Alys and María-Elena now sat with the old man, and presently Alec and Leopoldo joined them.

Leopoldo's grandfather was well acquainted with all their financial plans.

"We should not discuss business with the ladies present," he objected, as Leopoldo launched in, hoping to impress him.

"But my wife is deeply interested—she is a businesswoman herself." Alec touched Alys' hand gallantly, and Alys felt very proud.

"I ran salons—couture salons," she explained, "in London and New York."

"Women and clothes! Don't speak to me of it! Now, out here we have a world of needs and no one troubles about the fashions. But this might amuse you." He held up a catalog of stuffs from a local *venda* that supplied the farmhands.

" 'Blue or light-colored cotton trousers, merino shirts, calico suits, dress materials, handkerchiefs,' " he translated. "What could be simpler than that?"

"What are these?" Alys pointed at another page, trying to be interested, although she could see very clearly that Alfonso Ariños was belittling everything in her past life. Leopoldo leant over shoulder, and quickly translated the list for her, smiling encouragement.

"Brazilian cassinet, Fluminense gingham, Liberty, zephyrs—that's a light muslin—and Bocayuva cassinet. *Nossa Senhora!*" He started to laugh. Alys looked up enquiringly. "Bocayuva was an abolitionist. The description was used to appeal to ex-slaves—I suppose the use of the name Bocayuva became a tradition in the selling of textiles here."

"Oh!" said Alys, smiling as innocently as she could at the old Coronel. "So there *are* tastes and preferences among your country customers." She laughed. "Though obviously your advertisements are not based on luxury, as mine once were!"

"Nonsense!" Alfonso Ariños responded, distinctly irritated by her quickness. "People will always elaborate, when they have nothing better to do . . ."

Alys sat back, sipping tea and sampling the coconut and honey cakes. The Coronel was not a man to challenge or to make an enemy. But his dismissive attitude was hurtful; he had turned his head only degrees away to talk to Alec and Leopoldo, but she felt as if a door had been shut on her. It was irksome. And it suddenly seemed not enough that Alec cared for her and was happier than he had ever been. Coronel Alfonso Ariños made her feel irrelevant and second-place.

Alec and Leopoldo had moved on to a discussion about importing machinery from England for knitting and weaving. Alec wanted to sell some of his own inherited property in Brazil in order to finance a second plant, a printing works in São Paulo itself.

"Come and see the lemon trees," whispered María-Elena, bored.

In spite of the heat and her tiredness, Alys wanted to follow what was said.

"Can I just sit here in the shade for a little longer?"

". . . . diversify to meet various contingencies. With the war, it may be possible to develop an export market to the River Plate countries. We need high-quality textiles for that—perhaps Alys could help with her knowledge of English designs!" Alec suggested loyally.

Alfonso Ariños' patrician eyes flickered in her direction. She had no doubt that he lent no value at all to her possible contribution. It seemed unlikely she would ever persuade a man of his power to change his opinion.

"María-Elena, show me the lemon trees. *Con licença, O Senhor.*"

He acknowledged her attempt at social grace in his native tongue. Alfonso Ariños turned back to the conversation, forgetting her abruptly as she stepped down from the verandah.

María-Elena took her to the lemon groves, through the jaboticaba trees shading the private gardens of the house. *Quinta Elizabeth* was a large square building of three floors, with faded, powdery blue shutters at all the windows. There was a formal garden round all four sides, laid out in French style with pebbled paths and clipped hedges of some exuberant local shrub masquerading as box. They came to a well, the natural spring that had determined the site of the house. A bucket and ladle hung from the arch over it. The water was cool, a stony blue taste on Alys' tongue. In São Paulo, water was a brownish, flat liquid, drawn from clay storage pots containing charcoal filters. It was a sensation of freedom to drink a pure liquid from the earth.

"It's all very strange, very different for you," María-Elena apologized. "Grandfather is very much behind the times . . . Oh God, how I long to go to Europe or America again! Damn this war!" She dropped a pebble, to make a bell-like ringing in the water. "Do you regret coming here?" she asked Alys bluntly.

Alys shook her head. "It's understandable that your grandfather thinks as he does. He's a good man." She thought of the black boy, studying to become a man of letters, but decided not to mention him. Alys did not wish to say anything to María-Elena that might be repeated out of turn. "I have no regrets. Alec stood by me, and now I stand by him."

"But we're so backward here! My grandfather is a country 'coronel'—a 'big shot,' as you say, and that will help the mill at the start. He rules everyone's lives and will force people to buy his goods. But in this country now there are others who will take his place—opportunists, traditionless men."

"Do you include Alec?"

"Oh no!" She was too skillful to be caught by a simple question. "Foreigners, bred by the city—the Italians, the Turks, the Germans— yes, if you like, the other English. Our family must adapt to these new conditions."

Alys began to think that Alec was being used by the Monteira de Barros for their own progress, and hoped he would survive their various plunderings of his experience and fortune. She did not like the proprietorial way that María-Elena spoke of him.

"Alec is very excited by the potential here. He plans to bring over many more young men from England—after the war they will want jobs." Alys added.

María-Elena looked surprised. "Won't Alec go back with you?" she asked.

Alys was caught: "We've no intention of leaving!" she replied, knowing that was what Alec would want her to say, but feeling a sinking sensation as she thought of it. She was worried by the note of hope in María-Elena's voice; it only added to her suspicion that Alec was being used. And now that the words were out, she realized that, eventually, she would have to stop and consider her own future. The romance of fleeing from everything she had built up, her own solid life, was beginning to seem a little insubstantial.

A few weeks of riding, picnicking, and dancing passed amiably at the *Quinta Elizabeth*. The regular dusky drama of the thunderstorms, lightning and torrential rain, abated, and cool winds replaced them. The family moved back to the city, and Alys' carefully composed life of visits with Leopoldo, supportive work for Alec and formal entertaining for the *grã-finos* began again. Whenever she became restless, someone at the *palacete* on Avenida Paulista would descend on the *Chácara Santa Emilia* and take her off for a diversion. Alys felt hopelessly managed by the Monteira de Barros, but as Alec was often away on business at the Itatiba mill, she could not refuse their invitations. She even found herself traveling to the mountains, to Poços de Caldas to stay at the Grand Hotel with Madame Marie and drink the thermal waters. She sat alongside her hostess in the sulphur baths, feeling as if she had aged twenty years. Having never seen Switzerland, it struck her as a curious thing, to visit a health spa for the first time in the tropical highlands of a Brazilian state.

Settled comfortably with her embroidery, wrapped in hot robes, hidden between palm trees, she attempted conversation in French with Madame Marie. The old woman was immensely plump, and not as old as she liked to look. Her soft white skin was unwrinkled, her tiny figure made delicate by a complete lack of exercise and a constant diet of sweetmeats. Alec described her as a *"doña da casa* full of the old tradition," entirely occupied with the servants, spoiling her grandchildren and hardly ever leaving the house.

"It must be very hard for you," Madame Marie began sympathetically.

Alys sighed. They all treated her as if she were suffering so much, when she really rather enjoyed her idle life.

"You all worry far too much about me. I love being here, helping Alec." She could not tell Madame Marie that she and Alec made love every time they shared a bed; every time Alec went to the mill he came back even more delighted to find her waiting for him, and that the novelty, far from wearing off, seemed endless.

"No, *ma chère amie*, I meant that you have no family."

"Oh! But I do! I have the most beautiful daughter, married, with a child!"

"That's not possible!" Madame Marie looked deeply shocked.

"You're so young." Alys' tiny, neat figure was all too evident in her bathrobe.

"I married very young, and—"

"Before Alec? How sad."

Alys realized that the old woman imagined she was widowed, and thought better of giving her all the facts. Obviously María-Elena had avoided giving too precise a background to her friends.

"And you never had more children?"

"No. I never did." It simply had never occurred; with Alec, she had taken precautions, and he had never questioned her choice. It suited him to be free of responsibilities. Recently, she had even forgotten to protect herself; she was almost forty—a little too late to worry. Alys suspected that, ironically, her battles with William on this very matter had been entirely superfluous. She was certain something must have happened to her when Laura was born, and that she could never have another child.

"How simply dreadful for you. And for Alec."

"Not at all! We've been very happy!"

"How very brave you are, and how very good to you he has been." Madame Marie shook her head, infuriating Alys.

"We are very content, Madame. Very content."

But the old woman shook her head sadly, and Alys knew there was nothing she could do to convince her that it was so. To a woman whose enjoyment centered on family prayers and the perfect recipe for *goiabada* (the guava paste that all Brazilians adored), a childless marriage was meaningless.

But at home, Alec was supportive, affectionate and trying very hard to involve Alys in his new life. Because of his pride in her, she tried to be useful. Once, she suggested that the "colonos" wives, the farm workers, might like more variety in the great bolts of gingham and calico sent out to the *vendas*. The problem was storage; the roads were so poor that moving stock took a very long time. Alys' idea was to cut and package a *surtido,* or group of fabrics, and send these out from the warehouse direct. Sales of gingham rose swiftly as a result.

She also worked hard to develop Alec's idea that Brazilian cottons should compete with imported stock from America and England— with the war on, supplies were dwindling. Alec hired many new English technicians who had come out to Brazil before the war, and found themselves high and dry when uncompetitive businesses folded. They were only too glad to work for a partly English company. Alec found his print works, near the river Pinheiros, south of São Paulo center, and built a little office so that Alys could help with the textiles. Alys was very timid about turning her hand to fabrics on such a scale, but with the help of a clever young operator from Manchester she learnt enough about printing to make up a series of patterns on medium-grade cottons. Dots and bold stripes, exuberant and naïve florals, they began to sell, but only in the interior, which amused Alys. São Paulo city was far too smart for her "native" cottons; the wealthy only wore imported silks and lawns.

Those were her best days, sitting in her little wooden studio, wearing a thick calico smock to protect her dress, drawing designs for the Manchester boy, Bob Smythe, to transfer to blocks and take into the works. Sometimes Alys peeped through into the hot, noisy printing room, to watch the giant rollers beating over the cloth, to smell the acrid dyestuffs and human sweat. She always felt apprehensive and shy, but invariably someone would nod to her, "Doña Alys," and she would feel accepted. Unusually, several of the foremen were Brazilian. Alec knew enough about the prejudices of the immigrant workers to make sure that the Englishman really did train his crew, rather than disparage them. It was strange for Alys to hear broad Mancunian accents drop straight into a slangy Portuguese that she could still barely follow.

◆　◆　◆

For Alys' fortieth birthday, in 1915, Alec took her away from work for a few days to a smart country hotel at Campos do Jordão, so that they could ride in the cool air of the surrounding mountains. In the evenings, they watched other more proficient couples dancing to a palm court orchestra. On their last evening, one of the guests, who had noticed Alys' yearning expression, invited her to dance with him. Between waltzes, she came back to Alec, smiling.

"You're sure you don't mind?" Alys asked, eyes shining, extending her hand for Alec's permission to go on. He kissed it, then pulled her closer. "Not if you promise to come upstairs with me after the next one. Watching you makes me—"

"Possessive!" she laughed, but enjoyed his desire. The next dance was all the more enjoyable. . . .

When Alec took her to bed that night, she responded to him as if they had just found each other in love. She ran her hands slowly over his strong, bony back, down his firm arms, then kissed his soft belly, caressing his buttocks, before wanting to arouse him hard. The contrasts in Alec's body, between strength and weakness, force and vulnerability, made her want him most. She lay by his side, loving his face.

"Have you had a good birthday?" he whispered, pushing her hair from her forehead, gently smoothing it behind her earlobes.

"Of course I have. I love you, Alec."

"Many happy returns . . ." he smiled, rolling her into his arms.

In the morning, Alec woke her, and she heard the rattle of the breakfast table being laid by the parlor window next door.

"You're dressed! Have I overslept?" she exclaimed.

"No, not at all. It's just a little problem, I'm afraid. I thought our train left at ten-thirty tonight, but the hall porter tells me it's this morning instead. Sorry, darling—a *'bagunça,'* as they say."

"I know what that means—'a blunder!' They say it all the time at the factory! What a pity. Now I won't be able to seduce you again."

"Damn. I'd have liked that."

He turned, pulling his watch from his pocket.

"Nine-thirty—you've got an hour. Come and have coffee first."

A slip of paper fell by the bed: a crumpled telegram, which instinctively Alys picked up. Alec had not seen it drop.

NECESSARY YOU RETURN   IMPORTANT GUESTS TONIGHT   DINNER AT |
NINE   YOUR SUPPORT MOST VALUED   UN ABRAÇO   MB

Leopoldo: or, more probably, his mother, insisting that Alec fulfill his role as the family's advisor. It was all a fabrication, the change in their train time. Alys hid the telegram under her pillow. Alec had tried to save her feelings, not to fuel her resentment of his other loyalty, to the family business. She had to acknowledge that Alec treated her with tact, and she did not feel she could break their happy mood by accusing him of behaving like a puppet on a string.

◆　◆　◆

Two years passed, and the war seemed no nearer ending. Laura wrote to say that Jonathan was still safe, miraculously only once wounded, and that she and Jack were busy and well. Ned wrote infrequently, but they were most touching letters, describing his experiences and filled with small scribbled sketches. He had volunteered after Lily's death, and now had a not-too-dangerous job in reconnaissance, which gave him plenty of time to draw everything he saw. Taking note of it all had become an obsession with him.

Then Cecily Day wrote, no gossip at all this time, to tell her that Edward had been wounded when the Germans crossed the Marne, threatening Paris just as they had done in 1914 when Alys left England. He was back at home, recovering from his injuries—Cecily was not at all specific about these, which allowed Alys' imagination far too much freedom. Her own letters to Edward's address remained unanswered.

After a bold start, Alec's schemes in São Paulo began to grow more difficult to realize. A general strike, started by the textile workers for an increase in wages, caused the new printing works untold harm. The strike spread, leaving many poor families in the city on the verge of starvation. Some of the wealthier women ran soup kitchens in the slum *corticos*, but as the wife of a factory owner and a foreigner Alys was firmly excluded.

"They do it to spite me!" she complained to Alec. "It's so frustrating, not to feel useful when times are bad!"

"Yes, but Alys, these charitable rituals aren't right for you—for many reasons. You must see the embarrassment . . ."

"Propriety!" she exclaimed. "That's all María-Elena ever says to me!"

"Yes, but look at the other side. You're a modern woman. You're learning about the textile industry—you've given us some wonderful suggestions that have increased our trade."

"Yes, that's true . . . I'd no idea printed textiles could be so varied. I hope you'll let me experiment a little more when this fuss is over." For a moment Alys was positive.

"So, my dearest, don't hanker for the company of women with whom you have nothing in common. You know you'd be bored."

Alys pouted: an expression Alec had never seen in her face before. "You don't understand, Alec. I have to spend my time with these women when you're away, and I feel out of place."

"Then do what you know very well you can do: carve out your own society. You've done it before. Why not now?"

He made perfect sense, of course, and Alys was not at all sure why she could not rise to the challenge, why she felt uneasy and ineffectual. She was entering one of those deadening phases of emotional blindness, when she could not look inward at her feelings at all. She was old enough to recognize the signs in herself: apathy being the worst.

When the strike was finally settled, Alys held a small reception to celebrate Alec's third year in Brazil. (Her real reason was to give some small symbol of her approval for his efforts in forcing the Monteira de

Barros to provide good wages for their men.) Leopoldo, to defend his family's position, insisted on organizing gifts for a cotillion—gold-plated fountain pens, with each guest's name inscribed on them. After a supper served on lace tablecloths decorated with roses and borrowed silver (crested with the ubiquitous "MB") it was time for Alys' special entertainment. She had hired a young black magician from a vaudeville theater in São Paulo. He performed for the guests dressed in a frock coat, white gloves and tan leather shoes, introducing all his tricks in perfect French.

The audience was composed of the French and German consuls, two newspaper proprietors, some lawyers and industrialists known to Alec and those Brazilians whose names guaranteed them an invitation to any grand fete: a Prado, a Penteado, an Alves Lima and a Silva Teles.

They all applauded the magician, then drifted away to champagne and dancing in the candlelit salons. The young man packed up his magic, shiny boxes. He was as handsome as a puma, tall for a mulatto, with long fingers, glittering tight black curls and the softness, the gentle good manners that Alys had come to respect as the most remarkable quality of the true Brazilians.

She still spoke rather poor Portuguese, but tried to thank him for his performance.

"Gostei muifo as brincadeiras," she said, to please him.

"Merci bien," he replied, not lapsing into Portuguese. Alys picked an orchid from a large bowl on the table, and discarding his rose, fixed the spray in his buttonhole.

"A Senhora vai ficar furiosa . . ." He tried to laugh at her, but his nervousness showed when he glanced over her shoulder and bowed too low to a figure in the doorway. Alys turned: Madame Marie was smiling at her, standing quite still, surrounded by swirls of blue light, the cigar smoke caught in the candles. "Maria das Dores" was the perfect name for her, that night. Alys felt irritated and suspicious. The Monteira de Barros scrutinized her all the time, and knew all her activities, her opinions, even the details of her home. The doubts that Alys had pushed to the back of her mind began to plague her. She would never ever be accepted as part of the *parentela.* Brazil was a wonderful interlude, but if she ever expected to build any sense of permanence, she would be making a terrible error. The implications for her and Alec had always been there, but she had avoided thinking about them until now.

Her total dependency on Alec was the cause of her troubles. She loved Alec, but putting her life so completely in his hands angered her—and behind the anger was fear. She always had such a slight hold of her identity that living without goals of her own was making her become invisible to herself.

Alys saw resentment in her attitude toward Alec's world. She hated to be complaining, begging for more of his attention than was fair—more than she would ever have claimed in her former life! Alec was right, she should have made better use of her freedom, but somehow the inhibiting presence of the Monteira de Barros had drained her of vitality—made her own interests seem valueless. She was meant to be Alec's wife, and in that capacity Madame Marie considered her unsuitable—even worse, a failure.

"Good evening, Madame," she said, walking directly toward her. "I hope you've enjoyed yourself?"

"Delightful—it's wonderful how you Europeans enjoy our primitive performers. I'm sure London and New York have much finer entertainments."

"Everyone always enjoys illusionists—I suppose it's the child in us." Alys replied equivocally.

"You did know, didn't you, that there's an Italian company appearing at the Opera House? I could have arranged with the director for some of them to sing for you . . ."

"Oh, no! Madame Marie, you're very kind to think of helping, but it would have been a disaster! Alec positively *hates* opera, and would never have forgiven me."

"Ah, I see. *Pardon*, Madame, *il faut partir.*" Madame Marie bowed too graciously, and gathered up her clan.

When all the guests had left, and Alec had swayed a little drunkenly upstairs to bed, Alys felt restless and walked for a while in the gardens. Downstairs all was quiet. The servants, a slow-moving amiable black army in starched linens, had cleared the rooms, swept away the broken glass and crushed flowers and gone to their squat stone huts at the back of the house. Alys wandered through the emptiness. The house was a friendly, wood-paneled place, with intimate dark corners kept from the sun but now strangely illumined by a high yellow moon. None of the shutters had yet been closed. Alys heard laughter from beyond the kitchens—in a storeroom or in the ice-pantry perhaps. Someone should come to lock the windows. She went nearer the back of the house and saw that the door to the corridor between the kitchens lay open.

The young magician had one of the kitchen maids as a private audience. She sat at the end of a marble table on which the desserts had been set out on bowls of crushed ice. She wore only her camisole and petticoats for coolness; a wrinkled blouse hung on the back of the chair. Her hair was unpinned, the bushy mass held back by her lace cap and sticking out round her ears.

The magician was repeating his act, but describing it to the girl in his soft, unintelligible Brazilian. Thick African sounds and rhythms mixed with the nasal vowels of Portuguese. His voice rose and fell musically with emphases. He did not touch the girl, who sat with her chin resting on her hands, her plump shoulders and arms shining brown. When the young man finished, she laughed, covering her mouth with her palms to stop the noise and, when that failed, throwing her apron over her head.

They looked so casual in their fierce attraction for each other that Alys could not go on watching—but stayed just long enough to see the magician study the girl laughing, a broad grin spreading on his face. Then he poked one long finger into a trifle, and licked the cream. Alys could see that within minutes they would be in each other's arms, and not just for kissing. Thank God *someone* broke the rules, she thought, slipping off her shoes and moving as quietly as she could along the corridor to the main stairs.

She ran into the bedroom, where Alec was snoring, too much cigar smoke and small talk thickening in his head.

"Alec!" She shook his shoulders. "Are you asleep?"

"Absolutely not," he said. "How could I sleep when you attack me like that? How wonderful, Alys. I did not think you'd have the energy for it now . . . Come here, give me a kiss."

"Do you really love me?" she asked, holding him tightly.

"Of course I do. Don't be silly, darling—why does champagne always make you cry? It was a splendid evening—a social triumph. You'll see—*O Correio* will be full of us all in the morning."

By now he was wide awake and peeling off her clothes.

"I told Cida to go to bed, not to wait up for you, so I could do this . . ." he confessed, slipping his hands inside the layers of chemise and silk to place his hands round her breasts.

"Alec, listen to me. We don't belong here, I don't belong here, and I want to go home. Are you listening to me?"

But he did not hear her, and in the excitement Alys felt, already aroused by the beautiful sensuality of the girl and boy downstairs, she let him fill her mouth with kisses and slide her out of her clothes. They made love tenderly, not very skillfully, for Alec was more willing than able after a night of champagne. Somehow the very friendliness and trust in his apology ("Not entirely my best tonight, darling") made Alys even more unhappy. When she cried, he thought it was just the effect of the party, and fell asleep misunderstanding.

◆　◆　◆

The more Alys insisted on leaving, the more trenchant Alec became. At first he tried to pretend that she was exaggerating, just feeling homesick because of the endless sad news of her friends. He, too, was deeply affected by the losses of the war, he kept repeating, but it only made him even more determined to succeed with his new life. All the distance that had existed between them in New York rose up again, but this time it was much wider.

Alys' depression deepened with the very endlessness of the war. If peace was ever mentioned in the papers, or on newsreels, there was a reluctant hint that it would be an exhausted stalemate, a truce. The idea of all that struggle, for no real purpose, made her feel yet greater frustration.

She arranged to meet Alec at the Clube Hípico one day, after work at the printing plant. It was a cool wet evening; the *garoa*, a yellow blanket of fog like London's, thickened under the trees along the bridlepaths. Alec was late, so Alys went out for a ride alone just for the pleasure of the cool air, and to think over what she could say to him differently, or more forcefully, so that everything would be better between them. She could not hear any other riders, and realized that the fog was growing thicker, and it would be unwise of her to venture too far from the clubhouse. She turned her horse back sadly, dreading talking to Alec. She had tried so hard to share his life, and had so nearly succeeded. Guilt for her friends and a more personal sense of futility was making the task harder all the time.

Near the clubhouse was the riding school, where other members practiced dressage—a sport that struck Alys as even more useless than the rest. Alec still had not appeared, so Alys walked to the hall to watch the riders from the balcony. Alec met her as soon as she reached the top of the steps.

"There you are! I've been looking everywhere for you!"

"I went out for a short ride."

"That's what the groom said, but I couldn't believe you'd do such a risky thing in the fog. Really, Alys!" Alec turned away, annoyed that she had worried him. Alys was instantly repentant, for he had many responsibilities—and then just as instantly furious that she always had to be good.

Alec stood with his arms folded, intently watching the riders down below. The horses moved in silent, elegant circles, only the chinking of the reins and the occasional snorting from the animals breaking the silence.

"Stupid occupation," Alys said, sulking.

"Oh Goddamnit, Alys, nothing pleases you."

She could feel the tension rising, but did not stop it. "One thing would please me very much," she said, her heart thumping.

"Shall I guess? Are you really sure you would like me to make just one guess?" Alec sounded so exasperated and disappointed with her.

Alys looked down, and saw that one of the figures riding was María-Elena. While everyone else was maintaining immaculate posture, her perfectly formed face looked up, a white oval of female desire, staring at Alec. María-Elena did not care that Alys saw her, for she sensed that after years of waiting, her time was coming nearer.

"You really won't miss me, Alec," Alys whispered, and ran down the stairs.

"How can you say that!" he demanded, hurrying after her.

"Because there are certain people who will make damn sure that you don't!" she accused.

Alec was furious. "That's beneath you. Stop this madness. Don't flounce off like that."

"Oh, let me go! Let me go!" Alys shouted back, running through the fog to her waiting car. She heard Alec's quickening pace behind her, and for the first time since she had known him she did not want him to stop her. This time she would go away, forever.

"Alys!" Alec's voice was angrier, and more distant. He had stopped following her, and was just calling her to come back. "Alys!" But she kept on, not running now, because she was out of breath, but walking blindly toward the gates of the Clube Hípico.

When Alys got home, she locked herself in a guest room, and sat hunched on the bed, waiting for Alec to discover her. Hours passed and still she waited. The cold *garoa* seeped in round the shutters, making the sheets feel damp and her clothes cling to her. Alys shivered, but almost valued the sensation of cold and panic, as it kept her awake longer. At last, Alec returned. After an interminable delay, he climbed the stairs. She could tell by the sounds of the corridor exactly how near to their bedroom he went. Then the steps stopped abruptly. One, two, three; with her eyes closed, Alys pictured him turning uncertainly, looking down the corridor for a light under another door. He came nearer—she thought she would scream some dreadful abuse at him as soon as his hand touched the door. But he stopped, and she heard his hard breathing. The whole world was suspended in Alys' fear. She was well aware that this was the turning point in her life, and that if she did not call out to him, apologize for her accusations, he would consider it such a breach of faith that their life together would be over. She clenched her fists, forcing herself not to utter a single sound, getting dizzy with the effort of barely moving to breathe. Then Alec walked away, and she collapsed on the bed.

The next few weeks were nightmarish. Alys became obsessed with the idea that Alec had been conducting a long-term affair with María-Elena. She locked herself in the guest bedroom every night, lying there awake, thinking back over all the small incidents from the very beginning of her relationship with Alec that made it likely. María-Elena was beautiful; she had always been a little distant toward her—perhaps that might have been moral scruple, preventing her from being utterly two-faced?

Leopoldo had taken up the role of escort rather surprisingly, as he had always been a kind of younger-brother figure in Alec's life before. Was that out of pity for her ignorance? Perhaps the "Coronel" knew too, and despised Alys for not understanding her position. Perhaps Madame Marie secretly approved of María-Elena's schemes for Alec. After all, by Catholic rules she and Alec were not married at all, because of her divorce. The thought made Alys want to scream with fury. Seven years of attachment, affection, great change and tumultuous experience were being destroyed. Her isolation, without a single close friend near her, only added to her fantasies.

Keeping herself physically apart from Alec was the final blow to her marriage. They were forced to meet during the day to discuss work at the printing plant, or to attend social functions with the Monteira de Barros. Alec looked drawn, and nothing he said reassured her.

"Tell me it isn't true!" she would cry, trying to grasp his hand.

Alec pulled away from her. "I won't talk to you about it, Alys. If I take any of this seriously, there will never be an end to it. You will pursue me with your mistrust for the rest of my life. It doesn't matter what I say."

"Then it *is* true!"

"You see?"

"I see that you deny nothing, and don't care if I leave you!"

"I do care. I've always cared. Be honest, Alys; if you were happy here, would you have thought of it?"

"Oh, how can you say that! After all I've tried to do, to help you, to support you!"

"But how much you resent it. How very much you resent it." Alec shook his head and turned away. "I can't be eternally grateful for your sacrifice."

"You're twisting everything, I feel as if I'm losing my senses! Now you're suggesting it is all *my* fault!" Alys was so angry that she pummelled on Alec's arm. Alec hated that: he hated any show of violence, and she could see the beginning of distaste for her growing in his response.

"Please don't do that. You know I don't like it."

◆   ◆   ◆

All this time, the Monteira de Barros circled round Alys, offering to take her for a drive, inviting her to suppers on the Avenida Paulista, escorting her to gallery openings in the rua Libero Badari, where she and María-Elena used to go to buy trinkets. That is, Madame Marie and Leopoldo looked after her; María-Elena suddenly decided to go to Itatiba, to stay with the "Coronel" at the *Quinta Elizabeth*. It was all the confirmation Alys needed. Alec could visit the mill and call to see her there, unsuspected.

Alys was with Leopoldo, hypnotically functioning through a *matinée dansante* at the Rose Club, when the news that the war had ended came through to the streets of São Paulo. Firecrackers popped, streamers flew, and Alys swung round and round with Leopoldo. In spite of the madness of relief, she wished that it was Alec who held her, not a perfumed, taut-skinned boy in expensive clothes. She knew that instant would be forever in her memory; the day that the war ended, when she had danced with Leopoldo, tearfully gazing at his silk shirt and his long white neck, wishing he were Alec.

Leopoldo took her home to Santo Amaro. Alys did not expect Alec to be there and was surprised to see lights burning in all the downstairs rooms. As the Dodge drew up to the door, he came out and stood waiting on the steps. Alys wanted to fling open the door, run into his arms for a kiss to celebrate the end of all the struggles.

He smiled at her, seeing the eagerness on her face, and she saw that he was crying. He made no effort to wipe his face.

"Oh, don't, Alec. Please don't be so upset! It will all be all right now! Please!"

But before she could hold him, Alec put out a warning hand to stop her, and shook his head.

"I have to tell you. María-Elena does love me, and I have been unfaithful to you—not often, but a few times before you came out to join me."

"Never since?" She had to ask, mechanically.

"A few times."

"Oh, Alec." She hated him—but she wasn't insane with her suspicions! She had not lost her senses. She had been right, and felt nothing but freedom in the truth.

"But it didn't mean anything to me. At the beginning, I thought perhaps you wouldn't come." Suddenly he held her very tightly. Alys heard Leopoldo shuffling by the car, obviously listening. How she hated all of them, the Monteira de Barros. Then a terror seized her.

"Why are you telling me this? Something's happened. Is it Anne? Laura? Tell me! Tell me!" She broke free of Alec, and started to shake him, tearing the collar of his coat.

Leopoldo ran forward, and caught her just as Alec shouted the words, and Alys stumbled.

"Jonathan died. An explosion. Last week."

CHAPTER 20

A 1918 – 20

lys traveled straight to Bladeshill
when her ship docked. She had sailed back to
England at once, alone. Familiarly alone, with
Alec on the other side of the world, only this time
for good. María-Elena could have him if she
wanted.

Alys' reaction was not sexual jealousy. She
could not forgive Alec for expecting her to

change her whole life at his request, and then to betray her so casually. It was weak and treacherous of him. But anger always made Alys honest: her loss of face in front of the Monteira de Barros had counted almost as much in her decision, and in this she knew she was at fault.

She turned from such depressing thoughts to the view she knew so well beyond the carriage window. The greenness of the landscape overwhelmed her. After the violence of tropical colors, the subtleties in hedges, meadows and fields—all shades from gray and silver to olive and apple-green—filled her confused mind with healing, refreshing images. Women still worked on the land, alongside young Boy Scouts. Alys had the sudden realization that the lads she had watched in 1914 had probably grown old enough to die in the trenches before the end of the fighting.

All the family ran out to the doorstep when they heard the sound of her taxi arriving. Laura, standing erect, calm and smiling; Maurice, agitated, passing his walking stick from hand to hand so that he could wave and yet keep his balance; and little Jack, his father to the life with his clear blond looks, jumping up and down because the dogs were chasing the car wheels and barking.

He ran to her car door.

"Where's the monkey? My monkey?" he demanded.

"What monkey?"

"Grandpa said you'd bring me back a Brazilian monkey!" Jack began to see he might be disappointed.

"Oh, Jack, where are your manners!" Laura came forward to kiss Alys. "I'm sorry about the little fellow, Mama, I don't know how he could forget himself like that . . ."

"Goodness, he's a baby. Look here, Jack, kiss your grandma—that's better—now, let me see—pull those bags out, can you? Thank you, driver!"

"Oh, do come in." Maurice tottered a little, in protest at all the fussing about the child, but Alys would not stop until all her cases and boxes were emptied out on the path.

"It's perfectly natural for the boy to be excited. And I *do* have something for him—now look, John, look!"

From inside the taxi, behind several hat boxes, Alys produced the boy's gift. Disheveled from her journey, flushed with pleasure at the sight of her own dear family, she looked just as exotic as Jack had always dreamed his Brazilian grandma to be. There she stood, dressed in black velvet, holding a green parrot in a brass cage.

"Oh, Grandma! I can call you Grandma, can't I? Will you call me Jack? That's what you used to call me, isn't it, and Daddy did too, but he's dead, but I like to be called Jack now because I don't like John."

"All right. Jack it shall be then." Alys looked nervously at Laura across the boy's head, but Laura's kind smile did not fade.

"What shall you call the parrot, darling?" She picked up the cage and led them all into the house.

"I'm afraid it already has a name. *'Fecha boca,'* " Alys said.

"What's that?" Jack demanded.

" 'Shut up' in Brazilian," she answered, and Jack squealed with pleasure and jumped round her skirts. Laura laughed again.

Alys took her daughter's hand and held her back while Jack and Maurice went into the house.

"I'm so sorry." she said.

"Oh, Mama, it's so awful. So near the end. He wasn't even fighting—a storehouse blew up at the camp. I tell you, for a while I was so angry, I didn't think I could go on. But Jonathan was so good to me. We were very happy." She cried very suddenly and just as suddenly stopped. "Happens all the time. Can't help it."

"Here's my handkerchief." Alys cuddled her, and they were both silent.

"Come on," Laura said, at last. "I'm so glad you're back. You didn't really bring that bird from Brazil, did you?"

"Of course not. Harrods, where else?"

Laura laughed. "How perfectly splendid. Let's try to be cheerful, just for Jack. He's so pleased to see you."

"I'll try. I won't do half as well as you, brave girl. Jonathan would be so very proud of your courage. I am."

It was very hard. Jonathan was a presence all round the house, a memory of loving so strong that not only Laura but all of them seemed to be conscious of it. There was no sign of his former existence, no boots in the hall, no hats on the pegs or pipes left by the magazines. But Jonathan was still there in the comfortable warmth of his family's life.

"I'll see to lunch." Laura disappeared. "The others are in there. Go ahead," she called back. Her voice drifted along the hallway; Alys was so happy to hear it. She felt compensated a little for the misery of losing Alec. All that was entirely her choice, she could still forgive him and carry on with her married life. But continuing in Brazil seemed pointless if she would have to contend with the insecurity of losing him to someone else. It wasn't simply that Alec was untrustworthy. No one was perfect, and he had been devoted to her and tried to protect her from his mistakes. It was also that Alys would never really be convinced and hated to feel that she was compromising.

She walked toward the study, where little Jack had decided his parrot should take up residence.

Maurice straightened up as she came into the room.

"He likes it in here," he said. "This parrot is obviously used to living in men's company—did you buy him from a pirate, Alys?"

"Oh yes, from a pirate in the port of Santos," she agreed, taking Jack on her knee. "He was a black man, selling black crabs on a stick, tied on strings, like necklaces, and the parrot sat on his shoulder, calling to all the customers *'Siris-siris-siris-siris'* . . ."

Maurice leaned back in his leather chair, listening to Alys' traveler's tales with the same boyish pleasure as Jack.

For Alys, making a friend of a child was a novelty. When he was born, she had been full of her own success, unaware of the pleasure she now found in being a special figure in a child's life. She fell into her part, and began to sense that where she had been frustrated and impatient as a mother, she could now be more tolerant. Jack kept asking for more stories about far-flung places, and Alys imagined the pleasures in embroidering her memories.

Carrigrohane could become a garrison fort of elves and gnomes, fighting the banshees; Itatiba, the frontier between the white man and the hordes of Amazonian Indians. She even thought how she might tell him about her own infancy in Denver, enlivening it with adventures of Red Indians and the building of the railroads. Talking and daydreaming with Jack made it all come back: a safely distanced, stylized past.

The calmness and sense of belonging that Bladeshill gave her reassured Alys, and allowed her to look to her future. She was quite determined to start again, to prove to everyone, but especially to Alec, that her individual life was not important to her just out of vanity or selfishness, but because she needed to be creative.

Alys kissed Jack goodnight, and prepared for supper with her daughter. Laura's courage in facing her bereavement humbled Alys, but also strengthened her resolve to strike out, build up her work again, so that she could offer Laura support. Not finance—Jonathan had left Laura and Jack well provided for—but perhaps a companionable sense of enduring, struggling on, so that Laura would not feel she was on her own.

"William and Madeleine are here," Laura announced, when Alys came downstairs.

"Good God! Not for supper!" Alys sank into a chair.

"Mama, as if I would. No, of course not—I mean they're at Upton. I thought you should know. They gave up Richmond during the war—Madeleine grew nervous of the danger of invasion! Imagine! I visit occasionally, but—"

"Not William, too—no injuries there surely! He didn't fight?"

"No, a desk job. No, I don't find it so pleasant as I used to. Madeleine ignores Jack, and William criticizes his manners and —"

"They're happy as they are," Maurice interrupted. "I do keep explaining, my dear, that they have no children, and they like their house to be ordered. Old people do."

"You don't," Laura disagreed, contented.

"I'm in my dotage. Different."

"Dotage! The only difference is that you dote on Jack," Laura teased him.

Alys was well satisfied with the picture of Madeleine and William, fussing about Upton Park, positioning ancient plunder and Chinese vases precisely in front of cold, polished mirrors, traveling to London sales to acquire yet more fine objects for their private collection, their mausoleum.

"Madeleine always kept a beautiful house," Alys recalled, somewhat ambiguously.

"Mama! Oh, Mama, I do love your 'disapproving' face. No wonder women do just as you tell them when you look like that . . ."

"I don't know," said Alys, but the pleasure of being so easily understood flooded through her. She had been a foreigner for a very long time.

Emboldened by Alys' good mood, Laura asked her difficult question.

"Alec *is* coming back later, isn't he? I expect it was difficult for him to leave so quickly."

'No. I don't think so. I'm sorry, but I don't want to talk about it. One thing at a time, I think." Alys' tone was unmistakably final.

"Champagne?" Maurice offered, and they celebrated her return.

◆　◆　◆

But when Alys arrived back to London and considered her situation, she felt very grim. London was not the elegant city she had left. Ordinary people had taken it over. Everyone smoked in public, in the cafés and even on the streets. Everyone rode on the buses; once Alys saw an old lady pull the cord on a bus for herself, so that she would not miss her stop, and the conductor whipped round when he heard the bell ringing and shouted in her face. Alys understood that people's nerves were still bad from the exhaustion of the war effort. But, slowly, signs of release were beginning to appear. On Sundays, the parks filled with working girls in their summer-best clothes, cloche hats jammed down to their eyebrows, silk-stockinged legs jutting out below short skirts as they sat on the grass. Nobody cared about appearances or behavior.

All this shocked Alys. In the four years she had spent in Brazil, she had formed a slightly idealized picture of England, how it would be when she returned home. But a convulsion in English society had taken place, more obvious to her than to her friends because she had been on the other side of the world as it proceeded. She decided to see how her salons were surviving, under new management. Mr. Szenkier might have other attitudes to the new world, different from her own.

Mr. Szenkier was grateful to Alys for the opportunities she had given his daughters, when he himself was struggling to build his business. Now he was a rich man, one of the few who had made the transition from prewar handwork to a mechanized operation. But respect for Alys made him gentle with her, and he realized how different the running of the salon would look to her now. He bowed, folding his hands like a priest as he showed her his new lines in coats and machine-made beaded dresses.

"You see, Madame, these loose shapes we can do. Pre-war, you needed skilled hands to put in sleeves and all those darts at the waist! You had real technicians then, didn't you, Madame?"

She appreciated his flattery; it was kind of him not to regard her as "old-hat" in the fashion world. How utterly stupid she had been to sell everything up when an entire industry was just beginning.

"Trouble is, Mr. Szenkier, I don't know how on earth I could work in all this. Where are my customers now? Most of my ladies are widows, with old estates, no heirs and no money to speak of." Alys thought of Daisy Panton, who had lost both her sons. Word had it she barely stirred from the country now.

"That may be true, Madame, but your name has great attraction too. People still remember it, even the ones you never dressed before. If you want to come back—I'm sure we could come to some arrangement . . ." Mr Szenkier touched his rows of clothes a little protectively, almost apologizing to Alys for his success in taking over her company.

"You're very kind, Mr. Szenkier. But I'm not sure that I have anything to offer you . . . I need time. I have so many personal matters to attend to." Alys did not relish working in an alien atmosphere. "Salon Alys" still existed for a wealthy handful, but a larger proportion of Mr. Szenkier's clothes went out to the smarter London stores, where other labels were stitched inside them. Alys did not like the idea of such faceless production.

"Ah. Sad. And Sir Edward. A tragedy." Mr. Szenkier shook his head. "I tell you, it was not very easy, being in business with a name like mine. Sir Edward was very good to me."

"I don't understand."

"Oh, so many times we were accused of being German sympathizers, spies. The salon a cover operation. Me, from a long line of Polish tailors!" He wound his watch angrily, the memory of it stirring him. "Sir Edward published a disclaimer, and put his own name to it. In the *Times.*"

"That was just what he would do. I hope it helped?"

"Yes, a little." Mr. Szenkier did not wish to dwell on the subject. "And then all the bullet-makers' wives, the black-marketeers' girl friends, wanted our dresses, and we survived."

Alys was sure he exaggerated, but Mr. Szenkier had certainly made her see how little of her world was left. Any hope she had quietly entertained of going back to Berkeley Square, in any capacity, seemed futile.

She had to see Edward. The house in Berkeley Square was altered beyond recognition, requisitioned by one of the Ministries, and Mr. Szenkier would not go into details about Edward's health, only giving her a new, puzzling address. Alys recognized it as a small street in Kensington, not far from the park, and wondered why Edward had chosen such a quiet, modest place. She wrote, asking to see him, and was surprised when Charlotte telephoned to suggest an afternoon.

It dawned on her that Cecily had only written the briefest detail, that Edward had been invalided out of the army, and had given no hint of his condition. Alys had blithely assumed that he was recovering well.

"Didn't Cecily explain to you?" Charlotte asked in a crisp voice on the phone.

"I haven't seen Cecily. I went straight to the country when I got here, to see my daughter." She found herself apologizing. Alys was ashamed of her disregard for Charlotte during her affair with Edward. She only realized how self-centered she was now that she had been deceived herself.

"Edward can't walk, and he has trouble speaking clearly." As Alys heard Charlotte's direct, cool tones, all their past antipathy seemed justified. But then what Charlotte said pushed all that aside. "That's why I'm calling you myself. Do come, Alys. He'll be so very pleased to see you."

He was. Edward's great bulky figure straightened in his chair, and his hand shot out to hold hers. Even though he had lost weight, he still gave the impression of solidity and strength. But his head made Alys see how ill he was: his once handsome face, with its broad bones and florid features, was gray and drawn. It revealed all the harshness of his character, hidden before under a sensuous, fleshy fullness.

Charlotte left them alone. Alys knew that she had to hide her shock, and give Edward all the confidence she could to help him fight for health.

"Dearest friend . . . I'm so happy to see you, Edward. Thank God you came back!" she exclaimed.

She bent over and kissed him. He made an alarming guttural sound, like the noises he used to utter when they made love. He could not find words.

"I've only been back myself a few weeks—I went to stay with Laura, otherwise I would have come sooner, I so wanted to see you, and even more so when I spoke to Mr. Szenkier . . ." Alys chattered on as best she could, to give Edward a chance to form his speech. He signaled that he wanted to try, and spoke thickly at first.

"Damn sorry to hear—about Jonath-an," he whispered. His rich voice was still there, a broken instrument, irregular in pitch.

"So very many gone . . . that's why we're glad to have you, dear man. Look, I brought you something from Brazil. I'll unwrap it, shall I?"

It was a cherrywood box, painted inside on felt, a backgammon game. Edward managed a "Ha!," and his hands rested on the lid. He could not even open it, Alys realized. His hands were weak and the box too heavy. It was a useless gift. She began to apologize for her mistake, growing tearful, but Charlotte came in and rescued her, removing the box from Edward's lap.

"I've made tea. Alys, will you help me, please? It's Mrs. Browne's day off. We'll only be a minute, darling."

They left Edward, Alys stumbling after Charlotte, trying to regain her self-control.

Charlotte turned round to face her in the kitchen, the first time they had ever met alone.

"That was a bit of an excuse. I thought you'd like to leave the room."

"Thank you. I'm sorry. I'll do better now."

"Of course you will. Edward had a stroke, after surgery for a leg wound. His army friends call often, but he doesn't like to see them. You were—before all that. I think it helps."

"I'll do anything I can. You must get very tired, nursing him all the time?"

"We do have Edward's batman, he came with him. He helps lift and bathe him, that sort of thing. He won't be touched by a woman, as you can imagine."

"Oh, Charlotte." Any pretense at hiding her former feeling for Edward seemed unnecessary; Charlotte accepted it.

"Goodness. The tea's going to be cold. I'm hopeless at this sort of thing. I can't get used to no staff at all. It's easier in the country, but Edward won't go down."

Alys could understand why: Edward's grand home would remind him too much of his former pleasures, a ruined way of life.

They went in to take tea together, and after Charlotte helped Edward sip from his cup, the two women played backgammon for him, in front of the fire. The dice rattled in the leather cups; at one point Edward asked quite distinctly if he might look at them. He ran his big hands carefully over the tooled gilt surface. Alys had had his family crest carved into the sides of the shakers. Edward nodded at her, admired the cups, and handed them back to her.

"Very fine." he said.

◆　◆　◆

An unexpected pleasure came to Alys just when she was beginning to find London unbearably difficult and sad. Lisa Allen, once her mannequin, came back. She traced Alys through the salon, and turned up at the hotel in Dover Street, still the same comfortable corner of Mayfair where the model girls had once rehearsed in secret. Lisa was no longer beautiful. Her parents had died, her young husband had been lost in the trenches and she had ended up working in a munitions factory for two years. Her skin was badly marked with eczema, from handling TNT, and her always fragile beauty very much eroded by unhappiness.

"Can I stay with you for a while?" she asked. "You don't mind if I ask you, Madame? I always felt you cared for me, and you helped me very much, from the start."

"Good gracious. Don't think of it. It looks as if you've been a foolish girl, putting your health in danger like this."

"I'm only tired. Isn't everyone?" Lisa said, smiling wanly, the smile that always affected Alys as if she knew Lisa intimately, under the skin.

"I have grand plans, and you shall be my secretary," Alys pronounced, and from that day on, life improved.

Slowly, Alys gathered up the shreds of her past. Hardly ever did she talk about Alec. She did not even tell Laura the truth, judging her unprepared for more loss. Everyone she met in London was equally preoccupied with sorting out their relatives, their lives and their finances. A woman temporarily without her husband struck no one as odd.

But what to do? She positively rejected the idea of sliding into a graceful dowager's life, living with Laura and Jack at Bladeshill. She had enough money from the sale of her business to keep her well for a good few years. But inactivity and indulging herself did not appeal to her. She had already wasted too many previous years in Brazil—entirely wasted them—and she was determined to make up for lost time.

Alys felt very out of touch. Before, in London, without quite knowing how, she had understood the desires of her clientèle instinctively, and the colors and shapes that came to her then were exactly what women wanted to wear. Alys spent many days wandering through London, soaking up the atmosphere of the city and its people as it recovered from the stringencies of war. The freedom that women had fought so hard to win impressed her; young girls looked upright and full of themselves, compared to the demure young things in long skirts that she used to dress. Hard faces, flat chests, a swinging stride in their walk. The bright-red lips amazed her; and the perpetual smoking got on her nerves.

Supposing everyone looked upon her as a "voice from the past," when she still wanted to face up to new worlds, try to be innovative! Alys did not want to be sad, or think of her failures. How curious it was that although she hated Alec for his adultery, she could not help still loving him. Their good years together had so changed her, nourishing her with such a sense of her own lovableness, that she felt quite whole. Choosing to remember the best years, and not continuing to live with Alec once they had been stolen from her by María-Elena, was her way of being faithful to the spirit of her life with him. It was not a logic she could explain to anyone, but she held to it all the same. Alys was left with a curious sense of peace and freedom. She had made her choice, and was almost elated by the honesty of it. How hard it was, to feel so clear and strong, and yet to find that the world was beginning to treat her like an old-fashioned woman!

Alys did not feel even middle-aged—her heart and spirit were as searching and yearning for experience as ever. The only advantage of increasing years was that she had yet even more courage to do exactly what she chose to do—and the maturity not to mind what others thought. She did not give a damn for the world, and it had taken her until she was precisely forty-four to be rid of it.

Friends helped. Charlotte's devotion to Edward inspired Alys to put aside all nostalgia for pre-war times. Charlotte worked all day at an orphanage in Battersea, of which she was a governor, and in the evenings she organized suppers for Edward's closest friends, so that he would be constantly stimulated by company. She was very modern, Charlotte, in her short dresses and cropped hair—and she too smoked constantly. In the end, Alys succumbed to the habit herself, then, typically, became a collector of exotic cigarette holders. She would sit with Edward several times a week, in the early evening, at a small table, and play solitaire while they chatted, a long ebony holder jutting out of her mouth. One "White Lady," a stiff cocktail to last her until Charlotte came home, stood at the side of her cards. When Charlotte had dressed for dinner, the two women sat together and entertained Edward with their opinions until other visitors arrived.

Charlotte's clothes ceased to look ugly to Alys. The girl had never had her Aunt Cecily's passion for dressing. She had dressed *comme il fallait* before the war, and now it did not matter. Charlotte had the simplest shift dresses run up by a little woman who lived near the orphanage, relieved that she no longer had the social pressure to "dress up" as a Duchess once did. In her own way, Alys decided, Charlotte was the greatest lady she knew in London—moving with the times, intelligent, not frivolous, yet still full of charm. Her growing friendship with Charlotte surprised Alys, as well as a good few of their mutual friends.

One evening, Cecily called at Edward's house when Alys was visiting. She was no longer Mrs. Leslie Day, for her husband had "gone," as people said, when referring to those missing and presumed dead.

Cecily, left with a fortune (and very little regret for Leslie Day) had remarried a middle European. He was suave, *too* charming for Alys' experienced eye, and referred to as "Cecily's Count," though whether he legally had a title or not was a matter of dispute. Cecily certainly behaved as if she had one, and gave her husband the nickname "Legless." Alys did not find out if this was because he obviously was drunk quite often, or because the epithet approximated the sound of his real name, Lewinski.

Cecily looked characteristically glamorous, and Alys' eyes brightened at the sight of her.

"Paris." She suddenly thought of it. "Cecily, did you buy that in Paris?"

"Darling, you must come over with me. Legless has simply wonderful friends there, and we pop to and fro all the time. Stay with us—it would be such fun, like old times. Do say yes."

"I'll think about it—I'm waiting until Anne comes back, and then perhaps we'll come together—would you approve?"

"Dear Miss Hardy—quite a heroine she's become with all her war work. Built herself a good following."

Alys smiled beatifically. Only Cecily could imply that Anne's efforts had been purely an exercise in self-promotion.

"We're both rather good at drawing attention to ourselves," she responded, throwing Cecily momentarily off-balance by seeming to agree with her. Cecily recovered very quickly.

"Oh, I wouldn't say that! No one minds that you went away for the war at all! No one said anything—we all understood!"

"Cecily!" A deep growl from Edward's corner forced her to turn at once. "Did you tell—Alys—that you sold . . ."

"Ssh! Edward dear, don't rush so. No. I didn't. Of course, she visited the old place—how one forgets . . . Mmm, I must ask Legless to mix some more cocktails . . . would you like one, darling? Yes?" Cecily drifted away, trying not to appear eager to go.

"What was all that, Edward? You have some hold on her, I can tell!" Alys laughed at him, wishing to dispel the cruelty of Cecily's remarks.

"Bloody woman. Sold up Melbury before Leslie was stiff. Gone to a man in pea-canning."

"Oh dear. It was a beautiful old house."

"I'd rather it was a public park. Then everyone could make love in the bushes. What do you say? The lads that came back. Deserve it."

"Edward!" Alys blushed at the remembrance. When he laughed,

Charlotte (who had not heard a word) turned to look, so relieved and happy that Alys could not be embarrassed by his frankness. Charlotte had never found out—Edward assured her of that—but all the same, Alys had yet more reason to think she was a remarkable, perfect wife for him. Not to be jealous of the past was the sign of a generous woman. Or perhaps it was just the confidence of a woman loved, and properly loving.

◆　◆　◆

Alys still had a considerable sum left from the sale of her two salons to Mr. Szenkier. She used it to buy herself a little house in Kensington, in Spenser Street, not very far from Charlotte and Edward, and a comfortable distance from Berkeley Square, as if to symbolize that her links with her old home were tenuous, not broken. She and Lisa decorated it by mutual agreement, very much in the style of the old salon, with gray-blue silk walls, and small Louis Seize furnishings. They filled the windowsills with hyacinth pots to celebrate the first springtime of peace. Alys chose the house because it had room enough for her family and friends to stay with her—for Anne to have a London base. She knew well enough from her sister's letters that she had become entirely nomadic during the war years, touring France, or the regions of England, careless of personal considerations such as a home of her own. Anne was restless by nature.

Anne did not come back to London for a long time. She still had a great deal to do in France before she could free herself for commercial engagements, though many theater managers were pressing her with offers of leading parts. Everyone wanted to see Anne in comedies, light, happy vehicles to celebrate the end of war, and to pay tribute to her for all her moral support. When she finally appeared at Alys' door, it was to bring her news that Alys had dreaded. Ned too had "gone."

"I searched everywhere!" Anne told her. "No one has the slightest idea. He went out sketching, not far from his camp, and never came back. That's all that happened. No trace of him. There wasn't a bomb, there wasn't a special mission or anything like that. I would have been able to find out . . ."

"I don't believe it." Alys wept, clinging to her sister. "It's just impossible. He might be lying somewhere . . ."

"I asked in every hospital I visited. I looked at anyone who was suffering from amnesia, anyone badly injured, disfigured—even bodies that were difficult to identify."

"Don't. I can't bear to think of it." Alys tried to stop her tears. "Thank you. Thank you for looking."

Lisa came in, shyly shaking Anne's hand. "Miss Hardy? How do you do." She looked at Alys, sitting grief-stricken, rubbing her face like a tired child.

"I've made us some supper. I'm not much of a cook, but I hope you like it. I shall call it *Sole à la Mode Alys* because the sauce has gone your favorite blue-gray color! It was the mushrooms, I think . . . Come on, we've got to eat."

She forcibly led the two dazed sisters into the dining room, linking her arms with them. Lisa always said "we," as if her life and Alys' were one.

◆　◆　◆

Anne was soon immersed in a new London production, and Alys spent her days wondering how to start again. She took many weeks to come to terms with Ned's disappearance. Through Edward and through Edith Lyttleton, she instigated her own enquiries, but found that what Anne had told her was all there was to know—officially and unofficially.

She knew all those lost souls would want her to go on, to find herself and work again. But Alys felt all her good intentions waning, and a terrible apathy setting in. So many kind friends, familiar faces, were gone forever. She realized that others who had experienced the war at close quarters, like Lisa, Charlotte and Anne, had a steely spirit, tempered by reality, while she was all regret and guilt. She did not know where to begin.

Mr. Szenkier tried to help, personally commissioning some designs from her. Reluctantly, Alys tried to work. She made him promise to submit them to his private clients anonymously, because she did not feel at all proud of her efforts. She made *"robes de style,"* as they were called, reminiscent of the ornate evening robes of pre-war years, curiously still popular with newer customers. They were covered with embroidery, and had large panniers at the sides. Sometimes she made crinolines, tiers of net stitched with broad satin ribbons. Other creations were bedecked with long droopy tassels and streamers on the rich brocades of bygone days. Alys' new models were mere novelties in a fast-moving age, that made her feel even more left behind.

Inevitably, she began to suspect that her best days in designing had passed. She did not wish to repeat herself, though that was all that happened. The clothes of the twenties were altogether different from the complex constructions of the 1910s. Corsets had been phased out during the war, for the simple expedient that the metal used in their boning was needed for armaments. Women could not wear such things anyway, when manning ambulances, nursing wounded men or scrubbing floors. The freedom she had once advocated to make women alluring had become a fact of life without her.

Alys had never stopped being a believer, though her religiosity was not that of her Grandma Hardy, or even the quiet faith of her daughter, Laura. She did feel a need to be good, and sometimes, in the darkness when she could not sleep, wondered if she were being punished for escaping, in spite of her sympathy for Alec's moral objections to the war. The irony was that many others seemed to agree with his view, now that the cost was fully counted. The punitive treatment of the Germans at Versailles, where the treaty of "peace" was signed, confirmed a widely held opinion that the war had not been won but merely suspended. Edith Lyttleton told her that this was the feeling among parliamentary figures of all political parties, though few said so in public.

There was another war that had no resolution. While she had been hiding from the sun in São Paulo, the darkest clouds had gathered over Ireland. Terrorist outrages increased from 1916 onwards, and even at her great distance from Europe, the news of it had reached Alys, in film newsreels and in the papers shipped to Brazil from London and Paris. The French press gave a different report of events from London, which for the first time made her see the other side of the crisis.

In November 1920, the funeral of the secret service agents killed in Dublin on "Bloody Sunday" took place in London.

Alys was appalled by the violent scenes in the city streets, as the murdered men's coffins were drawn through the city on gun carriages draped with Union Jacks. They were buried with honor at Westminster Abbey, even though they had been responsible for many murders themselves. Reprisals followed swiftly. The Black and Tans opened fire on a crowd at a football match in Croke Park, Dublin, killing twelve spectators later that same month.

During the war, Alys' letters to Carrigrohane were never answered by Grandpa James himself. Sometimes The Inch wrote a short note to say that they were safe and thriving. Alec had reassured her often enough that the Republicans would not harm James Hardy. He had no tenants left at Carrigrohane, and was not an obvious target for attack.

That proved to be true, but it was Grandpa James' love for his city that caused his death. Alys heard the news when she was at Bladeshill for Christmas. By that time Cork was one of four cities under the rule of martial law. Following an ambush in which two of their men were killed, the Black and Tans rampaged through the streets of the city and set it on fire.

Layton Stayce sent Alys a formal account of what happened.

I regret to inform you that your grandfather James died of heart failure on the night of December 12, 1920. When told the news of the sacking of Cork, he grew very distressed. I believe his manservant, a Mr. Lynch, tried to summon help, but due to the troubles a doctor could not be found until it was too late. He died, with Mr. Lynch in attendance, during the night.

I must ask you to call at my office, when convenient, to discuss the Hardy estate. Please accept my sincere condolences.

Alys was more upset by Grandpa James' death than by any other loss she had endured. Perhaps it was because she had falsely assumed the worst was over. She had tried to spend her time learning to cherish those who remained close to her. Grandpa James' sadness in his final hours made her grief intense. In his old age, he had been contented, not solitary, and at peace.

Alys worried about The Inch, and what would happen to him now that his master was gone. She wanted to make sure he was provided for. On her return to London, she made an appointment for herself and Anne to see Layton Stayce.

How strange to revisit those old portals, climb the curved stone steps without the fear she had known in previous days! Alys had never been to see Stayce with a companion before, and held Anne's arm tightly as they were ushered in.

"The funeral was arranged by the Stoneys of Montenotte—old family friends, I believe?" Stayce said, leaning forward with his fingers tipped together. His hands were lean, almost transparent with age. Yet they still looked capable of cruelty, were a sign of his authority, as he turned the pages on his desk and studied her past life.

"Yes. Anne and I decided it was not wise to travel over. It was very hard for us not to be able to pay our last respects."

Layton Stayce looked deliberately at the beautiful, publicly admired face of Anne Hardy, much more vivid in real life than he had envisaged, and nodded briefly. She was too well known to make such a journey in the present crisis.

"I'm sure your grandfather would have wished you both to act with prudence." He squinted at the documents. The only real deterioration time had achieved was to weaken his sight, but when he looked up at her, Alys was still startled by the cold grayness of his eyes.

"There's nothing left, you know."

"Nothing at all?" Alys was surprised.

"Your grandfather's passion for gambling in recent years, and with only that old retainer—"

"Mr. Lynch." Anne interrupted sharply.

"Yes, Lynch; well, he appears willfully to have encouraged James. There are debts. Land and property are not worth very much in Ireland these days."

"And the will?" Alys asked.

"James left everything to you and your sister. But there will be very little once the charges on the estate are cleared. A great pity. James Hardy was once a rich man. But no one could control him in recent years. He was far too stubborn and wily to let anyone manage his affairs."

"I think you should sell the house," Anne said at once. "Don't you agree, Alys?"

"I suppose so . . ."

"Very good. But there is something else we should discuss." Layton Stayce sat back, and for a moment Alys thought he looked troubled. Surely not, she thought. He was above such feelings.

But there it was: a confession. With great difficulty, speaking very slowly, Layton Stayce made his admission.

"Your mother is—I have to tell you—alive. She lives in Paris."

"What?" Alys said, stunned.

"She wrote to ask me to release her from the agreement of silence she made with your relatives. I don't know why she has taken so long to come to this. I wrote to your grandfather some years ago, asking if he still wished to keep her at a distance. She didn't need the money by then."

"Money?" Anne asked, in a sharp voice. "Do you mean she was paid to stay away?"

Alys began to tremble. "Oh God, I remember, Anne! When I visited, Grandpa tried to tell me something, but I didn't follow him at all, I didn't really listen . . ."

"Perhaps he felt it was better to respect your feelings. This is, after all, history." Layton Stayce looked a little relieved.

"Mr. Stayce—" Alys began.

"Yes?" But Alys could not go on. She felt she might faint and she could not find the words she wanted.

"My sister means, explain yourself!" Anne spat at him. Alys did not know why she was so angry.

"It was a family matter. Your mother was very happy with the legal adoption. Without your grandparents' support you would have been raised in—in very poor circumstances, moral rather than physical."

"Do you mean our mother abandoned us?" Alys whispered. This truth was much harder to bear than the lies Grandma Hardy had told her. Alys had guessed that her mother had led a "wicked existence," and had died in agony from self-indulgence the way fallen women did in books. The notion that she had gone away willingly, had simply rejected her daughters by choice—for money—was repulsive. Even after all this time, Alys felt nothing but deep wounding. Anne sat tight-lipped.

"You must understand," Stayce added, "in those days a woman forfeited her rights to her children through immoral behavior. *You* almost ran that risk yourself, in your divorce," he said, looking at Alys, happy to feel superior again.

"Like mother, like daughter," he seemed to suggest. Alys felt a sudden self-loathing. If only Layton Stayce knew—she had indeed almost lost her own daughter once. She felt stifled, trapped in family wrongdoings, inherited selfishness. Perhaps she had been marked for failure from the start. She had never been worthy of love. It all came flooding back.

"Thank you, Mr. Stayce. My sister and I will inform you of our course of action shortly. Come along, Alys." Anne stood up and pushed a firm hand under Alys' elbow.

"Come along, Alys," she repeated, as if she were talking to a difficult child.

For many weeks, Alys was shocked into inactivity. The only positive action she took was to agree to Anne's proposal that they set up a pension for The Inch. It was to be expressed as "a legacy from the Hardy family" to make it easier for him to accept it and The Inch was to stay at Carrigrohane for as long as he wished.

Alys did not know what to do. Sometimes she wanted to rush across to France and confront her mother, to ask her how she had dared to leave her children like that. At other times, she would recoil from imagining what her mother must have become, all these years later. Better to live with a painful abstraction, a dream of someone beautiful, if wicked, than to deal with an ugly reality. She turned to her close friends and to her sister Anne, excluding all thoughts of the world around her. While order returned to everyone else's life, hers began to break in painful fragments. Worst of all, she regretted leaving Alec, but could not bring herself to write to him.

◆ ◆ ◆

A year passed. Alys sat at home reading fashion magazines. It was spring again; "Paris in the spring," they told her. Perhaps she should visit the salons in the rue de la Paix, and see the new *garçonne* fashions, the sparkling chiffon dance dresses for "boyish" girls. There were new names now that had become successful while she had been drifting aimlessly. With a distant, academic interest, Alys viewed the new styles. A Mademoiselle Chanel had launched the most unusual "chic" clothes in a knitted wool jersey. In the old days a wealthy woman wore only fine-grade wools or silks. Jersey was such a sensible idea. A Monsieur Jean Patou was making "separates," sporty coordinating skirts and sweaters. They were all immensely practical and attractive, and Alys admired their looks.

Paris: Cecily had written to her a few times, repeating her invitation. But every time Alys mentioned any of her spurious reasons to visit the city, Anne would look thunderous and come to the heart of the matter.

"I'm not going to run after her. You can, if you like. She's still no mother to me."

For a while Alys responded to the bitterness in Anne, drifting about her little house re-living the loveless days of her childhood. She could not put it all behind her, and slowly her will to go forward drained away.

Until the night that Anne came home from the theater very late. Alys still sat in her chair, smoking, looking out through undrawn curtains into the dark. She knew very well that Lisa was hovering in the hall, and overheard her whispering to Anne.

"I can't get her to come to bed. She's just sitting there. I'm really worried."

Alys was worried too, but in a calm, accepting way. She was useless, and knew it.

Anne came in, and turned on all the lights. Alys looked up quickly, startled by the brilliance.

"Gosh, Alys. You look terrible. You look as awful as I do when I cream off all my makeup."

"Thank you," she said.

"This won't do, will it?"

"No."

Anne put her arms round her sister.

"Do you miss Alec? So much? Why don't you tell him?"

"I can't. I just can't. That wasn't a real world for me. It's no use."

"But you can't go on like this. How can you be so sad, when the rest of us are saying thank you every day for peace? I know there are always things to regret, but also so much to be joyful about . . ."

"I don't know. I feel aimless. I don't understand myself."

Anne stood up. "Then go to Paris. I can't come because of my play. Not that I want to see her anyway."

Lisa came into the room. "I'll come with you. If you want me to," she offered.

A few days later, they sailed for Paris on the overnight boat.

◆　◆　◆

The streets were deserted, the villas formal and sunlit, in the streets near Versailles. Only a gardener sweeping leaves in a gravelled courtyard suggested domestic life. One pale stone house stood well back behind railings, gloomy sentinels of pine trees lining the path up to the door-steps. The shutters were thrown back, but the windows all closed. The garden gate groaned, an obtrusion in the silence, when they opened it.

"Shall I wait for you in the car?" Lisa asked, as she rang the bell.

"No, if you can bear to, please stay with me," Alys asked.

A neat maid with a frilled cap opened the door. Alys presented her card. Lisa spoke first, for Alys was again struck dumb.

"Is Madame de Tessier at home?"

With a murmur the maid disappeared. Louise de Tessier was a beautiful, grand name, Alys thought, bewildered.

But suddenly she could not wait. Through the stillness, she heard voices, laughter from the garden. Hurrying forward through the hall-way she came to double doors that stood open, leading down to the lawn.

An old man sat with his back to her, smoking a cigar, a Panama hat tilted back on his head, a crumpled gray alpaca jacket slung over his chair. In front of him sat her mother, gray whisps of hair a halo round the brim of her straw hat. The old people were tipsy, drinking champagne.

"Louise!" Alys called out. It was such a pretty name to say.

Her mother looked up, squinting in the light and shielding her face with her hand.

"My God."

The man stood up awkwardly; he was old and stiff. He turned as if he understood at once who she might be.

The maid fluttered behind Alys, arguing with Lisa, who had tried to follow her from the front door.

"*Ça va, Marie,*" the old man said. "*Elles sont amies.*"

As Louise tottered across the lawn, the old man steadied her, his hand under her arm. She looked slightly ridiculous, old and feeble, unable to withstand even a glass of champagne.

Louise stumbled on a step.

"Oh dear!" She laughed, and looked up at Alys. "It was Charles' birthday yesterday." she said. "We're still celebrating. Foolish."

The embarrassment of the moment was too much. Louise's hand went up to her chest, and for a horrified moment, Alys thought her mother might faint or have some sort of attack. But Charles lowered her onto a step of the terrace, and Louise leant back heavily against the iron balustrade. Charles untied her hat, murmuring all the time about her health and how she needed to be more careful of herself. Louise pushed him gently to one side, and suddenly smiled at Alys, as if they had never been apart. She patted the step next to her.

"Do sit down. How good of you to come, darling," she said.

CHAPTER 21

P 1 9 2 5 – 3 0

aris was as gay as Alys had ever imagined
it to be—but the excitement was nervous, a shal-
low brilliance. When last she had visited, before
the war, she and Anne stayed with the Baroness
de Falbe, in the rue de la Paix. She could still
recall the equipages and electric carriages drawn
up at the famous couture establishments, Worth
and Premet; *valets de pied* would stand beneath

the portes cochères waiting for their ladies, and drive them to discreet rendezvous elsewhere. Now, rich Argentinians fussed over furs, and the taxis might be driven by an ugly Russian prince. (The handsome Russian princes earned their living as gigolos in Montmartre *boîtes,* or sold antiques and books in St.-Germain-des-Prés.)

Louise told her so. Alys was fascinated by her mother. She was the embodiment of eccentric, prideful femininity, just as individualistic as she remembered Grandmaman having been. Meeting Louise again was like coming into contact with a newly discovered natural source of energy—like that strange creeping of the scalp when pleasurable objects are touched. Alys not only fell in love with her mother again, but discovered a wonderful new friend. Louise never called her "my daughter," fearing to provoke harsh words from Alys by claiming a relationship she had abandoned. She spoke to her in an affectionate, casual manner that was much easier to deal with than if she had been too familiar. A presuming intimacy would have been false after a separation of thirty years.

Yet there were no years between them. They had tastes in common, attitudes in common and a beautiful city to explore together. The days on the boulevards! Louise would take Alys to her favourite haunts, the *bouqinistes* on the Quai Montebello, antique dealers on the Ile St. Louis, art galleries in the avenue Montaigne, applying the same careful exacting standards that Alys had herself to everything she chose.

Louise was more of an eccentric, perhaps. She drank only from china cups or crystal glass, and never traveled on public vehicles. She still wore stays, never referring to them as corsets. Her skin was unblemished by any colorings or powders. Her back never touched any chair, as she perched upright, forward on the edge of her place. The smart house at Versailles was formally run, with a chilly perfection in its decoration that would have made Madeleine Wickham's efforts rustically cosy in comparison. Vases full of waxy flowers; shiny surfaces; ticking clocks; bare, echoing rooms. Louise was demanding, and her home had a visual elegance that Alys admired for its good taste but was happy to leave most times.

There were also the silent evenings. After dinner, Louise and her husband Charles liked to read, seated side by side but without speaking. When Alys stayed, she was expected to do the same. Louise liked the novels of Colette, Charles the poetry of the French Symbolists. Louise still occasionally played the piano, but now she preferred the music of Debussy and Satie to Beethoven.

It would not succeed, too close a contact with Louise: instead Alys took a little room in the rue de Rivoli, facing the gardens of the Tuileries. She knew now exactly what she wanted to do—spend time in Paris every season with her mother, and set up a little salon in a corner of the First Arrondissement, where the smartest ladies did their shopping.

Louise helped her furnish her little room. She got a young English artist of her acquaintance, Philip White, to paint very modern murals on the walls, and bought Alys a beautiful hand-woven carpet made by one of Paul Poiret's *Martines* (the poor girl apprentices who designed decorative objects for the couturier). Tasseled cushions, soft opaque glass lamps and curving pieces of white china made Alys' pied à terre welcoming. Everything spoke of her mother's taste; Alys experienced a child's delight in having Louise attend to her so assiduously.

Louise's only weakness was alcohol. Once in a while, unexpectedly, she would decide to unbend and when she did, her performance was electrifying. The evening would start innocently enough with wine at the dinner table, but then Louise would announce that only champagne would suit her mood, and become unhinged the moment she ordered the first bottle. Except for a few occasions, she confined these bouts to her home, much to Alys' relief. For when Louise drank, reminiscences sodden with sentimentality poured from her—the nearest Louise ever came to guilt.

Alys' infancy in America, and Louise's utter devotion to her babies in the wilderness of Denver, surrounded by marauding Indians, was a favorite topic. It was complete falsehood. Alys knew that Grandmaman had raised her almost single-handed. Even Papa had shown her more affection in an intermittent, charming way. Louise only ever gave love to the men in her life. It seemed there had been quite a few.

"As for those appalling people, the Hardys—to keep you from me, like that!" Louise ran her slim fingers over her disordered head, as if the whisps of gray were still a bronzed frame of hair round her lovely face.

"I cried when I left you. I was in misery for weeks. In fact . . ." She paused to sip champagne, her lips pursed while the bubbles burst on the roof of her mouth: "I never told you this before, though poor dear Charles knows the *truth*—I was saved from *despair* you know, on many occasions. At least I can thank *him*, the other one, for that."

On her many visits, Alys gathered fragments of the truth, and passed on all the details to Anne in her letters or when they met. Louise had traveled extensively in Europe with one lover after another, until she settled upon a wealthy banker, Daniel Newton. Allowing her some good points, Alys also believed the story that she had stayed with Newton even when he became sick and needed nursing for a long time before his death. Charles de Tessier was one of Newton's legal friends. He met Louise over the coffin.

Alys' discoveries only made Anne dislike her mother more, and there was pure jealousy in that opinion. Alys' trips backward and forward to France became so frequent that when Anne came home to Spenser Street, she missed Alys, and resented the attraction between her mother and her sister. She expected Alys to be there for her—since her return from Brazil, Anne imagined she ought to be more available than ever. It was her pleasure to sweep into Alys' life and shock her with stories of her leading men, or the latest improper proposal from an admirer. When the bravado stories were over, there were quiet evenings when they discussed their real concerns, and gave each other the kind of advice that only intimate knowledge of someone makes possible.

She would not go to Paris herself.

"Why don't you?" Alys asked. "Mother never mentions you, of course, in that way, she understands, but she regrets your refusal. You're wrong in not wanting to acquaint yourself. It wouldn't do any harm—and you'd like Charles, too."

"Oh yes, I like older men, darling, but as my admirers, not as parent figures. Too boring." Alys did not bother to argue with her. If Anne was only prepared to be flippant, there was no hope of convincing her. Perhaps Anne could let the past die. Louise had left Carrigrohane when Anne was still very small, just five, and Anne had grown up manipulating other people to give her satisfaction instead. Alys remembered how The Inch adored her, and how Grandpa Hardy always indulged her whims.

For the moment, Alys did not wish to introduce her own daughter Laura to Louise. If she asked herself why (and such questions were very difficult to answer, so she seldom did) she wanted to keep Louise to herself. In recompense, she spent a wild amount of money in the summer providing a holiday for Laura and Lisa—knowing that they would like each other, and determined to treat them royally. She took Laura to Patou, in the rue St.-Florentin, and bought her half a dozen outfits. She bullied the pair of them into a visit to Antoine's, the smartest hairdresser in the rue Cambon, where they both had the new deep waves crimped into their heads. While waiting for them, Alys fulfilled a private ambition and stepped into Chanel's enticing salon, in the same street, sensing a rivalrous enthusiasm as she paid a fortune for one of her simple knitted suits. Finally, she walked the two women straight through the Ritz to the Place Vendôme, up the rue de la Paix, and bought them both long strings of Tecla pearls.

Tea at the Hôtel Regina, quite near her apartment, brought the day to a satisfactory end. There was no room for Laura or Lisa to stay in her own little rooms, so she booked them into the hotel and left them to consider their finery in peace.

"Mama! Can't we see your rooms yet?" Laura asked before she left.

"No, not just yet, they're not finished, and I do want you to see the full effect. Next time you come, I promise."

Alys went home alone by choice, to that perfect little corner of Paris above a glove shop, with a view of the Jardin des Tuileries. It *was* quite finished, but she wanted it to be just hers. From her tiny round window, every day, she could see lovers patching up quarrels, shop girls practicing the tango in their lunch hours and governesses in smart English uniforms airing their charges. Beyond the park, to the south, was Versailles, where Louise and Charles would be sitting, reading in companionable silence.

The following day Alys had a meeting planned with Philip White, Louise's artist protégé who had decorated her pied à terre. Philip had suggested a small studio in the rue Duphot as a possibility for Alys' latest venture, and she wanted to have Lisa and Laura's opinion on the premises. Now that they had had a taste of Paris, they would be in the best frame of mind to see the possibilities of the place. She did not want to consult Louise about this decision.

Philip met them at the locked entrance to the courtyard, a heavy, gray grained wood, with a little door let into it for visitors to use. In the old days, the larger double doors would have gaped wide for carriages. Once, the building had been a *hôtel particulier,* the city residence of a noble family. It had seen many other uses since then. Its fine, high-ceilinged rooms leading off a stone spiral staircase were divided into apartments, for various enterprises. There were fabric wholesalers, fine paper merchants, a small lace-making school; a water-color teacher and an empty ground floor that Alys now considered, facing the small cobbled courtyard.

"What do you think?" she asked. "It's very close to the Faubourg Saint-Honoré and the Place Madeleine; cheap because it needs so much work, and perhaps the right size. I like the light."

Laura and Philip walked around each other in circles, admiring the tall arched windows, and the handsome marble fireplace. Lisa did not like the dirt.

"Do you know, Alys, everything in Paris has a certain—odor." she said. "I don't find this romantic in the least."

"You must imagine it redecorated," Philip said, to be encouraging. "I assume the same style that Madame de Tessier suggested for your—"

Alys cut him short. Laura was too busy thinking to have noticed the name. "No, not at all. I want this to be just like my salon in London used to be. Perhaps not quite so old-fashioned—in Paris, all that French furniture would look so unoriginal! But blue—my gray-blue, and silk for the walls."

"Not silk," he corrected, careless of contradicting her. "Try a heavy velour instead."

The three women circled round Philip, looking at the walls and trying to imagine what he had in mind. Alys watched her beautiful daughter, looking uncharacteristically smart in her new clothes and her shining coiffure. The "permanent" waves were curling up on her forehead. Laura always had such chaotic hair, now made worse because she had pulled off her cloche without concern for her appearance. Perhaps Philip would find her attractive—that would be nice for Laura, Alys thought.

Lisa wore her hat low on one side, with feathers floating at her cheek. This was to hide the last scars of her illness, though her health was slowly improving. She still walked with the grace that Alys had taught her, and her body was tall and slim. There would be ten years between them, Alys noted; Lisa was approaching forty, Laura thirty. They were both far too young to be widows.

Looking again at Philip, she felt hopeful. He had no money, of course, but he was attractive in a thin, sensitive kind of way—he might at least make Laura feel flirtatious again. He was obviously from a good family, and enjoying living as a bohemian. Even as she thought it, Alys gave up the notion. Jonathan was a hero, and Laura would never forget him. However, Philip was listening carefully to Laura, as she recalled the glamorous days of her mother's first opening in London. He bent low, awkward on long legs with no furniture near at hand to hang his body on. Arms folded across his chest, he looked across disbelievingly at Alys, as if Laura was exaggerating.

At first Alys was piqued, but then realized that this boy had only seen her in the company of "Madame de Tessier" without knowing that they were related. Alys knew that when she was with Louise, she behaved like an obedient mouse. She laughed, self-indulgent, and shook her head.

"My daughter, Mrs. Barclay, is not making it all up. I was extremely profitable in those days. It's in my blood—I can't wait to start again."

"How happy Anne will be to hear you say that," Lisa remarked. "But Paris—aren't you preaching to the converted?"

"Perhaps. But this is going to be very small, and very exclusive. People are always tantalized by that. And I like to think that I have a few friends who will be pleased to rediscover me."

She spoke confidently, but Alys *was* nervous. Suppose no one wanted to patronize her, thinking she was old fashioned, passé? Suppose she could not strike the right note—everyone said even the great couturier Poiret was past his best, though the old man struggled on against a tide of rising debts. But then, Paris was the place of the moment. Everyone wanted to be in the city to celebrate its freedom, its new life. That was why she had come, herself.

◆　◆　◆

Being a foreigner helped. Alys was more conscious of the general desire for novelty than some of the grand Parisian couturiers. No one wanted "substance" or "quality" any more: just "the latest thing," to catch the eye and amuse. She started work with a fresh eye, anxious to make up for years of absence. Her amazement at bold female manners was reflected in her first few sketches: boyish, witty figures wearing designs that were almost fancy dress, and mimicking the vamping mood.

Her own experience had something to do with it: Alys knew of a larger world, the vast simple market of Latin America, where a few bolts of gingham were enough to clothe the entire female population of country villages. "High fashion" seemed like a game compared to that. She wanted to work at something very intimate, to test herself. Paris presented an immediate, vital challenge—like going rather nervously to a smart cocktail party, and hoping to find the room full of old friends.

For this reason, she turned her back on large-scale manufacturing, and sought out small workshops able to produce hand work of a high standard. Alys had never found such fine resources in any other city: button-makers, embroiderers, beaders, specialists in chiffon and lace. There were whole streets of such professionals in the heart of the city (increased by an influx of middle-European refugees), all willing to try new ideas. In keeping with her desire for exclusivity, Alys ordered only a dozen of each of her designs. It was very small scale, but Alys was very happy with her new salon. She called it "Alys France," to distinguish it clearly from Mr. Szenkier's two properties, her former salons in London and New York, and followed his example by having small embroidered silk labels made for all her new garments. They were not "couture" clothes, in the old sense of the word; she created a "boutique," selling stylish designs off the peg and filling her cupboards and shelves with a wide collection of other pretty objects. Philip White hung his paintings; friends of his brought her limited editions of the new plastic jewelry that was all the rage, and she found flower-makers in the old Jewish quarter, the Marais, who made chiffon and satin flowers that were stitched onto knitted caps. Alys spent several weeks at a time in Paris, visiting ateliers to find new objects of interest to sell in her salon. Gradually the word spread, and many young designers came to her to find work, and execute her commissions.

Louise had an ambivalent attitude to Alys' success. She wanted to be proud of her, but preferred herself in the role of mentor and arbiter of taste. Inevitably this made her critical of some of Alys' decisions, and they found themselves in disagreement over many of her daringly short "frocks," splashed with patches of floral embroidery or using textiles of bold stripes. Although Louise preferred the languid laces and chiffons that were the style of her youth, she did her best to send her younger acquaintances to Alys, and helped build up her trade.

But the turning point came when a slight, familiarly dapper young man came to the rue Duphot, escorting a richly dressed dark girl in an engulfing monkey-fur coat. (It was September, and not particularly cold; Alys guessed as the couple approached that they were foreigners touring Europe.)

"Leopoldo!"

"Alys! I knew it must be you!"

In spite of the circumstances of her departure from Brazil, she was thoroughly delighted to see him.

"How are you? What are you doing here? Oh, is Alec with you?" Alys was momentarily fearful, not wishing her new world to be invaded by her past.

He shook his head. "No. I'm so sorry to disappoint you. I'm on my honeymoon. My wife—Isabella de Silva Teles . . ."

One of the Four Hundred—how it all was conjured up in a name.

"*Un praçer.* So now you are in Paris . . ." She wanted to add, "María-Elena must be envious!" but would not utter the name.

"I adore your clothes, Madame. These painted skirts—they look just like hibiscus flowers . . ."

Isabella swirled in front of Leopoldo, holding up one of Alys' dance dresses, bugle-beaded, with a drooping satin skirt. She flirted with him confidently. "Does it suit me?"

"*Da muito bem* . . ." Alys guessed they were buying up Europe as they speeded from capital to capital in one of Leopoldo's bullet-shaped silver cars.

"They're a new idea for me . . . exotic colors, wild patterns, I hope you like them." Alys explained.

"I shall buy six, and wear one tonight, and you shall come with us to the Bousca Bal—I love to meet Leopoldo's old friends." Isabella twirled again.

Alys did not like the "old" very much, but she did like the idea of the *bal musette* in the rue de Lappe. The Auvergnats danced, and the rich foreigners, slumming, were often dragged in. Leopoldo would enjoy the accordions, and the common pleasures of the street.

He smiled in understanding. "You'll come. Terrific! Do you know, Alys, I should have been the daughter, and my sister the heir. I do prefer to be idle."

Alys nodded toward Isabella, who was thrusting a jeweled hand into a bowl of satin flowers. "They gave you a handsome dowry, didn't they?" she commented. He laughed, not in the least offended. They were confidants, like old times. Leopoldo hesitated, then whispered back:

"She never got him, you know. Alec. After you left—"

"Please don't tell me anything! I don't want to hear of it!" Alys hurried away, her heart thumping quite uncontrollably with the remembrance of her married life.

Leopoldo was contrite. "I'm sorry. Whatever you wish, I will obey."

She turned on him in mock anger. "I wish you to bring all Isabella's rich friends to me, and tell everyone how wonderful my little boutique is going to be. Do that, and I forgive you, Leopoldo."

"Oh, that's easy!"

Isabella took the six spangled dance dresses with her in Alys' blue and silver boxes. Leopoldo kept his word. He invited her to receptions at the home of Louis de Souza Dantos in the avenue Montaigne, where all the Brazilian community gathered. She met artists, writers, society women with a talent for creating strong individual style (and who found that they had the audience for it in Paris that did not exist at home). Soon the rue Duphot received the Parisian colony of Latin Americans, and "Alys France" was safely launched.

◆　◆　◆

Unwittingly, Leopoldo helped Alys more than he realized. On one of his frequent visits to her little boutique, he brought her a slim, privately printed book of verse, his own contribution to *"modernismo."* There were more exclamation points and other punctuation marks than there were words, but a few phrases attracted Alys' attention, stirred a memory . . .

"Paisagems do mal gusto, espantosos . . . os homens se dependuran na vida mundana de São Paulo como se estivessem num bonde cheio." "*Landscapes of the most revolting bad taste . . . men hanging on to life in the city as if they were clinging to the platform of a full trolley bus."* These lines made the Praca da Republica come back to life before her eyes. Leopoldo had had his little book bound with a bold yellow and green cover—the colors of his country's flag.

He told her about his dabblings in the art world, the launching of the Modern Art Week in São Paulo that had attracted the world.

"And you know, this last summer, Villa Lobos came to the celebration in the Municipal Theater. A huge audience. Three years ago he was keeping himself alive playing piano for the cinemas. Anyway, now he is very successful, but that night the poor man wore a slipper with his evening suit. You know why? Because he had a corn on his foot, but everyone thought it was a brilliant futurist statement!"

Alys loved his stories; they reminded her of all the bold new things about Brazil that had enticed her, at the start.

"And do you know"—Leopoldo loved to chatter as much as ever— "I'm now on the editorial board of a new magazine, about art and industry. It's called *The Hooter*—isn't that what you would call—a hoot?"

She laughed; he was such a silly young man, but at least he had found his niche, and was pouring money into the hands of young artists and musicians as fast as he could. After he roared off in his motor with Isabella, Alys sat reading his little volume, her hands resting on the bold pattern of its cover.

Then it dawned on her. Printed silks! Printed *rayons*—even better! Frocks and simply cut jackets in related patterns—she would design a collection of modernist prints, much more sophisticated than her feeble attempts in São Paulo, and create a ready-made line in exclusive textiles. That was the missing inspiration she had waited for so long to find. If Leopoldo were to return to Brazil and tell Alec about her new work, she would be happy that he knew of it. He need not think that she regretted her choice.

Alec had never challenged her decision. Alys had quite given up hope that he ever would, because he had found his home in South America just as she had found a perfectly realized new life for herself in London and Paris. Alys imagined how very much Alec would enjoy the mixture of new industrial energy and artistic life that Leopoldo had conveyed to her in his gossip. Whatever had happened between him and María-Elena, Alec was surely becoming a Brazilian. But he had never asked her for a divorce, and she doubted if he ever would.

◆ ◆ ◆

Alys timed her visits to Paris to coincide with the main tourist seasons in the city. Every summer, in increasing number, Americans came to discover the ethereal spirit of Paris, and its more tangible cultural splendors. Its fashions were a minor but important part of the attraction. This was the right moment for Alys to show her mid-season cruising clothes and she sold large quantities to travelers passing through France. She returned to Paris for a few weeks every spring and autumn, to launch new collections. Just as she had hoped, "Alys France" was considered very chic simply because it was so small and original.

The salon in the rue Duphot became more picturesque each season, for Alys put back a large part of her profit into making it so. In 1926, its second year, she added striped blue awnings to the windows, and put bay trees in pots on the glass-doored steps. In the summer, small tables and chairs were set out in the sunshine so that visitors could take tea and ruin their figures with French pâtisseries. Alys never knew who might turn up from her past life, wondering if "Alys France" could possibly be owned by the person they had once known. Her pleasure knew no bounds when she came to the salon one day, and found the ample figures of Adelaide Hay and Mrs. Millsom, looking familiarly "New York" to her, but conscious of being unknown foreigners in this new setting. They sat chatting, generously spread on a banquette, admiring her clothes. Alys liked the idea that two women from such entirely different backgrounds had remained friends, all these years, after she had introduced them.

"It *is* you! I hoped so!" Adelaide exclaimed, but she could hardly stand to kiss her friend. Alys clasped her. Adelaide was indomitable. She had to struggle to her feet with two black ebony canes, but her eyes shone with affection, as if she were a young girl.

"Millsom's too busy doing business, so Adelaide and I came to buy paintings and 'do' Paris," Mrs. Millsom explained.

"I did so want to see the city again . . ." Adelaide added, not needing to tell Alys that this trip could well be her last.

"How wonderful to see you! How's that dear husband of yours?" Adelaide asked.

"Oh, busy, just the same . . ." Alys lied. Adelaide looked satisfied; she had always taken credit for the marriage. Alys decided she was far too old, and too dear, to be denied the illusion of its continuing success.

"He's in Brazil."

"Brazil—of course, he has interests there." Adelaide's encyclopedic knowledge of her circle was, as usual, helpful.

"If you are interested in art, I have—a dear friend who may be able to help you." Alys was eager to change the subject, and pleased to be able to think of a good connection. "May I take you to Versailles, this weekend? We could lunch with the de Tessiers—Madame de Tessier is quite an expert on the new galleries . . ."

"That would be just perfect." Mrs. Millsom pressed her hands in an enthusiastic grip. "Till Saturday . . . and send these things round to the Ritz, dear, will you?"

Alys' chief pleasure was to draw her mother into her circle, though she never publicly claimed the relationship. She did not feel ready to do so. But every time a link was made between the world Alys had created, and the private existence of Mme. de Tessier, Alys felt enriched. Louise thoroughly enjoyed helping such informed individuals as Adelaide Hay to meet the young artists whom she patronized. Alys' visits to Versailles with rich Americans, Brazilians or Cecily Day's middle-European connections, wove a thread of exoticism into Louise's life that suited her well. Of course, Alys could not deny to herself that she liked to show off her connections to her mother, just as much as she liked to display her to friends. Their secret relationship made it all the more pleasurable.

Meanwhile, Alys worked with Mr. Szenkier in London on her plans to make ready-to-wear clothes. New, cheap rayon fabric was cutting the price of fashion dramatically, and expanding the market. Mr. Szenkier was not at all sure that Alys understood the elements of styling that went into mass-production, so their progress together was slow, and he needed much convincing.

Lilian helped. She still ran the New York salon for Mr. Szenkier, and had made a modest personal fortune out of it. Now she managed a small factory, was active in the garment workers' union, the ILGWU, and even lectured at the Central Continuation School which opened that year to train young people for the growing fashion industry in Manhattan. Mr. Szenkier now marketed clothes in New York under the name "Lily Anne," believing that Lilian knew the domestic scene at first-hand more accurately than he did. It gave Lilian no small satisfaction to be asked for her opinion on Alys' plans. She approved wholeheartedly, relieved that Alys was returning to her former sureness of intention again. Mr. Szenkier began to view the situation with cautious interest.

"You see, Mr. Szenkier"—Alys grew in confidence, the more he listened—"I'm quite sure I'm on the right lines. I worked on printed textiles in Brazil, you know, I think I developed a knack for 'novelty prints,' something younger, fresher and less sophisticated than I've tried before . . ."

"Yes, but your cut is wrong," he ventured.

"Oh, I know! Young girls hate fussy things! You should see them in my boutique in Paris—they literally rip the clothes over their heads. They've a complete disregard for buttons and hooks."

"So have I. What it costs to stitch them on . . ."

"It's speed, Mr. Szenkier. Fast cars, fast lives."

"Fast manufacturing is what I'm after. This is going to cost a lot," he complained, looking at her samples. "You have to take account not just of cutting fabric economically, but of sizing. It's becoming more important. No one wants to wait for alterations to be made in the stores."

"I do try, Mr. Szenkier," Alys replied patiently. "I rather think this basic shape would work whatever the scale."

"Ha! Maybe so, when the customers put them *on,* but these things are too understated. You've got to make clothes that look good hanging on a rail."

"Oh dear. I do love the zigzag in this one, too."

"Zigzags . . . look at the trouble we'll have on the seams."

"Matching across?"

"Exactly, my dear—don't give me too many couture details . . ."

"No bows. No chiffon droops. No tassels. I know, Mr. Szenkier." She took up the cotton sample, and ripped it up the seams. "It will be perfect for you, I guarantee it. And furthermore, I have some good news. I've found someone to invest in us."

"Us?" said Mr. Szenkier, his voice fading a little. He found Alys quite intimidating when she had her mind set on a course.

"Yes. 'Alys Modes.' Your own wholesale line. No more of this anonymous manufacturing. You'll see."

"Are you suggesting that you buy your way back into my business?" he asked, trying to control his hesitancy.

"Don't you like my plan?"

"Well, dear Lady Colvin, I'm not at all sure. I've my daughters to consider, and my brother . . ."

"I could buy Sir Edward's shares." Alys was beginning to sense his reluctance, and it hurt her.

"Oh, he offered me those many years ago! This is a family business now, my dear lady!" Mr. Szenkier looked so proud that Alys was silenced. She would borrow the money that Mrs. Millsom offered her anyway, for the printing of her fabrics.

"Don't be too ambitious; let's take our time." He tried to console her. "I know it's not easy for you to work under someone."

"The idea! I can be as obedient and flexible as the next person!"

Mr. Szenkier did not bother to answer. He merely lifted up the torn dress and looked questioningly at her. Alys had to acknowledge that she did not like taking instructions from anyone. Succeeding again mattered very much to her.

◆ ◆ ◆

Jack came to stay with her in Spenser Street for a few days in his school holidays, and she took him to Paris to show him her corner of it. Alys acted the part of confidante and grandmother to the best of her ability, realizing that boutiques of flimsy dance dresses and sequined caps did not mean very much to him. Visiting the racecourse at Auteuil certainly did—while Alys studied the clothes, Jack learnt how to bet. Alys did not have to remind him that he was not allowed to mention such excursions to his mother, or the large sums spent on taking him out for meals in good restaurants. She wanted Jack to grow up with a zest for pleasure—never having found that in herself until much later in her life. He was only fourteen, but a handsome lad, and she loved him unequivocally.

But Alys failed to see that *everyone* was enjoying life far too much to the full. On October 29, 1929, the New York stock market collapsed and with it all the joys of the rue Duphot. The Americans hardly came to Paris that season, and orders from her Latin Americans, on whom she depended heavily, ceased to flow. There were exchange control difficulties, increasing delays in payments that suddenly threatened to drive her to the wall.

For the past few years, Alys had enjoyed her little "Parisian interlude"—to excess. She had spent nearly every penny she made, either keeping the salon beautiful, or on spoiling her friends. As her debts mounted through the autumn, Alys knew that her salon would have to close. The expense of living in both London and Paris was beyond her slender resources. She would have to economize and return to London. At least "Alys Modes" was a good prospect—Mr. Szenkier's caution was her saving grace. But Alys knew she would never be able to work independently again.

One evening she went to supper with Louise and Charles, to tell them of her decision. Philip White was also present. Neither Charles nor Louise had any sense of finance, and listened distantly, as if Alys' problems were a rare disease seldom caught.

"I'll lend you money," Charles offered.

Alice refused. "No. I think I should go back to London anyway. I feel more confident that I shall continue with my venture for ready-made clothes, and I think that is the best prospect. More of a challenge." She was trying to be optimistic; the real reason for refusing was that she was tired of carrying financial responsibility single-handed.

"The rue Duphot was my swan song," she admitted.

"Nonsense, darling." Louise poured her more wine. She was somewhat morose, sharing Alys' sad news. "Not at all," Louise repeated, waving an unsteady arm. "There's never an end to it. Never. While you breathe. My children . . . such talent . . ." she began to weep.

"Madame de Tessier—you never spoke of your family—" Philip began, surprised, hoping to revive Louise with his interest. He never finished his enquiry. Alys also burst into tears.

Dear, kindly Charles, never a man of many words, but an emanation of friendship, knew how to rescue such situations.

"Her children! I give you a toast: To Louise's 'children'—all the artists and sculptors, the jewelry makers and printmakers: the children of Paris, if you prefer."

They all drank to that, and Philip's question was never answered.

CHAPTER 22

A 1 9 3 0 – 3 5

lys France," rue Duphot, collapsed,
but left Alys a rich legacy. She might be useless
when it came to high finance, but there was one
change she was prepared for. In the autumn of
that same year, 1929, Jean Patou had defined the
change in Parisian fashion by dropping the hem-
lines of all his model dresses to within a few
inches of the ground, even for day wear. The

magazines were full of enthusiasm for this longer line, prophesying that soon "everyone" would follow it. Alys guessed that Mr. Szenkier would lose a fortune both in London and New York, because his shorter cut off-the-peg clothes were already being manufactured and could not be altered.

This was her chance to conquer his doubts. She had all her beautiful new modernist fabrics ready for printing, and quickly redesigned several prototype models in the new length. If Mr. Szenkier started work at once, a new collection could be made for a mid-season launch. Alys was more certain than ever, post-Patou, that her coordinated jackets and dresses would work. They were in keeping with the new lines, but simple in structure. Most of the new Paris couture ideas were difficult to reproduce, involving complex seaming that no wholesaler could quite master.

Mr. Szenkier *was* worried by a catastrophic drop in sales, especially as he had expanded into a second factory in Golden Square. He was grateful to Alys for presenting new ideas, and agreed to finance the manufacture of six of her designs. He would pay only a fee for her work: there was no suggestion that she would gain any foothold in his company. But he had bought her name, and done very well from the takeover of London and New York. It was a small favor to make her in return. "Alys Modes" came out with its modest first collection mid-season, bringing the latest Parisian fashions to London.

They sold very promisingly. Women were tired of the boyish, jazzy look. It was not just the effect of the recession—the new long skirts took up at least two yards more of fabric, and were actually more expensive than the clothes women had worn before.

Alys' fresh, tiny geometric prints, were screen-, not roller-printed, so that she could have short runs of each textile cheaply made. Natural, soft colors were new, too: eau de nil and navy blue, terra-cotta and white, browns outlined in black. Mr. Szenkier was getting high quality work for a very low price; Alys was getting only a foot in the door of mass-market fashion.

Their customers found there were some drawbacks, too. No one knew how to move in demure skirts. Long skirts folded round girls' legs as they walked to work. In the evenings, high heels tore into them at the front and men trod them down at the back. It was a mystery why the young should want to hamper themselves again.

Yet Alys knew that these subdued, softer, adult clothes were going to succeed, and stuck determinedly to this view, carrying Mr. Szenkier with her. She regretted leaving Paris, but she also looked forward to working in a new way—not for a sophisticated few, but promulgating ideas for a much wider audience. Paris had been a restorative, renewing time; now she felt she had her touch back, her fingertips responding to the pulse of life.

In the evenings, women still wanted glamour—not the whaleboned, jewel-encrusted grandeur of pre-war gowns, or the beaded tunics that only the very young had worn well in the twenties. The new slithers of bias-cut fabric fell to the floor, revealing beautiful brown backs, lithe bodies. Women who worked hard or economized all day suddenly wanted the hope of "romance after dark." Alys' three-guinea backless slips of crepe would make the dream accessible to everyone: "cinema satins," Alys called them, knowing from experience that ideas had to be evocative to attract a market.

"I could advertise these in the dailies," Mr. Szenkier suggested, "if you don't object to your name being used in such a commercial way?"

"Why should I mind?" Alys replied. "We all need the money, there's no shame in it."

"But 'Alys,' off-the-peg . . ."

"Sooner off-the-peg than out of work." Alys saw that Mr. Szenkier did not take her remark seriously. He assumed she had some kind of private income, but her finances were parlous.

"Let's try one more collection," he suggested. "I'll pay a designer's fee for it, then perhaps we could come to some more permanent arrangement."

"A share of the profits?" she asked at once.

"Maybe a bonus scheme . . . Lady Colvin, let's wait and see, shall we?"

He was unwilling to let her in. His loyalties lay entirely with his family, particularly Tina, who managed Berkeley Square very well (having learnt all her skill from Alys). Sometimes Alys wondered if she should take her talents elsewhere, but nostalgia kept her attached to her old business. It was still her name, even if she did not own it.

Alys sold the lease of the apartment in the rue Rivoli, but she owned the villa in Spenser Street outright, and just earned enough from Mr. Szenkier to give Lisa a modest allowance. Alys had to be satisfied with slow progress. She had not rebuilt her life without making serious errors, but there were good prospects. Losing control of her own little enterprise was sad—but then, responsibilities were tiring, and now she would have more quiet time.

The problem with freedom was that she was tempted to dwell on her emotions, and she had always hated that. Inevitably her thoughts centered on Alec, and the prevailing silence between them. Leopoldo must have returned to Brazil and reported all her activities; but still this provoked no response. On an impulse, Alys wrote for the first time, asking Alec if he had suffered very badly in the financial crisis.

She received no reply for weeks, but could not bring herself to send a second letter, in a less spontaneous mood. Perhaps Alec did not wish ever to renew direct contact. Finally, a letter came, and she was uncommonly glad she had been so impetuous, when she read Alec's response.

How kind of you to write. How many times I've wanted to do the same. Yes, I was hit badly by the Crash. But my interests are widely spread, and it was not the disaster that many others suffered. No one here makes me a spendthrift. . . . Your success in Paris was reported to me by many of my acquaintance, including Leopoldo, who retains a great admiration for you, as I do, you know that. Well done, Alys.

My deepest love to you, to Laura and young Jack. He must be a young man now.

Alec

Not one word about returning. Alys took the letter as signing her fate. A fascinating marriage reduced to civilized correspondence.

Others managed to live alone. Laura seemed content, and so did Charlotte. Alys did not dread old age, for Louise had shown her how full it could be—but then, *she* had Charles. The only way forward, Alys decided, was to have a plan, to take up a new, more leisurely interest. Alec had never been able to teach her to play cards, but now was the time to try again. Charlotte and Cecily moved in bridge circles; she would ask them—after a supper party that very night.

"You're just hoping to meet a rich gambler and 'reform' him," Cecily said, hitting close to the truth but making Alys laugh all the same.

"Cecily, I leave that to you . . ." Alys replied, and Cecily was reprimanded. "Legless" was becoming saturated with alcohol, but no one could prevent it.

Charlotte scolded them. "Please don't squabble. Alys will never learn if she's in a bad mood."

They began. But as each rule was explained to her, Alys became more and more confused, unable to remember what cards had been played, or how the bidding system worked. The air grew thick with her cigarette smoke.

Cecily became silly. "What about billiards? Why don't you try some ball games? Tennis, perhaps?"

"I don't see the point of all this," Charlotte intervened. "Either you play seriously, Alys, or not at all."

"I've always been hopeless. I thought perhaps I might have more time for it—to practice, that is." Alys smiled in apology.

"That's the trouble, darling." Cecily's scarlet fingernails pointed at the heart of the problem in mid-air. "You *will* build up these 'pictures' of yourself that have absolutely no bearing on reality. I mean, you're never going to be a serene fifty-year-old matron, playing bridge on a deck-cruise somewhere . . ." Cecily was enjoying herself.

"Oh?" Alys indulged her, mildly curious.

"No, of course not. You need a lover, that's all."

Charlotte blew smoke rings into the air. "Aunt Cecily, don't intrigue. At least, not in front of me."

"L.E." Cecily whispered.

"What?"

"Light entertainment."

"Ssh! Your bid!" Charlotte persisted.

It was impossible to concentrate on the game, Alys decided. Charlotte, frowning at her cards, made her feel rebellious, desiring wickedness. Some people found it easy to be good. Then Alys thought of Edward, lying deeply asleep upstairs, and of Charlotte's devotion to him. She was instantly ashamed of herself.

Charlotte, hearing her sigh, looked across with sympathy. "Bridge isn't the thing, that's clear."

"Let's have a drink," said Cecily.

◆　◆　◆

At Mr. Szenkier's new workroom in Golden Square the next day, Alys studied her new sketches with an unusually critical eye. A blinding headache from too much gin had something to do with it. Mr. Szenkier wanted to join the new London Fashion Group as a way of enticing buyers from abroad to his showrooms. Her new lines for "Alys Modes" would have to be particularly distinctive to satisfy his ambitions and put the company in the first rank. Inspiration . . . new patterns—where would she look?

Perhaps she should go to Paris again. But it was not a good time to suggest expensive jaunts—Mr. Szenkier was only just recovering from the Crash, had expanded into new, larger premises and was now regretting the outlay, convinced collapse would result from any extravagance. Alys wanted to see Louise again, to revive herself, but somehow she would have to draw upon her memories, and work on alone.

From her window she could see the plane trees in the square, bark peeling in patches to reveal creamy bare skin. An egg-blue sky was visible above the office buildings. A void—a blue void in which no new ideas seemed to materialize. A solitary pigeon swooped into the space. Alys suddenly wondered if this would be all the future held for her—a little office above Golden Square, among the tailors, nowhere near the glamour of Bond Street or the Faubourg Saint-Honoré. Alys quelled such negative thoughts—the world was changing, hundreds and thousands were on the dole. She was tired of pandering to luxury. It was far better to move on, leave the new rising stars like Schiaparelli or Vionnet to enjoy their moment. *She* had certainly enjoyed her own.

The pigeon fluttered loudly, taking off from the parapet just under her window. People were flying through that blue void, an idea that amazed Alys. Amy Johnson, in a tiny plane; transatlantic flights ending in disaster, like the R101. Mass travel would come—the newspapers predicted it. Then Alys wondered again if all her journeying was over.

Tonight she would go to an exhibition at Tooth's—new surreal things that would perhaps give her inspiration. On Friday she and Anne were going to an Equity benefit of Noël Coward's *Cavalcade*. For the weekend she would go to Daisy Panton's, to tell her the London gossip and cheer her spirits with the present of a new dress. Alys' life was very full—but Cecily was right. It was also very empty.

She began to scribble random notes on paper, diary dates, hopes, thoughts, gradually drawing her mind away from social diversions to pure abstractions in line and shapes. She grew happier within her unrest, more intensely focused, as the connection between thoughts grew stronger, and a theme emerged.

By the end of the morning, Alys' headache had cleared, and an excellent scheme for the autumn season had come into being. She would suggest neat suits with jackets like an aviator's, fur-trimmed at the collar. There would be rayon blouses and dresses printed in blues, grays and pinks, colors of the sky. Wide-winged birds, swallows, seagulls could be relieved with lines of clouds or waves between the pattern repeats. To launch it all, she would ask *Vogue* to photograph

Anne in one of the "Alys Modes" designs, for the September issue. She worked hard on her sketches for the rest of the day.

At dusk, alone, she crossed the square to take a taxi to the art gallery. The usual crowd was there, looking pallid under the early evening sky that dimmed above the glass roof, tinging the guests with gray. Sinuous sculptures, frosted curving glass objects, driftwood and steel stood revered on white plinths. The paintings were more fun—pastel abstractions of the sort that Louise admired.

She glimpsed Edith Lyttleton, smart in lace and a feathered pillbox, holding forth to the press in a corner, on the state of British art. Arthur Lyttleton was in the Economy Cabinet, so journalists followed his wife everywhere nowadays. Alys waved; heads swiveled to look at her, but the young writers did not know who she was, and turned away, uninterested.

Alys was tired after her previous late night, and went home early, although reluctant to leave company. When she arrived at Spenser Street, rain had started to fall, and she hurried from the cab, head bent, for the door. Alys stopped abruptly. A man was lurking in the entrance, silhouetted in the porch light. For a moment, she felt apprehensive— Lisa was away for a few days, visiting Laura at Bladeshill. She felt unprotected. But the figure unbent, and she recognized it instantly— Philip White.

"What are you doing here?" she asked, unlocking her door.

"I'm exhibiting in London—didn't you get my invitation?"

"*You* sent it? I thought it was from the French Ambassador. I've just been to see the show, tonight."

"Mm. I'm not impressed, Lady Colvin. You didn't recognize my work?"

"Well, to tell the truth, I wasn't paying close attention, the room was so crowded." Alys was not prepared to admit that she had left out of boredom.

"Come in. You look soaked." she added.

"So do you."

"I forgot my umbrella. Why aren't you dining with rich customers?"

"I promised Louise I'd invite you to come with me. She worries about you, your mama."

"You guessed." Tears welled up in Alys' eyes, though she did not feel actively unhappy. Just the mention of her mother was affecting.

Philip wandered round her room, touching things, opening books left on the piano. One was an old edition of prints, pictures of British flora and fauna. He flipped the pages casually.

"Do you miss Paris?" he asked her.

"Oh, yes, six months away is a long time. I loved the rue Duphot. It was doomed to failure, though."

"Mm. All right now, are you?"

"Oh, quite. An interesting venture. And you? Are you going back soon, or do you intend to stay for a while?"

"Well, that depends . . ."

"On clients, I suppose. How the gallery shows . . ."

"Look. I've nowhere to stay. No money," he blurted. "I spent my last bean tonight. Louise even gave me the fare to get here from Paris. Would you put me up?"

Alys appraised him. About thirty, poorly fed, too tall, an unkempt chin. Perhaps he had just had a row with his girl friend.

"Of course. Would you like a bath to get warm? I'll cook us something simple, an omelette—or do you really want to go out again?"

"Oh no! I mean, do you? Otherwise that sounds fine."

"No, I don't want to go out." Alys had to turn away to the kitchen, to control an urge to laugh at his transparent relief.

But an hour later, seated by the fire with young Philip, her mood became serious. She had never spoken to him about his work at length; in Paris, Louise was his mentor, and he had kept his distance from her. "Lady Colvin" was just another client. At least, that was how Alys imagined he thought of her, with a little regret.

". . . And so Mr. Szenkier employs you now?" he asked, wanting to have the precise details.

"Yes. Sometimes I think it's a bit of a comedown, but other times I am excited by it," Alys answered.

"Would you show me your work?" he asked.

"Goodness! I've never done that."

"I'm sorry—I didn't mean to intrude."

"No—no, wait. I have my latest with me."

Philip bent over her rough sketches. "How very interesting. I did some silk-screening myself, for a while."

"Oh, I know very little about the technical side." This was not true, but Alys wanted him to go on talking. His voice was so young, and his skin smelled warm from the bath and the fire. She knew she was being stupid, but she wanted to kiss him. Without quite thinking about it, she did, on his ear.

Philip looked up and grinned. "That was nice. Do it again."

"I'm most awfully sorry! I can't think what came over me. The gin." she adjusted her pearl necklaces, blushing furiously.

Philip wrapped his long arms around her, and stooping down, kissed her very hard, full on the mouth. Now Alys was amazed. Philip had a positive mania for never appearing to care about anything—he was always bored or flippant. She had never seen him move with any urgency, there was always a languid ease about him. Not only was he kissing her with fervor, he appeared to be opening the zip at the back of her dress with a knowing efficiency.

"What on earth are you doing?"

"Unzipping your dress. You want me to, and I want to, too."

"Nonsense."

"No, it isn't. You've always driven me mad, treating me like a boy, giving everyone else your warmth and affection, never taking me seriously. I think you're the most amazing woman I've ever met. Give me a chance, Alys."

"I'm old enough to be your mother!"

"You're not. Unless you were married at fifteen."

"You asked Louise about me!"

"A little. I worked it out."

Alys' little black dress was sliding down her arms, trapping her elbows at her side. She was exposed, and very shy. Philip was so young, his hair was silky soft, his hands everywhere on her body, and he covered her face and neck with kisses. Alys felt ridiculous, hysterical at first, but then his sincerity began to arouse her. What did it matter if he only wanted a warm bed for the night? She kissed him back with a generous spirit, edging her hands between the buttons of his shirt. His heart was beating hard; she could feel it in the tips of her fingers.

"Upstairs," he said. Pulling her by the hand, he led her determinedly through the hall, and Alys, nonplused to find herself willing, followed.

On the landing, he pulled off his tie, dropped his jacket on the floor, and began kissing her again. "Which room is yours?" he asked. She pointed, and he opened it first to look in.

Philip stood quiet. The room was neat and peaceful. A very feminine, private place, with a large portrait of Alys as a young girl with a child on her lap above the fireplace. He was abashed. He leant against the door with his head on his arm. She couldn't see his face when he spoke.

"Look, Alys . . . I—I haven't done this for a long time. Will you be upset if I'm no good?"

"But . . . ?" she had been mistaken. He was not running away from someone else, abandoned. Now she had no idea of his intentions. Yet she still wanted to make love.

He held her again. "I want to be friends, Alys. Will you give me a chance?"

"Don't. I haven't the nerve to talk."

"Come to me, then. Come here."

Alys closed the bedroom door, and started to slide out of her clothes. Philip stopped her.

"Let me do it, please." But first, he took off his own shirt, then shoes and socks, winking at her.

"Someone told me this, a long time ago. Nevaire forget ze socks . . ." He could not resist lightening the mood.

"Now . . ." with great ceremony, he unpinned her hair, letting down the soft roll at the nape of her neck.

"How beautiful you are," he said.

"How handsome *you* are, dear boy," she answered, with tenderness. His tall, thin frame was very finely drawn and clear-skinned.

But it was like making love to a talkative rabbit. Philip chattered at her all the time, commenting on her body, her hands, her feet, the shape of her ears (she had very small lobes) asking her all the time what she liked, how she felt, until the end. Then he moved on her with such a demonic, silent energy that she felt pummelled on the bed. Still, that was sweet, too: his enthusiasm helped her to respond, and she loved his almost unbearable tenderness toward her when it was all over.

◆   ◆   ◆

"What do you mean, do I mind?" Anne asked, looking stunned.

"Well, do you? About Philip I mean?"

"Honestly, darling, it's your house. I can move into a hotel." Anne went back to her script. She was to play Marie Antoinette in a new historical piece, translated from the French.

"That's not what I mean. I'd never let him live here. I couldn't do that."

"You'll pay for him to have lodgings, then? How piquant."

"You're being an awful prig."

"Honestly, Alys, I'm just concerned for you. How do you know he's not after your money?"

"Because I haven't got any!"

"Oh well. But what will 'Mama' say?" She mocked Alys, hoping to bring her to her senses. But Alys began to laugh, and Anne saw how inappropriate her remark had been.

"I'm so happy, Anne! I know I'm making a fool of myself, but I don't really care. I want to be special to someone again."

"Oh, I know, darling. I've always told you so—but do take it all as it is intended, won't you?"

"Oh, of course; I'm not a complete fool." Alys tried to sound collected, and wanted to think of Philip as a "fling," as Cecily would call it. But Philip did not behave thoughtlessly, and she could not help wanting to believe he loved her as much as he said he did.

He found lodgings in Chelsea—an attic room with north light. Alys paid the rent for the first quarter, wondering if she would have to go on doing so, and knowing that she did not care. But Philip's work was well received, and he sold a few of his canvases at Tooth's. His main enthusiasm was for mural work, and Alys had already seen, in Paris, how well he did it. Her living room and hall in Spenser Street were soon turned into a French rococo fantasy, with trellises and trompe l'oeil views between painted statues. Alys gave a little reception to celebrate its completion. Mr. Szenkier came, pleased to be invited but awkward at seeing Alys in her own undeniably modest environment. His other twin daughter, Kitty, whose career with Alys had ended with her "good marriage," accompanied him. Mr. Szenkier was considerably taxed by the irony of Kitty's suggestion that Philip should decorate her new house in Lowndes Street. Alys ignored the social vagaries. She was only too pleased that her acquaintances were willing to help Philip's career, and promised to ask him to consider it.

"It looks like a stage set," Anne commented, circling the sitting room, unable to think of anything more critical.

"Good! I'm glad you like it." Philip was delighted.

Anne was disgraced by his enthusiasm. "I'll ask a few people to come and see this," she offered.

"How kind of you—but could you leave it until after Christmas? I've several commissions to finish already and Alys has asked me to stay at Bladeshill."

"Oh. I hate Christmas," Anne said, stretching her fingers into her tight kid gloves. "The theater closes. I don't like that when the play is running well."

Alys shut her eyes, remembering another beautiful friend who used to say those very words. Remembrance of Lily descended on her like a blessing. She knew she would be happy with Philip, and that there was no point in being afraid of any of her feelings.

Life with Philip was not always easy. He could not understand why she worried so much about keeping their liaison secret from Lisa, and would roll out of bed only a few seconds before Lisa began to stir in the house. Alys would lie clutching the sheet over her head, eyes shut tight until she heard the door click gently, and Philip's whistle as he strolled off to his studio. It was entirely probable that Lisa knew exactly what was going on, but Alys preferred discretion. She did not want Lisa to feel less needed, or in the way. But in the end, Philip resolved the situation. The house began to fill with people—artists, sitters, gallery-owners calling to arrange new shows. While Alys (reluctantly) disappeared to Golden Square, Philip would hover over Lisa in the kitchen, begging her to make the coffee just the way she made it for Alys—"I really like it best"—or bring her flowers when she had typed letters for him. Sometimes Alys came home to find them discussing the menu for another soirée, or Lisa sitting radiant by the window, while Philip sketched her. Gradually Lisa's self-confidence, withered by what she imagined was the loss of her beauty, began to grow again.

At first, Alys had to force Lisa to join in the parties, not to spend the entire evening supervising the hired cook or butler. But when a gallery owner recognized her from one of Philip's pencil sketches, and asked her out to dinner, Lisa's gaiety returned, and she entered life once more.

Days grew busier, and nights remained full of love as Alys and Philip grew more attached to each other. She liked to sit in his studio, rolled in a rug on a battered sofa, flipping through the magazines, *Vogue*, *Tatler* or *Harper's Bazaar*, judging the competition and thinking of new possibilities. He never minded her interruptions, and although she had always worked alone in the past, she found his company helped her to relax and make new connections in her thoughts.

Sometimes she would think back regretfully to her days in Brazil, when Alec had wanted exactly this kind of life. Sometimes she felt a deep sadness that it had not been possible, and wondered why it should be effortless with a man fifteen years younger than she was. Perhaps it was the lack of social responsibility; there were no Monteira de Barros; no rules to obey, except the discretion London society still required. Everyone in her circle knew that Philip was her lover, and was pleased for her. But to the world at large she was still Lady Colvin, and Philip always left her house late at night with all the other guests.

He came back, after a stroll round the park, when the house showed no lights. He had his own key, and crept up to her room. Perhaps the secrecy appealed to Alys; stirred some memory of being alone in the dark, and finding herself held in the moonlight was a wonderful sensation.

Then there were the new ways to be loving. Alys thought of all the emotions Philip roused in her, and could not decide which sustained their intimacy most. She loved him because he was a beautiful boy, of course. She loved him because he took her body with a concentrated passion, a masculine vigor that aroused her wildest nonmaternal feelings. But most of all Alys adored Philip because he had the confidence to be sensuous, not merely sexual.

"I'm tired, darling," she whispered, curling against his hard, bony chest.

"So 'm I. Painted all the wall of the corridor today."

"Kiss me."

"I thought you said you were tired."

"I am, but you're stroking my back and I'm beginning to revive."

"Turn over, then." Alys smiled in the darkness, and lay spoonlike next to him. But Philip moved away, still holding her shoulders, and kissed her, licking the perfume and salt from her skin, all the way up her spine, and round the edge of her neck, where her hair tingled in her flesh.

"Make love to me," she whispered.

"No." He turned her gently to lie on her back, his lips wetting her skin, along her arms, over her breasts, lower, till his head rested on her belly. Cool and kissed, Alys smoothed his forehead, pushed back his hair, until she felt him grow heavy on her, and they fell asleep, promising to make love in the morning.

CHAPTER 23

1 9 3 5 – 3 9

The rapid success of "Alys Modes" made
her laugh to think how she had been afraid of
emptiness. Alys was in demand again—which
was how she liked to live. Her patterned textiles
were arty without being too difficult to wear, just
right for a wider sale in the fashion departments
of big stores all over England. The sales represen-
tatives brought back repeat orders to Golden

Square, and the company grew steadily under Mr. Szenkier's careful management. He stopped coming regularly to Berkeley or Golden Square, claiming old age and infirmity, but he directed his daughter Tina with an iron hand.

Alys found it hard to believe that he was nearing eighty; he had been grizzle-headed for as long as she could remember, prematurely middle-aged, and impossible to visualize as anything other than worried and working hard. Not until he retired, and Tina started referring to him as "Papa" or "Felix" did Alys realize that she had never known him as anything other than "Mr. Szenkier." The habit died hard, just as she would never be anything other than "Madame" or "Lady Colvin" to him.

"Alys Modes" was more than a label to her. It stood for her effort to be in touch with the real world, to make a mark on it in some personal way. Alys was delighted to find that she could work in a new direction, nowhere near the sophistication of her "Alys France" frocks, but equally saleable. It meant that her desire to create still had value. Alys did not question where this need sprang from, for she knew it was useless to deny its existence. To do so only made her very unhappy.

Philip understood, and did not presume to criticize her efforts, even though her métier was so different from his own more abstract work. There was one diversion where their talents met, and it delighted them both. In Berkeley Square, Mr. Szenkier had filled the main bay window overlooking the street with a somber felt backcloth, a single dummy displaying one of the latest models and a small label, "Szenkier: Alys Modes." Returning her to work one afternoon after an illicit engagement in his studio, Philip commented, "Here we are, back at the undertakers . . . all it needs is a sign saying 'Cremations and Funerals' " and his impression stuck in Alys' thoughts. She suggested to "the management" that the window should become a focus, not a disguise. Berkeley Square was one of the best addresses in London, though far fewer of the houses were still private residences—others were being turned into shops, offices and nightclubs. But it was busy—people crossed through all day long, on their way to Oxford or Bond Street, work and pleasures. She recalled how memorable the windows of "La Mascotte" in São Paulo had been. Dressing the space, like the boutiques of the French couturiers, would keep her name interesting.

Mr. Szenkier let her experiment, knowing that publicity was her talent more than his. At first Alys displayed a single beautiful dress in a strong color, decorated with baskets of flowers. Philip found this too conventional, and painted a set of screens with classic draperies for her. In front of these she hung an empty coat-hanger, with a card dangling from a blue ribbon, one word written on it; "Alys." In another week she filled the window with doves in gold cages, and a little banner in blue silk with the same name. For the King's Silver Jubilee in May 1935, the window was filled with a weaver's frame in stainless steel, silver cloth winding from it, "GRV" embossed on its glittering surface. The following winter, Philip erected an empty picture frame round a set of traffic lights, to flash across the square in the dark, a futurist image, with a scarlet dance dress heaped on the floor below. Alys enjoyed the game, and made the Szenkier building in Berkeley Square a notable sight for Londoners and visitors to the city throughout the seasons.

Soon she could afford her extravagant trips to Paris again. The time had come to take Laura and introduce her to Louise. Alys had a sense of years passing so rapidly that the links had to be made before it was too late—or before the looming dangers in Europe made it impossible to try. Rearmament continued, Mussolini invaded Abyssinia and the government began to consider air-raid testing over the English south coast. Hostilities had only been suspended, as Alys and many others feared. Their hope, to be proved wrong, was dwindling.

Sadly, Laura seemed to regard meeting Louise as a duty, something that meant little to her beyond a detached curiosity, and a concern for Alys' agitation.

"Really, Mama, I'll be so nervous. She sounds so grand—what on earth am I to say to her?"

"How can you think such a thing?"

"I'm just a boring countrywoman. I know how the French think of us . . ."

Suddenly Alys understood. "It's Maurice! I'd forgotten how anti-French he was!"

"Well, they did leave us in the trenches . . . Jonathan used to tell us the most frightful stories from the men."

"Oh dear. Look, she's nothing to do with all that. I promise you, you'll find her fascinating."

They traveled all together, Alys, Laura, Philip and Lisa, for a few days in the spring, and went on to stay at Versailles. Taking Lisa was not altogether wise, Alys realized, for she had developed Laura's prejudices.

The house was even chillier than Alys remembered, seeing it differently, through Laura's domesticated values. Modern walnut furnishings, bare floors, abstract patterned rugs—Louise was living devotedly in the present, even at her great age. Charles hovered lovingly, easing the awkward moment of introductions.

"A granddaughter! Splendid! We have wondered about you for a long time. Louise, she has your profile, and your height, too," he observed.

"How curious. But very English coloring!" Louise was unconvinced.

"I never thought of it," Alys said, marveling at her own lack of observation. They *were* alike. She found it hard to be pleased by the idea. Laura was all her own doing . . . those years at Upton, and then with Dr. Hardy, when they were alone together, and Alys unhappy, were strongly etched in her recollection. Now faced with her own mother, she saw that Louise's abandonment of her in Ireland had given her relationship with her own child a particular intensity, all through those early years.

"So London suits you, Philip?" Louise asked in a slightly chilling tone. "Quite why, I don't know. I always hated it."

"You never lived there," Alys objected. She could not help reacting as she knew Laura would, and then grew apprehensive. Louise was manifesting all her worst traits: arrogance, snobbery, pride, a chilly self-centeredness. Alys glanced at Laura, who was indeed looking wonderfully *English,* cool and reserved.

"I passed through London once," Louise continued. She obviously felt that had been quite sufficient. "Dirty, gray. How you can live without the sun for all those months . . ."

"But I work very well there," Philip explained, "and you know, the French may accept foreigners, but they think the English are too close to be indulged, and that they never make good artists."

"That's true," said Louise, ignoring his irony. "All the artistic spirit resides in the Celtic races."

"But you didn't like living in Ireland either," Laura dared to say. Neither Louise nor Alys failed to grasp the accusation in her remark. For a breathless moment, Alys wished she were miles away. Louise blinked rapidly a few times, then stared in frozen honesty at her grandchild. "No, I didn't. I nearly died of unhappiness. I had lost my husband and my world was at an end. You could not possibly imagine my feelings."

"No. I don't think I could, Madame. My world didn't die with my husband. I have always valued the love of my family."

Alys wanted to rush to her daughter, hold her tight in an embrace and thank her from the bottom of her heart for her loyalty. It was hopeless to expect Laura to accept her newfound grandmother at once; she was all antagonism and dislike, out of sympathy for Alys. Laura had understood and suffered for her mother all these years, not just the fact, but the consequences of Louise's desertion.

"Dear me!" Alys said, trying to be lighthearted, but unable to conceal the emotion in her words; "How very kind of you to say such things, but sometimes I was a rotten mother to you—far too overbearing. I'm quite impossible at times . . . Don't you . . . ?"

Her voice trailed away. Louise had moved to the window, unable to face the thoughts this dialogue brought her. She lifted her head defiantly, but her lips quivered.

"Laura and Jonathan came to Paris once before—before the war," Alys intervened in a desperate way. Louise was too old to be called to account for her actions. It did not matter now. It was of no consequence. "I don't believe you came out to Versailles—did you, darling?" she went on.

"No, we spent a very rainy weekend at the Louvre, before Jonathan went on active service. I remember a pretty restaurant in Montmartre, and Sacré Coeur, and Jonathan's appalling French . . ." she giggled, and everyone was conscious that, for Laura, Jonathan was always alive in her thoughts.

"How strange it is," Lisa broke in, more comfortable than any of them with Laura's way of "living" with Jonathan, "I can remember coming here with Alys, that first time, and worrying that you—forgive me, Madame de Tessier—would be very foreign, and that Alys would be disappointed . . . that was *my* first visit. And such a strange thing happened as I waited by the door. I only remember it now, coming here again."

"Yes?" They all wanted to know, to avoid more difficult topics.

"A gardener saw me waiting by the door, and came up to me, talking the most rapid French. I've no idea to this day what he said, and I did not want to embarrass him by not understanding a word, so I just nodded and smiled. Because he was in such a good mood, and only wishing to be friendly to another servant on a Sunday . . . He gave me a rose from a neighbor's garden."

"Perhaps it was our Théobald . . ." Charles laughed. "He has an eye for the girls. I assure you he's always gallant, my dear, and wouldn't say anything you could not have heard!"

They all laughed, and Lisa blushed. "No, I wouldn't have minded anyway. It was the idea of being thought French, on a doorstep, that amused me, and the way he kissed my hand. My Papa used to do it, when I was very young."

"Won't you come into the garden, now?" Louise invited, becoming animated again, and making Alys feel relief for her. "It is a pretty sight this time of the year."

They stepped outside, into a perfumed, sunlit pool of green, where insects humming in the flowers made a hymn to the world's glory, just for a moment. Alys heard it, and was glad.

"Théobald should have been kissed back," Philip said, admiring the beauty of it, and causing Lisa to blush even more furiously.

The tended beds, the opened summer house, made Laura, too, relent. It was a place of privacy and caring.

"You love your garden!" she exclaimed to Louise, enchanted by its color and profusion.

"I know practically nothing about flowers; Théobald is the expert, of course," Louise replied. "But I can't live without them."

"I am the same," Alys agreed, pleading with Laura, in her tone, to indulge Louise and discover some good in her. For she herself was able to see Louise now as a once beautiful, fragile woman, who had a knack for making men adore her, and no other prospect but one kind of love as the reason for her existence. She felt deeply sorry for her.

Hyacinths, narcissi, mimosa and lilac, old odors, redolent of the Belle Epoque, dissolved any harshness she had felt toward the vain old woman who had harmed her so much by her disappearance. Louise was walking round the flower bed, pointing out the names of roses to her granddaughter, and offering her cuttings from her plants. (She knew all of them by name, contrary to her words.) Alys did not need Laura to accept her mother, to help re-create some sense of family. Laura could respect just this much: show a little softening and affection for Louise's wonderful garden. It was all the more valuable to Alys, since she knew that, with Anne, the prospect of even so small a gesture was utterly hopeless.

◆　◆　◆

These years were busier than ever for Alys. The worse the world looked, the more hectic she became. The jobless marched all the way to London from Jarrow, fed tea by courtesy of Lyons from St. Albans to Radlett. Edward VII abdicated; Mrs. Simpson and her carefully pressed Mainbocher clothes were banished from the kingdom. Alys did not really share the feelings of her contemporaries, who looked upon the king's decision as a dereliction of duty, and the cries of 'Down with Baldwin!' that filled the streets, as so much romantic nonsense. Fascination with royalty had only ever mattered to her as a source of income. Still, she was relieved that for most of her old circle, such as Edward or Cecily, the subject was so painful that it was taboo within weeks of its happening.

The times reminded her of her days in Conduit Street, when she had sat and stitched while the young men went to war. Only now she sat and sketched cheap lines for "Alys Modes," not hand-made wedding dresses for the establishment.

Rupert Firth, long dead, released from a life of invalidism, came to her thoughts very often as she heard the reports from Spain of the Civil War. The faces of the farmers in the *Daily Herald,* bearing their weapons, brought back the image of the dead Boer Rupert had described to her. Rugged, rough men, more used to ploughing than fighting. Another dress rehearsal for a bigger war . . .

Alys reacted much as she had done in previous times of stress, but with a greater intransigence about those things that mattered to her. To supplement her income from designing for Mr. Szenkier, she began to write articles for a new women's magazine, *Style and Beauty*, one of the many that tried to show ambitious, socially insecure women how to dress and how to entertain as they rose in the world, usually alongside their husbands, but not always. There were a few professional young women, nurses, business girls, teachers, who enjoyed the self-parody in Alys' advice.

The continuing economic gloom made simplicity, even poverty, a fact of life. Fashion had to turn this into a virtue, and make classless, cheap things chic. There were new idols, besides the inheriting rich: the film stars, dancers and singers, who had found success with their looks, not their birth. Now it was true that appearances mattered, leveling everyone. A "lady" going to a cocktail party wore black satin; so did a waitress in a tearoom.

Alys' writings were unconsciously hilarious. Sometimes Philip or his friends teased her, not realizing that whatever her difficulty with writing style (Alys had had a truly rudimentary education), she could communicate, and she cared that readers took her advice. Her articles were the natural extension of her salon advisory teas, when she had dispensed good sense in private.

" '*An old aesthetical Lord I once knew advised his daughter, a very dear friend of mine who was playing "lady patroness" for a while on an English estate: "Give the old women a red petticoat; that'll cheer them up far more than a charitable bowl of soup." I must say I think this is excellent advice. If you must wear your little black dress for yet another season (and we so often must) add luster with a shining scarlet underslip or a satin bow . . .*' Lady Mary told me that story. She rather disapproved of her father, but I think he was quite right."

Philip looked up from his canvas. "What was that, darling?" he asked.

"I'm writing. Don't interrupt," she answered, lost in her thoughts. He smiled indulgently, though Alys' reminiscences were meaningless to him.

"Read it to me," he asked, wishing to be affectionate.

" '*A hostess should never outdress her guests. The toilette of a woman who is entertaining must be subdued, however rich, so as not to inspire envy or render a less fortunate person uncomfortable. Hazlett observes that a gentleman is one who never offends the self-love of others . . . one of the supreme advantages of white is that a gown may be exceedingly costly, yet never obtrusive,*' " she read.

Philip laughed outright. "I think 'haslet' is a kind of cold cut. They make it from bits of pigs' ears, up in the north, if you can imagine it," he said.

"Damn." Alys crossed it out. "Does Hazlitt have an i?"

"Yes, my sweet."

"And it doesn't sound 'too completely pseudo,' as your friend Bernard said of me last week?"

"Did he? How unkind. Not at all. You're quite right about white."

"Oh, thank you, Philip. Not that I care a fig for Bernard really."

"Well, you shouldn't. I don't say you write quite as naturally as you speak—and quoting Hazlitt is rather—"

"Look here, Philip, firstly I'm a designer, not a writer, and secondly, people love it. They may *say* the world's more democratic, but *I* know people read me for the same old standards, a touch of glamour, a peep into the old way of life. You know I'm not half as grand as I sound, and so do they! Besides, if you're unsure of yourself, it's wonderful to have such inspiration—makes a girl feel special! Now, what do you think?: Listen: *'The blonde and the brunette cannot wear the same hue— even white comes in various tinges, as anyone trying to match a piece of muslin will know. Blondes should wear a bluish white, brunettes a cream or yellow—and the more transparent the better. (I remember a wonderful Spanish contessa who knew just how to wear black: not heavy and overdone, but black net, her gold jewels shining through.)' "*

"I think you're amazing," Philip said, emotionally. "That's why I love you. I have to go soon. To the theater. I'll be late tonight, so don't wait up for me." He left his brushes where they lay and rushed off, kissing her good-bye. But when he had left, Alys grew thoughtful, and added a small note to her words on the page:

" *'An elderly woman should not confine herself to black when she is old. No one could accuse her of levity if she mingled a little pink with her gray, or even resurrected that wonderful pale blue satin gown ordered so long ago from Paris, and which has a unique charm now, against her white hair . . . To dress in harmony with one's years, one must know the meaning of the years.'* " Thinking how much she too loved Philip, Alys was quite sure that she understood. She had learnt to be happy with each moment, day to day, and to enjoy the passing on of her richness to others. She did not care if she sounded eccentric: she believed in the value of dressing well and she wanted every woman to enjoy her own beauty, poor or rich, young or old.

◆　◆　◆

Anne had asked Philip to design sets for a small theater club production she was launching in aid of the Civil War, an abridged adaptation of a novel by Galdos. Anne could always be relied upon to champion causes in her art, and had never ceased to amaze Alys with her political convictions when she held none whatsoever in her personal life. Lovers came and went, so many that Anne had long ago stopped telling her who they were. Anne's resistance to Philip was still a mystery, therefore. She admired his work, used him professionally, but always mistrusted his intentions toward Alys, even though two years had elapsed since they had come together.

After the first night of *La Fortunata*, Alys and Lisa plied the cast and attendant friends with bacon and eggs in Spenser Street, while heated discussions on Surrealism, Marxism, unemployment, and Marlene Dietrich in *The Garden of Allah* took place.

All the women in the room were draped in furs of sorts—small, snappy foxes with glass eyes, peering over their shoulders. Spotty veils pushed back from carmine lips and frizzy curls made Alys feel ancient (for she remembered the style when it was first worn by Edwardian belles). Alys was wearing her latest, a full-length evening skirt in plaid taffeta, with a glittery knitted sweater that Lisa had made for her. She had tied a pinafore over it while she served supper. A little velvet pillbox still sat, slightly crooked, on her forehead. Through the open door of the kitchen she could see Philip leaning against a wall, talking animatedly to some unknown young actor.

For some reason, although there was no reason on earth to doubt him, Alys glimpsed a time when Philip would draw away from her. She had no interest in talking to the young man who seemed to absorb his attention. They both had the world to conquer before them and she was becoming increasingly anxious about the menace, this time more serious than ever to her own loved ones.

Perhaps she just felt tired.

"I'm going to lie down just for a moment, darling," she called out to Philip. "Too much of something." Alys climbed the stairs to her room. She untied her apron with difficulty, realizing that she could not breathe properly. No one downstairs heard her call, the conversation and singing rang in her ears, and she fell forward, gasping.

◆　◆　◆

"The doctor calls it a 'nervous reaction'—too much work, that's all," Alys said. Lisa sat on the edge of her bed, rather white.

"Tell me the truth," she demanded.

"I've just done so. Don't fuss, dear. Just get me the newspaper and my glasses before Philip appears."

"Too late." They heard the door bang downstairs. Philip came rushing up, two at a time. The very thought of it made Alys exhausted.

"Here I am! What did he say?"

"He's recommended a holiday. Exhaustion, that's all. And not enough food."

"I'm always telling you, but you never listen!" Lisa was on the verge of tears.

"Ssh, I know, I know. I'm going to be a good girl. Don't fret now. Make us all a lovely cocktail, and I'll tell Philip where we're going."

"What do you mean?" Philip noticed the inference at once.

"You can't come. You've got too much to do, and besides, you'll only distract me." Alys put her glasses on, trying to look firm, and, perhaps less deliberately, old.

"I'll get the shaker." Lisa slipped away.

"I'm going to take Lisa and Jack. He's on holiday from college, broke, and will chaperone us. It might be the last time I shall see the South of France."

"Alys! What do you mean!" Philip looked terrified and rushed to the bed. But she could see that the panic was also caused by his fear of illness. The thought of sickness, even frailty, did not appeal to him.

"Silly, I only meant that things don't look good in the papers, do they? Mussolini . . . and now we've got Neville Chamberlain. He won't stop *il Duce*, everyone says so."

"Put like that, it all sounds catastrophic. It's unlike you to be so serious."

"I've seen it all before . . ." Alys did not care if she sounded old. She wanted to remind him of it. It would be better if he accepted a little separation, otherwise she would have to tell him the truth, and he might leave her altogether if he knew it. The doctor had told her she had strained her heart. "Go and tell Lisa I'm gasping for a drink, will you?"

"Are you telling me the truth?"

"Of course I am. We've never had secrets, have we?"

"No. I do love you, Alys. You mean the world to me."

"I know, sweetheart. I'll come back fitter than ever, and it will all be just the same."

Philip buried his head on her breasts, kissing her gently through the silk of her robe. He sneezed violently.

"I don't know why you have to wear these feathery things."

Alys teased, "Because it's my favorite old French wrap and it makes me feel whorish. Would you rather I looked like an invalid?"

"Of course not! Can I get into bed with you?"

"Philip! I'm supposed to be exhausted! That's why you can't come on holiday with me!"

"I'd be really good. Massage your feet . . . peel you oranges . . . buy you bunches of flowers . . ."

"Lisa and I will rub each other with suntan oil and Jack will read to me from the newspapers. Altogether more appropriate."

"I can't bear this! Stop teasing, Alys—you *are* going to be better, aren't you?"

"Oh yes. If you love me, don't make it hard for me to be sensible . . ." Alys spoke sincerely, and he was forced to agree.

◆　◆　◆

Those weeks in the hills above Menton were some of the happiest Alys had known. They were made memorable because she had to consider what she would do in response to the doctor's warnings. She did not want to change everything about her life, to survive for a sensible but reduced old age. The doctor said her "breathlessness" indicated a weakening of the heart, and that if she did not take care of herself, she could have a major setback. The dullness of it all irritated her. She was incapable of changing her ways. Alys saw that she would continue just the same and take the chance of what her body could manage. The only thing she *would* do was force herself to see less of Philip, to try to reduce their passion to friendship. Alys cared too much for him to have their good years spoilt by her infirmity—if anything were to happen, she did not want him to see it.

Perhaps she was being selfish, possibly denying Philip the chance to love her even better than he did already. But Alys was frightened that the reality would be different—that he would end by falling out of love, consider her a burden, wishing he were with someone younger, more contemporary. Whether this fear came out of mere vanity, or out of a loving protectiveness, was a question that occupied her night and day. She found no answer. She just wanted Philip to go on thinking her "wonderful" until the end.

Slowly, the calm of the house entered her thinking. It was a beautiful place, not at all the simple villa that Louise had described when she offered to lend it to her. It was very old, dating from the days when the English came to winter in the South of France. A square building on three floors, it had a winding stone staircase at one corner, and a long terrace at the back, covered in bougainvillea. Six tall cedar trees stood in the sunken garden, making deep shade, with a thick carpet of pine needles below, where nothing grew. At the side of the house was a sunnier terrace, where various ferns and pelargonia straggled in stone troughs round the edge of a small square pool that turned darker green as summer ended.

The house had belonged to Louise's former lover, Daniel Newton, and had been left to her in his will. Alys was mildly affronted to see aged sepia prints of Newton children and wives still dotted on bedroom walls. The weather never looked warm in these old photographs. Black-eyed girls in Panamas and wrinkled wool stockings, or boys in sailor suits holding fishing nets or cricket bats. The chest near the piano in the drawing room was filled with rust-spotted sheet music, copperplate signatures of various Newton family members and many other foreign names still legible on the title pages. It was a house where people had been happy, and done interesting things. Louise spoke of it with great affection, and this influenced Alys' imagining of the life it had held.

Jack looked after her dutifully, bringing her tisanes in bed or sitting at her feet, whitening his tennis shoes on the terrace and talking about "life." He was full of his first term at Cambridge, and pleased to share his gossip with her.

". . . so I got ten points at the end of the day," he rambled on about some sporting tournament. (Alys had not been keeping the score.)

"Marvelous, darling. But tell me, what *is* the shot put?"

"Oh, Grandma, you're so stupid! I say, let's talk about something you know *all* about. Tell me more secrets—" he grinned significantly at her.

"No more scandals! You know how cross your mother was when I told you about your birth!"

"Well, that was unfair. I'd worked out the dates for myself. I only asked you to fill in the details . . ."

"Well it *was* a love match. Of that you can be sure."

"Like you and Philip."

"Look here, young man!"

"Oh go on, Grandma. I've known for years. And wasn't there a Duke once? A friend at college told me. I'm quite ragged for having such a wicked grandmother you know."

"It's all lies. Though I *was* once propositioned by a famous artist. I refused him, and he took up with Lily Lavelle instead. Wonderful woman. Dead of course. Most of my friends have gone."

"Did you ever feel jealous, Grandma?" he asked, blushing.

Alys knew at once that he had lost his virginity sometime in the previous term. It gave her a twinge of sympathy for the rawness of his feelings.

"Sexually possessive, you mean. The sexual force is glorious, but it can be destructive too. Lily used to tell me to go on long journeys. Sometimes it works. It did for me."

"Oh, go on, Grandma, tell me more."

"You're quite mad about sex, young man!" she said, laughing. "How lucky you are I'm not disapproving! Listen." She leant forward and put her hands to his ear. "Never forget the socks. Otherwise, never mind about looking foolish. Girls like a man who can laugh at himself. If you ever fall off the bed, just make a joke and get back on it. She'll admire you for that."

Jack looked amazingly impressed and whistled.

"Tell me more."

"That's enough for one day. Perhaps I *had* better tell you a scandal instead!"

"Oh, all right. What about Cecily Day? I like the sound of her."

"Haven't seen so much of her recently. She went to Paris for a while with Legless. Got involved with a black bandleader; he was furious. Hardly surprising: everyone was doing it a few years ago, and she was always stunningly handsome. Made other women feel stupid. If everyone wore black, she'd be sure to turn up in white. If satin was the thing, she'd dig out an old sprigged cotton frock and wear that. Same with the men, I should imagine."

"Charlotte must have died of fright."

"*Aunt* Charlotte, if you please. Not as much as you'd think. The war changed many things . . . Charlotte certainly found herself, perhaps she understood Cecily better after it."

"God, Grandma, it's the young ones who are supposed to shock their elders. You make me feel a bit pathetic, as a matter of fact."

"You mustn't. Mine was an idle world. You should be more radical, young man. We're all irrelevant."

"When does Louise arrive? I'm dying to meet her."

"Don't be surprised if she fails to recognize you, will you? Family ties are not her strongest point. I didn't like becoming a grandmother very much myself, at the start. It's all rather a trial for her, the endless generations of us, that sort of thing."

"I know Ma's not very keen."

"That's a pity. Still, it's only my obsession, really."

"I understand, but I want her to like me, too."

"You're very kind to me, Jack."

Louise was not overjoyed. She responded to Jack as if she were a little deaf, a little absent-minded, so that she could avoid all discussion of the Hardy family tree. Jack was far too young, too blond, too affably English for her, and no one was old enough to have a *great* grandson.

After a few days enduring her distant behavior, Jack reluctantly decided to go to friends in Cannes—as had always been intended, once Alys was installed. But he was sad to leave her.

Jack and Alys played bezique on the terrace on his last evening. The air was cool after a rainstorm; for a while the cicadas had stopped. Hot drops of rain hit the creeper leaves, like the clap of babies' fat hands.

"Madame Denis will be sorry not to cook for you after tonight. The rest all eat like birds. I know she's made something splendid for your last meal." Alys said.

"I'm appallingly hungry."

"So am I," Alys agreed.

"You're feeling better, then, Grandma? I'm glad."

"I never felt better in my life. I'm as brown as a walnut, and just as wrinkled. A prune, in fact."

"No, you're not—you're a bean."

"And I've beaten you—look!"

Alys missed Jack very much after he left. She hoped Louise felt guilty for being so distant, although she was quite pleased with the idea that her mother wanted her more to herself. Louise had actually expressed concern when she heard that she needed to rest. Perhaps the sight of Alys sipping marc, smoking cigarettes and being mildly crude with Jack did not fit in with her picture of descending on Alys to provide maternal care. Still, Alys was angry that she had been cold.

Charles made peace between them, in his usual tangential fashion.

"Louise wants some snapshots taken of you," he suggested one day. "I've got a new plate camera. Would you mind? Have you the patience to sit for me, dear?"

"Of course, if you want me to."

"I'm very slow, setting it all up. Also, you'll be a very difficult subject. You have such vitality, so much movement in your expression and your body."

"Don't flatter me so! I haven't moved from this deck chair since three o'clock!"

"Ça, ce n'est pas ce que je veux dire," he disagreed, but continued to study her intently. "Will you wear this shawl? I don't want you to be chilled. The sun is moving round."

He gave it to her, a soft cashmere thing in beautiful colors. Alys recognized it at once. "Where's Louise?" she asked.

"Resting. She'll be with us later. Is it urgent? Would you like me to call her?"

"No. No. It can wait." Alys pulled the shawl closer round her shoulders, smelling the soft ferny perfume Louise always wore. She spent an hour with Charles in contented silence.

CHAPTER 24

1 9 3 9 – 4 5

*T*he following September, Alys was spending a weekend alone with Laura when the news of Chamberlain's peacemaking visit to Berchtesgaden was broadcast. Maurice was visiting old friends by the sea; Jack back at college. She and Laura tried to convince each other that nothing would happen, that war would be averted, but neither of them believed it. A few days later the French government called one million reservists to active service.

"What will happen to Louise?" Laura asked her. "Couldn't we persuade her to come and stay with us here for a while?"

"That's very kind of you. She wouldn't come," Alys answered with conviction. "Paris is her home. I know she'll stay there, whatever happens."

"I'm sorry, Mama. It must worry you so. But then, I'd never leave Bladeshill either."

Alys had no such strong sense of attachment to one place—except perhaps that small room in Paris, for a few years. Yet she appreciated what it meant for others, especially for Laura.

"I quite like my studio in Golden Square. But I shall have to give that up now."

"You've decided, then?"

"Oh yes. I haven't the stamina. It's collection time just now, and I feel myself getting tense . . . it won't do."

"What will you do?"

"Stay in London, write, just be there. I would like to."

London was forcedly gay, as she expected it to be. It suited her. The hotels and restaurants were full, the theaters crowded with the current mania for Austrian musicals, *Magyar Melody* and *The Dancing Years*. It seemed appropriate that the last performance at the old Lyceum, a theater that Anne had frequented in her early stagestruck days, should be that of John Gielgud in *Hamlet*. Helplessness in the face of growing evil echoed the general mood.

Balls, cocktail parties and weekends in country houses continued for her friends. Alys had already seen this determined and frenetic celebrating in two wars before, and it filled her with dread. No one seemed to want to face the signs in Europe. She felt helpless too, more personally. In the spring, Alys told the Szenkiers she would not continue to work for "Alys Modes" after the next collection. There was a fine young assistant, Freddie Collins, on hand in Golden Square to fill her place when she had gone.

Felix Szenkier responded to the news with genuine dismay. Freddie Collins was good, but nowhere near as original as Alys. After their initial difficulties, he and Tina had built up a very efficient working relationship with Alys, and he knew she had a real gift for novelties. In recompense for her years of service to the Szenkier company, he offered her a handsome sum, £5,000, and a pension, to replace her designer's fees and her annual bonuses. Considering that he had never let her become part of the management, it was a gesture of respect and generosity.

Tina accepted the news with alacrity; Alys knew that she would be relieved to have all connections with the grand old past finally removed from the building, so that it would become her own empire. White-winged at her temples, severe in black, Tina had waited long enough for her chance to be her own mistress, and Alys understood her feelings, although she would have liked a little regret at her own departure.

To make Philip understand her withdrawal was much harder to do. Alys had tried refusing to go to parties all through the winter months and made endless excuses so that he could not stay at home instead with her in Spenser Street. He was puzzled, and growing more insistent.

"I'll come back later, after the do," he suggested one evening.

"No, that's sweet, but don't. I'll only stay awake for you, and I've got a hard day tomorrow sorting through papers in Golden Square. Come to lunch instead. It's Lisa's birthday."

"But I want to be alone with you. You're always fending me off."

"Tomorrow then. Good-bye, you'll be late."

Philip kissed her. "Don't you love me any more?" he said, unafraid to be honest with her.

"I do! Damn, damn! This is hopeless! Don't you see, you should think of yourself? God knows what's going to happen! You should find someone younger to share all this ghastliness . . ."

"You *are* slipping away from me. I knew it. What have I done? Why?"

She had no choice. "You silly boy! You're wearing me out! I can't keep up with you any more! Leave me *alone*, Philip!" It was such an effort to say the truth that for a moment she hated him for making her admit it.

Philip stood quite still, leaning against the painted wall he had made for her. His face grew untypically hard.

"I think you should give me more credit. I'm not a plaything you can just throw aside. After all the times we've had . . ."

Alys was overcome with sadness. "Oh Philip, I'm so sorry! What have I said! Forgive me!" She burst into tears, shaking from head to toe, and utterly sensitive of her wrong.

"It's all right. Don't upset yourself so." Philip hugged her very close. "Why didn't you have faith in me? That's what hurts me the most."

"I—didn't—want—pity." Alys spat each word out, between sobs.

"I don't pity you. It's your decision. I'd have liked to be able to tell you what *I* feel about it, but there we are. I'll do as you say."

"W-won't you come tomorrow?"

"Oh yes. For Lisa's birthday. Good-night, Alys."

He was very angry, and it was her fault. Alys went to bed and wept her heart out.

Next day, it was very hard to concentrate on her work. Buyers were calling at Golden Square in half-hour sessions to make their purchases, trying to keep to normality and show enthusiasm for the future. Tina Szenkier hurried across to greet her. Alys was grateful that for once she seemed appreciative of her presence.

"There's a chap from Birmingham who is terribly keen to meet you. I hope you don't mind?"

"Not at all. I hope he likes this lot?"

"Oh yes. Don't you?" She looked surprised. Alys smiled.

"I think it's a little odd, people wanting all this, just now. It's only just struck me. How foolish we are."

The girls paraded in little Austrian bolero jackets, with tight-waisted wool dirndl skirts. Plain wool dresses with simple long jackets, lightly padded, were trimmed with white at the collar and cuffs. Tartan cotton with pleated skirts suggested only a little more color. They were all practical, well-cut, crisis clothes.

The man from Birmingham was called over. A Mr. Oates.

"I'm pleased to meet you," he said. "My mother often talks of you. She was one of your 'Dorcas girls' before she married my dad."

"Oh? That was a long time ago! Why, we stopped that kind of work after the last war, didn't we? All the girls went into factories instead . . . What was her name before her marriage?"

"Bassett. Ida Bassett. Do you remember her?"

This spruce, prematurely middle-aged man with a bristle moustache and a neat dark suit, at once took on a resemblance to an urchin child in a rough stained smock.

"The Bassett boys," she murmured.

"That's right. My uncles. Both died in the war, poor old boys. Mum never really got over it. But she's doing all right, living with me and the wife now."

"Your mother was an excellent seamstress. She made me some beautiful things. How nice to hear of her. She must be pleased with your success." Time fell away at the recollection of those barefoot boys who used to eat the buns at Upton lodge while their sister sewed.

"It was her idea. Me and the retail drapery business."

"Obviously good judgment. Remember me to her, won't you?"

"I will, Lady Colvin. It's been a real pleasure."

When the war comes again, Alys thought, he will do his duty just as his uncles did before him—as Philip will, and Jack too. Tina reappeared, looking somber.

"Anything wrong? I thought he liked the show, and I was very touched to meet him." Alys tried to sound encouraging.

"Someone called for you. She said to say only 'Charlotte rang.' She said you'd know why." Tina knew that it was the Duchess of Wye. Alys' private life was a subject of eternal interest at the salon, and Tina still had a habit for it, even though she ran the company.

There was only one reason why Charlotte would telephone in the daytime and leave her name in that way: Edward had been taken ill.

"Can I use your office?" Alys asked abruptly.

Tina seemed to understand her urgency without needing further explanation, and Alys slipped away to the telephone. Mr. Oates, left to negotiate with Tina, waved good-bye as she left the room. She was sorry to disappoint him by not staying to chat longer. She could see he had hardly believed his mother's old stories about life at Upton—at least, now, he would know it was all true.

"Hallo? Charlotte? What's happened?"

"He died. In the night."

"No!"

"He wouldn't be moved to the hospital again."

"He wanted to be with you. At home."

"I'm taking him to Burley for the funeral. It's on Friday. Will you come down?"

"Yes. Do you need me to come to you now?"

"No. No, thank you. I've my parents with me."

"Oh, of course . . ." Charlotte would retreat from her now. "If there's anything I can do, please ask. Oh, Charlotte, I'm so sorry."

"Thank you, Alys. I'm sorry too. Good-bye." The telephone click came very fast, as if Charlotte's hand had been on the receiver.

Alys hurried from the salon to Spenser Street, to celebrate Lisa's birthday. Laura had come down from Bladeshill for the occasion, and Philip was there too, waiting when she arrived.

"What's the matter?" Philip asked her, seeing her face.

"I don't want anyone to hear, especially not Lisa. Come into the hall." He followed her. "An old friend died, that's all."

"I'm sorry." Philip hunched up against the wall again, but this time he looked defeated, not angry.

"I'm sorry too. For everything." Alys lifted her face to kiss him. Philip sighed, then touched her cheek, very gently.

"Come on. Let's join the others."

◆　◆　◆

That spring was glorious. It was painful for Alys to make the journey through a landscape hazily covered with green buds, daffodils lolling under the hedges in long grass. Nature had taken Edward, one of its most ebullient, energetic creations, and cut him out of this world. Everything that Alys looked at reminded her how life would go on, lustily renewing itself without him. It would have been so much easier to travel to his funeral in rain and mud, not in the optimism of sunshine.

Edward had to be buried at home, at Burley, although he hated the place and hardly ever went there after his childhood. The house was too full of the presence of his stern parents. He rented it out to wealthy Americans most of his life, preferring to stay in London or spend the summer with the Days at Melbury, or wherever else he was invited. But Charlotte wanted his remains to be placed in the family chapel.

Its neglected stone walls and rusting windows were grim surroundings for an elegant man like Edward. Alys stood very quietly, aware of the vibrant perfume of its interior, the damp and green of disuse mixing spicily with the presence of warm bodies, and the cool scents of floral wreaths.

For an urban soul, as she was, natural things held a mystical power for remembrances and hints of another cycle of life. She felt comforted. The beauty of the flowers was not a reproach, as she had thought in the hour of funeral gloom. Instead their very glory and impermanence were inspiring. She was very happy to have known Edward, and to have loved him well for a time.

Alys sang her hymns with no sound coming from her lips. She was even more alone now. All the men, going: Alec lost to her, in Brazil; Jack talking of leaving college to train as a pilot; Philip accepting her pushing him away before it was too late. At least Edward would be spared the awfulness that was bound to come.

She glanced across at Charlotte, standing stiff and tearless between her aged parents. She was a dedicated, passionate woman by nature— Alys was glad to have seen her finest qualities. But with the death of the man who had brought out the best in both her and Alys, the friendship would not survive. It existed through mutual affection for Edward. Alys would miss Charlotte, too.

At the back of the church, someone sobbed. Although Alys had sworn not to do it herself, in respect for Charlotte's dignity, she felt great tears running down her face. She kept telling herself that Edward was fortunate to die before the nightmare began, but all the same, she wanted him to go on living forever.

◆　◆　◆

That same month, March 1939, the Germans occupied Czechoslovakia. To Alys it appeared to be the beginning of a series of demands made and concessions granted as Hitler worked for his designs on land in Europe. The months following were confused with conflicting reports about what would happen and who would do what. Alys listened to all of it with a deepening anxiety.

"Sweetheart," she asked Lisa one day at lunch, and Lisa knew she had a special request to make, "Will you turn the radio on?"

"At meals?" she answered. Alys had always been punctilious about certain things.

"Well. The news. Do you mind?"

"No. I understand." She would have preferred to talk to Alys.

"If we have to leave here," Alys said, after the broadcast, "You'd come with me, wouldn't you?" Lisa looked pained. "I'm sorry, silly question."

There was a pause. "We could go up to Bladeshill," Alys went on. "Everyone says people will move out of London soon."

"What about your magazine work?"

"They'll let me file it from there. I've asked about that already."

Lisa had been waiting her turn for some time, and seemed to listen to Alys with an air of satisfaction.

"Actually, it's all arranged. I've been waiting to tell you, but you know how you like to make your own plans all the time. Laura thinks they'll take Bladeshill for a Red Cross hospital. She's offered it, and may be made commandant. I'd like to help her on the management side, if it's agreed to."

"So we shall all stay together."

"You should never have thought we wouldn't. Also, I should tell you . . ."

"What?"

"Philip called while you were away. I've been waiting to speak when I felt you were a little stronger . . . *He* wanted me to tell you, when it was the right time to give you the news. Shall I, now?" Lisa's wide, brave face offered strength to Alys.

"Yes. Go on."

"He's been given something to do. Something secret, I think, and he's had to go away very suddenly. He won't be able to write to you, he wants you to know that he thinks of you and would send you his love, if he could."

"Why didn't he tell me himself?" Alys started to cry again.

Lisa came round the table and comforted her. "Because he knew you would be upset, and there was really nothing else to say. You should have trusted him, Alys. He really adored you, you know."

"You knew all the time."

"Of course I did!"

"You've never told him—all of it! What the doctor—"

"No. I'd never do that. Don't worry, Alys. He wouldn't want you to be ill again."

"I know. But it makes me feel I was very selfish."

"No, just foolish with him. But you did the right thing. There are other people who need you too, you know."

They packed up their favorite possessions and moved out in September, the month Hitler's troops marched into Eastern Europe and war was officially declared. At Bladeshill they were to live in a newly arranged flat above the kitchen wing, the main floors being used for the new hospital, with Maurice and Laura squeezed into the attics of the old house.

At first they took in evacuated cases from London hospitals. Beds were being kept empty there in preparation for casualties. But in only a matter of months, these patients were discharged, and the house began to fill up with wounded soldiers, sent back to hospitals in the regions where they originally lived. Alys, her friend and daughter spent all their time supplementing the care of the nursing staff, writing letters, listening to problems, fetching books or tobacco for the men.

Once more, Laura supervised the home farm—even the flower beds in front of the house were planted with vegetables. Alys could not work in the garden, but she made it her business to fill all the rooms with flowers, and took charge of entertainments. She hoped to persuade Anne to come up to the country; her play was going to close soon.

"Thanks for the thought, but I'm going to America," Anne said, her voice crackling over the telephone. "Goodwill tour, you know, fund-raising again."

"Haven't you had enough of all that?" Alys asked, relieved that Anne would be safe from the dangers and temptations of remaining in London. "Promise that you'll come here when you get back."

"Of course I will. London's getting so gloomy. Everything closing, with the blackout."

"Look after yourself."

"You too. Don't work too hard. Good-bye." There was no time for more; the line went dead.

Alys did not want to work hard. She found that willing her family to get through the nightmare took all her reserves of energy. At first Jack came home quite often on leave from his training place in Norfolk, looking immensely dashing in his uniform, and reassuring her with his heroic chat. But as the gaps between his visits grew longer, her anxiety for his safety increased. She wondered how Laura managed not to give way to nervous depression about him, but then Laura had always been more faithful, not self-centered, as Alys knew herself to be at times like these.

Louise wrote to her in June 1940, to describe *L'Exode:* all the roads south out of Paris were jammed with cars and queues of people fleeing from the advancing Germans. "I'm not going," Louise wrote. "I didn't desert Paris last time, and I'm not going to do so now. Colette is staying on, too. I hear her talking on the radio, and I agree with her. We'll stay and defy them. Do look after yourself, my dear. Charles sends his love, and you know you have mine."

Many others did the same. After a few months of the Vichy government, Parisians realized that there was less danger in occupied Paris than they had thought, and a reverse migration took place, as if nature had told all the birds of the city to ignore the hostile cold and fly back to their true home.

Alys had a similar desire. The Blitz had knocked holes out of central London. Berkeley Square had been badly hit, though so far her villa in Spenser Street was undamaged. Then Tina wrote to ask her to come and discuss a new venture, for which she was needed. In spite of her good intentions, she could not resist finding out what Tina meant. Ignoring protests from all the family, she traveled back to the city. In Berkeley Square, the debris had already been cleared from the top floors—glass, dirt and earth had been flung upward over several floors, the glass roof of the ballroom was shattered, and the bay window at the front, which used to give her and Philip so much entertainment, was destroyed. Now the basements were used for fitting rooms, work continuing in spite of the chaos above.

Tina explained the new working situation to Alys in what they both still regarded as Mr. Szenkier's office. The company had been designated as "essential" under the new government policy of concentration in the fashion industry. Only certain firms were allowed to stay in business, while others had to combine, rather than compete, to produce manufacturing units of a more effective scale.

Tina Szenkier could afford to be gracious, now that the company's future was secure! "We've been asked to contribute to the Board of Trade's scheme. It's an honor, really, for you." She handed Alys a letter.

"They want me to do 'Utility' clothes," Alys said, reading the details. "How kind. Hartnell, Molyneux, Amies—and me."

"Well, there's also Bianca Mosca and Olive O'Neill."

"I know, I know! I'm only teasing! I suspect Edith Lyttleton's had a hand in this." Arthur Lyttleton was in the Coalition government and had influence. It was a great kindness; Edith would know how much Alys would value a chance to contribute in her own way this time.

Reading the instructions, she realized that the task would be an absorbing one. All new clothing was restricted, not just in the amount of fabric, but in every detail, from the width of skirts, sleeves or pockets to the number of buttons. None were to be used for cuffs or lapels. The skirt had to reach just below the knee. No excess material was allowed for half belts or oversize pockets. Alys was well-versed in limitations, from her training with the Szenkiers. But she hoped that her own originality, the quality of her work and perhaps the influence of her name would inspire a less grudging acceptance of the new rules. Girls loathed having to wear dowdy, mean-cut clothes, however important it was to economize. It was a question of morale, which everyone agreed made a great difference.

"I'll stay at Browns while I work on them," she said, already considering vague ideas that she wanted to sketch.

"Are you sure? Laura won't like it."

"I'll tell her it was entirely my own decision—you had nothing to do with it."

She stayed where she had lived when her first salon was being opened: in Mayfair, where her dogs, Samson and Delilah, used to turn the corners in the streets before her, unbid. The florist's shop had gone, but walking on those familiar pavements brought back days with Edward most vividly. Alys wondered if the rest of her life would be like this, grappling with reality, while other forces, memories from her past, ambushed her at every corner. The war, her frightening impermanence, her physical weakness, made the future void; what lay behind was much more tangible.

Edward would have understood all this, she thought. The whole area was full of servicemen, Americans, Canadians, Englishmen, drinking away their off-duty time in nightclubs, flirting with the waitresses and barmaids. A vitality, a good-humored openness hardly concealed the sexuality in London's mood. "Hello, are you free for lunch . . . shall we stay the night . . . will you marry me?" Alys could see the possibilities in faces as she passed by. Sometimes it amused her, but at others she found being in London a nerve-racking effort. The almost nightly descent to the hotel basement shelter in air raids began to wear her out. Alys worked on the Utility designs struggling against her fatigue.

This was her last challenge; she knew that, for it was self-imposed. Alys never wanted to design anything after these were completed. Alone in her small room, she created and simplified, studying the rules as carefully as she could. It was a serious business—Tina had told her of a dressmaker prosecuted for embroidering butterflies on lingerie! She not only worked out the design, but cutting layouts and variations for all kinds of fabric. Supplies were going to be a problem, and the outfits needed to be flexibly planned. For the more expensive Szenkier clients, her suit skirts were designed using high-quality Scottish tweed so that they hung very well. For the cheaper "Alys Modes," they had to be cut on the straight grain and only kick pleats were allowed. Still, Alys found the restrictions added to her pleasure, stripping away the unnecessary and leaving only the essential elements of a balanced, clear design.

The only way she could add distinction was in the use of color balance, using small areas of contrast fabric, and in the practicality of her ideas. She planned to make tweed suits with yokes, using check fabric on the diagonal. Plastic buttons in different colors could be used on the contrasting stripes of a linen dress. A cape with a stiff collar could be made to sit perfectly on the shoulders because of its shape and seaming, without needing any fastenings. She thought of denim, cut like a pinafore, but made into a smart dress by its scalloped neckline; a style that could be repeated in good wool. Alys worked late into the nights, but never ignored the sirens. The honor she felt in her task made her want to see it through.

Alys supervised the making of all the muslin models of her designs in Golden Square. In spite of her enthusiasm for the work, the hum of war in London was beginning to assault her senses.

"Can't you get the lapels to sit better than that?" she complained. "It just doesn't work, especially if it's going to be made in a tartan."

"Lady Colvin," Tina said, barely restraining herself. "I really think you should leave the manufacturing to the workrooms. We're quite capable."

"But you don't understand, Tina. These have to be perfect." To make quite sure that her instructions would be followed, she ripped the collar bodily from the jacket. "Very well, ask Freddie to come and recut this piece for me."

Luckily, the telephone rang, giving Tina no time to protest. It was Jack.

"Grandma? What are you doing, back at work?"

"It's wonderful. I've been asked to make Utility models."

"I know. I phoned home and they said you were here. I bet you're pleased as punch. Look, I've got a couple of days' leave. Fancy a night out, to celebrate?"

"Laura's told you to spy on me. Send me home, I'll be bound."

"Nonsense. I wouldn't do that! I've got tickets for the Vic-Wells Ballet, and I'll treat you to a smart dinner, if you can stay awake that long, otherwise we'll go back to Browns."

"Stay awake, indeed! It's you who'll fall asleep, in the theater!" Of course Jack did just that, not being at all interested in the ballet, but willing nevertheless to give Alys her treat. He revived as soon as it was over, with the prospect of cocktails and taking Alys somewhere crowded. Alys knew he liked her to be cutting about the girls, and admiring about the young men, and she was in the mood to oblige him. Besides, she adored music of all kinds.

"Where shall we go? You name it. The Mayfair Club, the One Hundred—Milroys, what d'you say?" Jack invited.

"The One Hundred! That's the most popular! It will be fun to tell Laura I've been there."

"Right-o. Now mind the step, Grandma."

"Don't be silly, Jack."

They took a taxi into the center of London. Alys wondered if there had been any warnings while they were in the theater, but realized that Jack would have ignored them anyway. Londoners made a habit of nonchalance now, and she was in the same frame of mind, for once.

There was a traffic jam in Regent Street as they approached it, so Alys and Jack decided to walk the last few hundred yards to Leicester Square. Beyond the cars were ambulances, criss-crossing the lower half of the street. A bomb had fallen.

"I think we'd better go back," Jack said.

"No. I want to look." Alys succumbed to that atavistic urge to look at a disaster. People had told her one always did it: those who were not hit always had to suffer something, alongside those who were caught.

The glass dome of the Café de Paris had received a direct hit. Glass and ironwork lay in heaps everywhere, over the dead.

"Fools!" Jack said bitterly. "They think because they eat downstairs here it's safe to ignore the sirens. My God. It's just the opposite."

Bodies were oozing dark stains of blood; satin dresses were splattered bright red. Bow-tied necks were broken, men's heads rested awkwardly against bare shoulders. Only a few nurses and doctors had arrived and were struggling to help the wounded. There were many victims screaming in pain but left unattended. Alys saw a man in a dinner jacket stretched out, all his limbs shaking convulsively, his face turning blue-black. She had no idea if he were dying or could be saved.

A scruffy old man in a big overcoat stepped over the dead bodies lying in front of her. To her horror, Alys saw him bend down and unpin a diamond brooch from a woman's dress. At a table nearby, a girl who had died of bomb-blast sat unmarked, propped against a wall, staring like a waxwork at his deed. Incredulous, Alys saw another thief, a waitress, stripping silk stockings from an injured woman. The victim cried out as her legs were roughly handled. Without hesitating, the girl slipped the silk into her pocket.

"Come on, Grandma, let's get away from this," Jack said.

"Stop them! Do something!"

"I've got to look after you first. Look, the police are just coming."

Shaking herself free, Alys ran forward and grabbed the waitress by the hair. She knew she was behaving like a demented old woman, but she did not care. She started hitting at the girl with her handbag, and the sudden force of her attack caught the girl unaware.

"Let go of me, you old bitch!" the girl screamed, and turned round to give her a violent shove. Alys still clung to the girl's apron strings. She felt the strength in her hands failing her and a sharp pain in her shoulder as she fell. Then strong hands separated them and Alys found herself hauled into Jack's arms.

"Bloody hell, what are you up to!"

She felt herself lifted over the rubble. Alys was as elated as if she were fifteen and could do anything that anyone dared her to do.

"You're raving mad! What on earth do you think you were doing!" Jack scolded her.

"Stop her!"

"It's all right now—look, the policeman's got her by the arm. I've got to get you out of here."

Alys felt exhilaration in the midst of disgust. They were stepping back on the pavement when two stretcher bearers passed by with a man laid out, face down, his head turned to one side. The sight of him stopped her heart. The reddish hair—the thick beard—he looked exactly like Ned.

"Wait!" she called out, but the bearers did not hear her. The man groaned, and turned his head to the other side. Alys hurried forward to catch a glimpse of his face, but the crowd jostled in front of her, and he vanished.

"I know him." She pointed hopelessly at the ambulance across the street. The doors were shut and the van drove away at speed.

"Enough's enough." Jack was adamant. "Ma will never forgive me. Are you sure you're all right? Lean on me. Slowly now."

"It might have been Ned."

"I'll never hear the end of this. I'll never forgive myself. Bloody stupid exercise."

"Milroy's," Alys said in a daze. "Let's go to Milroy's."

"Not on your life. You're going home to bed."

Alys flinched. "It wasn't Ned. How silly of me. That poor man was far too young. Ned disappeared." She did not want to cry—Jack was already far too worked up about her to bear that. Her shoulder hurt badly.

Jack half carried, half walked her from the bomb site all the way back to the hotel. He ordered tea and sandwiches while Alys got ready for bed and made herself comfortable.

Jack sat on the corner of the quilt, sharing supper from her tray, incongruous in a thick-shouldered mackintosh that was far too big for him.

"Grandma, you're to promise me you'll go home."

"Of course, just as soon as—"

"Not likely. Listen to me. I want you to go back to Bladeshill tomorrow. I don't want to think of you—like this—when I'm flying. D'you see, old girl? It's no joke. Do you understand me?"

She saw at once by the light in his eyes, pleading with her, that there was someone else, a young girl whom he loved and worried about just as much as he did for her. She wanted more than anything in the world for Jack to come home to that girl unharmed.

"What does your girl friend do? Is she somewhere in London too?"

He nodded, not a bit surprised by her change of subject. Her intuition seemed natural to him. "She's an ambulance driver. You'd like her."

"What's her name?"

"Phyllis."

"I expect you call her Phil."

"Well, sometimes. But I like the name Phyllis, actually."

He lit a cigarette. "Do you mind?"

"What? Smoking? Not at all."

He laughed. "Talking about Phyllis."

"Show me a picture of her." He would be bound to have one in his pocket.

He took out his wallet. "There you are."

"Just a minute." Alys pulled out her reading glasses with great ceremony, so that she could give the face all her critical judgment. She heard Jack shuffling his feet, waiting for her word.

"She's ravishing, darling. What lovely hair. And a pointed chin, just like Vivien Leigh."

"Oh, you'll like her, you're sure to. Next time I come home to Bladeshill, I promise to bring her. But you'll do as I say, won't you, and go home as soon as you can?"

"I promise. Now run along, there's a good boy. I feel like a snooze. Good-night."

When Jack left her, Alys lay stiff in bed, sleepless, with a dull ache in her shoulder. The thick blackout curtains let not a chink of light in the room. She preferred to sleep with the vague impression of shapes about her, a little moonlight or a street lamp to show her where her clock was, or the radio, or the dressing gown hanging on the door. But it was utter blackness. If she put on her bedside lamp, the room would be flooded with maroon-pink and then she would never sleep.

In the vacancy of night, the sights of the last few hours darted in and out of her mind, jagged images with the sharp intensity of dreams. Alys tossed about, restless, eager to be rid of these visions, but they persisted to crowd in front of her open sleepless eyes.

She tried to focus on the incongruity of those apron strings, untying in her hands. She must have been mad. People were not often evil—just thoughtless, or stupid. They could be driven by necessity or selfishness to do cruel things. Some were kind—like Ned. He would be white haired, even bald, if he were still alive, not burly and red-headed like that stretcher case.

Alys had a beautiful dream, refusing to own that it was not a dream but a fantasy. Ned had simply walked out of his camp one day into the muddied fields of France, to think of Lily. In a small copse, he found a cottage like the ones in fables, where a pig farmer and his ancient wife waited for the war to end. Ned fell into conversation, stayed for a glass of beer and a piece of bread. He never went back to the camp, but hid out there in peace, while the Germans advanced past him, and months later fell back or deserted. After the war he went to Paris and painted.

Alys clicked on the light. Her hope was as real as the alternative, that he had stumbled from the camp in the middle of the night, in a mood of utter boredom with the misery of war and the emptiness of his life without Lily, and stuck his foot into a mine in an empty field. Now she knew what he would have looked like. Jelly, bloodied meat, bits of his friendly body just blown apart. Worst of all, a stillness in his lively eyes.

She liked her dream, that he was still alive and in Paris. Louise was still there too. She had written only once, through the embassy, since the Occupation. She and Charles managed quietly. They ate little—turnips, black bread, ersatz coffee. But it was enough. "We don't need so very much," she wrote. "One's stomach adjusts. We've taken in a few friends, and that relieves the boredom. I play the piano, and wait till we can see all our dear ones again. All my love."

Alys turned out the light, imagining her mother holding her little salon in Versailles; black bread, yet possibly accompanied by an old bottle from the cellars . . . the thought was good. Exhaustion began to seize her limbs.

Then, as she drifted, Alys felt as if she were dying too, stretching out her hands to reach all those people who looked down on her, continuing to care. Benign calm began to fill her body. It came clear to her in the pitch of night, that it mattered little if her friends were alive or dead. They were *with* her, in her, all forming her thoughts and actions as long as she breathed. Each person she had loved had touched her skin, leaving an imprint of their quality on her continuously forming self. She was like earth, pure clay that their warm hands molded and kept alive. Then she realized sadly that of all of the people she had cherished, only Alec was not in contact. She could not feel him at all, had no sense of his being. Her spirit of forgiveness might reach him. Alys fell asleep, drowning in the remembrance of him, as if that might summon his presence.

◆　◆　◆

Alys kept her word, went back to Bladeshill the next day, and decided not to go back to London again until the war was over. She contented herself with looking at the photographs in newspapers and magazines of her finished Utility designs, and with the complimentary letters about them sent by officials in the Board of Trade. Tina had been right: the designers at Szenkiers had completed them all exactly as she had visualized them, with no compromises.

By some strange working of logic that persisted from that last long night in Mayfair, she persuaded herself that if she stayed home and was obedient, Jack would be spared. Besides, gadding about was not so easy any more. Too much exertion caused the injury to her shoulder to ache again, and was better avoided.

There were many things to keep her occupied. She wrote a series of occasional articles, "Letters from Bladeshill," for her magazine, *Style and Beauty* which were a spirited evocation of the work that women like Laura, Lisa and the nurses were performing in many other similar hospitals. There were also her own unique observations about the visiting celebrities (friends, actresses she had dressed in past years) who came to entertain the patients, and made good copy.

Anne came back from America, and had more time to visit Alys, often giving a solo evening of verse, or helping with theatricals for the patients. She used her connections to summon other actors and actresses: "The Bladeshill Readings" became well known, and were broadcast a few times. When Anne stayed, she always shared Alys' bed, as they used to when they were young. She could have slept elsewhere, but liked to be close to Alys, and besides, the house was very cold.

"When this war's over, I'm going to live in a hot climate for the rest of my life," she grumbled.

"I'd be content with a bath a foot deep," Alys replied.

"Just like Carrigrohane. Freezing again." Anne laughed.

"Move over. You always take all the space."

"Oh do shut up, Alys." Anne did not move an inch.

"It's easy to see why you never married."

"I've had more men in my beds than you have, darling—be honest."

"Ah yes, but they didn't always spend the night!"

A loud, vulgar cackle from the pillow startled Alys.

"Do be quiet—you'll wake Lisa, and she has to be up early."

"So do I. I'm going back to London. Can I stay at Spenser Street?"

"Yes, if you must. I don't think you should be there."

"I've more radio work. It's good to have *something* I can do—never was practical. Tell you what else . . ."

"A new scheme. What is it this time?"

"After it's all over, I'll come with you to Paris."

Alys hugged her. She did not want to question Anne; the offer was enough.

◆　　◆　　◆

Alys spent her time running a sewing room for the hospital, on superior lines. She would have preferred never to touch a needle again, but gave in to necessity. Other Red Cross nurses in the area envied any girl sent to Bladeshill, for it was rumored to have its own "couture salon" on the premises. The nurses loved to have Alys refurbish their dance frocks or off-duty dresses, and she did so willingly.

The real difference in Alys' life was that she had no personal aim at all. She lived purely for others, for her family, her friends, and new acquaintances like the nurses. There was a young newly qualified nurse, Jennifer, who cried because she could not bear to do her "dirty duty" on the wards. She came to sit with Alys for a chat while she darned her black lisle stockings, and was cheered by Alys' scurrilous stories of grand names that she herself knew only from the papers. Alys also experienced the pleasure of watching Laura and Lisa becoming so close they might have been sisters. She had willed that, just for the love of a face . . .

Alys yearned for the war to end, as everyone did. The silence from

Paris was deafening. Every time a telegram arrived at the hospital, her heart fluttered in case it was news of Louise. Or Jack. It was a misfortune for her that telegrams and official letters arrived nearly every day at Bladeshill. It made the possibility of fatal news unrelenting, through all the dreary years of hostilities.

When Paris was liberated in 1944, Alys' first thought was to find out about Louise. She used every connection she had, through the Red Cross, through the Board of Trade, through the husbands of her friends such as Edith Lyttleton, to find out what had happened. No word came.

The Liberation brought other news, trivial but fascinating to her. Picture magazines showed the American soldiers entering Paris, being kissed by ecstatic French girls. Then came photographs of the elegant Parisiennes with their furs and turbans, modeling the autumn collections, the first to be seen in five years by the foreign press.

"Look as these ghastly shoes! The height of the heels! All that fur! Vulgar!" Jennifer chided Alys for too much interest in these pages but she looked over her shoulder all the same. Lisa came in to the sitting room as they sat by the fire enjoying burnt sugar and cinnamon on their toast.

"Don't you think it's a disgrace?" Jennifer asked her, holding up the magazine. Alys was amused. Jennifer had no idea of Lisa's former life.

"For a woman to wear a hat is a *défi*—don't you know that, young lady?" Lisa sounded strangely familiar to Alys. It was her own voice, unconsciously copied. "It's different. In France the women wore the best things they could, to show their spirit of resistance. It may look out of place to us . . ."

"It sure does when I have to paint a black line up my bare legs 'cos I've no coupons left for stockings," Jennifer complained.

"Shall we talk of higher things then, Nurse Smith? Like what to do with Lance-Corporal Biggs if he isn't back by seven?" Lisa asked.

"Biggs has money problems," Jennifer revealed. "His girl friend booked into the Golden Lamb last weekend. His wife expects him to be discharged next Friday—he hasn't even got her a Christmas present."

"Serve him right if she dumps him," Lisa said shortly.

"Oh, he's awfully upset about it. Sent the girl packing. But he's still got no money." Jennifer defended Biggs.

"I could deal with him," suggested Alys. "I'll show him how to make his wife a nightie case. He won't chase *me* round the table."

"Oh!" Jennifer's cheeks flamed. The laughter lasted several minutes until the bell rang to summon them to Laura's sitting room for the radio's six o'clock news.

◆　◆　◆

Two days before Christmas Eve, and to Alys' great joy, Philip White came to visit Bladeshill. He was on leave, in England for the first time since he had been sent away. Alys was filled with happiness to see him. His activities, whatever they were, had not altered any aspect of his appearance. He was just as boyish, soft-featured, clear-complexioned. Philip always moved with a deliberate lethargy; no amount of danger seemed to have affected that.

"Where've you been?" she exclaimed, hugging him. "I heard nothing for so long!"

"Here and there. France mostly." He would not say more.

"Oh. Did you ever get the letters I sent to you, about—"

"Louise? I was contacted to make enquiries, yes. I'm afraid I haven't much news. The house in Versailles is empty. But it was known to other sections."

"Do you mean that Louise and Charles were agents or something?" Alys was disbelieving.

"Charles had many Jewish friends. The house was a gathering place in the early days. My guess is that Charles and Louise went south, perhaps in the company of someone they were trying to help. I know the names of other Frenchmen in their circle who ended up in the Vaucluse, with the Maquis. Perhaps they're hiding out there. I don't know more, I'm afraid."

"But it's impossible! Louise isn't at all brave . . ."

"She may be wanting to protect a friend. Remember, she and Charles helped many artists, just like they did me. Perhaps someone came for advice or money. You know how generous they were. I wish I could tell you more. Even the details I know are in the strictest confidence."

"Oh. I see. That's why you came up here—just to tell me yourself?" She was grateful, but hoped there were other motives . . .

"Of course not. I also want to tell you—you were good to me. I couldn't do what I have to do if I wasn't alone. Do you understand? I think you do. I wonder if you knew that when you sent me away."

She shook her head. "Not if thinking made me do it. Perhaps, a feeling, I don't know. You were going to draw away from me."

"The night at the party. Remember? After Anne's play . . ."

"My God! That man I saw you with! They were sounding you out even then!"

Philip kissed her cheek. "I have to go. Chin up. Soon be over."

"Good-bye then. Good luck." She held him for a moment, then let him go. In the wards, the men were singing carols, and were waiting for her to join in.

It was a hard season at Bladeshill that Christmas. Alys wrestled with imaginings of her mother, hiding somewhere in the south. Laura's reserve was beginning to give way as the end of the war approached. Thoughts of Jonathan's death, so close to the end of the last Great War, haunted her. The house itself was very quiet, waiting with them. Most of the patients went home to their families, including the repentant Biggs and Jennifer.

There was someone else to think of, too. Alys had only a name, Phyllis. Jack never had the time to bring her to Bladeshill, and never mentioned her in his thin letters. Yet Alys fancied that the love affair went on. She identified with the young girl, waiting, wondering if she had a future with her love. Her own grandson. Alys willed with every ounce of determination that she possessed, that Jack would come back safe to his home.

One night in March, when Alys was in bed, she heard footsteps outside her door. She could tell by the tread that it was Laura, pausing to see if her light was still on.

"I'm awake. Come in." Laura appeared. "Is it the boiler again?" Alys asked.

"No. It's Jack. He was injured when his aircraft made a forced landing in Norfolk—he just made it down. He's coming home."

Alys snatched the telegram from her hands, though her eyes were so blurred that she could not read.

"Oh, Mama! I wish you wouldn't smoke in bed!" Laura stubbed out a cigarette with irritation. The edge of the glass dish tipped up as she did so, spilling ashes all over the floor.

"Oh damn!" Laura burst into tears, and sat down beside Alys with her head in her hands. "He was always so perfect. His skin. We've had pilots before with burns . . ." She started sobbing, a heaving, bottomless noise in her chest.

All the stored-up hoping produced a violent response in Alys. She grabbed Laura's hands away from her face, and gestured as if she wanted to hit her across the cheek.

"He's alive. Shut up! He's alive!"

Laura gasped as the skin on her wrists twisted in Alys' strong fingers. "Mama!"

Then she fell forward onto Alys' chest and they both cried. Alys wept in joy and fear. If it had given back her grandson, the war might claim Louise.

CHAPTER 25

A 1 9 4 5 – 4 7

lys and Laura stood anxiously in a cool wind as the ambulance arrived, bringing Jack to their home. He had managed to speak briefly from the hospital near his base, to assure them that he was not going to be disfigured, but beyond that they knew nothing. The doors opened: Jack stepped out, both arms stiff with bandaging, and a great deal thinner than he had ever been. He squinted in the sunlight, suddenly looking much older, no longer recognizable as his father's image, for he had outlived him.

Alys could not look at his hands when they were being dressed, but Laura stood over him, persevering in one-sided conversations to distract him from the pain, her gaze fixed steadily on his face. Alys would flit past the surgery door, watching as this tableau was repeated every other day for weeks. Jack grew impatient, having to be dressed and fed, having to have cigarettes held up to him, having books slide off his knees without being able to stop them from falling.

But then Phyllis came—and for her, he made the effort to be a good patient. Alys thought she was an overly competent, rather bossy girl, forgetting to make allowances for her fatigue after the war. As soon as Jack's hands no longer needed their casings, the couple got married in a Registry Office in London, near Phyllis' flat. They both wore their uniforms, and went directly back to Bladeshill, for Jack was too ill to travel anywhere for a honeymoon, and a night on the town would have exhausted them.

Alys liked to watch Jack, sitting on the lawn, holding hands with his bride, Phyllis' sleek head close to his fair one as she planned their lives. Just looking was a pleasure after his long, uncertain absence. Alys noticed that Laura would stare at the stringy, shiny marks scored down the back of Jack's hands, up his arms, just as she did herself, wordlessly dwelling on his former physical perfection. Alys was amazed how the texture and scent of her grandson's skin were known to her differently from that of the other boys she had helped. She did not need to ask Laura if she found the same, for the vacant sadness in her daughter's face, when she stared at those livid hands, told her that she did. Long fingers, exactly like his father's; Alys remembered how firm and gentle Jonathan's hands had looked when he held up his baby son. His fingers nearly met round a plump little body, brown against linen-white.

Jack convalesced, Phyllis began to lose her coiled-up presence, and Alys still waited for news from France. She denied all possibility of Louise's death for more than a year. Distant relatives of Charles de Tessier accepted the inevitable more readily than she did, and wrote asking her to come to Paris to take charge of her mother's few remaining possessions. She refused to do so. There was still a chance that Louise and Charles would be found in a hospital somewhere, or might emerge from a hiding place in a mountain village. In the aftermath of war, people often turned up unexpectedly. Alys read miraculous stories of such homecomings in all the newspapers.

Then Anne came to Bladeshill again.

"I think we should go. Together," she repeated.

"Why? You think she's dead, don't you? Then why do you want to go? I'm sorry you didn't have your chance. You would have liked her."

"Do you want me to tell you the truth? I regret it, certainly. I regretted it more during the war, but now—well, everybody's suffered much worse than me. It's the paintings. You told me she had a fine collection."

"Louise's paintings? Do you want them? As a—reminder? How strange. You've never cared for things particularly."

"No. Not as a souvenir, exactly . . ." Anne sounded purposeful, and Alys disliked the suspicions this aroused in her.

"You want to sell them?"

"Well, why not? I'm sure Louise would prefer you to have them, or me to do something good with the money, not let them fall into the wrong hands. Think sensibly, Alys."

"You've always got an answer! Perhaps they're sold. Perhaps she left them to the de Tessiers." Alys said. Nothing changed: she and Anne would argue over the same issues forever. But suddenly, with the same will that made her hold onto the idea of Louise's survival, Alys decided to give up hope. "All right. We'll go. If that's what you want."

Alys realized she could not tolerate uncertainty forever. Anne was her only sister—Louise's daughter, too. Her coming on this final journey had a sort of justice.

The house in Versailles had been stripped of all its contents; Alys knew that Charles' relatives had removed most of the valuable furniture during the war, after the couple left Paris. But she wanted to see it again and to show Anne at least the interior. The concierge in the house next door gave them a key, and they wandered through the empty rooms.

From the hall, Alys looked down into the garden. It was wildly overgrown, full of unpruned summer plants, black leaves hanging from yellow stalks like scraps of wet leather. Cool laughter, the notes of a Debussy song, the rustle of silk petticoats filled the emptiness behind her. Then Anne's high heels, clicking slowly on the bare staircase, destroyed her communion with a vanished scene.

"Nothing here. No locked cupboards. No loose floorboards," Anne announced, as if she were in a mystery play.

"There's no need for that," Alys said, irritated. "Charles was painstaking about the things he valued. He would have put anything precious in the bank—unless he sold it all."

"Oh, I hope not," Anne sighed.

They went to the de Tessiers' lawyers to sign various documents. Louise and Charles had lived for each other, with little thought for the future, but Charles had prepared a simple, precise will, leaving everything to Alys. There appeared to be very little for her to inherit.

"What about her jewelry? Did she leave anything of personal value with you?" Alys asked the lawyer.

He shook his head. "She disposed of many items during the war, to help her friends leave Paris," Charles' former partner explained. "There is a safe deposit box at the bank, waiting for you. I'll take you there."

Of all the ways to recapture the flavor of Paris and Louise, this seemed the least appropriate. To trail sadly through quiet streets, between solicitors and banks, seemed to Alys quite out of keeping with her mother's spirit, but it had to be done. Anne was growing more enthusiastic all the time at the idea of secrets, a paper chase through the remnants of Louise's life.

The lawyer came as witness and authority at the bank, in a quiet street near the Place de l'Alma. The strongroom was no bigger than a gentleman's dressing room, lined on one side with old mahogany safe-deposit boxes, neatly inscribed with italic numerals on brass discs. The manager remembered Charles' last visit as if it were only weeks past; he revealed his affection for Charles by the way he stood a little taller and spread his hands in a formal way as if he were actually conversing with his old client. He stood back to let Alys examine the box in privacy.

"The last time they came here together, Mesdames, they were very happy, not at all frightened. They didn't tell me where they were going, or with whom they were traveling, only that they had to take a journey. Madame de Tessier left just the one box, Monsieur Charles some letters, which I have waiting for you in my office—and these, to be given only to you, Lady Colvin."

A pile of paintings, stitched into rough canvas bags, stood in a corner. Alys saw Anne's eyes light up. For an instant she felt angry with her again. Then it occurred to her that Anne shared her mother's intense pleasure in certain situations: dramas, romances, the poetry of circumstances. In her excitement and her lack of grief, Anne became her mother's daughter more than she would care to acknowledge.

"Can they be taken upstairs?" Alys asked. "I'll carry the deposit box." It was small and felt light, very little inside it.

"This way, please." In the office, the lawyer and the bank manager stood at a distance while Alys unlocked the box. Inside was a tiny watercolor in a silver frame—Louise as a young woman—a long string of perfectly matched pearls and a few diamond pins. There was also a letter for Alys.

Darling,
　All this is for you. There are a few other things, you can dispose of them as you choose, but my pearls and my few little brooches I want you to keep, and give Laura and Anne. I never met Anne. There always seemed to be time enough to have her come to me, and I wanted to know you first. At least I succeeded in that, dearest. My love to you. Till we meet again, after all this. Faith, love and hope are in the waiting.
　　　　　　　　　　　　　　　　　　Your mother, Louise.

There was a gasp of wonder from Anne. She had pulled the covers from the paintings. Only ten canvases had been stored at the bank. They recognized among them an Olonetz and a Kosloff. All were of astounding brilliance in color and execution. One painting of a woman with a lace veil over the brim of her hat half obscuring her face, made Alys dizzy, wanting to faint.

"Sit down, Madame," the lawyer said, placing a hand under her arm. Alys sank down, recalling how that picture used to hang above the buffet in the dining room at Versailles. The woman in the new hat posed with her chin propped on the heel of her hand. She wore a long black glove. Alys could imagine the woman's voice, saying, "Do you like it? Do you? I certainly do, whatever you say!" There was appeal and defiance in her expression. It epitomized the tender and the harsh aspects of her mother—of herself, too.

"You take them all, Anne. Except that one."

"How wonderful! Is this legal?" Anne wanted to know. Charles' lawyer and the bank manager started to murmur agreement in the corner.

Anne kissed and hugged her, but Alys was inconsolable. The portrait's reappearance in the ugly, shabby office upset her. Alys had spent many crucial moments of her life in such brown and gloomy rooms. Legal chambers, bank vaults, smoky libraries—masculine citadels. Her bond with Louise had always been defined by such places. She had struggled all her life with the fantasy of a true mother. As she signed the documents the men presented to her, Alys accepted Louise's death and made her farewell to the imperfect reality of her caring. The fantasy was destroyed, and at the same time, the real person, with all her qualities and deficiencies, was lost forever. Alys grieved for her.

◆　◆　◆

Anne made a fortune from the paintings, which sold at Christie's for prices far in excess of her hopes. All Alys kept was the *Veiled Lady*. She suspected Anne needed the money for her retirement, as she had never saved a penny in her life. It struck Alys as entirely appropriate that the legacy of a woman who had avoided all maternal duties should provide security for a daughter who had paid scant attention to "domestic details," money or a home, throughout her own life.

Alys, on the contrary, had been giving the matter of her future a great deal of thought. Her little villa in Spenser Street had come through the war intact, though badly slipping on one side. The whole area of Kensington had increased dramatically in value, so even with this defect, her house was worth four times the price she paid for it.

It was her intention to leave the house to Jack and Phyllis, to set them up for their marriage. Not yet: they liked the freedom of their small flat at present, and Alys had her own strong wish to return to London. Country living had never been her favorite style of life. When Jack and Phyllis had a family, Spenser Street would be perfect! For children and old people it had all the amenities . . . it was close to the park and the museums, convenient for short expeditions to the stores.

Alys planned to move all her belongings to the ground floor, to avoid the stairs, and convert the upstairs into a flat for a housekeeper. She had sounded out a Mrs. Moore, an ex-matron from Bladeshill, who was willing to take the job. She knew that Lisa would be much happier staying behind at Bladeshill, for there had been lengthy conversations about her continuing to work with Laura, running the old house as a nursing home. Maurice was ailing too, and needed care.

Alys had seen quite enough of illness and she wanted to be free, to be at the center of things again. Laura and Lisa fretted about her decision, but she was determined to do what she wanted in spite of their concern.

"Mama," said Laura, in one of their many discussions about her plan. "How are you going to manage, all alone in London?" Alys was amused to be found "helpless" after all she had done.

"I've quite enough saved, thank you, and my little pension from the Szenkiers. I'm not going to be idle—people often write to me to give a little speech, sit on various advisory fashion boards. I think I shall enjoy being respectable for a change."

"It all sounds too busy. Aunt Anne should have agreed to share with you."

"We'd argue too much. Besides, she's never been able to afford something of her own before. She's enjoying house-hunting. If you want me to stay sensible and calm, Mrs. Moore's the thing. She'll spy on me for you too!"

"I'm only trying to help."

"I haven't got one foot in the grave."

A few months after she settled in, Alys invited Jack and Phyllis to celebrate her return. Looking forward to their arrival, she spent the afternoon fiddling with flowers and different vases, decorating the sitting room. She wanted everything to look its best for them. She looked around at the jumble crammed into her small rooms. There were her portable treasures—she had never grown used to owning large things. Ned's portrait of her; the two Delaunays she had bought years before and taken to New York; some of Adelaide Hay's photographs of immigrants in Manhattan, a world before . . . framed sketches of early "Alys" collections; silver-mounted family portraits. All the furniture looked exhausted, flattened by troupes of Anne's friends who had used the house during the past years. Gilt chairs, *louche* satin-covered sofas with the stuffing hanging out of cigarette-burn holes. She would not part with any of it.

The hall was a gallery of theater programs, Lily's posters, Anne's playbills, Philip's exhibitions, a parade of entertainments from many decades. Alys liked to have it all on show in preference to a more designed interior. No doubt Phyllis would do the place over in the future. For the moment, Alys rather liked choosing this or that to give to friends: perhaps Lilian in New York would like all her sketchbooks from "Salon Alys" for her lectures and her students, who might find them of interest. And Lisa could have some of Philip's pictures now that Bladeshill was to be her permanent home. Plotting such surprises was one of the pleasures of retirement, Alys had discovered.

Occasionally Mrs. Moore complained about "dusting round" but Alys always said, "Don't bother, Mrs. Moore. Ghosts don't mind dust and I'm making friends with quite a few."

She was utterly content, sipping sherry too early, cutting the ferns and roses. She anticipated the pleasure of young voices in her home—fresh and vigorous, like Philip's used to be. His voice came clearly to her then. Philip had married too, a French girl he had worked with at the end of the war. He had written from Belgium, promising to come and see her when his work was done. Alys felt no sadness or jealousy; just an intense relief that he still wanted her in his life, and that they would always be good friends. She remembered the hostility she had felt for Edward when she parted from him. It had taken such a long time for the strength of her feeling to dissipate. If age brought certain incapacities, it had its advantages: less passion, but less anger, too.

Jack would guffaw, his "Air Force laugh." Alys liked to tease him about it. Phyllis would talk all the time. She was a lot bolder than her pretty face suggested, Alys thought. Too argumentative, but perhaps that was no failing in the modern world. Alys admired Phyllis' independence, yet she could not help feeling disappointment that she was postponing having a child. Overlooking her own repugnance for maternity at the same age, she could not wait for a baby to dote on. The notion of Jack becoming a father was besotting, even though the couple teased her for being so old-fashioned. If only they knew . . .

The phone rang, and she hurried to answer it, hoping Jack did not have to cancel.

"Hello? Mama?"

"Laura! What are you doing in London?"

"Oh, I had to see friends. Could I come round? I'm quite close by."

"Your son's coming to supper. Won't you stay?"

"No, I've got to get back. Maurice hates me to be away overnight."

"All right, dear. I'll leave the door for you."

She arrived less than ten minutes later, looking agitated but not anxious. Alys was mystified.

"I can't think of a clever way to tell you this," Laura said, holding Alys' hands very firmly and guiding her to a chair. "Sit down first."

Alys began to feel an emptying out inside her, the first signs of fear.

"It's not Louise, is it?"

"No. It's Alec."

"What do you mean? Oh, Laura, he's not dead!"

"No. Now calm yourself, please. He's come back, on a visit. He'd like to see you, but he phoned me first, to see what I thought about it."

"He doesn't even know where I am." Alys was sad.

"Would you like to see him? Would you rather not?"

"Of course I want to see him! There's nothing wrong, is there, Laura? I mean, people often want to come back 'home' to England when they're sick, you know."

"Good heavens, no. He's in a trade delegation. I was so amazed I didn't really listen to the details."

"Why didn't he write first?"

Laura stared in a trance at the heap of flowers Alys had been arranging. "It was on impulse. He hadn't planned to make contact. But when he got here, he just had to do it."

"You're a hopeless liar. I think *you* wrote to him." Alys paled. "You're not hiding anything from me, are you?"

"Oh, I suppose I'll have to tell you. I've always written to him."

"Oh, Laura! You missed him very much. I always knew you did, though you never said anything about it."

Laura looked reflective. "I didn't, really. I was too caught up with other concerns for that. But it became a habit to keep in touch. He sent presents for Jack—he's a good godfather. We wrote notes of thanks. I didn't tell you, in case you'd be upset."

These words were very hard for Alys. Laura had not told her before perhaps because she did not want to look as if she were taking sides.

"I expect I would have been offended, in the early days," she admitted, feeling ashamed of herself. "I was very angry."

"Quite." Laura stood up briskly. "Shall I ask him in then?"

"You mean, he's here now?"

"At the pub round the corner. Dutch courage."

"Well, go and fetch him! How ridiculous!"

"All right, but do just relax and sit quietly now, won't you?"

Alys did no such thing. She hurried into the hall and peered at herself in the mirror. Her senses felt forced outside of her skin by panic, to see what he would see in her. An old woman, not very gray-haired, with too-prominent cheekbones, glared out of the mirror. The mouth was more pursed, and thinner than he would remember. She turned a little to the side, smoothing her lined cheeks upwards with her fingertips. Her hands were shiny and pale with age, and mottled on the back.

Alec appeared at the door, and she saw him reflected in the mirror. When he smiled, she realized he did not see the old woman staring out of the reflection; he recognized only his own once-loved Alys.

"Alec!" He brushed her cheeks, the Brazilian way, without touching her skin with his lips. It was all so strange that Alys was stunned into silence.

Nervously, Alec stepped past her into the little sitting room. He surveyed the chairs, not sure where to stand or sit. He held an ebony stick, and a silk scarf; he twisted the fringes on it while Alys, immobile, watched him. Alec looked surprisingly fit, not very much aged, except for thinning gray hair. He had the pale, lucid skin of someone used to living indoors in the tropics. His expensive, thin suit and new shoes made him look wealthy and foreign. That made Alys awkward, not knowing him, yet at the same time seeing that he was just the same Alec, in the atmosphere he brought into her room.

"I'm off to the station," Laura said, in an odd voice. Alys turned sharply, to see that she was crying.

She wanted to speak, but Laura flapped a hand at her and bolted, calling out, "I'll ring!" and the door slammed.

"Well?" he said at last. "Can I sit down?"

"Of course. Is it the mills? Is this really just a business trip or—"

"I sold my share in the mills. Vast profit, because of the war . . . I may come back, if this trip goes well."

"Retire here? Why?" She was suspicious. María-Elena was so tangible in the air that Alys felt she might materialize.

He avoided her eyes. "For many reasons . . . principally too many Nazis at the polo club." He leant back, embarrassed, coughed, then fluttered his fingers as if he wanted to give her another answer but could not find the words. "Could I have a drink, do you suppose?"

She fumbled with the glasses, pouring him a whisky without thinking. No water, no ice. He took it, murmuring thanks. Old gestures, old habits were so simple to revive.

"Look, Alys, it will take a long time to explain all of it. What I want to know is, am I in the way? Shall I come back another time? I will, if you prefer it."

"Don't be ridiculous. Jack's coming to supper, and Phyllis. I suppose Laura told you. I'll just tell Mrs. Moore to set another place. Mrs. Moore!" she called up the stairs.

Only now did Alec look her full in the face.

"Alys."

"Mm?"

"I *will* explain. Later. Believe me when I say you were the only woman who ever—"

"It's far too late for all that." Alys was not bitter; it was a statement of fact. "I don't want to hear any more just now. You're here, I'm here, we both chose to do what we did. Leave it at that, shall we? At least for a while."

Mrs. Moore appeared.

"Set another place, will you, dear? Someone unexpected . . ."

Mrs. Moore's bulky presence moving about in the dining room across the hallway provided a comfortable unknowing cover. Alec began to chat, relaxing a little, describing his journey back, his good fortune in selling his shares, and giving her the latest news about the Monteira de Barros. Leopoldo had four children; The old "Coronel" had died; María-Elena was still single. Alys listened politely, as if he were describing a routine business trip from a city office. Inside she felt a welling up of an old affection for a long-lost friend, and very little sense of betrayal.

Jack and Phyllis arrived, much more amazed than Alys had been by Alec's sudden reappearance.

"Jack—just like your father." Alec was visibly moved. They shook hands, and Alec bowed to Phyllis, such an old-world gesture that she laughed without thinking and embarrassment overcame him again.

They all sat at Alys' rickety table, eating good food together—three of them at least relishing a luxurious meal after years of ration books. Alys knew she should not be drinking—it was potent homemade stuff of Jack's concocting from elderberries at Bladeshill. Drink often had an unpredictable effect on her, sometimes making her sad, when she wanted to be carefree, or tense when she wanted to relax. She struggled with a growing anger. He was so effortlessly charming, already accepting that he could walk into her life again after so many years, as if he had some entitlement to her. All the wasted years, all the struggling without his support stood between them. She fell silent, thunderous as the meal went on.

Jack looked across at her. "Are you feeling tired, Grandma?" he asked, "Is it time for us to go?"

Alec started as if he had heard something extraordinary. He threw back his head and shook his napkin helplessly. Alys' eyes glittered at him.

"I'm so sorry," he spluttered, trying to control himself. "It's just—*Grandma!*" The idea made him laugh again.

"Alec! You're a disgrace!" Alys exclaimed. Now he saw fit to humiliate her because of her old age. She was too angry to accept what she knew really he intended: a compliment. To Alec she was a timeless companion, the woman in her prime whom he had married. But she was too confused and upset to let anything he said be pleasing to her.

"I'm going to bed." she announced. "Talk among yourselves—you needn't leave!" She turned to Alec. "You'll leave an address, won't you? It would be nice to see you again while you're here."

Alys stalked off, not bothering to wait for his reply. She lay rigid, listening to the sound of Jack's extravagant laughter and the clinking of glasses, feeling foolish.

When she awoke, she sensed it was quite late. Mrs. Moore was bumping slowly around the kitchen. It was after ten o'clock.

"Good morning! I hope the guests didn't keep you awake, Mrs. Moore. I expect they left quite soon after I went to bed?" she ventured.

"Oh no, Your Ladyship. They all left well after midnight."

Alys tried to sound accepting of this news.

"I'm glad they enjoyed themselves. Did anyone leave a message?"

"Only a number for you to ring." Mrs. Moore nodded to the sitting room. "I left it on the piano."

Alec had been to her desk, scribbled on her notepaper, and borrowed an envelope. Everything he did infuriated her.

> I'm at the Savoy. Can we try again?
> Thank you for a wonderful evening. Alec.

Not one word of apology. He really was an unforgivable man.

◆　◆　◆

For the next few weeks, Alec paid court to her assiduously. Sometimes she forgot to be angry and allowed herself to slip into reminiscences of happy times. It was difficult to be hostile to Alec when everyone else was so pleased to see him again. Laura was most evidently overjoyed, and he spent several days at Bladeshill while Alys cooled her temper as best she could in London. Every time she began to reconcile herself to the simple pleasure of his reappearance, something happened to make her withdraw again. Invitations addressed to "Sir Alec Colvin" began to drop through her door. When she handed these over, frostily, Alec apologized for the inconvenience, murmuring that it was an "understandable error."

Sometimes, when she suddenly wanted to see him, she would ring the Savoy to discover he had gone away for a few days to see other friends, without warning her. Of course, she had only herself to blame because she made it very plain that he was not to expect anything at all from her. No certainty of companionship, above everything.

Matters came to a head when she invited him to the theater and he had to cancel at the last minute because he had missed a train back from the countryside. He had been staying with Cecily Day and Legless

Lewinski. Alys was inordinately offended; completely forgetting that Alec was well-acquainted from childhood with most of her circle, and entitled to look upon Cecily as an independent friend. Cecily's enjoyment of the situation was another cause for anguish. The red roses Alec sent were kept in the kitchen "in case their stems bend in the heat in here," Alys said to Mrs. Moore, then went to sit in offended dignity alone in her sitting room.

Alec arrived punctually the following day to take her to a matinee instead. This only made her feel cheated of another chance to find fault with him. In the theater, he lifted her unwilling hand into his own, and turned his head to look at her. Alys kept her eyes fixed on the stage. The warmth of his gaze began to affect her, and she could feel his loving kindness like an aura transferring to her.

It was a trivial play, and for once the magic of the theater did not touch her. Alys was impatient to be home and talk to Alec seriously about his future. The other members of the "trade delegation" had gone back to Brazil weeks before. Alec still lingered, not quite sure what he would do. He talked about buying a little place in the country; he looked at various apartments in London. Then he mentioned going back to Brazil to settle more details first. She felt there was no conviction in any of his plans.

After the play, she stood on the steps of the theater while Alec searched for a taxi. It was raining, not very hard, a summer shower. The Haymarket was bustling with people on their way home from offices in the area—pretty girls swaying along with their ballerina skirts, white gloves, small hats—the "New Look" from Christian Dior imitated in a hundred cheap styles. Someone bumped into Alys, a young man who stooped to pick up the jetted bag that had fallen from her arm. As he handed it back he looked through her, barely pausing in his conversation with the girl at his side. Alys withered him with a long cold look, a witch throwing spells at his back as he walked away from her.

The crowd cleared a little, and Alys saw Alec raise his arm and jump up on his toes to hail a cab. His silvery hair ruffled up in the wind. He beckoned her. As on many other occasions, Alys made a decision in that moment of little consequence, just because of the tiredness she had felt when the young man jostled her, and because Alec look so very old when the wind lifted his thin hair. Alec came to guide her to the taxi door.

"Would you like to come back to Spenser Street?" she asked, a little weakly.

"What? I didn't catch what you said—the traffic—" he replied.

"Would you like to come back to Spenser Street? For good? I mean, why not? It would be quite convenient."

"Convenient. Is that all, Alys? You know I never stopped loving you. I was a fool to throw away your faith in me."

"You never married her. Why?"

"I knew as soon as you went back to England that I never would. I won't say we weren't—close—for a while. I was very unhappy. But she's a proud woman, María-Elena, and I couldn't give her what she wanted."

"You must have made her very unhappy." There was no hint of satisfaction in Alys' voice. It was a terrible fate to want someone as much as María-Elena had wanted him, to wait so long and be disappointed.

"I loved someone, too," she had to tell him. Alec looked very handsome to her at this moment—uncharacteristically serious, accepting her separation from him.

"I imagine you had a full life," he said lightly. "The point is, rather, can I make you happy now? I want to be with you. Not for the past—for a new life." He stopped abruptly. Alys knew better than to talk any more. Alec would understand by her silence that she accepted him. She sat back, deeply affected by his words. How sad it was that men so seldom spoke out from the heart. There had been a few times, she could remember each incident very specifically, when lovers had made a declaration of importance. They were stark moments, arrived at after painful times. How powerfully well Alec had made his offer. Like other such moments of truth, it humbled her.

◆ ◆ ◆

They were very happy in Spenser Street together. Alys enjoyed the new-found security of companionship with Alec. For the time being she refused to let him alter the furnishings or find a larger house to celebrate their new life. Instead, Mrs. Moore agreed to live nearby and come in daily. Alec had a bedroom and study arranged for himself on the first floor, and that suited them both. But there were many nights when Alys did not want him to go upstairs. In the end, she simply asked him to stay with her to sleep, as directly as he had offered to share her life. For many nights they simply held each other gently, and Alys often found herself crying, not unhappily, and not for long, just before she fell asleep. A phrase from her mother's last letter, which she knew by heart, often came back to her. "Faith, love and hope are in the waiting." She realized that the disappointments and separations of the past, with Alec, with so many others, were all her own doing. She wanted to love and to belong, but aspiration was easier to live with than achieving. Except in loving the very young, like Jack, where the grace of life was so evident.

Sharing her days with Alec was not at all easy, and Alys often had to remind herself why she had chosen to do it: because she was tired of waiting, and had lost the enjoyment of hope. She wanted her old age to be a time for absolute pleasures, to fill the days between memories, and strengthen her when she looked forward.

Alec gradually forgot to arrange any return trip to Brazil. She asked him when he would go back, knowing there were many things he would have to finalize in order to settle in England, but he always made an excuse—when he had seen all the friends he wanted, or after the summer, perhaps.

It was a wonderful season for Alys, not just because Alec was in a mood to entertain her all the time, but because she had no work, nothing but free days to spend with her family. Especially the boy, Jack, whom she loved more than anyone in the world. Alys believed that it was just her secret effort of will, her wish that Jack should survive, that had made him come back, even though it had exhausted her. A nonsensical, magical notion, but she held to it.

Anne invited everyone to see her new home. She had bought a cottage quite remote from company, in Essex, on the side of a hill with a view over open fields. Attached to it was an old barn which she planned to convert into a small studio theater. She would give classes in drama, and her students would stage new writing.

"Don't you think Louise would have approved?" she asked, as they walked from the warm, oaty-smelling room into the sunlight once more.

"Perhaps. She wasn't very rural . . ."

Alec and the sisters arranged a picnic on the grass in front of the house.

"I can't possibly sit on the grass," Alec said, opening the door to his hired car. "Could someone give me a hand with the hood? Careful, don't strain yourself."

Anne pushed back the canvas, laughing and flirting with him.

"Don't you find life difficult without a chauffeur? You're so used to servants . . ."

"I'm very adaptable. Alys will vouch for me, I'm sure. Last week I learnt how to make an omelette. The French way. Have some wine." Alec sat comfortably in the back passenger seat of the car, with the hamper open at his side.

"How are you going to bear it, being here alone at night?" Alys called out to Anne.

"I'm not going to be alone. I'll probably have students to stay," Anne said confidently.

"Don't lie on the grass like that, Alys. Take the rug." Alec fussed at her.

He threw it across, and the blanket landed like a tent collapsing over her head. It smelt of cigars, leather, a little damp and mildew. Alys rolled onto the sun-warmed lawn.

"I prefer it here, thank you. Fancy sitting in a metal heap on a day like this." Shading her eyes under the brim of her hat, she saw Alec shrug his shoulders, and Anne shake her head in sympathy.

"What a perfect picnic," Alys said, laughing. "We can all disagree and have a good time."

She lay back on the grass, the sun beating gold patterns into her eyelids. Then she tilted her Panama hat over her face, smelling the warm straw and the scent of her own hair. Her bones began to ache, but she wanted to feel the earth beneath her, the sky above and a now familiar suspension of self, bringing her peace.

◆ ◆ ◆

The days grew shorter, and the sycamores in Spenser Street dropped their spiraling seeds hopelessly to the gray pavement. Alys summoned her friends to meet Alec: new ones came to make his acquaintance, old ones to renew their friendship. Kitty and Tina Szenkier remembered him well, and so did Lisa. There was nothing Alec liked more than a gathering of women recalling old splendors and letting him flatter them.

Cecily and Legless often came to spend an evening and play cards with him, and sometimes persuaded Charlotte to join in. But Charlotte spent most of her time at Burley, Edward's old home, which was being sold to her orphanage, the Children's Foundation; after the war, there were many unwanted children. Then there were the surprise visitors, soldiers whom Alys had befriended at Bladeshill, and who kept their promise to come and tell her of their new careers.

One evening, Jennifer, her young nursing friend, returned to announce her engagement to a Canadian doctor she had met through the Red Cross. She looked older than twenty-four, more sophisticated than in her scrubbing days at Bladeshill. Her fair hair was piled up in a knot on top of her head, and a gash of dark-red lipstick hardened her face. Nylon stockings gleamed above her high suede shoes, and a tight belt held in the pleats of her gray silk dress. She looked graceful, if a little overdone.

Alys sighed, trying to overlook the excess, but unable to control the note of judgment in her voice: "Lovely color, darling, but not that loud scarf . . . come in here to me." She led Jennifer to her bedroom. "Just pull that out from under the bed, will you?" An old blue-and-silver striped bandbox, stuffed with silk scarves.

" '*Alys*'. How pretty," Jennifer said, untying the silk bow on the lid. Eager to please herself, she sat on the bed and rummaged through the box until she found a print in gray with pink spots. Alys tried to tie it for her, but lost patience because her hands were stiff. Jennifer did it, following her instructions.

"That's it." Alys stood back, admiring Jennifer's looks. "Softens your face." They heard Alec arrive and call out for her.

"Gosh, it's getting late. I shall have to go. What a mess I've made." The girl jumped up, turning round for Alys. "Is it better? How do I look now?"

She twirled and twirled, so hopeful, so pretty, even if she was a little silly and vain at times.

"You'll improve," Alys said, thinking of the times when Jennifer had sat up all night to hold some soldier's hand.

"I'll post it back, shall I?" the girl said, ingenuously.

Alys saw her pleasure in it. "Of course not. It's a present for you. Pink is your color—*strong* pink, mind you, not pastel. Like this—see?" She picked up another silk and held it close to Jennifer's cheek. She quite wanted to kiss her, not for her beauty, but more for the insignificance of the silk scarf that made the girl so intent and happy. Some pleasures never changed.

"Oh yes . . . You're quite right. Now I must fly. I really must!" Jennifer was awed by Alec's grand manners, and wanted to hurry into town to her fiancé.

"Good-bye, dear. Write to me from Canada."

"I will. Thank you for everything, Alys. You've been so kind to me." Jennifer hugged her, then hurried away, her pale hair gleaming under the lamplights.

After supper, Alys played solitaire while Alec murmured stories to her from his newspaper. He knew he could distract her, that she was only daydreaming. In Alys' thoughts, Jennifer's beautiful figure in her gray dress turned gracefully. The girl had a promising career and had worked hard to fulfill her dream. But she still wanted to be adorned, to create some new image of herself . . . Artists had their canvases, but women used their bodies to reflect every nuance of change in the world around them, in new lines, in the symbolism of coloring. The room grew quieter, warm from the fire, with just the clock ticking. Alec came and stood behind her, looking at her cards, softly whistling.

"Oh bother, I forgot to tidy away all the silks after that creature," she said. She liked the bedroom to be neat when Alec came to her. He patted her hand, recognizing the invitation in her words.

"Don't you dare to touch my cards while I'm gone," she said. She stood up, but staggered a little, clutching the side of her chair, and fell back against it, failing.

Speechless, Alys turned her head to look at Alec. All at once she was terrified, and very much in need of him. His face told her that he knew all that, and was as scared as she was. He had been waiting, a very long time, for when this moment came.

"Alys, oh my dear, I'm here . . ."

The room grew hazy. Figures in silk twirled before her. Now there was Jennifer, youthful, hoping; now there was Lily in cloth of gold. Laura, on a green lawn, and Anne in a pool of silver light. Another child, with roses in her sleeves was spinning round and round, and they all sang, "Do I look all right? Do I look all right?"

"*I* like it anyway," Alys said. Alec did not hear her words but held her till her heart stopped.

FRANCES KENNETT was born in London and went to Oxford University, where she studied English and designed costumes for university productions. After graduation, she worked as a fashion journalist and then as an editor and publisher. She has written several nonfiction books, mainly on the history of fashion. She has lived abroad, in the United States and Latin America, but is now settled in London with her three children, and is at work on her second novel.